*Getting a man on his kne
an opportunity...*

Ros doesn't accept excuses for falling short. Particularly not from herself. As CEO of a successful New Orleans marketing firm, she knows how to bring quality to the top. The same way she knows how to get it from the men who serve her in the bedroom.

Lawrence has been a SEAL since his teens. He doesn't know how to be a civilian. So when being a SEAL is no longer an option for him, he accepts a security job at Thomas Rose Associates to keep his edge. But from the moment he sees Rosalinda, his deep need to serve gets redefined.

He's never belonged to a Mistress. Ros is about to change that.

∾

Meet the Mistresses of Thomas Rose Associates. An intimate circle of women who embrace the challenge of domination—inside the bedroom and *the board room.*

AT HER COMMAND

A Mistresses of the Board Room Novel

JOEY W. HILL

At Her Command

A Mistresses of the Board Room Novel - Book #1

A spin-off series set in the award winning Knight's of the Board Room world.

Copyright © 2020 Joey W. Hill

ALL RIGHTS RESERVED

Cover design by W. Scott Hill

SWP Digital Edition publication June 2020

Digital ISBN: 978-1-951544-06-5

Print ISBN: 978-1-951544-07-2

ACKNOWLEDGMENTS

One of the most important things I learned early in my writing career was that the harder moments in life are the richest source of depth for my writing. This story brought me back to those roots. The way we not only survive and endure, but thrive and embrace life, is by never forgetting what matters most. Love. Even if we aren't as strong as its ideal, we can always strive to adapt and evolve toward it.

I also owe a thank you to a neighbor going through a difficult time, who reminded me of the personal and creative value of those harder moments, and helped sparked the core of Lawrence and Ros's story.

CHAPTER ONE

*S*he was being watched.

Watched by eyes hooded with thick, dark lashes and strong brows, like a bear's. The unrelenting black of the pupils pulled her in, but that didn't frighten Ros.

She'd never been lost in the dark. Quite the contrary.

The man was standing against the rail of Club Progeny's mezzanine level coffee shop and nursing a beer. His ironed button-down shirt was light blue, the sleeves rolled up to expose his forearms. The shirt was tucked into belted jeans. She pictured his underwear as black brief shorts that hugged his ass. She was betting he had a superior one that would flex at the bee-sting kiss of a whip. He wasn't a tall man, but he had broad shoulders and biceps that filled out the shirt. His mahogany-colored beard was neatly clipped, enhancing rather than obscuring the strength of his jaw and corded neck.

She inhaled. Despite the cocktail of perfumes, sweat and other provocative scents surrounding her on the ground level of the club, she vividly imagined the scent of his aftershave. She could do that. Tune out reality, bring the imagined into such sharp focus that it became real to her. It was a useful tool, professionally and personally.

Old Spice. If your grandfather hadn't worn it, you wouldn't exist.

Her lips curved at the remembered slogan. It would work for him. He looked like a complicated man with simple tastes. And he was fixated on her.

Or rather, her shoe.

It sparkled in its lightly bouncing position, because she had her legs crossed. He didn't appear to be absorbed by it in the foot fetish kind of way, though the Italian four-inch heels could inspire that kind of devotion. The delicate leaf pattern of the silver uppers molded to the top of her foot. Gladiator style, they were called. The purple soles picked up the matching hue of the lace sheath she wore. The long sleeves, scoop neck and mid-thigh hem showcased her firm body and excellent legs. The liner beneath the lace was flesh colored, adding to the ways she could tease a man.

The shoes had come from a boutique in a tiny West Virginia town. The operation offered unique designs that looked like works of art. Unfortunately, the place had been on its last legs. She'd given the store an effective, wide-reaching online presence and increased their annual profits exponentially, with the side benefit of a nice bump in tourist traffic to the town. The owner gave her the shoes for free, a personal gift on top of what her marketing firm charged.

"Have you ever had trouble getting a man on his knees, Ros?"

The question brought her attention back to her companions. The three of them were sitting at a table in the socializing area, which still offered a premium view of the club's spacious public play space. She cocked her head at the raptor-featured handsome bastard to her right.

"No. Because getting a man on his knees isn't a problem. It's an opportunity. I went by your building today, Matt. I think it was taller than when I saw it last. Don't you ever get tired of showing off the size of your dick?"

"I need a little more space and breathing room than you do," Matt replied equably. "We haven't added floors, but they have reworked the landscaping around the base."

Ros shot him an amused look. "No doubt. Manscaping *can* change size perception. Very clever of you."

Matt chuckled, but his only response was to take a swallow of his Kentucky bourbon. It didn't matter that they were sitting in a BDSM club and they were both sexual Dominants. Matt Kensington was never coarse in the presence of a woman. Not unless he had her in a state of near orgasmic torment and was whispering in her ear, telling her all the lovely, dirty things he was going to do to her.

"One of these days I'm going to drag a four-letter word out of

2

you," she informed him. "Bring you into the norms of 21st century male-female relations."

"Those norms are overrated. All women should be treated with respect." He swept his gaze over her, a compliment as well as a frank appraisal. "But particularly one like you."

He was relaxed in his chair, his long arm draped along the back of Ros's. The ankle he had resting on his opposite knee meant the bent knee brushed her thigh. The intimacy wasn't inappropriate. They'd been friends for some time, and Matt Kensington was the type of man who exuded unconscious sexual cues. Along with more consciously applied qualities, such as dangerous authority, powerful coldness or a biting sense of humor, capable of cutting up an opponent as efficiently as a guillotine.

He was also deeply in love with his wife, Savannah Tennyson Kensington. Savannah was CEO of another Fortune 500 company. If her husband ever strayed—which would happen *never* times infinity—she was the type of woman who would gut him from balls to gullet with a letter opener.

A truth that didn't conflict with Savannah being a 100% submissive who embraced her husband's dominance.

At one time a strong businesswoman with a submissive orientation would have mystified Ros. She'd also once thought most male Doms needed to bend over a spanking bench and give themselves a taste of what submission at a woman's hands was like. But time had taught her some compelling and often painful lessons.

They were all seekers. In their deep yearning to express themselves as Master and sub, toward one person alone until death do you part, Matt and Savannah had found one another. When a person found what they truly wanted and needed, particularly in this world, that demanded respect and acceptance.

Judge not, lest ye be judged.

After all, she didn't particularly care to be second-guessed by assholes who thought a Domme was a woman who hadn't found a man strong enough to top her the way she "really" wanted.

Her gaze slid back to the man on the mezzanine. He wasn't looking at her like that. She wasn't getting a full-on sub or Dom vibe from him, but definitely something intriguing.

She'd worn the high heels because she wasn't planning on playing tonight. Well, playing hard, that is. But if she changed her mind about that and needed more stability—in order to do things like accurately throw a whip against a willing body—she had square-heeled knee-high suede boots in her locker. A smart woman always kept the right footwear options close to hand for life's unexpected delights.

"I might have an 'opportunity' for you."

That came from the other man at the table, Dale Rousseau. While not a businessman like Matt, he was every inch a Master. A retired Navy SEAL, he ran a local animal rescue, and was married. To Athena, another businesswoman and committed submissive.

Ros smiled. "I suspected this wasn't a casual invitation. So what's up? Professional or personal?"

"Professional first, with a personal possibility," Matt said. "You asked me for recommendations to beef up your security for Laurel Grove. Dale has a man who could do that, and be a personal driver for you."

She sent him a narrow look. "I need enhanced security for LG. Not for me."

"The threat was made against you personally," Matt said.

The men now looked grave. Determined. Protective. White knights, the both of them. "This sudden testosterone surge is making me feel faint," she said. "Catch me if I swoon."

"When you tell a gang lieutenant to stay away from his pregnant girlfriend, the hiring of a bodyguard is good common sense," Matt pointed out. "Particularly when his gang has over a hundred thousand members in nine major U.S. cities, including New Orleans."

"I didn't do it in front of his underlings."

"No. But you also threatened to remove his undersized manhood with your fingernail clippers," Dale added. "A direct quote."

"Abby has a big mouth."

Ros said it without real heat, however, since she knew Abby was genuinely worried about her. She'd said the same things to Ros that these two were saying now. She and Abigail Rose didn't keep secrets from one another, which had strengthened not only their friendship, but the marketing firm they'd founded together, Thomas Rose Associates.

"Ros." Matt touched her shoulder. "She and the rest of your team are smart enough to realize he might come after you. And not just at home. You have thirty employees. Dale's man can upgrade your home and office security while being a personal driver and bodyguard, all for the price of one staff member." His dark eyes twinkled. "Nice for your bottom line. Plus, a driver saves you time and is a nice convenience in NOLA traffic. Keeping you alive just happens to be an added perk."

She sighed and poked at his large hand with her violet-painted fingernails. "Fine. I'm not agreeing yet, but tell me about him."

"He served on the last team I led before I moved out of field work," Dale said. "Exceptional operator. Been with the SEALs since his teens. He got an injury not too long ago. It's not the kind that qualifies him for a handicap sticker, but it knocked him out of being an operator. He decided to take the discharge, but he's been at loose ends since then. He needs a bridge to civilian life."

She'd had plenty of relaxed late-night conversations with Dale over drinks, after sessions. Since SEALs interested her, she'd asked questions. As a result, she knew that a man who made it through BUD/S training in his teen years was pretty damn exceptional. Add to it Matt and Dale's endorsement, and she didn't need anything further to confirm the man was qualified for what they were recommending.

But then Matt looked at Dale as if there was more he wanted the retired SEAL to say. The warning flags went up.

"We could have discussed this at my office, with Abby and the rest of my team's input. Why here?" She shot a sharp look at Dale. "Matt said professional *and* personal. What does that mean?"

His lips tightened into a line. "You're going to notice something else about him. Something that you may want to explore."

She blinked. "He's a sub."

"Maybe. Yes. No." At her raised brow, Dale shook his head. "I picked up on it when we worked together. He hadn't had any direct exposure to this world, so he had no context for it."

"Plenty of people have Dom or sub traits and go through life without the drive to pursue it in this kind of setting. What's made you certain he wants to go that way?"

When asked a complicated question, Dale usually took his time responding, weighing variables. His prompt response now told Ros the answer had already been through that internal grilling. "When I started to suspect it, I had him tag along with me to my regular club.

He wore the non-player bracelet, but I saw the way he watched. And we know it when we see it."

Yes, they did. An experienced Master or Mistress picked up on it like a matching heartbeat. That hunger, the leaning forward, the tension in the muscles. Sometimes a totally new-to-it sub would get so lost in watching what he craved, nothing could distract him. Except the attention or touch of the right Dominant, drawing him away from the window to bring him across the threshold.

She did like that kind of challenge, when it was real, when the sub truly wanted what she had to give. Matt and Dale understood that desire. Like her, their core identity was all about holding a submissive's pulsing soul in the grip of their will, cherishing it, testing it, asking everything from it in order to give everything back. A closed circle of pure sexual and spiritual bliss, when done right.

Her gaze flickered back to her intent watcher. He'd shifted, giving her a hint of the broad shoulder, a tapered waist. He had a body that looked ready to be stretched to the limits of peak endurance.

With reluctance, she brought her attention back to Matt and Dale and frowned. "You're concerned for my safety, but you want me to explore this man's sub side with him. Mixing security with pleasure sounds like a bad idea, and you two don't usually offer bad ideas."

"He'll put the mission first, because that's how he's trained." Dale's flat gaze told her he meant it. "Forgive the bluntness, but he could be balls deep in you, and if there was a threat, he'd be aware of it, on his feet and ready to meet it, faster than you could draw breath. SEALs are trained to notice everything, and evaluate and adapt accordingly."

"How useful. He saves my life and I get to punish him afterward for withdrawing without permission. A win-win."

That earned her a twinkle from Dale's blue-green eyes and a tight smile from Matt, but the men remained somber. They were ready to double down on their determination to persuade her to do what they thought was best for her. Because it was motivated by mutual regard, she wouldn't let it raise her hackles. However, with overprotective men, no matter how well-meaning, a woman had to make sure they understood which decisions were hers to make.

"You could have kept this out of the equation. Left it just business. You know I never lack for companionship when I want it. There's a missing piece."

"I care about the man," Dale said simply. "I think there's an emptiness to him, Ros. I've seen you take men who need what he needs and help them find it. You give yourself what you need at the same time. When you cut them loose, they continue the journey with a better, more balanced sense of themselves. Coming out of the SEALs is difficult. It's going to be harder for him than most."

Another warning flag there. "You think me teaching him to embrace his sub side would be a good distraction?"

"Not a distraction. A way to see himself as more than a SEAL."

"What's his backstory?"

Shadows crossed Dale's eyes. "Complicated. But he's straightforward in the ways that matter."

A complicated man with simple tastes. Well, shit.

"Dale," she said evenly, "is your man standing over near the coffee shop? Light blue shirt, jeans, drinking a Modela?"

Matt tapped his glass to Dale's beer. "Told you."

"I prefer to choose my own bedmates," she said testily.

Dale shrugged. "Since you've been eyeballing each other for twenty minutes, it doesn't sound like I've interfered with that."

"Or you two put the carrot in an optimal position to lead me where you want me to go."

Matt chuckled outright in his Texas-flavored deep timbre. "How long have we known one another? There's no obligation here, Ros. You enjoy a challenge. When you see one here that suits you, you indulge. If you don't wish it to go that way, then drop that element and focus only on the security angle."

She tapped her nails on the table. Despite his inescapable appeal to the opposite sex, Matt wasn't a charmer. He was honest and direct, whether at a board room table or sitting in a club, like now. His evaluation was accurate; she'd been intrigued by the man the moment she noticed him, well before knowing he was here at Matt and Dale's invitation.

But the most significant deciding factor had nothing to do with any of that. Dale was appealing to her as a friend. His concern for his man was genuine.

"Didn't he think it was a little odd, you wanting to do a job interview here?" she asked.

"Didn't tell him it was a job interview." Dale grunted. "I told him

7

you were looking for a security guy, and that he could come along with me tonight, get a sense of you. If it worked out on both sides, you could set up an interview at your company. He's gone with me a few more times to my regular club, though always as a non-player. He never asks to go, but if I offer, he tags along. So tonight probably didn't raise any flags for him."

Ros sighed. "What's his name?"

"Lawrence Barrera Gatlin."

Lawrence, a name whose Latin roots came from a town known for its laurel groves. She knew that, because the mythology behind the laurel was why she, Abby and the rest of the ladies of her executive team had named the domestic violence shelter they'd founded Laurel Grove. It meant refuge, safety, protection. As well as triumph over adversity.

It had also been named after the woman they'd loved. That they couldn't save.

Well, shit. She wished she wasn't the type of person susceptible to signs from the universe. But the universe liked to stick its mega-sized foot up your ass when you ignored those signs.

"All right. Invite him over. Then you two take a hike."

"Yes, Mistress," Matt murmured. She wrinkled her nose at him.

"Mess with me, I'll tell Savannah you flirted outrageously with our big-breasted waitress."

"She won't believe you."

"I'm in marketing. I can convince people to trade their last dime for dogshit."

He chuckled again as Dale made a gesture toward the mezzanine. Ros glanced that way in time to see Lawrence straighten with a nod, another lingering look at her. Then he disappeared into the shop, shouldering past a couple subs she knew. That comparison in body types told her she'd been right about his height. He wasn't a towering six foot plus. He might be about five-seven, five-eight. She was just over five feet in her bare feet, so with her heels, she'd be close to eye level with him.

She preferred to take control of a man far more physically powerful than herself. As he emerged onto the main club floor and came toward their table, she knew that wasn't going to be a problem. The shirt straining over his shoulders and biceps had told her the truth. He was solidly built, all compact muscle. He worked the jeans well with his confident stride. He moved exactly as she expected, a man trained for one of the most elite special forces in the world.

There were more shadows here, so the smooth, close-cropped beard was darker, a roast coffee brown. It matched the simply styled but well-cut hair, layered and clean on the sides and nape. She suspected he'd acquired that style recently, because most active SEALs seemed to keep their hair a little shaggier.

As he reached the table, his eyes brushed over hers, held.

"Munch, this is Rosalinda Thomas," Dale said. "She goes by Ros."

As they regarded one another, Matt and Dale rose. Matt gave her one last slight nod. Then it was just her and Lawrence.

Munch. An interesting nickname. She'd figure that out another time.

As she studied him without saying anything, Lawrence did the same. Maybe it was the venue, or maybe Lawrence took his time studying someone before saying hello. She appreciated the silence.

His eyes were green. Traces of gold highlighted the color, some darker flecks. She wondered if she'd also see glints of blue-gray in there, depending on the light. True green eyes were rare, and usually a compendium of color shades.

As a Mistress, she could study a submissive however long she wished. She wondered what would happen the first time she told him he couldn't look at her until she gave him permission. The thought made her glossed lips curve. The instant flicker of awareness in his gaze ignited an answering tingle in her chest. The anticipation of a beginning.

Ros offered her hand. "Hello, Lawrence."

His closed over hers the way a strong man's did, carefully, but with a firm surety. His fingers were blunt and warm, the cuticles kept trimmed but not manicured. She noted a certain speculation in his expression, as if he were absorbing the way her fingers folded and fit inside the grip of his. She liked being held by a man who knew how to do it. With the right mix of sexual hunger and respect.

"Hello, Rosalinda," he said.

Her smile deepened at the hint of challenge. He'd deliberately ignored Dale's direction about calling her Ros.

He was a sub all right. Just the kind she liked.

CHAPTER TWO

She gestured to the three empty chairs at the four-chair table. "Have a seat."

He pulled out the one to her right, turning it so it was facing her. As he sat down, the spread of his knees flanked her top crossed leg. He was leaning forward, one arm on the table, the other hand draped loosely against his thigh. It was within fingertip reach of her shin bone. Electricity ran through her skin as she thought of him stretching out one of those fingers, running it down that straight line. But she gave him an unamused look, deliberately surveying his proximity.

"Fancy yourself a player, Lawrence?"

"No, ma'am. Lot of white noise out here. Didn't want you to have to strain your voice to be heard." He gave her a half smile. "Didn't want to shout at you, either."

"I rarely have to raise my voice to be understood."

"I expect that's so." He cocked his head. "What can I do for you, ma'am?"

A question with so many answers, particularly in this environment, but she pushed their surroundings away. Instead she focused on what his body language was saying to her, the tone of his voice, his expression. There was an edginess to him, the nerves working beneath the skin. From how intently he was regarding her, there was a deeper drive to his question, whether he realized it consciously or not.

"What do you want to do for me, Lawrence? I don't mean the job. Don't waste my time by playing dumb or claiming you've no personal interest in the things that happen here."

As Dale said, they'd been eying one another for the past half hour. She didn't believe in pointless small talk. He didn't say anything right away, but his expressive eyes inspired her to adjust, drag her nail across the top of that dangling hand. It left a scrape mark, and his gaze flicked to it before coming back to her face.

"Ask me for what you want," she said. "The way *you* feel it."

His mouth tightened. So did his shoulder muscles, his fingers half curling. A man poised, receiving a signal that put him on alert.

"I'd like to know what you want," he said. "The way you feel it. If you're of a mind to tell me."

"I do love the way you deep South boys phrase things," she responded. "I want you to be quiet until I answer your question."

Curiosity crossed his expression, but she noted some of the edginess eased, a good sign.

She relaxed deeper into her chair, her hand now resting on the table at her side as she returned to her leisurely perusal. Those shoulders and biceps were worth an additional look. A side trip across his chest noted the shirt was open one button at the throat, revealing the hint of chest hair. With his shirt sleeves rolled up to the elbows, she could enjoy the close-up look at his forearms. His hands looked strong, the nicks, tan and skin texture indicating a working man. The top knuckle and fingertip of his left-hand pinkie was missing.

He saw her looking. "Dale was a tough Master Chief. Quick to make an example if we dragged our asses."

The sober delivery was diluted by a little sparkle in his green eyes. She smiled. "That seems harsh."

"Naw. I was lucky. You should talk to the fellow on our team with one ear."

Her gaze held his a significant beat. A reproof he understood without words. He went quiet again. She waited another couple beats before speaking.

"You want to know what I want. I want to stretch that beautiful, powerful body of yours against something you can't break. I want to wrap braided rope over your muscles, tie it tight so it will leave marks on your skin when I finally take it off."

She stayed relaxed in her chair, remote. "When you can't move, I'll touch you exactly as I desire. Your voice will get hoarse from cursing, or begging. It's all the same. I won't let you go until you're so exhausted you'll fall into my arms when I take away the bindings. You'll let me care for you in the same way I worked you. Making you give me all of yourself."

He blinked. "Except for that 'fall in your arms' thing, it sounds like my BUD/S instructors. They do their best to kill or train us—whichever comes first."

"So I've heard. I've told Dale next time one of them takes a vacation, I'll be happy to put those boys through their paces."

He chuckled. "They'd flat out let their hearts burst before disappointing you, ma'am."

"I'm not seeing the problem."

His green eyes stayed fastened on hers. Even with the banter, she could see the wheels in his mind turning, replaying her words. He nodded.

"Let's do it."

Her pulse leaped, but a good Domme became good by controlling her impulses. Until it was the right time to unleash them. This wasn't it.

"Not tonight," she said. And waited to see his reaction.

Disappointment, which was gratifying, but also a little set to his jaw that suggested other, less pleasing things. "Is that part of this game? Bait the hook, but leave the fish wriggling on the line?"

She'd been stroking the stem of her wine glass with idle fingers, but now her hand stilled. The shadow that crossed his face told her he recognized he'd just fucked up. But that was fine. It was better to get this out of the way early, before deeper misunderstandings could occur.

She injected coolness in her tone. "Sometimes a man conceals his discomfort with what he's really feeling by saying stupid, kneejerk things he knows are wrong. I don't have a lot of tolerance for a man working out his own shit by taking it out on me."

She paused, but he didn't interrupt her. Points for him. "Some men think this is a good way to have a woman jerk him off, a little kinky play to joke about with his friends later. I'm not a prostitute with an *a la carte* menu. Nor am I a pro-Domme who has to make her client's desires the focus of her time with him. Everywhere I go with a sub is where I want to go. The first time a man tells me to get him off or fuck him, no matter how it's worded, the session is ended as surely as if he safeworded."

"My apologies," he said stiffly, but with real chagrin, which was the only thing that kept her where she was. "I don't know this world."

"You might not know the mechanics, the spoken language, but I think you feel it," she said frankly. "Else you wouldn't have been staring at me the way you were. You feel it deep, where it's never seen the light of day. Am I wrong?"

He shifted. The set of his shoulders looked stiffer. "I don't know, ma'am. I want to say you're wrong. But I'm not sure that's true."

Her gut eased some. If he'd denied the truth, it would have been game over, because it wasn't a game. Not that kind.

"Okay. Are you up for a little exercise?"

"Yes, ma'am."

No hesitation there, though she could see the wheels turning behind his eyes again. Only experience revealed that to her, because he actually had an excellent poker face.

"Show me respect, the way you feel it." She leaned forward in her chair, increasing the power of the lock between their eyes. "The way you *feel* it," she repeated.

Dale and Matt were a few tables away, engaged in conversation. She wanted to see how much their perceptions of him mattered against what his gut was telling him to do.

For a nice, long simmering pause in the universe, his gaze didn't leave hers. Slowly, he backed the chair enough to give him room. He didn't look around to see if Dale and Matt were watching him—first test passed.

Then he went to one knee in front of her.

He put his hand under the purple sole of her shoe, the other curving over her calf. The heated palm slid against her skin as a gradual glide, a man not rushing anything, taking in the sensation.

He eased her leg upward, straightening it from its crossed position. Dipping his head, he pressed his mouth to her flesh, a few inches above the silver leaf design molded around her ankle.

A kiss, a tasting.

Cherishing, worshipping.

Then he added a touch of teeth.

Claiming.

Electric current passed from that contact to the hairline at her nape, and all the right places in between. She laid her hand on his bowed head, fingers and knuckles capturing and stroking the short thickness of his hair. She let herself trace it around his ear, to the pulse point just beneath it. A steady thud, like war drums, focused, intent. Powerful.

There was a subtle vibration to his muscles, a faint trembling. The nerves of a sub who'd made his first step. She thought of that tremor as the collision between the mind's *what-the-fuck* and the heart and soul's whoop of *you-go-boy*.

He lifted his gaze to hers, his mouth still on her. She saw fire, darkness, desire. It made her lips move against one another, a moistening that had his fingers tightening as he saw it.

What was it Dale had said? *SEALs are trained to notice everything, and evaluate and adapt accordingly.*

The energy pulsing between them was more than enough for her to channel, twist and play with it, turn it into something even more marvelous. He kept her leg in those reverent yet possessive hands when he spoke, his voice low and rough. "Why can't we do...what you want to do tonight?"

She managed to sound calm as she tapped her wine glass. "I've had two of these. With a man I already know, who wants soft or medium play, in a familiar scenario, two glasses are a non-issue. For a new man, where it could go a lot of ways, no. My head has to be fully clear."

"I wouldn't let you hurt me." He was as sure of it as men usually were. Underestimating just how easily a Mistress could tear them to shreds.

"If I do what I want to do to you, take your mind where I think it wants to go, you wouldn't be able to protect yourself. I have a responsibility to you, and I take it very seriously. Trust and surrender are what it's all about. Do you like the sound of that?"

His gaze shifted back to her leg and foot. Not like he was lowering it, but as if he was thinking and needed a less distracting focus than her eyes. "I don't know much about any of this,

Rosalinda. It feels a lot different from flirting with a woman in a bar."

"I certainly hope so." She did smile now, changing the energy between them. Glancing up and seeing it, he offered a wary smile in return.

"You have a very nice mouth," she told him. "I could do a lot of wonderful things with it. But think about what I just told you, the specifics. Is there any of that you can't do?"

"I'm capable of a lot of things, ma'am." He paused. "But I really prefer to skip the being tied up part."

Disappointing, but not a deal breaker. "Control issues? Past trauma?" Since he'd been a SEAL most of his adult life, it was very possible he'd been captured, more than once. Imagining that made her gut spike with a low-level anxiety, no matter that he was sitting before her, safe and sound.

"Control issues, yeah, probably. Of a sort. But you won't need to restrain me. Whatever position you want, I'll hold it. No matter what you do to me."

She wondered how long it would take him to realize that every word he spoke gave her vital information. "What does 'of a sort' mean?"

"If I'm tied up, I can't protect you from what comes through the door."

She didn't typically seek out the protective he-man type, but his frank sincerity made her stomach do a nice roll. "Who are you expecting in the middle of an exclusive club where the membership is vetted?"

"Anyone," he said simply.

"Okay. What about sensory deprivation? A blindfold?"

He considered, then inclined his head. "With conditions. In a private room, door secured."

She nodded. "Put one hand on your thigh. Put your other hand on the table, palm up. Don't move it."

He gave her a curious look, but complied, hand slipping away from her leg. Once it was on the table, she rested hers on it, noting the difference. His fingers weren't much longer than hers, but they were broader, the overall look masculine against feminine.

"I understand you have an interest in managing security at my company," she said. "I'll need to talk to my executive team, and they'll want to interview you as well."

"This was an interview?"

"Yes."

"An HR department might throw a fit at your approach."

She thought of Vera, who handled HR and legal matters at their firm, and pressed her lips against a smile. "Maybe. I'm not a fan of the word, Lawrence, because I think it's vastly overused. But do you have any triggers, other than the military based control issues? Chinks in the armor where I could hit a vulnerable place in the wrong way?"

She saw the wall go up, his expression as smooth as glass. "SEALs don't tolerate triggers. We handle what we're given, and we get the job done. No mission failure."

It was the first time he'd lied to her. But that was okay, because it wasn't conscious. The biggest lies people told were the ones they told themselves. She suspected "SEALs don't tolerate triggers" was one he used routinely on himself.

He registered that she considered the response bullshit. A muscle flexed in his jaw, but he said nothing. Just waited.

"All right." She rose, and he rose with her. "Come to my office Thursday morning. Eleven-thirty, if you're still interested in the job."

"If you're leaving, I'd like to walk you to your car. If you'll allow it."

"And if I don't?"

That firm mouth tugged. She really wanted to take a bite of it. "I'll watch from the door, make sure you get in it safe," he said.

When she'd first met Matt Kensington, she'd discovered he had old school habits. If he was seated when a woman approached him, he'd rise. No woman ever touched a doorknob around him. She also had to have a ninja's reflexes to pick up a dinner check before he did.

Calling him sexist didn't change his behavior a bit. She'd realized soon after becoming his friend that Matt loved, respected and cherished women. The Dom side only added to it. He knew who he was, and made no apologies for it.

Since she had a lot of that in herself, she'd come to accept that part of his personality. Over time, it even became part of why she trusted him at her back.

She saw a good deal of those chivalrous qualities in Lawrence, though they had a different twist to them. The kind that had put him at her feet tonight. But she respected that version of it just as much.

"I'll get my things and you can walk me to my car. Thank you, Lawrence."

As she moved away from the table, Lawrence following her, Dale and Matt looked her way. She gave them a nod that conveyed things were going in a good direction, but no real decisions had been made yet. She didn't want the two of them thinking they'd accomplished their goal too quickly.

Matt saluted her with his drink, and then she and Lawrence were headed for the locker rooms. As they descended a short set of stairs, she held onto the banister, but she noted Lawrence's hand near her elbow, just in case.

"Those shoes don't look very stable," he said. "Though you walk like you were born in them."

"My poor mother, if that were true," she responded. "And for your information, Broadway dancers can spin and bound in shoes this high."

"So you're on Broadway, too? Has your mama ever come to watch you on the stage?"

She shot him a mock glare as he offered an innocent smile. "Do you want to walk me to my car or not?"

He lifted his free hand, a truce, and she suppressed the desire to smile back at him. "Dale said you recently left the SEALs."

"Yes, ma'am. Right time for me, I guess."

The stilted brevity confirmed Dale's assessment that the transition hadn't been an easy one.

She went into the locker room, leaving him in the hallway, and retrieved her clutch with her phone. A Domme had a natural craving to turn over every stone in her sub's mind. While she enjoyed navigating the maze of action and reaction, this one was giving her a more intense charge than usual.

As she checked her lipstick and hair in the mirror, she was joined there by Lady Z, a regular at the club, and a self-defined BBW—big, beautiful woman. Her red latex dress enhanced her ample curves. A pattern of bats fanned out from the right hem and spiraled upward, across the waist, up to the shoulder. Black lipstick and makeup enhanced Z's pale skin. She'd topped the look with a headband sporting small, glitter-covered red horns. A voluptuous demon.

Lady Z sent Ros a conspiratorial look. "If that one waiting outside was mine, I'd be smiling like that, too. And if he's not yours, let me know, because I'm going to pivot and head back out there so fast I'll risk whiplash."

Ros chuckled and tucked her lipstick back in her bag. "Not mine. Not yet. He's wearing a non-player bracelet."

"Yet he's waiting for you." The Domme winked at her. "I'll keep my hands off until he decides what he is. And whose."

"Your restraint is much appreciated, Lady Z."

"I can't speak for the other bitches out there, eying him like vultures. Best not leave him alone too long."

What was it that SEALs said? *Roger that.* And good advice, because a non-player bracelet didn't forbid socializing. Yet on principle, Ros made herself take an extra moment to touch up her hair before strolling back out.

Sure enough, two Mistresses were talking to him. Probably asking his background, what brought him here specifically. Things were straightforward in a BDSM environment, no dancing around. They were likely asking the same questions she would have been asking.

So, you're wearing a non-player bracelet. Are you considering the Dom or sub side, or possibly playing as a switch?

They'd listen carefully, looking for cues in his answers that spoke to their own interests, while revealing more about him.

They would assume he was mostly or all hetero, because gay men typically preferred their own exclusive club venue, though a few played here. Her guess was that Lawrence was going to be uncompromisingly straight. Having a sub play with another man was a visual treat, but Lawrence could provide equal stimulation to her without that ingredient in the mix, if it turned out to be a hard limit.

When he saw her, he ended the conversation. Though he did it politely, he looked relieved to see her. Lawrence might be ready to let his alpha sub side out of the closet, but she expected he'd prefer it to happen initially in private. Ideally, in a bedroom. The room closest to that closet.

He'd have to settle for a private club room, because she wasn't in the habit of inviting men into her home. Yet surprisingly, when she visualized him in her bedroom, it spiked her blood and imagination.

The Mistresses looked her way. They tossed her different versions of Lady Z's knowing smile and wandered on. Lawrence came to her side, putting a hand under her elbow again as they started up the stairs. Not a direct touch, just the awareness that his support was there, available.

"Are you married, Lawrence?"

He shot her a startled look. "No, ma'am. I'd be kind of an asshole if I was. Right?"

She shrugged. "We have married people here who can't fulfill this need at home. Some come with the consent of the spouse. Others don't feel they can tell them."

"So you've had relationships with married men?"

She tsked. "A lot of judgment in that wording and tone."

"Intended, ma'am."

She stopped at the top of the stairs and faced him. "That sounds personal. Has someone cheated on you?"

That muscle flexed in his jaw. "Yes and no. There were extenuating circumstances."

"Hmm." She resumed walking toward the exit. "I don't engage in sessions with married submissives whose spouses aren't in the loop. Their reasons are their own, and may have validity for their own circumstances, but it's my personal preference. I demand total honesty from a sub. If I'm dealing with someone who doesn't view 'love, honor and cherish' as a mandate to be truthful with their significant other, then I know we don't share the same life philosophy."

His expression relaxed. As he pushed open the door for her from the locker area to the foyer, his hand grazed her lower back. She nodded to the submissive at the front desk, a woman dressed mannishly in Victorian butler wear, her hair slicked back tight to her head.

As Ros stepped outside the club, she glanced down, a personal grounding ritual she did when entering or exiting Progeny. The decorative steppingstones embedded in the concrete walkway formed an arrow that started wide at the parking lot and narrowed to a point in front of the entryway. On each of the stones was a saying or instruction relevant to what happened here. One of her favorites was the one she stood upon now.

Regard. Respect. Care.

He'd followed her glance. "When the owners of the club re-poured this walkway," she said, "they decided to put in the stones, let contributors pay for them and choose the content. As people move between the parking lot and the building, the words plant ideas to keep in mind when we're engaging with one another."

"SEAL training has something like that." His eyes tracked the different quotes. "Laying down the principles as they're breaking you down, so that you know what ropes will hold you when you're hanging over the abyss." He nodded to the one before him. *"'Love covers a multitude of sins.'* That's a good one. Unexpected, considering it's from the Bible."

"Why? Because there are some Christian sects that treat sex as a sin? Particularly alternate expressions of sexuality?

"Yeah, pretty much."

"Do the SEALs operate on any biblical premises?"

Lawrence's eyes turned to hers, steady, unblinking. "Yeah. Plenty. John 15:13. *'Greater love than this no one hath, that one should lay down his life for his friends.'"*

That odd gut punch of reaction again. She didn't like imagining him in harm's way. She had her hand on his forearm. "I'm glad you haven't had to prove your greater love in that way."

"Me too. I would have missed tonight." He nodded toward the parking lot as they moved in that direction. "Which one are you?"

"That one." She gestured to the red 2017 Ford Mustang convertible.

"Muscle car. Figures."

"How so?"

"Controlling all that power with the lightest of touches."

She sent him a smile. "I like you, Lawrence."

"Same goes, Rosalinda."

"You're not going to call me Ros, are you?"

"No ma'am." He turned to face her as they reached the car door. "Some names give you the feel of something. You can't call a willow 'will,' and see this graceful tree in your mind." His gaze swept over her. "You're a Rosalinda, head to toe."

"Hmm." He wouldn't give up control easily, but he wanted to do so. She could feel the craving pushing against her. Not just for her, but for what he knew she was, what she wanted from a male. She knew the difference between a man who challenged the queen because he thought he could knock her off her throne, and the one who did it because he needed her to compel his bended knee in front of it.

She unlocked the door with a quick chirp of noise, and he opened it for her. But before she slid into the driver's seat, she decided to move closer to him, lay a hand on the resilient curve of his upper arm.

"Stay still," she murmured. "I want to taste you, but you don't have permission to taste me back. Not yet. No biting, either."

He gave her that slow, closed-lipped smile, before her own lips were on it, testing the firmness, the taste of him. Her cheek brushed the slight roughness of his five o'clock shadow above his beard line. She tasted butter mint, felt heat, a quiver under her palm as his hand lifted but then lowered, obeying her order. She moved in closer, thighs brushing his, and slid her touch along his lower back and up, following the valley of the spine.

She wished he wasn't wearing a tucked-in shirt so she could have tested his reaction flesh to flesh, but this would do for now. That quiver of tension increased, particularly as she rubbed one thigh deliberately against his. Her breasts brushed his chest. Just the tips.

His lips parted under the pressure of hers, and she sampled the mint and heat directly. When she eased back, he leaned toward her before he realized what he was doing and stopped. His green eyes were filled with heat.

"A man is always ready to come to bed with a woman," she noted. "But knowing he accepts that he has to wait, that's a heady feeling. Particularly if he doesn't give himself any relief at all, until she tells him he can. Or she takes that release for her own pleasure."

The green eyes flared, and she pursed her lips. "It's up to you, Lawrence. Imagination and reality are equally wonderful things. When I touch myself tonight, I'll think of you taking yourself in hand, coming all over your fist, as you fantasize about all the things you want to do for me."

Just visualizing it gave her a shiver. He saw it, his eye for detail as good as any Dom's. She liked that, though she put a hand on his chest, anticipating his movement forward and reminding him of boundaries.

"As much as I like that," she said, "I like the idea of you denying yourself even more. Because that's also something you can do for me."

She slid into her car and closed the door, lowering the window when she turned over the engine. He put both hands on the edge, his gaze all over her, the desire in his face plain. She resisted it, though it wasn't easy putting the car in drive, letting it start to roll, watching his hands slip away from her.

"Your choice. No penalty for giving in to your imagination." She tossed him a look. "But denial might earn you something even better."

CHAPTER THREE

*a*s Lindi finished her presentation on her strawman client, Ros was slowly somersaulting her pen over her fingers, touching the ends to her notepad. Back, point, back, point. Abby sent her a subtle look that included both amusement and admonishment. She always knew what Ros was thinking. Since that was a two-way street, Ros knew what the admonishment was.

Go easy. She's an intern.

Several years ago, they'd entered into a co-op work agreement with the area colleges for three business internships per quarter. On the interns' first day, Ros always injected a caveat into her welcome speech.

"Criticism is a teaching tool. If I make you cry, go to the bathroom and cry. But prove to me you're worth my time by drying your own tears and learning from the feedback. Skill comes from experience, which includes failure and mistakes."

Today was the mid-point of the quarter. Two weeks ago, the interns had been challenged to choose a "client," and offer a viable marketing strategy for their product to the executive team at TRA.

The preceding two presentations had been decent, the students demonstrating that they'd absorbed a satisfactory level of information from the first six weeks of the internship. Now it was Lindi's turn.

Ever since Bambi, giving girls names that sounded too precious should have been outlawed. In Ros's opinion, it sentenced them to a life of not being taken seriously by anyone, including themselves.

Lindi clicked off the laser pointer she'd been using with her painstakingly prepared Power Point presentation. She beamed at them with an earnest mommy-always-loves-me expression that said no one in the world would ever pee in her cornflakes. Ros half expected her to take out her phone and do a selfie for social media. *"Here's me, rocking the presentation at my co-op job."*

"Lindi, your product is a cheap Barbie knockoff," Ros said. "The hair falls out after about a month of use, and the movable arms and legs break in half that time. Correct?"

Lindi's smile faltered. "I guess so. I didn't really..."

"Didn't think about buying the product off the shelf and seeing what it was really like? Comparing it to online reviews?"

"I studied the client's product site. Learned the specs."

"But you didn't put your hands on it. How do you sell something you haven't physically touched or used yourself? Let's move past that. Based on my description, is this a product you would buy for a niece or nephew?" Or herself, since Lindi looked barely old enough to be past the doll stage.

"Uh..." Lindi's dark brown gaze darted around the room, a flush tinting her bisque-colored cheeks.

"Stop looking for cues for the right answer. Tell me what you *think*. Unless your brain is just to maintain a head shape for that cute hair style."

Lindi swallowed. Abby stepped in, toning it down. Their usual balance of good exec, total bitch exec.

"Ros isn't trying to put you on the spot, Lindi. When we think about representing a client, we start with our own opinion of what they're selling. Tell us what you think about this product. Would you buy it for a loved one?"

Lindi settled some, a frown capturing her frosted lips. "No. Probably not. Unless I had a child who wanted a Barbie, but I couldn't afford one."

"A lower income demographic will find this kind of doll at the dozen types of dollar stores out there. They don't need our marketing skills for that." Ros stabbed the table with her pen, a pointed rap. "Marketing tells a potential customer why the product is worth their money. If we don't believe it's worth anything ourselves, then we don't sign the client. Honesty isn't just a moral compass. If you truly believe in a product, you will work that much harder to ensure its success."

Despite what she'd said to Matt about convincing people to buy dogshit, that was exactly the type of marketing Thomas Rose Associates didn't do. "Now, let's move on to your strategy. The rollout is sound, but you're missing some foundation blocks. The client has social media platforms, a newsletter, advertisements. Before you put this together, did you review all of those, to see how they've been marketing themselves, what kind of style and voice they're projecting?"

"Um, that would take a lot of time. In my model, they're only paying for twenty-five hours of marketing."

"That's correct. But if you're working for me, then you'd be salaried. Which means a certain number of your forty plus hours a week should be dedicated to getting to know your client, to make sure those twenty-five hours are top quality work. If their profits increase from your efforts, it ups the odds they put us on permanent retainer. At which point you get a percentage bonus for achieving that goal."

Ros was pleased to see the girl trying to digest that, despite flushed cheeks and a hyperawareness of the five sets of eyes on her. Changing direction during a presentation when the client wasn't responding well to it required information processing while under intense scrutiny. She gave the girl one more hard push to test it.

"The more you give, the more you get. Whereas the less you give, the more corners you cut, the more likely it is your client will decide they've received a generic, cookie cutter effort. And your employer will decide you're better suited for a mindless job to pay for your cappuccino addiction. Got it?"

Lindi swallowed. The laser pointer was clutched in tense fingers. "Um... Yes, Ros."

"Good. I want you to re-work this, present it again next week. If you have any questions, ask Abby."

"Um..."

"And for God's sake, surgically excise that syllable from your presentation skills," Ros said flatly. "It makes you sound like you're apologizing for existing."

"Um—sorry, I mean..." Lindi's eyes had that pre-cry glassiness to them, but she pushed the question out. "If you're the one who has issues with my presentation, shouldn't I ask you the questions?"

"A good point, Lindi," Abby said. "But often you might not have direct access to the top executive. You have to ask the right questions of a go-between."

"Agreed," Ros interjected. "But in this case, I can make the time. Shoot the questions to my email. If we need to talk over the phone, we will."

"Yes, ma'am." Lindi collected her laptop and fled. As the door to the board room closed behind her, Abby swiveled her chair toward Ros. "She'll be in the bathroom for the next half hour, texting her friends about how awful her internship is."

"Maybe not." Ros pursed her lips. "She held it together, and that was a good question there, at the end. She shows promise. Of the three of them, she had the best command of marketing mechanics and analysis."

Now Lindi just needed to understand the heart of it. Ros wanted to see her succeed. Her team knew that about her, which was why they gave her crap. Like right now.

"Actually, Ros wasn't nearly as bitchy as usual on a presentation day," Cyn pointed out. "I think she got lucky at the club the other night."

"Haven't we discussed keeping these inappropriate comments to a minimum?" Vera sighed.

Cyn crossed her eyes at her. "I bet Ros got well and truly fucked. Better?"

Vera rolled her eyes and Cyn raised her brows. "What? Where I grew up, 'fuck' isn't a bad word. Respect my culture, bitch."

Ros pressed her lips against a smile. "Skye, you with us over there?"

As Skye's fingers flew over her laptop keyboard, a mannerly Michael Caine-esque British accent emerged from the computer.

I think you met someone. No sex or chains yet. Just a meet and greet.

That was Skye. Always intuitive.

"Yes and no," Ros said.

Four pairs of shrewd eyes turned her way, coupled with expectant expressions. "I've received a recommendation for a vetted security expert from Matt Kensington and Dale Rousseau," she said. "I met him at Club Progeny. He was their guest. Former SEAL."

She glanced at Abby. "Did you really think getting the two testosterone towers to gang up on me would work?"

"Not at all," her partner said. "But I had a feeling you would listen to logic and sense, as long as it didn't come out of my mouth."

"Or if it came out of the mouths of two testosterone towers," Cyn said, and ducked as Ros chucked the pen at her. "Has Matt come to his senses and decided to try the submissive side of the whip?"

"Absolutely. In your most wild-ass fantasies." Ros looked toward Abby again. "I'm considering using this recommendation of theirs as a personal driver and bodyguard—temporarily—until the gang nonsense blows over. Just to make you all feel better."

The intercom on the board room phone buzzed. Even without the annoying leap of adrenaline, Ros knew why Bastion, their office manager, was giving them a heads up.

She punched the button with another pen. She brought several to meetings, probably due to the likelihood of them being thrown at her executive team. A crescent of tiny dimples in the table marked her spot at the head of it, thanks to her habit of using them to punctuate her more emphatic points. The way she'd done with Lindi. "Yes, Bastion?"

"Lawrence Gatlin is here, Ros."

"Excellent. We'll be with him in a moment."

"No rush at all," he drawled. "I'll get him some coffee and keep him company."

"I'm sure you will," Ros said dryly and cut the connection. At the curious looks around the table, she explained. "Mr. Gatlin is easy on the eyes."

She paused, rolling the pen over her fingers one more time. The others waited her out. The benefit of having a management team who were all sexual Dominants was that they caught a lot of subtle details, personally and professionally.

"Dale believes he's a closet sub," she said. "After meeting him, I agree. We're going through the initial steps of the dance, but if it goes down that road...he's mine."

She wasn't calling dibs like an overeager adolescent. Not exactly. If he was going to pursue this, it would be with her. They'd already made the connection.

"Is that another reason Matt and Dale..." Abby began.

"Yes."

Abby frowned. "I don't want him distracted when he should be watching your ass. For security purposes, that is."

"It won't be a problem. Dale assured me of it. If anything, that might make him more diligent."

Abigail didn't look completely convinced, but she shrugged. "Well, let's have him, then."

"On the table, with chocolate sauce," Cyn muttered.

"I was thinking a creamy alfredo," Skye's British choice intoned. "Nice and hot. Make him squirm a bit."

"Please don't instigate sexual harassment claims today," Vera said, swiping through screens on her tablet. "Me and my team are already buried under employee evaluation forms and client contracts." She aimed her stylus at Abby. "You owe me five evaluations, and you're three days overdue."

"Is it sexual harassment if we haven't hired him yet? And won't he be more of a contract employee?" Cyn said.

"I'm pretty sure there's nothing in employment law that says harassment is okey-dokey if it's only an interview candidate or contractor," Vera retorted.

"Well, that's very short-sighted." Cyn sniffed. "They should think about changing that."

Ros noted Abby's creased brow and worried expression and suppressed a sigh. She wished Abby would get married, have kids, so she could unload all those overprotective instincts on them. Unfortunately, Abby was never going to do either of those things.

Remembering that, and why, was enough to soften Ros's irritation with her best friend. She hit the intercom button.

"Send him up, Bastion."

"If I must."

Ros chuckled. "Maybe you need to have that discussion with Bast," she told Vera, who just shook her head.

"There are some causes that are hopeless," she said.

When they heard the two men approaching, Ros adopted a mask of purely professional interest.

After shooting Abby a cross-eyed look, and sticking her tongue out the side of her mouth like a crazy person. Which meant her too-serious partner was chuckling as the door opened.

~

Lawrence had never spent so much time thinking about a job interview. He told himself that it was because it was his first one in the civilian world, post-SEALs.

Yeah, right.

The day after meeting Rosalinda at Club Progeny, he'd stood in front of his closet twenty damn minutes, to pick out khakis and a casual jacket to go over a white dress shirt. No tie. New Orleans wasn't a formal suit world, most of the time. He gave the shirt an extra ironing, hung the whole ensemble in the corner of his closet, and turned his attention to more important things.

Dealing with Rosalinda Thomas and her security required upfront intel gathering. During the time between the club meet and the upcoming interview, he did some serious research. On a security job, there was no such thing as too much information on your assigned VIP, or who might be after them.

This time, that research had a different component he couldn't ignore. From the second he'd seen her at the club, she hadn't left the top level of his mind.

Those shoes had caught his attention first, like the glint off a rifle scope. The multicolored lights that artfully spotlighted different areas of the club had created sparkles on them.

He'd never seen shoes like that, and the woman who wore them... he'd never seen anything like her, either. White-blond hair with dark tips that curled under and rested on her shoulders, straight wisps framing eyes shadowed and mascaraed to enhance their glittering mystery. They'd looked dark, but when he'd gotten close enough, he'd found they were a deep blue, a stunning but natural enough color to be her irises, not contacts.

Her mouth... Jesus, that mouth. Wet and full, yet round and contained and pretty much perfect, like a half-opened rose. Rosalinda Thomas. She was aptly named.

She had killer legs. Any man who could look at them and not

imagine them wrapped around his ass as he drove into her was gay, or a monk so devoted to God he qualified for immediate sainthood.

She was around forty years old. The short lace dress she'd been wearing had shown off nice-sized breasts and sweetly flared hips, both in proportion to her toned body. Everything about her said she was self-contained, self-disciplined, and very sure of herself. And she had the track record to support that confidence.

Rosalinda Thomas and Abigail Rose made their reputation as a marketing team when they designed and executed plans for several companies who, before that, hadn't been household names. Now they were. After that, they could have set their salary with any of the biggest firms in New York City, including the one where they'd worked. Instead they'd chosen to leave that company, come to New Orleans, and open their own firm.

Since then, interestingly, they'd rejected more clients than they'd accepted. The *Wall Street Journal* joked there was a waiting list to be represented by TRA, but Lawrence suspected it wasn't really a joke at all. They improved the bottom line of any client they signed.

No marriages, no kids, for either one of them. They also had no family history in New Orleans, though Abigail was born in Baton Rouge. Since Rosalinda had gone to NYU, Lawrence assumed she was a New York native. Her accent wasn't Southern, but it wasn't strong north of the Mason Dixon, either. It was smooth, melodious, like she was rolling a sugar cube over her tongue as she spoke. He suspected she had purposefully softened the northern angles of her speech to accommodate her southern environment. Over time, that had become a permanent change.

He found what had evidently brought her and Abigail to NOLA in a society column from some years back. It was a wedding piece for Todd and Laurel Markingham. Todd Markingham was a grandson in an old New Orleans money family. A photo taken at the reception showed Laurel Markingham, formerly Laurel Bourbon, with Ros and Abigail. The caption beneath read: "Mrs. Todd Markingham, with NOLA area marketing executives Abigail Rose and Rosalinda Thomas, bridesmaid and maid of honor, respectively."

Laurel Grove. That was the name of the domestic violence shelter they ran. As he went looking, he was already bracing himself, because he'd known the second he looked at a shot of the wedded couple. The set of the guy's mouth, the way he leaned into Laurel as she had a hand on his chest. Most would focus on the intimacy cues, the way the day's happiness was reflected in their expressions. But when you knew the signs, grainy newsprint couldn't blur certain details. Sure enough, several years later, Laurel and Todd hit the papers again.

"Ah, shit."

"Society wife drowned by husband; Todd Markingham confesses to murder."

The Markingham family expressed their horror in typically guarded ways, but Todd's grandmother wasn't as cagey. *"He always had trouble when he drank. He's a good boy when he's sober."*

At that point, Lawrence took a break from surfing to prop his elbows on his kitchen table and scrub at his face. He had to drive things out of his head that had nothing to do with him taking this job.

Laurel was why Ros and Abigail had started their shelter. The shelter that was now the source of Rosalinda's security issues. Thanks to Matt's connections to key members of the NOLA and Baton Rouge police departments, Lawrence was able to read up on the gang that could be gunning for her. Reading that file had parked a ball of ice in his gut.

Before Hurricane Katrina, New Orleans hadn't had much in the way of organized gangs, but since the storm, that had begun to change. Over the past several years, the Death Dealers out of Atlanta had been establishing a presence.

Snake Sampson was fairly high in the gang's pecking order. Pria, his pregnant girlfriend, had decided she didn't want her baby growing up in that life. She'd told him he could leave the gang to be with her, or they were done. His response had been to have two of his buddies hold her still while he punched her in the face several times, knocking out her teeth and breaking her nose. To protect the baby, he'd studiously avoided hitting her below the neck.

Who said chivalry was dead?

What concerned Lawrence was how calculated the act had been, intended to send a wider message while giving Snake a controlled outlet for his rage. Snake thought his violence through. According to his contemporaries, he'd earned his street name because he struck when his enemies weren't expecting it. It was why he was a righthand lieutenant at the ripe old age of twenty-five. He'd also moved here from Atlanta, a job relocation plan for the Death Dealers. He'd grown up in the gang life.

After reading that file, Lawrence gave serious thought to camping on Rosalinda's doorstep until the interview. Fortunately, a follow up call to Dale and Matt helped him tone down that reaction.

During their initial push to get her to beef up her security, reinforced by her business partner's concerns, Ros had followed their advice to scramble her work and social schedules. She'd also tartly revealed she had a concealed-carry permit for a Walther. She'd taken and aced several self-defense courses.

Abby had confirmed with Matt that Ros wasn't one of those people who never activated her installed security system; if she was in the house by herself, it was on. Because of her bond with Abigail, she'd promised to take extra care in her daily movements, and Abby believed Ros wasn't just paying her lip service.

She doesn't bullshit me, Abby had told Matt and Dale.

Sometimes gang members were smart enough to know when they shouldn't make a big deal of something. This might or might not be one of those situations. But her insult had been personal, which meant retaliation, if it was coming, would be, too. Snake would want to do it himself.

If he lived up to his reputation, Snake's plan for that would be sometime in the future, when he deemed her guard was down. But not so far in the future that he'd leave the insult hanging unanswered for too long. Or let his girlfriend slip beyond his grasp.

All of which gave Lawrence a narrow window of opportunity to augment and restructure her security in a manner that would derail Snake's plans. Hopefully long enough he'd lose interest and move on.

Or make a mistake that landed his worthless ass in prison.

~

So, yes, he'd had to handle the time until the interview managing the unease that came with waiting for an op to start, hoping no variables changed drastically before the planning for it went to waste. But he'd made it to the day without turning into a stalker.

He didn't stop thinking about her, though, and that was all right.

It was a nice change of pace from the incessant thought treadmill concerning the things in life he couldn't change.

He arrived at the Garden District location for Thomas Rose Associates early and parked his 2010 silver Dodge Charger a couple streets down. As he approached on foot, he studied the building.

Thomas Rose Associates operated out of a ten thousand square foot home built in 1860. According to the engraved plate on the wrought iron fence that surrounded the property, the building had been designed by Henry Howard, the same guy who'd designed the famous Corn Stalk house.

The iron fence had flowers in the design and sharp top spikes. While the gate could be climbed over—carefully—there was a code latch on it, which he approved of.

In this pricy part of NOLA, the police patrolled regularly, and neighbors paid close attention to who was wandering about. Mostly. There were always groups of tourists, so this house and those around it saw plenty of foot traffic.

It had a slew of windows, upper and lower level. The lower ones were a good eight feet tall, with rounded tops. They had sheers, but people could be seen moving around inside.

Snake might consider rattling her with a drive-by. Spraying those lower windows with assault rifle fire would do a lot of rattling. But it would also start a total shitstorm. His gang had businesses to run, after all, and that kind of thing would result in a city-wide shakedown of criminal elements.

The grounds inside the gates were a lawn-and-garden magazine spread, with lots of frowsy azaleas, live oaks dripping with Spanish moss, and artful flower arrangements in pots and dotting the natural areas.

When he pressed the button at the gate, the response was immediate.

"Welcome to Thomas Rose Associates. Do you have an appointment?"

That had to be her office manager, Bastion Lake. The deep voice possessed a heavy Southern accent that reminded Lawrence of that kid in the *Tokyo Drift* installment of the *Fast and Furious* franchise. The one who went on, ironically, to star in *NCIS: New Orleans*. What was his name? Lucas Black.

Lawrence was pleased the intercom wasn't being manned by some perky Southern magnolia secretary who wouldn't give a gang member the slightest pause. Except to consider how fuckable she was. His analysis wasn't sexist. That Southern magnolia might have a black belt, carry a nine- millimeter and be able to kick a gang member's ass. However, the most successful security measures discouraged an attack up front. An ounce of prevention was worth a pound of cure.

"Lawrence Barrera Gatlin. I have an appointment with Rosalinda Thomas."

"Yes, you do. Glad you're here. Come on in."

The latch buzzed and he was through. When he let the gate go, it closed with force. No creaky half-assed swing where the lock didn't catch.

The uneven brick walkway had probably been repaired at some point, but they'd maintained the pre-Civil War look. Along the short path to the door were a couple stone benches, and a fountain where a concrete fish emitted a graceful spout of water over its head. He noted several paths disappeared through the screen of azaleas on either side of the house.

Detouring to those areas, he discovered additional sitting spots, maybe for staff breaks or client meets on pretty days. One of the spaces had a statue of a male with a very strategically placed spray of leaves over his groin. More sculpted vegetation climbed up his leg and thigh, forming a nest for the squirrel perched on his open palm. The plaque beneath said *Sylvan, Nature God.*

Taking in the coy dip to the man's head, the sensual smirk on his face, Lawrence decided an appreciation for Greek mythology wasn't what had attracted Rosalinda to that particular piece.

Returning to the front, he mounted the stairs to the porch. The wide pair of double doors had glass panels on either side that didn't thrill him, but they were narrow, and the door looked as solid as he could wish.

There was a security panel here as well, this time with the installing company's logo on it. Not top of the line, but good enough to discourage run-of-the-mill burglars. There were monitors on the window latches. As he stepped in, he heard a soft chime from the one on the door frame.

The foyer was the front desk area. Open French doors on either side revealed spacious rooms. Those original living or dining areas had been converted into office space, a puzzle arrangement of desks, populated with about a dozen people on each side. They were busy at computers, on the phone, or meeting in clusters in front of white boards, discussing things with an amiable enthusiasm.

He liked the space. It reflected warmth, beauty and comfort, mixed with success and pride. That opinion didn't change as he brought his attention back to the foyer. The staircase to the upper level curved along the wall, the chandelier dropped down beside it like the stamen at the center of a furled flower. It wasn't in use at the moment, though, the cream-colored walls transformed to butter yellow by the sunlight coming through the windows.

The floors were polished dark wood, the walls mounted with colorful, eye-catching pieces by local artists. The largest one was behind the reception desk, a painting of the French Quarter. Carriage horses, street players and the buildings were portrayed in bold, dynamic colors.

"Gorgeous, isn't it? It's a Dianne Parks."

Bastion Lake rose from behind the desk. He was six feet tall, with assessing brown eyes and dark hair tied back in a neat tail. His slacks and dress shirt showed a body that didn't look afraid of a fight. Good.

Before Lawrence could respond, a young woman came hurrying down the staircase, her shoulder-length mane of gold and black curls quivering around a strained face. She was clasping her laptop to her chest, and her eyes were suspiciously bright. She cut her gaze away from the two of them, made an abrupt right turn and disappeared into the office space on that side.

"Now that Ros has finished decimating one of our interns, she should be ready for you soon," Bastion said, unruffled. "Did you bring chocolate?"

"Will it help? Or will it just give her an excuse to get close enough to bite me?"

The male's eyes warmed on him. "That's not always a bad thing, Mr. Gatlin."

No, it sure as hell wasn't.

CHAPTER FOUR

*B*astion invited him to have a seat in one of the comfortable chairs and offered coffee or pastry, which Lawrence declined. Though Bastion didn't disguise his appreciation for Lawrence, he quickly returned to his other responsibilities.

Lawrence wasn't surprised that a dedicated Mistress like Ros hired a man to be her office manager. But the deciding factor in the hiring decision had to have been his competence. The admin bounced between phone, computer and the continuous flow of random requests from the offices effortlessly. If the guy had a crew cut and was a lot less fashion-conscious, he'd hold his own with a SEAL team logistics officer.

Staring at people made them act abnormally, so Lawrence leafed absently though a New Orleans lifestyle magazine. Instead of reading what was on the pages, though, he logged the faces of the staff, the names he overheard, the bits of data that their conversations gave him.

Lawrence imagined Ros's voice among them, that same rolling-sugar-in-her-mouth purr, maybe with a more business-like edge. Thinking about it got him more than a little worked up. After the club, he'd really wanted to take himself in hand, release a couple times in the shower. In his bed. Instead, he'd made himself a late-night sandwich and found a marathon of B-horror films to watch, because he was too restless to sleep.

She'd left him the choice, after all. Just looking at her, talking to her, had given him plenty of fantasies. Yet as strong as those were, he couldn't get past thinking about what she'd consider a reward for denying himself.

Something deeper also kept him from doing it, something beyond reward or punishment. He'd decided not to plumb that too deeply. From what he'd learned, both personally and as a SEAL, certain types of analysis could just drive a man batshit.

"Mr. Gatlin, they're ready for you. Please follow me."

Bastion rose, signaling to a woman just inside the French doors on the right side. She raised a hand in acknowledgement, even as she kept talking on the phone. Since she had a direct view of Bastion's command center, she must be taking over front desk duties until he returned. Another tick in the approval box. The monitoring might be casual, but at least they didn't leave the front entrance wholly unsupervised.

Lawrence followed Bastion up the elegant staircase to the third level. The wide hallway was laid with more dark wood floors and protected by a Persian-style carpet runner. Bastion stopped at a pair of antique double doors with solid blue, green and red stained-glass panes. One of the doors stood partly open. Lawrence heard women talking, a ripple of laughter punctuated by Rosalinda's. Heat stroked over his skin.

He really should have given himself that orgasm. The last time he'd been this terrified of getting a full erection in front of a bunch of people was junior high school.

Bastion gestured to him to enter the room, shooting him a cryptic smile and a parting reassurance. "Don't worry; we keep a first aid kit on premises."

Lawrence raised a brow and watched the guy stride off. He walked with the confident, long strides of a pro-wrestler, not an office drone. Yet he was already tapping his earpiece to answer another call. "Thomas Rose Associates. How may we help you?"

Lawrence turned away and stepped over the threshold of the board room.

"Mr. Gatlin. Thank you for coming."

It was Abigail Rose who spoke, warm as a home-cooked meal. She had left her chair to come to the door and now, as she gestured to the

37

others, she laid a light reassuring hand on his arm, a gesture of welcome.

The woman's website photo wasn't a touch-up. She was insanely beautiful. Shimmering red hair, cat-shaped hazel eyes. Her trim business suit molded a body that looked intended by God's design to wear satin lingerie that barely contained the curves, all while she sprawled with sensual abandon amid a nest of white pillows, a come-hither look in her eyes.

Yet it wasn't her that held his attention after the courteous greeting. At the head of the table, Rosalind met his gaze. She wasn't smiling, but her eyes were intent upon him, and he was far too aware of the many different things that gaze could mean.

Show me respect, the way you feel it.

He was facing a test here, offering proof that he could keep business and pleasure separate. And not just to her. As Abigail made the introductions, he could tell she was doing her own assessment. Abigail was the one most concerned about Rosalinda, the most protective of her. Enough to push security on her boss even when Ros didn't think she needed any. That push had been backed by this team, all of them closely bonded to Rosalinda.

Cyn Marigold, Veracity Morgan, Skye Sumner. Veracity handled legal and HR. Skye was their IT and communications person. Abigail did the books and shared some responsibilities with Cyn, who managed the project teams. Rosalinda oversaw all of it, as well as being the lead on sales, acquiring and managing new accounts.

No other woman in the room had Abigail's movie star looks, but every one of them was a head turner.

Veracity's chestnut skin contrasted with the black curtain of hair that fell down her back. She had it cropped short to the crown on either side, revealing ears framed by a cuff of rings. Her silk blouse and tailored slacks mixed the professional with the provocative. Her tasteful silver jewelry included a gleaming pentagram pendant that rested above her cleavage. She had light-colored eyes and wet crimson lips.

Cyn's riotous curly brown hair framed wide, thick-lashed brown eyes. Her direct gaze held a man like a hook through his testicle sac, a promise that she'd tug or yank without warning. Her slacks and sleeveless cotton shirt hugged lean curves. The several necklaces of varying lengths dangling from her slim neck bore fleur-de-lis charms made from different colored metals.

Skye had spiky blond hair, longish on one side, shaved short on the other. It enhanced the childlike look of her moon-shaped face, until he met her dark, fathomless eyes. They belonged to a Fae spirit, one who could lock a man into her gaze and whisk him into her world for a century.

As he logged input from each very brief face-to-face, an unsettling realization was building in the back of his mind. The feminine power-saturated air tapped him on the shoulder like an insistent monkey, saying, "Do you see it? Do you see it?"

Yeah, he saw it. And felt it, with a hellishly distracting certainty.

Every one of them was a Domme. *Goddamn.*

They pinged his radar in that familiar-to-the-soul way that Rosalinda did. He was in a room with five women who'd be happy to strap him down on this table and make a full course meal of him. Bastion's parting remarks about first aid kits might not have been a joke.

When Lawrence met Rosalinda's gaze once more, his pulse rate had increased. The slight curve to her lips, her blue eyes sharp as a knife edge, told him she liked that he'd figured it out so fast.

"Please have a seat, Mr. Gatlin." Abigail said it with enough emphasis that he guessed it was the second time she'd said it.

Way to go, Gatlin. He jerked himself back on point. He needed to get his damn head in the game and keep it there. Or call it game over and turn the job over to someone else. Because even if Rosalinda didn't think she needed better security, he and everyone else in this room knew she did.

He didn't like the idea of anyone else taking charge of her protection, which was an alarm flag on its own. But down range, abandoning the mission was the last resort. Until then, you worked the problem, figured it out.

Yeah. But you're not down range. You're here, in the back-home world. Which is where you usually get your ass handed to you.

He shut that voice down with extreme prejudice. Abigail had pointed him to the chair beside Skye, which put him at the opposite end of the table from Rosalinda, surveying all of them. Once he was seated, Abigail continued to lead the discussion. "Being vetted and endorsed by Dale and Matt is a strong plus," she said smoothly. "However, we prefer to make our own judgments. Do you have family in the area?"

He should have been prepared for that one, but maybe because of everything attached to it, he hesitated. Only a minor pause, but everyone noticed it. It was like being a bug in a roomful of cats.

"No, ma'am. I was born in Texas, spent most my younger years in Baton Rouge. My daddy was quite a bit older than my mama, so he's already passed, some time ago. They moved back to Austin, her birthplace, while I was in the SEALs. She lives there now."

They went from there. Fortunately the personal questions moved fairly soon into the professional, plumbing his thoughts on their current security, which made him glad he'd taken the time to look it over. He'd already formed a rough plan in his mind and appreciated the chance to go right to the plan of action.

"It'd be good to have a couple sit downs with your current staff," he said on the tail end of it. "Explain what the situation is, and what precautions should be taken. Snake Sampson isn't known for letting a challenge pass unanswered. He takes time to plan his response, but he also likes to mess with the heads of his targets before executing that response."

The women were serious and attentive. Rosalinda's expression was the hardest to read. She was leaned back in her wheeled chair, legs crossed. Her hands were on the arms and she was swiveling the seat slightly side to side, like a ticking clock.

Cyn looked toward Ros. "You should lie low for a while. Get out of town, take a vacation trip."

Ros shook her head. "Nothing has changed since the first time we discussed that idea. We have three major campaign rollouts this month. All of them new clients I brought into the firm."

When Cyn opened her mouth, obviously to argue, Rosalinda cut across her, shooting Abby a look. "Despite having ambushed me with the idea, I accepted the security consultant as a compromise. Someone to watch my back and advise additional precautions while I go on with my life in the way I fully intend to live it."

Cyn and Vera exchanged a silent look of frustration that clearly said *told you*. Rosalinda's tense posture said she was aware of it and wasn't unaffected. If things got sticky, he might be able to use that to leverage her cooperation. But there was another way as well.

"You don't strike me as a woman who wants to have smoke blown up her ass by anyone. Even yourself."

All eyes turned toward him. Lawrence clasped his hands together on the table, locking gazes with Rosalinda. "You're tough. But you don't wake up in the morning knowing that the day's going to include beating up your pregnant girlfriend, running a drug deal, and making a rat in your crew disappear in the Mississippi, only to have him wash up miles away with his eyes eaten by crabs." Which had been attributed to Snake but couldn't be proven.

He was aware of Abby's sharpened gaze on him, but he kept his focus on Rosalinda. "You're beautiful, ma'am, and you can send every bit of blood to a man's lap with no more than a look. But if you want me to be effective, you're going to have to listen to me."

She was in the same position, but she wasn't doing that little tick-tock. She was as still as a barn owl. He could work with that.

"I'm going to treat you with respect," he continued. "I'll take your input seriously. However, bottom line, if you don't follow my direction, then the job's over. I won't have you killed on my watch because you were too stubborn to listen. I assume you don't hang onto clients who don't listen to you. Seems a waste of their money and your time. Your reputation gets sacrificed on the altar of their stupidity or stubbornness."

Her lips curved. If she'd had fangs, he expected the bottom tips would be showing. "Which is more likely to get me killed?" she asked sweetly. "My stupidity or my stubbornness?"

"When the end result is a corpse, they don't look much different." He leaned forward. In that moment, for his intents and purposes, it was just the two of them. "If you follow my orders on your protection, Rosalinda, I'll follow yours on everything else."

He couldn't call it clearer than that, but there was no reason to, if he'd judged this room accurately. The silence was deafening as the others waited to see what their boss would do.

Ros folded her hands together on the table, a feminine mirror of his pose. "As my employee?"

"Doesn't matter to me what you call me."

Now an actual smile appeared on her rosebud mouth, though her eyes remained laser sharp. Abigail laid a hand on Rosalinda's, drawing her attention.

"You are my dearest friend," Abby said. "My sister of the heart. The head of the family sitting at this table. Do you understand?"

The look between the women spoke of their long history. Ros's expression reflected exasperation, but before she could respond, Skye reached out a hand, linked it with Vera's. Vera clasped Ros's other hand. Cyn and Abigail linked up and the four of them looked toward him, a human chain with Ros at the center.

Her expression was tight, holding back a surge of emotion he decided she hadn't expected. No more than he'd expected a gesture like that in a formal business setting. But then he remembered this wasn't the first time there'd been a threat to a member of their circle.

Last time, they'd been too late.

Abby turned a somber expression upon him. "You swear if you take the job, her safety will be your top priority. If you don't think you can do that, now, or at any point, you'll stand down and find the right person who can."

"Yes, ma'am." He could live up to that promise. "I'd do that, even if you didn't ask it of me."

A frown crossed Rosalinda's face, but when her lips parted, Abby's hand tightened on hers. Lawrence saw the nails dig in. Hard enough to win a warning look from Rosalinda, though Abby didn't back down from it, locking eyes with her friend.

"No," she said, in a voice he expected very few people used effectively on Rosalinda Thomas. "I support what we do at the shelter, why we do it. We fight monsters. But not the way he does. It's smart, not weak, to admit when an additional skill set is needed."

Another significant pause, then Vera spoke. "With Dale and Matt's recommendation, no need for a background check. Sounds to me like he's hired. Ros?"

Rosalinda turned her attention from Abby back to Lawrence, but gazed at him several more moments without speaking. He recognized the exact moment her expression went from businesswoman to Mistress, because it became about three times as hard to hold that look. Something in it was trying to compel him to look down. Kneel. Put his mouth on her calf again.

Unexpectedly, the idea didn't conflict with what he'd just told her.

But no matter how unorthodox this conversation had been, he decided that would likely strain the boundaries of a business environment.

"All right," Ros said. "I can accept that. As long as you accept I won't just fall in line on your say-so. I need to understand why I have to do something."

"If there's time to explain, that's a reasonable request."

"I won't be pushed around. I push back."

Now he couldn't help but smile. "I hadn't noticed that, ma'am. Thanks for pointing it out."

"She's also a real bitch when she doesn't get her way."

The automated British voice sounded remarkably like Kate Beckinsale's sensual purr. "But she doesn't mean anything by it. If you prove her wrong, or she feels like she owes you an apology, she'll buy you a cupcake. In your favorite flavor."

He looked toward Skye, where the voice had originated. She typed on the computer again. Now the voice that came out sounded like Reese Witherspoon in *Sweet Home Alabama*.

"Since she pisses people off regular, it will be real nice to have you around to watch her back, Lawrence. Thank you."

Ros sent her a searing look. Skye blinked guilelessly.

Damn. His research hadn't revealed Skye was mute. She didn't appear to be deaf, though, which made him wonder what had taken her voice. Childhood defect, illness, or an accident?

"If you want the job, it's yours," Rosalinda told him brusquely. "Vera will take you to her office to go over salary and paperwork."

"Okay." As the other women rose, Lawrence did, too. Before he followed Vera, he shook Abby, Skye and Cyn's hands, made eye contact. It wasn't a chore, though the Domme vibes challenged him to keep his focus. Then he reached Rosalinda, offered his hand.

"I'm looking forward to working together," he said to her.

She put her hand in his. "I'm looking forward to having you work for me."

The promise was there in her eyes. A promise for him, feline anticipation for her.

He wondered if they paid overtime. But almost at the same time he had that thought, another overlapped it.

Did he really fucking care?

After Lawrence accompanied Vera out of the room, the other women sat down again.

"Did you notice it?" Cyn asked Abby.

"I did."

"What?" Ros demanded.

Cyn ignored her. "She flushed a little when he took her hand."

"Could be a hot flash," Abby noted. "She is forty now."

"Fuck you. All of you."

Cyn chuckled. "If we went that way, honey, I'd be at the front of the line."

"Get tequila in you, and you'd be at the front of the line to copulate with every knee in a cypress swamp," Abby retorted.

"There's a reason Vera says we're an HR rep's nightmare and a labor litigator's wet dream," Ros said. "Thank God we hire primarily women."

Cyn made a *pfft* sound. "We hire fewer men because if they were all like that one, we'd get no damn work done."

"Oh, dearies, we wouldn't have to." Skye's computer voice was now a startling falsetto, an affectionate Miss Piggy. "Just choose all female clients and send him out with the contracts. They'll sign with no questions asked."

Ros chuckled at the youngest member of her executive team. But her mind went to that moment in the kitchen, when Lawrence had held her hand for a lingering beat. And then to what he'd said in this meeting, in front of all of them.

"If you follow my orders on your protection, Rosalinda, I'll follow yours on everything else."

She could and would do that, even though she still believed her staff was overreacting. If the personal made the security issue sticky, that was his concern, not hers.

Had he denied himself for her these past couple days?

If he had, it would heighten her interest in him considerably. Without fear, there was no courage. Without effort, the finish line was a meaningless goal. So many sayings that meant the same thing. An unearned gift was far less valued than one you'd busted your ass to deserve.

In her world, without suffering, denial, self-restraint, there was no pleasure.

Well, correction. There was what she called bottom floor pleasure. A quick release and done. For some submissives, that bottom floor was enough. Even for Doms, that could sometimes be enough. Like fast food versus a sit-down dinner.

There were other subs who could make it up to the fourth or fifth floor before they got cranky about the denial, or lost interest. It was only fun up to a certain point. They found Doms interested in a similar level of effort.

But every once in a while, a special submissive came onto her radar. He'd feel the bite of the arousal, and the deeper it sank its teeth into him, the more he'd deny himself. He would never ask his Mistress for release, not when she'd made it clear that decision belonged to her. He'd only ask for more ways to prove himself to her. Even if he took the ride all the way up to the penthouse and kept going, Willy Wonka'ing the elevator to the clouds, he'd still wait on her word.

When a man gave her that kind of control, offering him release was a charge equal to closing her hand around a lightning bolt. She was the kind of Mistress who wanted everything, without apology. If a sub gave her that, she'd give him everything in return.

She wondered how long she could hold out before indulging in that pleasure with Lawrence Barrera Gatlin.

CHAPTER FIVE

*M*eeting concluded, Ros rose and headed out of the board room. She needed to check in with Cyn on a couple things, and Cyn had gone down to the second level to talk to one of the project team leaders. The executive offices and their board room were on the third and top floor, with the project teams scattered between the first and second floors. On the second floor, the office spaces were converted daily living spaces and bedrooms. They'd kept the embroidered wallpapers and historic-style window treatments around the tall windows as a whimsical reminder of their earlier use. They'd remodeled the bedroom and parlor doors, replacing them with wide, molded archways to open up and connect the space.

She paused in one of those archways at the sight of Lawrence, sitting on the edge of Lindi's desk. The rest of the girl's team must have left for lunch, since the five-desk room was empty. Lindi had apparently chosen to stay and work.

"Why do people have to be so mean?" she said, with a little sniffle. She was drying her eyes with a tissue. "I'm working as hard as I can."

"Working hard is important, but working smart is what gets the job done." Lawrence said. "People who know how to work smart will help you with that. Ms. Thomas obviously thinks you've got talent."

"What?" Lindi flicked startled, wet eyes up to him.

"You think she'd waste that kind of energy on someone not worth her time?" Lawrence shook his head. "Lot of companies, they don't offer internships, don't give people the opportunity to learn hands-on the way you're doing. Real world business is tough. That's what makes it feel so good when you succeed. You know you've done something. It hasn't just been handed to you."

Lindi set her pert chin. "I'm going to start from scratch and find something really good to market. Maybe TRA will consider signing them on as a new client."

"That's the spirit."

Looking up, Lindi noticed Ros. She turned red as a beet, but rather than fleeing, she executed a polite if stiff nod, and went back to looking studiously at her laptop.

Lawrence didn't turn immediately, which told Ros he'd known she was there. Probably from the moment she'd leaned in the opening. As he rose and came toward her now, she enjoyed the movement of his body, the look in his steady gaze. She stayed where she was, a shoulder propped against the smooth wood. When he reached her, he braced a hand above her head, the cant of his body forming an alcove of privacy between them. She tilted her head to the side to glance at him.

"Why aren't you with Vera?" she asked.

"She had a conference call. I told her I needed to talk to you a few minutes." He angled his chin subtly toward Lindi. "Her brain is to keep her hairstyle in place?"

"I am not known for being nice. Only good at what I do. Being good's better."

"No argument there. Would you like to have dinner with me tonight?"

"No. I want to come to your place and do what I said I was going to do to you when we parted ways at my car." Her gaze slid down his body and back up again. "Any objections?"

He blinked. "You don't believe in getting to know one another first?"

"I absolutely do. I just have a different approach. One that doesn't involve eating an overpriced salad I don't really want. Or a bunch of empty carbs that will make me too lethargic to do what I'd rather be doing after the meal."

His firm mouth quirked. "You are a very direct woman, Rosalinda."

She shifted so they were shoulder to shoulder. She still faced

JOEY W. HILL

Lindi's office area, while he faced the hallway. It was an intimate pose without the distraction of being eye to eye. "You seem relaxed, Mr. Gatlin. Almost too relaxed." She glanced sideways at him. "Shame. I was looking forward to handing out that reward."

"A SEAL excels at following orders, ma'am. We're good at making the toughest ones look easy. At least on the surface."

His relaxed veneer vanished, revealing a reaction hot enough to burn. Though they'd been pitching their voices low enough Lindi couldn't hear them, he leaned in and murmured in her ear.

"I took a lot of cold showers these past couple days. As that freezing water was pummeling my ass, all I could imagine was you, wearing those silver shoes and nothing else, while you gave me orders, told me what you wanted me to do to get you off. You said I'd have to do it a dozen times, and do it right, before I'd earn the same privilege even once."

For a man who'd never submitted formally to a Mistress, he'd obviously done a lot of fantasizing about it. He was way too good at his delivery. As he'd spoken, she'd closed her eyes. His breath shivered along her nape.

"Hmm." Opening her eyes again, she saw Lindi looking at them. Though the girl couldn't hear their conversation, their body language was giving away more than she wished. Ros pivoted, leading the way back up the stairs to her office. She did it at a stroll, studying the New Orleans street scenes on the wall as they walked together. She needed the focus, the extra beats of time, to ensure her voice didn't come out breathless. "Text me your address. I'll be there when I get there tonight. But no later than eight."

"I was going to wait on you, drive you home. I need to see your place. Do a security assessment from the inside out."

"You're not officially on payroll until tomorrow. I have one more day to leave my office without a shadow. And that means I don't want to see you waiting to shadow me, either."

"You wouldn't. Unless I've gotten slack."

She wasn't going to bend on this, not without a fight. "I heard what you said in the board room, and I will live up to my word, but tomorrow. Give me one more day to wrap my mind around it."

He studied her. "Okay. If you promise to make sure you're not the last to leave, and you text me before you exit the building. I know

48

you've taken self-defense classes, but there are some things I want you to do to increase your situational awareness, keep you safe on your way to me."

"Fair enough."

"I can still meet you at your place."

She shook her head. She wanted to see the man in his natural environment, and she didn't care to wait on that. "I'll be safer at your place, where they won't expect me to be. You can assess my place tomorrow."

He paused. She could tell he really didn't want her at his place, but that alone told her she wasn't going to give him wiggle room unless he took a hard pass on it.

He relented at last. "You want me to make you dinner? Something low carb, protein rich?"

"Something other than you?"

His laughter had a distracting deep throatiness. Close to a growl. "Yeah."

"No. I'll eat before I get there." She slid her gaze over him. "I like it when a man wears jeans and nothing else. The kind of jeans that aren't too tight, but snug in the right places, worn in the crease points, coaxing me to touch."

He blinked. "Okay. If it matters, I don't care what the hell you wear. Just so you get there sooner rather than later."

"I'll take my time, then."

His sexy chuckle followed her as she left him, striding into her office and closing the door.

At six twenty-three, Ros texted Lawrence to tell him she was on her way, and to request the address he'd not yet sent her.

Sure you don't want to go to your place instead? I could come pick you up, drive you there.

Interesting. Another attempt to dissuade her. *Do I strike you as someone who is ever unsure of what I want?*

624 White Gate Circle. Waverly townhomes. Unit B.

Victory. She knew the neighborhood, a multi-family neighborhood, upper middle-class townhomes. They were adjacent to a less pricey, more blue-collar scale apartment complex. Waverly was located on the outskirts of central New Orleans, where historic charm gave way to subdivisions. The nice but cookie cutter styles represented most of the neighborhoods built in the past twenty years, the design of choice from developers driven by coastal housing booms.

He also texted her a list of things he wanted her to do before, during and after she left. Since they were common sense driven, nothing ruffled her feathers. She sent him a raspberry emoji as her confirmation text when she was safely in her car and on her way.

As she pulled out of TRA's paved entranceway, she saw a police car parked in front of the building. The driver, a youngish looking officer, lifted a hand as he saw her emerge. He pulled off as she headed down the street. Lawrence hadn't tried to surveil her, but he'd called in a favor with the active police presence.

No matter how much overkill it might be, she couldn't fault how seriously he took his job. She stopped by the house to freshen up, pick up some things and give Freak, her cat, his dinner and one-on-one time. She sent Abby a text, asking her to check on him later tonight. Several bouncing eyebrow emojis and a couple cartwheeling cheer-leader ones came back, with a three-word note. *We expect details.* She shot her another raspberry answer, then she was on her way.

She hadn't expected Lawrence to have a house, since a SEAL with no wife or kids would have little reason to own a place with ample maintenance needs. However, the townhome, with a managing HOA for the outside, made sense as a sound resale investment. Though she thought he was about a decade younger than her, Lawrence had had the maturity to think about his future. Maybe an older SEAL like Dale had offered that kind of guidance, and Lawrence had been smart enough to follow it.

Or the story might be something entirely different. That was part of what she looked forward to figuring out tonight.

When she drove up and parked in front of his place, she saw little to differentiate it from the ones flanking it on either side. Brick façade with vinyl trim and a small square of grass out front. No wreath on the door, but two pieces of statuary by the walkway. A horse, fairly nondescript, with its concrete hindquarters turned toward the person coming up the three short steps to the postage-sized front porch. The equine was half buried in the shrubs lining the walkway, so whether coming or going, the hind end was the notable part.

Horse's ass. She wondered if it was a joke from some of his SEAL buddies. She had no doubt the other piece of lawn art was. A garden gnome with a toy assault rifle strapped to him, and the gnome was in fatigues. Then she realized he wasn't a gnome. He had his non-gun encumbered arm stretched out and pointing, his earnest face and parted lips obviously supposed to be saying the words scrolled cheerfully on the plaque mounted on his feet.

Follow the yellow brick road!

Munchkins. From the *Wizard of Oz*. Munch. Dale's nickname for Lawrence.

She had a smile on her face as Lawrence opened the door. The first thing she noticed was, while his jeans fit her requirements perfectly, he still wore a shirt, shoes and socks.

"Sorry," he said immediately, though she suspected the apology wasn't for the excess clothing. He looked stressed, which suggested the requirement had slipped his mind.

"For what?"

"For not meeting you at your car. I was watching for you, but I got a phone call I had to take and—" He broke off. "Doesn't matter."

"Care to explain?" She gestured to the horse. "A joke?"

"Yeah. Something like that." He managed a half smile without real wattage. "Glad you're here."

"No, you're not."

The smile faltered, but he lifted a shoulder. "I'm glad to see you. That's the truth."

She nodded. "The truth is what keeps my attention. So tell me more truth. Like why you don't want me here."

Her attention slid pointedly over his stiff body language. He'd remained in the threshold, his arm braced on the doorway, an unconscious block. He twitched a shoulder.

"I lived here with a woman for a while. For quite a while, off and on. Since I was gone a lot, in a way it feels like I've invited you to my ex-girlfriend's house."

"Does she still live here?"

He looked reassuringly startled by the question. "No." He took a breath. "I still deal with a lot of shit from that part of my life. But it's fallout, not hanging on."

Complicated backstory, Dale had said.

Lawrence shook his head. "A first date shouldn't be this involved. Why don't I grab my keys and we can go out for a drink or something?"

"Instead of what I told you I wanted to do to you, with you? I don't think so. Unless you're giving me an absolute no on that."

Before he could say more, she closed the distance between them, planting the toe of her shoe on the threshold between his spread feet. She put her hand on his waist, just above the belt of his jeans, so she could finger that strap, play a little beneath it. She rested her other hand on the doorframe, just above the latch.

"How about this? How about you stop worrying about everything you think you need to control, and let me have my way? See where it goes. See if you can trust me to know my own mind."

"I do. I just want this to be...what you wanted. I don't want to make you uncomfortable."

"Stop trying to take care of me. Protect me."

"That's what you hired me to do."

"You're not on the clock yet."

His jaw set in a distractingly stubborn way. "Your firm hired me to protect you. But me deciding to protect you, watch after you, that's a decision I made when we met at Club Progeny. Even if the 24/7 doesn't start officially until tomorrow."

He had a knee-weakening way about him. But she had her own way, too. She followed her instincts.

"Invite me in, Lawrence. I promise to drain all your blood, steal your soul, and have you thank me in the morning."

Now his eyes crinkled at the corners. Humor returning, even as it had to push its way out of the shadows. "So you're staying the night?"

"It depends. On what shape you're in when I'm done."

On how much aftercare he'd need after he gave her everything she demanded. She held that thought to herself.

Clouds could cluster thickly around a man's soul and mind. When she found the way to part them, to glimpse the fire and need that lay behind that screen, it told her even more clearly than words what needed to happen next. Her fingers tightened on his belt and this time she didn't ask. She stepped forward, executing gentle pressure.

Five foot seven or not, the man was a brick wall when he didn't want to be moved. But just when she thought he was going to give her that hard *no* after all, he relented, letting her in.

Once inside, she eased him arm's length from her so she could close the door. She flipped the latch with a decided thunk, remembering what he'd said about needing to be sure their space was secure before he gave over control to her.

As she turned her back to him to do that, he gravitated toward her. A predator was good at taking advantage of an unguarded moment. Though his torso didn't touch hers, she expected there was less than a hand span between them. He confirmed it, by resting his forehead against her shoulder. She went still, waiting to see what he thought he had the liberty or implicit permission to do. His hands crept to her waist, dug in, and then he laid a kiss on the bare collarbone offered by the scoop neckline of her silk shirt.

He stayed like that, his forehead against her shoulder again, his hands at her waist. Holding her, but also holding himself, she thought. Giving himself strength by drawing from her presence, her strength. A simple, subtle sign of trust and faith in that power. Or hope for it.

The man could overwhelm her, not just with the power of his need, but with how strong a hold he had on the reins to it. When she convinced him to hand those reins to her, it was very possible her world might change in ways she didn't expect.

Easy. Slow it down. For both of you.

She'd had a brief impression of a living room with a flatscreen, an open floor plan that led to a kitchen, but none of that interested her. Not right now. She didn't want any distractions. She wanted her entire focus, everything filling her senses, holding her attention, to be him.

She put her hand over his on her waist. "Show me where you spend the most time when you're here."

If it was the bedroom, she expected he'd choose his second most preferred living space, to avoid being obvious. Or to avoid temptation. She didn't disagree with that.

Taking her hand, he led her to the kitchen. The island there doubled as his dining table. A sliding glass door led out to a small patio. Through the half-open vertical blinds she glimpsed a tiny backyard enclosed by wooden panels on the left and right sides. While it was open to the woods behind the townhome, the panels provided semi-privacy between his patio and that of the neighbors.

No dishes in the sink, all surfaces clean. The kitchen was mostly white walls, brown and white granite counters. But along the back-splash of the stove were a line of brightly colored tiles, each with a Day of the Dead sugar skull design. Matching skull saltshakers on either end. A cast iron skillet had a permanent spot on one of the burners.

Hanging from the handle of the stove was a dish towel that looked hand-embroidered, likely a gift from a family member. It was the SEAL emblem, a fierce-looking eagle with a bowed head, the talons grasping a trident. It was flanked by two solid blue functional towels.

Lawrence stood a short step behind her left shoulder. Because she knew he was watching her reactions, she let her gaze travel at a leisurely pace over the room again, for a different reason. She wanted to check out her options.

There was the refrigerator, the handle of the stove. Cabinet handles. She liked breaking a sub's control, so none of that was sturdy enough. Her gaze returned to the refrigerator, and she marked the broom and dust mop tidily tucked in the space between it and the counter. Then her attention returned to the kitchen sink. Double-sided, fiberglass.

Done.

Moving to the sink, she tilted her head in that direction, indicating he should follow her. The small area made her hyperconscious of his scent and heat. They were closed into their own private world, no work requirements here for either of them. He didn't disrupt what was building between them with the offer of a drink, the option to sit down or other such nonsense.

What she'd felt standing next to him in the doorway to Lindi's office space, what she'd sensed when he had first come into their board room, was a mere echo of the force of attention she felt from him now. It told her how much he'd been suppressing behind that façade. The increased heat in his gaze, the dense energy that surrounded her, reminded her that he had a woman he wanted in his home, and it was just the two of them. He was more than capable of overpowering her and taking what he wanted. Not that he would, but he would push her awareness of that, see how she would react, to give the sexual energy between them a dangerous edge.

That edge, if they both gave into it, could turn this into just sex, offering quick relief. The bottom level. But she was banking on him knowing, just as she did, that so much more was possible here than that. Even if it was still mostly subconscious for him, that knowledge, when the conscious mind got out of the way, became far more powerful.

"Face the backsplash. Put your hands on the edge of the sink, shoulder width apart."

He kept his eyes on her as long as was possible before full compliance. When he did, her hand was there, in front of him. "Lean forward until your chest meets my palm."

As he adjusted to the new angle, his shoulders flexed out, ass, back and thighs taut. A standing push-up of sorts.

"Until I say otherwise, you'll do what I say. You won't speak unless I ask you a question. Everything is about what I want, what I demand you give to me. Do you understand?"

"Yes, ma'am."

"Ma'am is what you give to any woman. Mistress is more acceptable."

"Yes...Mistress." His voice roughened on the word as if she'd given him a gift.

"Have you ever called a woman that?"

"No, Mistress."

"Good." She meant it. She liked an experienced sub, one who knew what to seek what he wanted within the club walls, but Lawrence was a lake of submissive possibilities, just waiting to be channeled.

"If at any point something concerns you, you may use a word to tell me to take a beat, slow it down, explain. Touch base. Don't fight me on that. This isn't about macho endurance bullshit. It's about my intention to take us both where we want to go. That word helps me know if I've made a wrong turn on that journey. What word will you use?"

"Gray."

"Good. If something needs to stop immediately, you will say what?"

He had to fish for that. After a pause, she placed a palm on his back. "How about 'sanctuary?' A reminder to you that if you call a halt to things, it's not a bad thing. It's a safe thing, and I will respect it, and keep you safe."

She expected the resistance in his eyes, and increased the pressure of her touch against his back. "You think I can't hurt you, Lawrence, but I can. There are so many ways to fuck up a person's head. Especially when doing this, and accepting how much control I want. I'm looking for things way deeper than just two people getting off. You want more than that too, don't you?"

"I think so. I know the things I've thought about since I saw you, they weren't just about sex. Though I'm not averse to that."

"I'm not surprised. Straighten for me, but keep your hands on the sink."

When he complied, she ducked under his arm, came up in the small space between him and the sink. She propped herself against the edge, her elbows in close to her body. She rested her fingertips on his chest.

"What did I tell you I wanted you *not* to wear, Lawrence? Earlier, at the office."

True chagrin crossed his face. "Oh, shit. I intended—"

"We're in the beginning stages," she said firmly. "It was a suggestion, a glimpse of my preferences. I didn't issue it as a command."

But she saw what she wanted to see in his expression. It bothered him, a lot, that he'd overlooked something she'd wanted. She suspected he was a full-on anticipatory sub. Once in that headspace, he'd take whatever she said as a command. If he fell short, no one would be harder on him than himself.

There were a lot of perks to that kind of sub, but it had to be monitored so he didn't take it to excess. "In the future, if I order you to do something and you forget, or interpret it according to your wishes, not mine, the choice of punishment is mine. When that punishment is done, it's done. Punishment is entirely my area, Lawrence, not yours. I have a feeling you'll need to be reminded of that. But not today. Understand?"

She could see him warring with it. "When you were a SEAL, did you waste time apologizing for a fuck up?" she asked, more sharply. "Or did you fix it, and make sure it didn't happen again? Because actions speak a hell of a lot louder than words."

She'd found the right path. Things settled, and he nodded, though the gesture still came with the tight jaw. She caressed it, enjoying the smooth feel of the clipped beard. "Good. Quiet now. You're mine to play with."

Proving it, she unbuttoned the shirt, her fingers brushing warm muscled flesh. She spread the fabric open, conscious of his arms braced on either side of her as she fanned her fingers over lightly furred flesh. The male biceps pressed against her arm quivered, while the heartbeat under her palm increased.

She slid her hands up, under his collar and then out toward his shoulders, taking the shirt off of them, pushing the fabric down and keeping it there, from elbow to elbow, fabric folded against the lower part of his back. He didn't lift his hands without permission, which some men would have done, incorrectly anticipating her wanting to remove the shirt fully right now.

Good boy, she thought, though there was nothing boyish in front of her. A man this fit was a work of art, a beautiful display of well-earned muscle, his upper torso as graceful a shape as a stallion's arched neck.

"Lower your right arm so I can get around you."

He did, and she slipped behind him, trailing her fingers along his side beneath the open shirt, then across his hip bone. Now she took the shirt all the way off the one arm, and with a quiet word, had him do the same with the other. After laying the shirt over one of the kitchen stools, she had him put his hands back on the sink. "Remember not to move them unless I say so. You're doing well, Lawrence. I'm pleased."

That quiver increased, a man's power and ferocity, leashed only by her demand. She had no idea why anyone ever did drugs, when something like this could be created merely between the give and take of two people's wills.

She moved to the island, to the stool that was farthest from him, because he could see what she was doing in his peripheral vision, if he strained. She wanted him to see, even as she wanted him to fight to keep his head still, obeying her order to face the backsplash.

She removed the scoop-necked blouse, revealing the dark blue demi-bra beneath it, cups low enough to hint at her nipples. She left on her skirt, but inched it up enough he could see the garters. The fasteners were jeweled purple roses. She heard the intake of breath, saw the ripple along his back and shoulders.

She took her time unhooking the garters and skimming off the stockings. Then she slid her matching panties off her legs, offering a quick glimpse of hips and shadowed places before she had the skirt in place again.

She rolled the panties into a soft ball, and returned to him. No head movement, but his eyes were everywhere, pupils dark and full. They moved over her face, the brush of her hair on her shoulders, her mostly bare upper body. His attention paused on the scar over her left breast, a five-inch crescent that had healed to a deep mauve groove. It was widest near the sternum, tapering to a threadlike shine past the swell of her bosom.

She shook her head slightly, a warning. It drew his attention back to where she wanted it.

"Open up," she said, and his lips parted. She tucked her panties in there, effectively gagging him. "Easy to spit out and safeword, but just in case, lifting your right hand will mean gray, left hand will mean sanctuary. Closest hand to the heart. That means lifting it and keeping it in the air. Not getting startled by something I do and shifting your grip, or momentarily pushing away from the sink because you can't control your reaction."

He watched her as if nothing in the universe could be more important than her and what she was telling him. It was a heady feeling, even as she reminded herself it was all new to him, the actual doing.

At some point, she wanted to hear all those fantasies he'd had about a woman dominating him. Every detail. But right now, she had other pleasing things to do.

She'd brought in her Louis Vuitton purse, shaped like a monkey, furred with brown sequins and possessing rhinestone ruby eyes. She tucked her hose and garters into an interior side pocket, then removed what else she'd decided to bring when she'd chosen her clothes for tonight. She laid it out on the island.

Multi-colored pieces of quarter-inch jute, all rolled into one ball. A pair of EMT snippers. She read the sudden tension in his features and answered it.

"No restraining your ability to move in my defense. I remember."

She moved behind him again. This time she reached around him, unbuckled his belt, freed it with a few firm tugs that brushed his canted ass against her upper thighs. She slipped the button of his jeans, worked them off his backside.

"Toe off the shoes. Stand on the end of the socks and pull them off, too."

He did. She worked the jeans down, putting her hands inside the denim to help the slide and enjoy the heat of him caught in the cloth of the seat, the resilient flesh against her palms. "I have a cat who likes to curl up in the seat of my jeans after I take them off," she commented. "He'd like yours better. A nice, tight circle."

He grunted at that, making her smile. When she had the jeans down to his calves, she lifted her touch away from him. "Kick them off."

He did, and she set them aside with the shoes and socks. Now he only wore black shorts that clung to his ass. She trailed her fingers down one buttock, flipped her hand over and did the other cheek with her knuckles. A shiver went up the middle of his back, and she followed that trail. He had no tattoos, but way too many scars. She traced them with her fingers.

"Is this how you imagined it, Lawrence?"

He shook his head.

"Is that a bad thing?"

He shook his head again and then, in a surprise move, he let go of the sink, reached back and clasped her wrist, the one against his waist. She would have admonished him for the infraction, gently, since it was his first session and he was new to it all, but she held off and focused, reading the significance of the gesture.

He moved to interlace his fingers with hers, hold tight. His head had dropped, while his breathing had elevated.

"Okay. Sshh, it's all right." Her brow creasing, she ran her hand up and down his back. "Easy. Whatever it is, it's okay. You're all mine. I've got you. Now let go of my hand and behave, before I have to get rough with you. Trust your Mistress."

It was rare she used a possessive like that, particularly in a first session, but in this moment, she was *his* Mistress.

He reluctantly loosened his grip, returned his hand to the edge of the sink.

She kept her hand on his back, making easy circles as she

murmured to him. "There's a part of you that has probably wanted something like this for quite a while. You didn't know how much until now. That tempts me to push you hard, Lawrence. Break you down, strip you raw, teach you to beg. But not tonight. Tonight's not for that."

He listened to her so intently. She wasn't sure she'd ever had a man's attention so fully. Even in session, a submissive's mind could fragment, go in a lot of different directions, even as they orbited around the Mistress's demands. His focus was gratifying, intoxicating.

He'd unlocked something in her with that yearning, spontaneous grip, a strong man desperate for what she was. While she recognized the euphoria of an exceptionally good beginning, there was more to the way he grabbed onto this. Like he'd been floundering in deep water and had finally, after so long, been tossed a lifeline. That reaction connected to the man himself, not just the sub side.

She wouldn't chase that down tonight. Tonight's timing called for a lighter handed approach. Yet even knowing she was right about that, it was more difficult than expected to rein herself back. The more limitless the needs of her sub, the more the most demanding parts of herself came to the surface. Since she was getting the feeling Lawrence's needs were going to be the deepest well she'd ever drawn from, it was hard to resist going deeper than she should tonight.

Abby had said once that it could take a lifetime to get to the bottom of that well, with the right sub. And maybe not even then. When you went that deep, you might hit the core of the Earth itself, where fire was an endless, liquid need, boring through the soul.

All right, enough of that. She was getting carried away. In another moment she might hit Domspace, for God's sake. Pushing away the disturbing realization that Lawrence's simple gesture and the close energy contained in a small kitchen had pulled her that deep, that fast, she realigned herself with the moment. To do that, to settle them both down, she focused on the physical.

She hooked his briefs and pushed the back fabric down to his upper thighs. Mother of God, that was an ass. All flexing muscle, it begged for teeth marks.

Cyn was a biter. Ros could see her going after that perfection like an erotically starved piranha.

Reaching under his arm, she unhooked the band of his briefs from the head of his erect cock. It was so thick the removal of the cloth confines barely changed its position, hard and tight against his belly, pointing up and out.

She let the side of her hand graze it, enjoyed the convulsive jump. *Yeah, you eager beast. You're going to get to know my touch very well. You'll learn how to behave to get my approval, and everything that goes with that.*

She pushed the underwear down far enough they dropped, and he could step out of them. "Straighten up and turn around," she said. "But put your hands back on the sink on either side of you. As far as you're concerned, your hands are chained there."

As he complied, faced her, his gaze had shifted to the left.

"Look at me."

He did, a little reluctantly, and she knew why. "You don't have trouble looking at me with lust in your eyes," she observed. "The conquering hero, restrained by my word and your will, an acceptable masculine pairing. Meeting my gaze while my panties are stuffed in your mouth? That's something different. But your discomfort, that kind, is irresistible. This moment is about what I want, and you won't hesitate when I give you an order, sailor. So you keep your eyes on my face unless I say otherwise. Even when I look elsewhere, when my attention comes back to your eyes, I expect you to be looking me full in the face."

His gaze rested there, high spots of color in his cheeks. She'd flustered him, but he'd obeyed. She wasn't into humiliation; this wasn't about that. When she had a man under her control, she knew every trick and evasive maneuver. She left the soul and mind no retreat points. Full surrender was the only option. Full submission.

The lace of her panties teased his lips, making her think about the heat of his mouth on the flesh the sheer fabric had been covering.

"Can you taste my arousal, Lawrence?"

He nodded, another spark of heat going through his eyes.

"Good. Stay still."

She propped her hips against a stool and settled into a full study of his warrior's body. Like everything about him so far, unexpected emotions came with the exploration.

More scars. Deep ones that even her eyes, untrained in medical knowledge, knew had been life-threatening. A long gash across his pec, a slice on his collar bone, and a tiny nick on his throat, below his ear. If connected, they would have formed a diagonal line. It brought to mind a blade slicing upward, him falling back so it slashed across his chest but caught his collarbone and ear, rather than cutting his throat.

Round, shiny scars, which had to be bullet holes, below the shoulder and in the thigh. Dropping to her heels, she took a closer look at a scar that ran from the widest part of his calf to just above the ankle. It looked like a jagged edged knife had sawed the flesh away. But in the middle of that was a surgically precise line.

She was used to evidence of childhood injuries, like a broken bone from falling off a swing set. Active, athletic men could certainly have their mishaps, too. White water rafting, playing basketball with buddies, wall climbing in a gym, an afternoon run on a greenway. They left small scars, bragging rights.

She'd even had an active member of the military or veteran under her control a time or two, but never one from special forces, with years of service to his credit. Maybe because one willing to relinquish control, even at this level, wasn't common. Or maybe they were, but most didn't have the salary to afford Club Progeny, her usual fishing pool. Still, she suspected a SEAL with a submissive orientation, comfortable enough to embrace it, was as rare as a snow leopard.

She laid her hand on his calf, felt what was beneath it. Reached for the other one. There was a difference, for certain. "I'm thinking you have some issues with this leg, as well as some random aches and pains from the other scars. We'll talk about that before I demand anything very strenuous from you, but you can use your safewords if we run into issues sooner."

When she glanced up at him, his eyes were straight ahead, his body tense. He wasn't avoiding her gaze because of the gag this time. He'd forgotten that. Her touching his calf, that jagged scar and the surgical one in the midst of it, had unlocked something else.

She remembered Dale had said an injury had led to his leaving the SEALs. *Not the kind that qualifies him for a handicap sticker, but it knocked him out of being an operator.* She suspected she'd just located it.

Most men didn't care to admit any physical limitations, and ironically the ones who pushed their bodies the hardest were the worst about it. She knew how to handle that, but it wouldn't be in this meet-and-greet session.

She straightened. "Lawrence, you're not looking at me. Do you have trouble following my orders, sailor?"

That same jerk and chagrin combination. She could tell he was mentally cursing himself, telling himself to get his act together. She caressed his face, his stretched mouth, with a fingertip.

"Don't forget again," she said softly. "Or I might show you what I can do with that metal spatula." She dipped her head toward a clay container full of kitchen utensils, by the stove.

Maybe his fantasies hadn't included that kind of play. But the flash in his eyes, the curl of his hands on the sink, said it had definitely gotten his attention.

She liked the hair on his chest. Brown with a gleam when the light hit it right. Curling up toward the throat and spread out in a light mat that would become straight dark strands when he took a shower. The arrow of hair bisecting his six pack went to a trimmed thatch of the same brown hair over his attentive cock. Impressively sized balls cushioned the base.

"Stay." Retrieving the broom and dust mop, she unscrewed the cleaning ends and left those tucked in next to the fridge before bringing back the two painted wooden dowels.

She threaded the broom handle behind his back, under his straight arms, in front of the elbows. "Lift your hands, clasp the pole."

He complied, the position arching his back and making his chest profile more prominent. She put the mop handle on the island and unrolled two pieces of colored jute from the ball she'd left there. Eyeballing it for the proper spacing, she tied a loop around two different spots on the rod. She put it on the floor, nudging it with her shoe until it met his bare toes.

"Look down," she said. "Adjust your feet so they line up with the two loops and put your feet inside the loops, the rod under the balls of your feet, weight on your heels."

As he followed her direction, she continued. "As far as you're concerned, your wrists are bound to that broomstick you're holding, and your legs are locked in place by a spreader pole. Do you understand?"

One short nod. Another element was rising in his gaze, one she'd hoped to see. Acceptance of her control was there, but the man, the inner beast, was growling against the bars of the cage.

"You want to fuck me, don't you? An angry, powerful part of you wants to put me on my back, spread my legs, show me who's boss, the strongest predator in this room." She reached out, traced a line over his pectoral, did a sinuous track to his navel and back up again. "You don't scare me. I know I can put my arm through your cage bars and be all right. Because there's another part of you, just as focused."

Her gaze rose to his, held. "It wants to prove you'll serve me however I demand it. That's how you'll show your true fierceness to me. You'll tear anything apart for me, for the clasp of my hand on your cock, calling it mine. Calling everything attached to it mine. I could ask you if I'm right, get you to say it. But I don't want that. I want you to show me."

His green eyes reflected an incredible mix of emotions, showing he was as much in his own head as he was trying to figure out hers. Despite her earlier self-cautions, she knew she was going to be a little more intense than she usually was in a first session. She wanted to cut him loose from the swamp of debris she sensed was in his head, that had made him grip her wrist like a drowning man. In the protected bubble of a session, when everything was going right, such idealistic thoughts came easily, without doubts.

Everything was definitely going right.

"Stay still," she ordered, and turned back to her ball of jute.

She unrolled lengths of red, blue and green, laying them out on the counter. A glance at the sugar skull tiles told her she'd come close to the color scheme. Aesthetics mattered, and were a particular pleasure, when she could incorporate them.

She noted his growing arousal only seemed to increase his focus, not the usual thing. But she was handling a man who was trained not to blink, particularly as things became more chaotic, because loss of attention had life-altering consequences.

Hypervigilance. That was the term for it. While she liked that close regard, her Domme side knew he needed to learn to dial it back some. This wasn't a mission, there was no enemy to fight. Everything in this space was safe. He could relinquish some attention and control. A blindfold might help, but that would take time and negotiation. For now, there were other ways to get him to ease up.

Picking up a longer blue piece of jute, she turned to him and

64

looped it around the base of his cock. She began to twist and tie, create the knots and diamond pattern she wanted.

Jute was prickly. She watched him adjust to the mild discomfort as she worked her way from base to head. Her knuckles were brushing him, her fingertips, so his cock was twitching under her touch, getting admirably harder and thicker, which pressed him tighter against the rope. She'd allowed for that, so it wouldn't dig in too much.

Her head was bent beneath his, his mouth so close to her temple, and she let her lips curve, showing him she was aware of that. His chest rose and fell, his hands curling and uncurling against the broom handle. She let the energy between their bodies build, and submerged herself in that dense heat, savoring his self-restraint.

After she was done creating a rope sheath, she ran her hand over it, gripping him fully. His eyes closed briefly, then opened again, obeying her command. Muscles flexed in his abdomen, his shoulders, his upper thighs. A bit of lace fluttered from the panties in his mouth, stirred by his breathing.

She ran her thumb over the head of his cock, pressing her nail against the slit, letting the bead of arousal pool on the top of her nail like a drop of thick honey. When she brought it to her lips to taste it, he spoke a muffled word against the lace gag. Her blood heated.

She liked the way he said her name. All four syllables. She liked when he called her Mistress even more.

Turning, she removed a metal rod from her bag. It was about the diameter of her pinky, and eight inches in length.

His pupils dilated, eyes slightly widening. She suspected the guttural sound against the panties this time translated to a *fucking hell no*. She suppressed a smile, kept her expression bland and waiting. Wanting to see what he would do. His gaze flicked from the rod to her face, and then he said nothing. He didn't raise a hand to safeword. Just looked at her with a challenging expression.

That only lasted a moment, though. In the space of a breath he shifted from intrigued, engaged, aroused under her control, to detached, ready to fight. Another turn of the dial, and a deeper response gripped him. His gaze traveled between her face to her hand, back to her face, back to her hand, and then straight out, staring at the wall.

Resignation. Ready to endure. A martyr to someone else's pain.

He'd been hurt by a woman. A lot. Not physically; she doubted that. But one had emotionally battered him, so that this reaction could be triggered when he thought he was being tormented in the wrong way, for the wrong reasons. He wouldn't back down, even as it tore his soul apart to be treated that way by someone he wanted. Loved.

She knew that expression, those feelings. Seeing it in him shot uneasiness through her. She took an involuntary step back. She despised that look and everything that created it.

His gaze snapped to her face when she moved away. She closed her eyes, shutting him out for a second. Raised a finger, an order to him to maintain. Then she breathed. Just breathed. Grounded herself in the present. When a sub was under a Domme's control, there was no other place she should be.

She imagined every glorious inch of him, how she had his irresistible body arranged, the beauty of his hungry expression. Meet-and-greet, damn it. This was not going to go down that road for her, and she sure as hell wasn't going to let it go that way for him.

She opened her eyes, met his. "It's all right." Placing her feet on either side of one of his, she gripped his bound cock again. She stroked it and felt that quiver return as he looked down at her, their faces so close. His gaze was troubled, so she shook her head at him, leaned in, her breast cupped in lace against his chest.

"This rod isn't what you think it is. But more importantly, you need to learn a safeword protocol isn't like calling *uncle* in a wrestling match. It's not an admission of defeat, a declaration that someone has bested you, or is stronger than you. Would you like me to explain more about what it actually is?"

Wariness lay in those green eyes, but those troubling things were receding. She wondered if he'd been surprised she'd picked up on his change of attitude so quickly. SEALs weren't the only ones trained to watch people closely, anticipate what they were going to do, what they were thinking. And though her sessions weren't supposed to be life or death situations, the disruption of a session, of an emotional flow that intimately connected the two people in it, was a loss that could wound deeply.

He nodded. A slow up and down, once. "Good." She let him see her approval, and felt him relax a slight bit more. It helped her do the same.

"Say you and I decided to go hiking," she said. "We're going to climb to a mountain top, where the view is phenomenal. But if I need to take a break to rest and watch wildlife, or you think we should detour to swim in a creek, because it's such a hot day, those pauses make it a day to remember. That's what a safeword is. A timeout to make sure the experience is worthwhile, and we get where we want to go, together. I said this is a journey. I meant it."

She lifted the small rod so he could see it. "This doesn't go in your urethra. Sound play can be very pleasurable, but it's also a pretty advanced play that I wouldn't spring on you the first time we're together." She lightened the moment with a playful smile and a tap on his cheek. "But I will be chuckling over the look on your face for awhile."

He gave her a narrow look, but there was amusement in his eyes as well. "Let me show you what it *is* used for," she said.

Dropping her hand, she threaded the rod into the rope sheath around his cock. Despite his increased thickness, she'd gauged the harness size well. The ropes were snug, but not cutting into him unbearably. She had to work the rod into the diamond-shaped openings, but she managed it. Looking up at his face again, she adjusted the rod half a turn.

The movement tightened the sheath and the rough knots lining his cock. To a man, very conscious of the vulnerability of his parts, that piece of mindfuckery could feel like gravel being pressed into a roadbed by a passing truck.

His jaw flexed, muscles in his arms constricting as his hands clenched the broomstick. Yet he held. He didn't move, though his expression wasn't detached anymore. She'd gotten through. He was with her again. She raised one hand to his shoulder, slipped it over to cup his nape, as she kept the other hand on his cock and that rod. She turned the rod back, releasing the tension. His gaze had dropped to it, so she sharpened her tone, just a little, keeping it to a low purr.

"Where did I tell you to keep your eyes?"

They came back up to her, but she was ready to reinforce the lesson this time. As tempting as the spatula was, it was farther away from him than she wanted to move. "So you'll remember..." She turned the rod again, this time for more than half a turn.

He stiffened again, a groan coming through the panties. As his gaze clung to her face, she showed him what his obedience, his straining, powerful body, his unflagging cock, despite the discomfort, was giving her.

"Excellent." She glanced down to thread the ends of the rod into other openings, causing minute pulls on the ropes that had growling moans coming from his throat. The head of his cock was glistening. The pain was arousing him, something a Mistress like her loved to see.

When she was done, she removed her grip on the rod. It would stay in place, keeping the ropes tight. She cupped his heavy testicles, squeezing and playing. His hips quivered, his thigh muscles flexed. He was fighting not to thrust forward.

"You're working so hard to be good, to meet my expectations. I appreciate that very much, Lawrence. You don't know what that does for me. Or maybe you do. If I'd taken the panties off now, they'd have been soaked all the way through."

Putting her hands beneath her skirt, she ran her fingertips over her damp cunt, and brought them back out, putting them under his nose. His nostrils flared as she painted the dampness on his stretched lips.

"Drop to your knees."

She stepped back, enough to give him the room to do it, while staying close enough to spot him if he needed it. The mop handle under the balls of his feet made the maneuver challenging, but he did it, showing impressive command of the muscles in his thighs, his core. When his knees were on the floor, he straightened up for her again, his hands still clasped on the rod under his arms.

She removed the panties from his mouth, set them aside. Then, putting a hand on the island to balance herself, she lifted her left leg and braced it against the sink, over his shoulder. The skirt creased up toward her hips, the position putting her sex within inches of his face.

And look at that, he'd remembered to keep his eyes on her face, though the effort showed. "You have my permission to see how wet I am. You may put your lips where you are wanting to put them, ease your tongue out to take one taste. Then I expect you to sit back on your heels again."

She curved one hand around the back of his head, enjoying the feel of the short, thick hair as he leaned forward. This wasn't an exercise in control only for him. From the first touch of his mouth, all the arousal she was containing rushed toward that contact, making her want to rub, drive his tongue in deeper, work herself against his face.

Instead she remained still as one of the bar stools, even as everything beneath her skin was vibrating madly. Oh...God. His tongue slowly, slowly penetrated her, took one slow swirl before sliding away. When his nose was pressed against her clit, the quivering care of his movement translated into a full fondling of the aroused area.

"Very good," she managed in a breathless voice as he sat back, and she returned to standing on two legs again. Now the hunger in his gaze was threaded with a male satisfaction, knowing what he was doing to her. She picked up the panties, put them between her legs and rubbed, pushing the fabric partly inside to saturate the silk as much as possible. Then she nodded to him. "Open up."

His lips parted, and with him staring up at her as she replaced the gag, her cunt throbbed. It might be one of those words only used in romance novels, but it didn't make it any less true. When a man this tempting was at her feet, offering himself, the flesh between her legs throbbed, ached, clenched, quivered.

"Stand up."

As he complied, she studied her handiwork, steadying herself. His blood-flushed cock was a dark contrast against the colorful jute. His hands were tight fists on the broom handle. His legs, spread for the pole, only accented the lean ropes of muscles in his thighs, the set of his hips.

She removed her phone from her bag and laid it on the counter. As she crossed her arms, she projected a relaxed attitude, as if she were having an office conversation, rather than talking to a naked, self-restrained man.

"You know my executive team are all Mistresses. Did you imagine them putting you on our board room table, spreading you out, locking you down? Going after you in so many ways that you'd lose count of how often you'd come? There's a reason we keep a full pitcher of water in there. Dehydration kills."

Amid the boiling lust and need, she relished the slow warming in the eyes fixed on her face, the hint of humor.

"I would like to take a picture of you for them, Lawrence. I won't include your face. If you don't want me to take the picture, I won't. If you want to think about it before I share it with them, that's fine. But may I take a picture now? Before I share it with them, I will ask you again. If you say no, I will delete it from my phone."

He considered it, gave her that slow nod. She took the picture, careful to capture only his bearded jaw and mouth above the neck, because she simply couldn't leave his mouth out of it. Too many wonderful fantasies associated with a man's mouth. Especially gagged with her panties.

"Hmm. Nice." She looked at it for a long moment, then she let her gaze travel back to him, moving up his torso. Part of it was to savor. Another part was to log important things. His shoulder with the bullet mark and scar across the pectoral was looking tight. The broom handle was starting to bother him. Not enough to safeword probably, but she didn't want to give him the wrong kind of discomfort. She noted the leg with the scar tissue was also looking a little restive, the ball of his foot shifting slightly, back and forth.

She moved forward, put a hand on his chest. Applied pressure so he moved back, off the handle. She dipped the toe of her heeled shoe over it, sent it rolling back to the island behind her. She kept moving him back until his bare ass met the cabinet below the kitchen sink.

"Brace your feet again. Wherever they're comfortable for your balance. Lean against the sink."

She reached up, removed the panties from his mouth. After she mopped up some inevitable saliva, she rubbed her thumb over his lips, smoothing any lingering irritation. She tucked the panties in her bag.

"Sorry," he said, probably about the spit.

"Nothing to be sorry for," she said. "Except speaking before I gave you permission to do so. How are you doing? Anything requiring the word 'gray'?"

"Not yet."

"But maybe soon."

The strain in his voice told her he was feeling the rod's constriction on the cock harness, fighting the urgency of his erection. She'd been keeping her eye on the color of his flesh, and it was getting close to time to give him some relief.

He flashed her a grim smile. "Maybe. Mistress."

He'd acknowledged it for her. Didn't deny it with a foolish stoicism.

"Good." She leaned against him, running her hands over his restricted arms. As she let her fingers make their way down his belly, slow and easy, his breath accelerated, and his cock moved against her upper thigh, the tip fully wet now. When her hand closed on his cock again, there was no fabric to muffle the part growl, part groan that came from his lips. But he had learned well. His gaze was fastened to her face as if she was the last thing he'd see before death. Sometimes her subs saw that as a gift from heaven. Other times, a curse straight from hell. The sweet spot for her was the perfect balance between both, where he loved and hated her equally in the same moment.

She slid the rod free, which pulled on the ropes and knots an uncomfortable second before their hold eased. His chest rose and fell in a breath of relief. His fists squeezed the pole as the pain washed through him and away.

She closed her hand over him again. Flexing her grip, she worked the knots against him. The abrasion was balanced by the friction, a rubbing she enhanced with her thumb on the knot that had been placed at the V-point of his coronal ridge.

His body surged with the response she'd been anticipating, perhaps more than he had, since she'd kept him focused on her demands. Staring her in the eye, holding the panties in his mouth, managing the discomfort of that rod, listening to her talk. During all that, he'd been banking his arousal, pushing it back, pushing it down, and then she'd locked it up tight with the rod. Suddenly it was ready to spill forth, coming up fast and nearly violent, all that need.

Hard to control, even for a male with his discipline. Which was exactly what she was intending to prove to him. Show him he could let loose, give her the control, the authority to say when, so he didn't have to worry about the control, the saying when. The staying in charge.

He was teetering on the edge, so she was ready for his look of desperate disbelief as she began talking again, casual, as if she had all the time in the world.

"I like watching you when I'm doing this." Her gaze flicked down to his fists, white-knuckled on the broom handle. "Your hands out of the equation, everything up to me. It gives me so much, Lawrence. It

71

makes me want to demand everything from you now. But right now, I'll settle for this."

Because she loved being a Mistress, she had a hell of a lot of practice at it. She could gauge where a man was at, how close his release was, and she could deny it, bring it back, so close, deny it again. She did it to him, several times, until his hips were bucking hard, the movements of his body rattling the cabinet doors beneath the sink. That desperation had grown, the primal beast rising.

"Are you going to come before I say so?" she asked, her voice deceptively soft.

He shook his head, violently. "Fuck...God..."

"That's not a proper response, Lawrence."

"No...Mistress."

"Hmm." She took him up again, so close, so close. His fevered gaze held her eyes.

"Do you want me to be merciful, Lawrence? Do you want my mercy, or my cruelty?"

"I want..." His voice dropped to a guttural rasp, his green eyes savage as only a warrior's could be. "You. Anything you want to give me."

The impact of that went from heart to cunt, a ripple shockingly close to a climax. Her knees trembled, but she steadied herself, kept working the jute over him, her fingers.

"Do you want my cunt?"

He nodded, that quick, violent jerk again. "Fuck, yes."

It only took a sharp look this time, the bite of her nails.

"Yes, Mistress."

"Willing to earn it?"

A groan broke from his throat as she took him toward that edge, past words. Her body was flush against his side, the broom handle pushing into her rib cage, his fingers gripping the stick against her upper arm.

"Tell me," she snapped sharply.

"Yes...Mistress."

"Then come for me."

If he had an ounce of will left, she suspected he might have tried to hold back, prove that he could hold out even longer if she demanded it. But she'd pushed him well past that point. He'd done far better than she'd ever seen a first-time sub do. While being fully engaged in the moment, responding to her on all levels.

His hips jerked, his toes curling hard into the floor tiles. She'd positioned herself to the side, so as his cock jetted, she watched the white fluid pump out of him, bathe her hand as he groaned under her stroking grip.

His head dropped back, jerked forward. His whole body tensed, arched, then bucked forward again. Violently enough the handle running under his elbows, across his back, couldn't take the stress.

The wood snapped with a sound like a gunshot.

She hadn't expected that, but in protective reflex, her hand immediately left his cock, pressed against his chest as the reaction tipped him forward. With the same kind of instinct, his arm fell around her, gripping her hip, holding her as the two pieces slid free, clattered to the floor. All while his hips were still working.

She returned her hand to his cock, milking the last of it out of him. His climax was on the downward slope, the fluid coming in short spurts instead of thick fountains. They leaned into each other, the counter bracing his body providing an anchor for them both.

As he finished, his head was down, his chest rising and falling fast. After one more gentle squeeze, she released his cock and laid her palm on his chest again.

"Okay," she murmured. "I've got you."

His gaze went to her, and she saw surprise there. Shadows, surprise, and other things. His arm was around her still. Tight. Holding on.

"Let's get you to one of these stools." She moved him forward.

Her attention was on him, on his well-being. She'd forgotten about the handle she'd left on the floor. Her shoe hit it, rolled over it. The resulting loss of balance yanked her body backward.

Or would have, but almost the second it happened, the arm around her constricted, lifting and righting her. All with his head still down, his mind and body reeling from the climax, still quivering from aftershocks.

He could be balls-deep in you...

Just like Dale had said.

It unsettled her, like no man had in quite some time. She gave a hundred percent to her chosen subs. Loved them in the moment, as

73

Abigail would say. In session, they had her full attention, her regard, all the way until the end. Afterward, they also had her affection, warmth and humor. Even an almost maternal protectiveness. She kept tabs on every sub at Progeny she'd ever been with.

At times, she'd made enough of a connection with a man in session that she considered taking him home. Or meeting for dinner, having an actual date. Those ideas usually never left the consideration phase, idle fantasies she didn't pursue. She didn't have the time or energy for that, and really, it wasn't necessary. She loved the outlet the sessions gave her. The intimacy of those couple hours was a gift a relationship might not accomplish for months, if at all.

Your heart doesn't get involved, Abigail told her. *That's why it's relatively easy to make that decision.*

It's not a shortcoming, Abby. Not if I prefer it that way. I like my life, and my relationships, the way I manage them. I want my focus to be on you and our business.

Yet with one protective gesture, when his mind should have been incapable of it, he'd sent her spiraling among some crazy notions.

She pushed that away to focus on more practical things. He'd made a mess on the floor. She would have put a condom on him, but she'd wanted him to feel the knots on his flesh directly, and when he'd chosen the kitchen as his preferred area, with its tile floors and cleanable surfaces, it had confirmed her decision.

Everything she'd seen so far showed he kept a tidy home, far more so than most men she knew. She'd leave it to him to handle clean up later. She liked imagining him finding spots over the next couple days he might have missed, and remembering their time here.

"Thank you," she said, a simple acknowledgement of his extraordinary effort to keep her safe from a fall. Unfortunately, she couldn't say the same. When she eased him onto the stool, her hand slid over a sticky spot on his back. Glancing behind him, she found out why. "Damn it."

"It's okay," he said. He had his elbow on the island, his other arm still loosely around her waist. "Hey, come here. Don't worry about that yet."

He gathered her into his arms, dropped his head on her shoulder. Comfort for him, yes, but his arms around her were strong, supportive. Giving her the same back. A different kind of thank you. Not very aligned with Dom-sub protocol but, with a faint smile, and an unusually tender feeling in her breast, she figured she'd allow it, this once. She curled her fingers in his dark hair, and leaned into the embrace. His beard was soft and rough at once on the tender rise of flesh above her bra cup.

"I didn't do anything for you," he said. "I'd like to."

"On the contrary, you did quite a lot for me. When I want an orgasm, Lawrence, I'll demand it." But it pleased her that he was considerate. "I made a mess of your kitchen," she said.

"I think I did that."

"So you did." Her smile deepened as she brushed her lips against his temple. "I'll tuck you into bed, and you can deal with it tomorrow. I won't even order you to clean it up with a toothbrush, on your hands and knees naked. I'd only do that if you'd misbehaved."

He snorted. "That would have been a hard 'sanctuary' call."

She chuckled. So he wasn't that kind of sub. At least not at this point. That was okay. That had never really been her kind either. Though it did bring to mind Whistler, a Progeny member who ran a very adult cleaning business. Male or female subs, according to the client's preference, would clean their home while wearing almost nothing. Additional bonus? They did an exceptional job for a reasonable price.

Vera had enjoyed a couple sessions with Whistler, who was a sub himself. When he gave her house a very personal one-man cleaning for her birthday, she'd acquired some memorable pictures.

"I'm going to take a look at this." More insistent this time, Ros slipped from Lawrence's grip and made him lean forward so she could see. When the handle had snapped, it had broken the skin almost at the center of his back, but fortunately the wound was shallow.

As she pulled her bag over the counter to her and removed her small first aid kit, he raised a brow. "Not the usual thing in a woman's purse."

"It's not my purse. It's a session bag, a small one, for spontaneous or offsite sessions like this."

He examined the monkey design. "I didn't take you for the whimsical type."

"It was a gift from Skye." A reminder not to let the shadows in life block out the light.

She opened an alcohol wipe and cleaned the wound. She put her hand on his shoulder, fingers stroking in a soothing way as the topical burned. Other than a slight tensing, he didn't react to it. "I've had powerful men under my control," she said quietly. "Maybe not quite as strong as you. Next time I'll go for rebar instead of a mere broomstick."

"Good call. Your fault, though," he grunted. "The way you tease things to the top, it gets a guy's testosterone raging."

"This is my gentle mode, but if that was your reaction to it, we'll need a place less susceptible to damage next time. Particularly if restraints are a hard limit."

His lips curved in that serious smile. She used magnifying glasses to check the cut for splinters, then taped a clean gauze pad over it.

"You have any bottled water?"

"On the counter, there beside the fridge. I prefer it room temperature."

"All right." She brought him one, cracked it open, and handed it over. "Slow sips."

He obeyed. His head was still down, as if he were thinking. She kept her hand on him. First time aftercare was no less of a discovery zone than the session itself. Some men liked to talk, touch. Some needed their physical space. Others went to sleep almost immediately. Some zoned out, not sleeping, but not really phased in, either.

Lawrence seemed more meditative. She supposed that wasn't surprising, since SEALs had to function through physical stress—lack of sleep, food, water...under torture. She didn't want to think about that last one, not at all.

"So...are you staying the night?" He lifted his head to meet her eyes. As he did, he covered her hand on his shoulder with his own. She considered him.

"Since you've never done something like this, I think I better."

"Will you sleep in my bed? With me?"

He'd anticipated a Mistress's mindset well enough to make the distinction. On the very rare times she had slept at a sub's house, she took his bed, but made him sleep elsewhere. Like the floor. If he'd been good, she'd let him have a pillow and blanket.

But if she knew something different was needed for the man in question, she didn't go that way.

"Maybe." She already knew she was going to curl up behind him, stroke his hair, watch him fall asleep. Make sure he did fall asleep, and determine how he slept. Deeply? Restlessly? Or so light it was almost not sleeping at all?

"Do you sleep in your bed, or do you crash on that man-sized couch in the living room?"

"Yeah, mostly. The couch."

"Then we'll start there. After we do this."

She adjusted to stand between his knees and began to untie the harness. In his cock's sated state, the hold was loose, so freeing the knots wasn't difficult. His organ stirred some beneath her touch, especially as she petted and stroked while removing the jute.

With a cock having so many folds, it wasn't as noticeable, but normally she enjoyed tracing the lines that had been left in bound flesh. Once she'd tied a man from shoulders to thighs. He'd struggled so much during the session, he'd still had the marks when she'd demanded to see them at the club the following night. She'd experienced the kind of satisfaction an artist felt, gazing upon a deeply personal work.

She extended a hand to lead Lawrence to the couch, but he hesitated. "Are you sure I can't... It feels wrong, not to give you pleasure, Mistress."

"As I told you, you did give me pleasure, Lawrence. I'm in charge of that part of things. I will tell you what I want, when I want it. Understand?"

He shifted, then nodded, even though she could tell he didn't like the imbalance. Part of it was that he was a good man, a generous lover. He'd already proven that to her, in many subtle and not-so-subtle ways. But there was something deeper to it, a quid-pro-quo that didn't have a place in the Dom/sub dynamic, because it was a passive way for the sub to hold onto control. Even if he wasn't aware of it, she was.

Fortunately, he seemed willing to accept her decision, but he had another concern. He glanced at himself ruefully. "I'm a little sticky. Don't want to superglue myself to the cushions."

"A good point." One she herself should have noted. His back had distracted her. But then she remembered tripping over the handle. She was usually good at keeping her mind on the details herself, and he'd put her off her game some. He was so damn absorbing.

Good thing she wasn't in charge of *his* security.

"You can put on the underwear," she decided.

He retrieved the black shorts and slid them on before offering his hand. When she put hers in his grasp, they moved out of the kitchen, into the living room. She noted a bed pillow tucked beneath a throw pillow on one end of the couch, and a blanket folded along the top.

"Lie down like you normally would, to sleep," she told him.

He stretched out on his side, facing the TV, putting the throw pillow on the floor beside the wide couch. She slipped off her shoes, and his gaze logged the height reduction. "Without my shoes, you're taller than I am," she said.

"Might make us good dance partners."

"Do you dance, Lawrence?"

"My father taught me. He said a woman can gauge a man's love-making ability by the way he dances." A dreamy smile touched his lips, his eyes half closed as he looked at her. "The first time he saw me dance, before he taught me, he said, '*Mijo*, if you want a woman to take you to bed, never dance in front of her.'"

She chuckled. "Scoot forward."

When he obliged, she put her bare foot on the couch near his shins and lifted herself over his legs, lithely stretching out behind him. "Hand me that throw pillow."

When he complied, she propped it on the sofa arm and put herself where she could see his profile as she stroked her hand over his hair, the broad point of his shoulder. She brought her legs up enough to fit the shallow spooning position the couch allowed, the hem of her skirt brushing the backs of his bare thighs. His eyes were open, not looking at her, but she could tell he was tracking her movements.

She spread her fingers out close to his throat, flattening her palm so she could absorb as much of him through her touch as possible. His warmth, the pulse in his throat a steady thud. She teased the hair at his nape and settled closer, pressing the satin cups of her bra high against his back. She wanted her pelvis cradling his firm backside, but keeping this vantage point was more important right now.

"I don't want you to talk right now. I just want you to relax. Sleep."

She picked up the remote off the side table and clicked on the TV. Finding a documentary with an even decibel range, she lowered the volume so the show provided a soothing murmur.

"*Ancient Aliens*," he said. "Good choice."

"I will put those panties back in your mouth. Don't think I won't."

He smiled again, but she saw his eyes, the movement of his mouth where he almost said something, but didn't, which resulted in a little ripple of tension through his shoulders.

"What do you want, Lawrence? You have permission to ask me."

"Will you take off the bra, so I can feel you?"

"Only if you don't turn around."

"No, ma'am."

She unhooked it, slid it off, passed it over. She noticed he held it a moment, fingers sliding along the inside of the cups in a way that had her nipples tightening. Then he nested one cup inside the other and laid it on the coffee table, stretching forward then coming back. As she pressed her breasts against his shoulder blades, above the gauze pad she'd taped over his injury, she decided to indulge herself. She rubbed her upper body against him, her knee sliding along his buttock, leg stretching over his thigh.

His shoulders rose and fell in a sigh, releasing something that had been tightly caged.

"Thank you," he said.

She'd slipped the hand that had been caressing his nape under his arm and he clasped it, his head dipping as he pressed his mouth to her fingers. Ros stayed curled up against him, no room between their bodies. With his hand on hers like this, her sandwiched between him and the couch, she felt two emotions she hadn't experienced together in a while.

Safe. And aroused.

She tightened her arm around him, and he settled in, holding onto her hand. She didn't ask for it back.

He fell asleep first, but he was a light sleeper. The slightest twitch on her part would stir him, open his eyes. She'd see the momentary calculation, figuring out who was here, who had his flank, then he'd drift off again. So eventually, to help him stay asleep, she kept her hand moving over him. It gave her pleasure to do so. Touching his hair, his skin. Feeling the rise and fall of his body.

He was a quiet sleeper, no snoring. But a couple times she felt tension slide over his body, tighten it, and he'd growl out words, low, urgent, impossible to understand. She continued to stroke through his hair, over his ears, behind his neck. She outlined every scar, marked every muscle. Admired the man, suffered at the thought of what had caused his wounds.

He'd seen things her eyes never would. Her day job was marketing. His had been doing things that maybe kept the world safer. Or at least some corners of it. She'd no doubt he'd been asked to do things he didn't think kept the world safer. Maybe even made it less so. Every job had those snag moments where one didn't agree with the boss. Though it wasn't usually over who to kill or not to kill.

Those possibilities gave him a different kind of core. That was what made him so intriguing to her. Once she plumbed that mystery, she would find a man beneath it, like any other man. Engaging, worth her time, someone she'd remember with deep affection when the time came to let him go.

She was inviting him to serve another purpose in her life, which could take this into deeper areas. However, once everyone else realized that Snake had more pressing things to do than chase her down, she wouldn't need extra security. Relationships worked far better with natural expiration dates, ones that everyone involved knew were coming.

She put her head down on the throw pillow. He still had that grip on her hand. She thought of loosening it to run her touch over his backside, his cock. She'd put her hand under the stretched cotton, clasp him. Hold and fondle him, slow and easy, as he slept. As she fell asleep. But she decided to stay just like this, her one palm on his chest, the other tucked under the pillow for her head, her fingers close enough to his head to play with his hair.

Watching a man sleep after she'd worked him over was almost as much a pleasure as the working over itself. However, since this was her first opportunity to study her surroundings more closely, she took it.

He had a good-sized flat screen, but not movie-theater big. His sofa didn't match the other two pieces, a two-person recliner and an easy chair, but their upholstery picked up the blue in his sofa. Pictures on the wall were mostly abstract color blends, like one would see in the lobby of a corporate office. An office not run by people like her. She loved her local art picks, and enjoyed cruising the galleries and street vendors to change it up a couple times a year.

These were pleasing, but not really pictures of anything. They were hung against a wall painted a mild blue-green.

That was the word. Mild. Everything was mild and almost generic. Mild colors, generic, functional furniture choices. Personal items included a cheap vase on the bookshelf next to the TV, like something left over from a flower delivery. It was placed next to a stack of books. Suspense, a couple NYT literary choices. A short stack of comic books set apart from them, though she couldn't see the titles. A stuffed bear leaned against a transparent rectangular book end holding the books upright. The bear had a stuffed heart in its paws, and the heart was stitched with Happy Valentine's Day. Maybe it had come with the flowers.

She noted a scrape on the sheet rock that disappeared behind the bookcase, a few gouges around it that suggested something had been thrown at the wall. She expected the bookcase hid the worst of the damage.

He'd said he'd lived here with his ex. He kept it clean, but she saw no indication he'd claimed the space, making it his. Except the couch. The couch, in a bold dark blue, with teal green edging on the arms, was his. She believed that because the vibrant color choices reminded her of the tiles in the kitchen. Maybe that was why the couch felt so comfortable. That and being pressed up against the man lying upon it.

She nestled down deeper against him, and his fingers tightened on hers.

"S'okay," he murmured. "I've got you."

She studied his profile, the tension in the features, and caressed his cheek, his jaw. Then she put her mouth to his ear and reminded him.

"No, Lawrence. I've got you."

CHAPTER SIX

*U*nlike Lawrence, she wasn't a light sleeper. Not at all. Abigail said Ros slept like a person capable of a self-induced coma.

"Sleeplessness is a sign of a guilty conscience," Ros had informed her.

"If that's true, then your sleep is the opposite end of the spectrum," her friend had retorted. "Conscienceless sociopath."

Ros woke to the smell of coffee brewing and bacon frying. She was still on the couch, but she was by herself. However, she was wrapped up in the very warm and comfortable fleece blanket that had been folded on the back of the sofa. Blinking, she realized it not only carried Lawrence's scent, but had Wizard of Oz munchkins marching all over it. Another gift from his team members, she expected.

Pushing herself up to a sitting position, she ran her fingers through her mussed hair. Skye had nicknamed Ros's makeup brand "The Day After," because it purportedly held up for a full twenty-four hours.

Even knowing that, it was still disconcerting to wake in a man's home and know he was going to get to see her before she saw a mirror. For a woman, forty plus was an age most evident upon waking.

Screw it. She wasn't the type to scurry off to the bathroom like a frightened animal because a man saw her nestable hair and face creased in sleep.

A clean folded T-shirt was on the coffee table next to her bra. She donned it over her bare upper torso. Another Lawrence-scented item.

With his broad shoulders and deep chest, the shirt was loose and comfortable. It fell to her upper thighs. Just. She still wasn't wearing anything under the skirt, so she left that on. She put her heels back on. She didn't walk around barefoot much, and she wasn't uncomfortable wearing her high heels as bedroom slippers. Particularly when a glance toward the kitchen showed he was already tracking her movements, his attention lingering on her legs as she slipped on the strappy heels.

When she wandered that way, she found a few good things to look at herself. His sweatpants hung low on that high, taut ass, and he wore a T-shirt similar to hers. Dark blue.

"I don't remember saying it was okay for you to wear clothes," she said.

"I had a medium contact you in the land of the dead. You said it was okay. No splattered bacon grease against my sensitive parts."

"Funny. Smartass." A place setting, complete with a placemat, plate and utensils, was set up on the island. A bowl of assorted sugar and sweetener packets rested next to a small pitcher of milk. Sunbeams streamed pleasantly through the vertical blinds over the sliding glass door.

As she took a seat on the stool in front of the placemat, she blinked at the steaming liquid he put at her elbow.

"That's coffee, dark roast. I also have tea if you drink that for breakfast."

"Nope. Coffee is great. I prefer dark roast." As she dumped in the milk and sugar, she noticed him paying close attention. She'd bet good money next time she wanted coffee, he'd have it for her, with her preferences already added. An anticipatory service sub with overwhelmingly alpha tendencies. In her world, he was a treasure worth guarding like a dragon.

"Do you really know a medium?" she asked.

"I do. This is New Orleans, after all." He sent her that quick smile. "She reads palms, tarot cards, the whole bit. Most of that is an entertainment thing, but she actually has some mojo. A few years back, I lost something I'd left on the top of the car. She told me exactly where to find it. It had tumbled off on a stretch of highway, rolled down a slope and gotten hung up on some shrubs. She landmarked it with a pond, a red maple, and an old eagle's nest in a dead tree. Since it was a route I took regularly, I remembered the eagle's nest."

"Good to know. Abby is the world's worst for misplacing things. She'll put your medium on speed dial." She wondered what had distracted her detail-oriented sub so much that he'd left something on the top of the car. But sensing that might hit a complicated emotional snarl neither of them would welcome untangling right now, she gestured at the backsplash with the colorful tiles. "I like those."

"Thanks. My daddy was a street artist in Mexico City, and he would paint the tiles for the tourists. My mama was an interior decorator. Eventually they turned it into a business together, him creating the tiles and her integrating them into her customer's jobs."

"Wow. So he was a painter *and* a dancer."

Lawrence chuckled. "He lived in the moment and enjoyed his pleasures. They eventually caught up with him. Heart disease. She runs the business now with my younger brother and sister. They're twins."

"I'm sorry. The colors are beautiful."

"He taught me to appreciate beauty. Mama taught me to be practical and watch my money."

"Romantic and pragmatic roots. A good balance." She took a sip of the coffee and closed her eyes. "Perfect. How did you go from that to the military?"

"My uncle, Mama's brother, was in the Rangers and first got me interested in the special ops route, because I wasn't the least bit artistic. I also had a close friend whose dad wanted him to serve. He joined the Army."

As he spoke, he'd moved from bacon to eggs. She watched him spread the cracked eggs over the pan's interior surface with deft movements of his wrist, a flexing grasp on the skillet handle. Dancing wasn't the only way women knew a man would be a good lover. It had a lot to do with how patient he was, how much time he took, and whether he had too much or too little focus on the things that mattered.

So far, Lawrence was getting high marks on everything.

"Mind if I ask you something?" he said.

"Depends on the question."

"Why aren't you married? Are you not the marrying kind? I know it's not a given these days."

"You've been checking up on me. You didn't ask me if I'd ever been married."

He lifted a shoulder, not denying it. "Part of the job, knowing the background of my clients. But it doesn't always give me the why."

She pursed her lips. "No man ever turned my mind in that direction. I've been career-driven since my teens. I've also been a practicing Mistress for a long time. Like any craft that engages your attention and imagination, it's a passion. I assume you had options other than being a SEAL, which takes up so much of your personal life."

He lifted a shoulder. "Never wanted to do anything different."

"It gave you what you needed," she confirmed. "Truthfully? Being a Mistress satisfies that relationship craving. Each time I meet a sub who clicks with me, it gives me that charge of falling in love and lust. The structure of the relationship keeps it from disintegrating the way so many relationships do. When it runs its course, then it's done and no hard feelings. Even if there is some grieving for the end, it's not the same thing."

"So you don't pursue relationships outside that structure."

"Not usually. No."

He held her gaze an additional blink. "You don't ever wish for something that will last longer than that? Get messy?"

She raised a brow. "What are you after, Lawrence?"

His expression altered, showing her a mix of guarded emotions. "Last night was a first for me. You knew things that I wanted...that I didn't realize I wanted. But when you asked for them"—a wryness touched his lips—"demanded them, it was like they'd been sitting there on a shelf right in front of me all along. Kind of took me by surprise, so maybe I'm asking you questions, trying to understand who you are, to determine what this is in me that has responded so strongly to it."

"I appreciate that." It impressed her, that he was thinking about it so clearly, not shying away from what some men would have had a problem digesting.

"The bond you have with everyone I met yesterday," he continued, in a more careful tone. "Is that part of it, too? Why you don't really care about pursuing a relationship?"

"With that kind of intuition, you could be a Dom yourself."

Though she knew he wouldn't want to be. "It started with Abigail," she said. "She's my heart."

And Laurel, she thought. But Laurel was gone.

He nodded. "That's pretty clear, the way the two of you are with one another. Full body language conversation without any words spoken."

"All the women in that room are links in a chain," she said. "We're bound to each other for the usual reasons. Shared experiences, crossed paths, opening up avenues you didn't expect. Eventually you reach a deeper level that commits you to one another. No going back."

He brought the bacon to her with tongs, arranging it on her plate, and then scooped fluffy eggs out of the skillet and deposited them with equal care for their arrangement. He might not be an artist, but presentation was important to him. He picked up another plate off the side bar, put his food on it, then joined her on the opposite side of the island. He offered salt and pepper to her and when she shook her head, he used them on his food instead.

"So are the SEALs like that?" she asked. "Filling that gap for an intimate relationship? Providing companionship with those who know you soul-deep, are there for you?"

"Yeah." Lawrence sent her a half-smile. "Probably would be enough, if women didn't have some pretty spectacular things to offer."

She answered him with a light smile of her own, but she wasn't going to be put off-topic. "What do you do after years of having that and now you don't?"

He stopped, but he didn't look up from the food, telling her he was concealing his reaction before he spoke. "You go find a hot Mistress, of course."

"Lawrence, look at me."

When he did, the shadows in his eyes were heavy and dark. "I still have the team. We're still friends."

But it was way different from when he was with them. No longer read into the missions, no longer aware of all the nuances and insider stories. It was there in the short answer, the sudden tension in his shoulders.

"Maybe that's why you were so open to what we experienced together last night," she observed in a light tone. "Leaving the SEALs left a void. A particular person or experience can shine a light on that emptiness, guide you to seek something different for it."

"Maybe." He grunted, returning his attention to his eggs. "Does that happen to a Mistress, too? A session gets a bit deeper than you expect, because there's an emptiness that can't be filled by what you already have plenty of?"

Last night hadn't been one sided. He'd picked up on it, but he'd had the manners to pose it as a question. She was comfortable enough with who she was and what she wanted that she could accept the observation with a short nod. And a question of her own.

"I noticed you were very courteous toward my team," she said. "But with Abigail, there was a hesitation of sorts. A different reaction."

He shrugged and rose, putting his dish in the sink. She'd never seen a man put away food so quickly, with such impeccable manners.

"It's an impression," he said. "Likely a wrong one."

"You said that to spare my feelings, not because you actually believe that. So spill."

His face altered subtly. Regret perhaps, at being read on the subject and called out.

"She's strong, but she's also got that kind of fragile beauty that goes hand in hand with pain," he said. "I've run into people with the look she has, mostly on missions. Their world is limited, and they're aware of exactly where the boundaries are. They've accepted that, but they still always look like they're standing on a dock watching a ship sail away, carrying all their dreams with them."

She looked down at her coffee mug. Stared at the contents. His hand slipped over hers. "I shouldn't have said anything," he said.

"I asked you a question and required an answer."

"I should have lied."

"No." Her eyes snapped up to his. "You shouldn't. Not ever. Understand? I'm *not* fragile. I can handle what decimates most people. Even if I can't, the choice to be destroyed is mine. The only thing I can't bear is the betrayal of a lie. Because that's what a lie is, even a well-meaning one. It's a way of telling someone they don't have your trust, your confidence that they can handle the truth."

His green eyes were reading between the lines. "Or that they care about you so much, an evasion is an act of love," he said. "Of protection."

"I don't need that kind of protection," she said brusquely. "If you don't understand that, this relationship ends right here. Personally *and* professionally."

Maybe it startled him, her going there in a blink, but the point was that important to her. She wouldn't let there be any confusion about it.

He straightened, took his hand away. But it wasn't a rejection. It was assuming a stance that told her she had his full attention, and his response was equally committed.

"I understand, Mistress. Truth always."

"Good." She glanced at her breakfast. She still wanted it, though it was going to go down a little less easily. As she picked up her fork, she noticed him still watching her.

"Yes?" she said, a little testily. "More truth to impart?"

He leaned forward, brushed her tense lips with ones that were soft and fragranced with breakfast smells. His moustache teased her skin. "You don't have a fragile beauty. You're strong as hell. Mesmerizing. Addictive." He kissed her with each word, at a different angle. Then he lifted his head, pinned her with a breathtaking heat.

"You didn't choose to have a climax last night. I understand that. But I want to give you one. I want to carry you to my couch, put my mouth on your cunt and bring you pleasure, Mistress. When I'm on my couch by myself, I want to remember your scent, pleasuring you there."

She blinked. "And if I say no?"

"Then you say no. But you asked for the truth. That's my truth, and every time I look at you today, that's what I'm going to be thinking."

She set down the fork. "You know how to turn truth into an irresistible incentive, Lawrence."

He nodded, not denying it. After a moment's consideration, she turned the stool away from the counter and sent him an expectant look. She was interested to see how he'd respond to it.

She didn't have to wait long. He moved around the island and lifted her beneath the arms, so she could wrap her legs around him.

The movement pushed her skirt back to her upper thighs. She left her shoes on.

He had no problem carrying her, one hand curved under her backside, the other around her back. When he lowered her to the sofa, he eased her there gradually as he brought himself down to one knee beside it, hands braced on either side of her thighs.

Under his kindled gaze, she leaned back on her elbows and waited. He dipped his head, looked at the way his shirt stretched over her breasts, the aroused nipples. He kissed between her breasts, eased the T-shirt hem up to put his mouth on her navel, play there. He shifted his hands, dipping them in between her thighs, under them, lifting, as she fully reclined against the cushions. The skirt folded back under the pressure of his touch.

Though he had the blinds closed over the double set of windows in his living room, there was a crescent-shaped window above them that wasn't covered. She could see the bluish-gray, rose and gold colors of a morning sky, heralding the rising sun.

He pressed more kisses on her upper thighs, then worked over to her mound. From there, he traveled to the insides of her thighs. Nuzzled in between them as she drew in a breath, a nice, anticipatory, shuddering breath. Then he put his mouth fully on her.

Slow, easy, a nuzzle becoming a dragging lick, a swirl, pressure in the right places, a deeper exploration that wrested a small moan from her throat. Her hand went to his head, fingers digging into his hair. She lifted her legs to rest her calves along his back, avoiding the area below his shoulder blades where the broom handle had broken. Her high heels bit into the upper rise of his ass revealed by those loose sweats.

Oh, he was good at this. Taking his time, moving his mouth in a slow rhythm that matched the insistent stroke of her fingers in his hair. There was a reason for the crass term "eating pussy." Done right, it was like the doer was enjoying a good meal, never wanting it to end.

She tightened and eased her touch by turns, lifting herself to his mouth. She dropped her head back, and drifted on clouds of bliss, sharp and soft at once. Her hips strained for him and he dove deeper, with an animal growl of enjoyment that made her cunt spasm beneath the clever ministrations of his tongue and lips. She heard soft, wet sounds as he enjoyed her, and it took her even closer to that pinnacle.

She could come whenever she wanted. This was all about her plea-sure. He wasn't pushing her, so obviously immersed, taking his enjoy-ment from the journey itself, the clawing of her fingernails on his neck and shoulders as sensation built, the humming sounds in her throat...

She could have done it forever, too, stayed on that precipice, holding onto the simple and almost miraculous experience of a man with only one intent. To follow her lead while anticipating exactly what she wanted as she wanted it. Projecting nothing but powerful male satisfaction that he was the one giving her that experience.

A man who, with everything he did, made her want to make him hers. Whose eyes said, in that peculiar dichotomy of service and possession, that he was already well on the way to considering her his.

His question about marriage had opened strange things in her mind. Strange thoughts, mixing with this rising spiral of desire. She'd never thought she'd want to belong to a man, or have one who belonged to her, after the session was over. But maybe that was because she'd believed those words meant something else. Not what they meant when she saw them in Lawrence's eyes, felt them in his touch.

She believed in the instant obsession, the overwhelming crush. Flashes of lightning in the sky, here then gone. She let go of the absurd feeling that this was more than that, and held onto what always made sense.

That spiral was getting tighter, higher. She gripped his hands, nails digging into the area behind his knuckles as her body shuddered. She locked her legs over his upper body and bowed back as the climax swept through her, her flesh pulsing against his heated, wet mouth, the firm tongue and lips, lashing and flicking, thrusting and swirling.

He moved with her as she bucked, as the cries tore from her throat, as lights exploded behind her eyes. Her body shimmered and locked, the power of the release holding her in tight fists for wave after potent wave. Even when they started to slow, they were as sweet and easy as riding a rocking sailboat to shore.

"Oh..." The syllable came out with a long breath. Her hand had dropped off the side of the couch, and she felt like a cat as she gazed at him from under half-closed lids. "Put your cock in my hand, Lawrence. I want to know how hard you are."

He straightened and shifted, so his hand was still braced against the back of the couch, him leaning over her in that way that felt like a shelter. As he clasped her wrist, he brought her palm up against the rock solid heat beneath the sweat pants. What she felt was impressive enough her sex rippled with an aftershock. His eyes glowed with more heat.

She found her way under the fabric and gripped him fully. He shuddered but didn't thrust, gazing down at her.

"I'm not letting you come this morning," she said softly. "What do you think of that?"

"I think I'm going to have to work extra hard to keep my mind on the job."

"You do that. Consider it a test of the self-control Dale said I could bet my life against."

The smile disappeared from his eyes. "You don't ever have to worry about that, ma'am. Not ever. The mission comes first."

The switch was startling. He spoke as if she wasn't touching him intimately at all. She wasn't sure if it was off-putting or arousing beyond belief, and decided the choice was hers. She reached up, touching his mouth. "Come lie down with me while I catch my breath."

Before she could shift to make room for him, he'd slid an arm beneath her. The world turned smoothly, and he was stretched out on the couch beneath her, her body partly sprawled across his, her hips cradled between his thighs as he wrapped an arm around her back. His way of moving her around with so little effort was decidedly breathtaking.

She wouldn't admonish him about putting her in such a cosseted position without permission. After that performance with his mouth, he was allowed to cosset. And she didn't mind the feel of his hard cock against her stomach at all.

"So how did you become a Mistress?" he asked after a bit.

"I owe it all to my history teacher."

He was playing with her hair. With her head on his chest, it made it easy to close her eyes, consider drifting back to sleep with him as her body pillow. After all, he was doing his job, wasn't he? They were at his place, where no crazy gang members would expect her to be. He was as close as any bodyguard would need to be to serve as her human shield.

She didn't like the direction that thought took her, so she pushed it away in favor of something better. She imagined what it would be like, lying in his bed after she'd had his body. The sheet tangled over his mostly bare leg, a bit of hip showing. She'd eat him alive all over again.

She had no meetings this morning, after all. And she was the boss.

"That's all you're going to say?" His voice held humor. "Just leave me visualizing your history teacher as your sex slave?"

She laughed. "Okay, Mr. Ray may have been Mrs. Ray's sex slave, but since I was fourteen and he was *soooo* old, at least thirty—*eww*—that never crossed my mind."

Lawrence chuckled, the deep sound vibrating through her. "Okay. So how was he responsible for you becoming a Mistress, then?"

She adjusted so she was next to him, still within the curve of his arm. The change in position let her pull his T-shirt up, and find his nipple and muscled pec with her mouth. As she stroked and tasted, she rubbed against the iron bar of his cock. A soft oath escaped him.

"I can torture you like this all day, Lawrence. The more you take, the more you please me."

"I was taught to withstand torture under interrogation. That was easier."

Had that teaching ever been put into practice? She traced the bullet scar near the nipple, but held the dark question. Instead, she answered his.

"Like most teenagers, I knew everything. I did a very self-right-eous, self-important speech about how history was written by, for and about men. So Mr. Ray gave me a project. By the Christmas break, I was supposed to write an essay about ten powerful women in history the school's curriculum didn't include. So I did."

Her caresses on his chest slowed as she remembered. "As I read about these women, I noticed they didn't waste a lot of time screaming about men being horrible and unfair. Finding a group to blame or hate wasn't they were about. Just the opposite. They saw what they wanted, moved forward and made it happen. They had a firm grasp on their own personal power."

She chuckled. "I'm not sure I made such an articulate conclusion at fourteen, but the exercise planted the important seeds. As I grew up, it came together in my mind. And then..." She drew out the syllable for dramatic effect, "When I was a senior in high school, I watched the movie *Story of O, Part 2*. Where she's far more in charge of what's happening than in Part 1. It gave that seed sunlight, water, a desire to grow. I started to know what I was."

"I'll bet you were a handful and a half for your teachers."

"And then some." She smiled. "Even though I wasn't actively practicing at that point, there were some budding submissive male types who picked up on the vibe in high school. When the senior yearbook was published, someone had put me down as *Most Likely To Have An Army of Male Sex Slaves*."

"An army, huh?"

She grinned as his fingertips slid over her shoulder, along her collar bone and beneath the band of the T-shirt, sending tingles along her skin. "As every ruler knows, it takes a lot of resources to care for and feed an army. Though for some reason, I'm now thinking about the 'Army of One' campaign the U.S. Army did a few years back..."

He laughed when she ran her fingertips down his abdomen, a ticklish move that had him grabbing her wrist, even as he brushed his lips over her forehead.

"Too bad I'm a SEAL," he said.

"I expect the same principles apply, regardless of the branch of service." She closed her eyes, pressed her palm against his heat, the thud of his heart. Then she removed her hand from beneath his shirt and propped herself on her elbow to look at him. His eyes were smiling, his lips slightly curved. She'd seen hints he could be a wiseass, playful, maybe even a prankster in his less serious moments. She didn't think he'd had too many of those moments of late, so she was glad to give him one now.

That said, she hoped the smile would still be in place in a few minutes, but she wouldn't put off the necessity of the next conversation they needed to have.

A sub she chose needed to know up front the way she conducted her relationships. If there were going to be hurt feelings or tantrums, she wanted them out in the open. The reaction would inform her whether she could go forward with the man in question or if she needed to go ahead and cut him loose.

All the emotional twists of last night, capped by those unexpected thoughts a few moments ago about belonging to a man, told her it was time to have that conversation. For herself as well as him.

"I need to draw some boundaries between us, ease back some," she said. "The way this is progressing isn't my preference."

"Oh." The smile disappeared. His hand had curved around hers when it came out from under his shirt. She extricated hers smoothly, sitting up in a manner that indicated she wanted him to do the same. She adjusted her skirt back over her thighs.

He tipped his head toward the bedroom. "I have a feeling this is an engagement that's going to require more body armor. Mind if I get dressed?"

She glanced down at her T-shirt, no bra beneath it, her wrinkled skirt. "I think we've got an equal amount of protection."

"Still."

"Oh." He wasn't asking. A decided shift in the give and take that had seemed so easy between them a moment before. She inclined her head. "Do what you've got to do."

A look of frustration crossed his face at her cool tone, but he rose and disappeared up the stairs to the townhouse's second level she'd yet to see.

Two could play that game. She retrieved her blouse and bra, donned them in the downstairs bath. Straightened her hair and touched up her face with her bag contents.

During that time, she gave serious consideration to just finishing her tasty breakfast and making last night the beginning and the end of it. On all levels, including the security detail. Since she'd agreed to that only for Abigail, she could smooth that over with some additional reassurances to her friend.

But then she thought through what had happened last night, what she'd felt from him as she'd taken control. It took a lot of self-discipline to walk away from the candy case when it was open, the contents within grasping distance. Especially when her senses were full of that candy's scent, its texture so freshly imprinted upon her fingertips, the taste still lingering on her tongue.

She had that kind of discipline. But her instincts told her not to walk away. He had a submissive craving, but he was a hundred percent alpha male. Used to calling the shots, even if he craved to give that up in the bedroom. Instead of calling an end to it, she could view his guarded reaction as more of a reason to greenlight things.

She'd returned to the island, intending to sample her eggs and bacon. Even cold, they would still be good. The man could cook.

Before she could lift her fork, he'd returned, and the plate was gone. He put it in the microwave, hitting the re-warm. "Not as good as right out of the skillet, but better than eating them cold," he said shortly.

"They weren't that cold." She eyed him. "What's going on, Lawrence?"

When he said nothing immediately, she crossed her arms on the counter but leaned forward. A combination of open and closed body language. "Do you want to chalk it up to a good night and leave it at that?" she asked quietly. "It's not an ultimatum."

He held her steady gaze for a long minute, and then he shifted. Not in a way to the visible eye, because he didn't break the lock. She felt it in a change of energy between them.

"If I say yes, you won't employ additional security, will you?"

"You think giving me your body is a condition of the contract? Vera would spawn an army of kittens if she thought I'd given you that impression."

His lips quirked. "No. I don't think that. I want you safe, Rosalinda. I also want you. But I don't know how to take some of the things you say. We had a good night, right?"

"A very good night."

"I agree. I don't care for games. We had a good night. It was something special. Waking up and acting like it wasn't, that I'm something on the to-do list for the day, doesn't play as honest to me. It plays like you're protecting yourself."

She raised a brow. "I'm honestly and absolutely protecting myself. Maybe you're used to women who say one thing while they feel another. I don't. My relationships have been in a club structure, a session, where these things are laid out up front. If you're not a club guy, it's not a deal breaker, but I still prefer to make it clear what I want and don't want, when we get together."

He thought it over. Sipped his coffee. Glanced outside. He had a birdfeeder, she saw, and a mob of finches were feasting on the seeds, tossing the hulls this way and that like confetti.

"Okay," he said at last. Not a clear signal to go forward or retreat, but she interpreted it as him wanting her to continue, explain further.

"Your desires are as important as mine. The rules aren't intended to diminish that, but to anticipate problems or misunderstandings. Exploration in Dom/sub dynamics is very focused, which is what gives them the ability to go deeper and wider. Not giving it any structure is like asking a flag to fly, without any wind to provide direction. Do you understand?"

He blinked. "No. I'm not sure I do. But it sounds...it sounds like I misunderstood. My apologies for getting the wrong idea."

"What was that wrong idea?"

"That last night didn't mean much to you. I'm not being a little bitch about it, asking for more than you want to give. I just..." He set down his coffee and grimaced. She could almost see him picking up the stick to beat himself with it. "I thought you were fucking with my head," he admitted.

He looked like he was still staring at the coffee. In reality, she suspected he was staring, in his mind, at whoever had done that routinely to him. Which brought back what had worried her last night.

However, he was being forthcoming now, showing he wanted to overcome whatever baggage was dogging him. She wouldn't penalize him for that, due to her own worries.

"Nothing is further from the truth," she said. "Come around here. To me."

"I'd rather you come to me."

"Would you *really* prefer that?" She arched a brow.

A long moment of silence as they regarded one another across the counter. At length, she uncrossed her legs, started to get off the stool. He shook his head, a sharp jerk. Then he moved around the island to stand in front of her.

"You remember at Club Progeny, when I told you to show me how you felt it, and you put your mouth to my ankle?"

He nodded, slow, those eyes opaque, revealing nothing, though energy vibrated from him. He wanted so much from her, but she had a feeling it was like a briar thicket to him. He was sure he was going to get torn to pieces when he plunged in. Even as she was sure it wouldn't stop him.

96

It was another unexpected thought, one that had her reaching out and cupping his face, stroking his beard, running her thumb over his lips, the line of the soft moustache. The man was as hard as a brick wall, but his beard was thick and soft, like a winter-coated wild animal.

"I loved last night. I loved what you gave to me. I loved that I'm your first Mistress. I want more of what we were discovering last night. Do you believe me?"

He was analyzing her expression almost as closely as she had done his, when she had him under her command. He wasn't taking it on faith, glossing over it. She'd thought last night a woman had hurt him badly. It showed.

"I want to," he said at last.

She'd take it. She was glad she hadn't decided to walk away from the candy case. "That's why the rules need to be there. Dom/sub sessions can be very powerful, very amazing, when in reality you know very little about one another."

"You said my desires are as important as yours."

"Yes. Always. Though they don't always look quite as straightforward as desires typically are." At his confused look, she smiled. "If I withhold an orgasm from you so you can prove you serve me, not yourself, that will turn you on far more than just having an orgasm whenever you decide it's okay. Disagree?"

"I take the fifth."

She chuckled and returned to eating her breakfast, pleased when he slid onto the stool next to her, his thigh brushing hers. When he resumed drinking his coffee and a companionable silence drew out, she knew they were good.

At length, she wiped her mouth with a napkin. "So, you wanted to go by my house for a security assessment."

"Yeah. What's your work schedule today?"

"I was going to work from home this morning and go into the office in the afternoon."

"Okay. I don't want to assume Snake is going to give you more of a grace period than he already has." He frowned, thinking. "For the foreseeable future, whenever you're coming or going anywhere, clear it with me first. I'll escort you or advise your best method of getting safely from point A to B. If someone is watching you, they're going to know from here forward you have a protection detail."

In a blink, he'd become her security advisor. Even his body language shifted, so there were a few inches between them. It felt like they were in her office, rather than his kitchen, enjoying a morning-after breakfast. It was making it harder to taste her breakfast, let alone swallow it. She tried not to let it affect the mood, telling herself she needed to listen closely, not get her hackles up about it.

He continued, either oblivious to her internal struggle or accepting it as an expected reaction from a new client. "The further in advance I can know your plans, the better. I know that's not always possible, but whenever it is, it helps. I also need to know who knows your schedule, other than me. I'd keep that to a minimum, and whoever does know needs to watch what they reveal and where."

She raised a brow. "No one in my firm is going to betray me to a street gang."

"It's not that. Say Bastion is stopping to get his morning coffee, and he runs into a co-worker. They're chatting, and Bastion happens to say, 'Yeah, our boss is going to be at so-n-so at ten this morning.' If Snake is smart enough to have people tailing your people, gathering what intel they can, he's just given a heads up to the gangbanger two people back in line, hanging onto every word."

She frowned. "You *really* think they're going to put this kind of energy into this? Or are you just placating my team?"

He didn't smile. "From what I've read, this isn't a guy who just lets things go."

"I really think you're all overreacting."

"Said a dead person never." He didn't miss a beat when she made a face at him. "We'll take your car this morning and I'll drive. That way I can determine if you're being tailed."

It was too much, too soon. She slid off the stool. "I'm sorry. I'm not doing this. I'm not going to turn my life into a constant looking over my shoulder. I don't jump at shadows."

"Rosalinda." He touched her face, but she drew back. She'd left her hand curled tensely on the island, though. Undeterred, he let his hand land on it, though lightly.

"When I had a bad reaction to what you said, a few minutes ago, you took the time to lay it out for me, help me understand. This is no different. When a person first realizes they might be in the crosshairs, a couple things happen. Denial heads the list. Not knowing where the threat is coming from, or who will deliver it, is a huge loss of control, and strong people don't like to lose any control. You're a strong person. Kickass, take-charge people hate to feel fear. Again, that's you."

He tightened his grip. "But fear, much as it sucks, can help us make as many smart decisions as it can dumb ones. Especially if instead of reacting to the fear with denial, you take a look at what's causing it and plan how to manage it. I'm your fear-manager."

She glanced down at their linked hands on the counter. It hadn't escaped her notice that the more he'd spoken, the less she'd felt like pulling away, raising a wall. "You're very good at this. Do SEALs do a lot of protection details?"

"A fair bit. Depends. But keeping people calm in the line of fire is one of the most vital things we can do to keep them alive. Sometimes it's even more important than having superior fire power."

He lifted her hand to his mouth, brushed an easy kiss over her knuckles. It didn't change the steady calm in his gaze, nor the oddly reassuring coldness in his tone. They told her he wasn't in unfamiliar waters on this, the way she was.

"I have two full bathrooms, if you want a shower on your own after you finish your breakfast," he said. "After that, we can head for your place."

CHAPTER SEVEN

*T*hough he wouldn't have turned down an invitation to shower with her, Rosalinda had confirmed what he'd guessed, that she wanted some space. She'd chosen to take one on her own in his guest bath. As he headed up to the master to take a shower and shave before they headed out, Lawrence hoped he'd been able to help even out her negative reaction to the security measures.

Apparently, he had.

He'd figured if she finished before him, she'd hang out in the living room, watch the morning news or do a million things on her phone to run her universe. Instead she came upstairs, in one of those just above the knee skirts of hers in an ivory color, paired with a copper colored silk blouse and matching bronze jewelry. She wore another strappy looking sandal. From the hint of black lace at the neckline, he knew she was wearing a different kind of underwear. She gave him a better glimpse of it and her cleavage by stretching out on one hip on his bed.

While that was distracting for so many reasons, all of them having to do with sex, the position gave him a hint of the scar over her left breast. He wanted to ask about it, but figured they'd hit their quota for touchy subjects. From the instant warning look she'd given him about it last night, that was obviously one.

Now she merely watched him get ready, with those mysterious blue eyes. She didn't require that he talk, and she wasn't excessively chatty. He liked that about her.

He was kicking himself for getting pissy with her earlier in the morning, when she'd merely been laying down some ground rules on the Mistress stuff. He'd reacted to her like she was someone she wasn't.

Past baggage should be goddamn past baggage. Especially since she wasn't like anyone he'd ever encountered, male or female. She spoke her mind straight out, like a man. But from the top of her blond-streaked hair—soft as a whisper across his skin—to the tips of her insanely high heels, she was a hundred percent female.

He thought of the shoes digging into his ass when she'd clamped her legs against his back and he'd pleasured her sweet folds, coaxing forth that slippery, heated release. Thinking of how she'd kept her shoes on during that made him hard again. Maybe he did have a shoe fetish—if she was the one wearing them.

He'd kept a towel wrapped around his waist while he shaved, and that, plus being pressed against the counter as he did it, contained the reaction. Not that he thought she'd mind seeing it. But he normally donned a towel when he touched up his beard and shaved at the mirror. Plus, she seemed to like the look. Her gaze, sliding over the terry cloth clinging to his ass, reflected blatant appreciation.

Jesus. Maybe women's coyness had an evolutionary purpose. Around a woman like this, all a man would ever think about was fucking.

Eventually he went to his small walk-in closet to pick out a shirt and pull a pair of nice jeans off the shelf. He was on the job, so needed to look professional, but if he was going to be checking the security at her place, he might be tunneling behind bushes or going up a ladder.

She rose from the bed and wandered in behind him. As he turned her way, her buttock brushed his thigh. She trailed her hand along the rack of shirts. When she moved in close enough for a deep inhale, it was all he could do to act casual, as if a Mistress came into his closet every day to enjoy his scent, like a cat attracted to catnip.

Her eyes met his. "Olfactory memory is one of our sharpest senses. Even more if you use it a lot."

She moved back to the doorway of the closet, but the distance did nothing to cool his erection. He could be self-conscious about it, but since it was the effect he expected she wanted, and she was standing there, heel hooked around her ankle, arms crossed beneath her silk-clad breasts, he shed the towel, put it up on its hook. He reached toward the basket that held the neatly arranged rolls of his clean underwear.

"Stop. Turn toward me." When he obeyed, she closed the distance between them with one sauntering step.

His jutting cock was pointing at exactly what it wanted. With easy grace, she dropped to her heels. His hands clenched. She hadn't given him permission to touch her, which told him he shouldn't. The self-imposed denial only made his cock pulse harder.

As she applied the curled moist heat of her tongue to the tip of his cock, she took a couple kittenish licks, teasing. Then she went down to the root, a slow glide. He swallowed an oath as she followed a sucking, leisurely path back up.

She released him, straightening to stand again.

"I love to taste a cock begging for its Mistress," she said matter-of-factly. "All day today, I want you to remember how my mouth feels there. And think about how you could earn more of it."

Even without the direction, he was damn certain the memory would run through his head all day, like stocks ribboning along the bottom of a news channel screen.

She returned to the bed, stretched out again. He made himself focus on getting dressed. Underwear, jeans, shirt. Belt, shoulder holster and nine-millimeter. Knife in the ankle holster. He put a short-sleeved open button down over the cotton T-shirt beneath it to conceal the gun.

She noted all his preparations, but said nothing until he indicated it was time to go. Only then did she speak, rising from the bed.

"Don't shoot my cat," she said.

She didn't live far from her office in the Garden District. On the drive over, Lawrence put a hand over the console, offering. Ros glanced at it dubiously.

"Not a hand holder?" he asked.

"I guess I think of it as what teenage lovers or really old couples do, something sweet. I'm not all that sweet."

"I'd disagree with that, but it's not about sweet."

"What's it about, then?"

"A way to say I care, for reasons more than to get in your pants."

She considered that. "Can I hold your hand, even if I do just want to get into your pants?"

"I'm okay with that."

She put her hand in his, felt his fingers close over hers. She noticed that even as he was talking to her, holding her hand, he kept surveilling their surroundings, what was ahead, behind and along the sides of the car. He included a brief visual touch on her with every cycle. She put her hand over both of theirs as he rested them on the console, indulging herself by tracing his rough knuckles.

While she wasn't one of those people overly sensitive about someone else driving her car, it had felt odd to hand over the keys. She had no problem with his driving skills, though. The Mustang and he were getting along like a cowboy and his horse. It must be the Texan in him.

"What fantasies have you had about being dominated by a woman, Lawrence? And don't say 'things like last night,' because that's a cop-out."

"If I tell you about mine, will you tell me about yours? About topping a guy that is, not being dominated by a woman. Though if you have those, I'm not averse to hearing the details."

"I'll bet." She snorted. "I'm a woman of action. I convert my fantasies to reality, as soon as the opportunity presents itself. Stick around long enough, you'll get to experience exactly what my fantasies are."

He glanced her way. "All of them? You're telling me you don't have fantasies that go way past the line? Woman 'most likely to have an army of male sex slaves?'"

She tossed him a glittering look. "You're evading."

He lifted a shoulder, not denying, and returned his attention to the road. It was about a thirty-minute drive to her place from his, depending on the traffic, so there was time to get a good answer to her question. She wasn't concerned that she was interfering with his security priorities. She felt sure he'd tell her if she was, and she didn't think there was anything to be concerned about anyway.

"Let me help," she prompted. "Very first movie you ever saw, or book you read, that got you thinking about it."

That distracting mouth twitched. "Easy one. Wonder Woman comic. When I was about eight or nine."

"Hmm." That definitely deepened her attraction to him. Some men's craving for submission evolved as adult life shaped them. But some men were born with the urge. Lifting the hand she had resting on the top of their clasped ones, she traced a line along his thigh. She studied the shape of his body, his competent, easy movements as he navigated the car. Her attention drifted to the spread of his thighs, the curve of what lay beneath his inseam. His testicles had filled her hand with a solid heat and weight last night.

Having a submissive near, even if it wasn't the appropriate time to actively play, was like having a nice tall glass of wine to sip upon at her leisure. The shimmer of electricity under her touch told her he'd noted her attention.

"When did you become aware that Domination and submission was a thing?" she asked. "And connect it to your thoughts?"

"Not sure I ever did that last one." He frowned, obviously thinking. "Not consciously, until I started going with Dale to his club. It was just a way I felt, when I looked at certain things. I laughed it off, considered it just a typical reaction to anything about sex. Guys joke all the time about having some hot woman tie them up and go down on them, you know? But in my gut I knew that wasn't the way I was fantasizing about it."

Because in that scenario, he was being served *by* the woman. A submissive, particularly one like Lawrence, wouldn't fantasize about that.

"In school, I had this one girlfriend," he continued. "Which was kind of a miracle, because I was a chubby, awkward kid, especially around girls."

She poked the firm muscle of one buttock where it pressed into the seat. "You got past it."

"The weight at least. Some women can still get me tongue-tied." The smile he sent her was almost shy this time. She told herself she was unaffected by it, even as she flicked her nails along his nape in playful admonishment.

"Stop flirting and tell me the story."

AT HER COMMAND

"One day, we were in her parents' kitchen. They were gone for the day. Like any other guy, I should have been all about jumping her as soon as she gave me a green light. Instead, I remember asking her, all polite, but in this rough kind of voice, if I could take off her panties. She said yes, had one hand on the counter to keep her balance as she watched me slide them off from under her skirt. So quiet, her eyes so big. Crazy, how I remember the details."

He'd changed lanes in the middle of painting that scene for Ros. Now he switched back, glancing in the mirrors. Whatever he saw satisfied him, because his expression relaxed slightly, and he resumed. "As I went to my knees to take them off, I remember thinking, I want her to lift her foot, put it on my shoulder, hold me there when I start to get up. Instead of me standing again, she'd tell me to put my mouth between her legs, prove how much I could turn her on. Course, she didn't do that." He slanted her a wry look. "She was fifteen, I was sixteen. I was the guy, she was the girl. She was waiting for me to take the lead."

"So what did you do?"

"I did. I took care of her. Not as good as I would have liked to, but hey, when you're kids, you're kids. Afterward, I thought maybe whatever was going on with me was lack of confidence, wanting her to tell me what to do. So I pushed past it, made sure I knew what to do. But it stayed in the back of my head for a long time. There were always these scenarios unfolding in my head when I was having sex. Her being on top. Her holding me on the edge. Me having sex with a girl while another woman sat in a chair nearby, watching me, threading a belt through her fingers, like she was going to strap me with it, if I didn't fuck her good enough..."

He broke off, shot her a look. "Hell, you know how to get a man going on this shit."

Though that was true, so was Dale's assessment. Lawrence's awareness of their surroundings—her care—hadn't faltered, not once. She'd never been so turned on by a man's ability to multi-task.

"I didn't tell you to stop. Keep going, Lawrence."

Since they were at a stoplight, she let her finger drift down her throat, over her sternum, and into the V-neck of her blouse, where she could tease the stiffening nipple beneath her bra. His gaze followed her hand, watched it grip the right breast fully beneath the silk.

He cleared his throat. "I had visions of them tying me up, one of them straddling my face. The woman with the belt telling me to make the one on my face come while she traded out the belt for a crop, beat my cock with it. Then she wrapped it up in chains, because it only belonged to her."

She'd seen hints of it last night, a craving for some level of pain. Hearing it show up in his fantasies was very good news. "Ever thought about having a woman fuck you, Lawrence? Put a strap-on up your ass?"

She saw the flicker in his gaze, the flex of his hand on the wheel. It told her the answer, even as she saw him calculating her feelings on it.

"Just honesty," she said. "That's all you owe me."

"No," he said frankly. "That's not really my thing."

She liked fucking her subs, but if they weren't into it, there were plenty of other things she enjoyed. Still, she wouldn't consider it a true hard limit until they'd had other sessions together. Lawrence was very new to all this. A sub's limits more often than not changed, the more experiences he had with a Mistress he could trust.

"Even a little strap-on? Pinky-sized?"

When she wiggled hers at him, he chuckled, looked her way again. Did a bit of a hitch. She'd opened her blouse one button, and had lowered the cup to more thoroughly enjoy caressing the nipple. Now he could see it, caught between her knuckles, being tugged. Since the car was in motion, and people didn't typically look in other people's cars, she wasn't too worried about privacy.

"You have good focus," she observed. "Do you want to hear one of my fantasies?"

He muttered something that might have been *Jesus Christ*, but nodded.

"I'm eating breakfast. My sub is naked, on his hands and knees beneath the table. My feet are propped against his side, toes curled into his warmth as I read a book, finish my breakfast. I use a vibrator on myself and come. My feet are pushing hard against him, but he doesn't move an inch, an anchor so I get the full measure of satisfaction. Then I put the vibrator, still wet with my arousal, against the head of his cock, strap it there. I drink the rest of my mimosa while I call my mother, letting her know what I'm doing with my weekend. Gardening, catching up with some reading."

His thighs flexed, his ass shifting in the seat. The telling movement speared her with satisfaction. "I've gagged him, so she won't hear his groans. As she tells me about her weekend, I watch him come, his hips jerking. But he still fights to keep his body still, not wanting to disturb his Mistress's footstool. When he's done, I have him sit down by my feet, put his head in my lap. Because he's done so well, I allow him to curl his arms around my hips, and I stroke his hair, enjoy the feel of his heated breath on my damp pussy, while I finish the call."

The look in his eyes was pure, nerve-tingling fire as she drew her hand from her breast, slid the button closed and adjusted her blouse.

"You know," she observed, "Matt was right about one thing. I'm going to enjoy having my own driver."

Lawrence had decided *she* was right, what she'd said that first night to him. She could be a BUD/S instructor. Particularly when they tested a candidate's focus under extreme duress.

He couldn't imagine anything more distracting than Rosalinda Thomas's vibrant imagination. She'd pulled his own fantasies out of his head and embellished them in ways he hadn't considered. Then made those ideas coalesce into an urgency to do them all. Now, now, *now*.

He pulled up to her place, a two-story historic home painted salmon red with cream trim. The sprawling live oaks in the front yard provided generous shade, a pugnacious magnolia tree thrust up among them. The house had a raised basement, in deference to the moisture-rich sub-surface clay that made subterranean structures in New Orleans challenging. A jungle of hydrangeas and azaleas clustered around the cement foundation on both sides. The foliage grew up high on the narrow, non-driveway side, providing a screen that obscured a clear view of the first level windows.

The balcony on the second level was a full wrap-around, like the porch below it. Getting from the first level to the second with the screen of the bushes would be as easy as having an intruder in good enough shape to do it.

"You're frowning," she said. "What is it?"

"A couple things." But the one that concerned him the most was coming from his gut. He let the car roll slowly along the driveway, past that first cluster of azaleas. No active flags, until they parked in back.

A pane of glass was broken out on the rear entry door, just above the brass-looking knob.

When she followed the direction of his gaze, she saw it too. Her hand shot to the handle of the car door, but he gripped her forearm, holding her in place.

She struggled against him. "Abigail was coming by last night to check on my cat, Lawrence."

Fuck. Something she should have told him. Something he should have asked, the second she told him about the damn cat.

"Call her," he said evenly. And didn't let go of her.

Giving him a look that would have cut most people off at the knees, she yanked out her phone and made the call. Her expression was white, tight-lipped, and didn't ease.

"No one is answering."

"She could be in a meeting."

"Or she could be lying on the kitchen floor," she snapped. She went for the door handle again. This time when he grabbed her wrist, her fingers curled into a fist. Tension, not a threat, but from her forbidding expression he suspected that could change. "Lawrence, I am *not* waiting."

The right step was to call the cops, wait on their arrival. Letting local law enforcement do their job was the best way to stay on their good side, and only an idiot risked clearing a house without waiting for backup. The only justified reason to do it was if someone inside was in imminent danger.

Which she'd just pointed out might be the case.

He muttered an oath. "You're going to stay in the car and call the police," he said. "I'll go check out the house."

"I'll stay behind you, but I'm going." Her tone said the topic wasn't open for argument.

It wasn't.

"Remember our deal," he said. "You listen to what I tell you, or

108

you find someone else to do the job. Someone who will let you set the terms and get you both killed."

Her eyes flashed, her mouth curled in a snarl, but he gave her credit; her mind didn't stop working under stress. In less than a blink, she executed a curt nod. "Fine. Let go of me."

He complied, though he was ready if she was trying to fake him out. He could guess some of the worries pummeling her mind, making her body tight as a spring. He couldn't alleviate any of that until he knew what the situation was, so he didn't waste time on anything but what was necessary.

"Lock the doors after I get out. Call the police. If anything happens you don't like, anything at all, lay down on the horn until I show. Are you carrying your gun?"

"In my purse." When she spoke through stiff lips without looking at him, he put a hand on her shoulder.

"Look at me, Rosalinda."

Frustration wreathed her expression, but she did it. "You know the average time for most police and bad-guy gunfights, beginning to end?" he asked.

She shook her head.

"About three seconds. So I mean it. You see anything, you hit that horn without hesitation, take out the gun and get low. Promise me."

"Why are you still here?" she grated.

He tugged her hair, touched her face with a fingertip. "Because you're paying me to protect you. Abby and the cat are extra."

The grim humor served the purpose he intended. It broke her concentration on worst case scenarios, at least for a moment.

He exited the car, waited until she'd engaged the door locks, and then headed for the house.

Ros dialed 911. As she relayed the details in terse syllables, she watched Lawrence approach her back porch.

He'd drawn his gun and had it at the ready. A moment ago, he'd used a gentle tease to break up the avalanche of worry burying her. Now, if he'd been dropped in the middle of a war zone, she expected this was how he'd look. Focused. Deadly. Which was surreal, since he was moving along her petunia-flanked walkway and headed up the back porch stairs, lined with glossy black planters of dark red, wheat-plumed ornamental grass. Garden stakes with metal pinwheels shaped like daisies embellished them. The light wind had them spinning gaily.

Her heart thudded against her chest, a hammer of accusation. When he'd gone over his security precautions, like giving him her schedule as far in advance as possible, and making sure Bastion wasn't too chatty when he was picking up morning coffee, he'd rattled her. Which had annoyed her, so she'd reminded herself how everyone was overreacting, and that she was doing this mostly to placate Abby. Playing with him in the car, seeing if she could distract him like a tourist in front of a guard at Buckingham Palace, had helped restore order to her universe.

She'd been an arrogant idiot. She hadn't given a second thought to having Abigail check on Freak. She had a security system, after all, and there was no alert on Ros's phone, saying the system had been compromised. But how many times had she heard that a sophisticated criminal, one with more than just random burglary in mind, could jam or get around run-of-the-mill security systems? Now she had a broken pane of glass, suggesting someone had been—or still was—in her home.

If this had happened while Abby was here... And what if Freak, being Freak, had drawn their attention?

She was still on with the 911 operator, but when her phone buzzed with a text, she pulled it from her ear to glance at it. Abby.

Just got out of a staff meeting. What do you need?

Abby was okay. But that meant the break-in had happened after Abby was here last night. Freak was outgoing. He would come investigate someone in the house. Which meant they would have hurt him. She knew it.

She couldn't stay here. She just couldn't. If Freak was injured but could still move, he'd hide himself away in one of the spots that only she knew. He wouldn't make noise unless she was looking for him. She had to get in there.

She was a smart woman, and though yes, she was arrogant, she could admit when she was wrong and adapt accordingly. She understood why Lawrence had told her to stay put. But what if Freak was minutes away from being beyond help? What if he was dying, and thought he was all alone...

She told the operator she was going in, for the police to hurry, and cut the call while the woman was sharply admonishing her not to do that, and to stay on the line. She stuffed her phone back into her small crossbody purse, bolted out of the car, reached the back porch and came through the kitchen door.

Lawrence was in the living room. She expected her shoes on the steps had told him it was her, because he had the muzzle of the gun pointed away from her. The look he gave her was as lethal as a bullet, though. They'd be talking about this later.

With a curt movement of one hand, he gestured her to slide in behind him. She complied. "Be my second set of eyes," he murmured. "You look wherever I'm not looking."

She nodded. Hesitated before showing him the text on her phone, because what if he tried to take her back outside until the police arrived, since she'd confirmed Abby was okay? She couldn't leave without finding Freak.

He glanced at it. His jaw flexed, he met her gaze, but then he nodded and proceeded deeper into the house, her staying close behind him and alert for movement as he'd ordered.

Since she deduced it was best to have only the most experienced gun hand in the mix, she left her Walther in her purse and instead grabbed the letter opener off her secretary as she passed it. The point was wicked sharp. If needed, she'd ram that thing home, fuck from ass to eyeballs whoever had broken into her house. She wanted so much to call out for Freak, but since Lawrence had restricted himself to hand gestures and whispers, she followed his lead. Coming up the stairs, across the porch and into the kitchen in her high heels had likely been as subtle as firing a nail gun.

With an internal wince, she could imagine his sarcastic response to that.

You think?

Fortunately, it ended up being a moot point. He moved through her home more swiftly than she expected, while being infallibly thorough. A smooth, methodical check of every room, closet, and hiding spot, including under the guest and master beds. When they finished, they were in the upstairs guestroom at the back of the house. He holstered the gun, gave her a look.

"Find your cat," he said.

As they'd moved through the house, she hadn't noticed anything in disarray. No vandalism, which was a relief. But when she returned to her bedroom and entered her shoe closet, she smelled cigarette smoke. Someone had stood in this spot, their presence marked by the caustic scent. The thought made her stomach drop to her feet.

Her laundry basket, full of clean towels, was pushed close to the back wall under her hanging clothes. The position formed a hidden alcove between the wall and the basket. She'd put a folded fleece blanket in that spot because it had been Freak's favorite hiding spot when he first moved in with her. It still was, when he was unsettled.

"Freak," she said softly. "Hey, buddy. Are you there?"

The tension that could crowd into a single heartbeat was like the nightmare version of a thousand angels dancing on the head of a pin. But by the time she'd squatted, she heard his croak, and he was hopping out to see her.

"Oh, thank you," she murmured. "Thank you."

The black and white three-legged cat had a wary expression, his pupils the size of moonpies. That alone told her someone had been here who shouldn't have been. Freak was not a wary cat. He was the master of his universe. Prior to losing his front leg, he'd been the terror of birds, squirrels, and at least one neighborhood dog he'd cut down to size.

"I'm sorry, Freak." With relief, she noted he looked unharmed.

Freak's head twitched right, those big eyes focused behind her. She turned on the balls of her feet to see Lawrence staring at the contents of her closet. "I've never seen a shrine to shoes," he said.

She made a face, her gut loosening a little. "This is a normal shoe collection for a fashion-conscious woman."

"Just what I'd expect any self-respecting shoe-hoarder to say." He offered her a hand to help her up as Freak disappeared back into his spot. "He okay?"

"Yes. Seems to be. Very spooked, though. I smell cigarette smoke in here."

He sniffed, a brief frown crossing his brow as he concentrated. "Good nose."

"Cigarette smoke gives me headaches and stomach issues. I bought a used car once. Though no one else could smell it, and the car lot had given it a professional cleaning, I got nauseous every time I drove it. Had to trade it within a couple months."

She was biting off her syllables in a short, sharp way. He ran a light hand down her arm, a reassurance. "Do you usually leave your shoes like that?" he asked quietly.

She'd been so focused on Freak, she hadn't paid attention to the shoes. Now she did.

Every shoe in her collection had been reversed, so the toes all pointed outward.

A dickless asshole with nicotine-stained fingers and the stench of cigarette smoke lingering on his skin, his clothes, had touched her shoes. She made a mental note to contact whatever cleaning service could come in and wipe down all her footwear.

She tried to focus on that, and ignore the chills the act sent through her. It creeped her out more than a full-scale toss of her home, which she expected was why it had been done. The thought snapped her spine straight and firmed her chin.

"No," she said. "I don't leave them like that."

The police arrived a couple minutes after that. They had her walk through the house again, make sure nothing else was out of place. Nothing seemed to be, until she reached the living room.

The wall-mounted shelves held pictures of her family, trips, friends. The frames had been laid face down and stacked up in a tower.

As she talked to the police, she couldn't take her eyes from it. A variety of emotions were gripping her, but what was simmering the closest to the top was rage. She felt Lawrence's regard and crossed her arms over herself, rubbing her hands briskly along her upper arms as she answered the questions.

In time, Lawrence took over that part of things, which maybe wasn't the best thing, because it left her in her head. As she thought about those pictures, her shoes, Freak's nervousness, the possibility of

Abby being in the house, her volatile reaction to all of it continued to expand.

She thought about when she'd been in the closet and they'd heard the sirens approaching. Lawrence's hand had dropped to her wrist, given it a light squeeze. A reminder she still had the letter opener clenched in her fist. He took it, set it aside, and had quietly escorted her back downstairs.

She could hold it together. At least until the police were done.

The officer who took the report was shrewd enough to recognize this wasn't a typical break in. She recommended Ros stay with friends for a while, indicating that even with the best precautions, bad things could happen.

Ros thanked the woman politely, told her that she'd hired additional security, indicating Lawrence, and left it at that. Lawrence took some shit for coming into the house before the cops arrived. He handled it stoically, his expression saying he'd expected to take the hit. But he'd done it for her, and to ensure Abby and Freak were okay.

Ros would have stepped in to point that out, but he made a slight gesture during the dressing down that told her to let it ride. She wouldn't normally have done so, but her temperament was uncertain. She wasn't so far gone that she'd unleash her temper on the police who'd responded to the call.

As he showed the woman and other officers out the front door, a prickling started along Ros's skin, preceding the flush of heat, a shortness of breath. Fortunately, now she could deal with it the way she wished.

She strode out of her living room, past that stack of pictures, to her kitchen. Jerking open the utility closet door, she found what she wanted, gripped it.

There was another door in her kitchen, one to the basement. It had a deadbolt lock that required a manual key, and it had a security pad all its own, with a different code, hardwired. Her house security had been circumvented and deactivated, but this panel was still red-lit. That, and the undisturbed keyed deadbolt, was why she assumed Lawrence hadn't needed to open that door the way he had all her closets. She'd told the police there'd been no breach of the basement, but it wasn't the deadbolt or security panel that told her that.

It was the translucent thread she kept between the door's jamb and knob. It was unbroken, until she did it now, deactivating the panel, unlocking the deadbolt and yanking open the door.

She moved down the steps to the basement level, kicked off her shoes and waded in with a snarl. If she didn't deal with the wave of rage crashing down, it would drown her.

Her exercise equipment was closest to the stairs, specifically her punching bag. It took the brunt of her first swing from the baseball bat she carried, a solid thwack that made the bag rock. She hit it on the rebound and kept hitting it, letting the fury build and crest, until her arms were burning and her breath sobbing in her throat.

They could have sat in her chairs. Lain on her bed. They'd touched her shoes. Scared Freak.

She stopped, closing her eyes as she caught her breath. The bulk of her anger was at herself. The physical exertion helped her drain it out, until she could grasp a more measured response. She'd fucked up. It was done. Time to get a grip and realize no one had paid too dear a price for her mistake. There was time to adjust her thinking and do better.

Opening her eyes, she saw Lawrence sitting on the bottom step, watching her with eyes that didn't judge. She expected he'd seen every possible version of rage, helplessness and despair there was. He had her pair of discarded shoes sitting next to him. Neatly arranged, toes pointing the way they should.

His expression was quiet. He wasn't about to tear into her about anything. She couldn't say the same.

Dropping the bat with a decisive thud, she came toward him, unzipping her skirt and kicking it off, leaving her in the pair of filmy underwear beneath it. This pair was black, a lot of mesh and lace that rode beneath her hipbones and barely covered her mound.

She'd reclaim the personal sanctuary of her home, starting in the spot the intruders hadn't soiled with their presence. She straddled him on the stairs, cupped his strong jaw, fingers digging into the beard as she jerked his face up so she could put her mouth on his, demanding, invading.

She relished the startled look in his green eyes. Yes, she didn't react in the typical female way to things. She was angry, and needed to mark something as her territory. Or someone. Someone strong and hard to control, someone willing to submit to what she demanded.

Who would hand her that control because she could make it worth his obedience.

It was the wrong attitude, she knew that, but she also knew he was strong enough to fight back if she went too far over the edge. That was what she wanted right now. A fight, a tug of war, something to pull her mind from everything that would be waiting for her on the other side of this.

"Take off everything above the waist and get the jeans out of my way." She backed off, opening the buttons of her blouse while she gave the command. He rose, his eyes resting on the black lace bra she revealed as he unbuckled his belt, pulled it free. He handed it to her, a gesture that made her want him even more. She doubled it in tense hands, running it through her palms as he stripped off the overshirt, shoulder holster and T-shirt. He set them aside, keeping the gun close to hand before he unfastened the jeans and pulled them open. He didn't shove them down his thighs yet. Instead he bent, picking up her shoes.

His gaze met hers before he came to her and dropped to a knee. He bent his head as he laid his hand on her calf, her ankle. She lifted her foot, put it into the heel. The Manolo Blahnik ankle tie sandals were a chestnut color that picked up the color of the open blouse, the trim on the ivory skirt she'd left on the floor. He ran the tie around her ankle, adjusting it, his steady touch pulling other, less violent things from her. Things that could ground her.

She'd never been a switch. She'd always been a Mistress who wanted to hold the reins. So watching him wrap the strap around her ankle and cinch the tie just right, not too much, not too little, his fingers caressing her, soft leather around her ankle, sent an arousing message. It could be complicated, but only if someone wasted time trying to translate it into words. He did the other one, and then rose.

His breath was warm on her face. She thought of him holding the gun, the startling lack of emotion in his eyes, the coolness and the concentration. She also remembered the kinder note in his voice when he'd said "Find your cat." He could have bellowed at her for not following his direction and waiting in the car.

He was a man who had masterful control of his impulses, but who wanted her to command his passions. It showed now, a close-to-the-surface aggressiveness that suggested his potential for violence.

She didn't say a word, but what she wanted was in her expression. He lifted her, one arm banded around her back, the other around her hip. His broad palm cupped her ass as he moved them to the wall. The thud against her back was like a paddle against flesh, the reaction shooting through all the right nerve endings.

She wrapped her legs high on his hips. Because the erotic gods were smiling on this moment, her heel inadvertently slid through the belt loop at the back of his jeans. She pushed against it, pulled down. Impatient, her hands skated over his shoulders, gripped his nape as she pulled him forward, captured his mouth anew. She wanted to devour him, all his heat and strength.

"Fuck, wait..." He tore his mouth away, but held her pinned to the wall with his body.

He found the condom, freed his cock from his briefs. He sheathed himself, with a quickness and dexterity that made her wonder if he practiced that as often as he practiced his marksmanship. When he pulled the crotch of the panties to the side and tested her body's welcome a brief second before he thrust into that gushing wetness, ready for him, she thought he did.

She wouldn't have chosen this to be the first time she had him inside her, but she wasn't going to deny herself. She began to climax the second he started thrusting, and she saw his surprise at that as well.

I know what I want, when I want it.

He'd adjusted his forearm against her back, hand flat on the stone behind her head so she was pressed against his knuckles and wrist, not the unyielding surface. Caring for her even as he shoved into her, obeying the demand of her flexing thighs and locked heels. The climax drew moans from her throat, her nails raking down his neck, high on his shoulders. She avoided the place she'd bandaged last night, but she didn't stop herself from drawing blood elsewhere.

While he continued to move with her and she rode the intense aftershocks, she let other sensations in. She inhaled the clean smells of stone, of velvet and wood, because this room was more than her home gym.

It was her dungeon.

She was looking over his shoulder at a wall of impact toys. A St. Andrews Cross, a dungeon horse, queening chair. BDSM classic favorites, because they could be used in so many ways. While she hadn't brought home many subs, she'd done a lot of things to those few trusted and trusting males here.

She wanted to use all those things on Lawrence. But despite the visual stimulation they provided, all she wanted right now were his arms holding her as she took her pleasure from the working of his powerful body and thick cock.

As she gripped him within and without, holding him in a claiming vise, his rigid muscles, the increasing force of his thrusts, told her he was ready to follow her over the edge. Gripping his shoulders, she opened her eyes, stared at his face.

"Don't you finish," she whispered. "Not until I say. And don't do a damn thing to hold back."

His green eyes flickered and mouth tightened. Frustration, yes, but her words lit the fires of a challenge, to serve her the way she demanded.

As he kept going under her unblinking stare, his thighs and buttocks, the muscles of his face, started to quiver with the strain of stopping his release. She did everything to make it more difficult, contracting her inner muscles on him, letting him feel the wet, heated stroke of her pussy. It continued to spasm with aftershocks. She arched her back, lifting away from the protective arm behind her and giving him a prime view of the wobble of her breasts in a nest of silk and lace.

His palm slammed into the cement wall next to her head, fingers clawing as he cinched her waist in the other arm, his buttocks rising and falling under the clamp of his calves.

"Ask me, Lawrence. Ask me nicely." Her voice was breathless, but no less demanding. "To make up for when you're going to scold me, for not staying in the car."

His eyes flashed and his lips parted. She teased them with her own, licking at them, and a part groan, growl came from him. "Ask," she demanded. "Or I'll make you do this for hours. Until I've come three times."

"Wouldn't take hours to give you...that."

She bared her teeth in a smile. Biology was going to override his will and her command eventually, but he was fighting it with everything he had. For her. He wanted something beyond what his body wanted.

She would test it, even though the answer might unlock things in her she wasn't ready to have unlocked. Her lips formed the words anyway.

"Do you want to come, Lawrence?"

Green eyes flared. "If you want me to come."

"Who am I, Lawrence?"

"My Mistress."

His Mistress, for this incredible moment, when the whole world, everything they had to deal with, would wait on her command as well. No matter that it was an illusion, the thought could steady her.

She laid her hands on his face. "Keep looking at me, Lawrence. Come."

She'd added a layer of difficulty to it, because no one wanted to look right into the eyes of another when they released. It was an intensely private moment, a cutting free from self-consciousness into pure sensation. But that was why she wanted to see his eyes during it, hold his gaze. She wanted him to release while fully tethered to her, aware that it was her will that released him, dictated to him, here, in this space in particular.

His hips bucked, friction and heat against the tender skin of her inner thighs. She watched that glaze come over the green in his eyes. He'd had an intense but relatively quiet climax the night before. Now what came from him was a jagged-edged roar. He pounded into her, and she let out a gasp as the heat filling the condom translated into tiny featherlike strokes inside her channel.

He held her gaze manfully, all the way to the end. When the climax reached its strongest peak, and his body shuddered in the clasp of her arms, his eyes trying to close, he didn't allow it. He didn't cut himself free from her.

At last, they were both done. She coiled her arms around his head and shoulders, drawing him in, letting him rest his forehead against her shoulder as she pressed her jaw to his temple. He put both arms around her, pulling her fully off the wall. His jeans had never dropped further than his thighs, so he could still walk. Though he appeared as if he had the strength to hold her up for days, she knew strength was something men would push past the point of stupid. Lawrence might not do that, but with endorphins running through him right now, he might need the reminder.

"There," she gestured, and he followed her gaze. He carried her over to the queening chair. It sat on a raised step, so it could also work as a throne, a man on his knees before her, his wrists bound to either armrest. She could put his face into her lap, to service her or simply let it rest there while she stroked his head and shoulders, like she'd described in the car.

She didn't give Lawrence specific direction on how to arrange himself. She simply had him lower her to the chair and waited to see what he would do.

After he put her down, he hiked his jeans and underwear back on his ass, covering everything, but left the jeans open. He sat down between her feet, putting his back against one of her calves. When he rested a loose hand on his knee and dropped his head back on her knee to look up at her, she leaned against the inside of the throne, one hand on the arm rest, the other on his shoulder, stroking.

"I like your threat response mode," he said.

She gave him a tight smile. The moment was passing, and other emotions were closing in. But before they had a full grip on her, his post-climactic lassitude shifted to an expression so laser sharp it rivaled the knife he carried.

"You ever not listen to me like that again," he said, "I will quit. But I'll wear your ass out first with my belt, so maybe you'll listen to the next guy better."

He meant it, which gave her a heart-thudding insight into the hand-in-hand nature of the man and the submissive. It didn't displease her to see it.

Before they'd pulled into her driveway, she would have responded with more rancor. But no one knew how to punish a mistake like a Mistress. Especially when she was the one who'd made it.

She moved her hand up to his hair, stroked without replying. At least not until a few minutes had passed and she could say it aloud. "I could have gotten Abby killed."

He closed his hand over hers. "But you didn't. I should have asked you if you had anyone who came to the house regularly. Especially after you mentioned the cat."

He didn't deny she'd done something stupid. But he took his own share of the blame. She wouldn't argue with him, since he had his own professional standards, but privately she felt the primary fuck up was hers, due to her unwillingness to take this seriously, until now. He'd had no reason to suspect anyone was stopping by her home during her absence, especially with a gang threat against her.

"Two questions?" he asked, after another pause.

She nodded, steeling herself for something that highlighted her lack of judgment more acutely.

"Why the thread over the door?"

She deduced he must have noticed it when he was clearing the kitchen. His attention to detail might not be a surprise to her at this point, but it didn't fail to impress.

"A friend of mine had something awful happen in his dungeon, some years back. It made me think about it. I wouldn't ever want to use what's in here again if someone I didn't invite tainted its purpose, or the energy that is supposed to exist here."

"Like someone pissing in a basin of holy water."

"Yes." She liked that he understood. "Since no one but me and people I really trust know how to get into the room, that probably sounds foolish."

"No. We may think we go overboard to protect the things that matter, but if a threat happens, it's not overboard, is it?"

Her lips pressed together. "Touché."

"I wasn't intending to draw parallels." He tapped her knee, gave her a hint of that hard look again. "I already said what I meant on that."

"Okay." She curled a strand of his short hair over the top of her finger, rubbing it with her thumb. "Second question?"

"Did you come up with the cat's name? Seems mean."

She understood the reaction. In addition to the missing leg, Freak had a missing ear. He also had digestive issues, so that she fed him a vitamin-added home cooked rice and chicken mix. Though she gave him generous helpings, he was naturally skinny, and his fur was thinner, without the shiny luster most housecats had.

"It was a compliment," she said. "I called him Freak from the day I moved in. You know how sometimes a person gets called a freak because they're different, or they go their own way and don't give a shit what anyone else thinks? Well, that was him. When I moved into the house, he already lived here, in the backyard, on the porch. He refused to move with the previous occupants. Kept coming back.

"At that time, he didn't want to be an indoor cat. I fed him, but he caught and ate squirrels, moles, the occasional bird. He was an incredible hunter. And fighter. He once chased a German shepherd who got out of her yard all the way back to her house. After he launched himself onto her head and scared her half to death. One night his luck ran out."

"It happens," Lawrence murmured.

She nodded. "The vet thinks he got attacked by a pack of loose dogs. In escaping them, he also got hit and rolled by a car. Lost the leg, and the ear was torn up so badly, the vet clipped it down to the base. I didn't know if he'd be okay, being my indoor cat from there forward, but he settled in like he was always meant to be a house cat. I sing Super Freak to him sometimes. He seems to like it."

He smiled, and his hand fell to her foot, playing with the ankle tie of her shoe. The touch sent tendrils of sensation up her leg. Since she'd sat down with one knee bent, her foot on the edge of the seat, and the other leg behind him, it gave the air the chance to dry the dampness of her folds through the thin fabric of her panties, now readjusted back over herself. His gaze had drifted to that part of her, a look of hunger passing through his green eyes. When he moistened his lips, she flicked his shoulder.

"Lawrence Gatlin, you are a total pussy hound."

"Guilty, ma'am. May I kiss you there?"

His voice was rough, the request delivered in a stilted way that reminded her she really was his first Mistress. He was finding his way in a manner that was damned irresistible.

"Yes. Just one kiss, though."

Pressing his hand into the seat of the chair, he lifted up and put his lips on her cunt. Heat and the cushion of his firm mouth sent more of those pleasant ripples through her. She cupped the back of his head, holding him there. He didn't interpret that as a change to her directive, so she had the deep pleasure of his mouth resting upon her without movement, his breath bathing her with further heat.

At length she let her hand slip away, and he correctly interpreted that as an order to ease back. He rose, fastening his jeans, and offered her his hand. "Time to deal with it," he said.

She gripped his fingers and stood. As he picked up his T-shirt and the short-sleeved button down he'd had over it, she moved away and retrieved the belt she'd dropped. When he had the shirts back on, and had donned the shoulder holster and gun, she threaded the belt through the loops of his jeans. He watched her, his hands falling on her upper arms. When she buckled the strap, she grazed his abdomen beneath the shirt he'd left untucked, his warm skin and the silky arrow of hair. She set her jaw, nodded.

"Time to deal with it."

CHAPTER EIGHT

$\mathcal{T}$hough Lawrence hadn't wanted the break-in to happen, there was one immediately obvious benefit. The chance that Abigail or her cat could have been hurt had resulted in a one-eighty on Rosalinda's attitude. The potential threat to others motivated her in a way that the real risk to herself hadn't.

Based on what he knew of her so far, that didn't surprise him. From his brief exposure to the women of her inner circle, he could tell she saw herself as more than their boss or friend. She was the head of the family, as Abby had said. She reacted to a threat to them the way a SEAL would, or a police officer, anyone in charge of the safety of others.

On the other hand, her personal reaction to her house being broken into had surprised him. *Holy Mother*. She'd gone at that punching bag with the ferocity of a pissed off polar bear, and then, casting the bat aside, she'd looked for the second-best way to burn off aggression. The look she'd thrown his way was one he'd never experienced from a woman. Pure, violent possession.

You're mine, her mouth on his had said. *I want what's mine*, her body had said. And her eyes...

He was going to be thinking about the way she'd stared him down for a while, trying to understand everything there, and what she'd called forth from him in response.

When Dale had first taken him to a club, let him watch, Lawrence hadn't been sure how to react. After getting over his initial shock that his Master Chief was into that kind of thing—and then recognizing Dale was such an obvious Dom he felt like an idiot for not seeing it sooner—something had happened. He'd taken a long, deep breath in a world that didn't feel alien at all. It was like landing on Mars and discovering it had been his home planet all along.

It was as he'd told Ros. Throughout his life, the clues had been there. His cock pretty much took notice of anything related to sex, but when it involved a woman taking charge, it had a whole different gear, and those things stayed with him, far longer than a naked girl picture on the Internet did. Hell, he'd taken extra trips to see the school nurse in middle school because of her firm, no-nonsense manner and touch.

Him jacking off as a teen, thinking about Nurse Conrad, was not something he would be telling anyone, ever. Even Ros. The woman would be his grandmother's age at this point, and she'd been overtly not sexual, with her sturdy body in white slacks and smock, her chapped hands. She'd had a nice, soft-looking bosom though, and generous thighs he'd imagined...

Yeah, not going there.

During all those club trips, Dale had never said straight out that he knew that Lawrence might like the sub side of things. He *had* dropped hints that if Lawrence was interested in trying anything, Dale would help him get there. Lawrence had shrugged, neither confirmed nor denied. Even when it was pretty obvious the Dommes were who he always ended up watching the most.

Some of them had noticed, watching him back. They talked to Dale about him, he knew it, but as long as he wore the symbol of a non-player, they let him be. A couple tried to engage him in social chitchat, but he kept it purposefully high level. It wasn't that he'd been intimidated by them. He was figuring this shit out for himself, and had needed more time. It had evolved from that into a waiting for something, undefined but specific.

It was like that on missions, a gut feeling that said, *Yes, this is the right moment. Go.* Or *Stop here. Retreat.*

Then Dale had invited him to the Club Progeny and he'd sat down at a table with Rosalinda Thomas.

This is the right moment. Go.

Someone who could hold the reins, but also...someone he could take care of. Who needed his care. A woman in the crosshairs of a pissed-off gang member.

Shit. Like that avenue didn't have big-ass warning signs for him.

Nurse Conrad had a club foot. He remembered holding doors for her, offering to carry her medical supplies to her car. Busting Rob Orwell's nose for making fun of her limp.

He decided to set aside the confusing swamp of past and present and focus on something easier to understand. Like his reaction to the things Ros kept in that basement room. Things that could tease and torment a man, not only while he was in the room with them, but for days after.

Much more pleasant thoughts than what faced him now, but the mission always came first.

As Lawrence watched Rosalinda feed her cat, he thought about the creepy shoe and picture adjustments. He wished she would take Cyn's advice, or the female officer's, and head off to some remote corner of the planet until this asshole was locked up. Whoever had broken in might have been a lackey doing the mindfuck stuff based on Snake's orders, but that didn't read true to him. This was Snake himself, doing a personal "I'm coming for you, bitch."

And he'd been careful enough that none of her neighbors, an attentive group with a community watch, had seen a damn thing.

Until Snake did something overt to her and got caught, the only thing between her and him was Lawrence. They'd bypassed and deactivated her standard security system, great for repelling garden-variety criminals. Her password was a string of unrelated letters and numbers —she earned points for that, instead of using something obvious, like her cat's name. However, she kept the monitoring service's confirmation code on a post-it on her refrigerator. Hidden under a magnet, but even so. Once he started looking for it, he'd found it in less than a minute.

He'd reach out to Max, another former SEAL team guy who lived in the city. Max worked as security and head limo driver at Kensington & Associates, Matt's company. The system there was far more sophisticated. The company who installed and monitored it could quote her on an upgrade for her house and her business. Max maybe could work a package discount.

Hell, from what Lawrence knew about Matt Kensington, if the CEO got wind that someone had broken into Rosalinda's house, he'd foot the bill to have a system upgrade installed same day. Not that Rosalinda would let him do that. His lips firmed against a smile. She'd tell Matt to shove his money up his ass.

Fortunately, though, when Lawrence laid out the plan to upgrade her security system with Max's help, Rosalinda merely nodded. Putting the bowl of what appeared to be home-cooked food on the floor, she gave Freak a quick full body stroke.

"That's fine. Let me know the estimate, but go ahead and schedule them as soon as they're available."

She straightened and pulled a loaf of bread out of a wooden box she had resting on her granite countertop. In the same smooth movement, she flipped on the oven controls. "Do you want your sandwich toasted? I have peanut butter and three flavors of jelly. Blackberry, strawberry and grape."

"That's lunch?"

"PB&J on toast is my favorite quick meal. The bread is homemade, from a local who sells it at the farmer's market at Jackson Square."

"Maisy Wellington?"

She beamed, a welcome break in the tension that had returned to her demeanor when they left the basement. "You know Maisy?"

"I buy her cookies way more often than I should," he admitted.

"I look at those things and pack on the pounds." She pointed the knife at him. "We're not telling Abigail or any of the others that my house was broken into. I'm not going to have them hammering at me to come stay with one of them, or take a month's vacation on a remote island in the Pacific. As if a guy who was part of a national gang network couldn't afford to hop a plane, same as me."

He lifted a neutral shoulder. He was standing on the other side of her kitchen counter, hip propped on her tall bar stool. His eyes tracked the knife until she set it down.

She cocked a brow. "Thought I'd use it on you?"

"No. But it's habit, to evaluate all threats, active or passive." He flashed her a grim smile. "That's not a habit I want to lose. And the answer to your question is no. They need to know, Rosalinda."

She scowled. "I wasn't asking a question."

"That's true. But I'm not asking your permission to keep them informed. Do any of your executive team use your car, ever?"

"If one of them is having her car serviced, they might grab mine to run out for lunch."

He met her eyes. "If you were in a meeting, would they let you know they were doing that, or grab the keys and go?"

"They don't have to check with me on something like that. They know..." She trailed off, and her lips firmed. "And if someone knows my car, they expect me to be driving it."

"Yeah. If your people are aware of just how much of a threat you're under, then everyone stays mindful of the risks that overlaps like that can cause. Everyone stays safer."

She tightened her lips. "Just because you've figured out that a risk to people I care about will get me to go along with more security doesn't mean you can use that whenever you want to get your way."

She was handling the situation well, but the nerves were just below the surface. The pressure built up before she went after the punching bag was rebuilding.

"Tell me any part of what I just said that was incorrect," he said.

She glared at him, then sighed. "Fine. I'll set a meeting for four o'clock. Then you can discuss anything you want them to do that will help keep everyone safe."

She picked up the pan of sliced bread and put it in the oven. When she did, she slammed the door with a resounding metallic clang. Freak took off in a scramble of three legs, upsetting his water bowl and sending the contents flooding across the floor.

"Damn it." She snatched up a towel and dropped it. He came around the counter, touching her arm.

"Let me do it." *Mistress.*

He had to bite it back, unsettled by how it wanted to come to his lips. He wondered if she heard it anyway, the way her gaze settled on him as he dropped to a knee and wiped away the liquid. Her hand fell on his shoulder, sliding up to his nape, fingers tense.

"Can you..."

She stopped without finishing the sentence. He waited, his head dipped to look at the floor, but now there was no liquid to mop up. He was simply waiting, his head bowed, on one knee beside her. And while being taken over the way she'd done it in the cellar had made him hard, this roused different things in him, but surprisingly no less intense.

Yeah, it's about more than the centerfold, buddy. You already covered that.

Her nails scraped him, and then she squeezed his shoulder. "You can get up now. Thank you."

He pressed a light kiss to her thigh just above her knee before rising. She moved away, keeping her back to him as she pulled the jelly out of her big stainless-steel fridge. The kitchen had modern appliances while the ceiling was pressed tin, small squares with dotted patterns of flowers. A mix of the old and new.

The smell of toasting bread was starting to fill the room. He checked it, saw it was a light brown.

"Light or dark?" he asked.

"Light."

He picked up a potholder and pulled the tray out, putting it on the stove. She handed him a plate and he transferred the four pieces of thick bread on it, giving it back to her. As he watched her put peanut butter on the bread, he shifted so their shoulders brushed. She stopped when she'd done a reasonable layer of the spread. "Enough for you?" she asked.

"Yeah." He leaned in, brushed his lips against her temple. "It's going to be okay," he said. Quiet and simple.

She nodded, not looking at him, but nudged the jars of jelly his way. "Thank you, Lawrence."

~

They'd eaten their light lunch, Lawrence had fixed cardboard over the broken window, and then they'd headed to TRA. Ros had packed up a go-bag for Freak and brought him along. He'd become a regular fixture at TRA when she'd done some renovations last year, and he also was as comfortable at Abby's house as he was at Ros's. She wasn't risking him being home alone until things were settled. She'd ask Abby to take him home with her tonight.

Once at the office, Bastion immediately took possession, since he and the independent cat were fast friends. Ros expected Freak would be petted and spoiled by everyone on the first floor for the rest of the day.

On the executive floor, there was a small room in the back corner that might have served as a reading nook for the turn-of-the-century occupants. Abby had once told Ros she imagined it as a place that the woman of the house could go in the middle of a restless night. It would have kept her close to the master bedroom, or the nursery, but it would have been considered her space, where she could read, write down her thoughts, or gaze out the narrow window into the moonlit gardens as she managed any worries she had. Vera had agreed, indicating the space had a female energy to it.

After TRA took over the building, they'd converted it to a cozy office space that visiting clients could use when they needed privacy to make calls or do work on a meeting break.

Ros indicated to Lawrence it could be his office if he had need of the landline or computer installed in there. So when they reached the top of the stairs and he excused himself to start on the security upgrade tasks, she figured that was where she'd find him. Before they parted ways, he told her he'd be available for her meeting at four. His not-so-subtle way of reminding her she couldn't get out of that.

She didn't want to think about it right now.

She'd had her violent outburst. She should be in control of her emotions. Yet dealing with this was proving harder than she'd expected. Maybe because until today, she really hadn't dealt with it at all, so suddenly it was in her face, replaying over and over. The moment where she'd threatened Snake, the meeting with Dale and Matt, the concern they'd shown that she now realized had been legitimate. The broken window, her frightened cat. Then there was Abby, whose stress and worry factor Ros was about to increase tenfold, goddamn it.

Slap on top of that was the mixed bag of Lawrence's presence. She expected he was hard at work right now, planning to mummify her in more layers of security.

He was doing the job she was paying him to do. She could recognize that, even while being battered by waves of helpless irritation. She'd go into her office, close the door, and get the damn things down to ankle biter level, instead of being smacked in the chest and face with them every few seconds.

As she passed Cyn's office, she saw her account manager was on a call. Her heeled boots were propped on the edge of her desk, her black slacks and blood red blouse a businesslike contrast to the relaxed pose. Cyn saluted her with a wink and gave her pen a Ros-like twirl, finishing with a mock stab into the stress ball on her desk. It was shaped like a heart. When Ros made a rude gesture, Cyn grinned, without breaking the even professionalism of her tone.

"You can go that route," she said. "I'd actually recommend it. Especially if your quarterly sales goals can be met by guilting your grandmother and closest friends into a pity purchase."

Cyn was excellent at matching the client's temperament to the right TRA project lead, but when those leads hit a snag, they could always depend on Cyn to step in and back them up. She had a gift for helping their customers understand what changes had to happen for a product to be successfully marketed, a mix of no-nonsense frankness, charm and a winning brand of sarcasm.

Ros remembered Sy had given Cyn the heart-shaped stress ball on Valentine's Day a couple years back, the male sub showing a keen if tongue-in-cheek insight into Cyn's sadistic happy side.

Normally Ros would stop and figure out which client Cyn was handling. But not today. She kept going toward her office, relieved to see Abby in a meeting with Mel and Toni, their accounting support people. Her friend gave her an assessing glance that Ros met with a solid smile and a quick lift of her hand. Sometimes working with a circle of intuitive Dommes was a pain in the ass.

But she was past the gauntlet. She'd made it to her door.

She closed it firmly behind her, hanging her purse up on the back hook. Moving to her desk, she sank down in her chair, turning it toward the bank of windows behind her.

The midday sky was bluer than her eyes, though a wispy gray cloud floated across an expanse of fluffy white ones. She didn't look down at the central gazebo and garden area in the back, where semi-private spots had been landscaped for her employees to enjoy breaks or lunch. She wanted to rise above all of that, so she kept her gaze on the tangled canopy of gnarled live oaks, dripping with Spanish moss. When they had their semi-annual leaf drop, sometimes they were thin enough for her to see larger portions of other houses in the Garden District.

Usually this time of day, she would get herself an afternoon wakeup coffee from her K-cup machine in the corner. She'd make a couple calls, read the updates that were uploaded from their project software, handle a hundred little details that could use her touch, backing up her employees however they needed. If they didn't need her input, she'd chase down and develop leads.

Most of her workdays began with anticipation for the challenges the day would provide. She embraced the chance to succeed, achieve, win over another client, deliver everything they wanted, or change direction on one that wasn't doing so well and make it work.

Maybe she and Lawrence were alike in that regard. She didn't believe in mission failure. The answer to most problems was action, or taking steps to keep the problem from happening. She played offense, not defense. She sure as hell didn't wait for the clouds to become a full-on hurricane before she got off her ass and did something.

She was angry. Frightened. Unsettled. Emotions she absolutely hated. She'd burned some of it off with the punching bag and the bat, and then with Lawrence, but it was trying to crawl back into her gut and set up shop there. He might be right about keeping her staff informed, but in this mood she was likely to rip the head off of anyone who tried to tell her what to do. Which was what worried and concerned family members did.

If she closed her eyes, she saw Abby on her entryway floor carpet, bleeding. Or Freak, picked up and hurled against a wall, left broken, for no other reason than he was vulnerable, and this asshole liked hurting things that couldn't fight back.

The shoes. What had been done to her shoes bugged her, and she couldn't dismiss it, because it had bothered Lawrence the most as well. Damn it, this waiting for things to happen bullshit wasn't for her.

Snake's minions dealt off of Canal, down one of the side streets. Snake often set up shop there himself, in the back room of a hole-in-the-wall tourist trap, a business flanked by a head shop that had been there forever. She was going to deal with this. A man who beat on a pregnant woman was a coward, and him slinking into her house, playing with her shoes when she wasn't there, underlined it like a fat Sharpie.

Cyn had a client meeting at two-thirty she'd asked Ros to be available for, if they hit a bump. But even if that happened in Ros's absence, Cyn could handle it or text her. Either way, Ros was pretty sure what she intended to do could be done in about an hour, including travel time.

Done thinking about it, and shoving away any voices in her head that weren't her own—Abby, Lawrence—she retrieved her purse, exited her office. She strode down the hallway without looking left or right. It was unfortunate that she couldn't leave unnoticed, but then again, she wasn't going to slink around and hide from her own fucking staff.

As she marched down the curved staircase, Bastion looked up, assessing her mood in a blink. She shook her head at him, holding up a hand. "Back in less than an hour," she said in a voice that tolerated no questions. Then she was down the hall, passing through the kitchen break room to the back door, out to the parking area.

Lawrence had kept her keys, not in a controlling way, but because he was her driver today and she'd seen no reason to ask for them back. However, she had a spare.

She'd applied for an exemption from the city to have the gravel area paved, because no way were clusters of little rocks ruining her shoes. As a result, she didn't have to slow her stride as she crossed to her car, unlocking it with her fob.

She'd put her hand on the door handle when a man's shadow darkened the pavement to her left.

Her heart leaped into her throat and she whirled, the keys clutched in her fist. As she swung the handful of spikes, her lips pulled back in a snarl. She wasn't thinking, she knew she wasn't, and yet she did it anyway, the adrenaline and nerves fueling the fight response.

Lawrence stepped away, his hand closing on her wrist and his body angling to ease her against the side of the car before she overbalanced. She jerked back and he let her go immediately, though he was well inside her personal space. Like a handler unwisely standing inside the tiger's cage and, even worse, coming with attitude. His flat gaze said he was ready to tear her a new one, though his tone was neutral.

"Going somewhere?" he asked.

Fuck off was the first thing that came to mind, but something entirely unexpected came out of her mouth.

"There is nothing about this that works for me."

Her voice startled her. Strained and high. "I'm not going to sit here while he breaks into my house. I'm not going to pay good money to keep myself locked in while he wanders free, trying to unnerve me or hurt those I care about."

"So what's the plan? Go shoe shopping to prove you won't be intimidated?"

This time, she swung with full knowledge of what she would hit. The result was the same, though. He blocked her once more, but still let her wrist slide out of his grasp without holding it when she yanked back.

"You dick," she spat. "I'm going to go where his people deal and tell him to cut this shit out. He's a criminal. He'll back down if there's a public scene. If he attacks me in front of witnesses, then I can file assault charges against him, the way Pria should have done but won't. If anything happens to me after that, everything will point to him. I can get him to lose control, give it all to me."

She was an expert in that, too.

"Rosalinda—"

"My name is Ros," she snapped. "And you damn well know it."

The green eyes stayed flint, his controlled reaction just adding to her anger. At herself, as much as him. She tried to open the door, but he leaned against it, crossing his arms and hooking a foot around his ankle as he faced off with her.

"You know, I haven't seen you in action at Progeny yet."

The segue startled her, and he moved smoothly into that pause. "I'm guessing when you've had men tied up at the club, there's a whole thing that happens. Where you wait, and study, and figure out how to get what you really want from them. Takes patience, study, but the sweet spot is what results from that. Something much better than instant gratification. That's why you reward denial."

He cocked a brow. "Yes or no."

She closed her eyes, turned away from him. She rested her hand on the top of the car, gripping the frame over the window, hard. He'd shifted, was right behind her. Normally she wouldn't have tolerated anyone in her space when she felt like this, but it didn't feel like he was trying to take up room she needed to breathe. It was as if he was trying to give it back to her.

"I know this is tough," he murmured. "When we had to wait for something to happen during an op, the anticipation, anxiety, worst case scenarios, can crawl into your gut and drive you nuts. Until you do it often enough to figure out how to handle it, how to wait for the right moment. That's why the team leader is a big help, and the other more experienced guys. They help you manage that anxiety, understand how choosing the right moment is key to any kind of success."

He paused. "You've learned how to handle pressure in your life, Rosalinda. This is just a new and different kind. That's all."

She understood better than most the dangers of suppressing strong feelings. Her preference at the club were powerful men with pent up emotions that needed to be drawn to the top through sexual expression. They craved a woman's touch for it, a woman they believed was strong enough to hold the reins on them. Channeling and releasing those feelings required a delicate balance to keep everyone safe, including her.

"You were supposed to be in your office," she said.

From the direction he'd appeared, he must have chosen to work in the gazebo. It was private enough for him to conduct calls without being overheard. It also gave him a direct view to the parking lot, her car and the more screened approaches to the building.

"You should quit," she added. "I'm not good at this. I'm going to break your rules, over and over."

"I have more faith in your learning curve than you do." He was kneading her shoulders, so slow and easy. "You've never been threatened by someone like this. I told you that people react to it different ways. Give yourself a break. You're doing better than most."

"How many try to go after their attacker without any useful plan other than 'I'm going to fuck him up?'"

He chuckled. "It's a mixed bag. Some don't want to acknowledge there's a threat. Total denial, like I mentioned before. Others refuse to work with their security at all; security has to work around them. Every protection detail is different. You're the best-looking assignment I've ever had. Except maybe this Latin American cartel princess who flipped on her prince..."

She shot an elbow back and almost got him that time, except he shifted to the right. It pressed his hip bone against her buttock, his thigh sliding against hers.

He was making her smile, even when she didn't want to do so. She leaned back into him, against his solid chest. He adjusted, but resumed the massage, now moving to her upper arms, the round part of her shoulders. He was paying attention to what he was doing, too, working out kinks. She relaxed a little, despite herself.

"I apologize for hitting you. The second time."

"You didn't," he said. "You tried to hit me."

"Ass." She tilted her head left and right. "Oh God. You're good at this."

"I've learned a lot of ways to handle stress. Though I like some of your methods better."

A movement at the back door caught his attention, his head lifting. Ros followed his gaze. Abby was on the back porch. She moved a few steps down the slope of the handicap ramp, obviously looking for Ros. When she saw her, her gaze coursed over them, Ros standing by her car, Lawrence behind her, his mouth so close to her ear, strong hands massaging her shoulders.

Ros wasn't surprised to see her. No matter her attempt to mask it, Abby would have picked up on her mood when she marched by her office. Bastion might have buzzed her, too.

Fortunately, Abby's lips curved in a smile, making her worried frown disappear. Though her face was alive with curiosity, she went back up the ramp and disappeared into the building. Respecting Ros's privacy.

At least in theory. Ros wouldn't be surprised if her friend sprinted to the third floor and pressed up against a window to keep watching. Along with anyone else of their circle she could alert that their all-business boss seemed to be in an intimate conversation with the new security contractor.

"I hate that most of all," Ros said. "Having them worried about me. I'm the one who looks after all of them. I like it that way."

"I'm betting you all look after each other. You just haven't come up on the rotation as needing it before now. Which unfortunately is going to make them a little more protective than normal. It freaks everyone out when the boss is vulnerable. But that's where having me around is useful. Convinces them they don't have to be so worried. That is, if the boss acts like her security has it all handled, rather than charging off to face down gangs by herself."

"Stop being so damn reasonable, or I really will punch you in the face." *Or try to.* She backed away from the pleasure of his hands. Pivoting, she faced him. "I downloaded my calendar to your company account."

"I got it. You're working out with Cyn on the odd days, Abigail on the even ones. So tonight you work out with Cyn."

"Yes. And it's not on my calendar, but one night a week, I go to Club Progeny with the others. I've been moving it around, so it's tonight. I usually ride with Abigail, so you don't have to drive me."

"Yeah, I do. Unless Abigail is qualified for protection detail duty."

A fair point. She eyed him. "You don't have to accompany me inside. Unless I invite you. Do you want to be invited, Lawrence?"

She was trying to regain some sense of control, she knew that. But it was a far healthier path than what she'd been about to do.

He sighed. "When you're on familiar ground, you're pretty much irresistible."

"And when I'm not?"

"I'm still standing here, aren't I?"

She gave him a tight smile, but the million intriguing things moving behind his thoughtful eyes held her attention. "Yes," he said at last. "I would like to be invited."

"All right. I'll give it some thought." Turning, she walked back toward the building.

"Rosalinda."

She paused, turned. He met her gaze. "Are you a woman of your word?"

"I try to be."

He grimaced. "I need to go and do a couple things while you're at work, before the four o'clock meeting. I can't do those things if I think you won't stay here and inside, while I'm gone. Can you promise me you'll do that?"

"Are you going to tell Abby and Bastion to keep an eye on me to make sure of it?"

"Sometimes these feelings come in waves," he said. "If you don't mind, I'll take your car for the errands."

"You're not answering my questions directly," she said.

"Neither are you."

She crossed her arms over her chest. "You can use my car. But don't think that means I'm giving up my right to drive."

"Nothing in the Constitution about a right to drive."

"I'm sure the founding fathers understood the right to pursue happiness included having access to a horse and buggy. And you having my car doesn't guarantee anything. If I wanted to leave, I'd borrow someone's car. Or use New Orleans' ample public transportation options."

His gaze swept down her legs to her feet, a spark of male interest in the otherwise neutral expression. "I'm not seeing you on the bus in those shoes. Plus, when you tell off the bad guy, there's a cool exit requirement. Marching thirty feet away from him to wait at the nearest trolley stop would ruin the impact of your public smackdown."

Then he sent her a smile that was almost as reassuring as his touch had been. It was a new sensation to her, being able to rely on a man's care and attention. It had been her choice, structuring her relationships to minimize that possibility, but now she thought her reasons for that might not have been the most important ones.

A nice-to-have could transform into a must-have, faster than a chocolate addiction.

"But if you go that route," he continued, "the trolley goes right through the Square. Pick us all up some beignets on the way back. Since you want to do my job and yours, I'm sure Bastion would be happy for you to do his as well."

Her sharp two-word response had no problem making its way past her lips this time. It deepened his grin in a distracting way. "I'll get right on that," he said. Then he closed the distance between them, gripped her hand and looked her dead in the eye. "Rosalinda."

She sighed, reached up, touched his face. "I promise," she said. "I'll be right here."

CHAPTER NINE

Snake had pulled off a Garden District home break-in, but Lawrence didn't see him attempting something ballsy at TRA during operating hours. Not while Rosalinda was surrounded by thirty-odd staff members.

Max had come through, putting things in motion fast. Lawrence met Kensington's security company choice at Ros's house to get them started on the upgrades, and they picked up on what he wanted immediately, requiring little supervision. Since he had a little time before he needed to be back at TRA, he knew what he'd do next.

Juggling an ever-changing schedule for years meant he regularly shifted his daily workout around to accommodate other demands. He carried a go-bag most everywhere, and today had been no different. As he pulled it out of the trunk to change into his workout clothes at Ros's house, he texted Neil and Max, letting them know his ETA at the park, in case they wanted to join him.

As an active SEAL, Neil could be called up at any time, but as of last night, Lawrence knew he was in town. Max had work at K&A, but his hours weren't always nine to five. The three of them had a standing agreement to work out together whenever their schedules lined up.

The habit had started when Max had to leave the SEALs to care for his sister. With his usual gift for saying a lot with a little, Dale had suggested it to Lawrence and Neil. Their Master Chief had lost a leg below the knee when he was with the SEALs, and had finished out his twenty teaching, helping with tactical and logistics.

"Not being part of the team, with you guys down range, left me feeling like I'd had something far worse cut off than a leg," he'd told them. "I wouldn't have made it without you guys being such persistent little assholes, never leaving me alone when you were home."

Dale's prosthetic worked so well it was hard to tell he even had one when he was wearing jeans and his boots, and he was as balls-to-the-wall now as he'd been when he led their team. However, Lawrence did remember those low days when they'd seen a bleakness in their MC's eyes, a loss of spirit, in a way that was damn terrifying.

So he and Neil had responded to the advice, meeting up with Max whenever possible, working out together, staying connected. Then Lawrence's number had been called, and he was getting a front row seat to the hellish transition Dale and Max had been through.

Working out wasn't critical to his survival, or that of his team members anymore. He didn't like thinking that thought, even in his head. Moreover, he didn't accept it, even if it was staring him in the face every day. He couldn't shut down that part of himself yet. Maybe he never would. The routine helped with a lot of things beyond fighting form.

Having two close friends who'd weathered the storm should have made it easier. They both had good lives now, satisfying ones. But he guessed he was still too new to it. Emptiness had a voice, and staying busy was the only sure thing that took it down from a scream to a dull roar.

Which was why when Ros took things over and that roar simply disappeared, he'd noticed. It felt good, right, but the enormous relief of not feeling that emptiness, even for a short period, could make him compromise things with her he shouldn't. He needed to be careful of that.

Problem was, he wasn't sure if that was an option when she went into full blown Mistress mode.

As he started the six-mile loop at the park, he let his thoughts drift where they wanted to go. Mostly they drifted to her, but that was okay. A workout was a mental timeout, his energy on the physical side of things, keeping his body conditioned.

He liked the way she touched him, looked at him. He saw his body as a tool and a weapon that required proper care, like his guns, but her pleasure gave him additional reasons to maintain what he had, as best as he could.

That last little tag was a reminder of why he was no longer an operator, and cast a shadow on what was otherwise a good thought. Fortunately, his intuition provided him with a distraction. He was being stalked.

Though he knew he had to be careful about pushing too hard, he still increased his pace. Neil, long-legged bastard that he was, caught up, tried to edge past him. Lawrence matched him, and then Max fell in step as they went over the ridge. Things in Lawrence's chest eased and tightened at once.

Not the same as it was, but being together, it was something.

They didn't need much conversation. After they did two miles together, they hit the interval workout area, did their reps there, squats, pullups, pushing themselves, working up a sweat, and then they were off again.

Neil started to pull ahead, but then eased back again. Max was maintaining a steady pace, stride for stride with Lawrence. Lawrence wasn't going to stand for it.

"Fuck you, go on," Lawrence growled at Max. "You're not taking a stroll in the damn park."

"He's starting to sound like Dale," Neil said.

"I mean it," Lawrence said. "Go. Damn it, Max. Work him out. I want to see the sweat dripping off him."

Max and Neil exchanged a look, but they couldn't argue it. Neil needed to be at his best. Because Max's departure from the SEALs hadn't been due to an injury, he kept himself in pretty much active duty condition. All of them did, if they could, because that requirement was wired bone deep.

The two of them started to pull ahead. They tried to make it gradual, but from the way they eventually lengthened their strides, they could have left him in the dust in a matter of seconds. Now Max was doing what he should, pushing Neil to keep up. Former SEAL or not, Max was a bitch to match. Neil would have some aching muscles before it was over. But the kind that would be fine after a good cool down.

In contrast, the ache that had started in Lawrence's ankle was working its way up his calf, a burn turning into a full-on acid strike. His knee was joining in on the chorus of pain. He needed to slow it down, or he would be in trouble, but the further they pulled ahead, the more the emptiness inside him expanded and he tried to push himself. Then he cursed as the injury caught fire. He was an idiot.

He passed mile six at a jog that wouldn't have gotten him past a three-legged bulldog, and was relieved to be able to slow it to a walk. When he reached the part of the park where he'd left Rosalinda's car, Max and Neil were still there. Max was perched on the top of a split rail fence, sipping water, while Neil was doing some idle pull ups on the monkey bars of the small playground in this area.

"So how's the job going?" Max asked, tossing him a bottle of water. His level look said he'd kick Lawrence's ass if he tried to apologize for making them wait. Thank God, since Lawrence had been about to say something pathetic to excuse his slackness.

Lawrence shrugged. "Biggest challenge is getting her to understand what's best for her protection. The usual with a strong-minded VIP."

The term fit Ros well. So did HVT, high value target, though he expected she wouldn't appreciate the target part. For his part, he equated it with something far more intimate, like the center of a bull's eye. The goal worth reaching.

"Is she hot?" Neil asked. "It balances the aggravation if they're hot."

"Yes, she's hot," Lawrence said. "Rosalinda is a very take-charge kind of person."

Why he'd added that as a component of her relative hotness, he didn't know. An enigmatic smile crossed Max's face. "I'll bet."

Dale wouldn't have said anything to Max. Lawrence was sure of it. Yet Max looked like he knew things.

Of course he does, dumbass. Lawrence's throbbing leg was interfering with his cognitive processes. Matt Kensington was a Dom. From what Lawrence had picked up on what Dale felt comfortable revealing, apparently so was Matt's four-man executive team, just like Ros's. Doms apparently liked to clump together for work *and* play. Max was their head limo driver, for both business and social demands. Like dropping them off at clubs. Which meant he had exposure to the BDSM world.

"Something wrong with this woman?" Neil said, looking between them.

"Not even slightly."

Now Max grinned. The smug prick did know, at least about Ros. That knowledge didn't necessarily include Lawrence.

Neil grunted. "I don't mind a take-charge woman. In our line of work, a woman who doesn't fall apart when you're not around is a plus."

"Not exactly what he meant," Max said.

"So say what you mean, Munch." Neil frowned.

Though Max was deliberately prodding Lawrence, his annoyance with it was balanced with an extremely petty spurt of satisfaction. There was something he and Max knew that Neil didn't. Neil was privy to so much they used to carry around together, like the air in their lungs.

But then Lawrence thought of how that must be for Neil, not being able to share those need-to-know things with his two former teammates, and the pettiness was gone. Things would be so much easier if they could just be team guys for all their lives, but their way of life was too fraught with peril. It just didn't happen.

While she wasn't broadcasting it for her clients, Ros didn't seem to make a big secret of being a Domme to her friends and close associates. Therefore, if Max already knew about Ros, and with Neil being one of his closest friends, Lawrence didn't necessarily feel he was betraying Ros's trust. If he ever did get around to talking about this stuff as it related to him, personally, it would likely be with these two. And Dale.

"She's a Domme. As in sexual Dominant. She prefers to be in charge in the bedroom."

And pretty much everywhere else. The Mistress side colored all the way to the edge of the page.

"Wow." Neil digested that. "I think I just got even more aroused."

Lawrence shook his head. "Ass. You have no idea what you're talking about."

"Max probably does, though," Neil rebounded. "Janet is as scary as MC on his toughest day."

Lawrence snorted. "No disagreement here."

Janet didn't take shit off anyone. Lawrence knew firsthand how ballsy the woman could be. Other than that experience, he hadn't spent much time around her, but that brief window had suggested Max's relationship with Matt Kensington's imperious executive admin was a lively one.

Was it possible Janet was a Domme? He let the startling thought hit him, absorb. Lawrence's limited interactions with her had been about something else entirely, no time to get that vibe from her, but now that he thought about it... He didn't know. What he did know was Max didn't have a sub bone in his body, at least not in any way Lawrence had ever detected. So how would that work, if Janet was a Domme and Max wasn't a sub? Max wasn't the sharing kind.

Neither was Lawrence. He'd been trying not to think about Rosalinda at her club tonight, what she'd be doing if she didn't invite him inside.

Max gestured with his water bottle and fortunately changed the subject. "Dale and Athena will be doing First Sunday barbecue again this spring and summer. It'll start after Memorial Day. He wanted me to remind you guys you have a standing invite. So do Matt, his guys and their wives. You might finally get a chance to meet the rest of them."

"Are the other wives as hot as Dana and Marcie?" Neil asked.

"I have no idea what you're talking about," Max said, deadpan.

Neil chuckled. "That's a yes. Looking forward to it. I'll take any chance we can get to flirt with Athena, rile old MC."

"You call him old, or flirt with his wife one too many times, Dale's going to use his garden shears on your dick," Max warned, though his serious gray eyes twinkled.

Lawrence checked his watch. "I better hit the showers here." The park had an aquatic center, which provided a fully equipped locker room. "It'll give me time to pick up a burger and get back to Ros's office. I'm supposed to be available for a four o'clock meet about the break-in."

Max slid off the fence. "Let me know if you need anything else. On the security stuff, or whatever comes up."

"Same here, Munch," Neil said.

Max gave Lawrence a level look as he made the offer. Since his gaze slid down to touch on Lawrence's still throbbing leg, he probably meant that. Maybe.

It didn't matter. Down range, there was zero time to indulge Oprah moments. Didn't matter if you'd seen a toddler blown to bits by a dirty bomb, you pushed forward, held it together, made it all work.

But that kind of stuff could tear you apart in the down times, so they all learned to hold it together with whatever glue worked. Which meant Lawrence could tell the two of them anything.

Message received. Just still not there, on most of this shit.

"Appreciate it. Both of you."

His phone buzzed with a text. He considered it good timing until he pulled the phone out of his shorts, glanced at it. He put it back in his pocket.

"She texting you again?" Neil asked.

Lawrence lifted a shoulder. When Neil and Max exchanged a look, he shook his head. "That's been over for some time. Doesn't matter if she's still texting or not."

"Yeah." Neil's expression was a mix of things, including a warning, but Lawrence didn't need that. They'd gone down that road with him, and he wouldn't be dragging them down it again. He wasn't going down that road, either. Not the same way. He'd established distance, but it just wasn't possible to cut all ties. Not with so much history between him and Valentina.

The phone buzzed again. It was going to be a multi-text afternoon. Fuck. He couldn't shut the damn thing off while working this job for TRA and Ros. That sick roll in his lower belly kicked up and made the ache in his leg worse, too. Which connected to the emptiness, and an all-round fucked up feeling.

"Munch," Max said.

He shook his head. "It's fine. I got a handle on this."

"Yeah," Neil said, but he'd shifted so he, Lawrence and Max formed a closer loose circle. "Want to grab that burger together?"

Lawrence shook his head. "Can't. Gotta be on the go, because I have to get back to the take-charge client."

"Roger that. But let's do beer and softball this weekend if we can all make it. Semi-final championships at the park. Bring your take-charge woman if she wants to come," Neil said to Lawrence, then nodded to Max. "Yours too. Low security risk with all the games happening and a million parents there. Plus the players could whip a lowlife's ass in a heartbeat. Hell, I think they could whip ours."

Lawrence chuckled. Neil was a serious girls' softball fan. He'd managed to convert them into fans by dragging them to wherever the games were held, when down time allowed. Eventually they'd all gotten into it, hollering encouragement, insulting the umpires. Those girls played a hundred percent, and were tough as badgers.

He wondered if Rosalinda had ever played softball.

He'd overdone it on the damn leg. He couldn't conceal the limp, so after torturing himself on the stairs, he came to a full stop in the hallway when Rosalinda emerged from her office. She was on her way to somewhere. Since she had two eager project team members scurrying next to her, one holding a tablet and chattering, he expected she'd pass him without comment.

Instead her brow creased. Damn it, she'd seen the way he was moving. She sent the other two staff members ahead of her.

"You all right?" she asked.

"Yeah. Just overdid the workout."

"Do you need to—"

"If I can't do my job, you'll hear it from me first."

Coolness entered her gaze, but she nodded and left him there, striding away.

"Fuck," he muttered under his breath.

He hobbled past Skye's office. She had four monitors forming a command center around her, and her fingers were flying over the keyboards as her attention moved between all of them. She spared him a glance as he went by. When he looked over his shoulder as he passed, she had code on one screen, and what appeared to be a video conference happening on another. The other two monitors displayed an ad spread and an array of images which she seemed to be swiping on and off the ad page, trying them out.

Every woman on this floor was scary.

He went to the office they'd given him and checked on a few things, keeping an eye on the time. Three-thirty. Ros had told him she wanted to break the news to the team by herself, but he'd be ready to be called if they had questions.

A movement at his door drew his attention. Skye was standing there, her video conference apparently over. She wore a pair of billowy black slacks that flowed with her movements, and a clingy pale green shirt. Her necklace of black and green stones matched what was on her wrists and ears. It worked in a creative professional environment, but had an earthy enough look to go with the trendy hair style, all straight and feathery over her face on one side, shaved sharp on the other to reveal the delicate line of her neck. Her dark gaze reminded him of goshawk's.

She had a tote bag on her shoulder, a stylish vinyl-looking thing printed with a sloth hanging from a tree branch. The branch bloomed with blue flowers. As she stepped into his space, she slipped the bag off her shoulder and removed a bottle of over-the-counter pain pills from it. Uncapping it, she shook out two of the contents and put them on his desk, next to his half-empty energy drink. She tapped the can, then pointed to the pills. Her way of saying "Take these."

Then she pulled something else out of the bag. A heat pack and a cold pack, the kind you cracked to activate. She gestured to the heat pack, held up ten fingers, then five—fifteen minutes—then the same thing to the cold pack. Fifteen more minutes. *Alternate heat and cold.*

Something he should have done himself, but he was trying to ignore the pain like it might go away on its own.

She rolled over the guest chair and, with perfect posture and balance, lifted her foot, put it in the chair, then put it down again. *Elevate.*

"I'm good. But okay. Thanks."

She tapped the drink again, the pills. Folded her hands and waited. Gave him the stare.

"I will. Go away. Ma'am."

The piercing goshawk look increased, significantly.

"Christ, fine." He picked up the aspirin, tossed them back with the energy drink, then dropped the heat pack on the chair, letting his calf and ankle follow, land on it. The heat was instant bliss on the scarred tendon area, but he schooled his face not to show it. Like that worked with these women.

Stepping forward, she patted him lightly on the head, pivoted and departed, leaving him scowling.

Good boy. Yeah, got that one. He could have brushed it off except the way she did it, the look on her face, was an echo of that deeper thing which caught this attention and held it, even when it came in the guise of nursemaiding.

Cue a vision of Nurse Conrad. *Jesus.*

His phone buzzed again. Twentieth text since the park. He wouldn't look. He wouldn't. He shut the fucking phone off. Ros was in the building. He didn't have to have it on right now, not until just before the four o'clock meeting.

But even with it off, the intrusion had achieved its usual result. The garden bathed in sunlight below his window now looked covered in gray cloth. The bird song he could hear through glass was far more plaintive, far less cheerful.

But it was what it was. Goddamn it.

∾

"So was Freak ready with his usual complaint list of things I did wrong?"

Abigail asked the question as Ros entered the board room for their four o'clock. Her friend said it brightly, in a voice and with an expression that reflected it was so *not* what she wanted to talk about. She wanted to talk about what she'd seen in the parking lot. As well as what had happened last night, when she'd sent Ros those cheerleading emojis.

Ros dearly wished that was what this meeting was going to be about. While she'd figured out a way to manage her mood after her meet with Lawrence in the parking lot, she was still a little raw around the edges. Lawrence snapping at her a little while ago hadn't helped. Though in fairness, she'd seen the regret in his eyes right after he did it.

Men could be distracting. The right ones for certain, and she'd had more than her fair share of right ones. Which included sessions that lingered in her mind for days afterward. But they didn't interfere with her business, and what she remembered were pivotal moments when they relinquished control to her. Not so many specifics about the man himself.

Throughout the afternoon, with her exceptional sense of olfactory recall, she'd inhaled the lingering scent of Lawrence's aftershave, remembered the heat of his body pressed against hers. Especially this morning, while thrusting into her like a beast.

Other moments had snuck in as well. Him covering her hand on the car. That phrase again, "Find your cat." Maybe because it was an acknowledgement that no matter how pissed he'd been at her, he'd known what she needed the most before she could hear anything else.

Crap. She was daydreaming. Not-so-secret smiles were being exchanged around the table. Bastion's blatantly guileless look from the corner, his usual post to record action items and oversee anything else admin-related for their meetings, made it official. Abigail had spread the word about Ros's whereabouts last night *and* the embrace in the parking lot.

Because her team knew her, the daydreaming and parking lot thing would raise a lot more eyebrows than the overnight. They'd all known she'd likely have a session or two with Lawrence. Exchanging intimacy and physical affection outside of that? A far less typical thing for her.

At least none of that would have been shared beyond the people inside this room. For all their Vera-exasperating innuendos with one another, they were infallibly professional with the rest of the staff. If anyone else had seen her and Lawrence in the parking lot, any speculation over it would have been shut down with a firm admonishment to mind their own business.

Ah, the hypocrisy perk of being upper management.

She pointedly ignored all the nonverbal communication happening and responded to Abby's spoken question. "Freak gave that up long ago. He said the list of things not right about you is much too long."

"Kind of like staff meeting agendas," Cyn said. "Particularly when they include Vera's latest HR requirements."

"Firing you would cut at least fifty percent of those," Vera said placidly. Cyn sneered at her, but not unexpectedly, she was the one to take the bull by the horns. She turned her dark brown eyes to Ros.

"So what's on the agenda for this unexpected end-of-day meet? Hopefully a confidential, highly detailed discussion not meant for ears other than ours?"

Ros really didn't want to do this. She knew Lawrence was right, she needed to. But that didn't matter. She was still standing, and one hand had closed into a fist as she pressed her knuckles into the top of the table. It was a rhythmic motion that happened when she was putting together difficult things in her mind. The others zeroed in on it, one of the ways she'd learned it was a stress tell for her. But around the people she trusted, she didn't try to control it. Particularly when she needed them to pick up on the cue and change the tone.

"We need to discuss security issues. Bastion, you'll be in charge of relaying the relevant points of our discussion to the full staff."

"Yes, ma'am," he said, now just as serious as the others.

"First, I do not need anyone overreacting." She shot a pointed look at Abby. "That won't be helpful, and it will make me angry. I need to not be angry today. Trust me, I'm dealing with enough of that already."

Abigail frowned. She was absolutely going to overreact. As would the others. Ros stifled a mental sigh. Might as well get it over with. It was the blessing and curse of having a family, even one you'd chosen for yourself. Maybe especially one you'd chosen yourself.

"My house was broken into last night."

"What?" "When?" "What happened?" "Fucking hell."

That last one came from Cyn. Skye looked at Ros with alarm and the fiery expression of a battle angel.

Ros fielded the questions, giving them the relevant details. Not much different from a business meeting, after all. Except she didn't normally have a ball of nerves in her gut like this. She assured them the security upgrade at her house was already in process, but that didn't satisfy Abby.

"I want Lawrence in here to talk about this," her partner demanded. Almost before she finished, there was a knock on the board room door. Ros sent her a smug look. She'd sent the text about two minutes ago, when points were being rehashed and pointless what-ifs discussed.

"Wiseass," Abby muttered.

Lawrence slid in, nodded politely to the women. For the next few moments, he handled their questions. While Ros took a seat in her chair, he stayed on his feet, arms crossed in a relaxed way across his chest, feet braced. She expected he'd had to answer questions fired at him by ambassadors, high-ranked superiors, or foreign dignitaries, standing on their home turf. Her group wasn't going to rattle him.

That confidence was reassuring enough to calm them down significantly, even as they asked the serious, intelligent questions she'd expect from them. When the meeting was ready to conclude, they were all mostly on the same page, including Abigail.

"So is Club Night off or on for you this week?"

Skye was using the computer voice she used to talk to clients. If Skye could talk, Ros imagined the mild Southern accent, a musical feminine hum threaded through it, would have been the closest to her real voice. Firm and pleasant at once, it captured the attention.

"Can't think of any place safer than a private club populated by Doms and management, all focused on the safety and well-being of everyone in there," Ros said. "Also, Lawrence will drive me there and take me home."

Abigail's gaze slid to Ros's, held. The unspoken question, *Will he also be accompanying you inside?* was there. Measuring glances were sent toward Lawrence, the Mistress in each woman coming to the top. She wondered if he was aware of the subtle change in their scrutiny. From a light flush on his nape, his first indication of discomfiture so far, she thought he was.

Ros didn't have an answer for them yet. The invitation was still pending. If she offered, she needed to be in the right headspace to enjoy the hell out of the experience.

As if reading her mind, Cyn spoke. "First things first, then. Time to go get hot and sweaty. And not in the fun way."

CHAPTER TEN

*W*hen Lawrence had first checked Ros's calendar for the location of her preferred workout place, he'd expected some shiny fitness locale, populated by women in colorful leggings and sports bras. She and Cyn would be chatting or listening to audio books on their earbuds as they worked out side-by-side on treadmills or ellipticals.

Instead, they worked out at Roughnecks, a fighters' gym. If Stallone had wanted to make *Rocky* in the Big Easy, the sweaty hole-in-the-wall would have been the perfect set location.

Roughnecks had been here a while, but it had evolved with the times from a traditional boxing gym to a place that included MMA training and all the fight styles in between. A good marketing decision, Rosalinda would probably say.

He wouldn't be surprised if she'd been involved in that in some way, even if only to give advice to the proprietor. Good marketing was more than just a paycheck to her. It bugged her when her preferred businesses didn't present what they could offer to their best advantage.

Cyn was already standing at the entrance when they arrived. Ros gave her a wave as Lawrence turned onto a side street and parked in between a beat-up Toyota Camry and a shiny Ford 150 pick-up with expensive rims and a gunrack in the back window.

Cyn followed, moving around the corner to join them. She was dressed in black leggings and neon-orange Danskin workout tank, and carried her workout bag slung over her shoulder.

The outfit revealed what he'd already suspected. Cyn took her workouts almost as seriously as he, Max and Neil did. The muscle definition in her shoulders and upper arms had required dedication. She still had enough body fat to maintain an attractive pair of B-cup breasts and an eye-catching firm ass, but she had a trained athlete's way of moving. Or a professional assassin's.

Something about Cyn said she had a power over men she could wield like a sledgehammer when she had a mind to do so.

Lawrence rolled down the window and she leaned in, propping her elbows on the frame before speaking to Ros. "So how is it, being chauffeured everywhere?"

Ros held up her phone. "Another twenty minutes of work knocked out. I could get used to it."

"Lucas says the K&A limo service saves them so much time it pays for itself. Since he's Matt's CFO, he should know. Maybe we should consider it. We could pick up clients in the limo, really impress them."

"Or make them think they're being overcharged," Ros said dryly.

Cyn's gaze moved back over Lawrence. "Is he coming inside?"

He quelled the urge to say, "*He* is right here." He'd been undressed by women's eyes before, but Cyn's look wasn't exactly that. It contained that additional component, an unsettling throwback to the meeting, when he'd realized they all knew what else he might be to Ros.

He was witnessing a conversation between two Mistresses. When Ros's hand settled high on his thigh, his body responded accordingly, with a little mental jolt that vibrated to her, because her gaze intensified on him.

"Yes," she said. "He is."

"Good. He can watch you get your ass kicked." Cyn straightened from the window, the energy dissipating like the fizz of a good beer on the taste buds. A lingering taste that would make a man crave more.

Lawrence knew Ros acknowledged a modern world where BDSM required rules of consent and clear structure, so everyone stayed safe. But there were times, particularly when the women were together as a group, the energy shifted. It made him think of an alternative universe where women like these held all the power, men there to serve them. Possessions that they rode hard and never put away, wet or otherwise.

Lawrence considered himself an even match with whatever a dirtbag like Snake could throw at him. With these women, he might be in over his head.

Well, at least he was a SEAL. He could handle an immersive experience. With Rosalinda and her Mistresses, the water seemed nice and heated most of the time.

"I should have suggested you bring workout clothes," Ros said, unbuckling her seat belt. "But you can likely scare up an extra set here."

He shook his head. "I'm on the clock right now. And on that note, I'm sorry I snapped at you earlier today. That was unprofessional."

She lifted a shoulder. "Did the ice packs help?"

"That was your doing?"

She shook her head. "All Skye. She misses very little. But she let me know she did it."

"Yeah, they helped. I'll thank her. I wasn't very gracious to her either. But I didn't try to take her head off like I did you."

"Hmm." She glanced down at his leg. "Did you sprain something during the workout?"

"No. Not exactly." He sighed, glancing in the mirror to confirm they were alone in the alley. Cyn had disappeared through a side door. "I shattered my knee during a mission, got a disconnected patellar tendon. Recovery took about three months. When it was all done, there was no way I could be in the field again."

During the first part of it, he'd been in a VA hospital. His mom had been all set to come up and nursemaid him when they discharged him, and he wasn't putting that on her. Even though he had no plan for how he was going to handle basic things he couldn't do at that point, like shower or pull on a pair of pants without help.

Then Dale had pretty much told Lawrence he'd be living with Dale and Athena until he was past that part. His Master Chief had helped with most of the hands-on stuff, and there'd been no better place to handle Lawrence's recovery than with a retired SEAL amputee. It had kept Lawrence's bitching down to a grumble, most days.

He also had enough self-awareness to never take it out on Athena, knowing Dale would have busted his other knee for that. Lawrence would have done it himself first. Athena had unobtrusively supported her husband in Lawrence's care, with class and kindness, without making Lawrence feel emasculated, stupid as he knew that reaction was.

"So snapping at me wasn't about a sore leg," Ros said.

"Yeah. But leaving the teams was a choice I made. I could have done training, logistics, whatever, but being down range with a team was what I loved. Didn't have a real feel for the rest. Dealing out, figuring out the rest of my life, was the track for me."

"Is there anything you ever thought about doing, other than being in the military?"

There actually was. He'd dragged his feet on it after his recovery, and Dale had told him that was normal. *You need time and space to work things out before you plunge fulltime into something that requires a lot of emotional fortitude.*

"Yeah. I like working with kids. At-risk teens. Me, Neil and Dale volunteer with one of the local centers. When the social workers come in, counselors, court advocates, sometimes I've thought I'd like to get the schooling to do that. Help the kids figure shit out. Common sense and life experience help, but the training would guide me on the less obvious stuff. Give a kid with everything going against him more firepower in his or her corner."

"I like that." She glanced toward the gym. "We have some kid groups that come here. Maybe you could talk to the owner about an outing for your center's kids."

"Yeah. Maybe." It actually sounded pretty good, but he was ready to be done talking about things that related to his leg. "Wait here."

He exited the car, checked the area once more, then opened her door. She had picked up on his unspoken cue, for she gave him an easy nod, though her eyes were thoughtful. She led the way to the side entrance Cyn had used. The swipe card gave her access, but he changed places with her to precede her through the door, doublechecking before he brought her in behind him.

The not necessarily pleasant aroma of a primarily male-member gym brought back his surprise about her being here. Yet as she moved toward Cyn and the locker rooms, leaving him scoping the room, she bantered with the other regulars, showing she was at ease here.

She'd said most of her workout happened on the ground level, versus the gym's second floor, so he found the section of wall that gave him the best vantage point. In his current attire, jeans, open button-down and T-shirt, he stuck out some, but he wanted to do so. If this was her regular workout place, it was possible one of Snake's gang or their family members might drift through.

It was hot, so he shed the button-down, draped it on one of the hooks available along the wall. Losing it revealed the shoulder holster, which meant he'd deal with the reaction to that shortly. He leaned against the wall, his arms crossed over his chest.

"Got a permit for that?"

Right on time. The guy who approached him in a black sweatshirt with the sleeves cut off and gray sweatpants was obviously a cop. The eyes and body language broadcast it, even if the NOPD emblem on the breast of the shirt hadn't. Lawrence reached for his wallet, intentionally placed in the pocket opposite from the holster for just this kind of moment, and pulled out his necessary carry permits and service card. The guy, who had a face that looked like it had been hammered by life but he'd just kept hammering back, nodded as he looked them over.

"I'm Grizzly," he said. "That's what they call me here. Sergeant Grissom on the job. Saw you come in with Ros. Any problems we need to be aware of?"

"You own this place?"

"Part-owner." He gestured toward an older, equally rough-hewn version of himself. The gray-bearded man was eying Lawrence from the main boxing ring. "My dad founded and runs the place."

Lawrence nodded toward Grizzly's daddy, then glanced at Grizzly. "Now I'm doubly glad she came here, instead of a frou-frou place with a no-guns-permitted sign on the door."

The sergeant shot him a look. "Because we all know what crooks call those places, right?"

"A target-rich environment," they said at the same time, and Lawrence allowed himself a grim smile. "I'm security for Rosalinda Thomas. She's had some gang threats. Got between one of the lieutenants and his pregnant girlfriend he was using as a punching bag. Seen anyone in here you think might be connected to any of that?"

"Not a chance. This place has way too many current and retired cops, fire fighters, military. But now you've told me, we'll keep an eye out, just in case. Why didn't Ros just cut the shitbag off at the knees to bleed out in the street?"

"So you know her, then."

"I do." Grizzly grinned, but his eyes got a hard light. "No one will put up with someone giving her a hard time. She'll be safe whenever she's here. Guarantee it."

"Appreciate that."

When Grizzly wandered back to his dad a few minutes later, likely to bring him into the loop, the subject of their conversation appeared from the lockers. Dressed in an outfit similar to Cyn's, except her top was a sky blue, Rosalinda stood out like a blue rose in a dirt field. She'd put her hair in a ponytail, a charmingly girlish look.

She looked for him, which gave him a surprising charge. Then Cyn spoke, and Rosalinda moved away with her to start their workout.

Good security was wallpaper until needed, not interfering with the client's behavior unless there was a safety conflict. Yet another reason for the warnings about emotional involvement. Because being totally ignored by his rose while she bantered with a bunch of sweaty alpha guys who obviously enjoyed flirting with her could get the wrong guy twitchy.

If she knew he'd called her that in his head, Rosalinda would probably give him her enigmatic look. Good thing her ability to crawl into his mind and pull things out of him he wasn't expecting hadn't evolved into full-on mind reading.

Though he had no reason to doubt Grizzly, Lawrence studied everyone in the place. There were only about five women, including Rosalinda and Cyn. One was doing some serious competitive training in the corner with a personal trainer. Lawrence evaluated her and the other two women as closely as the men. A gang camp follower could be every bit as deadly as a member with a dick. They were also good intel-gathering plants.

In the meantime, Rosalinda and Cyn were running through a pretty grueling regimen. Body-weight exercises, including squats and push-ups, then they alternated on cardio, one working with the jump rope while the other handled the dodge bag, then they swapped. They didn't hold back, both showing a damp line of sweat down their backs and at the top of their close-fitting workout pants.

After they finished with all that, they donned gloves and started in on the speed bags. They did those side by side, but they worked a double-ended bag together, one punching, the other nimbly moving back in, circling, not getting in one another's way.

When Rosalinda had gone after the punching bag with a bat, he'd noticed she'd been ready for the recoil, dancing back a step, then forward again to land another blow. He saw those footwork skills here. The graceful display of coordination caught more than one man's attention.

Lawrence saw even more than that, though. There was a trust between the two women. They anticipated one another's movements like dance partners. As he thought of where they could have developed that synchronicity, he couldn't help but imagine them sharing the same sub in a complicated dungeon scenario. If that was true, how did he feel about that? *Christ.*

They were done with the bag. In what he figured was their final step, since Rosalinda had told him the workout would be about ninety minutes, they headed for one of the marked-out sparring areas. A VIP's comfort or skill in defending themselves was an additional tool in the security arsenal, so he looked forward to seeing that.

A metal staircase led to the second level. The signage posted next to it indicated additional cardio equipment and battle rope were up there. Each time the door to that level opened, he'd noted who'd emerged. Now he saw a familiar face. Matt Kensington.

The K&A CEO wore loose shorts and a muscle T-shirt. The sweat he was mopping off his face and well-cut upper arms and shoulders suggested he'd completed his workout. Matt was around Dale's age, but like Dale, looked as fit as they came. No desk paunch on the man considered one of Louisiana's most successful business owners.

Matt hailed Rosalinda and Cyn casually with a lifted hand as he moved past their sparring area. Since Lawrence had relocated closer to it, he heard Cyn's taunt as she bounced on her toes. "Ready to do a round with us, Matt? Or are you still too scared?"

"Petrified," he responded, unruffled.

"Give it up," Rosalinda bussed her gloves against her friend's. "You won't live long enough to see Matt spar with a woman. At least not physically."

She shot Matt a smile and he touched his forehead in salute. He'd also noted Lawrence's presence, for as the women re-engaged, he wandered over to stand next to him.

Lawrence saw the sharp dark eyes note his armed state. Matt leaned against the wall, lifting his water bottle to take a swallow. "Security company do their job?"

So Max had brought the head of the company into the loop. It didn't surprise Lawrence, since Rosalinda was a close personal friend of Matt's. "Yeah. Couldn't ask for better. Appreciate it."

"Good. Anything she needs, you let me know. Even if it has to be on the down low to get it done. I'll take her alive and pissed with me, versus happy and dead."

"Roger that. Though I'm keeping it honest with her up front, so I'll take the brunt of that temper. That's part of what she's paying me for."

"Good man. Brave man."

Lawrence smiled. As Cyn and Rosalinda circled each other, he noted they'd gained even more male attention. Two hot women going toe-to-toe? Yeah, every straight guy in the place was going to look.

The two women were quick on their feet, and could land a solid punch. However, though Rosalinda might give him shit about it, Lawrence was glad for Matt's refusal to get into it with her or Cyn. Matt Kensington's physique and fists looked capable of sending a punching bag rocking, and even the most careful sparring matches could get rougher than intended.

"This wasn't the workout experience I expected her to go for," he said.

Matt grunted. "When she and Abigail first founded Laurel Grove, Ros took victims home to collect their things. They always tried to do it when the abuser wasn't there, but things don't always work out as planned. One afternoon, the husband came home while they were still there. This was before Ros learned to fight the way you see here. Big bastard, but she got in his way enough to let the spouse escape the house. Thank God, the wife ran to a neighbor, called the police. She also came back with the neighbor and his two high school aged sons, both athletes, to pull the husband off Ros. Otherwise he might have killed her."

Lawrence thought of the scar on Ros's breast that she didn't want to talk about, and wondered if that had happened then.

"Broken nose, cracked ribs." Matt said, suggesting it had been about blunt impact weapons that day. Probably the prick's fists. Matt nodded to Grizzly.

"He teaches self-defense classes for women, but after that, she wanted more. She wanted to learn how to fight, offense or defense. She said she needed to know how to take full-on hits from a man and stay in the fight. Grizzly taught her. He made her use full protective equipment while he did, but still." Matt shook his head, his jaw flexing. "I couldn't watch it."

Lawrence knew women could kick ass in combat situations, but he didn't like imagining it for his Mistress, with her delicate features and slim bones. However, he couldn't deny the training showed. She moved with competence and purpose. Dodging, feinting, good foot work.

Cyn must have joined her in those classes, or maybe she'd already known how to fight, because her style seemed more self-taught. And more street-dirty.

Once they'd gotten started, they hadn't engaged in much trash talk. They were focused on their moves, and they pushed one another. He glanced at Matt to see him studying them closely. "Cyn needs to get her guard up. She has—"

Rosalinda landed a solid blow to Cyn's face, fortunately protected by the padded helmet, but the force knocked her down on her ass. A collective, sympathetic groan rippled through the watching fighters, but Cyn rolled and was back up on her feet in a blink. She waded back in, alternating kicks and punches.

Lawrence straightened. "Getting a little enthusiastic."

Matt nodded. "Cyn has a temper. They'll get into it pretty heavy. I believe it's cathartic for Cyn. Whereas the more aggressive Cyn gets, the more Ros feels it's a worthwhile workout."

Interestingly, Cyn's temper improved her skills exponentially. Whatever Rosalinda's punch had unleashed increased her focus and force. Cyn was quicker on her feet than her boss, and knew sneakier moves, but Rosalinda stuck with the classic basics and flowed away like water from the rushes and jabs. She never stopped thinking, whereas Cyn was a gut fighter. Lawrence guessed there might be about ten years difference in their ages, but Rosalinda was tiring out her opponent, even as she never stopped looking for another opening to put her down.

"Marcie spars here," Matt said. "I believe you know her."

Lawrence sent him a quick peripheral glance. Neil had joked about Dana and Marcie being hot, and that was true, but they'd met the two women in circumstances that were no joke. Lawrence was certain Matt wasn't going to bring up that situation, but he'd probably mentioned Marcie as a heads up. Lawrence might cross paths with her here, something that hadn't happened since that fateful day.

Dana and Marcie were prime examples of women who could be just as badass as a man in a physical fight. Dana was the wife of Peter Winston, Matt's operations manager. She was also a former Army sergeant. Though she was blind now due to an IED, it had made her no less capable in the precarious situation Dale had pulled Neil and Lawrence in to help manage.

Marcie was the wife of Matt's top lawyer, Ben O'Callahan. She'd done corporate investigations work, but Max had mentioned she'd enrolled in the NOLA police academy.

"Ben sometimes works out with her here," Matt said, "but he can't be on this level of the gym when she's doing her MMA sparring. She prefers male opponents, and if someone knocks her down, which has happened, he can't sit on the protective instincts."

Lawrence thought he might feel the same way if he had to watch some guy's fist hit Rosalinda's face, knock her head back on her fragile-looking neck.

Matt's voice reflected faint amusement. "My wife says it's a shame that women can't *actually* be helpless, just to make men like me more comfortable.'"

Lawrence smiled. "Sounds like she and Rosalinda would get along just fine."

Savannah Tennyson Kensington. Lawrence knew who she was, too, though they'd never met directly. CEO of another successful company, she and Matt had alternated between being business rivals and joining forces on ventures of mutual interest. Until those interests had merged in the most important ways, resulting in their marriage.

Well, hell. For a guy who was trained to ferret out details, make connections, he seemed slow when it came to things in the Dom/sub arena. Rosalinda had said there were married club members whose significant others weren't part of that world, but that wasn't the impression Lawrence had been given about the kind of Dominants Matt's inner circle were. Which meant Marcie, Dana and Savannah... they all had to be submissives.

Who people were behind closed doors wasn't always easy to figure out from who they were in front of them. Turning that mirror on himself, he was an operator trained by his government to be a very effective and deadly weapon. No one would coin him as the type of guy who hungered for a Mistress. What he felt toward Rosalinda, and his fantasies—he didn't call it being topped or dominated inside his head. But he supposed others would.

Ever since Dale had introduced Lawrence to Rosalinda, he'd been wrapping his mind around the realization that Dale knew exactly what he wanted, even if it had never been talked about in the open between them. If Dale had pulled Matt into the intro with Rosalinda, then Matt probably knew, too.

Cue the ball of tension, wondering what else Matt would bring up. Fortunately, the CEO didn't seem like he wanted to talk about anything else. He just held up the wall with Lawrence, watching the women until they finished their workout and headed their way.

As they passed the community fridge, Cyn grabbed a couple of bottles of water from it and handed one to Rosalinda. As she did, she said something that made her boss smile, shake her head, cut a glance at Lawrence. Then Cyn was giving him the same kind of assessing look she'd done at the car, only this one was even more blatant. Her blood was up from the fight. Lawrence could see it in the flush of her cheeks, the catlike saunter as they made their way over.

"Matt." Rosalinda smiled as Matt lifted a closed fist and she bumped hers against it. "Good to see you. Thanks for the assist on security. Though I wish it hadn't been needed."

Lawrence detected the slight edge in her tone, but the thanks was genuine. His Mistress had class.

"We'll do anything for you and your ladies, Ros. You know that." Matt offered her a return smile. "Who else is skilled enough to rebrand my image when the local papers officially dub me the Predator of the Bayou?"

"It's a lot easier to do when you don't take actual pride in the title," she replied.

Cyn propped an elbow on Ros's shoulder and gave Matt an up and down. "Don't pay attention to her, Matt. I'd be happy to rebrand your image personally." Then she tilted her head toward Lawrence. "So is your bodyguard like a therapy dog, Ros? Do I need your permission to pet him?"

Lawrence stiffened. Matt sent him a hard-to-read glance, but nodded to Ros and Cyn. "I need to get changed and head home. Ladies. A pleasure as always."

The reaction told Lawrence that yes, Matt definitely knew what dynamic was happening between him and Ros, but no, he had no interest in embarrassing Lawrence about it.

His temper spiked, thinking his current employer had no such concerns, but before he could figure out how to react to that, he noted Ros's expression had cooled about twenty degrees. She slid smoothly out from under Cyn's elbow and gave her a quelling glance. "I'll join you in the locker room. Give me a minute."

Cyn's expression went from playful to shuttered in a blink. With a nod, she left them.

To her credit, Ros didn't try to gloss over it. "Everything all right?"

"I think we need to pull this back," he said. "I'll handle your security until your problem blows over. We revisit the rest of it, if there's anything you want to revisit, when the job is done."

It burned his gut to say it, but whereas he thought he could handle his own emotions and not let them interfere with the job, he had overlooked how it could impact human variables farther outside his control.

She spoke carefully. "If you really feel that way, okay. But did what she say really bother you, or is it that she said it in front of another man? A Dom on top of that? In a public venue that isn't a club or dungeon?"

"I expect basic respect for what I'm here to do. That's all. I'll wait for you outside."

He headed out the main door, taking up a watch post there. The fresh air might have done him good, but in this part of New Orleans, the air wasn't so fresh.

His gut was tight, because *yes* was the answer to all of her questions. Though his personal reaction wasn't the primary problem, it did make an impact, so he made himself look at it.

When he was with Rosalinda, just the two of them, and that Mistress side reached out to him, all those dark fantasies and urges surged up like she was some kind of summoner. But he wasn't ready to be sucked into a world where a label was slapped on him that made other Mistresses and Masters treat him like Cyn had just treated him. He wasn't a goddamn pet because he was getting turned on by Rosalinda taking the upper hand. If that was what this deal was truly about, then it wasn't for him.

Shit. Who was he? What did he want? It was hard enough to be facing those questions since he'd left the SEALs. To deal with that and a sexual identity crisis was too much.

Except, even as he had the thought, he also remembered being with Rosalinda in his kitchen, his body restrained by nothing more than her commands and a couple household items. During that impromptu session was the first time that the incessant "Who am I now?" question had shut the fuck up.

The front door opened. Matt had put on a dark blue sweat suit, the jacket unzipped over his muscle shirt. He carried his gym bag over his shoulder. Lawrence noted a pink unicorn hairclip, shiny with glitter, clamped over the top of the gym bag strap.

Matt noted his glance, and a light smile tugged his firm mouth. "Discovered it in my car this morning. My daughter's. Probably pulled it out when she was in her car seat. She prefers her hair down. Easier to get sticky things tangled in it."

He stopped next to Lawrence, put down the bag, and fished in his jacket pocket, emerging with a pack of gum. He offered Lawrence a stick. Lawrence shook his head.

Matt surveyed the street. "You were right, about Ros and Savannah being on the same page when it came to women's strength. But Ros didn't get along with Savannah at first."

Despite the awkward tangle of emotions inside him, Lawrence's interest was caught. "Why not?"

"Sometimes it's tough for female Dominants to understand female subs." Matt shrugged. "Same way it's sometimes tough for male Doms to understand male subs. For those of us who have the Dom or sub orientation from an early age, it's an instinct. But instinct isn't skill. It can't reach full potential until the rules are learned and training happens. Mistakes create experience.

"It seems like a no-brainer, knowing a hetero male sub won't react to a male Dom the same way he does to a female one. Or that a sub in general won't react to another Dom the way he or she does to their own Master or Mistress. But we're human, notoriously thickheaded."

What Lawrence was willing to discuss with Rosalinda was definitely not in the same category of what he wanted to talk about with another male. Still, he wasn't being asked to respond, and intel was intel.

Matt put a piece of gum in his mouth, chewed. "When mistakes happen in that environment, they're often because we make assumptions about who someone is. Dom, sub, switch. A woman tells me she likes candy, that tells me nothing more than she has a sweet tooth. The vital info is what kind of candy, and why does she like it. What's her favorite way of experiencing it? Does she trust me enough to take it from my hand? At what point has she had enough or too much? And what's the best timing to offer it?"

Matt finally looked toward Lawrence, his dark eyes and hawk-like features reflecting understanding, man to man, in a way that eased Lawrence's gut. Then Matt directed his gaze toward the street again, as if he knew this discussion worked better that way for Lawrence.

"An experienced Dom will identify a submissive pretty quickly, through personality traits we recognize, how they perform their jobs, or conduct their relationships. When their deepest submissive responses, that core hunger, bonds with a Master or Mistress, it's a gift that a Dominant of either gender should recognize, respect and protect."

Matt tilted his head toward Lawrence. "Give Ros the chance to do that. Cyn is young, and she's an aggressive Mistress. She overstepped, but Ros will address it. That said, if you get pushed like that, and she doesn't address it, or isn't there to address it, you have every right to push back. Ros would agree with me on that, a hundred percent."

He picked up his gym bag. "I wasn't going to say anything, but in this world, mentoring, getting good advice, is a vital part of making the most of it." He met Lawrence's gaze squarely. "I'm a Dom, Lawrence. You're not. You have a desire for a Mistress. That doesn't make me see you as less of a man. Not all male Dominants will feel that way, but every culture has its assholes. Don't let that stop you from being who you want to be, or from being with who you want to be with."

He stepped off the curb without saying anything further, and strode toward his Escalade. Lawrence glimpsed the baby seat in the back.

He was still thinking over the conversation a few minutes later when the door opened and Rosalinda and Cyn emerged. Rosalinda's face was as smooth as water, which told him the total opposite might be happening below the surface. Thinking of how quick he'd issued that cut between them had his gut knotted up, particularly after hearing what Matt had to say. Cyn had overstepped, yeah. But maybe he'd overreacted.

Cyn put a hand on her boss's arm, spoke a low word. Ros met her gaze, made a face, but nodded. To his surprise, she stepped back inside while Cyn moved toward Lawrence.

"I told her you'd probably be more comfortable if she was standing inside the door while you and I talked. So she's not vulnerable out on the street."

Good instincts. He wouldn't have been willing to have a conversation with Matt or Cyn while his client stood out on the sidewalk, a sitting duck.

"I fucked up, Lawrence," Cyn's dark eyes were sincere, her face reflecting genuine regret. "I apologize. I get worked up when we spar. Even when that's not the case, sometimes I have a problem leaving the dungeon behind, and remembering the real world has different rules."

She extended her hand. "You're protecting someone who means a lot to me. To all of us. That deserves my respect and support. You have it, from here forward. I'll kick the ass of anyone who doesn't follow my lead on that. Will you accept my apology?"

Straightforward, no excess discussion or analysis of it. He had to appreciate the style. After a moment of thought, because he didn't want to say so if he didn't feel it, he reached out to clasp her hand. And offered his own olive branch. "From what I saw, you hand out a pretty good ass kicking. But watch that left side. You leave it open too much."

"Thanks. Matt's told me the same. Takes me a little longer to learn." She tightened her grip, holding the link.

"She doesn't know I'm offering anything beyond an apology, so she'd bust me for this, but I'm going to say it anyway. I hope you don't cut things off with her. It's been awhile since she's been with someone who holds her attention the way you've managed in such a short time. You're new to it, and that's another thing I should have taken into account. But if you're not offended by me saying so, and don't take it as an excuse, it makes you even more irresistible."

She winked. The gesture held such straightforward mischief, he couldn't help but want to smile.

"Fine," he responded gravely. "I can accept that. As long as you keep the suggestive comments and ass grabbing to a minimum. Otherwise I'll call in the big guns. Report you to Vera."

Her brown eyes twinkled, the tension around her mouth easing. "Her and her endless supply of forms could circle the globe ten times, just like the plastic bottles." She released him. "See you later."

She didn't specify whether that would be tomorrow, at the office, or tonight at the club, even though it was obvious Rosalinda had told her he wanted to dial it back.

He'd been given a way to backtrack on that, if he thought that was an acceptable idea. Jury was still out, more than one side and argument jockeying for position in his head. Security risk, gut risk, comfort zone blowout...all were in contention.

Cyn turned the corner to the alley where he'd parked. A couple moments later, she emerged in the driver's seat of the glossy black pick-up on all-terrain tires. The one with the gun rack in the back window. He should have known. She waved and pulled out.

The door opened once more, and Rosalinda stepped out. He moved to her side, and they didn't speak as he escorted her in the same direction, opening the passenger door at her car. The sun had almost set, making the buildings clustered around them extend shadows over the hood of the car, on the street, like giants looming over them. Maybe it felt that way because of the feelings looming over him, weighing him down.

He got into the car, closed the door. Put the key in the ignition but didn't yet turn it.

"I overreacted," he said. "I think so, at least. I'm not used to not knowing who I am or what I'm doing. The only thing in this situation that's familiar to me, that I feel like I know for sure, is how to protect you. But I can do that whether I'm in your bed or not. So I'm going to stop using it as an excuse."

He turned to look at her then, straight out. Her blue eyes were fixed attentively on his face, but otherwise, she was giving him no cues, which was impressive, since he was trained to read people pretty deeply. He expected she was too, only her training had come from a different source. "I'm sorry I walked away from you, issued that ultimatum, gave Cyn the cold shoulder. I shouldn't have done that."

"No, you shouldn't have," she said, surprising him. But there was no anger in her voice, no accusation, which settled his immediate defensiveness. Her gaze on him was even, calm. A Mistress's gaze. "But do you understand why?"

When he thought it through, a parallel emerged in his head that startled him. He wasn't sure if he was right, though, so he said it out loud, slowly, testing. "When we came back from an op, sometimes the higher ups would attend the debriefing, talk shit about how one of us handled something. If our team leader gave us the cue to explain, we did. If he didn't, we didn't say anything, because he was going to handle it, usually after the rest of us had been dismissed."

Maybe she hadn't expected the analogy, but from the flicker in her gaze, he thought he'd gotten it right. "So you're telling me you handed her ass to her in the locker room?" he ventured, to confirm it.

She answered that with a question. "Did your team leader tell you what he said to those higher ups after you left?"

"No. Not usually. Respect for the chain of command."

"Correct. Cyn is a Mistress. A Dominant in her own right."

So she had exchanged words with Cyn in the locker room. Thinking about that took him deep in a whitewater current of conflicting emotion. Topping the list was regret.

They had only just started down this road. They had no solid basis for trust between them yet, yeah, but no solid basis for the kind of distrust he'd demonstrated, using the job as an instant retreat. That had to do with his shit. Just like when he thought she'd been fucking with his head this morning at his place.

"You haven't ever been involved with a woman who will champion you, have you?" she asked softly.

He'd never really thought about it like that, but soon as she said it, that tide of emotions surged toward her, yearning. Even as he told himself that wasn't something he should be asking of her.

She reached over the console, put her hand on his arm. "Do you want to continue down the road we've started, Lawrence? Now. Not after the job is done."

He met her gaze square. "Yes, ma'am."

She gave him a cordial nod. "I want you to join me in the club tonight. As my guest, and my submissive. Will you?"

Just like that, they were back in sync, because she let it be that easy. Her hand lay lightly on his arm, but it was her eyes that pulled him in and held him, drawing everything up inside him. Because that made far more than his cock stir, he had his answer.

"Yes, Mistress. I will."

Her blue eyes sparked, and she tightened her hand on his arm, letting him feel the bite of her nails. Some perverse part of him wanted them to pierce him down to the bone.

"Good. I want that too. But I need you to hear this as well. As a Mistress, it *is* my job to protect my submissive in certain ways. Just the same way it's your job to keep me alive and in one piece. I take that job every bit as seriously as you do yours. Do you understand that?"

When he paused, thinking it through, the sensual heat in her eyes deepened. "It's fascinating to watch you process," she murmured.

She really was like a sorceress. She had the ability to stop time and gravity and anything else that moved in the world around the two of them.

He cleared his throat. "What was the question?"

Her eyes smiled, even as her lips stayed serious. "Do you understand that I take your care as seriously as you take mine?"

"Not as deep as I think you want me to understand it," he said. For the reasons she'd said, another quagmire he didn't want to face here and now. But as he'd told Matt, he was doing his best to always be honest with her. "I'm trying. Ma'am."

She sat back with a satisfied nod. "That's good enough for now."

CHAPTER ELEVEN

*T*he security company had replaced the backdoor window when they were there to do the upgrades. Everything had been completed as he'd specified.

Lawrence showed Rosalinda the new features of her system, but then he had to address one potential wrinkle in tonight's plan to join her. Whatever she had planned for him at Club Progeny would be distracting. He wouldn't take the chance of that compromising her safety, and he let her know that up front.

"Being your guest tonight is dependent on me finding a backup to watch things on the outside. So I need to make a call or two. I'll make sure it's someone like Dale, who already knows your preferences, or can be trusted to be discreet about them. I'll also pay him out of my check, so it's nothing extra to you."

"You'll do no such thing," she responded instantly. "You're not doing this pro bono, and you can't watch me 24/7. As for the discretion, I appreciate it, but you don't have to limit your security options. I don't go around announcing that I like to tie men up and beat them, but I don't hide that I have a membership at Progeny. I am who I am."

Hearing that eased the small twinge of guilt he'd felt about talking to Neil and Max about her. But he couldn't let the other thing ride. "I pay for this one," he said. "If I'm with you, and not doing my job, then I pay for the person who is. Consider me an old-fashioned guy."

She cocked a brow. "The equivalent of picking up the dinner check, because you're the man?"

"Something like that."

She gave him a female look. "Fine, then. But don't give me your stubborn look. It makes me want to strap your ass."

He snorted. "Set the security. I'm going to run home, grab a change of clothes and clean up some."

She glanced at the clock and then at him. "What you're wearing works just fine for the club. No sense in you having to get home and back through NOLA traffic. Eat a light supper out of whatever you like in the kitchen. Nothing too heavy. Use one of the guest bathrooms to clean up."

It was peculiar, how he could tell the difference between when she was making suggestions and when she was giving orders. The latter held his attention as if she'd suddenly appeared before him dressed like Wonder Woman.

Pausing at the base of the stairs, she glanced back at him through her long lashes. "The clothes aren't important, because you won't be wearing them long."

She winked and continued up the steps. Her hips swayed left and right, her hand trailing along the banister. The erotic impact wasn't exaggerated or calculated. Not exactly. Rosalinda Thomas just enjoyed the sensual way her body moved and sank into the indulgence, the way another woman would forget herself while dancing.

She disappeared down the hallway, and he listened to her enter her bedroom, close the door. They hadn't really talked about doing things in front of people, like being naked. Progeny had private rooms, but what if she...

He had his safe words, and though she obviously liked pushing his comfort zones, she was really sharp about picking up on when he might be trying to accommodate her in a way that didn't work for him.

You've never had a woman champion you.

Every time he thought about her saying that, a can of worms tried to crank itself open in his chest, so he wouldn't be thinking about it now. But the words themselves, they held him almost like her arms did. With an unsettling strength.

He turned his attention to making that call for backup. Though

Rosalinda's openness about her sexual preferences did widen his choices, him being in the club with her tonight, as her actively participating guest, limited the number of people he felt comfortable calling to a grand total of one.

It was the eleventh hour, so if Dale couldn't do it, he'd just bow out of the guest stuff tonight and stick to being her security. While that thought should be a relief, another, far bigger part, didn't feel that way about it.

"Hey, Munch. What's happening?"

Acknowledging things like this for the first time made him feel a little more squirrelly than expected. But he forced out the words. "I was wondering if you wanted to make a little money tonight. Rosalinda invited me to...join her, in the club. As her guest. I don't want to do that unless I know I have focused eyes on the outside."

"Sure. I can do that. Athena is handling a business dinner, so I was just doing some woodworking in the shop. No emergency birdhouse projects."

"Great." They worked out some other details, concluding with Lawrence's estimate of their arrival time. "I'm thinking we'll be at the door by eight."

"Sounds good." Dale paused. "Lawrence, I've known what's what with you for awhile. You get that, right?"

"Yeah. I'm still wrapping my head around it."

"Roger that. But let me lay one thing out for you. I didn't disrespect your privacy or Max's, but I told him there was an operator I knew checking out the sub end of things. Who might need a sounding board from another team guy. Max gave me the greenlight to say what I'm about to say to you. Janet is a Mistress."

Since thinking about it at the park, it wasn't really a surprise to hear it. But Max...

"Max isn't a sub," Dale continued. "Not in the traditional sense. But he and Janet make it work."

Nothing he'd seen about the couple made Lawrence doubt it. Max hadn't made noises about them getting married, but they lived together at her place, and it was clear Max had found the person he wanted to be with.

"Okay." He cleared his throat. "Maybe I'll talk to him at some point."

"I think you'll be glad you did. But it's up to you, son." Dale's voice became quieter. "Your team knows who you are. Nothing's going to change that opinion, and this is definitely something that shouldn't, anyhow."

He wasn't sure how to respond to that, so he went with keeping it simple. "Thanks, Master Chief. Gotta go. Thanks again for helping out tonight."

"Always happy to have your back. See you there."

Lawrence put the phone away and rose, headed for the guest bathroom. Time to clear his mind, steady himself.

It didn't take long. He stripped down, ran through the shower, dried off, put his pretty much clean clothes back on. No razor, but the five o'clock shadow on his neck and above his clipped beard would likely be okay. Just light sandpaper.

He grabbed a sandwich in the kitchen, using Maisy's great bread and some cold cuts, then turned on Rosalinda's flat screen to give him some background noise while consuming his light dinner. The New Orleans-based *Pit Bulls and Parolees* was on, so he stuck with that while eating at her kitchen island, not risking crumbs on her couch.

He kept an ear tuned to the upstairs. When he at last heard the bedroom door open, her heels clicking on the carpet runner, he'd finished his meal and moved to an easy chair. Now he turned off the television and rose.

She'd told him his casual outfit would work. The moment he saw her begin to descend the stairs, a sense of anticipation built inside him, because his Mistress had definitely not chosen casual for herself.

Tonight's shoe of choice was a closed-toe pump in Valentine's Day red, the four-inch slim heel wrapped up in a jeweled gold and rose-colored vine. A similar piece, looking like an opening rose, was molded along the back heel.

As she descended, his gaze slid up her beautiful legs. She wasn't wearing stockings, but there was something coating her flesh that gave it a faint, glittery sheen. Then, pretty as all that was, his gaze lifted higher and he got lost. So fucking lost.

The glitter worked with the dress she was wearing. He'd never seen anything like it. The fabric was sparkling gold, the gathered skirt accentuating the roundness of her hips. The hem traveled diagonally from mid-thigh on the right side down to her left knee. A split opened up a view of the left thigh nearly to her hip bone.

The point of the V-neckline began a few inches above that slit and swung upward in a curve. The V-shape widened as it went between her breasts, revealing the hint of curves. The covering over the left breast was held by a strap that passed over her opposite shoulder. It concealed her crescent scar. The right side didn't have that strap, the glittering fabric seemingly molded around her breast without anything holding it. He assumed the same creative wiring that handled women's push-up bras kept it in place.

It was a dress that had been created to pay homage to a woman's shape. Particularly this woman. She wore nothing on her throat, though she had on earrings, twisting gold wires dotted with tiny rose-gold blooms. They dangled and brushed against her throat.

Her blonde, dark-tipped hair was soft and loose, lots of sexy tousled curls to her shoulders, which made his hands want to touch. Her lips were a soft rose, her eyeshadow a glittering gold. Her mascara gave her vivid gaze a fringe of black mink.

His self-consciousness during his conversation with Dale vanished. Along with his worry about what she'd want from him at the club. Hell, pretty much every worry he had vanished. Some things were so incredible, so overwhelming to the senses, they demanded that the universe and all the bullshit stop, so that a man could savor the gift he'd somehow been given. Even if it was only for one damn moment.

When she reached the bottom of the stairs, he was there. Taking her hand didn't seem to be enough. Only one thing matched what he was feeling.

He dropped to his knees.

Ros had seen men look at her with all different kinds of hunger and need. Some of it calculated, though not in a bad way. They understood if their true hunger and need were properly embellished or presented in a dramatic way, she'd be more receptive to their service, apprecia-tive of their efforts. She'd savored it, channeled it into memorable experiences.

She'd thought a while before wearing the René Hurt original

tonight. Just like her shoes, she kept a change of clothes at the club in case she decided to get more down and dirty in a session, or needed more flexibility than her formal wear allowed. Having that backup allowed her to start the night wherever her mood took her. So she'd followed her intuition, and chosen the dress she'd most wanted to wear. She'd wanted something that said Mistress, with a capital M.

She'd never had a man look at her the way Lawrence gazed up the stairs at her. There was nothing calculated about it. When she reached the bottom step and he went to his knees, this man who'd had no formal training as a submissive, who was following only the wishes and needs within him, she knew the message she'd intended to send had been clear. Her own reaction was less planned.

She took a moment, her hand gripping the banister, to school her face to calmness. But her heart had tilted in an alarming way. Her heart didn't do that. It might beat a little faster, but it certainly did not do somersaults in her chest.

She modulated her voice to a low purr to keep it steady. "Eyes down, Lawrence. I need to adjust my shoe, and I'm not wearing anything under this dress."

He'd gripped one of the balustrades as he'd knelt and she saw his fingers tighten, but he lowered his eyes. His tension was a palpable thing as she braced the sole of the pump on his shoulder, leaned forward. The shoe needed no adjustment. Her only intent was to torment him with the thought that if he flicked his gaze up he'd be looking under the skirt at her bare pussy, which had been as honey dusted as the rest of her body to help with the fit of the dress.

The silken liner was thick enough to keep her skin from being irritated by the sparkling gold texture on the outside, and the wiring maintained the bodice of the dress so she didn't have to worry about gapping. But any man looking would be teased by the deceptive accessibility of the right breast. From the side or above, the curve was almost fully exposed except the nipple, while the front was almost modestly covered with a half shell of gold.

He didn't look up, but she could feel the effort it took. "What are you thinking, Lawrence?" she said. "I want your thoughts, unfiltered. I want to hear them as you're thinking them."

"I want to look more than anything. Except to please you. I want that more. So I won't look."

"Obedience from a powerful man does please me, Lawrence. More than you know. Stand and look at me."

When he did, since she was standing on the bottom step and wearing the heels, she was slightly taller than him. The green eyes were on fire. She laid her hand on his forearm, because he'd put his hand on the banister. Heat emanated from his flesh, blood pounding hard beneath the surface.

His foot was on the bottom step next to hers. He'd moved into her personal space when he stood up, and bracketed her with his body. A move that might seem at odds with the compulsive deference that had taken him to his knees, but he was conveying a different sort of message to her now. Readiness. Ready to serve how she desired.

"Tonight, I want you to absorb the things you see at the club," she said. "Think of everything as a submissive who is there to serve his Mistress's pleasure."

She'd given so much thought to the things she'd like to do to him. Starting with having him strip off his clothes as soon as he crossed the club threshold, so she'd be able to touch a lot of bare flesh. She'd let him keep the dark brief shorts she knew he was wearing, merely to watch his cock stretch the limits of the threads, the way she was sure it was doing now.

That was the simplest of her desires, and that alone would be a big step for a man who hadn't played in a BDSM club environment before. Or had a formal session with a Mistress, inside or outside of a club, except for the time in his kitchen with her.

"If I ask you a question tonight, if I require an answer right then, I'll tell you. Otherwise, many of the questions I ask will be designed to have you think about your response. So look, listen, feel. And think."

She trailed her fingertips up his shoulder, grazed his jaw. His hand came up, gripped her wrist. He turned his mouth to her palm, nuzzling. She curled her fingers in, scraping his face with her nails. "But don't think too much. I like the animal in you, Lawrence. The pure response. I can enjoy it when it's welcome, and punish you when you cross the line with it."

His gaze slid to hers, held, and her lips curved. That fire had just gotten hotter. He liked the idea of punishment.

Most bad boys did.

Once they left the house, her sub shifted back into security mode. Which included waiting until she'd fastened her seatbelt to leave the driveway. This morning, she'd tested his focus because she hadn't been taking his job as seriously as she should. She didn't make that mistake tonight, but since he had assured her he could multi-task, she used the drive to prep him for the basics. Once they arrived, she wanted to immerse him in the club experience as soon as feasible.

"You probably noticed the general rules when you came as Dale's guest. Not interrupting a session, that kind of thing. When we go in tonight, I want you to read those rules through again. This time, you'll follow them as an active submissive. There are protocols in place to maintain the power dynamic atmosphere. Like if I'm talking to another Dom, you are not part of the conversation. Even if we're talking about you. If you want or need to say something to me, you ask my permission to speak before you do."

She didn't expect he'd do that too often. He was a listener, an observer, his impassive expression not fooling her. He was always gathering information.

He changed lanes, his eyes moving to the mirrors. "Yes, ma'am." He took a turn they didn't need to take, then rejoined the main road a couple blocks later.

"Are we being followed?"

"The maneuvers I'm doing are a way to figure that out." He reached out without looking, closed his hand on hers where it rested on her lap. He didn't fumble for it, telling her he was aware of her, how she was sitting, how her body was positioned in relation to his.

"If we have a problem, I'll tell you," he said. "Don't let it worry you."

"Okay." Even as she felt that familiar tinge of resentment, because it did. It made her feel out of control of her environment, having to trust the changes in it to someone else.

She'd make an appalling submissive, wouldn't she?

The wry thought settled her. Self-awareness could be a blessing and a curse. She reached out and caressed his nape, earning a quick glance. "If you have questions now, you may ask them."

"I know you want me watching things, but what's your preference when I'm near you?" he asked. "A lot of subs don't sit with their Doms. They kneel at their feet, or hold up a wall nearby."

"I'll decide as we go along. I might pick a corner booth, straddle you, order you to put your hands out to either side, since many of the booths have handles along the back for just that purpose. Then I'll kiss you as long as I like, rub against you, take things at my own pace. Until I'd like to see what your pace is like. Or how much what I'm doing to you affects it."

A short nod, his body a little tauter than it had been a second ago. *Shit.* She was doing it, playing with his focus. It was that bitchy side of her, annoyed that she couldn't be completely in control.

"I could be okay with that," he said, making a turn.

He'd given her an opening she couldn't pass up. She dug a fingernail into his biceps, enough to leave a crescent mark. "How would you feel if I said 'I don't care whether you're okay with it or not?' Would that turn you on? Or make you uncomfortable? Nervous?"

"Yes."

The ripple of pleasure was a welcome distraction that balanced things for her again. "Yes to all, then. Before we go down that kind of road, Lawrence, I need an answer to one all-important question."

"Okay. If you don't mind, can it wait until we get there? Sounds like it needs my full attention."

"I thought SEALs could make critical decisions no matter the situation."

He chuckled. "Apparently, being punched by bullets and avoiding exploding grenades is less distracting than this discussion."

Bullets *had* punched through his body. She'd seen the scars. Maybe to men like him, that was routine, but she quelled the urge to recapture one of his hands, hold on to it. Every time the subject came up, no matter how casually, she seemed to have that reaction. She was a protective Mistress, but her response to him being in harm's way still seemed out of proportion.

Easy, girl. You really are getting too overboard with this one. Virgin subs could be overwhelming. She reminded herself of that, even as her gut told her he was different. She ignored it.

They were only about ten minutes from the club. She honored his request, holding the vital question and occupying herself with checking her work messages on her phone, inhaling the warm male heat and pleasant fresh soap smell that was Lawrence. Then, as they stopped under a streetlight, she noticed a difference in how the light filtered into the car. Which made her realize just how distracted she'd been.

"When did my windows get tinted?" she asked sharply.

"This afternoon, as part of the security upgrades. It's temporary and can be removed if you don't want to keep it long-term, but for now it makes it difficult for anyone to draw a bead on anyone in the car based on identity."

Evasive maneuvers, tinted windows. Security upgrades at her home. A nebulous uneasiness gripped her as he pulled into the club parking lot. She was seeing all the shadows, places someone could be ducked down...waiting.

No, damn it. She was not that kind of person.

Lawrence gripped her hand, drawing her attention. "A protective detail is unsettling, at first. But then you get into the flow, and accept that it's my job to watch for threats."

He sent a text. Within a few seconds, the phone beeped. He glanced at it, then put it inside his pocket before unsnapping his seat-belt and turning toward her. "That was Dale. He's here and has us covered. You have my full attention, Mistress. What was the impor-tant thing you needed to ask?"

He had his hand on the wheel, fingers loose, body language atten-tive to her. His green eyes were patient. He understood her reaction, was giving her time to manage it. "You really have had experience with this," she said stiffly.

He shrugged. "I've protected a handful of pretty different folks. Like a fourteen-year-old Saudi prince who tweeted every detail of his day, including how many times he took a whiz. Believe me, you're handling having a protection detail far better than him."

"How did you deal with him?"

"I tossed his phone in the toilet and told him if he didn't straighten up, I'd take my belt to his spoiled little ass. We got along just fine after that. Well, after he found out his dad wasn't going to cut off my head just because the kid told him he should." Despite the humor, Lawrence's expression remained serious, his eyes on her.

She sighed. "This is really pissing me off. I have a certain mindset on Club Night. This disrupts it."

"I get that. It's why I called Dale. I can't guarantee some part of me won't be assessing threats to you, even with his backup, but now that he's here, I feel more comfortable giving you more of my attention than anything else. But..." She saw the regret in the set of his jaw. "If this really does ruin your groove, I get it. I can go back to wearing my security hat tonight and you can do your usual thing."

She was a very disciplined person. Under normal circumstances, she would already have reached that conclusion herself. But she recalled his look as she'd come down the stairs, that yearning. She could still feel that vibration through her bones when he'd dropped to his knees.

"No. You're here tonight as my guest. *My* submissive."

His hand flexed on the wheel, the only cue she needed. She laid her hand on his thigh. "So, back to that important question. We've talked about your safewords, but tell me what you think a safeword is."

"A way to tell you I need to stop or slow down."

"Yes. But it's critical that you understand the significance of a safeword. It doesn't matter what we're doing. If I've spent days setting up a scene, if I'm a breath away from climax, none of that matters. If you safeword, I will stop what I'm doing, out of respect and caring for your well-being. For you."

She tapped his bent leg. "If you tell me you have a hard limit, I might test the edges, but I will not cross that line until you tell me that it's no longer a hard limit. Limits do change in this world, as trust grows, and the feelings of the moment take on a life of their own. That can be a positive thing. But here's the negative one."

This was a vital conversation with any submissive, but with what she'd picked up from him already, the possible unhealthy nuances from his previous relationship, she suspected it had additional import. "In vanilla relationships, there's a lot of saying you're fine when you're not. Going along to get along. We're not immune to that in the kink world, because people are people, but any Domme worth anything will tell you she respects the integrity of a safeword, even as she never fully relies on it. In the middle of a session, when emotions and lust can be possessing the mind to unimaginable levels, there are subs who would literally die before realizing they were in trouble."

His gaze flickered. "I don't think you have to worry about that. I can't imagine letting go of that much control."

She loved when a sub unwittingly laid down a gauntlet. With effort, she kept her expression neutral.

"There are other, conscious reasons a sub can get into that kind of trouble, too. Like if they think they have to prove something to the Domme. That's why a Domme seems so intensely involved in a session. A good one, we're watching everything. It's all in our hands, and we love that sense of full responsibility. We revel in it, even as we want you to watch out for yourself if we miss a cue. You are that important to us. During a scene, you are the most important thing in our entire world."

That had an impact. She saw his emotions rise and fall, touching on those past scars. She'd seen that same turbulence when she'd recognized no woman in his romantic relationships had ever stood for him.

"So here's the question, and there's no wrong answer, except a dishonest one. If you safeword, I need to be sure you understand I am not going to see it as a sign of failure or weakness. Not in the least. The protocol is there because we are extremely complex human beings, and there is no way I can anticipate or know everything that works or doesn't work for you, as much as I'd like that to be true."

She held his gaze. "If you safeword, it will not end our relationship as Mistress and sub. Not unless either or both of us decide the scene has been ended because our desires as Dom or sub are incompatible. If that's the case, we part amicably, no judgment. We just didn't fit. I expect you to care for you. Not let me pull you forward into something you don't want, out of some misguided notion that my desires of the moment are more important than the integrity of your heart and soul. Can you tell me, truthfully, you understand and believe that?"

He did that thinking thing she'd told him she found so fascinating. Now there was a different tension to him, as he struggled with details of his past she didn't fully know. But when he spoke, the conflict in his voice had to do with the here and now. "What if I don't know exactly what I want?"

She made sure to let the surge of approval show in her expression, let him hear it in her voice. "Then it sounds like we're starting an intriguing adventure together. We'll figure it out that way."

He came around and opened her door for her, took her hand. As they crossed the parking lot, she was aware of eyes upon her. No surprise, with what she was wearing. She was even more aware of him, how he kept a lookout around her, noting every set of those eyes, their intent. Dale was out there somewhere, but she decided if she was going to make this work, she was going to have to do exactly as he'd recommended. Trust him to handle her security. She'd handle him.

The night she'd met him here, she'd drawn his attention to the quotes stamped into the different shaped and colored stones embedded in the concrete walkway to the entrance. Their significance extended beyond the words, however.

Progeny had started as little more than a co-operative grouping of lifestylers who'd wanted to invest in a club that met their needs. Now it had a primary ownership and management, but the continued success of most BDSM clubs rested with its core membership, and what they could contribute to the shaping of its environment.

Each year a couple of those who'd volunteered time, skills or money to improve the experience for everyone were chosen to add their favorite quotes to the as-yet blank stones. Scene names of those volunteers were etched in a discreet corner of the stones. She liked seeing the Dom/sub combinations. Some were actual names, like Alicia/mike; others used their scene names, Lion/kitten.

She stepped over the one Lawrence had mentioned, *Love covers a multitude of sins.* 1 Peter 4:8. As she'd told him, the entranceway was a way to prepare for the experience past the threshold. When a person read the words on the stones, they built a foundation in their mind, shifted perspective.

Tonight reading a few helped her do that, including moving further away from that mental snag the security issue had created. Her mind centered where it needed to be. On the intriguing man new to being an active player.

As they entered the club, she was enveloped by the hints of erotic heat, the vibrating music just past the foyer, cloaked by the conversations of couples arriving just like them. Their movements and voices were weighted with sensual intent while they funneled through the foyer toward the arched opening to the main club. A stargate, Skye called it.

Ros put a hand on Lawrence's shoulder, nodding toward the posted list of rules for him to review as she'd directed. It was also another kind of reminder. They'd crossed the threshold. Those rules were now in place.

She turned to the desk sub. Her name was fairygirl, and like many submissives, she preferred the lowercase reference for her name. She had a fairy tattooed high on her pillowed breast, accentuated by the hold of her pink corset, the color matching her hair.

"A silver bracelet," Ros told her. "I registered a guest for tonight."

"Yes, Mistress."

She scanned Ros's own permanent membership bracelet. The rose-gold band was custom made, a perk to life members, and logged her presence in and out of the club. The silver bracelet was activated to do the same, with Lawrence's name attached to it in their system. Progeny had done some security upgrades in recent months. Ros had been indifferent to them, since she'd never had any problems here, but tonight she was glad for them, because it would help Lawrence do as he'd said, trust Dale and give her more of his focus, without worrying that he wasn't doing what he considered his most important job.

Lawrence was reviewing the rules as she turned. When she put the bracelet on his wrist, she caressed the pulse tripping beneath it. "The silver base says you're a submissive," she said. "The red light on it says you're attached to a Mistress tonight. Anyone who addresses you will be socializing, not looking for a play partner. Understand?"

He nodded, then glanced back toward the board. "Yes, Mistress."

A submissive asked a question by any club Dom will answer Yes, Master or Yes, Mistress, unless the Dom prefers another honorific that does not disrespect the sub's ownership by another. He did follow direction well.

She remembered when the rules had been developed. Newer subs or Doms might feel self-conscious, hesitant to manifest their power exchange personas in the ways they desired. The rules encouraged them to do so, to make the transition to Dom/sub headspace easier, from the moment they walked through the club doors.

He'd discarded the gun holster and short sleeved button-down in the car, so only wore the T-shirt and belted jeans. As she let her fingers play over his chest, palm smoothing the fabric, she saw a question in his expression. She stepped closer and he dipped his head to speak into her ear.

"How do you want me dressed, Mistress?"

Despite her earlier thought, she'd intended to let him stay dressed for a little while. But the atmosphere changed things. The look on his face, the anticipatory body language, told her he was on board.

"Take off the shirt. Go to the locker area. They'll give you a place to put it. I'll meet you at the Green Room public play space."

He began to move away, but her grip on the shirt front stopped him. As she leaned into him, he touched her hip, gripped to steady them both.

"Pay attention. I said it in the order I want it done, Lawrence."

She saw the ripple of anxiety, a knee jerk reaction to being called on a mistake, but then it was gone. He kept his eyes on hers as he pulled off the shirt, revealing his muscled upper body. She was aware of other appreciative glances, but those eyes would note what bracelet he was wearing.

Look. Enjoy. Don't touch without permission.

That bracelet kept him so safe from unwelcome advances inside the club, she wished there was a version of it she could use outside these walls on herself, so he wouldn't have to worry about her protection.

She turned away, with effort. As she moved toward the "stargate," she saw Skye, leaning against one side of the archway. She'd gone with a mix of soft and hard in her wardrobe choices tonight, a dark blue lace top over black latex and thigh-high boots. Her longer fall of blonde hair on the one side had a matching blue streak.

Her gaze had been resting on Lawrence, same as Ros's, but when Ros turned to her, Skye's gaze swept over Ros and her dress. She made a "wow" gesture.

"Oh, shut up," Ros told her with mock irritation.

Skye did her silent chuckle. Though in the office she used her computer speech programs, and she carried the same software on her phone so she could do it in public, Skye also knew sign language, useful in the noisier environment of the club. Thanks to their time together as friends, Ros had become almost fluent in it, as had the rest of the group. So she followed what Skye told her now, as she drew close enough that people passing wouldn't interrupt her line of sight to Skye's gesturing hands.

You're going to drive all the boys crazy.

The sign for crazy, that hand brought up to the side of the head as if holding a seashell and tilted back and forth, was accurate. Ros wanted to drive one particular man crazy tonight. Giving him the space to figure out things, being patient, was going to be far more difficult than she'd anticipated. Having him take off his shirt was going to torment her all the more. She wanted to tie him so she could feel his muscles quiver with restrained strength against the things she could do to him. She wanted to leave permanent marks on him. It was an unsettling thought.

She wasn't the sadist Cyn was, but right now she understood her friend's nature better than she ever had before.

"I'll join you all shortly," she told Skye. "Soon as I set him on the path I want him to take."

CHAPTER TWELVE

*I*t was a weeknight, so the Green Room play area was busy but not overly crowded, which she'd intended. A member could usually access whatever equipment or room she wanted, even if she had to wait a bit for it.

Though she didn't watch for him, she knew when he'd rejoined her. His heat was at her back, and she reached behind her, finding firm, bare flesh. Pivoting on the ball of her shoe, she hooked her fingers in the waistband of the jeans. That intensity in his eyes sent electricity through her, every time.

"They don't all have it, but there's a fire to some of them, a warrior spirit. They will fuck you until they have nothing left, and then, if you demand more, they'll find a way to give it to you."

One of Vera's insights, spoken in her "high priestess" way, as Cyn called it. But they'd all known what she was talking about. It was rare. Ros had it right here.

"You can use your eyes to navigate, but I expect you to lower your gaze to my feet when I'm talking to you."

She enjoyed the jolt through her system as he complied without comment, yet he briefly brought his hand up, closed it over her wrist, a light squeeze before he dropped the hand to her waist. It wasn't impertinence. He was a toucher. She liked that.

She cupped his shoulder, exploring the shape of it. She wanted to take him into a private room and eat him alive, but she'd show enough control to let him experience the club in the public areas first.

"Keeping your eyes down enhances other kinds of sensory input you might miss otherwise," she explained. "Nuances in my touch, what you're smelling, hearing. What you're feeling through senses you don't think about. Focus is everything."

"May I ask you a question?"

"You may," she said, quietly pleased. When he'd asked her what she wanted him to wear, he hadn't first asked permission to ask her a question. But now, as the atmosphere was sinking in, so was the embrace of those rules. Or his embrace of them. While she expected the structure fit well with his time in the military—*permission to speak, ma'am*—when a submissive picked up protocols quickly, it often meant they craved that structure. Which was exactly what the Club Progeny rules intended to make even easier for them.

"What kind of submissive is your fantasy?" he asked.

A normal question for a sub to ask. Usually because they were eager to please, and they wanted to prove to her they could meet that measurement. It was a way of holding onto control by being competitive, something she channeled into more positive directions. Letting a sub alter himself or his behavior the wrong way to meet her approval wasn't the goal. There was a lovely organic evolution to it, where her fantasy could change from sub to sub, fitting what treasures that man could give her, that fit who he was, and who the two of them could be together.

"After a few sessions together, I'll ask you that question," she said. "See if you've figured it out."

There was no one man who could be everything she wanted and needed. One who would curl around her at night, who would think of serving her before anything, make her the center of his world, who would not leave or let something else become more important.

The reasons she'd left behind the childhood imaginings of such a man far quicker than her school mates were psychology 101, a girl who grew up with a functioning alcoholic for a father, one who went to work and pulled his weight to pay the bills, but who routinely satisfied his emotional needs with beer and the lifestyle attached to it, rather than his family.

That was a permanent part of the soil in the landscape of her life.

Thanks to time and experience, she'd learned how to grow a life from it she fully embraced. One where she could change the plantings and look as the mood took her, see which things fit and responded best to her desires and needs.

Abby had smirked the first time Ros used that metaphor, because Ros could kill anything green except weeds. She didn't even have houseplants.

Her response to that? *I pay a landscaping company to handle my actual yard. It gives me time to grow a lush metaphorical one.*

Ultimately, it was the basics that mattered most. Protect yourself, respect each other, and enjoy the ability to play and be together until fate called an end to the game.

"I'll be over there." She pointed Lawrence's attention to the booth where Cyn, Skye and Vera were waiting on her. They looked like they were sipping sodas, indicating they intended to play at a level requiring clear heads. Taunting her to do the same, the bitches. She suppressed a smile.

"I want you to wander around this room, check out the scenes. Take your time. Think about how you'd feel in the sub's place in each of them. When you're done, you'll come sit or stand beside me, whichever I prefer. Do you understand?"

"Yes, ma'am. Mistress."

He wanted to watch the sessions, but gratifyingly, he also looked reluctant to be away from her. She ran her knuckles along his arm, then pivoted, leaving him there.

Her attention would be as closely locked upon him as if she was standing at his side, even if she looked like she was chatting with her friends. She wondered if he'd realize that.

She acknowledged greetings from Doms she knew, noted the unattached subs she or others of her ladies had played with. Those along her path greeted her deferentially. She grinned at comments about her dress from a couple Mistresses, and laughed outright as Trey, one of her semi-regular subs, pretended like he was having a heart attack when he saw her.

When she slid into the horseshoe shaped booth, Cyn lifted her glass. "Our queen arrives. What an entrance. That is a serious 'wouldn't you just die to fuck me' kind of dress."

"Accessorized with her 'touch me without permission and I'll stab you through the heart with my pretty shoes,' attitude," Vera noted.

Her legal advisor and HR manager had chosen a vintage look tonight. The red linen sheath contoured to Vera's body, the neckline a straight vertical cut between her breasts that revealed tempting hints of the black bra and generous curves. She'd paired the dress with red pumps and an intriguing pillbox velour hat that had black net lace pulled over her long-lashed eyes. Elbow length red gloves completed the look, fingerless to display her crimson nails. She wore a lethal-looking curved vampire nail on her forefinger.

Cyn usually preferred all black, and tonight was no exception. Black slacks and a tight black T-shirt highlighted her Kate Beckinsale *Underworld* body type.

Vera nudged Ros. "What's your boy doing?"

"He's in study hall. Learning what's possible, seeing what will rouse his interest."

"Bullshit," Cyn said. "You're watching to determine what will get *you* going, based on his reaction."

"Potato, potahto," Ros said. She pulled her eyes away—briefly—to meet theirs. "Where's Abby?"

"She's coming. Probably literally. She got in the swing of things early. Took Tiger to a room."

Ros frowned. If Abby went into a private scene early, she was venting tension, cocooning herself from her emotions. From the knowing glances the others sent her, they shared the same concerns. But in the scheme of things, it was a healthy way for Abby to handle bad things in her head.

"Trey's available tonight," Ros mentioned to Vera. "And he looks more than ready to play."

"Hmm. Might be a good choice. I'm not in the mood to break someone in. Just want a good time."

"That's what I figured." Ros tipped her head toward Skye. "You know Abby likes to tag team. She might work Tiger up and want you to take him through to the end."

Skye confirmed it with a gesture, tapping her phone to show she was waiting for Abby's cue. Abby enjoyed getting a sub worked up into a frenzy, but she often stopped there, letting one of them take over the finish. A lot of Mistresses preferred to be in charge from beginning to end, but as a man reached that frenzy level, the need for complicated oral communication diminished considerably. So she and Skye were able to make that work, when Skye didn't care to orchestrate her own scene.

Ros returned her attention to Lawrence. He was making a counterclockwise track through the spacious Green Room's offerings. Five separate theme areas provided a meandering maze of equipment, mats, tables and suspension hooks. The walls were mounted with boards containing a generous variety of toys, if the Dom hadn't brought his or her own. When done with them, they could be dropped in one of the art deco style gold and black containers placed in discreet locations. They would be sanitized and reconditioned before re-use, or discarded and replaced.

In between those boards were large erotic prints, the subject material veiled with a gold tint overlay. The pictures were bracketed by wall lights that threw out warm, glittering light. The illumination gave the bronze paint on the crown moldings and chair railings a sheen. A black and gold theme, the colors of New Orleans.

Lawrence was watching a woman bent over a spanking bench. She wore a kitten head mask, complete with ears and whiskers. Her Dom had just finished administering a firm paddling and was easing an oiled plug into her backside, which had a faux fur cat tail attached to it. Silver chain strung with red jewels embellished the tail, and the blotched red of her paddled buttocks complemented the color nicely. She wore black kitten heels, of course. Her Dom uncuffed her and lifted her to her feet. As he bent to kiss her exposed lips, he dropped a hand, clamped it over one cheek with a purposefully bruising grip.

Her heels lifted out of the shoes, her body squirming with the discomfort even as she kept her head still for the kiss. But her hand was resting on his chest. As he soothed the area he'd just offended with a calming stroke, she nestled against him and they wandered away, making room for the next Dom who wanted to use the bench. It was always popular, positioned on a dais to satisfy the exhibitionist tendencies of the users.

Lawrence moved onward as well. The next session involved a male sub and his Mistress. Lady Alberta had Marc Agony—his play on Roman hero names— up on his toes, his arms chained over his head. He was naked, and the short red lines on his backside, thighs and upper back told Ros he'd been caned. He was in the zone, swaying, his head tipped back. Lady A, in a black lace bodysuit, had the look of a Mistress absorbed in the task before her. It made Ros want to get there herself. Patience brought its own reward, but the wait could be a bitch.

She wished Lawrence was okay with being restrained, because she would dearly love to wrap cuffs around his wrists, immobilize him from head to toe. She'd do things to him that would make his body contort, all those beautiful muscles rippling as she transformed him into a rutting beast. If she did it exactly as she wished, he'd be torn between the overwhelming primal desire to fuck, and the soul-deep need to serve her.

Lady A drew a strap-on out of her personal bag of tools, and Ros did a mental high five. She'd wanted to log Lawrence's reaction to that kind of play. Some people thought strap-on fucking meant a man was gay, or wanted the experience of being fucked by a woman, the way he could fuck her, but it could also be a lot more complicated than that, differing from sub to sub.

Alberta buckled the strap-on in place and adjusted it. Since there was a faint sheen around the seam of her submissive's buttocks, Ros deduced she'd already lubed him up. Lady A brought herself up against Marc now, rubbing the tops of her breasts, straining under lace, against his back. Reaching around, she gripped his cock at the base in a hard pinch between thumb and forefinger. He quivered, his lips pressing together in concentration.

She said something to him. From the death grip on his cock, Lady A had likely told him he better not release. He had a condom on, a requirement for this kind of play, and Ros thought it unlikely he'd be able to hold back, since he looked like he was on the edge now. From the satisfied glint in Lady A's eyes, the Domme knew the same. Those cane marks were likely to double.

Ros's gaze moved to Lawrence, standing so still and watching them. His body language altered subtly during the interaction between Lady A and the restrained male. The whispers of conversation, the brush of a hand to create a shiver. The press of the male's lips, evidence of both frustration and effort. Those types of things seemed to pull him in the most, more than the mechanics and trappings, the restraints and strap-on.

Cyn, Skye and Vera had been chatting, but they were watching now, too. They saw what she did. Lawrence moved slightly forward as Alberta sank the rubber phallus into the sub's ass. She kept her grip on Marc's cock while feral pleasure took over her body language. Ros knew that moment. When you were totally in control, and you wanted to take and take. The more he gave himself into her hands, the more she wanted to reward the gift, even as she wanted to push him to the edge and beyond.

Her gaze slid between the two and Lawrence. Back. Forth. Back. Forth. Reading two books at once. He was so still that, without his jeans and shoes, he would have been mistaken for one of the erotic statues scattered through the club and flanked by lush tropical house-plants. When Alberta had pushed that phallus in, Lawrence's jaw had flexed, his shoulder twitching. If she closed her eyes, Ros could imagine the pair of them standing where Lady A and Marc were. Her hand closing over his hip, a firm reminder of her presence, as her other hand gripped his ass, fingers playing between his buttocks, testing the slickness of the oil she'd placed there, worked in with her own fingers.

She'd press against his back, rub her cheek over him, feel the muscles flex against the chains holding him. Her hand would slide up his chest, cover his heart.

Her eyes opened. Alberta had started thrusting, her hands on the male's hips. She was a tall woman and her sub was not, so she hadn't needed a stool to align their bodies properly. Interestingly, once it became about the simple act of fucking, Lawrence drifted onward. Because he didn't want to get too worked up? Or because the part that absorbed him the most was the moment of surrender, the emotional transformation that happened then. Difficult to say, but she filed the information away.

He went to the rope play area, studying the several couples doing suspension. Again, he seemed to stay long enough to note the connections, what was making the scene work for the participants, before he moved forward. He spent a longer time watching a rope artist create a harness for her submissive, one that didn't restrict his hands, but had enclosed his chest and shoulders in the intricate pattern of knots. She'd already enclosed his cock in a sheathe of smaller ropes, the way Ros had done to Lawrence in his kitchen.

Now this Domme threaded the trailing rope ends of the harness up between his buttocks to secure them to the net she'd formed between his shoulder blades.

Interesting. Ros leaned forward. The young woman wasn't done. From her toy bag, she removed a handful of...barbed wire? Yes, barbed wire, cut in varying lengths. She wove them under the tight harness holding her sub's torso. The Domme must have been given permission to do blood play, because if her sub writhed too enthusiastically, the sharp tips were going to tear flesh.

Lawrence's attention meter jumped a whole couple levels at the sight. Ros's lips curved. A SEAL, by his very nature, needed challenges beyond the limits of normal human endurance.

She could give him that, without adding to his scars. Cyn might be their sadist, but Ros was the ballbuster. She used pain if it served the purpose. He responded to a certain level of it. But his craving for challenge went deeper than the physical.

She couldn't imagine the things he'd seen in his time with the SEALs. The missions might have helped keep the emotional fallout swept to the corners, but he no longer had the ability to go down range for that housecleaning. Then there were the problems in his personal life. Though the details were still out of focus, their significance was evident. The heart could become a seething, restless place of disappointments, sadness, failure, regrets. Under her control, he might find a place to purge it, let it all go. That was the ideal, the surrender point she wanted.

"He is something, Ros," Vera murmured.

"Yes. He is," she said softly.

There was a reason they were her closest friends in the world. They knew how to take this walk in their heads. Even Vera, saying she was just looking for an easy night of it; she'd still claim a taste of that for herself tonight, whether with Trey or someone else. They rarely chose a man who didn't have it in him to give that.

Doms needed to take, subs needed to give. It was how they provided what the other craved in ways that defied explanation. Every time she felt it, it proved to Ros there was a Divine Power that knew what the fuck It was doing.

Vera and Cyn were watching her as closely as they were all watching Lawrence. Skye had left them, probably signaled by Abby that she was ready to hand off Tiger. Ros hadn't even noticed her departure.

"Sure you want to go down that path with him?" Cyn asked.

"You have concerns?"

Cyn tilted her head left and right. "Yes and no. Your reaction to him is more complicated than usual."

"I've had difficult and complex submissives before."

"Yeah. You have. I said the complicated part is you, not him. He's the abyss that beckons you to jump off the edge. Just never gotten the impression that you want that."

"Then you weren't paying close enough attention."

That observation came from Abby. She'd worked Tiger and herself hard, because she still had a faint dew of perspiration on her forehead, along her delicate throat.

Despite her sharp corporate style in the office, at the club, she went for contrast. Fashionably faded jeans were belted low on her waist, and coupled with a sleeveless gauze white tank. The black lace bralette beneath gave her breasts an appealing range of movement that would tempt any man with a pulse to want to rest his head there. And hope for permission to put his mouth on the faintly outlined peaks.

She took Skye's place across the table from Ros, and their eyes met. "Is Tiger still walking?" Ros asked pleasantly, pointedly ignoring Abby's observation.

"Mostly. Skye will finish him off." Abby's attention slid to Lawrence. "Cyn's right. He's complicated."

"This one, not so much," Cyn said, drawing their attention to another male coming toward their table. Built lean and roped with muscle, he had his locs held in a top hairband, their dyed gold color a contrast with the black color of the buzzed fade on the rest of his skull. He nodded with respect to all of the women, and then dropped to a knee, his attention lasering to Cyn. He wore nothing but loose jeans and a few intriguing tribal tats on his arms, mixed with an array of strike brands.

"Mistress," he said. His voice had the deep, dreamlike rumble of a train moving over tracks at midnight. "Feel like dishing out some hurt?"

Cyn's lips curved. "Always. Are you volunteering for the

honor, Sy?"

"Always. If it pleases you."

"Abigail." Cyn gave their friend a pointed look. "If you don't mind, move your fine ass out of my way."

Abby chuckled and complied. "The room I reserved is a double," she mentioned. "Skye won't mind sharing."

"My thoughts exactly." Cyn tossed her a wicked look.

While subs didn't usually approach Doms, if they were familiar with the Dom in question, they knew when the timing might be right for an opening. Case in point? As Cyn wandered away with Sy, Trey brought Vera a drink refill.

At six feet, with a shaggy mane of golden-brown hair and friendly sky-blue eyes, Trey was a favorite club sub. Tonight he wore black jeans and a muscle shirt printed with a logo for the Dream Palace. The shirt was old enough to be a collector's item, because the Frenchmen Street music club was now called Blue Nile.

Outside the club walls, he worked at one of the lube and oil places, a job that gave him the money he needed to pay his share of an apart-ment with three other roommates. They were also his fellow band members, who played local venues whenever they could get them.

Ros had heard him play, and he was a hell of a musician. She'd given him tips on marketing the band that had increased their expo-sure and cash flow, but that was enough for them. They didn't want to be the next big thing on tour. They were more into the craft and their easy-going life as NOLA musicians. As long as they could pay the bills, make music and enjoy beautiful women, they were content.

He'd known he was a submissive for most of his thirty-something life, and so hoarded enough of that money to maintain his member-ship at Progeny.

Along with a refill for Vera, he'd also brought Ros her preferred non-alcoholic drink, a pomegranate-blueberry green tea fusion. He knew it was equally possible Ros or Vera might choose him tonight, but he wasn't hedging his bets. Trey was a mature, experienced sub with his shit together, and he wasn't pushy. He genuinely enjoyed their company, and the feeling was mutual. On nights they weren't here to play, they'd more than once invited him to join them for socializing.

At Ros's nod of invitation, he slid into the booth, his thigh companionably brushing hers. "That is a hell of a dress you're almost wearing," he said, his blue eyes twinkling.

"I see no one has reminded you of your manners tonight." She clinked her glass against his bottle of O'Doul's.

"Did a session with a newbie earlier." He flexed his tattoo-sleeved shoulders. "She was sweet. Think she'll be about my speed in a year or so, if she sticks with it. I steered her toward Olman. So, you going to tell me who he is?"

"Who?"

"The guy who's thinking about eating my face."

Surprised, Ros slid a glance toward Lawrence. Sure enough, Lawrence's attention was zeroed in on Trey. Not with a bodyguard assessment look. It was pure male-to-male, hands off.

"He needs to dial that back," Vera commented. "Or Ros is going to teach him pretty fast she's no one's possession."

"Men are men," Abby said. "Territorial nature doesn't turn off." In her eyes were a mix of emotions Ros didn't want to see there.

"But it can be channeled in some delightful ways," Ros rejoined. "Vera."

Vera nodded, understanding perfectly. "Trey. I have a mind to have your mouth on my pussy for about a half hour. While I teach you those manners with a flogger."

Trey's behavior shifted to perfect formality and deference. "Yes, Mistress. You honor me."

He rose and offered his hand. Abby took it to stand, letting Vera slide out of the booth. Trey gave Vera his other hand to support her as she rose, and gallantly pressed a kiss to Abby's knuckles before letting her go. When he and Vera moved away, Abby didn't retake her seat.

Ros gave her a look. "Abby—"

"He's coming this way." Abby nodded. "Enjoy him. And don't you dare hold back."

Lawrence had studied the scenes as Ros directed—as a submissive. On several of them, he'd been pulled right in. They gave him a hard cock, elevated blood pressure, and a mix of emotions that didn't make logical sense.

This stuff got into his head, no argument. But faced with extreme shit involving toys, cuffs and whips made it harder for him to reconcile that absorption with who he was supposed to be. When Ros talked to him, and when he fantasized, it all made perfect sense. No need to question it in his head. But when things got too deep, it unsettled him, and he got unbalanced.

Looking at her helped. Until he saw her sitting with a tall blond. He was sitting too close, his hip and thigh brushing hers in that dress Lawrence told himself she'd worn for him, even though he knew she wore it for herself.

That was part of what appealed to him. She liked the way it looked on her, and it made her feel good. She didn't give a fuck if he liked it or not, even as she'd not only known he'd like it, but had wanted it to have the effect on him it had.

The blond left with Vera. Probably a good thing, as Lawrence had started across the floor before he knew his feet were moving. When he told himself to rein it back, he was successful enough to turn it into a more casual approach. Or so he thought.

Abby had slid out of the booth and was moving his way. As she passed, she put out a hand. His forearm muscles quivered as he recognized a Mistress's touch, even if his focus wasn't on this Mistress in particular. He managed to stop and give her a courteous look. "Ma'am?"

The faint smile didn't reach her eyes. "You have her interest. Don't blow it by being a typical male dick."

Then she was gone, stepping by him with a waft of feminine scents, including a musk of perspiration and lingering female arousal. It was a heady combination that didn't settle him in the least.

Ros glanced up as he arrived. He curbed the desire to sit next to her, in the spot Trey had vacated, like a dog marking his invaded territory.

"May I join you?" It was a way of asking how. Standing by the booth, kneeling at her feet, sitting with her. Across from her.

"Beside me." She pointed next to her, on the inside.

It wasn't his tactical preference, but he sat down on the other side of the booth and slid around the horseshoe shape until he was next to her. He didn't press up to her the way Trey had, but put his clasped hands on the table and gave her a look.

"What's on your mind, Lawrence?"

"I'm wondering what's on yours."

"You're evading." She dropped her hand beneath the table, slid her knuckles along his thigh, dragged them over his fly. Her gaze glinted with satisfaction at the hardness she found there. "While you tell me what's really on your mind, you'll open your jeans so I can play with what's in them."

She propped her elbow on the table and twisted toward him. The right breast swelled under the unstrapped side of the dress. Even as he hoped to see all of it, the part of his mind that could still think was sure he wouldn't. The whole ensemble was intended to tease a man into being stupid.

Or humble. Because it reminded him this magical creature, this imperious goddess, was bestowing her time upon him, her attention. And while she was both of those things in his fanciful imaginings, she was also a woman, opening herself up to him in cautious ways.

He was poised on an edge where he could be the dick Abby had warned him against, or he could be something else. Something Rosalinda needed. That thought took away anger and defensiveness, and left something far more appealing.

He opened the jeans one-handed, pushed down the zipper. She kept her gaze on his face. "Arms out to either side of you, along the top of the booth. And they don't leave there, no matter what. You don't move against my hand. I'm not some sex worker jacking you off for money."

"No ma'am."

The fervency of his response earned him a look of deep approval. Her hand slid along his thigh. Up. Down. Along his inseam, following the shape of his balls pressed against it. Then up and up, inside the opening. When her nails scraped against his shaft through the thin stretched fabric of his underwear, he curled his hands against the top of the booth. Finding those handles she'd described earlier, he latched onto them. She noted the flexing of his arm muscles, but when she glanced at his face, her eyes held sharpness.

"I'm not big on waiting for certain things," she said. "Just say it as you're thinking it."

"I'm not big on being part of a harem." He swallowed as those nails pressed in a little deeper and she dragged them up toward his glans. He was sure there was already some fluid staining the dark cloth at the tip of his cock. "If I'm only going to get you while you're interested, I want to know the interest isn't divided."

She hummed in her throat as she stroked downward, gripped him firmly. He pulled in air through his teeth, his lower body tightening up, trying to remain still.

"It might last longer if it is," she said practically. "It means I come to you willingly. Not because I don't have other options."

Despite the stimulation, irritation made it through. "Lack of options. Never heard commitment and exclusivity called that. So if I see a Mistress that interests me here, and you're otherwise occupied, it's okay for me to do a scene with her?"

She paused, her blue eyes flickering. He noted a slight tightness around her mouth. "Yes and no," she said after a moment. "I won't tell you what the yes means right now. That's a far more advanced discussion. But the no? That's a definite. I do not wish to share you with another Mistress."

"And I don't want to share you with another sub. Or any other guy. While we're exploring whatever this is."

Her hand started moving again. Massaging, stroking and teasing again. His cock was getting all kinds of iron hard under her ministrations. And thick. He sucked in a breath as she squeezed, scraped, teased. Was she trying to seduce him into changing his mind? No way, even though he was pretty sure he'd do anything else for her at the moment.

She eased her touch some, going to an idle stroke. "Okay," she said at last. "For the duration of us exploring this, I will only play with you. Fair enough?"

"Yes. Thank you, Mistress."

"Don't thank me," she said. "I'm very demanding. You may change your mind and want me to have more men than you at my fingertips. I have a fairly insatiable appetite."

He smiled, showing his teeth. "Stamina and endurance are SEAL specialties."

Her eyes glinted at him. "Good to know."

Christ. If she kept doing what she was doing, he was going to rip those steel handles right out of the back of the booth.

"Are you ready to follow me to a private room?" she asked. "Submit to what I want?"

He thought he'd do anything for her as long as her hand was on his dick. But she expected better from him than that. *I'm not some sex worker jacking you off.*

What was getting him so aroused, more than the movement of her fingers, the curl of her palm, were her words. She considered his cock something that belonged to her, and knowing that got him even more worked up. Her voice seemed to have changed, become throatier, more dangerous, her eyes piercing right through him.

Here she was a queen. He was...he was her subject. Hers. If he only let go enough to let that happen.

"I don't know how it works. What to expect."

"Do you need to do so?"

"I don't know. Maybe."

Another pursing of that wet, rose-shaped mouth. "I want to pleasure myself using your body, your submission. If you accept that and come with me to a room, from this moment forward, you follow my orders as I issue them, without question. You won't talk unless I give you permission or if you need to safeword. Gray or sanctuary, remember?"

He almost jerked away when a woman paused at the table. One of the waitresses. "Mistress, would you like another drink?" she asked. "Or one for your sub?"

Her gaze slid over Lawrence, then immediately returned to Ros. She was a submissive staff member, but even so, the two women were having a discussion while Rosalinda was stroking him. She behaved as if he was hers to play with, however and whenever she wished.

It was an odd feeling, to be deliberately talked about, with no requirement to participate in the conversation. More than that, no permission to do so. Which made him worse than hard. He was worried he was going to...

He caught Rosalinda's wrist, no time to tell her, and closed his eyes, fighting for control. Fuck. Fuck. *Fuck.*

It was a near thing, but he managed to hold back. He wasn't a teenager.

"You like it when people watch when I'm dominating you. Good to know."

He opened his eyes. The waitress was gone, and Rosalinda was looking at him. Her eyes seemed darker, her mouth a firm bow. When he made himself let her go, her gaze dropped and he almost groaned, because her staring at his erection with that expression was as potent as a stroke.

"Fasten and zip the jeans, being careful of what's beneath. We're going to a private room, Lawrence. I want what's mine. Follow me if you accept my terms."

No more looking, or watching him looking. She wasn't waiting. He had no idea what to expect, but nothing would keep him from following her.

Into the dungeons of hell, if necessary.

CHAPTER THIRTEEN

*H*e had plenty of ideas about what the private room would look like. He didn't expect the chamber to remind him of an observatory. Dim lights and optical illusion made the ceiling look like a domed version of the night sky, stars and planets slowly rotating. On the walls, projected silhouettes of trees moved, as if touched by the wind. The faintly cool air movement in the room added to the feeling, as did the aroma of pine. A black draped rectangular shape in the corner was likely a cabinet with supplies, and it screened the doorway to a washroom small enough he could see the interior at a glance, no hidden corners.

In the center of the otherwise empty room were a bench and two vertical poles. The two poles were a few feet from the bench. If lines were drawn between the three items, the poles would be the bottom corners of an isosceles triangle, the bench the top point. The poles looked like tree trunks, with rough brown bark. Eye hooks were embedded along them. The wooden bench had been polished to a golden hue, providing a silky surface for the one sitting upon it.

Rosalinda moved behind the black draped area. The sound of a door opening confirmed it was a tall cabinet, likely holding the supplies she'd requested, or whatever stock items were provided. She emerged carrying a handful of cuffs.

"No restraints," she confirmed. "Unless you find these acceptable." She showed him the D-rings on the cuffs. "When I clip a chain to these, you'll have enough slack to unclip them yourself," she said. "And the door is locked. There's a tone that happens before the door is opened, and it can only be opened from the outside by a staff member with a master key. Otherwise, I have to open it. Acceptable?"

The muscles in his shoulders twitched. One part of him rejected any bindings upon him. Another was stuck in that scene he'd watched, the girl bent over the spanking bench, her wrists and ankles held there.

"I don't know," he said honestly.

"Fair enough. Remember your words. Gray and sanctuary. We can go from there. Same rules apply. No speaking unless I ask you a question. You obey everything I tell you to do." Her blue eyes gleamed. "You're handing over control to me, Lawrence. You break the rules three times without using the safewords first, the scene is over."

"A punishment."

She nodded. "Discipline is key to the goal here. I expect you to demonstrate that."

She was pure Mistress right now. While a chasm was opening up between the two people they were outside this room, the people they were within it were getting more intimately close. He wondered if that was the goal she meant.

She moved to the bench, sat down in her gold dress, crossing her legs. The position showed one thigh all the way to the shadowed curve of her ass, reminding him she'd said she wasn't wearing any underwear.

"Take off everything," she said. "And stand between the poles."

He complied, folding and setting aside his clothes, his shoes on top. Standing between the poles put him square on display before her. And she took her time looking.

Damn, it wasn't as easy as he would have expected, standing still while she perused him from top to toe, as if she were covering every inch of him with an invisible touch. His cock was already stiff and at attention. Her gaze touched on it without a change in her expression. Her being remote as a statue made his gut coil and his cock harder.

She picked up the cuffs. "Extend your arms to either side of you. Remember your safe words."

She rose from the bench. She wrapped the first cuff around his left wrist and buckled it, made it snug enough he couldn't slip it over his hand, but not so tight blood flow would become an issue. She ran her fingers under it to be sure, and his pulse rate bumped up in tingling reaction to her touch. As she put a cuff on his other wrist, she moved slow, watching his expression the whole time.

Most special ops guys were aware they had danger zones. Situations that could trigger a response so deeply trained into them it could be called an instinct. The limits he'd given her mostly had to do with that, his desire to protect her from such a response. She was respecting those rules, even as she flirted with them in a way that kept him on edge. So far the good kind of edge.

A chain dangled from one of the hooks on each pole. She lifted one and attached it to his left cuff's D-ring. He had enough slack to curl his hand inward, reach the clip and detach it, as she'd promised.

She did the right one the same way and returned to the bench. As she crossed her legs once more, the red shoe with its jeweled heel reflected the dim light. She indulged herself with another good, long look at him, now bound between the two poles.

It was his nature to collect details. In this case, the more details he gathered, the harder he got. She was feeding on the visuals, her lips parted, her body language saying she had one focus. Him.

Now he understood what she'd meant about the differences between Dommes and pro-Dommes. The professional was being paid for a service, which meant her domination, at some level, no matter how well-concealed, or genuinely offered, had to be about serving.

He was in this room because her Dominant side wanted him. His submission was a gift she was giving herself, like her decision to wear that dress because she liked it. He felt the import of that even more keenly, now that she had him restrained and naked, displayed before her.

She rose. "Don't move."

She disappeared behind the black drape. He listened for her movements, heard a rustle, like clothing being adjusted. Or removed. He swallowed.

She emerged in a short black silk robe, loosely belted. If she bent over, and there was a God, he'd not only see her gorgeous ass, but the sweet folds of her cunt.

She didn't return to the bench right away. Instead she stood before him, and when she spoke, her voice was direct as a commanding officer's. "Don't move."

Her fingers with their sharp, shiny nails descended. She hadn't said he couldn't look, so he saw her pass one fingertip, then two, over his wet slit, rub, use that pressure to probe, get more. He steeled himself not to move, even as a quiver ran through his muscles, that electric reaction.

She returned to the bench, sank down on it. Legs crossed in that board room executive way. He bit back a groan as she slid her other hand beneath the right panel of the robe, eased it back so her breast was exposed. Then the other side. The skirt of the robe was still in place, the sash tied, but the top part of the robe was open to expose both breasts. His gaze touched on that crescent scar, but he put aside the question it kept raising, and moved on to what she was doing. She rubbed what was on her fingers into one nipple, and then the other.

She tilted her head to examine them. "Now they have a little bit of shine. Do you like that, Lawrence? Knowing it's you that has polished them that way?"

He nodded, then found his voice, which came out rough. "Yeah. Fuck, yeah."

He froze at the icy blue gaze. Her tone shot spikes up his spine. "Am I a stripper? Waiting for you to stuff dollar bills in my G-string?"

"No ma'am," he said. "I meant to say, 'Yes, Mistress. I like that. I like it a lot. Thank you.'"

She rose again. Under the bench was a matching stool. As she placed it before him, he could tell it was solid wood, stable. She stepped onto it, bringing those magnificent breasts with their glistening nipples level with his face.

"Taste yourself, Lawrence. With proper table manners."

The reminder kept him from going after her like a feast laid out before a starving man. From the assessing gleam in her eye, he knew it gave her pleasure, keeping him straining at the end of a chain. Literally, in this case, because he had to step forward, which erased the slack in the chains, drew his arms back. It sent a strong message to his entire system. She was in charge in here.

He put his lips over the left nipple. He did taste the musk of his semen, but that sheen on her skin had a honey taste to it. He pulled her deeper into his mouth, gradually, a lot of slow suckling that had her murmuring her approval and pleasure. His lips passed briefly over her scar, learned the texture of it. He didn't linger, once again sensing the tension that said she didn't want his focus there. When he moved fully back to her nipple and the area directly around it, her hand cupped his head, telling him he would stay there for a time.

He gave himself to it. His arousal, his need to fuck her, was growing hotter, more dangerous and needy, with everything she did. But his desire to follow her commands, please her, was keeping pace with it, forming a crazy tug of war inside him. It disrupted rational thought and made everything about sensation.

She moved him with insistent pressure to the other nipple, and he gave that equal, reverent attention. She had beautiful breasts, firm, but not too firm. A man could bury his face in them, hope she would let him sleep that way. His mouth would rest so close to those tempting nipples he could wake in the depths of the night and taste them.

Her fingertips were stroking through his hair. Her sporadic tight grip on it told him she was aroused, too. Lawrence had a feeling she was an expert at stretching that out for herself, since making him work for it was part of the charge for her. Her breath was a little unsteady as he suckled, and he improvised, using not only his lips and tongue, but his beard and the rougher area of skin above it, teasing her with the contrast of light sandpaper and smooth hair. The bone-like wiring of the dress had left an impression on the right curve, and he passed his lips over that, soothing, offering care.

He wanted to give care. He wanted to give her pleasure. He wanted to give her more of both of those things than that blond bastard could. Than any man had ever given her. There was a well of it in him, begging to be given, and though he knew the danger of it, knew it for a weakness, he wanted to believe he could give her all of that and it would be okay.

"Stop. Mouth off of me, eyes down, but stay where you are."

He drew back the bare minimum needed to lift his mouth from her flesh. The sash around her waist was so loose he didn't know how the fabric was keeping her covered below the waist.

The condom she pulled from the pocket of the robe gave him a leap of hope she dashed with a knowing chuckle. "You're nowhere close to earning that. But we have to make sure you don't make a mess."

"I'm good, Mistress. I can control myself." He wasn't a teenager, for God's sake.

"Did I ask you a question, Lawrence?"

Shit. She hadn't.

"No, ma'am."

"That's one rule broken. Two more and the scene ends."

If he broke three rules and this ended before he'd given her pleasure, he might just lose it. She rolled the condom on him with an efficiency that made him hot with jealousy, thinking how many dicks she would have had to handle to do it that well. He struggled to get on top of the crazy mix of emotions, wondering if she was intentionally stirring that kind of feeling inside him. He didn't like thinking of that, so he turned his focus to better things.

She adjusted so his mouth was over her sternum, not touching her. But it put his downward gaze up close and personal as she lifted her hands, cupped her breasts, and began to play with the distended nipples. Her thumbs passed over the top of the swelling curves as she pinched the tips using her knuckles. He noted one thumb unconsciously swept over the groove of the scar. He wanted to soothe that with his mouth the way he had the dress's impression on the right side. He didn't want anything to hurt her, ever again.

He also wanted to be touching her, his mouth on her. The saliva gathered under his tongue like he was a hungry predator. But still she just played with herself while he had to watch, straining at the ends of those chains.

She made a humming noise in the back of her throat, and her hips jerked as she pinched herself with particular enthusiasm. The sound he made was a strangled growl. A plea, if he was being honest. Her low chuckle sent a jolt through his cock as she stepped off the stool, sliding it out of her way with one push from her foot.

"Soon, baby. If you're good."

He could be so good he'd make her see real stars. She'd have the most powerful climax of her life. But he had no doubt she meant what she said about earning it. Particularly when she reached down and slapped his cock. Hard.

Sensation rocketed through him. There was some pain, but mostly it was like right after climax, when the head was so sensitive that it could barely handle anything other than a firm grip. A caress could become torment. This was like that. Uncomfortable and arousing at once.

"Stay still, sailor," she said sharply, the right word to have him tightening up, steeling himself to follow orders. Whatever those orders might be.

She went after him again. *Slap, slap, slap.* Up and below, to the sides, and she never missed. With his eyes down, he could see every impact. Watching her slim hands, those polished nails, whacking his cock with such force, her bare breasts quivering with her movements, resulted in an unstoppable reaction. *Fuck.*

"Mistress...gray. *Gray.*"

She stopped, her hand paused in mid-stroke. *Shit.* That wasn't what he'd meant. She cupped his bowed head, kneading his nape. He kept his head down, eyes lowered, short breaths escaping through his flared nostrils as he fought for control, swaying against the hold of the chains.

"Tell me what the problem is, sailor."

It took him a second to answer, all his focus on what he was trying not to do. He found himself suddenly ashamed to admit it, as if it was weakness.

"I thought...I was about to come."

"Did I tell you that you couldn't do that?"

"No, ma'am." He pressed his lips together. "I thought...I was supposed to wait until you say it's all right."

"You thought you were supposed to wait for that, or that's what feels better to you? For me to say it's okay first?"

He nodded. "Both, Mistress."

"You're right, Lawrence. You need to wait until I give you permission. So I'm going to keep doing what I was doing, and you're not going to come. Am I understood? Your yellow light word is intended to pause the scene because you're experiencing the wrong kind of distress or anxiety." Her tone went ball-busting hard again. "It is not to give you the chance to take a tighter grip on your self-control. You learn to do that while I'm doing what I wish to do to you. If you fail, you're punished. That's how you learn not to fail."

Hell, he was right. She *was* a BUD/S instructor.

"Do you understand?"

"Yes, Mistress."

"I better not see those eyes close. You keep them right where I want them pointed."

He didn't want to fail her. He didn't. He steeled himself to think of anything else, and she started again. Harder this time, more frequent. Fuck, fuck, fuck. Beating off had a whole different meaning.

He tried tightening every muscle in his body. He tried thinking of other things, but he was hopelessly visual, and there were her beautiful breasts, wobbling with her movements, the nipples still glistening from his mouth. Her elegant hand continued to briskly spank his cock. It vibrated and cringed from every blow, all while getting so pulsing hard and heavy that the bob of it shot sensation after sensation to the root.

He held out way longer than he would have expected, to the point he wondered if she'd intended him to fail.

"Hell...oh God..." Breath escaped him and his hips jerked, his arms pulling against the chains with hard clanks. She moved back as the climax jetted out of him into the condom. The condom he'd insisted he didn't need.

He missed that touch keenly, but it didn't stop the climax as he humped the air with powerful movements that engaged every muscle. The lack of her touch made it far less satisfying, but it was still intense enough his vision got fuzzy around the edges, and groans tore from his throat.

He came so hard he wouldn't have been surprised if the force of the spray shot the condom on the floor with a wet splat, but fortunately the manufacturers took that kind of thing into account. Or it just felt possible to the guy in question, an inflated sense of one's virility.

Even though he expected she'd pushed him this far on purpose, that didn't really penetrate as much as the knowledge that he'd fallen short. He wanted to say he was sorry, but he wasn't supposed to talk unless she asked him to do so.

"We have some work to do, obviously. A SEAL can do better. Can't he, Lawrence?"

"Yes, Mistress."

"Yes. That's true. But there's something important for you to learn in this room. In any session with me."

He groaned again as her hand closed fully over his semi-erect shaft, clasped it tight. Her bare breast pressed against his side as she murmured into his ear.

"I am the strongest thing in this room. You can surrender it all with me. You can be everything and anything. A man, a boy. A SEAL, a criminal, a boy scout. Every version of yourself, and some you haven't even considered. I will deal with all of it. So what's the lesson?"

His brain was still muddled, but maybe that was why the answer came to his lips, unfiltered. "You wanted me to fail. You wanted me to come, to prove you're in control here. So you can punish me."

"Good. That's part of it. The rest will come to you in time. Move back so you're standing between the poles again."

She walked away, back behind the drape, and returned with a square of thick foam. She dropped it at his feet and moved the chains holding his arms two hooks lower on either side, which drew his arms down, further relieving the ache in his shoulders. She'd adjusted the robe so she was fully covered again.

"Down on your knees."

He realized the mat was to cushion his knees. She'd remembered their conversation about his injury. As he dropped, he noticed she slid behind him, her hands providing support at his waist to ensure it was a controlled descent. He had the leg muscles to do it, but right after climax, it wasn't as smooth as usual. It did odd things to him, her watching after him that way.

"You're used to being the caregiver, aren't you, sailor?"

"Yes, Mistress." He didn't want to go down that road. He hoped she wouldn't.

Back behind the drape she went. His imagination could conjure a warehouse of possibilities, items from terrifying to arousing, something she was proving to him could be one and the same thing.

When she returned, she was carrying another, thicker foam cushion. This one had a wedge shape, and when she dropped it several feet in front of him, he had a sudden mouth-watering idea of what it was for. But she was also carrying something that looked like a short, stiff whip with a wooden handle.

Black thin gloves followed her arms up to the elbows like a second skin. It startled him, how erotic he found that. She moved around him, studying him with that detached yet avid appraisal, as if this position was a new painting in the gallery of images she was creating. Which made him think of the photo she'd snapped in his kitchen. He'd agreed to let her share it when she was ready to do so. The realization rippled through him, that she might have already shown it to the women who were here with her tonight.

"Back on your feet, sailor."

She stopped behind him as she gave the order. The end of the whip played over his back, starting at his shoulder blades and trailing down to the seam of his buttocks. Her hand followed it, cupping and squeezing.

"Beautiful," she said. "Every time I see your ass, Lawrence, I want to touch it. Maybe one day you and I will play tourists for the day in NOLA. I'll enjoy fondling it wherever I want, in front of anyone I want. A man can't do that to a woman without inviting disrespect for her. But a woman doing it to a man? It invites stares, speculation. A lot of fantasizing. Some delightfully disapproving *tsks*. A double standard for certain, but in this particular case I'm willing to celebrate our differences."

He didn't know if that was a yellow or red zone. Or maybe neither. Right now, everything she talked about was green for go. Even though his cock was still drained from the recent climax, she was going to have it up and stiff as a board again in no time. She wanted him to suffer for her. He wanted that, too, though he couldn't explain why.

Her gloved finger probed between his buttocks. She'd lubed it up, so the digit rubbed his rim with distracting ease.

He tightened his cheeks instinctively. A part of him said *no*, strongly. He didn't even mess with that part of himself when he was alone.

"You said a strap-on wasn't your thing. But I want you to think about that scene you watched earlier tonight. Lady Alberta, taking the ass of her devoted sub. Imagine what that felt like. Opening up a place to her that you haven't opened up before. It's not just about fucking you like a man, Lawrence. It's about something else entirely, and you know it, deep down. Relax and let me in. Whose ass is this?"

He wrapped his mind around it. Just the two of them in this room. "Yours," he said, low.

"Louder."

"Yours," he said.

"Exactly."

She kept playing around the rim, stroking, sending out tendrils of sensation that wound around the base of his cock and balls, tugged. His cock really was trying to come back to life, as if her command could override the rules of anatomic sanity.

She put the tip of her finger in, pushed and eased until it was a little deeper, moving it around so those sensations jangled through his nerves. His cock twitched in response. He bit back another oath as her thumb kept teasing his rim, the inside of his buttocks. "Lovely," she said quietly.

She withdrew then, and stripped off the gloves, tossing them into a bin nearby as she circled back before him again in her rose and gold heels, the thin robe. She twirled the short whip over her fingers. He recognized it as the way she twirled and twisted her pen when she was at her board room table. He'd never see that the same again.

"Having you bound, all to myself, being able to look at you all I want...I need a release to take the edge off. I have a lot of options." She nodded to the wedge. "I can lie on that, use my fingers, do it myself. Or use a vibrator, quick and easy. Blindfold you, so you can hear me do it. Smell my arousal as it wets my fingers."

"My mouth can serve you better."

He said it with a fierce insistence. He could have bitten it off, but it was worth the price.

She cut her gaze to him. "Second infraction. One to go. But you calculated that, didn't you? You think you have a buffer of one more. You're underestimating my ability to break your self-control, Lawrence. On your knees again."

She moved closer. With him kneeling, head bowed, her thigh brushed his jaw. He flexed his arms, an unconscious testing. The chains clinked, because he had a lot of slack right now. But that was only in the chains. Her hand on the reins was tight and unwavering.

"Making me come with your mouth must be earned. You've broken two rules, one deliberately. You misused your safeword. But I'm in an indulgent mood."

She moved to the cabinet. This time she returned with a handful of connected metal rings in one hand and a black cloth in the other.

Shit. He'd visited enough BDSM websites to guess what the rings were. She gestured with the cloth.

"I'm putting a head mask on you. It's thin. You can see through it, somewhat. It has an opening for the nose, but it covers the mouth."

Over the mouth? But didn't she want him to...

"No direct contact between your mouth and my pussy," she said, his sadistic Mistress. "But you'll be able to get the cloth wet and press against the fabric to prod and lick as much as you're able. Any safe-word issues with the mask?"

He thought it through. "No, Mistress. I don't think so."

"You know what to do if that changes." She put it over his head, adjusted it. A Velcro strap around the throat held it in place. She was right. It took some effort to get his eyes open, and it put a dark shadow over everything around them, already dimly lit. It made things darker, though he could see where she was, and every lovely curve of her.

"Don't look down."

She gripped his cock next. She put a fresh condom on him, and then she brought that handful of metal rings into play. He winced as she pushed most the rings over his cock, and put his balls through the opening of the remaining one, tugging them out the other side. A connecting strap between the ring clasping him beneath the head of his cock and the one around his base was tightened, curving his cock up toward his stomach. Now the rings held him snugly, all the way down his shaft to the stranglehold on his testicles. With some alarm he realized that, as he thickened, those metal rings weren't going to give.

"This keeps you focused on your Mistress's will," she said. "But I do like to test the resilience of those rings. If you start to feel real pain, you tell me. I won't let you abuse what's mine out of some misguided testosterone display. If you hurt my toy, I won't be playing with it. Tell me you understand."

"Yes, Mistress."

The person he was outside this room, the SEAL, the guy in charge of her protection and security, really seemed to be disappearing. Everything was being swallowed by what she was doing and saying to him. It was also winding him up like a clock, the mechanisms getting tighter and ticking faster, his heart hammering in response to her demands.

"Good." She checked something on the chains holding his arms, making an adjustment. "You're going to show me how much better you can do than Trey, Lawrence. Trey, who you were shooting dagger looks at while he was talking to me. He's had his mouth between my legs, and yes, he knows what he's doing down there."

He froze. The swirl of good emotions turned to rock in his throat, his chest, his lower belly. He told himself to get a grip, to not do this, to mask his reaction, but he couldn't. He'd gone rigid as stone in truth. His erection literally floundered, even worse.

She'd noticed. He shot her a helpless look. He didn't want to break the third rule, but he had to reassure her, cover it. Say something. "It's...I'm okay. Sorry."

She touched his face, the mask so thin it should feel as if it wasn't between them, but it was. He could read her blue eyes clearly, suddenly full of a lot of different things. Reproof yes, but more. "Say gray to me, Lawrence. This is a gray moment."

She'd anticipated he'd feel like a failure for having to say it, but even knowing how she'd warned him against feeling that way, he struggled with it now.

"Say it," she said quietly. But with force.

"Gray, Mistress."

"Okay." She nodded, pressed her hand to his chest. Dropped to one knee, so the two of them were almost eye to eye. "We're all right. I taunted you with Trey because often that rouses a competitive streak in an alpha male. Purely sexual. But when someone you trust or love has used that tactic like a rusty knife blade, then it does nothing but open the wound again. No, stay with me."

She curved her hand around his jaw. He wanted loose. He needed his clothes back, some kind of defense. He knew it was evident in every tense muscle, and he was ashamed for being so out of control, but she dealt with that, too.

"Look at me, Lawrence. Study my face, my eyes, what they're telling you. Get your own head out of the way."

He forced himself to do it, feeling like he was having to crank his eyes up to her visage with a forklift. It took a moment, because she was right, he had to get his own head out of the way, but then he really looked.

Warmth, caring. Pride. In him. Arousal, pleasure. Pleasure with him. That edge she could call up and wield like the whip was momentarily absent, showing him clearly that she'd told the truth. Yeah, she'd been fucking with him, but purely in the spirit of play and pleasure, not to screw with his head in the wrong ways. Not to make him feel less.

He wet his lips. "May I...may I speak, Mistress?"

"You may."

"You won't even remember his name when I'm done."

Her lips curved, and then she leaned forward. She cupped his skull with both hands so she could bring his head down, press her lips to his forehead. She held there as he breathed her in, as he steadied, tried to let her pleasure with him wash that garbage in his psyche away.

"I'll hold you to that, sailor."

Then, showing her faith in him was instant and sweet, she stretched herself out on the wedge cushion, draping herself before him with grace and ease. Untying the sash, she let the robe fall away from her body. Her entirely naked body, her legs falling open to show him her wet pussy, the neat hair shaved around the pink petals, their appearance veiled by the black mesh over his face. His nostrils were distended, seeking her scent. He wanted to fall upon her, but he made himself wait until she gave him the nod, her eyes fixed upon him. That edge was back, and it was a relief. She'd given him the hand to pull him out of his own shit, and even better, she was showing him she knew he was a big boy. He could clean himself up and move forward.

He bent down, and discovered a challenge. The chains let him lean forward on his knees, but they would only let him get so far. When his mesh-covered mouth reached her sex, his arms were stretched back at a straining angle that would become a hell of a workout for them. He could do that. Tightening his core and thigh muscles to balance it out, he went to work.

Though *work* was the last word he would have used to describe this. In order to pleasure her the way he'd boasted he could with an unrestricted mouth and tongue, he had to figure out how to use the impediment as an asset. So he started by rubbing his mouth slowly over her, pushing his tongue against the fabric, using that pressure against her clit, the labia. His breath and tongue quickly wet the fabric, as she'd said, and that helped.

At first, she didn't move, and he sensed she was holding herself still, using as much control as she was demanding from him. She wanted to goad him. Mission accomplished. He put himself even more into it, letting something take over that wasn't human at all.

Then she started letting her body rise up to him.

He growled in response, pushing his tongue into her as far as he could, which wasn't fucking anywhere far enough. But he played his lips over her quivering petals, the flushed clitoris, savoring the soft breaths, the little moans that started to come from her lips. He wanted to encourage her, wanted to tell her how much he loved this, but he was now hyper-mindful of breaking her rules. It was another form of restraint she'd put upon him.

The more she started to writhe, her breasts moving with her body, her leg hooking over his straining shoulder, the more his cock swelled and stretched. And those rings at the base started to pinch like a son of a bitch. Fuck...no, he wasn't stopping. He would endure anything to see her rise to him like this, tip her head back, that moan caught in her throat, but as he shifted, something shifted with him, and Jesus, oh, hell...

He lifted his head. "Gray, Mistress. Fucking hell. I'm sorry. Gray. The ring at the bottom..."

Because she was so aroused, he would have expected some reluctance, some lethargy to her movements, and had steeled himself for the delay. Instead, she moved as quick as one of his team members responding to a threat. She was up off the cushion, her hands between his legs. When she straightened out whatever had been pinching the fuck out of him, it was a good thing he was on his knees. The relief was strong enough they would have given out in response to it. Her fingers rubbed him, soothing while also adding to the arousal. She had her other hand on his shoulder, the side of his throat, and he realized she was testing the strain to his shoulders there, from the angle he was leaning forward.

"I'm...May I speak, Mistress?"

"You may." Even through that mesh, he could see the glow in her eyes. His cock gained another degree of thickness, just from that approval.

"I'm okay. I want to finish. I want to give you pleasure. Please let me finish."

"Hmm." She ran her hands carefully over his shoulders, but then made her decision, nodded. Laid back down. "I'm very pleased with you, Lawrence. You took good care of your Mistress's property." Reaching up, she ran her fingers over his mouth, and then those long nails hooked the mesh, tore it, so his mouth was free. "That kind of care is rewarded."

She laid her arms over her head, a decadent siren eying him out of half-lidded, fuck-me eyes. "Continue."

It was a good thing the chains still held him back, because he really would have fallen on her like a starving wolf then. Instead, he went after her as if he had the mask still in place. At first. Nuzzling, quick stabs of his tongue, a teasing pressure of his lips that became more aggressive. The clank of the chains became a coital rhythm, driven by the movement of his head and the rise of her body. She smelled and tasted like every good thing in the world, and he wanted to stay right where he was for the next decade, listening to her. The helpless note of her rising cries made him even harder, knowing his Mistress was trusting him with herself.

He renewed his assault, this time thrusting his tongue deep, sealing his mouth over her clit, licking and sucking, playing over her folds, rubbing his face in her cunt so that her cream joined the moisture of his mouth, sinking into the mesh around it, filling all his senses with her taste and scent.

She bowed up, her leg clamping down on his aching shoulder as the climax swept her, but he could handle that. He growled his approval, his cock straining against the rings. The sounds she made when an orgasm took her were feminine and sweet, the badass Mistress offering the treasure of her vulnerability. Lust tangled with emotion. He wanted to gather her up in his arms and hold her when she was limp and dewy, sated.

Except he had a raging hard-on, those rings biting, and his arms were bound. He was fully erect again, wanting to plunge inside her, find the release he needed so much he'd kill for it, especially with her hands on his shoulders still, nails digging in, probably drawing blood, as she quivered through aftershocks.

She stared into his eyes. "Come for me, Lawrence. With the rings on. I want to see you make it happen."

"It won't be me making that happen, Mistress. It's you."

Her lips parted, her eyes still dazed with lust, but not so much so that the Mistress wasn't still there. "I didn't ask you a question, Lawrence. That could be strike three."

His mental reaction was violent. If she thought she'd end things now, she'd lost her fucking mind. He would...

He closed his eyes, fingers flexing, arms testing the chains. The clanking was more erratic, his body twitching. But there was a still center to it, the eye of a hurricane.

"What do you think I should do?" Her voice filled that void. He opened his eyes to find hers locked on him. "What would your SEAL instructors do? Would they just let it go?"

Forming the words was more difficult than he could imagine. He was a mass of wild emotions and physical need, but when she lifted her upper torso to lay a hand on the side of his face, that stillness increased. He was in that moment when he brought it all to a halt so he could think, make the right decision, no matter what kind of shit was blowing up around him. Or within him.

When she'd said what she had about Trey, he'd technically broken the rule for the third time. She'd overlooked it then. That alone told him what his answer should be.

"No, ma'am." Every word was a blow. "They wouldn't."

"No. I suspect they'd remind you of the lesson in a very memorable way. So it didn't happen again."

She eased the cushion forward, until it almost touched his knees. She curved one leg around his waist, then the other, calves crossed over his ass. She leaned back on her elbows and, with her gaze still on his face, lifted her hips enough to put herself over the tip of his bound cock. "Don't move," she said. "Not the slightest bit. Resist the pull of my legs to stay exactly where you are. To my count of three."

He saw her stomach muscles flex, felt her thighs tighten on his sides as she guided herself onto him. Now he understood why she wanted him to anchor himself. She was using him, a counterbalance so the constriction of her legs would allow her to push herself down on him. Slowly, since the rings made the entry a little trickier for her own comfort.

But she took him, one ring at a time, her lips parting as she did it. To feel the slickness of her cunt closing over him, but with the interference of that fucking cage, and without being able to move, was pure torture. She went all the way to the hilt, then slowly moved back up. Her stomach muscles showed their definition, evidence of her personal discipline, as she did the maneuver.

"So good," she murmured. "Every inch of you feels so good. My cock. My sub." Her eyes glinted. "My slave."

A reminder about the high school yearbook joke. Only the way she looked at him, hell, the way he responded to her, it didn't feel like a joke at all. Because he didn't want her to let him go. She was torturing him twelve different ways, yet he'd bear all of it, to stay like this with her. Be the center of her attention, have the chance to give her what she needed.

"Two," she breathed, coming down to the hilt again. Her muscles flexed on him, he could feel it on the sensitive head, and he gritted his teeth. His cock pulsed hard. He couldn't do it. Couldn't do it.

No. She'd said no.

"And...three." She withdrew and gazed up at him, her fingertips drifting along his chest, to his waist, tangling in the trimmed hair above his cock. If she touched him, he would go off like a rocket.

"May I speak, Mistress?"

"You may, Lawrence."

"I want to hold out for you, but I think...if you touch me, I can't." He hated to admit it, but his body had reached its breaking point.

"It takes practice to learn that kind of control. You've done well, for your first time. I'll expect better next time." She curved those nails into his side, a reminder. "But that leaves us a dilemma. I have to remove that, Lawrence. You want me to, don't you?"

God, yes. He nodded. "Yes, Mistress."

"To do that, I have to touch you. So if you want me to remove it, you're going to have to dig deep, find a way not to climax. I expect you to exceed expectations, sailor." She gazed up at him, all blue eyes and pale flesh, her nipples tight and dark, her curves laid out before him, her mouth soft. With his spinning head and the mesh of the mask interfering with his vision, it made her look dreamlike. But that voice was crystal clear. "Do you understand?"

"Yes, Mistress."

She wasn't cruel about it. She took the rings off with gentle but brisk efficiency, not caressing him the way she had when she put them on. It was probably the only reason he made it. She left the condom on him, just in case, and he couldn't argue with the smarts of that.

She rose, drawing the robe around her, and attended to his shoulders, easing him back onto his heels. With a touch and quiet word, she adjusted where the chains were fastened so when she had him get to his feet, his arms hung naturally at his sides. She pulled the stool behind him, checked his shoulders, arm and back. Massaged them some more.

She'd retrieved that short whip and slid it between his legs, with enough pressure to separate his balls with its length. She put her hand on the center of his back. "I've decided you're going to come for me, Lawrence, because that's what *I* want, despite your infractions. But when you're about to do so, you better ask me for permission."

When she pressed herself against him, she'd opened the robe again. He shuddered at the pleasure of her breasts against his shoulders, her lower body against his buttocks. She smoothed one hand down his side. "You like pain, Lawrence. You like sacrifice and effort. You like to prove to your Mistress you're strong enough for her. I like that, too."

She backed off, leaving his skin aching for more of that warmth. Curled up in a bed behind him. That set off a stranger, lower belly ache, but all of this was like that. Lust spiked into a bucket of emotional shit, tied up with the past and present, lost and hoped-for futures, beliefs and dreams. Dreams that had been discarded and replaced, or shattered and gone forever. So he'd thought.

The whip struck his ass, and he flinched. She was putting more behind it this time. "This is my will," she said, landing another blow, between his shoulder blades. Then down to his buttocks again. "Come for me, Lawrence. Every blow is me telling you what I want."

His hips jerked forward with each strike. She didn't leave it there. She circled him, an erotic dream through the veil on his eyes as she flicked the whip over his hip, his upper thigh. Then a glancing blow on his cock itself. It reminded him of her hand, slapping him there, and that was all it took. His hips were pumping air, as she kept the dance going with the bee sting kisses all over his body.

His thighs quivered, his feet rocking forward and back. She hit him really hard on the ass, leaving a trail of fire, following it up with a barrage that kept him bucking, a friction of movement that took him to that edge, and...

"Mistress," he gasped. "May I come?"

Two more hits, that he groaned through, the boiling in his balls so close. He was going to fail. No, no he wasn't. A SEAL didn't fucking fail...

"Yes, Lawrence. You may."

He probably looked like a puppet, jerking against invisible strings. The chains clanged against the poles as his cock jetted once again. It was a rough climax, all his muscles tight, his body bowed forward, then snapping back, and then his knees gave out.

She was there, in front of him, her arms around him, easing him down onto the square cushion. As she held him, she deftly unclipped the cuffs from the chains so they swung free. He barely managed to do his part not to overbalance her as she eased back onto the wedge, him collapsing between the cradle of her thighs, his arms spread out over her sides like wings. Then, bliss, because she brought his head down to her breasts, let it rest there.

Strength was gone, all of it was gone, as he lay on the best bed he'd ever felt in his life, every curve pressing into the right valley, her scent surrounding him.

Somewhere far away, he knew this might just be the result of the extreme paces she'd put him through. Another, closer part wondered if she'd merely busted through all the doors and found his center. Because that part of him spoke the simple truth in his heart and mind, and left it there.

He was home.

CHAPTER FOURTEEN

O ver time, that feeling receded. He knew it would, and he tried to get a handle on it. Tried to place himself in the here and now, get perspective.

"I didn't know it felt like this," he said. His head couldn't get straight, and that was a problem. The tightness in his chest said he was vulnerable, which meant his team was vulnerable. He couldn't get pinned down. He couldn't find his weapon. That was bad.

Sometimes it boiled down to the kindergarten basics. This good, that bad.

"Lawrence." The voice penetrated, like a wind that had been somewhere off in the distance but was moving closer, coming through dense forest. It covered his movements, but it covered the movements of the enemy as well.

Stop it. You're not down range. You're in a BDSM club, and you've just had the top of your head blown off by a Mistress who is in the room with you right now, needing you to keep your shit together.

"Easy," she murmured. "I'm touching you. Is that okay, Lawrence?"

She was smart enough to ask. He needed to marry this woman. She knew more about him in the space of thirty minutes than...no, he wasn't invoking that name. Not here. He wasn't touching this with that.

"Yeah," he said at last. "What's wrong with me?"

"Not a thing," she said, in that sexy purr. She'd taken off the hood, and was passing her fingertips alongside his head, a gentle stroke, but with enough firmness to remind him she had strength. Holy God, did she. Enough strength to steady him, tell him things were okay. Lawrence hadn't fucked up. This was exactly why he'd had Dale guarding the perimeter. He'd anticipated.

"You were amazing. Beautiful," she told him. "Everything I could want. You're like a meal and a dessert. One I just finished, but I want to start all over again. And we've only scratched the surface."

Some of that penetrated, but mostly he followed the music of her voice, and brought her face into focus by at last lifting his head. Her tousled hair. So soft. His hands still lay limply on either side of her.

"Want to touch." He shouldn't lift his hands without permission.

Her eyes warmed with approval. "Then ask me."

"May I touch your hair, Mistress?"

"You may."

He lifted a hand that he noted was shaking. She gripped it in both of hers, brought it to her face and let it go, so he could tunnel his fingers into her hair. Warm and thick, and he had both hands in it before another moment passed, and then he put his mouth on hers. He knew he hadn't asked for that privilege, but he needed it so much he hoped he wouldn't be denied.

He wasn't.

Her hands were on his face, his hair, his chest and shoulders. Soothing. He'd lost control under her command. And that was okay. It had pleased her. He'd pleased her. That meant everything. He devoured her mouth, his hands still in her hair. He had to be getting heavy. But the tightening of her arms said she wanted him where he was.

When at last her hold eased, he shifted his arms so they were threaded around her back and waist. She let him pillow his face against her breasts. She stroked his flesh, murmured to him. His heart was thumping at a less erratic pace.

"This is normal, Lawrence," she said. It was as if she knew he needed intel now. A way to understand. "Not only for a first session, but one that became more intense than you probably expected. It works that way sometimes. Especially when you've needed it for so long."

She kept it easy, so that personal insight didn't jar him, raise defensive walls. With that kind of timing, she would have made a hell of an interrogator.

"You didn't have this kind of relationship with your ex," she said. A statement.

"No. What's the term you used...we were vanilla."

"*She* was vanilla. You adjusted yourself to that."

"Yeah. I guess. She needed...a lot. Before now, I really hadn't visualized how this looked. I mean, fantasized, yeah. But taken that to a strategic, real-life plan, no. Not even close."

"Even when Dale took you to clubs."

"Looking seemed to satisfy me, in some ways. The first time he took me...I was still with her."

Or rather, in their volatile on-again, off-again relationship, it had been an "on" period.

When he was with Valentina, he would imagine a relationship between them like this. When it was difficult to make things happen by staying in their reality, that imagining would help him satisfy her, get himself off. It was a private guilt he hadn't shared, and he wouldn't share now. But Rosalinda seemed to understand, regardless.

"Service can stand in for submission. Sometimes, with a personality like yours, service is the more important part."

The words eased the jagged feeling the thoughts were provoking, but he really didn't want to feel any of that.

"Can we... I don't really want to talk about the past right now. Don't want to ruin this."

She paused, then she nodded, her chin moving against his head. "All right. For now."

"May I ask you something?"

"Yes. I don't promise an answer."

"You said you haven't ever been married. Have you ever been with someone...that you call yours?" Not just a club hookup, but someone she took home, wanted to keep.

She was quiet for a long moment. The slight tension told him it wasn't an easy-to-answer question. "No," she said, before he could retract it, show her the same consideration she was showing him, not taking this into murky waters. "I have Abby."

"You keep saying that. Some version of that. Are you two..."

"No. Not exactly. And don't try imagining what I know you want to imagine. Your cock has had enough of a workout for one night."

He chuckled against her silken flesh. He liked the way she was stroking him. So easy and gentle, yet she always kept that sureness in her touch. In control, confident. Not weak.

Yeah, pure poetry, his thoughts. Thank God she wasn't trying to get him to talk much.

"Rest," she said. "Just be at ease. When I know you're ready, we'll head home. You're not on duty right now, sailor. I am."

~

Those words should have galvanized him to pull his shit together, but he ended up dozing in her arms. He had no idea how long. He also couldn't remember the last time he'd let himself relax enough to let it all go. She made him feel like he could do that without the world falling apart.

When he surfaced, it took him a moment to figure out where he was, since waking up naked, lying upon the soft and willing body of a woman, wasn't his usual experience. Let alone in a room that smelled of pine forest and had a starry-sky ceiling.

"There you are," she said, with a light stroke of his back, his shoulders. She'd been doing that for a while, because the impression of her touch lingered on his skin all around that area. "What do you say we get dressed? I'll drop you off at your place."

First time he'd ever wished a security company had been less diligent. If they hadn't done the upgrades yet he could have made a valid case for staying with her tonight. However, her tone, as well as the pointed words, said she wasn't offering that. He hadn't done anything wrong, as far as he knew, and she didn't sound mad. She was just doing that thing she'd done before, setting boundaries, reminding him of them. This kind of stuff could lead to assuming too much, too soon. He got it. It didn't mean he wasn't disappointed.

But he was a grown-up. He could deal. "Roger that," he said, clearing his throat and pushing himself off her. She wasn't dropping him off first, though. He'd make sure she was secure at her home before he called it a night. Even though he felt like he'd been run over by a street sweeper.

An eternity ago—otherwise known as before what had happened in this room—Lawrence had intended to let Dale go home after they emerged from the club. Yet when Lawrence had been in the locker room, storing his T-shirt, Dale had sent him a curious follow-up text.

You've got me for the night if you need me. Whatever happens in there, don't rush yourself. Don't even worry about me until you're ready to come out. Then give me a heads up.

So Dale knew it could be like this. Lawrence had seen subs after a session, looking dazed and out of it. But he hadn't really understood what was going on, why it looked like they were floating on a different plane from everyone else. Now he did.

He wanted to pull it together enough that he wouldn't have to make Dale's night longer than it had already been, so he started focusing on ways to bring his head and feet back to earth. Clothes would help.

But first he offered his Mistress a hand to help her to her feet. He had one last glimpse of her bare body, the tempting curves and sweet folds between her legs, before she released his hand to belt the robe. Not tight though, so the cleavage held his attention an extra beat. Or two or three. Fuck, he was drifting again, swaying on his feet in some dreamlike lazy erotic haze.

She touched his arm, breaking him out of it, and he cleared his throat, turned away. As he found his clothes and started to put them on, using the bench when it was time to put on his shoes, she moved back behind the black drape area. He assumed she was putting her dress back on, but instead she returned in a dark blue T-shirt, a knit mid-thigh skirt in a blue and green striped pattern, and a pair of white sneakers. Not plain white sneakers, though. Not his shoe-conscious Mistress. They'd been painted with a blue and green swirl on the side, anchored with an arrangement of rhinestones like a blue and green petaled flower. Her dress was in a garment bag, the shoes likely tucked in the tote over her arm. He offered to take the bag from her, and she handed it over. She gave him an easy smile.

"No reason not to be comfortable, right?"

She wasn't wearing a bra under the T-shirt, so he didn't think he'd be comfortable for long, watching the movement of those curves, the hints of her nipples. She shrugged on a short jacket, which helped. But he couldn't stop watching her do...anything. Free her blonde hair from the collar of the jacket, shake it back. With her in sneakers, he was taller than her, and that made things tight in his chest, the way she looked up at him, standing so close he seemed to shelter her.

As he opened the door for her, she ducked under his arm to go through it, shooting him a smile. She was relaxed, content. Happy with him and herself. But he also saw the attention in her gaze. Still watching after him.

They stopped at the men's lockers so he could get his T-shirt, put it on. While he was in there, he texted Dale that they were heading out.

When he returned to her in the hallway, he anticipated she might want to go by the main floor, say good night to her friends, but instead she headed for the lobby. He guessed maybe she'd already texted them that she was leaving, though he thought he better confirm it with her. He'd seen how much Abby worried. The words were thick on his tongue, but he got the question out.

"We texted while you were resting," she said. "Abby headed home a while back. As did Skye and Vera, after they finished their sessions. Cyn is still with Sy, but she's a night owl. She'll work a man through his paces all the way up to closing, if she's in a mood to do it."

His focus wasn't sharpening, that haze not dissipating. Not as much as he would have expected. He also realized, with a far-too-mild surge of horror, that it was more like she was escorting him, her grip on his arm a guiding force.

He stopped her in the lobby, checked his phone again. Dale had texted back the all clear. He had them covered.

She had the keys and shook her head when he reached for them. "I'm driving," she said. "Trust me."

He wanted to argue, but he couldn't. In this situation, focusing on their surroundings and driving would divide his already degraded attention. He wouldn't risk her for pride.

Dale was leaning against his truck, which he'd relocated a couple spots away from her vehicle. He watched the mostly empty parking lot, the building, and anywhere else that might produce a threat.

Male pride got Lawrence to the car and opening the driver's side door for her. Rosalinda waved at Dale before she took the offered seat. Lawrence zoned out another second, enjoying the sweep of her legs as she folded them in with her.

"Lawrence?" She touched his hand. "Get in the car, honey."

Fucking hell. Before the uneasiness could flood him, she had gripped his other hand, dangling loose at his side. "This is normal," she repeated, in a tone that held him like a climbing rope. "Dale is here. I'm safe. You took care of me, Lawrence. Let me take care of you. Your mind will clear as you do normal things. Don't fight it, don't get anxious about it. Just let it happen naturally."

That made sense, and thinking about it any other way was going to cause him and her problems. When he turned to move around the front of the car, his gaze passed over Dale. His Master Chief offered him a firm, reassuring nod. Everything was fine. He wasn't falling down on the job. That helped even more.

Once Lawrence came around and sat himself in the passenger seat, fastened his seatbelt, he went over logistics for past missions, did a few multiplication tables. Exercises he'd used in what should have been far more unsettling and focus-eroding situations. Active conversation would help bring his mind out of this unsettling fog. Since he liked hearing her voice, that was an additional perk.

"Is that a Mistress thing, anticipating control triggers?"

She'd turned over the ignition and pulled out of the parking lot into the late evening traffic. "Yes and no. Some of it is intuition and experience, but in your specific case, I sought additional information."

He looked at her profile, the slim neck, precise chin. The movement of her hands on the steering wheel. The length of exposed thigh as she shifted between brake and gas pedal to accommodate traffic. "You talked to Dale."

"Of course." She glanced at him. "I've never been in session with a special ops person, let alone one so recently active. Vigilance is the norm for you. I had to make sure if I took you into subspace it wouldn't trigger any dangerous defense mechanisms, for you or me."

Really smart. Though he had thought about it, he hadn't reviewed any of those variables with her. He'd thought he could keep a handle on it himself, by setting parameters like no hard restraints. He'd failed to anticipate.

"I'm sorry," he said. "I should have been the one to have that conversation with you."

She shot him an amused look. "Lawrence, if I was in the middle of a war zone, I'd be stupid not to rely on your experience to get me out of it. Right?"

His brow creased. "Yeah."

"During a session, you should be able to rely on my experience and judgment. I'm the Mistress." Now her tone and her glance became firmer. "It's my job to ensure everything I do in a session is safe for both of us. Doesn't mean I won't fuck up, which is why there is the safeword backup, but I sure as hell learn fast from my mistakes. Otherwise, I wouldn't be as good at this as I am."

"It's more than being good at it," he said. "You love it. So much it becomes you. Who you are."

A reminder that prodded that *who am I now?* emptiness in him, which had once again been notably absent during most of their session.

He was tired, and she was saying it was okay. She had this. Had him. Instinct had him wanting to resist relying on that, but she reached out, her palm up. For maybe the first time in his life he put his hand into a woman's grasp. Rather than thinking of it as her putting her hand in his.

"Do you like pie?" she asked.

He blinked at her, and she squeezed his hand. "There's a little place nearby. I like a piece of pie after a good session, and I think the normalcy will help ground you."

"Is it always like this?"

"If we do it right." That smile again, part sex kitten, all woman. She tilted her head toward the rearview mirror. "We can invite Dale to join us."

"Dale?" Lawrence twisted around. "He's still with us?"

Stupid question. He hadn't exactly given Dale the all clear to head home, had he? But Rosalinda answered his question smoothly.

"He decided to tag along. He'll follow me home after I drop you off at your place. Make sure I get inside, where my new and fancy security system can take over for both of you until I next decide to grace the world with my presence."

She'd slowed down to a crawl as she looked for a parking space, and was texting one-handed, barely glancing at the phone as she kept her eye on the road. "I told him you were still a little out of it. Don't," she warned as he opened his mouth. "I'm the Mistress, right? But you tell me. You think you're in any condition to provide competent surveillance right now? Handle a weapon?"

He'd definitely qualify as under the influence right now, though he'd taken no other drug than her control over him. Apparently, that was pretty potent stuff.

He responded with a semi-grumpy look, just for form's sake, but she didn't get offended. Merely slanted an oddly tender look at him as she pulled into a side street space.

Dale pulled past them, finding one several spots up. This time of night, in this section of New Orleans, it wasn't too difficult to park near the front of the diner.

"Wait there," Lawrence told her. "You did leave me enough brain cells to open the door for you."

"I won't next time." Her blue eyes glittered as she let her hand drift along his leg. "But you'll still have to come eat pie with me. This place is my personal little ritual after a satisfying evening at the club."

If she could do better than tonight to knock him off his feet, he'd be lucky to sit upright in a booth and not drool on himself while she enjoyed her key lime, or whatever her preferred pie type was. He told his stupidly stirring cock to go back to sleep and got out, lifting a hand to Dale as he circled around to her side.

Being in a home environment, grappling with a totally new experience, could impact his training and experience. Yet he'd been in situations where he'd been close to hypothermia, dehydration. Wounded. In danger of discovery by the enemy. That training and experience, the vigilance so hard to turn off when he came back from a mission, were all designed to not let him or his team down.

Which was why he'd only made the first stride around the front grill of the Mustang when the significance of her words penetrated. He came to a full stop, his gaze darting toward Dale. When their eyes met, their combined decades of that experience and intuition came together in a blink.

Lawrence snapped his head around toward Rosalinda, and bellowed the words.

"Get down."

Gunfire ripped across the Mustang's side panels and shattered the driver's window.

Adrenaline surged through him, shoving aside any cloudiness and propelling him back to the passenger side as the rounds rocked the car's body.

Yanking open the passenger door, he dove in and found she'd listened. She was flat on the seat, head covered with both arms and a lot of glass. She'd dropped before the window had exploded, thank fuck. He popped her seatbelt latch and seized her hands, shoving the belt harness off her shoulder before he hauled her toward him. "Come on."

He heard return fire, three rapid and precise shots. Dale had located the shooter's hiding spot. Lawrence pulled Rosalinda to the pavement on the far side of the car, wrapping himself around her to hold her tight to his side, even as he made a cursory check to verify no bullets had punched through the door and found her vulnerable body. He heard the few late strolling pedestrians screaming, but no more gunfire. Over in less than a handful of seconds, just as he'd told her.

Then one of those screams became the kind of a wail he knew too well. His gut seized up. Ros's head came up at the same sound, the shock in her eyes replaced by awareness. She located the source at the same time he did. She would have scrambled that way, but he wouldn't give an inch, even as she fought him.

"You're the target," he snapped. "You go out there, you put them in more danger."

That penetrated, but her eyes were wild, her face a mix of fear and fury. Normal reaction for the fucking abnormal.

Sirens pierced the air. They were in downtown NOLA, so police support wasn't far off, thank God. Fuck, the night was about to get longer and more complicated. But none of that mattered so much as what was on the ground thirty feet from them.

A kid, maybe about eighteen, likely headed for the diner and same pie Rosalinda had been seeking. His girlfriend was on her knees next to his prone body, his blood on her shaking hands. An older man, a tourist by the look of him, had her putting pressure on the wound below the kid's right shoulder while his wife called 911. Either the kid had been facing his girl when the shots rang out, or he'd turned to protect her.

Dale jogged across the road, his eyes hard and face set. The expression told Lawrence the shooter was gone. Master Chief stopped by the two teens and the tourists, made sure they had it under control and were doing the basics to keep his vitals up. Then he came to Lawrence, squatting on the other side of Rosalinda, the two of them and her car forming a bulwark around her.

"I hit him," he told Lawrence. "But the piece of shit was in an alley with a back way out."

"Is he okay?" Rosalinda asked. The direction of her gaze said she was talking about the kid on the ground. Her voice was hoarse and unsteady, but her clutch on Lawrence was fierce as a hawk's.

"Took a good chunk out of his shoulder, but it was on the outside," Dale said. "They'll find the slug in the building brick behind him."

"Ambulance is on the way," Lawrence told her.

Her face had become as cold as marble. "That bastard," she said, between her teeth. "That motherfucking bastard."

CHAPTER FIFTEEN

*R*os paced her kitchen. They'd talked to police at the scene, but a detective, Miles Rosetti, had come to her house to go over the same info with her. In addition to tonight's event, he went over the information the police had taken for her earlier break-in. He said he would be the primary on her case going forward.

It was good news that she would be considered a priority case, but she was relieved they'd been able to leave the diner before any ambitious late-night reporters arrived on scene. She'd been assured her name wouldn't be released to the press, though leaks happened. The last thing she wanted was TRA or her getting that kind of attention.

She'd been straightforward about where they'd been before they headed to the diner. To his credit, Rosetti took it in stride, didn't act like a BDSM club was a nest of criminal behavior that might be connected to the shooting. It didn't hurt that Dale and Lawrence filled in the blanks about Snake, and lent the weight that their military service could bring to the situation, her credibility and theirs.

Her glance went to the cheerful pink box on the counter. The diner owner, a veteran named Big John, had boxed up a whole blackberry pie for her, her favorite, and given it to her on the house. His Vietnamese wife had patted her hand. "Pick up some ice cream on the way home," she advised. "Pie and ice cream will make everything better."

She hadn't done that. She already had some Breyer's old-fashioned vanilla in the freezer, but her stomach couldn't have handled a gumdrop at the moment, let alone pie and ice cream.

She'd left Rosetti talking to Dale and Lawrence in the living room when it was clear they were going over things she already knew, and Rosetti had no additional questions for her. However, whenever she turned her gaze that way, she found Lawrence's upon her. He'd been visually checking on her every few minutes. A reassurance. Watching over her.

She didn't want to be watched over. She wanted to find herself a big, nasty weapon, like a flamethrower, and roast Snake with it. Starting with his useless testicles.

Quick footsteps on the back deck briefly drew the men's attention, but Dale spoke a word to the detective, and the men returned to their discussion. Lawrence's gaze held hers an extra beat, telling her the late-night visitor was his doing.

Abigail came in through the kitchen door. She wore black leggings and a tunic top printed with Monet's water lilies. With her hair pulled up in a quick tail and no makeup on her face, she'd likely stripped off her pajamas, thrown on some clothes and rushed out the door. In a heartbeat, she had her arms around Ros and was holding her, in a waft of fragrant bedtime moisturizer.

Despite her low-level urge to be pissed at Lawrence's presumption, the anger that had Ros stomping around her house became other things she hadn't been allowing herself to feel. So she held her friend back.

"It's okay," Abby murmured. "I know you're angry. I know you hate this so much. I love you."

Ros closed her eyes, sighed a deep breath. When she drew back, Abby was ready with the second thing she needed. A grim sense of humor.

"I have limb loppers in my car," her CFO said stoutly. "We find him, castrate him, let him bleed out, be done with it."

Dale cleared his throat. They looked his way to find her declaration had captured Rosetti's attention. "Much as I agree with your plan," the detective said dryly, "best not to say it right in front of me."

Abigail shot him a less friendly look. "Get this piece of crap off the street and he won't have to worry about his tiny little dick."

"They have no proof it was him," Ros said. "Didn't catch the shooter, though Dale did hit him. They found blood in the alley. So they'll check the hospitals and maybe get lucky. But it was probably one of his guys."

Giving Abby the details helped, though saying it aloud was no less frustrating.

"Well, shit." They sat down at the table together. Freak skirted the living room, eying the unfamiliar men, and hopped into the kitchen. He wound around Abby's legs, since he was almost as devoted to her as he was to Ros. Abby adjusted as the cat jumped into her lap and started kneading. Ros gestured to the fridge.

"Want a soda? I just picked up five cases of your favorite for fifty percent off. You can take them home."

"Where'd you score that price?"

"At the pharmacy, when I was getting Freak's compound. Whole pyramid of them."

Totally irrelevant to anything going on, but it made her feel good to talk about something normal for a second. So did looking toward Lawrence again. She was doing it as much as he was. Touching base. He felt her regard, held it a second before they both turned back to their respective people. It was like having a string tied between them, a little tug every few seconds. *Hey, I'm here.*

Abby laid her hands on Ros's, and Ros turned back to her friend. Having Abby here brought other things to the surface. "He saved my life, Abby," she said, low. "He anticipated it a moment before it happened. I don't know how he did that, but he did. And he's beating himself up because he didn't figure it out sooner. Because I scrambled his head in a scene. I'll bet good money he's going to try to pull back, say we need to keep this professional."

"Is he right?" Abigail sent her a shrewd look. "It has to have been a pretty damn good scene if you don't want to wait to resolve this situation before pursuing things with him."

"It was," Ros said. "Timing is everything. When this job is over, whatever he and I are doing probably is, too. You know my attention span doesn't last that long."

Abby's eyes darkened. "I think he's different, Ros."

Ros drew her hands away. She wasn't going down that road. Abby registered the shift, and fortunately didn't pursue it. But maybe that was because she knew her next topic would annoy Ros even more.

"I have an idea that might fix that discussion before it happens," she said. "I've got the Rainbow Foods meeting in Indiana this week. I was flying up there tomorrow."

"Yeah. They're supposed to have snow this week. You can visit the family cabin, do some snowboarding."

"Or you can go instead."

Ros frowned. "Why would I—"

"Because it takes you away from here for a couple days. I've run it past Lawrence, and he supports it, but he said I should talk it out with you first. If you agree, he said not to discuss it beyond you and me yet."

Ros's hackles rose, but she didn't get to retort, because the detective had stepped into the kitchen. Fortunately, it was to wind things up. Rosetti gave her his card, exchanged the obligatory assurances about them doing what they could to work the case. She noticed he spoke the words firmly, though. They weren't rote, and he made sure to make eye contact with Abby to underscore them.

"Call me if you think of anything else," he said, to all of them. Dale walked him out.

Ros pivoted to face Lawrence. He'd drawn closer and had a hand lifted, probably to touch her shoulder. When she twitched back and leveled a glare on him, he stopped.

"Thank you for asking me if you should call Abby," she said in a saccharine tone. "And for discussing our next steps with her first."

Abby stood, letting Freak tip to the floor before she rapped the tabletop. "He didn't bring up the trip; I did. Don't take it out on him."

Ros opened her mouth to snap, but Dale had stepped back in, in time to overhear the exchange. "The trip is sound thinking," he said. "Snake's brought down a shitstorm, doing a drive-by in that part of town. The police will be on his ass big time for the next few days. Maybe even be able to crack something loose on the shooter if someone reports him getting treatment. With any luck, by the time you get back, the threat could be resolved."

Ros remained stone-faced. She kept her attention locked on Lawrence. His green eyes flickered, and he started to respond, but a buzzing from his phone stopped him. He pulled it out, noted the number. Surprise flitted through his gaze, even as his mouth tightened and he glanced at Dale. "I need to take this," he said.

He moved back into her living room. The hunch to his shoulders, the tension in his grip on the phone, even the stiff tone of his voice, said the call wasn't welcome. Impossible to postpone, apparently, but not welcome.

Dale's eyes had gone flat, telling Ros he knew something about who might be calling Lawrence, and he wasn't thrilled by it. Ros started toward the living room, but was brought up short when Abby gripped her arm. Her friend couldn't care less about Lawrence's caller.

"You just told me you don't want this situation to influence the personal relationship between you, end it when it's just started," Abby said, low. "But if you keep reacting like this, it will do just that. He called a friend to support you after a trauma, something a security person would likely do. *I* was the one who brought up the trip and suggested you going instead of me. *He* told me to discuss it with you. Got it?"

Ros knew she was right, but fuck, she didn't respond well to being handled. Abigail knew it, which was probably why her tone was more firm than angry.

"Fine. Got it," Ros said, and extricated herself. She was being abrupt, but she'd ask Abby's forgiveness later. She needed to know what was going on. Dale had dropped to his heels and was making friends with Freak. Since Dale ran an animal rescue, Ros expected her cat could tell he was trustworthy material.

As she moved into the living room, Lawrence had his back to her, was looking out the window. "I don't know where she is, Zoey. No, I can't go look for her right now. I'm sorry. I've got other things going on."

He flinched, as if he'd been kicked. "Yeah, they are pretty important. Listen, you know how this works. She'll turn up. Or she won't. I've got to go. I'm sorry. Maybe...maybe later I'll come by. Okay?"

He listened another second, then cut the connection. Ros watched him stare out the window. He'd handled her being shot at with smooth efficiency, an enemy he knew how to fight. But this phone call defeated him. She saw it in the slump of his shoulders, how he rubbed a hand over his face.

That kind of weariness was something she recognized, so clearly she took a step backward. She'd seen a hint of it at his apartment, that first day. But now a montage of past and present rose in her mind. They crowded in on the images of her session with Lawrence, bending the walls around it like cardboard.

The scene had been perfect, in every way that mattered. But people weren't perfect. That was why she kept things at the club. In a rigidly controlled structure, she didn't get hip deep in the messes that were other people's lives. She couldn't afford to do that. Because of Abby.

She always told herself that, and usually it was true. Right now, it was possibly about self-preservation. It didn't make it any less a good decision.

"You're right," she said quietly. "What you're thinking about us."

He turned, startled to see her there, the man who was always aware of his surroundings. Except after strenuous scenes with a Mistress, or a phone call from someone she knew had to be associated with his ex.

"This is probably too complicated to do right now." With effort, she ensured her tone was brisk, efficient. No baggage. Just practical. "You're wrong to think you failed tonight, because you didn't. Even if Dale hadn't come with us, you knew about the ambush before it happened. You would have gotten me into the restaurant and figured it out, protected me. But it's a lot to ask of both of us, to try and explore what we explored tonight with all the rest going on. Let's let it rest, for now. I'm going to bed."

His expression had gone blank. A lot was going on behind that mask, which said he was thinking. Though some ego-driven part of her would have liked an immediate protest, he wasn't a kneejerk response guy.

"Are you all right?" he asked.

Of course he'd ask her that, and mean it. He was a good man. The genuine concern in his face could unhinge her, so she sat on the emotional reaction that wanted to reach out to him. It made her tone even more flat.

"Yes. Angry, frustrated. Rattled. All very normal and expected, I'm sure. Nothing a shower and a good night's sleep won't handle. How about you?"

She saw the despair, deep in his eyes. He'd glimpsed something he'd truly, deeply wanted, earlier in the evening, and she was putting an end to it, possibly for good.

But just as she'd locked down her own desires and presented herself to him as Ros, the in-control independent businesswoman, he did the same. He stood before her as the man who considered himself responsible for the mission. Whether it was to protect his country, his team, or the woman standing in front of him.

He nodded at her. "I'm good, Ros. You can count on me. No matter what. Sleep easy."

It was the first time he'd called her by the name everyone else did. She hated it.

Lawrence had had Dale bring him a fresh go-bag from his place. After the evening's events, he wasn't leaving Rosalinda. Fortunately, she didn't insist. If she had, he'd merely have been sleeping in a car right outside the house, rather than on her couch, but he preferred the latter.

Before she'd disappeared upstairs, she'd agreed to the trip to Indiana, another good thing. This morning they could focus on those preparations, keeping the awkward silences about personal shit to a minimum.

Abby would be telling the regular staff Rosalinda was sick at home, and that Abby had cancelled her trip to Indiana to help manage the office. Only her inner circle, including Bastion, would know the truth. With any luck, Snake would pick up the chatter. The cops watching her place might get a crack at catching him, or flipping one of his guys to nail him for last night's shooting.

At seven a.m., she came through for coffee and an absent hello. He was on his phone with Matt, but he didn't get a chance to tell her that before she'd returned upstairs. Though she put on a vaguely pleasant expression, she was stiff as a board. A night's sleep hadn't helped her feel better. He suspected she'd spent the night stewing and had woken more aggravated. The energy hovering around her reminded him of an undetonated landmine.

So many things about last night had gone right. Then she'd pulled back from him hard, but he couldn't argue with her decision. When threats were coming this hard and fast, nothing else made sense. But he'd wondered a couple times during his own restless night if her decision to pull back had more to do with his phone call about Valentina's latest bender.

It didn't make the security issue any less relevant, though. And none of it sat any better with him, especially when he thought of how nice it would have been to go to bed curled around her. After enjoying pie at the diner, listening to her talk and seeing her smile.

Neither of them were smiling today.

He needed to bring her up to date. Bracing himself for stepping on that landmine, he mounted the stairs. He heard her voice, knew she was on her phone before he arrived at the threshold to her home office. It gave him a moment to just look at her.

She was concentrating on something on her computer while talking on the earpiece. She wore a pair of blue lounge pants and a clingy white tank over it. Her feet were bare, one of them curled on the seat edge, her bent knee pressed against the arm of the office chair. Her hair was down, tumbled across her shoulders. She hadn't yet put on makeup. She was tired, and stressed, but it didn't make her any less beautiful to him. If anything, that hint of vulnerability drew him to her like a magnet, with the urge to comfort and reassure. Make her breakfast and tell her she could go back to bed for awhile and not worry about anything.

None of which was a security guy's job, he reminded himself.

She still looked touchable in a way that had him wanting to reach out. So he crossed his arms, leaned in the threshold and closed his eyes, listening to her voice. He didn't really care what she was talking about. He'd experienced it in a very personal way last night, but it captivated him, how she chose her words, how she flavored them with humor, firmness, confidence. An easy flow.

Then she stopped, ending the call. He opened his eyes, finding her gaze upon him. For just a second, she was looking at him the way he'd been looking at her. In theory, once the threat was contained, they could pick up where they left off, but he wasn't sure they really could. There was something about her demeanor that suggested the window of opportunity was closing. It was enough to make anyone cranky. He straightened.

"I checked back in with the hospital. Brian Albert, the teenager who was shot, he's good. They'll discharge him this morning."

Her expression eased, so he was glad he'd led with that. Then he jumped into murkier waters. "Matt Kensington has cleared the schedule of his private jet. We'll be taking that to Indiana."

A variety of reactions crossed her face, none of them all too pleased. But thank God she didn't argue. "I'll reimburse Matt for the expense," she said.

Lawrence lifted his shoulder. "That's between you and him."

She looked at the computer, a dismissal. But as he started to straighten, she spoke again. "I'd prefer it if you didn't keep Matt in the loop on everything happening with me."

"He called me last night. Saw the news report about the shooting, recognized your car." A car the news fortunately so far hadn't connected to the shooting's target, since he knew she didn't want that kind of attention. "Should I have lied?"

He made it a question, not a retort, keeping his voice even. She set her mouth in a firm line, shook her head, then tapped the keys again. Making another call. "Don Adams, please. This is Ros Thomas of TRA."

He got it. In her shoes, he would feel just as out of sorts. In fact, in her actual shoes, his arches would be killing him, reinforcing the bad mood.

What he really wanted to do was come up behind the chair, put his hands on her shoulders and his lips to the top of her head, as he told her again it was going to be all right. But since he valued his hands and his ability to chew food, he didn't follow through with that plan.

With a grim smile that didn't reach his heart, he headed back downstairs.

At eleven, she was ready to head for the airport. She'd packed what she needed, and he'd put it in the rental car, which had been dropped off by the company in the alleyway of the house next to them. Rosalinda had called the neighbor and asked if it could be parked there. His Charger was in her driveway, a replacement while hers was being repaired. Leaving it here was part of the plan to make it look like she was still at home.

"I want to drive," Rosalinda said, as they got ready to leave.

He shook his head, but before he could say anything, she crossed her arms. "I need to drive," she said. "I need to feel I have control of one fucking thing."

At her stony stare, he evaluated the risks and determined her being behind the wheel would make little difference. An unmarked car would be trailing them partway to the airport to confirm they weren't being followed. He didn't really need it, well-trained himself in detecting a tail, but he had no problem with the police offering their resources. "Okay, you can drive."

"I wasn't making a request."

He was right. Her mood was precarious, any attempt at civility a strain. But when she threw down that gauntlet, he'd reached his limit for walking on eggshells.

He'd been inside her body. She'd been inside him, a lot deeper than that.

He closed the two strides between them. "Rosalinda," he said quietly. "I get it. You're angry. You feel out of control. You want to be pissed. You want to hurt someone."

She stared at his chest, a peculiar stillness coming over her. "You called me Rosalinda."

He gave her a puzzled look. Didn't he always? Because it looked like she wouldn't implode at a single touch, and he couldn't keep himself from it any longer, he put his hands on her upper arms. "You and me, Dale, Rosetti, the police, your staff—we're all doing what we can to stop him, change this situation. The waiting is the worst part. I know that."

At last she met his gaze directly, looking for understanding, connection. "How do you deal with it?"

"I figure out ways to let go," he said. "To accept I'm not in charge of every fucking thing in the world. There are others out there just like me, trying to figure it out, balance the scales. We all do our part." He tightened his grip. "You did your part. You're doing it. Snake's girl and her baby are safe, thanks to you. Your shelter is helping more like her, getting them away from monsters, changing their future."

"It's never enough," she said.

"Never feels that way, does it?" He ran his hands up and down her arms, an easy stroke. "It's okay. Battles are won a day at a time. And by not letting the losses take you out of the fight, or make you lose sight of where you do good."

He paused, then said the words she'd said to him, before that unforgettable session. "Focus is everything."

Grim amusement flickered through her eyes. "True. But I'm still driving."

"We can make that work." He touched her chin. "But stay away from the ultimatums when it comes to your protection. I'm past the walk away part if you won't listen to me. I may be more personally invested than I should be, but that isn't always a bad thing. I won't hesitate to toss you over my shoulder and lock you in your basement dungeon to keep you safe."

Her eyes narrowed. "That might work out better for you if you locked yourself in there with me."

Though she looked like the only thing she'd want to do in that room was tear him a new asshole, it didn't matter. His dumbass cock still took it as foreplay.

He managed to conceal that reaction, but showed his teeth. "Interesting as that sounds, we have a plane to catch."

She'd indicated she needed to make one stop on Canal Street, to pick up some touristy thing that would amuse the client. The unmarked car had peeled off, after calling Lawrence on his cell to let him know they hadn't been tailed from the house. The officer at the wheel was the woman who'd covered the initial break-in, and she wished them safe travels.

It was a sunny day. Getting out of the house and the thoughts that had filled up that space overnight seemed to help Rosalinda, since she seemed to relax more as she drove. While he kept a lookout, she made a couple business calls on her hands-free. It impressed him, how smoothly she engaged with clients and co-workers alike. She listened well, provided good input and guided them toward the best solution for their goal or problems. More personally, he was glad to see her settling into it. Keeping her focus on business would help her deal with what he'd described, the torturous waiting for something to shake loose.

Canal Street had its usual foot traffic congestion this close to the casino and major hotels. She parked near the corner of the alleyway where the tourist shop was. The gaudy looking place advertised pralines, cheap NOLA T-shirts, and the kind of tchotchkes the tourists took home by the suitcase loads. She waited without being told for him to come around, scope things out, then open the door for her. When they reached the sidewalk, she put her hand on him, squeezed, met his gaze.

The relaxed demeanor dropped, her features warrior ice.

"I need to do this," she said.

She pivoted and strode away, moving past the head shop next to the tourist store. A jungle of tie-dyed shirts hanging along the eaves fluttered at her passing.

He'd been played. Suppressing a violent oath, he went after her. Hell, she could move fast in those damn impractical shoes. Today's pair had a bunch of slender black straps, each one sewn with a line of pearls. The wider strap around the ankle bore a sexy studded pattern of pearls alternating with clear sparkling rectangles and white stitching.

Canal Street was a melting pot of tourists and locals. Like most crowded city boulevards, criminals could conduct business within a rock's throw of couples buying a novelty voodoo doll to take home to their kids. Sure enough, hanging out near the front of the tourist place were a couple lookouts, probably for the low-level drug deals happening within. Which told him exactly why she was here.

Unfortunately, those lookouts were damn alert. By the time Rosalinda marched up to the front of the shop, Snake was emerging.

He had the right bad boy look to attract a teenage girl. Dark shaggy hair, a lean, muscled body garbed in trendy jeans. A silver chain strung with religious charms hung from a belt loop and one pocket. He wore fancy athletic shoes and his black muscle shirt showed off tattoos.

While Snake had been alerted to her presence, he hadn't expected her to meet him toe-to-toe, put both her hands on his chest and shove.

He wouldn't stay surprised more than a blink. Lawrence closed that final distance as fast as he'd ever done anything, bodily moving people out of his way. When Snake recovered, his eyes firing,

Lawrence was at her side. While evaluating the new variable gave the bastard pause, it didn't slow Rosalinda's roll in the slightest.

"You think breaking into my home will scare me?" she demanded. "Threatening my people? Shooting a kid? That's who you are? Don't have the balls to bring the fight to me?"

Foot traffic slowed, tourists and locals alike ready for a show. That landmine he'd detected in her earlier was set to go off. If she hadn't been grabbing a tiger by the tail, her courage would have awed him. But he knew too well the fragility of the body containing that force of will.

Snake was barely twenty-five, but he had those too focused eyes that said his world was coated in blood and tears, because that was the way he liked to paint it. Lawrence didn't doubt Rosalinda saw it. She just didn't care.

"Why don't you break into my house while I'm home, Snake?" she said. "Or did you just like playing with my shoes when I wasn't around?"

Fucking hell. Lawrence yanked her out of the way as Snake made a jump at her. It was show, though, because as soon as Lawrence had shoved him back and put his hand on his gun, making it clear he would draw, Snake stopped the forward lunge, spreading out his hands. He gave Lawrence a *fuck you* look, but motioned to the several lowlifes who'd joined him, a signal to hold back. This wasn't coming to a head here. Too public, too many cameras and people.

She'd known what she was doing. To a point.

Snake grinned, a nasty expression. "Oh, I'll come see you, bitch. On my own schedule, not yours."

"I'm not afraid of you, you piece of shit."

Lawrence didn't think the lock between her fiery blue eyes and Snake's cold dark ones broke until he backed her far enough away he could get her headed to the car. Once there, he shoved her stiff form in the passenger seat and closed the door.

Snake had come to the edge of the curb in front of the head shop and was talking trash, making rude gestures in their direction. Now he was striding toward them.

Lawrence put himself between the car and Snake. The man intended only to have the last word, to save face in front of his crew, Lawrence was sure, but he'd keep himself between them.

"When I come for her, I'm going to go straight through you, *cholo*," Snake said, low. "You might want to get out of the way. That cunt ain't worth it."

Christ, he was going to strangle her. Lawrence heard the car door open and held up a hand, hoping it would keep Rosalinda behind him.

"This isn't worth your life," he said. "That's what you're going to lose, you keep on this track. Let it go."

Snake sneered, but shrugged as if the conversation didn't interest him anymore. He turned and sauntered away. Lawrence watched until he disappeared back in the tourist shop before he glanced over his shoulder at Rosalinda. As he suspected, she was standing by the passenger door. She'd been ready to intervene if Snake tried anything with him.

She gave him a challenging look he answered with stone-faced calm. "Will you please get into the fucking car?" he said pleasantly.

A muscle twitched in her jaw, but she responded with an icy nod and compliance, thank God for small miracles.

He got in the driver's seat, started up the car and pulled away from the curb. She said nothing, her hands in her lap, clenched tight as she stared out the window. He didn't say anything either.

Fortunately, they'd left before Snake could have anyone follow them. Her confrontation shouldn't completely ruin the at-home-sick ruse, since she could have personal reasons for being at home that wouldn't exclude such a foolish act. Like being so rattled by the attempts on her life she'd taken a couple days off as sick days.

When they reached the private airport, he parked the car. They were early, though, which gave them time to sit there a few moments. He supposed each of them was doing their own version of settling down.

"I know everything you're going to say," she said at last. "But I needed to do it."

"I know." He saw her flash of surprise as he put a hand on hers. "You thought it out. You confronted him in a crowded public space to minimize the risk. You goaded him, because you want to keep his focus on you, not your people. You also want him to come after you himself, since that makes it more likely he'll be nailed in the act."

On top of all that, she'd shown Snake he wasn't going to back her down. Certain predators fed on fear, and she wasn't giving Snake any extra meals. He could kill her, but he couldn't intimidate her. He would never get that from her, which for some of these guys was half the fun.

The problem was, if someone had something to lose, fear could always find a way in. And she had the kind of life with lots to lose.

"Okay, so maybe I didn't know everything you were going to say," she said after a moment. "I'm sorry, Lawrence. I trust you, but I don't know how to stand behind someone else to fight my battles. It's just how I'm made."

"I get that. But maybe you could trust me to stand at your side." He gave her a hard look. "Don't leave me a step behind like that again. I can anticipate a lot of things, but if I'm dealing with a really smart client who likes to fight her own battles, and a really smart bad guy, then I'm having to watch two fronts."

He'd used logic, and it was the right way to go. Her jaw flexed, then she nodded, a concession. "All right."

"I also want you to remember something else. As smart as you are, Rosalinda, he's a guy who's okay using violence to get his way. His mind operates on a whole different level from yours. You dying while refusing to show him fear? Yeah, that's a form of courage. But so is being smart, letting yourself be protected, so you can keep on living and helping people long after he's rotting in prison or killed on the street. His way of life doesn't come with a long lifespan."

She studied him. "How much effort is it taking you to be all calm and logical like this, rather than shouting at me and shaking me until my teeth rattle?"

He managed a smile, and then he struck. He yanked her over the seat and put his mouth on hers, hot and angry, his grip shifting from the collar of her pretty blouse to the back of her neck as he plundered. When he plunged his hand into her hair, he didn't care that he mussed or tugged on it, hard. He held tight until he'd taken as deep a draught of her mouth as he needed to settle the nerves she'd set on end.

She let herself be kissed, not fighting him, her hands on his face, his shoulder. Through that touch, the way she opened to him, he knew she'd missed having him in her bed last night, as much as he'd hated not being there.

He drew back. "You *ever* do something like that again, I swear to

God I'll go after you with one of your own fucking paddles. That answer your question?"

She curled her hand over his forearm, and her eyes were soft. "Yes, it does. Thank you, Lawrence."

He let her go, rubbed a hand over his face. "Let's go."

CHAPTER SIXTEEN

*G*etting on the private plane was uneventful. The seats were arranged in comfortable groupings, like a living room. Ros spent a portion of the flight on the phone, handling business matters, though she was careful to make it sound as if she was still in New Orleans.

Lawrence chose a seat that kept her in his direct view, but gave her space to work. He didn't get restless. He took a nap. She expected that was a learned skill, recharging when the circumstances allowed it. For a security detail, those circumstances didn't get more optimal than inside an airborne private plane. She wryly reflected that the pilot and flight attendant didn't appear to be on Snake's payroll.

When the attendant checked in to see if they needed anything, Ros was on a call. However, she saw Lawrence gesture to her as he spoke to the woman. When her call was done, she had a fruit, nut and cheese plate at her elbow, along with a fresh Diet Coke over ice.

"Have you been through my underwear drawer to determine my preferences, or just my pantry and refrigerator?"

"I didn't anticipate needing to pick out underwear for you," he said. "But I'll be happy to do that, if you leave the choice in my hands. I try to anticipate my client's needs."

He was more relaxed up here. So was she. She noticed the flight attendant's discreet smile at his response and then she disappeared into her compartment. Ros gestured to Lawrence and he obligingly left his seat, taking the one next to her as she leaned in, forming an intimate bubble around them. "Your client's, or your Mistress's?"

An intriguing light kindled in his eyes, but then she saw him remember last night. "Might not be the best idea to open that door again," he said evenly.

"Tell yourself that. You kicked it open in the car. My lips are still vibrating." She cupped his face, her fingertips sliding along his throat, teasing his beard. She moved forward, brushing her mouth over his. His lips parted, but she tightened her grip on his throat, telling him to stay still as she let her lips play over his. His eyes half-closed, his hand curling on the chair arm.

"So are you anticipating your client's needs, or your Mistress's?" she asked again. "A true answer."

"Not sure there's a difference."

She eased back, her hand lingering at his throat before she plucked at his shirt front, the crisp button-down he was wearing over his well-defined upper body. "I was curious about one thing," she said.

"If you're only curious about one thing, you're way more on top of all of this than I am."

She picked up a cube of cheese. "You might struggle with the personal versus professional question, but you don't seem to have a problem with the sub thing. Many men do at first. You get uncomfortable about it in front of male peers, like Dale or Matt, but that's different. In the room, just you and me, there's very little of that."

He shrugged. "Being in special ops pretty much eliminates most debates on whether I have enough testosterone to carry the man card. I don't struggle with that. Plus my dad taught me that while I should fight for what's right, protect those who need protecting, fighting isn't what wins a woman's heart."

"Oh. What does?"

"Sorry. Trade secret. Can't know unless you have a dick."

She blinked, reached over, and cupped him through his slacks, rubbing her thumb over what was beneath. She suspected he'd already been reacting to their low-level banter, but his cock noticeably responded to her touch. The muscles in his arms twitched, his eyes heating.

"I believe I do have one. Right here." She picked up a cashew in her free hand and offered it, close to his mouth. "So, what's the secret?"

He held her gaze as he took the nut. She caressed his mouth, while fondling him through his clothes. The slacks would make it difficult to hide his full erection if the flight attendant came back. Ros liked that idea. Liked another woman seeing what belonged to her.

She'd shut down so completely last night, she'd suppressed the things she'd wanted to do to bring a proper finish to the night. But they were right there, waiting, just as ready and eager to open things back up again. "Lawrence?"

He gave her a rueful look. His fingers had dug into the chair arms. He knew not to touch her without permission.

"'To win the heart of a woman, *mijo*, prove yourself to *her*, not to those watching.'"

Bless his father. He'd raised his boy right.

"Fair enough." She offered him a piece of melon. This one he took with his hand, but he caught her fingertip briefly between two of his, a gentle tug, before he sampled the fruit. The gesture flavored their sudden erotic intensity with a reassurance. One she appreciated, after the stress of the past day. Far above the earth, balance was easier to find.

She was going to risk upsetting it, but that same balance might make it easier for Lawrence to comply with her next request. "Tell me what that phone call last night was about."

Another kind of tension gripped him. "That an order?"

"Yes. It is."

He tapped the arm of the seat. "You're a pain in the ass."

"Why, yes. I am. Literally and figuratively." She leaned in and spoke against his ear, making sure her bottom lip brushed his throat beneath the lobe, before she closed both lips on it, a nip. "I've given a great deal of thought to the kind of pain I can dish out on your ass. How much depends on how much you keep trying to play this game of responding to me while holding yourself out of reach."

When he stiffened, her hand landed on his forearm, tightened. "No. I know you're not doing it on purpose. You don't have that kind of manipulation in you. Something in you wants what I can give you. Backing away from it last night wasn't about my security. Not for either of us. It was about that phone call, and my anger at being out of control."

"Our personal shit could still impact my effectiveness."

"It won't. Want to know how I know it?" A grim smile curved her lips. "It's a trade secret, but I'll tell you anyway. If you ask."

He gave her a wary look. "Okay. I'm asking."

"Other than us, there were four people in the waiting room for private plane departures. Who posed the greatest threat?"

He studied her. "None of them were a physical threat. But the teenager in the back corner was pissed his parents were making him go to the Bahamas instead of on a ski trip with his friends. His dagger looks could have taken out everyone in the waiting area. Mass collateral damage."

She gave him a satisfied look. He shook his head. "You really are a pain in the ass."

"Still waiting on an answer. Phone call."

He sighed, ran a hand over his mouth. "How much grief can I expect if I refuse to tell you?"

"I'll punish you for it, to restore the balance you'll need from denying me, but I'll leave it alone until you're ready to tell me. That's not the major issue, though."

She met his gaze. "I've had some time to think about it since last night. I'm done with the half-in, half-out conflict. I'm not going to let my irritation with uncertainty, with feeling out of control of the Snake situation, dictate you and me. You need to make the same choice. Either you're fully committed to exploring your submissive side, the way I can tell you want to do it, which includes opening up the sticky emotional stuff, or you turn this job over to someone else. Because I want you, and I won't be around you and not be able to have you. Think it through. You can start talking whenever you're ready, but stay where you are."

With that, she returned her attention to her refreshments and her tablet. While she ate, she added markups to the presentation Abby had prepared.

Lawrence stayed quiet, but she was keenly aware of his thinking process as the minutes passed. It vibrated from him like an electrical field.

At length, she laid her hand on his thigh. He had his legs slightly open in his resting pose, but she added some pressure to her grip, just to see what he would do. A stillness, a couple heartbeats, and then he adjusted, spreading his thighs wider. Still a casual sprawl, but the response it sent to her hit all the markers. She curled her fingers under the inseam, digging in, the heel of her hand on his inner thigh. Not indecently placed for the attendant's comings and goings, but it showed she had intimate knowledge of the body she was touching. She wanted anyone watching, particularly him, to know it. A mark of ownership. A ripple went through his thigh muscles as he received that message.

She continued to work until he shifted. She glanced his way, and he offered a slight nod. He didn't look comfortable, but he did look resolved. She put the tablet in energy-saver mode and gave him her full attention.

"My ex-girlfriend..." he began slowly. "We were together about eight years, off and on."

It confirmed her original thought about his townhouse being another woman's nest, except for the kitchen. "You seem like a traditional guy. Marriage didn't come up?"

"It did. Valentina never wanted to. Said she didn't want someone to control her, and that's how she saw marriage."

"How do you see it?" At his quizzical look, she tightened her grip on his leg. "The nice thing about a conversation like this is that it doesn't have to be a straight line. We can take it a little at a time, keep it relaxed."

That kind of meandering gave her more data. But those detours were necessary for another reason. From the second he started to speak about Valentina, his body language changed significantly. Rigid, closed. A lot of pain there.

"I don't see marriage like she does," he said simply. "But even dating a SEAL long-term is tough, let alone being married to one. Except for Valentina, I never got that far in a relationship."

Ros guessed Lawrence was in his early thirties. Eight years with Valentina meant he'd spent a large part of his adult life committed to the same person. Not much time to cultivate another long-term relationship.

"What broke you up after eight years?"

A flex in his jaw, another shift that showed his discomfort with the conversation. "She drinks too much."

She'd hoped she was wrong. She'd wanted to believe she'd misinterpreted the familiarity of his behavior. A coldness settled in her lower belly, but she pushed that away for now. The situation might have key differences that could result in a better outcome. She wouldn't close herself down to that possibility. But she couldn't deny a pall had fallen on the conversation, now that she knew for sure.

"She's an alcoholic," she said.

"Yeah," he said after a minute. "Yeah, pretty much."

If he hadn't been able to say that, she might have called it quits right there. But she could tell he'd held back to be kind to his ex, not because he denied the truth.

"It's been going on a while," he continued. "Everyone knows the drill. They've put it on TV enough, the whole progression. Funny how that doesn't change anything. The person still does the same pointless things; lying, blaming everyone else, or arguing they don't have a problem."

While friends and family members struggled with the same pointless efforts to deal with it. But she held that thought. "Was she the one who ended things?"

"Yeah. And no. It became a cycle. It would get bad, she'd take off, send me a text she was done. I'd get on with life, and she'd cycle back. Since I was away a lot, sometimes I was here for it. Other times, the cycle fell more on her mom. Zoey. That's who called last night. Valentina fell off the wagon, took off again. She wanted to know if I'd seen her."

"Does she still have access to your townhouse? A key?"

"Yeah. Until I left the teams, I was gone as much as I was there, so I let her keep living there, even when we weren't together."

Ros took her hand away. "So you're still together."

His jaw flexed again. "No. I don't see her as my girlfriend anymore. She pretty much...she killed that, the ninth, tenth, or eightieth time she did this. I don't really respond to her that way. But I do see her as mine to look after."

"You said you've never done what we've done, yet you have an incredibly well-developed innate response to it," Ros said slowly. "Did she top you?"

"No...not that way. I took care of her."

"You served her. The harder you tried, the more she demanded. Her difficulties, the way she detached herself from you, made her seem like a Mistress in your mind. You structured it that way mentally, to find what you needed in the relationship."

He lifted a shoulder, obviously not wanting to look where she was pointing.

She settled back, though nothing felt settled inside her. She pushed the rest of the food to the side, took a sip of the soda. "Do you know about Laurel?"

He inclined his head. "I put the pieces together from newspaper articles. Wouldn't mind hearing the story from you, though. If it's not too painful."

It was. When it had happened, the agony had been unbelievable. Breath-stealing. Only Abby and the rest of the women of their circle had helped Ros survive it. But she could talk about it now, because his ex, the specter of who and what she was, called up Laurel like a mirror image.

"She, Abby and I were a trinity. Since college." Ros withdrew a slim metal case from her bag, like a credit card container, only this one held a dainty chain with a triquetra on it. She rarely wore it, but she kept it with her. Abby had one. Laurel had been cremated with hers.

When she showed it to Lawrence, he touched it gently with a fingertip, his green eyes full of care for her, because he read way too much from her features. He could do that so easily, turn things away from himself, focus on her and what she needed. She had to contain her reaction to that, too, as she tucked it away again.

"She met a man and fell in love. She was like us, a Domme, but being a Domme doesn't make you any less susceptible to the vulnerabilities that come with love. He was more vanilla, an alpha secure enough to bottom for her, but he never had a true sub orientation. That works for some couples, the same way a lot of submissives are married to spouses who aren't Dominant, but they figure out ways to make it work. Just as some don't."

She paused. "Their problems didn't have anything to do with the Domme/sub side of things. He had a temper, which was worse when he drank, and he drank more and more. But she loved him. She kept thinking they'd figure it out, kept giving him chances. When he left bruises on her, broke bones, she'd leave him. But she always went back. It drove a wedge between us. I told her I couldn't be around her when she was with him."

What had she said, about the plane being high enough above the worries below to restore balance? His response to her question, what she was telling him now, made it feel like they were about to take a nose-dive. Her voice had gone flatter. Lawrence's ex was filling her mind, a faceless void.

"Rosalinda." He had his hand on hers on the chair arm. She closed her eyes, accepting the reassurance even as the cold ball in the pit of her stomach told her she was perilously close to this same damn shit, all over again. "You don't have to do this."

Wow. It was as if he'd directly answered her thought, causing a precipitous sinking sensation within her. She wasn't ready to let him go, but she might be tethering herself to someone who would drag her toward that same cliff.

Damn it, she'd started the story with a purpose, so she'd finish it. She needed to see how he'd react to it.

"Abby would still meet Laurel for lunch, go to movies. She kept me up to date on what was happening with her. Whenever Laurel wasn't with him, we were a trinity again. If she went back, it would be just her and Abby. So in time, the trinity felt far more fragile, because there became an ever-widening gap of things we wouldn't talk about. I analyzed and analyzed what the fuck was wrong with her until I was exhausted by it." She glanced at him. "You read the article about what happened to her."

"Yeah. The end result."

"He lost his temper, hit her in the head. He stormed back into the house. She tried to get up, was disoriented, and fell into the pool. So she drowned. Neighbor heard him crying and they found him holding her, saying 'I didn't mean it. I didn't mean it.' Like that meant a fucking thing."

Useless anger was always there, pressure behind a dam. Letting it out did nothing but temporarily ease the pressure before it refilled. "Abby...she has a better time accepting it, though that's not the right word. He's in prison. One day he'll be out on parole, maybe. I don't keep track of it, because I can't trust myself not to do something crazy, like stand outside the prison to shoot him in the head the second they let him out."

She took a breath. "Abby was the one who came up with the idea of Laurel Grove. We started it to help not just the typical victims of domestic abuse, those trapped financially or by lack of education, or learned family behavior, but those like Laurel, too. Those who *could* walk away, but they just don't. Loving someone is about more than sacrifice. It's also about caring for and protecting yourself. Not in a selfish way, but in a way that honors what love is supposed to be between you."

She turned her attention outward, to him. A handsome, strong man with scars, with pain in his eyes. Laurel had been beautiful and strong, too. And fatally flawed. "Do you get that, Lawrence? Have you learned that lesson?"

His brow creased. "I'm not sure that's the same scenario."

"Of course it is," she snapped. "If you love someone, what do you want for them? For them to be happy, healthy. For them to find joy in life. To not be a drain on them emotionally, physically, if you can do anything possible to avoid it. Right?"

Her tone was shutting him down. A moment before, his desire to offer her comfort, help her deal with her pain, had been plain to see. Now that she'd turned the spotlight toward him, his expression was guarded, a wall forming. Remembering Dale's expression from the other night, when Lawrence's phone had rung, she knew this wasn't the first time someone had had this conversation with him. But she apparently wanted to be foolish, and persisted anyway.

"You have a responsibility to safeguard those things for *yourself*, if your partner stops being able to value them," she said. "You give yourself the love they're supposed to. Protect and care for yourself."

She gripped his forearm. "It's what someone who truly loves you wants you to do for yourself."

Alcoholics had no control over their impulse to drink and yet, in one of those perverse things about human nature, they were expert manipulators. Hook them up with an alpha male sub, equally driven to protect, to serve, to submit to their needs, and they could empty him out to the bone.

But as she knew too well, it didn't work only on a sub. It worked on anyone, top, bottom, vanilla, kink, who loved someone else past the point of self-care. Which was pretty much anyone who truly fell in love.

Laurel's loss had committed Ros to the ideas she'd just expressed, but it was her developing feelings for him that made her want to hammer those ideas into him with untold levels of ferocity. She wanted to stretch him out on a rack and tear him open, purge all the bad feelings associated with his ex and give him the freedom to submit, surrender, without that baggage.

But she didn't see any change in his defensive body language. He was a man who took the time to consider information. Her desire to see him do a one-eighty on self-destructive behavior wasn't realistic.

But she couldn't go down this road again. Just the thought of it made her feel sick. He was here, right under her fingertips, yet what vibrated from him told her he'd fully withdrawn. He didn't want to talk about this.

Okay. She forced herself to rein it back. She'd had plenty of practice keeping her feelings within controlled boundaries since Laurel's death, since the promise she'd made to Abby. She could be a Mistress to him and not let herself step too far outside those lines. She reminded herself she and Lawrence had a timeline. She hadn't promised him forever, and he hadn't asked. They were safe for one another.

"We're not in a long-term relationship." She was grimly proud she was able to speak the words in an even tone. "I recognize it's your life and choices. But I do care about you, Lawrence. So I hope you'll think about it."

She'd gotten his attention with the long-term comment, a flash she couldn't read. Unfortunately, his relief when she backed off the subject of his ex was clear as a neon billboard.

She went back to her tablet, to all appearances fine with everything, even as what was inside her didn't feel fine at all. But it would be. She would lock it down, drive it out of her head, heart, gut; wherever she found the infection that led to caring too much for someone hell-bent on self-destruction.

Lawrence would be exactly what she'd intended him to be. An intriguing male sub she'd enjoy to the fullest, within safe boundaries. Those boundaries were a little wider and fuzzier around the edges with him, admittedly, but after accepting the value they each had to offer one another, she'd cut him loose with affection, nothing but the pleasure of fond memories left behind. And that would be that.

When they reached the hotel room tonight, she'd take them both to an easier place. She was the one in control. She could do that.

～

She kept that resolve through the arrival in Indianapolis, and picking up the rental car. She let him drive to Bloomington. Conversation between them was pleasant, though he was mostly quiet and she worked.

At the hotel, she handled check-in, requesting two card keys. Abby had set them up in a suite, which had a king-sized bed plus a foldout sofa in the separate living room area. Keeping Lawrence close, but giving Ros the choice of how much space to put between them. Her friend knew her well.

They went up in the elevator without saying anything, but she noted he positioned himself not at her side, but slightly ahead of her. As the elevator opened on each floor, she had a human shield in front of her. When they reached their floor, he stepped out, glanced around, then nodded to her.

Now she took the lead, headed for their room. But at the door, he extended his hand for one of the key cards, obviously intending to clear the room first.

"Do we really think Snake is Jason Bourne?" She shot him an amused look. "We've done a lot to cover our tracks coming here."

"If we treat him like he's that smart, then it's less likely he'll be able to sneak up on us, right?" Lawrence checked the room, then returned to her, picking up the luggage items he'd put down in the entry way, moving them to the bedroom. "Gangs like his aren't just a bunch of street corner thugs. The grandkids who know how to re-program the cable box at age three grow up to be street criminals as well as straight A students. And they watch a lot of the same crime and reality shows, which do give away some trade secrets."

"Okay." She gave him that point. "But...we're safe for the moment?"

He nodded. "Do you want to do room service? Or we could do delivery or go out. Your preference."

"Are you hungry?"

He shrugged. "I could eat. Whenever you're ready. No rush, though, if you have other things you need to do. I'll stay out of your hair until you're ready to go somewhere."

She nodded. He turned to go do whatever she expected staying out of her hair entailed for him, but she brought him up short with a hand that landed on his shirt front, curled in the fabric.

When he glanced back at her, he shifted his weight, anticipating her drawing him to her. She didn't. She held that distance, but kept her grip.

They'd both shown their ability to maintain a casual façade. She was done with it. She didn't like the weight, sitting low in her stomach like a bad lunch.

He knew the discussion on the plane had changed things between them, but he wasn't sure how to deal with that. She could see it in his eyes. Fortunately, she *did* know how to deal with it. It might make the problem better or worse, but it would change the feel of it, and that was her immediate goal. Sediment couldn't be removed as long as it was packed at the bottom of the lake.

"Take off the shirt and give it to me."

A couple potent heartbeats. He opened his mouth, closed it, and she saw the flash of need in his gaze.

"You want to make it better, Lawrence. Your obedience will do that."

He met her gaze, and that weight between them pulled on her heartstrings, made her want to say things she couldn't say. She tightened her grip instead, a silent reinforcement of the command.

She knew how to break down walls while holding onto a shield that would guard the most vulnerable parts of them both. It was as he'd said. She loved being a Mistress, and she was damn good at it. A good scene could take out the emotional garbage, even if it was only temporary.

As he moved his fingers to the buttons of his shirt, he paused briefly over her hand clasped there, caressed it. He'd decided to believe her. Trust her. That was half the battle. Her gut loosened and her senses sharpened, narrowing her focus to what mattered most in this moment.

He opened the shirt and shrugged out of it, handing her the

garment. She closed her fingers tight into the fabric, carrying his body heat.

"Take off all the rest. Kneel in front of the coffee table. Your ass on your heels, your knees spread out, hands laced behind your head. Head up and eyes straight ahead, staring at the wall. Stay that way until I tell you otherwise. It could be awhile."

She moved away, crossed the threshold into the bedroom. And shut the door.

Once there, she leaned against it, taking a long, steadying breath. Being by herself for a few minutes would help. She didn't have to guard her expressions and body language against an overflow of feelings. She could let them rise to the top, spill away. Leave only what mattered.

She put her suitcase on the bed and opened it up. As she'd proven the first night in his kitchen, she didn't have to have a lot on hand to execute an effective scene. The most intense playground was within his mind and hers, anyway. But the right props could make it far more pleasurable.

She decided what she would wear, laid it out, along with a couple other things. Flying via private plane had allowed her to bring some items she wouldn't have brought if she'd had to deal with a commercial flight security check.

She sat on the end of the bed, needing a couple minutes to get her mind right. If she approached her desire from the wrong direction, driven by the unhappy feelings the plane conversation had raised, she could damage his trust. Yet he also needed her extremes of emotion to release his own feelings. So she'd walk that tightrope and see where it took them.

Seventeen minutes later, she'd changed her clothes, checked herself in the mirror, and deemed herself ready. Head and heart in the right place.

She opened the door.

CHAPTER SEVENTEEN

*L*awrence was caught off guard, first by that unexpected command, then her departure from the room. He watched her stride into the bedroom, ass twitching under that form-fitting skirt she'd worn with her blue blouse and matching heels, total sexy woman business wear. The closing of the door resounded in his chest.

During the painful cordiality since that unfortunate plane discussion—several hours that had felt like several days—he'd been thinking of ways to restore their earlier ease with one another. Like getting a pizza, watching some TV.

Her mind had obviously been running on a different track from his.

Some part of him must have been aware, however. In the time it took her to issue the order and disappear, his muscles tightened, and a raw coil of desire low in his belly told his cock to ready itself for whatever she needed. Even if what she needed was simply to torment it with what she wasn't going to give it.

He hadn't wanted to talk about Valentina, damn it. And worse, he knew his reaction had bothered Rosalinda, dredged up bad things for her. Maybe this was a way he could make up for it, return things to a good footing. Even if that was the wrong answer to it. But wasn't that always the way he felt about Valentina? Unsettled, inadequate, frustrated, unhappy.

He really didn't like what Rosalinda had said, so decisively, about them not being a long-term thing. Not that he'd made any plans but... that was the thing. He hadn't planned for an ending. It sounded like she had.

Thoughts like that made his erection flag. He considered knocking on her door, coming up with some security-related excuse to take a raincheck. Or he could safeword. That was the deal with this stuff, right?

But he didn't. He told himself he didn't want to disappoint her, but he wondered if he was also choosing to believe what she'd said, that his obedience could make things better, for both of them. He was putting his trust in her. A new and unsettling thought.

He'd been standing here about five minutes, thinking. She might come out any minute and see he hadn't followed her direction. They could talk it out, but the moment would be lost. He would have disappointed her. He'd done enough of that for one day.

He stripped off his clothes, put them neatly by a chair and went to the coffee table. As he knelt there, heavy anticipation settled over him, but also, remarkably, a tentative calm. The promise of peace. When he laced his hands behind his head, straightened his back and stared straight ahead at the painting over the pale blue sofa—a quarry at sunset, likely a Bloomington landmark—that feeling increased. So did his arousal, his cock jutting out from between his thighs. Just from complying with his Mistress's desires.

He hoped she was pleased. He didn't want to think about anything other than that. He stayed in the position she'd dictated as the minutes ticked by and damn, if he didn't keep getting harder, every minute he spent waiting, stripped, in a subservient position. It was almost as overwhelming as having someone rubbing his cock while he stayed motionless like this. The things that happened to him under her command continued to surprise him.

The door to the bedroom opened. He knew to keep his eyes straight ahead, even though he wanted to look at her. Fortunately, she rewarded him by coming to stand in front of the sofa, the coffee table between them. The sight of her was enough to have him swallowing, hard.

She was wearing her pearl-studded heels, his shirt, and nothing else. She'd buttoned the middle button, just beneath her breasts, so it

263

gaped, showing him ample amounts of what was above. The tails shifted below as she moved, revealing trimmed pussy, silky thighs. He thought of her legs in those sharp heels, wrapped around his waist. He thought of how she'd clamped them over his back when he'd served her with his mouth, a moment both too far away and pretty damn recent.

A little while ago, she'd asked if he was hungry. Now he was ravenous.

Her gaze slid over him, judging. He instinctively straightened his back, tightened the lacing of his fingers. He kept his gaze in a straight line, even though she'd likely caught his slight movements as he'd taken in her full appearance. She'd dropped something on the side chair as she came out of the room, but he didn't look.

She moved from behind the table, circled around behind him. When something touched his side, he realized she was now holding a crop. "Very pleasing form," she said. "You follow orders well, sailor. You may respond appropriately."

"Thank you, ma'am."

A tap from the crop, and he corrected himself. "Thank you, Mistress."

"Hold the position."

Slap!

She hit him across his back, then his ass. She was good at snapping it there, creating a stinging sensation that warmed the flesh. His balls drew up, and his cock got stiffer, especially when she moved to his front, giving him that choice view again. She flicked the end of the crop over his dick, those tiny little snaps over it, around it. He held, even as his skin flinched at the contact. Then she brought the crop up to his face, caressing his throat and shoulders with it. She put it under his jaw, and locked gazes with him.

"Mine," she said. "Every inch of you. Every part of you. Nothing held back. Is that what you want? Do you want me to take it all?"

There were a lot of layers to the question. It was a scene, a session, whatever the fuck they called it. Some level of fantasy and play, but it really didn't feel like play at all when the two people engaged in it wanted it to be real. He knew she wanted honesty.

"Part of me...yeah. I want that. Another part...not sure. Not sure if I know how to do that. Or if it's something you'd want. I feel like I need to protect you from how much I want. Or protect myself. And I want to say I'm sorry. For not being able to be...what you need."

Christ, that last part hurt to say out loud. But did any of that make sense to her? Aside from that, how did she pull this out of him? There was so much that an operator had to keep inside to make everything work, to get the job done. Keeping it inside became ingrained. Yet somehow, when she put him on his knees, turned on this part of him, it made the words come in a way he didn't expect.

But it was apparently the right response, because her blue eyes became even deeper blue and her mouth, while still that firm bud-shape, eased enough to make him want to taste her there. And everywhere.

"I decide if you meet my needs sufficiently, Lawrence."

But he wanted to exceed expectations. Always.

"You know your safe words. Say them to me."

"Gray to slow it down, evaluate. Sanctuary to stop."

"Good." She came around the table, sat herself down on it. There was very little room between him and the table, so when she spread her thighs to flank him, her knees pressed against his sides.

When his eyes shifted, she tsked. "Eyes straight ahead," she reminded him. "You're a statue until I tell you otherwise. I want your shoulders aching, Lawrence, those powerful muscles in your thighs straining."

She opened a packet and rolled the condom on him, and he savored her touch, even as functional as she made it. "Don't want you to make a mess on this rug, if you lose control. Your immediate reaction is to deny that you will. That you won't do anything I don't command. But my will may be for you to lose control, Lawrence. Remember that. You follow my leads on this. Not your own."

She tapped his hip with the crop. "Spread your knees wider. Back up far enough so if I have you bend forward, your head will be in my lap."

He complied, though his knees out wide like that made movement awkward. He felt the pull in his groin, the increased exposure of his cock and balls. She held the crop up in front of his mouth. "Kiss this and thank me for what I'm about to do."

The end of the crop had a short tassel of slender strips of fabric, rather than a loop. As he put his lips to it, he saw a metallic glint to the strips, explaining why they had a bite like multiple tiny knives. "Thank you, Mistress."

It got into his head, doing that. That crazy flopping in his lower belly made him want to kiss the crop again, thank her again. She took it away, but she praised him.

"Good." She started up again, doing those teasing stings on his cock, his inner thighs, spread wide for her. She went after his chest, his nipples. His body shuddered, twitched. His dick kept getting harder, seeming to feed on the pain. Or maybe it fed on her avid attention, the way she wet her lips as she left marks on him.

She changed the intensity, feathering the end of the crop over the head of his cock, down the shaft, his balls, hanging free and vulnerable between his legs. She thumped him there, lightly.

"Did you know a woman's clitoris and the head of man's cock are essentially the same thing, Lawrence?"

"No, Mistress."

"Some men get hung up on the whole gay versus straight thing, but our bodies don't care. They're made for sex. Are you a man who gets hung up on things like that, Lawrence?"

"I don't know, Mistress. I'm not attracted to men."

"No, you're not. Your eyes make a meal of me, every time you look at my body. It's a good thing it's done with the proper amount of respect or reverence, or you'd be blindfolded right now, to teach you better manners."

He bit back a muttered oath as her clever strokes with that crop had his hips wanting to follow its movements. He thought about what she'd said, about putting his head in her lap. He wanted to eat her pussy again, even though it would only make him harder. She liked to deprive him, and something in him got off on it. But she had something different in mind.

She rose. Staring straight ahead as ordered gave him an incredible view of her breasts, the hint of her hips again, the folds of her sex. Then she disappeared, circling behind him. "Lean forward toward the table. Brace your hands on the corners."

When he did it, her crop followed the valley of his spine to his buttocks and then probed between them. Since she'd had him widen his stance, the feel of it teasing his rim sent further jolts of sensation through him. She trailed the tassels down one cheek.

"Beautiful," she murmured. "You are incredibly beautiful, Lawrence. Every muscle defined, your thighs and arms, all of it so strong. I want to taste it, every inch. You care for your body, because it has had to serve you in some incredibly difficult situations. You have to make sure it's ready for that. Don't you?"

"Yes, Mistress."

He couldn't figure out where she was headed on all of this, but he expected that was what she wanted. For him to stop trying to anticipate, and simply respond. He was used to planning a few steps ahead, but he was equally ready for things to turn out different from the plan. He'd never realized the skill would be useful under a Mistress's control.

Now her hand was on him, and the contrast with the crop was so significant his whole body wanted to gravitate in that direction. He'd lost count of how often he'd thought of the palm of her hand slapping his dick, and the way he'd practically come just from that.

"Maybe you think this will put that emotional mess I raised on the plane back in the box where you have to keep it. But I don't serve your needs. You serve mine. And I don't want those emotions tucked back in a box."

She leaned in, spoke against his ear. "I want to lay them out, flatten them like paper, and then set the whole lot of them on fire, burning them to fucking ash. Close your eyes, Lawrence. Keep them closed."

He was thankful she didn't want a response in words. As he shut his eyes, she stepped around him, close enough her body brushed him. The shift of the table suggested she'd moved behind then onto it, perhaps kneeling on the surface, close to his face. His lips wanted to part, show his willingness to taste. Then something touched them, something that made him flinch and draw back before he could stop himself.

He froze, fighting a tug of war between safewording and disappointing her. He hadn't let go of the table, though. He hadn't fucked that up.

"What did I tell you a few moments ago, Lawrence? About a woman's clitoris and the head of a man's cock?"

"That they're the same thing." His voice was tight.

"But you don't believe that, do you? Yes or no answer."

"No, Mistress. A dick is nothing like your sweet pussy."

She chuckled warmly.

"I disagree. I'm wearing a strap-on, Lawrence. Every time your mouth touches it on the outside, I feel it. That's because it has a dual head. When you put your mouth on the outside shaft, the inside one pushes deeper inside me, like your cock. There's a clitoral stimulator, so that pressure also plays on my clit, gets me even more excited."

Her hand was on his hair, stroking, and her thigh slid against his side as she put one foot on the floor next to him, between his spread arm and the table. Her other leg was still bent, knee braced on the table, because he could feel it pressed against his other forearm.

He'd expected a rubbery scent, conjuring an image of packaged dildos in a sex toy shop. Instead the strap-on smelled like aroused female, her honey scent. What had brushed his cheek was smooth and hard.

"It's stainless steel, Lawrence. Like you, since your cock is steel hardness beneath a thin velvet sheath of flesh. This strap-on is also warm. But reversible."

His brow creased, and he heard her throaty chuckle. "The warmth is an internal setting, a nice feature of this model. What I mean by reversible is, when I know you're ready, I'm going to pull out the part that's inside me, turn it around, put it inside your tight, stubborn ass. It will be coated in my arousal. So open your mouth and lubricate this end, because that's what will go inside me next. You want to tend to your Mistress's comfort, don't you?"

She was spinning pictures in his head, and she was damn good at it. Having his eyes closed helped. When his lips parted, reluctant, she made a little purring sound that diluted that hesitation.

"There you go. Play over it like you did my pussy the other night. Use that clever tongue. Remember, the head of a cock is like my clit. Every movement you make against it I can feel. And if you swallow it to the root, your mouth will be on my pussy, won't it?"

She was the devil. The kind of devil a man craved. Even though what he had his mouth on was shaped like a man's dick, she'd planted the right visuals. He licked, stroked, imagining it as her pussy, the hard nub of her clit, getting more and more swollen from arousal.

She'd given him an irresistible incentive to take the thing into his throat. He slid down to the base, and his lips touched her cunt, her honey taste. He inhaled her scent up close and personal, which gave him additional incentive to move his lips over the steel cock, getting it lubed up as he strained for every contact with her flesh. The effort almost choked him, but he fought his gag reflex.

She tightened her hand in his hair, holding him, and he could hear her little gasps, feel the movement of her hips, her legs, bumping against him. So caught up in her pleasure, he didn't realize for a few seconds that she was actively fucking his mouth with the dildo. When he did, he was in a part of his head he wouldn't willingly abandon. Giving his Mistress pleasure, every lick and push sending a reaction between her legs. He could imagine the undulation of her body, the quiver of her breasts. It wasn't about him sucking a guy's dick. It had never been about that at all.

"There we go. My very, very good boy." She didn't say it in a patronizing, weird way. More like how a guy said, "Who's your Daddy?" to a girl he was fucking senseless. He understood that a little better now.

She withdrew, caressing his hair, his neck and shoulder, and then she was making some adjustments. Probably reversing it, as she'd said. Which gave him a really strong desire to open his eyes, watch her bring that thing out of her, turn it around, put the other side in.

"I'm not entirely cruel," she said. "The side that was inside me is smaller. I won't stretch you too hard this first time. Since I expect you've never had anything up there except a doctor's finger, we'll take it easy on you. It doesn't hurt, sailor. Not if you stay relaxed and listen to your Mistress. Understand?"

"Yes, ma'am." Then his fingers clutched the table as her hand circled his cock, a tight, squeezing grip that wrested a groan from him. He tried to stay still, but his hips jerked, and he paid the price for it with her sharp tone.

"Do you have my permission to move, Lawrence, let alone act like you're fucking something?"

"No, ma'am. No Mistress. Sorry. Just...couldn't help myself."

"No, you can't. Because you're all worked up. But I expect you to exercise better control. Don't let it happen again."

She ran her hand down his back, in between his buttocks. She was putting something inside him, her own fingers. Two of them, easing in. He realized she had some type of finger glove on, because her nail didn't feel sharp.

"You've slicked the steel up nicely, but I'm also adding some lubricant to make sure. I don't want to hurt you, Lawrence. Not that way. There are better ways I can make you hurt."

A quiver ran through his arms. This wasn't anywhere near the most physically demanding thing he'd ever done, and yet his body was acting stressed. As if the places she was taking his mind were breaking him down in unexpected ways. She seemed to know it, because her free hand caressed his back and shoulders, soothing. What was going on between his buttocks set off spirals of sensation that had his thigh muscles bunching with the effort of not moving.

"You told me this was a limit, Lawrence. Do you want me to proceed? Do you need to safeword?"

He drew in a deep breath through his nose, let it out. "No Mistress."

"Good. Now, relax. Push out against me. Easy, easy..." she almost hummed it. That slick hard heat went past his muscles and then it was there, all in, all so full. A faint burning, but nothing bad. Not at all.

As she pushed herself in to the hilt, she was flush against his back, laying her body against him. She'd removed his shirt so it was all her. Her nipples were firm, her breasts soft. He closed his eyes even tighter, a sound coming from his throat.

"You like that, hmm? The feel of my breasts against your back, my hips molding to your ass, my thighs sliding alongside the inside of yours. Who is fucking you, Lawrence? Is a man fucking you?"

He shook his head.

"When it's good, when it's right, this is how it feels to a woman, too. Like he's got you, he's deep inside you, helping you feel everything. You're safe and flying at the same time, holding onto him with everything you've got. And you have to use your words, sailor. Is a man fucking you?"

"No, ma'am. It's sure as fuck not."

"No, it's not." She pressed in deep and hummed in her throat, as she wrapped her arm around his chest, the other hand on his hip. "It's a Mistress. I plan to fuck and use you hard until I come, Lawrence. You're not going to come until I say so, are you?"

"No, ma'am." Though he might have to make a deal with Satan to live up to that intention, because Satan's Mistress knew exactly what she was doing. He expected she could make him come in a matter of strokes. Any control he imagined he had was merely illusion.

"Good. No more talking at all. I want to use you, Lawrence, get lost in my head, in working you. You stay still and take it."

He braced, but there was no bracing for this. She kept up the thrusting, a rhythmic rise and fall that drew sensation up through his balls and cock, through his whole body, with every stroke. Her gasps, her moans, her muttered curses at how fucking sweet he felt, how tight his ass was, how much she wanted from him, tested his control as much as the physical stimulation.

Her nails scraped his chest, leaving tracks. When she went over his nipples, tingles jolted through him as well. She put her teeth to his neck, his shoulder, and then she ramped things up. She started to hammer into him, so forcefully he had to brace himself. He was going to have rug burns on his knees.

His cock was doing a drum beat against his sac with her movements, shooting all sorts of want through the base. He fought off the eight million messages that rhythmic movement sent to his brain. All saying the same thing.

Come. Come. Please, fuck, let me come.

She knew what she was doing, because among her own whispered words of pleasure was praise for him.

"So good... So good for your Mistress. Such control. I'm so proud of you. I've got you, Lawrence. I've got you..."

And then the one that meant everything. "Mine. All of it is mine. Your body, your responses. All of it. Tell me."

"Yes," he managed in a hoarse voice. "Yes, Mistress. Yours."

"Then come for me."

The climax took him violently, his hips jerking as she pumped into him, hitting whatever she was hitting inside that practically made his eyes roll up into his head and pass out from the power of it. The table ended up against the sofa, the wall behind it the only thing strong enough to stop their forward motion. He groaned, cursed, bellowed. He'd never made a lot of sound when it came to sex, and now he sounded like a rutting bull, but he couldn't stop himself.

Nothing could stop him but her, and she kept him going, long past the last spurt of semen into the full condom. Even when she slowed, she kept stroking as he shuddered in her arms. His chest was burning, telling him she'd scored him with her nails. His knees were raw from the rug. And his ass was burning because she'd fucked him just as hard as she'd promised. His shoulder ached where she'd bitten him. His Mistress had left her marks on him again.

All he wanted was more of them. But he couldn't speak. His lips weren't working right, and somehow he'd gone from being braced over the coffee table to having his cheek down flat against it, his hands still gripping the corners, but his elbows slightly bent, like a bird in flight.

She pressed kisses on the back of his neck, his shoulders, along the valley of his spine. She eased out of him, whispered, "Stay here, don't move." Then she was back, with a warm washcloth she rolled up and placed against his rim, his buttocks holding it as she removed the condom and took care of it, cleaning him up there as well.

"I can..."

"Sssh." A reproving tap of the crop she'd apparently kept close to hand. "I didn't tell you to speak, Lawrence. Be still."

With the pressure of her hands, she moved him away from the table. "Follow me, love. You can open your eyes." She kept her hand trailing on the back of his neck, a little tug on his hair. She didn't intend for him to get to his feet. He followed her where she led, moving on his hands and knees, until he reached the easy chair. She'd put the shirt back on, this time a couple more buttons done, though he still saw cleavage and hints of her legs. She'd added a lacy pair of panties. She sat down in the chair, curling her legs up, and patted the space of cushion by her folded shins. "Put your head here. Lean against the chair."

When he did, she had brought bottled water, a pack of crackers. She gave him some of the water, let him drink it himself rather than feeding it to him. He wasn't as out of it as he'd been on the club night, but he was affected enough to wonder why he'd been on missions far more grueling than this where he'd been able to find more brain cells at the end. This was like being drugged, in a good way, but nothing responding the way he expected.

Subspace.

He'd heard of it. Read about it. Seen it, but hadn't really believed it. He'd decided it was a scenario where the person experiencing it had decided to surrender everything, was "allowing" themselves to let the brain stop working. Trusting the Master or Mistress enough to do that, but still a conscious decision.

Now he wasn't sure of that part of it. Even right now, all these thoughts, they were like bubbles going by, him poking at them with languorous movements of his mind, not really caring if they burst or kept on floating. Pretty, shiny things.

He chuckled at himself. It was the first easy smile he'd had since the plane. Her hand paused on his hair, then continued, that slow, easy stroke. He thought if he looked up, she'd be smiling at him the same way. That was good. He wanted her smiles.

His temple was against her thigh, and he coiled a hand around her calf, fingers stroking. A sigh lifted and lowered his shoulders.

"There we go," she said quietly. "Just let it be, Lawrence. Let it go. It's enough for now. For both of us."

After a time, she clicked on the TV. He may have slept. He was good at sleeping in unusual positions. He should have woken cold, but instead he found a blanket around him. She couldn't have left without him knowing, because his hand was still on her calf. Maybe she'd brought the blanket earlier, draped it over the chair and then put it over him. Caring for him. He'd given her everything, and she'd cared for him. Told him with that blanket he'd pleased her.

She was right. It was enough. For this moment in time, it was everything. The other things, earlier problems, could remain dormant.

"I'm moving to the bed," she said, a sudden break in the dreamlike haze. She touched his face. "Come with me, Lawrence. You can sleep with me tonight."

Another reward. Life was just getting better and better.

∼

He'd had the presence of mind to re-check the locks on the door, and put his gun in the nightstand. They'd fallen asleep with him curled around her. She'd taken off his shirt, so she only wore panties. She'd rested her fine ass in the cradle of his hips and thighs, that intimate spooning position.

He couldn't help getting hard again, but she didn't seem to mind falling asleep with his erection pressing against her. Which made sense, for a Mistress. She probably preferred to fall into dreams knowing she'd left her sub wanting more. The contentment that thought brought, coiled around that sexual tension, told him he was good with it, too.

When her cell phone rang at two twenty-six in the morning, he woke to full alertness. He was trained for that, but Rosalinda answered it as if she had the same kind of practice, ready for whatever life was going to slam into her.

"I'm here," she said to the caller in lieu of a greeting.

She sat up, leaving the curl of his arms. Her bare back was a pale curve. Despite her calm, tension threaded the matter-of-fact tone, so he reached out to caress.

She rose, his hand falling away from her as she picked up the hotel robe at the foot of the bed, belted it on. The unsettled glance she sent his way, masked with an absent smile, told him she didn't routinely have a man spending the night in her bed.

He'd have liked learning that, if her body language now wasn't so clearly "get out." He decided to play dumb, and stayed where he was as she sank into the guest chair at the window. She could have pointed him toward the couch in the living room area to give her more privacy, but she didn't, and she didn't leave the room herself. He took that bit of info as one of two possibilities. She preferred to handle whatever this was in her bedroom, or she found some reassurance from having him here.

Or maybe she simply realized he was going to overhear her, no matter where she was. The suite wasn't that big. Plus, she'd sent her Mistress's message with the dismissive body language. *Don't touch. Stay back.*

He remained where he was to tell her he understood, even as he tuned into the side of the conversation he could hear.

"Did you turn on all the lights? Okay, I'm here now. Turn them on... No, they're not there. I promise you. I'd never bullshit you, would I?" She glanced toward Lawrence. Not to meet his eyes, but almost as if the conversation was suddenly involving him. "About anything important."

Ouch. He'd be pissed off, except words were the best defense mechanism. Evade, distract, deceive, deflect. Feelings and actions were the only place truth lived. Real truth. He knew what he'd felt from her, only a couple hours ago. Maybe it bothered him that she'd said something like that now, whatever her reasons, but it would have torn some things apart in him only if she'd meant it.

"They're not there," Rosalinda repeated firmly. "You're so afraid of seeing them, you create them in your head. It's like a false positive test."

Her voice stayed no-nonsense, but the streetlights from the parking lot showed her pale face was strained. A little fear in her eyes. He wasn't sure, but it seemed a faint sheen of tears were gathering. She swallowed, keeping the evidence of them out of her voice.

He needed nothing else to tell him exactly what to do. Whatever was going on beneath the surface of this was something that pushed aside whatever puzzle pieces he was sifting about her intentions toward him, or the things getting his hackles up. Pride and being right often meant so damn little in the world.

He left the bed. She'd leaned her shoulder against the chair back, her forehead pressing against the curtain and the window frame beneath it. When he dropped to his knees at the arm of her chair, she glanced his way. Following some kind of submissive intuition, this shit he was learning he had in heretofore untapped reservoirs, he wrapped his hand over the chair arm, next to her hip. He did nothing but sit there quietly, on his knees next to her.

She didn't tell him to go away. Instead, as she continued to persuade the person to go from room to room and check what they feared was in the shadows, she shifted her hand to his shoulder. Kneaded, a rhythmic movement to slow the erratic pace of what was galloping through her head. Whenever the person responded, her hand stilled, tightened on him, released. Now it formed a fist and beat a light tattoo on his shoulder.

"Okay, stop. We've checked all the rooms. Take a breath. Listen to my voice, honey. Hold onto it. How many rooms? No shadows. Nothing in them. Head back to your room. You left the lights on, right? No shadows. Nothing in them. See? Double check as you go back through the house."

A long pause, as she listened to the voice on the other end of the line. Her nails dug into him, but he didn't move. He wanted to cover her hand with his, but remembering that she'd shaken off his touch twice, he stayed as he was.

"Okay. Good. That's that." Her tone became more relaxed as she shifted smoothly to discussing normal things. The office. The club. Then she paused. This time when she glanced down at Lawrence, he saw a glint in her gaze. "No, I am not going to talk about him. You're trying to emotionally blackmail me. If you were really in crisis, I'd tell you everything, but this is just panic, so you'll be lucky to get breadcrumbs."

Finally, there was a smile in her voice. "You're calling me a bitch like I don't know it's your pet name for me."

His shoulder was getting caressed, more of her attention on the gesture. She played with the hair on his nape, drew circles there. He turned his head to rub his jaw, his beard, along the inside of her forearm. She allowed it, her fingertips teasing through the hair, then moving up to his temple. As he raised his face, their eyes met.

"Yes, he is here," she said quietly. "He bedded down on the sofa."

She handled the lie without faltering, but he wondered how intuitive the caller was. When you cared about people and they cared about you, the emotional effort to tell a lie—an important one—came through the voice. Hearing it confirmed his guess on the caller's identity.

Abby.

"Are you in bed now?" Rosalinda was asking her. "Want me to sing to you? Girl Scout camp songs, commercial ditties, pop or country chart?" Abby's response made his Mistress swallow, her fingers drop back to Lawrence's shoulder. They dug in once more, like something had hurt her, deep inside. But her voice stayed light. "Okay, but if I sing that, you sing it with me. You don't stop singing until you fall asleep."

Rosalinda hummed the first few bars, closing her eyes. And then she started to sing. He didn't know the song, but it was soft, sweet, something about lost things and where to look for them, and learning they were never really lost, just misplaced. And those misplaced things could be found in dreams. Or inside your own self.

She was an okay singer, but her intent wasn't to be Celine Dion. It was more like a mother, singing a child to sleep after a nightmare. Her voice was laden with love, gentle reassurance on top, a core of steel beneath, telling the child she was there. She would always be there.

I've always had Abby... Abby is my heart.

Whenever he asked her about relationships, she always went back to Abby. Suddenly, that answer had far more serious implications.

He could faintly hear Abby on the other end, singing with her. After a time, the voice faded to silence, but Rosalinda sang a while longer. She let the song drift off, listened carefully. Then she disconnected and put the phone on the side table.

"She's not to know you were in the room," she said.

"I got that."

"I'm not going to tell you what that was about."

"Not my business if it doesn't threaten your safety."

She glanced down at him. Her hand rested alongside his neck, her fingers twitching over his skin, his hair. "When I told her you were sleeping on the couch, she said, 'I think he's kneeling right by your chair.'" A painful smile crossed her face. "Even I didn't anticipate you doing that. She knows you were here, but I want her to have the option of believing you weren't. Understand?"

"Yeah." He laid a hand on her thigh, and she didn't draw away. There was a need inside him, bigger than anything in the room. It told him she rarely let anyone watch over her, even when the things she safeguarded took their toll. "Everything okay?"

She propped her head on the chair back. "Abby wakes to fears of things in the shadows, whispering to her. You can be so afraid of a monster, you create one. I always insist it's not what she thinks it is. My surefire way to prove it is always within reach. 'Never happens during the day, does it? Only at night. Only when you're alone. Always in those shadows.'"

Her attention turned back to the parking lot. He saw a bleakness in her eyes that punched him in the gut, because he knew that look. It came when you knew something couldn't be changed, no matter how much you wished it.

"But one day, the monsters might come during the day," she murmured. "I won't have a way to fight them."

"Yeah, you will. There's some part of you always working the problem. You'll figure it out."

She gave him an absent nod. After a moment, he offered a quiet suggestion. "Want to go back to bed?" He ran his hand lightly along her thigh. "You're cold."

She looked his way, and something shifted in her eyes as she realized someone was worrying over her. A painful smile crossed her face. "Okay."

"Mind if I carry you?" he asked.

"That would be kind. You're a kind man, Lawrence."

"I know how to be kind. There's a big difference between that and being a kind person."

"Knowing when to be kind is even more important."

He slid his arms under her, lifted and took her back to the bed. It was always a surprise to find how light she was, since her personality and strength had a gold brick density. The thought gave him his own painful smile.

She didn't remove the robe right away. He spooned around her, pulled the covers up, draped his arm over her waist. She tangled his hand in the robe sash, wrapped it around his wrist, then her fingers over his, and let out a small sigh.

"Do you know that feeling..." Her voice drifted off.

He found her fingers through the loops of the sash, overlapped one of hers with one of his. "What feeling?"

"There's this mural, on an abandoned building where Cyn grew up. At first glance, you think it's Moses parting the Red Sea. The ocean is split, a narrow path of sand between the two walls of water. People are walking on that path. All different types of people. The strip of sand and the invisible walls holding back the water have a name. *Hope.*

"It sounds like an uplifting message, doesn't it? Yet I wish I could unsee it. Because I can't get past the ocean, swirling around, turbulent, pushing against that invisible barrier of hope, ready to crash down upon them. Hopelessness."

Her hand tightened on his forearm. "The people are all holding hands. Which makes me wonder. Is the wall held back by that, the connections they maintain with one another? If they let go, break those connections, does the wall fall? Or is it a reminder to each one of us, that it's when we let go, refuse those connections, make ourselves feel alone and isolated, that hopelessness has its biggest chance of drowning us? But what happens when we can't *feel* those connections, can't believe in them, even when we're holding as tightly as possible to one another?"

Her voice cracked a little, and he wrapped both arms around her, held her close. He didn't say anything, because he didn't sense that was what she needed. She needed arms around her in the middle of the night, a listening ear. Comfort, connection. His Mistress knew her truths without needing them confirmed. She just needed them to be heard, by ears other than her own.

Another sigh after a time, another wrap of the sash around his wrists. "Lawrence."

"Yes, Mistress."

"The plane. I can't change my feelings about it, but... I'm sorry."

He nodded. "Me too."

That settled, they both went quiet. She kept him bound to her with the sash, and dropped back into sleep. As he lay behind her, holding her, he thought she should cut herself some slack on the kindness point. She obviously knew when to be kind, too. Just like she knew when to be cruel, in ways that could keep him thinking about her, not sleeping, the rest of the night.

But since he needed to be fully on his game in the morning, he let those things go and nestled his face in her soft hair. Doing that, inhaling her female scent, he was able to follow her into dreams.

Where lost things could be found, even if for just a little while.

CHAPTER EIGHTEEN

*I*n different ways during their short association, Lawrence had told her that she was able to pull things out of him he didn't usually discuss with anyone. Last night, when he'd knelt next to her, carried her to bed, Ros had wanted to tell him things, too.

She hadn't, because she respected Abby's privacy. But without that concern, she might have told him what was really going on. Some strange part of her said she could trust him with anything. Any part of herself.

Ros had shared a lot of intense moments with submissives. Every once in a while, she was tempted to draw one deeper into her life, even beyond a dinner date or inviting them to her home dungeon. Sometimes it was easy to resist, the temptation of a cupcake. Other times, it was something with a far stronger pull, such as the loneliness that gripped someone in the deepest part of the night.

Whether the desire fell on the cupcake or loneliness end of the spectrum, the urge disappeared in the light of day. Like Abby's monsters.

Yet the sun had risen on a new day and the pull was still there. Almost as strong as it had been in the middle of the night.

He'd been up and taking a shower when she rose and poured her first cup of coffee. He'd had it ready, thanks to the in-room carafe. As he left the left the bathroom, his lower half wrapped loosely in a towel he held together with one hand, she'd headed that way. The universe required she trail her hand over his slightly damp skin. As he watched her do that, he raked a hand through his hair, finger combing it.

The sidelong look out of the green eyes made her want to do a lot of things. But the most unexpected one was the urge to take time for a leisurely in-room breakfast. They could sit at the table and two chairs in the living area, her bare feet playing with his as they talked and she stole things off his plate. Whimsical, horrifyingly girlish behavior. Thank heavens the client meeting was this morning.

But after she emerged from her own shower and preparations, she didn't stop herself from indulging the things she *could* allow herself. He'd donned his ironed shirt and was belting slacks. She slid her hand down his back, to the taper at his waist, hooking her fingers briefly over the belt before she molded her palm to the curve of his ass. "No tie?" she asked.

He smiled at her. "In a hand-to-hand fight, it's pretty easy to grab a guy's tie and choke him with it, throw him off balance."

"Marketing meetings rarely get that violent."

The smile deepened. Her gaze went to his shoes. Dress shoes, yes, but not the conventional ones with slick bottoms. These were black oxfords with dark rubber soles. Her bodyguard wouldn't be losing his footing in that hand-to-hand fight. Or be slowed down if he had to run.

She had a mental checklist she reviewed to anticipate what might happen in a meeting; questions clients might ask, information that would be useful to support their confidence in TRA's ability to meet their needs. Lawrence obviously had a similar list.

She shifted her attention to the dining table. While she'd been in the bathroom, he'd visited the concierge suite on their floor and brought her back a breakfast plate with a variety of things. Along with a fresh cup of coffee, the right amount of cream and sugars stacked on the side.

He took care of her, anticipating her needs. If he didn't know one of them, he asked, in unobtrusive ways she appreciated. She'd never had such a useful travel companion, one capable of giving her the space to do what she wanted, when she wanted it. It made for an irresistible combination, the decisive man taking the lead from a security standpoint, and the submissive providing her steady support, care and attention.

She loved her job, but today she realized what she anticipated the most was having him at her side. It wasn't a bad feeling to start the day with.

Even if feeling it so strongly was a little unsettling.

~

In the rental car, she asked him to drive so she could update some notes, but under the guise of doing that, she stole a lot of glances his way. She liked looking at him, knowing he was hers. At least for now.

He wore a brandy-colored suit jacket and matching slacks with the slim belt. His sharply ironed dress shirt had one button open at the throat. He smelled of a spicy and tempting aftershave he'd put on after his morning shower.

She leaned her temple against the headrest in the car, giving herself to that haze of pleasant thoughts, even as she continued to review what was ahead, workwise. Abby was still primary on a handful of accounts she'd brought to the business. Since this was one of them, an additional run-through was needed.

Rainbow Foods. The company inhabited a turn of the century brick building in downtown Bloomington. They shared the three-story structure with a variety of other businesses, though the entire third floor was theirs. Ros liked their CEO, Theodore Nichols, a thirty-something who'd graduated from chef of a food truck to head of a small convoy of them, and from there to this enterprise. He was diversifying into a boxed meal delivery service, and TRA was helping ensure the success of the rollout.

His employees had mostly come from the food truck world, though he'd recently filled several key positions with people from corporate backgrounds, with experience in managing expanding enterprises.

When Abby had been introduced to those hires on an earlier visit, she'd discovered one of them was a college acquaintance of theirs, Salma "Sally" Smith.

Back in college, Sally had had somewhat of a Domme vibe. At

least, that was what Ros remembered of her. During the marketing visit, Abby had taken the woman to dinner. On her return, she'd confirmed Salma was confident, and sexually assertive. She was incredibly direct about her hook up intentions at the bar where they shared drinks after the dinner. However, Abby's opinion was that she wasn't a Domme. Discreet questions on the topic revealed Salma had never taken it in that direction, and Abby hadn't felt the urge to open her eyes to it.

"I just didn't really connect with her," she'd said. "But she's very good at what she does, management-wise. Theo made an excellent choice."

Ros didn't find any disagreement with Abby's opinion when Sally met them in the lobby. The corporate executive's greeting was warm as she squeezed Ros's hand with both of hers in a firm handshake. In college Salma had had long hair. Now it was a professional, sleek shoulder bob that framed her intelligent brown eyes and attractive features she enhanced with expertly applied makeup. She wore black slacks and a red blouse with tasteful gold jewelry.

"I'm so sorry Abby couldn't make it." Her steady voice complemented the aura of corporate confidence. "But I'm delighted that you did, Ros. It's been too long. Maybe we can grab dinner tonight."

Her gaze moved past Ros, touched on Lawrence, came back to her.

"My driver and bodyguard, Lawrence Gatlin," Ros said. "I had some troubles down in New Orleans, so I've contracted his services. Likely nothing to be concerned about, this far from home."

Sally's expression creased with concern. "I'm so sorry to hear that. New Orleans can be a dangerous place. But Bourbon Street's music and margaritas make it worth the risk." She flashed a grin at them both, making Ros chuckle.

Sally had been an energetic and ambitious force in college. Which made Ros wonder why she was here, at a grassroots-based business only a handful of years away from start-up, rather than at one of the mega-conglomerates where there was more money and prestige. Since she and Abby had made a similar right turn, it would be interesting to learn what had changed Sally's stated plan to be a VP at a Fortune 500 company by age forty.

They all had experiences or met people capable of changing their course in life. Laurel flashed through Ros's mind. So did Lawrence.

No matter how she tried to ignore the thought.

~

Lawrence followed the two women onto the elevator, after courteously holding the door for them.

Salma Smith was hard to read. She kept glancing at him with curious eyes. Lawrence couldn't tell if that was because of Rosalinda's purposefully brief mention of some "problems" in New Orleans, or because she hadn't explained why he was accompanying them to the meeting room, rather than staying in the lobby or just dropping Ros off like a driver would.

In theory, he could have done either of those things. The chances she'd run into a threat inside this building were slim to none. However, ever since he'd seen those meticulously rearranged shoes, he'd had an uneasy feeling about treating Snake like a garden variety thug with limited imagination. No harm in being thorough. He'd check out where she was going to be doing her meeting stuff and then find a quiet place to occupy himself on the same floor, where he wouldn't be disruptive.

While he was sorry if it made things awkward with her client, smoothing that out wasn't his mission. Yet Ros hadn't questioned him in the car about how present he intended to be, and she didn't seem perturbed now. She and Sally were chatting about their college experiences in a way that seemed natural, as if Ros was fully immersed in that walk down memory lane. Only the things he'd learned about her in such a short time told him that it was the practiced skill of a woman good at putting a client at ease about any bumps in the road. Including the silent presence of a watchful bodyguard.

No surprises on the third-floor meeting space. He reviewed risk points, exits and entrances for the floor, and then found the optimal spot for himself. Since the office had an open layout, the padded bench by the elevators gave him a view of the conference room door, the elevator corridor and most of the workspaces, so he put himself there.

It was a busy place, with people in clusters around screens and having a lot of animated discussions about food. The dress was more relaxed than a corporate office, but still work-appropriate. No flipflops and cut-off jeans, but there were jeans, designer tees with humorous motifs. Sally was a bit overdressed, but he'd picked up that she was here for her corporate viewpoint, so her appearance reflected it.

He'd reviewed the business's background and knew the creative environment matched the head of the company, a guy who'd started out running a food truck on construction sites. There was colorful art on the walls, no cube farms separating the employees. Everything encouraged interaction. The staff was mostly on the younger side.

They must have a test kitchen up here, because the floor smelled like fresh bread sprinkled with nutmeg. Ros had said they'd be providing lunch, a sampling of the boxed meals they were promoting. He'd have to snag something for himself when that time arrived, because he suspected his thorough boss would want his reaction to it.

She'd disappeared into the room and the door was closed. The meeting had begun. He did some work on his tablet, checked some things, then sat, listening and watching the comings and goings, seemingly relaxed on his bench. He could handle a lot of nothing time when he was on a security detail, because he knew how to keep his mind alert. He listened for Rosalinda's voice with half an ear, pleased whenever he could detect the rise and fall of it.

It did things to him, seeing her go into professional mode in her high heels and trim business clothes, usually the kind that showed off her legs and curves in a classy way. His reaction amused him, even as it created a low level buzz of arousal, just being around her. When her eyes had met his in the lobby, while Sally was talking to her, he thought she'd felt it, too. That connection that said they were together.

They hadn't defined what they were doing as a relationship, but he always thought that was kind of stupid, how people thought that meant something. If you were intimate with someone, a relationship was happening. The real question was what kind of relationship.

Not long-term. She'd said that straight out yesterday, and it still wasn't sitting great in his gut. To be fair, she'd made it clear from the first night she kept her relationship with a sub within defined boundaries. But with everything new they shared, the shape of that kept changing.

He knew his relationship with his ex was a serious problem for her, but she hadn't cut him loose over it. Not yet. He expected they'd face that question head on later, after the security issue was resolved. However it was dealt with, he knew he wanted whatever was between him and Rosalinda to keep going.

But that might not be his call.

The employees who went by the elevators initially offered pleasant greetings and slightly quizzical looks. However, as word apparently spread about who he was and why he was here, his "I'm working" vibe resulted in passing nods and less attempts at engagement.

Until it was close to lunchtime. Then he was surprised when Ms. Smith slid out of the room and clicked toward him purposefully on her breezy heels. Shorter and sturdier than Rosalinda's, but his Mistress had exceptional balance when it came to those creations she wore on her pretty feet.

He rose to meet her. "Yes, ma'am? Do you need something?"

"Yes. Ros said you might help me." She offered a friendly smile. "I know it's not your job, and if it interferes with it, feel free to decline. However, I could use just a moment of your help, getting something out of storage. We need to show Ros the VIP swag items we used for the Vegas trade show." She pointed to a pair of double doors no more than a dozen feet from the elevators where he sat.

The careful check-in process on the main floor and the measures taken to ensure no one knew Ros was even here meant he could spend a couple minutes pulling a box off a shelf, less than a stone's throw from the conference room. So, obligingly, he nodded and followed Ms. Smith to the storage room. She paused at the doors, giving him a smile as he opened one for her.

"Thank you. Chivalry is not dead." She closed the door behind them and took the lead. The storage room was much larger than he'd expected, lined with several aisles of shelves, piled with an eclectic mix of file boxes, kitchen and office supplies, non-perishable food items and more. A couple giant cardboard displays shaped like food trucks were against the back wall, along with folded pavilion tents.

"It's that one there, up on the third shelf." She pointed, and he saw a big box, *Vegas swag* written on the side in purple marker.

"You got it." As he moved there, she followed him.

"Be careful. It's a little heavy."

He reached up, sliding his hand beneath it to test it, and found it did have some weight to it, but he should be able to balance it on the way down. "Don't stand too close in case there's stuff piled on top that could fall off," he warned.

"Thank you. You're very kind." She took a step back.

The woman was pleasant and professional. Her manner now was no different from how she'd acted toward him and Rosalinda in the lobby or the elevator. Which was why, as he brought the box down, he froze in shock.

Soon as it cleared the shelf, she'd closed the distance between them. In that same breath, she reached beneath the load from the side and cupped him through his slacks, with an assertive, firm and caressing hand.

He managed not to fumble the box, but the thing was heavy, so he had to endure her touch a few seconds too many to ensure he got the thing down to the worktable in the center of the aisle without bobbling it or dumping it on her head. But once he did, he moved decisively out of her reach. Then had to block her when she reached out to continue.

"What are you doing?" he said sharply, barely managing to edit out *"the fuck"* he wanted to inject into it.

Her expression didn't show shame, embarrassment or uncertainty. From the amusement it revealed, the bump in interest, he was reacting as she fully hoped he would.

"You're one of hers, aren't you? It's in the eyes, the way they follow her. Boys couldn't get enough of her in school, but she only had time for the best of the crop. Very choosy, even then." Her gaze had a probing force that made him feel like her hand was still on his balls. She stepped closer, and he realized she almost had him backed into a corner. She wasn't a threat, not like that, but he didn't appreciate being maneuvered.

"Ma'am." He tried to wrap his hand around her wrist before she could cop another feel. She jerked back.

"Don't touch me," she snapped, a teasing mockery to the serious admonition. "You wouldn't want me to say you grabbed me, took advantage. Would you?"

She smiled, easy and pleasant again. "Settle down and don't overreact. It's just touching. I want to play a minute with one of her toys.

Who's to know but us?"

She cocked her head, eyes bright, mouth in an *it's all in fun* smirk. "Pick up the box."

His mind had been sifting the contingencies and choices here, but he jumped at the suggestion. Whatever got him out of this room and situation worked for him. Except that he realized, too late, she'd been speaking in the present tense, not the past. *I want to play...*

He'd picked up the box, but before he could take step one toward the door, she was in his path.

"I need to get back into the meeting, so I only have a minute or two," she said. "It's not much to ask of you, and what man doesn't like being appreciated by a good-looking woman? I expect you want to keep your job."

From the calculated light in her brown eyes, the flash of meanness she'd tried to cover with that smirk, he had no doubt she'd do as she said, accuse him of being the one who'd taken advantage. He was an idiot for going in here alone with her.

He didn't want to give Rosalinda issues with her client. Not over a little ass grabbing in a closet. Salma didn't give him time to make up his mind one way or another, but stepped close to his side again. When she reached beneath the box and touched his cock again, stroked, making it stir, he felt vaguely sick. Her eyes were on his face, her lips parting. She found his discomfort arousing. Which only made his stomach more unsettled.

"Good boy," she murmured. "You should keep your options open. She's never kept one for long, after all."

Her other hand slipped around, fondled his buttocks. "God, she has the best taste, though. You could bounce rocks off this ass. Just keep holding that box. You don't have any choice while you're balancing it, do you? Just have to do what I want. You're helpless, really. Helpless to whatever I want to do to you. A big strong man. Caught... under... my... thumb."

She did a broad stroke with that thumb. He'd rallied enough to tell her to get her hands the hell off him, but just as he opened his mouth to do so, she stepped back, apparently satisfied. "Thank you, Mr. Gatlin. I appreciate a reasonable man. When you're presentable enough, just bring the box into the conference room and leave it on the side table. Don't disrupt the meeting."

She touched her well-styled hair with a casual hand and then she was gone. He had an acute awareness of time, and barely a minute had passed from the time he'd taken that box off the shelf.

He set it on the table again. He was rattled, but not terrorist-level rattled. He was a grown-ass man who'd let her manipulate him into being her plaything, for a minute.

She obviously harbored some resentment of Rosalinda. That pissed him off on his Mistress's behalf. But there was other shit roused by her actions, stuff he didn't want to affect his behavior. He didn't want his gut hurting and his head caught up in Valentina, but he couldn't deny the similar feel to the way Smith had played him. Valentina had been good at turning his best intentions into guilt, self-blame and failure.

Just like Rosalinda had described it on the plane.

He shook it off. An opportunistic, horny bitch with wandering hands had no power over him. Less than a minute of his life, he reminded himself. Shit happened. He'd been in far worse situations.

He picked up the box. Being "presentable" wasn't a problem. Her touch had gotten a sluggish reaction at best, though her achieving any reaction at all repulsed him. It made him feel like he'd betrayed Rosalinda, even though he knew logically that wasn't the case. If that female viper was the last woman on earth, he'd have taken a vow of celibacy.

As he emerged, he saw a slim mixed-race kid in khakis and white shirt walking by with an armload of files. He was watching Salma Smith disappear back into the conference room. At the sound of Lawrence's approach, he turned.

If Lawrence hadn't just dealt with that shitshow, he wouldn't have seen it. But as the young man met Lawrence's gaze, recognized that he'd come from the storeroom, same direction as Salma, it was as if the two of them were an open book to one another. The kid's jaw flexed, he lifted an awkward, resigned shoulder, and moved on.

This was probably his first job. A job he needed enough to put up with some shit like that. *Damn it.*

"Lawrence?"

Rosalinda's voice was usually a balm to his nerves, but now he jumped. Worse, her hand brushing his forearm made him flinch.

Stupid as it sounded, he felt like he needed a shower before she touched him.

It was a damn grope in a storage room. *Shake it the fuck off. Team guys like Neil would laugh their asses off at it bugging you. You've gotten soft.*

"Yeah. She said you needed these files."

"I know. We just took a break." Her blue eyes searched his face. "What's the matter? Is there a security problem?"

"No ma'am. I'll go put these down for you."

The other people were filing from the room. Salma was with Theodore Nichols, chatting in an I-have-the-boss's-full-confidence kind of way. She barely glanced their way, but he knew subtle surveillance tactics. She had him in her peripheral vision, evaluating his response. She'd determine if she needed to get ahead of things before that meeting re-convened, level some accusation at him and make things difficult for Rosalinda.

He'd managed a credible composed demeanor, because as he shouldered into the conference room, the final gaze Salma flicked his way contained a satisfied light.

Rosalinda had stopped outside to talk to a couple other members of the group, so he found the room blessedly empty. He put the box down. Stared at the wall. They'd brought in that lunch, and normally it would have looked and smelled good. Right now it was turning his stomach.

He was mature enough to take responsibility for the choice he'd made, and his reasoning for it had been sound. He didn't have to say a damn thing about any of it.

But the kid's look bugged him.

"Lawrence."

How did the woman manage to sneak up on him better than insurgents could? Because she had a habit of coming up on him when his head was messed up. No brainer there.

Her hand was on his wrist, his fist braced on the table. "Something's wrong. Tell me."

Not a question. A command. Not exactly her Mistress mode, though there were always intriguing hints of it in her demeanor. This was the CEO of Thomas Rose Associates, wanting to know what the hell was going on.

He'd promised her honesty. "Something I'm trying to decide

whether I need to tell you or not," he said frankly. She was still in his peripheral vision, because he hadn't taken his gaze from the wall yet. "It could cause you issues with this client. Or not. I don't know how you'll deal with it. My job isn't to cause you problems if it doesn't involve your safety."

Saying it aloud helped make his decision. He shrugged, rearranged his face into a more relaxed expression before he turned and met her eyes. "Don't worry about it. We'll talk about it at the hotel. It's nothing important."

He wasn't going to destroy her groove while she was closing a deal. And there was more than that to think of. This was Abby's client. He didn't want to cause problems for Abby, either. Especially when it seemed Abby was having some serious problems of her own.

Rosalinda's gaze searched his. Learning to lie without any tells was also a special ops trait, but he'd had married team guys say that shit didn't work with their wives. Curiously, he'd never had a problem doing it with Valentina. But now he knew what they meant, because he had to work to keep his eyes on Rosalinda's face, not falter.

During their eight-year relationship, Valentina had never demanded he crack open his soul the way Rosalinda did. On top of that, he'd willingly done it for his Mistress, used the sledgehammer she'd handed him.

The pause between them had a thousand-pound weight. He would have moved past her, tried to disengage, but she shifted so they were square, making it clear he wasn't dismissed. "If the problem was security," Ros said at last, slowly, "Then I'd accept the delay, and your judgment. Because that's your area, your call. But if it's not about security, it's about something that is my call. You. And everything about your body language says it is."

Her voice had taken on an edge. Like a hunting hound on a scent, she'd picked up the personal note. Shit. She touched his chest. "Meet my gaze, Lawrence."

Pure Mistress voice. Christ. How did she do that? He shouldn't be in that mode at all, not in this environment. But the voice, the firmness of her touch, switched him there in a heartbeat. A lot of things came rushing up from last night, so fast he felt startlingly lightheaded.

"Whoa. Hold on there." She put her hands on his upper arms, moved in close. Close enough she took up most his field of vision.

Now he met her eyes, and saw a million things in those depths. But there was one really important one that caught and held him.

This was a woman as capable of taking care of him as he was of her. She'd said that to him, hadn't she? But hearing something and knowing it were different things.

He'd never sought that, never thought to ask for that. He wanted a woman to care about him, but he'd never ask her to care for him. He was a man, he didn't need that. Yet seeing that potential in her pulled the rug out from under his world.

She was good at that, too.

They were alone in the room, everyone else off taking that break, but it wouldn't last long. He needed to pull it together.

"Lawrence." Her tone was still ball-busting firm, but gentler. "I didn't expect things to go as deep as they did last night, and the residual effect of that kind of subspace can hit you for a couple days afterward. It's normal."

A soft smile crossed her face. "I guess I should have warned you ahead of time, that it could impact your state of readiness, but I honestly didn't expect it to unsettle you here. It's hard to predict."

She thought it was that. He had an out. But what she'd said during that first session came to mind.

...there's no wrong answer, except a dishonest one...

We are extremely complex human beings... There is no way I can anticipate or know everything that works or doesn't work for you, as much as I'd like that to be true.

Him letting Salma touch him hadn't been a betrayal. But if he wasn't honest with Rosalinda now, telling her what was happening, the omission would be.

Even acknowledging that, it was difficult to correct the impression. But as he was figuring out the best approach, she did a whole new evaluation of his face and body language. That light smile vanished. "Did Salma do something?"

Wow, hammer hitting the nail dead center. When his gaze flickered, she had him. Her expression tightened.

"It's okay," he said. "It doesn't have to be a thing. You're here for a meeting—"

"Shut up," she said, and he did, startled at her tone. It was pure, glacial ice, just like her expression. "Tell me what she did."

292

"She got overly friendly in the storage room, that's all. I handled it."

"I want what she did, what she said." Ice could cut like a razor. "Just pure facts. No cleaning it up."

"There's not time—"

"Not as long as you keep dodging the question. Report, sailor. *Now.*"

She could crack her voice like a whip, and without raising it any higher than that murmur. He stared into her eyes.

He'd been trained to withstand torture, as far as any person could avoid being broken, because everyone could be. Yet now he opened his mouth and he told her. Flat, wooden. How the woman had touched him, what she'd said. He hated saying it, hated that his gut curdled like he had food poisoning.

So a woman grabbed his junk, convinced him to stand there and just take it. Big deal. He hadn't been forced. He'd chosen, consciously, not to cause a drama over it. He could have knocked her hand away.

But the re-telling reminded him of her smirk at his discomfort. Trained to anticipate threats at levels most people couldn't imagine, and he hadn't seen her coming. Because she had this act down to a science, even down to covering her ass. Which hammered home the significance of the last part, when he'd met that kid's eyes.

Ros's expression remained in that frozen mode. When he was done, she dipped her head, a curt acknowledgement. "Thank you, Lawrence."

She turned toward the side table, which held the lunch stuff that had been brought in. As he watched, bemused, she made a sandwich with fresh sliced bread and a Waldorf chicken salad, and put it on a paper plate with a couple sides, one a rice dish and the other a fruit salad. She added a cookie the size of a saucer, then chose a cold Coke out of the drink selections and handed the lot to him.

"Go back to where you were waiting on me. Eat your lunch. I'll be out shortly."

He wasn't hungry, but he wasn't going to tell her that. "Rosalinda—"

Two people came back in, so he bit back whatever he was going to say. But as he stood there, feeling miserable and uncertain, she reached up, touched his face as if the people weren't there. He met her gaze and what he saw there, though he couldn't define it, settled something in him.

He might be able to manage the cookie. It was pecan shortbread, after all.

"I'm sorry that happened," she said quietly. "We'll talk more shortly. I'm asking you to obey my direction. Please."

She turned away, engaging the two people in conversation. He moved toward the door, though his feet dragged some. Now that it was out there, he didn't really want her to do anything. He wanted to forget about it. If she acted upon it, he expected it would be a private meet with Theodore after the meeting. Maybe he could intercept her before then.

As he slid out of the room, Salma came back. She was with several others, and he kept his expression empty, disinterested in her presence. The security guy doing his job. She reciprocated with a professional smile and nod, but her eyes couldn't hide what she was. Once a mask slipped, there was no forgetting what lay behind it.

Most people living in a world like this were clueless about their vulnerability. He knew a dozen ways to kill her, right here and now, using what was within reach. Not one of those methods would take more than a few seconds to execute. She might take an extra minute to die, but the outcome would be inevitable. Or he could indulge himself, put his bare hands around her throat and wipe away that fucking smugness forever.

Not a helpful thought. It made his stomach buck again. Even stripped naked with no props around him, he was classified as a deadly weapon by the U.S. government. Which meant he couldn't afford violent impulses. He'd go sit on the bench, get his head right. The only job that mattered was the one he'd accepted. To protect Rosalinda.

But from a personal standpoint, protecting her wasn't just about Snake Sampson. Had he messed things up for her here? Or would she ultimately decide to let it go, to keep things smooth?

Fuck, he wished he hadn't told her.

~

Ros placed her tablet and files in her laptop bag, clearing the space in front of her. She did it as she was chatting with the CFO and Theodore, who were replenishing their coffee. She courteously declined their offer to pour her a cup.

She was well aware of where Salma was, talking to several other staff members. The skilled corporate executive; a smooth, professional demeanor, a careful listener. Before the lunch break, she'd had some outstanding ideas to increase the profit range of the boxed dinners. Not all of them had struck Theo's fancy, some of them being too predictably corporate and large scale, but a couple had fit his vision for Rainbow Foods well. Sally was obviously the most experienced businessperson in his company, an asset. The queen bitch in this particular pond. Except when someone like Ros was here.

In college, Salma had been competitive, and they'd been friendly in that "don't really want to be friends but we'll get along" way that could easily have turned into something more sharp-edged. But they'd never crossed swords. Had Salma felt the need to one-up Ros in some manner, due to their shared college history?

No. Sally might have used that as the excuse, but from what Lawrence had described, her behavior was well past a college grudge. She had used her knowledge of Ros's personality, the hints of who and what she was with men, to get past Lawrence's guard.

As Salma spoke, her hands were gracefully waving, illustrating points. Those hands had been on Lawrence. Without invitation. Without consent. Because Ros sure as fuck didn't consider coerced compliance as permission. Even if Lawrence could break her neck with less effort than it took him to brush his teeth.

As a CEO, Ros considered her employees under her care when they were on the clock—and sometimes off. But Lawrence wasn't just her employee, contract or otherwise. And she wasn't just his employer. She was his Mistress. It took her reaction to a whole different level.

As she spoke to the CFO, she managed that reaction, calming herself down. Righteous rage and mayhem had its place, but a cooler approach often resulted in a far more effective solution to the problem.

No matter how satisfying using an ax and the Jack Nicholson *The Shining* approach would feel.

"If everyone is ready, let's get going again," Theodore said. The several people in the room still standing took their seats at the table. Theo's admin, a middle-aged woman with dyed red hair, settled into her spot at a corner table near the lunch spread. She'd been diligently recording action items, just like Bastion at home.

"Ros." Theodore nodded to her. "You want to continue with Phase Three of the campaign we've been discussing?"

"I do. But I need to address another issue first."

She rose from her chair, putting her laptop bag in it. Salma, sitting on the opposite side of the table, leaned back, her expression attentive, legs crossed.

"This account is important to us," Ros said, meeting Theodore's open, friendly expression. "I like your product, and the way you treat your customers."

"You've helped us take even better care of them, while increasing our sales," Theodore responded, curiosity in his gaze at her posture, the deliberate placement of her bag in her chair, as if she was preparing to leave. "I'm looking forward to your ideas for the upcoming trade show."

"I appreciate that. However, I'm afraid I can't continue this meeting at this time. How you respond to what I'm about to say will determine if we'll have a professional relationship going forward. Because no matter how important a client is to me and my firm, no one is going to manhandle a person in my employ without repercussions."

Her gaze slid to Salma. The woman went white. She hadn't expected to be confronted in front of Theo's executive staff, but she rallied fast, snapping up in the chair.

"I wasn't going to bring it up here, Ros, but your bodyguard came on to me when I asked for his help in the storage room."

Ros lifted a brow. "Did I say it was you, Salma?"

"I...you..." Salma sputtered, then visibly tried to reclaim her composure. "You looked at me, and the incident just happened. I assumed he talked to you and tried to cover his ass about grabbing mine."

"Hmm. Yet you didn't immediately go to your boss, before the break was over, and tell him my employee was inappropriate with you. Before we went back into a meeting that involves Rainbow Foods paying my firm a great deal of money. Curious, don't you think?"

Salma started to speak, but Ros turned back to Theodore, point-edly ignoring her. "She's doing it to others here," she said frankly. "I'd meet with your more vulnerable team members individually, find out the truth. And—"

"I'm not going to be accused of things I haven't done. We'll sue your company." Salma surged out of the chair. Her face was flushed. "She's just pissed because she thinks the guy she's screwing was attracted to me. She was this way in school, too. I should have warned you, Theo, when Abby said she was coming instead of her. We never had this problem when Abby met with us."

"I expect because Abby didn't bring a male bodyguard," Ros returned, keeping her expression cold, controlled.

"Go to hell." Salma straightened, crossing her arms over her chest. Ros had rattled her, but she could tell Sally was already trying to rein it back into the right parameters, exude the proper level of outrage.

Theo's gaze was shifting between the two women. He wasn't the most experienced of CEOs when it came to personnel issues, but he had a good mind. He was rattled by the turn of events, though, so it would take him a few minutes to figure out how to handle things. The others showed a mix of embarrassment and uncertainty, but when Ros's gaze touched on the admin, she noted the woman's gaze was fixed on Salma, her expression flat but guarded.

She knew. The support staff usually did.

Ros returned her attention to Theodore. "I'll send you references for some excellent marketing firms that can take over this job from us. They'll get what we've developed thus far, so they can run with that. You've paid for that expertise, and you won't be starting from square one, getting ready for the trade show. But I will be warning them about Ms. Smith, so they can protect their male staff members."

She shouldered her bag, giving Theodore a courteous nod, as well as the other members in the room. She saved Salma for last. The marketing manager had gone tight-lipped, shrewdly recognizing her best bet was waiting for Ros to leave. A million calculations were going on behind her eyes as she figured out how to salvage the situation. Ros stared her down, with a look that wisely kept Sally's tongue in her mouth. At least for the moment.

"Shame on you," Ros said quietly. "Trust is a gift."

Then her attention moved back to Theo. "I'm sorry to lose our relationship," Ros said. "But if someone abuses one of my people, my top priority is living up to their trust in me. And I will do that, with extreme prejudice. I wish you the best, Theo."

CHAPTER NINETEEN

*S*he stepped out of the room, closing the door behind her, and gestured to Lawrence. "Time to go," she said.

His gaze was troubled, but he rose. She shook her head, lifted a quelling hand when he looked as if he were going to say something. *Not here.*

He nodded, understanding, and pressed the elevator button. When it arrived, he held the door open as he had on the way up. A gentleman.

They rode it down in silence. She kept a foot between them, because she needed the space to breathe, get control of her emotions. Fortunately, he seemed to respect that.

After they reached the lobby, she excused herself to go to the restroom. She touched up her makeup, her hair. Braced her hands on the edge of the sink, tightening her grip until the granite left marks in her palms. As she imagined Salma in the storage room with Lawrence, Ros wanted to put the woman on her ass, leave her bloody. She also wanted to put Lawrence on his knees, show him what mattered in this situation. It sure as fuck wasn't her reputation with a client.

When she emerged from the washroom, she was calmer. It had been about fifteen minutes, so Lawrence was only a few feet outside the door, probably debating checking on her. His expression was still troubled, though he smoothed it out when he saw her, nodded.

As she moved across the lobby, he fell in to walk by her side.

Maybe half a step behind, which might be for the security vantage point. Or maybe instinctively, for other reasons. It was a more pleasant thought to dwell upon than most of what was going through her mind.

They'd almost reached the front door when the reception desk hailed her.

"Ms. Thomas?" The man was standing, as if prepared to chase her down, in case she hadn't heard him. "Mr. Nichols asked if you would mind waiting on him for just a moment. He's on his way down."

"Certainly," Ros said pleasantly. The lobby wasn't large, but there were several comfortable chairs. Ros took a seat in one, crossing her legs. Lawrence moved to her back, remained standing. He was watching the doors, she noted. Ingress and egress points. She wondered what else was going through that complicated mind. She was willing to bet he was concerned about telling her what had happened, feeling if there was any negative fallout from this, it would be because he couldn't just put up and shut up.

She would address that. In due time.

Theo emerged from the stairwell out of breath. Lawrence shifted. With surprise, Ros realized he was going to intercept the CEO's path if it looked like his intent was hostile. She rose, putting an easy hand on Lawrence's shoulder. She could already tell there was nothing to be concerned about.

Theo was out of breath, and not just because he carried the extra pounds of a man who enjoyed and celebrated food. He'd obviously hurried, not wanting her to wait any longer than necessary. His expression was somber.

"Ms. Thomas," he said without preamble. "I apologize. To you both. And particularly to Mr. Gatlin, though he deserves far more than an apology." He extended his hand to Lawrence.

Lawrence, after a beat of surprise, accepted the firm handshake. Theo nodded to him, then turned his attention back to Ros. "Ms. Smith is currently clearing out her desk. I've suspended her, pending a thorough investigation with the employees under her supervision."

Regret passed through his gaze. "I'm not going to talk about specifics, but she didn't do much to help her case after you left the room. And there was some...corroboration, from my staff. You gave them the opening I wish they'd been comfortable taking before it reached this point." He sighed. "I guess now I know the real reason she took such a serious salary cut to come here."

Theo scrubbed a hand over his short, bristly beard. "Running a company this size is a lot harder than operating one food truck. But TRA has made it a lot easier. If I confirm her dismissal when it's official, would you continue our relationship?"

"I'll have to discuss it with my executive team before I say for certain. However, when it comes to me and my team, I can say good behavior is almost always rewarded."

She put out a hand, and Theodore took it, with a look of relief. "Don't beat yourself up too much," Ros said, more kindly. "The ones who are really good at it know how to cover their tracks. Being a woman, she had extra camouflage."

He shook his head. "Thanks, but the buck still stops here. I should have been paying better attention. Apparently, it wasn't much of a secret among our junior staff. We need to work on winning their trust on things like this."

"I have a feeling the steps you're about to take will do that. It's a pleasure to work with that kind of management, Theo. Thank you."

Theo and Rosalinda spent a few more moments in discussion, shifting over to business and where they'd pick up if the relationship continued, which looked like a good bet.

When she made that "good behavior" comment, Rosalinda had flicked a glance his way. He'd taken the subtle tease as a reassurance that she wasn't pissed at him. That and Theo's handshake, the man's direct look saying he didn't think less of Lawrence, had helped ease what was in his gut.

But most importantly, it sounded like that kid wouldn't be coming to work anymore with that sick feeling Lawrence had seen in his eyes. That he'd experienced himself, to a far lesser degree.

Lawrence excused himself to go get the car. When he returned, he anticipated having to wait on them a few more moments, but Rosalinda was alone, waiting on him inside the lobby. As he escorted her to the car parked at the curb, opening the passenger door for her, he noted she seemed more relaxed, too. He didn't want her to feel like she had to do follow up with him, so when he got in, he was the first to speak, trying to put things on a more even footing.

"You handled that like you've dealt with it before."

"Almost every working woman has," she said. "With women far more common in management now, men are having to deal with it too. People think gender is the driving motivator, but it's not. It's power." She grimaced. "Something every Dominant knows. It's a shame that a course on power exchange protocol and dynamics isn't required in high school. Might do wonders for cultivating a workplace culture of mutual respect."

She smiled, touched his hand, but then she withdrew, sobering. "I had my share of it in my early days, in New York. It's good to have HR departments more on top of it these days, but I would have handled it myself back then regardless. I'm fortunate that I've never been in such a financially desperate situation that I have to make a choice between being sexually harassed and paying my bills. Or feeding my family."

Lawrence shook his head. "I'm surprised you dealt with it at all. You project the 'don't fuck with me' vibe. You're not the usual target of those kinds of predators."

"Which should make you ask yourself the question, why are you?"

"Excuse me?" He sent her a startled look. She cocked her head, swept her gaze over him.

"There's something about you. Knight in shining armor. You'll stand up to terrorists, but a woman in need...that's your vulnerable point. Serving a woman. You thought you'd jeopardize this account for me if you set her back on her heels. She used your strength against you."

He wanted to deny that was what happened, but that was reactive, and her words *had* echoed some of his own thoughts, when it was happening. He needed to think it through. So he didn't say anything to that. Just shrugged. "Regardless, it's done."

She gave him that unfathomable look again but fortunately changed the subject. "We've just bought ourselves an extra day. We could go home, but Abby wanted me to consider staying a couple extra days at her cabin at Monroe Lake."

"Cabin?"

"She inherited it from a great-uncle. It's just this little place cobbled together out of a modular home and a log cabin kit. But it's perched up on a hillside in the forest, and has an amazing lake view. There's a fire pit and a big deck, and the interior is really nice. None of which matters to you. What matters is that no one except Abby and Bastion will know we're there. For a day or so, you won't have to worry about keeping a target off my back."

That concern never took a day off, but he admitted it would reduce the risks to her considerably, being completely off grid and schedule. "I'm hearing a lot of things to make me happy," he said neutrally. "But how will you survive without people to boss around?"

She sent him a look that had a pointed heat to it. "You'll be there, won't you?"

Yeah, he'd opened himself up to that one. Maybe on purpose. He didn't want her treating him with kid gloves because of what had happened earlier. Things had been resolved in a good way, so with a little time, he'd shrug it off.

Yet he needed something from her. He needed her touch to erase where Smith had touched him. He needed that catharsis of her dominance that drove things out of his head.

Maybe she got that and was playing along, because she closed her hand on his thigh, her eyes a mix of things. "Don't drive too fast," she said, teasing. "We'll have time to do everything I want to do to you, Lawrence. And plenty of things you won't expect."

Like that was going to help him drive slower. But first things first. His stomach was noticing he hadn't eaten much of that sandwich she'd made him.

"Should we pick up some food before we get there?"

Because the cabin was remote, they not only picked up lunch for him, they stopped at a grocery store to cover a couple meals and snacks. He enjoyed wandering around the grocery store with her way more than he'd expected, and he thought she did, too. He watched her pick out a bottle of wine, eye a flat of finger-sized devil's food cakes in the bakery section. He slid it into the cart when she wasn't looking, and gave her an innocent look when he unloaded it on the belt. Her rosebud mouth pursed in a suppressed smile, but she let it go through. She insisted on paying, which didn't thrill him, but she pointed out it would all be expensed as part of the business trip.

Then they were headed for the cabin. It wasn't too far outside Bloomington, where the regular road quickly turned into a winding route among the hills around the lake. Eventually they ended up on an even more twisty side road that became a gravel path, ending at their destination.

As she'd said, the place had started life as a double-wide mobile home, then it had acquired a foundation, new siding and roof. The newest part—and new meant in the last twenty years—was a log cabin add-on built against it. A deck jutted out over the steep hill where the house had been planted. Through the trees, he saw Monroe Lake, sparkling in a cold late afternoon sun.

Based on the outside, he would have expected seventies décor on the inside, a harvest gold fridge, shag carpet and paneling on the walls. Instead there were granite countertops, tile floors and soft ivory walls that absorbed a lot of sunlight through the plethora of windows in the open living area. During certain times of day, Rosalinda told him it turned the room a mellow lemon color.

"Abby's great-uncle was a regular Martha Stewart," Lawrence commented as he unpacked the groceries, stocking the side-by-side refrigerator.

Rosalinda chuckled. She was in the master bedroom, unpacking her bag, and he could see slices of her as she moved around. "Abby could have sold the place for a mint, because the land itself is worth a great deal, but she liked it here. It's very peaceful. So she decided to keep the structure as is, except for some updates, like a new roof and reinforcement of the deck, but renovate the inside to suit her tastes. She likes to say she should have torn the whole thing down and started from scratch, that the cost would have been roughly the same, but she has good memories of visiting here, and she was very fond of her great-uncle. I think she likes pulling up the driveway and seeing it looking mostly as she remembers it from childhood."

She emerged from the bedroom, adding, "There's a little path cut in the hillside so we can get down to the boat house and dock. She has a fishing skiff and a pontoon. If it wasn't so cold, it'd be a good time to go out."

Rosalinda had changed her office clothes for a long-sleeved black sweater that clung to her upper body and fell to her upper thighs. She'd put it on over a pair of teal-colored leggings that matched those painted tennis shoes she liked. Her hair was carelessly pulled from her face with a barrette, so little pieces wisped around her face.

He'd poured her a glass of wine and offered it. She took it with a thoughtful look and dipped her head toward the deck. "Join me when you're settled. Don't make me wait long."

Her steady eyes, the set of her mouth, told him that was an order from his Mistress. "Yes, ma'am."

She closed the sliding door behind her. The sweater hugged her hips and trim ass. Though he wasn't a big fan of leggings on women, preferring the fit of jeans or one of her snug skirts, the cling of the leggings did remind him of how nicely her legs folded around his body.

He changed into faded jeans and a flannel shirt, took a Miller Lite from the refrigerator, and headed for the deck.

From the way she was curled in one of the handful of Adirondack chairs, he could tell her sweater wasn't warm enough. Before he headed out the sliding glass doors, he backtracked to the bedroom to retrieve her coat. What was laid out on the bed gave him pause.

Her rose and gold shoes were there with a pink corset, matching panties. He touched the bit of lace edging on the corset. She intended to wear that. For him. Or rather, for herself. Maybe she'd allow him to show her how much he appreciated it.

Thinking of something so good yanked the chain on that other shit boiling inside him about today. He needed to figure out how to get rid of it, so it didn't come into what he wanted to give to her.

He returned to the deck, set his beer aside and offered the coat. She uncoiled, leaned forward, and let him put it around her, giving him a smile. "Thank you."

At her gesture, he took the chair next to her. He sprawled in it, stretching out his legs, and followed her contemplative gaze. For a few moments they sat in companionable silence, enjoying the lake view.

He didn't feel like he had to talk around her. Just a couple years back, he'd been far more of a talker. A joker, the smart-ass with the quip when shit hit the fan. He could still find that part of himself when the moment was right, usually when he was with Dale, Neil and

Max. But his injury and things coming to a head with Valentina had increased the value of easy, quiet times for him.

But there was another reason he was being quiet. She wanted him to be. She was projecting that "don't speak until I say" vibe. After seeing what he'd seen on the bed, hearing her tone in the kitchen, he was ready to obey, to be what she needed. A bite in his gut wanted her to get moving on it, let him jump into that with both feet, get loose of the other stuff. Yet the first thing she'd ever taught him was that everything was at her pace, not his.

He wouldn't want it any other way.

"There's this misconception about submissive women." Her voice was crystal clear in the cold air. "It sometimes applies to submissive men, too. That they're looking for someone to take care of them."

When he looked her way, she captured his gaze, held it. "The statement itself is actually true. But not in the way that most people think. The strongest submissives, they're the ones that have the most trouble letting themselves be cared for. Within that submissive structure is the only place they can be trained to let go, enough to allow someone to care for them. It's there they finally find a balance they often lack in their real lives, where the demands placed upon them by others, and by themselves, can be extreme."

If she'd been a sniper, she would have hit her target dead-on. It sure hit something in him. He studied his beer. "Why do I feel like this isn't just an academic discussion?"

"Because it's not." She put down the wine and dropped her feet to the deck so that she could perch on the edge of the chair, rather than relax in its reclined shape. She gave him a steady look. "Why the hell did you let her touch you?"

He stiffened. "You were there to meet with a client—"

"You're not listening. Take me out of it, take any other consideration out of it."

"The question doesn't have an answer without those elements. You can't subtract—"

"It does have an answer. And I want it. Think, Lawrence. Why did you let her touch you?"

Stripping it down that way left him feeling exposed, raw. He rose from the chair, moved to the rail. It was a defensive move. He knew it was, soon as he did it, and so did she.

"The kind of submissive I just described, the one handling extreme demands, needs very clear signs of ownership." She spoke quietly. "Boundaries that tell them what is and isn't their issue to handle."

"My world doesn't work that way," he said sharply, turning toward her. "The lines blur. You can't just say something isn't your job if it connects to the things that are. If it connects to people you care about. I'm not that cold-blooded."

"And I am?" She cocked her head. "You're challenging me on purpose. You want me to put you on your knees, pour gasoline on you and set you on fire. Burn it all away."

He didn't have a response for that, but apparently she wasn't looking for one. She rose, came to stand before him. "You remember that fantasy we joked about, early on, about me having a sex slave. About you belonging to me?"

Her appraisal slid over him, thoroughly, before coming back to his face. "Imagine a world where that's the norm. My brand on your ass, my collar on your throat. Maybe it's the only thing I let you wear, so even if you're out in public, buying your Mistress things she sent you out to buy, it doesn't matter that all that fine flesh is on display for others to see. That brand, that collar, shows that you belong to someone else. So if the lady selling cabbages wants to grab herself a handful, what do you do? Say it, without thinking."

"I stop her."

"What if she says she won't sell cabbages to me, and they're my very favorite food?"

"Cabbages are no one's favorite food," he said.

He'd placed his beer on the rail, and only his reflexes kept him from having his ear slapped through his head. He caught her wrist. She stayed that way, her slim bones in his grip as she stared up at him. He saw a tidal wave of emotion in her face.

"Mistress," he said quietly.

"Never," she said through her teeth. "Never again. You care for what's mine, by caring for yourself. There is nothing in my life more important than taking care of those who matter to me. Got it?" She reached up with the free hand, cupped his face. "I need to hear it."

"Yes ma'am." He gripped the wrist of that hand as well, so when she put both hands on his face, he was holding her arms. "I'm sorry."

He closed his eyes, let the weight of her palms hold him. "Protecting you matters to me, too, Rosalinda. Whether it's you or anything connected to you. She took me by surprise. She wasn't a threat I knew how to meet, which means she wasn't really a threat to anything I was protecting. Except your reputation, your standing with your client."

A muscle flexed in her jaw. "You're still not getting it," she said, not unkindly. "But that's my job to address. Not yours."

She freed herself, moving toward the sliding glass doors. "In the car, you said you need to check the perimeter before dark. Go do that, while I update my notes and handle some email. But after that, come find me."

∼

He needed the mental break, as well as to familiarize himself with the surrounding area. She'd scrambled his brain, left him wondering about that mysterious comment. *That's my job to address. Not yours.*

They were a mile or so from the nearest neighbor by road, about half a mile as the crow flew. This time of year, however, the properties were likely to be empty, since most of the real estate here were vacation homes. Access to the house was limited to that gravel path for a car, on foot through the woods, or by boat, from the lake.

The sunset was disrupted by a gathering of clouds that quickly became a gray, heavy-hanging sky that reminded him of the snow forecast. It wasn't unexpected for Indiana this time of year. The roads should stay reasonable enough to get to the airport when she was ready to fly home.

Until then, holing up here with her didn't sound bad. There was a fireplace inside the log cabin, already stocked with wood and tinder. A generous supply of additional fuel was stacked inside the storage shed adjacent to the back door. Abby had called her property manager to ensure the house was prepped. Most of the staples for cooking—spices, condiments—were already here; the grocery trip had been to get the things they'd specifically want to eat. For dinner, Ros had wanted a steak, with a fresh salad. A good choice for him, too.

Now, as he stepped back inside, he found she'd already started the fire, making things toasty after the cold outside. She'd finished her work stuff and was sipping wine as she sat on the couch and gazed at the fire.

She'd also changed clothes. She was wearing the outfit she'd left on the bed.

The corset had a whole different impact when it was wrapped around his Mistress. It molded her figure in a severe kind of way, nipping in at the waist, her breasts swelling at the top. The hem along the bottom, emphasizing the flare of her hips, was a smooth line covering the top of her matching lace panties. The rose and gold heels sparkled, reflecting the flames.

He shrugged out of his coat, hanging it up by the door, never taking his eyes off her. She kept looking at the fire as she spoke.

"Take everything off and stretch out on your back on the floor beside me. Hands laced behind your head, legs spread out. I expect your cock to be right below my fingers, here."

She let her hand dangle off the edge of the couch. Now she did turn her head, her gaze sliding up to him.

"I know things are out of balance for you," she said. "You're going to give me what I want. And that's going to make it better. Do you know why that is?"

"Because you're my Mistress." Why the hoarse note continued to surprise him, he didn't know. "And I want to give you everything."

Her blue eyes sparked with that vibrant light of approval that turned him on even more than her commands and her touch. Crazy, but true.

She glanced down, a slight smile on her lips. "This style of corset is called an Agent Provocateur. With your special ops training, I thought you'd appreciate it."

"I do, ma'am. Appreciate it. Appreciate all of it." His gaze rose to her eyes. "Appreciate all of you."

Her mouth softened, a hint of vulnerability that matched the moment. Emotions rose up, hard and fast. He hadn't been in the board room, but what Theodore Nichols had said to her in the lobby made it clear she'd stood for him. No matter what he'd said or thought about it being best if she'd just let it go, he realized he would have felt differently about her if she had.

It didn't have to make sense. A lot of things that were right didn't have to be explained. What was happening right here, right now...it was two people who claimed the Mistress and sub feelings for themselves, respectively. But they also claimed each other.

He moved toward her. She'd told him what to do, but that slip in her expression needed a different answer first. When he was a stride from the couch, he dropped to a knee, adjusted to close the distance. He wouldn't loom over her. That felt wrong to him.

As he had the first night, in a move that was becoming a defining gesture between them, with all the right meanings, he pressed a kiss to her leg, just above her ankle. He cradled her shoe in both hands as he did it. When he lifted his head a few inches, he couldn't help but follow with his gaze the avenue her legs provided to the tempting triangle of lace and the bottom of the corset.

"I'd like to take off your shoes, Mistress. If you're okay with that."

"You don't like the heels?"

"I do. I just like it when you're in your bare feet, too. Kind of feels like you're at home when you do that."

"Hmm. So it's not a foot fetish." Amusement in her voice, but tenderness, too. She stroked his hair, teasing the short ends above his ear.

"No, ma'am." He smiled. "They're just pretty feet. And it means a lot, that they're walking the same earth as me."

"Well…" She paused. "I was thinking of digging my heel into your testicles as you lay on the floor, but I can hold off on that for now. Unless you'd like to save your request for when we go to bed. You could take my shoes off then."

Maybe most guys would have leaped at taking the shoes off now, hearing that she planned to apply something that looked like a spike to his nether regions. But she knew him too well. His mind imagined the picture her words were painting, and leaped in a different direction.

"If I earn your pleasure, I'll look forward to that, ma'am."

It was so natural to him, these things he'd never said to a woman. As if he'd been waiting forever to say them. To the right woman.

A sexy little smile appeared on her lips. "Then get undressed, and follow my directions. In fact…"

She pointed to the area in front of the fire. "Undress there, and take your time with it. I like the way the fire flickers over your skin. And Lawrence?" Those eyes glowed with the blue of the flames. "No more talking unless I require it. From here forward, you listen, and feel. I want you to understand the meaning of everything I'm going to do to you, demand of you."

A reminder of that statement, *That's my job to address.* He wanted to assure her she didn't need to worry about what had happened earlier. It was past, all was good, but he wasn't supposed to talk, and something kept him from it. Maybe the remembrance of Smith's hands on him.

"Lawrence."

He'd moved to the spot of floor she'd indicated and had his hands on the buttons of the flannel shirt, but he'd stopped. He had his eyes down, and was fighting the unpleasant feeling. He didn't want any of it mixing with this.

"Look at me."

When he did, she was in that same relaxed position, but there was a demand in her expression that drove out anything else.

"She touched what was mine. I'm going to take care of that. Trust me. Can you trust me?"

"I can try, Mistress."

"All right. Take off your clothes. Show me what's mine. And look at my face as you undress. See how you please me."

He opened the shirt and shrugged out of it, but he took his time with it, for her. He unbuckled the belt the same way, opened the jeans after he took off his shoes. As he did all of that, he watched her, just as she'd demanded.

It was like stepping into a heated pool after spending hours in the cold. Her gaze tingled over his skin, closed over it, pulling him in deeper. He felt her hold on every part of him he exposed. His shoulders and chest, his waist, every hair, every inch of skin. His cock was already swelling in response to her attention. He could say she hadn't even touched him, but that wasn't true. For his Mistress, touch was far more than a physical thing.

He stood before her in his boxer briefs that showed her his erection, the line of hip and flank. Her gaze covered all of it, lingered, then she gave him a slight nod. He removed them and stood before her naked, bathed only by the heat of the fire behind him and her gaze in front.

"Put your hand on yourself. Grip and stroke. Slow."

She settled back into the cushions, dropping a hand over her head, a decadent siren in pink lace, her body shaped in those severe hour-glass lines.

"I still don't want you to speak. But I'm going to ask you questions, and I want you to think about them. What would you do, Lawrence, if I brought you into my board room, and told you to do this in front of my executive team? Every one of them a Mistress, every one of them knowing you're mine. They'd be thinking about what they'd do if I gave them permission to touch, to play."

The knife blade edge gripped her tone again. "But they know that permission is mine alone to give. That day at the gym, Cyn stepped over a line, teasing you as a sub in the wrong moment and setting. That's why she apologized to you. Those things can happen, because the five of us are very close, and sometimes mistakes are made. But she would never, ever do what Salma did to you. Because respect toward me as your Mistress is an umbrella over respect for my care of you. My respect for you."

There was passion in every word, so much he thought the strength of how she felt it startled even her. But he saw her roll it over in her mind, and own it. His cock got thicker and heavier in his grip, his chest and throat tight.

"When we get done tonight," she continued, "there will be no doubt in your mind. If anyone *ever* again tries to do to you what that bitch did, you will immediately shut them down. If someone attacked me, you would defend me, with whatever means were necessary to end the threat quickly, decisively. I want you to have the same attitude toward yourself, because *you are mine*."

The three words were as targeted as a barked command across a battlefield. She meant he was hers, not just in a session. Not just D/s play. She'd crossed a line herself, and his response was a hundred percent acceptance. Feeling surged from a huge well within him, wanting to show her in a million crazy ways she was right. It was a good thing she was still in charge, helping to contain it, so he didn't burst at the seams. The energy of it vibrated off him.

She pointed to the floor. "Down here. On your back. Hands above your head, clasped together to keep them out of my way. They stay there, no matter what I do to you. You don't get to come until I say, and it's going to take a very long time, Lawrence. I'm going to see how close I can push you to savage before you break."

"Not until you say, Mistress," he managed.

Her expression turned feral. "Speaking without permission. Break enough rules, and you may not be allowed to come at all tonight."

"If I can give you all the pleasure you want, Mistress, I'll take that as the consequence."

He was pushing her deliberately, and he had no idea why. She seemed to know, though, because she merely pointed to the floor again.

He came to her, stretched out as she'd described. Hands laced behind his head, legs spread, everything open to her.

Her expression became smooth as a statue's, like the popular Aphrodite everyone had seen at least once. Remote, as a goddess would be, yet so present her attention was like electricity when lightning struck.

She straightened, swung her legs down from the couch. She put her heel into the joining point between his testicles, and pressed inward, until it felt like she was against the base of his cock. It was uncomfortable, but she did it gradually, the effect more psychological than painful. But then she started moving that heel around, random rotations that made the sensitive area more so.

His lower body quivered, and he had to steel himself not to twitch. With the heel still deep in between his balls, she shifted forward, so the toe pressed on his erection. She rose, keeping most her weight on the opposite foot. Even so, for a brief moment, he felt that compression increase almost to the point of pain, but then she removed it, to straddle and stare down at him.

Christ, what a picture. All those curves above him. Through the lace of the panties, he could see the shadows of her folds. He wanted to kiss his way up her thighs, show his hunger for what was between them. But she wasn't in a giving mood right now.

"Set the house security and follow me," she said.

The cabin had a basement with a wine cellar, a storage room, and another room. She'd told him it was Abby's playroom, and had declined to open it until now. It was padlocked, and she produced a key from the bodice of the corset when they arrived. She handed it to him, a slight smile crossing her otherwise remote expression.

"I know my sub likes to check a room before I enter it."

If someone was hidden in there, he'd get a field test for his earlier thought about how lethal a weapon he was when stripped naked as a newborn. Fortunately, the only threats contained within were those to his self-restraint.

As he opened the door, he saw this room had the most modern upgrades of any other space in the house. But Abby had also included touches that reminded Lawrence of Rosalinda's historic Garden District home. The walls were done in beadboard, the ceiling pressed tin.

Several wall mounted screens came to life as Rosalinda flicked switches and adjusted the lighting. The screens offered live feed from cameras on the outside of the house. Snow had started to fall, and through the trees the lamp posts that followed the trail down to the lake set off a glitter on the water. She started an ambient noise sound-track from the music player that fit the view. Night sounds, including the random chirp of a bird, the rustle of wind through the trees. The lap of the lake against the shore.

A comfortable couch was here, as well as a bed in the corner. The rest of the room could have come from one of the pricey private rooms of Club Progeny. Glossy wood on all the equipment. Gold studs to hold washable, rich-looking red upholstery in place. It was stretched over the wood frame of a spanking bench, the padded pieces of an X-shaped cross, and the seat and back of what looked like a throne. A queening chair.

"On your knees, Lawrence."

He dropped, setting his ass on his heels as she went behind a decorative screen, coming back with a handful of things she didn't show him. But she did move to the door, drawing his attention there with one word. "Watch."

Though it padlocked from the outside, inside it had a dead bolt option, no key access to it from the outside of the room. She turned the latch, putting the bolt in place. "The security is set, and the system has a panel down here." She gestured to it. "If there's any interruption to it, an alarm will go off. All right?"

He nodded.

"Good. Your eyes should be on the floor. Don't look at me. Not even my shoes."

He complied, his gut tightening as her tone became harsher. "You've disappointed me, Lawrence. Made me angry. And you know it, so you're pushing for punishment. I want to step across your hard limits. I want to bind you and blindfold you. Make you completely helpless to me. This room has chains. There's a part of me that wants to see you in them, metal biting into your skin. I want to hear the clank of those links as you pull against them, trying to reach me, wrap me up in them with you."

She paused. "I won't use those tonight, but I do intend to use other things in the room that can restrain you as securely. If you don't want that, and you safeword, I will do other things, and there will be no negative repercussions, because I respect your safeword. But I believe you need what I can give you, past those limits. The choice is yours."

She tossed something at him. A collar landed in front of him. And a leash.

A mix of emotions shot through him. Kneejerk distaste for the leash, but his gaze settled on the collar and wouldn't let go. The sub part of him knew just how much one of those things meant. Even a simple service one. This one was three inches wide, with a heavy buckle. And a lock.

She strode across the room, and perched on the queening chair. He was mostly obeying her directive not to look at any part of her, but he was staying aware of her movements. "If you don't want to safeword yet," she said, "then put that collar and leash on yourself, come to me on your hands and knees, and put the leash in my hand. If you do need to safeword, then leave the collar and leash on the floor, go to the X-frame and put yourself on it, gripping the handles. I will proceed accordingly. You have thirty seconds to decide."

She pointed, and he followed the direction of her extended finger to the wall clock. No boring disc with simple black numbers for this room. The time piece was artwork, with a vintage-looking face of Roman numerals surrounded by a steampunk style assortment of gears and an ancient map style depiction of the earth.

She lifted something else in her other hand. A cane. She flicked it back and forth, almost like a metronome, only more lazily, and settled down in the chair. He couldn't chance that direct of a look, but he wouldn't be surprised if she'd closed her eyes, like she was meditating.

He studied his two choices. Thought about what she said. If he started feeling things weren't safe, he could stop. But she'd addressed all his security concerns, knowing that keeping her safe kept things inside him safe, undisturbed.

What she was proposing was intended to test his limits as a submissive, not as her bodyguard. She was planning to tear things open, let them all spill out. If he backed away from it, it was about that, not about protecting her.

He'd never wanted anyone to get that deep inside him. But even as he thought it, he knew that was a lie. He did want someone to get that deep inside him, not to dismantle it all, but to be there in it with him, in his head. His heart. His soul. He just hadn't ever thought that was fair to ask. And he'd been worried about what it would do to his effectiveness if he did. How it would change him.

She wasn't waiting for him to ask. She was demanding entry to that part of him. It was his choice, and she'd accept it if he denied her, but she had a way of angling his mind toward the repercussions from his own gut and soul if he did.

He picked up the collar, the leash, held them in his hands. He started to lift the collar to his throat, but then he stopped. Thought about it. What he wanted. Sometimes when she took him deeper like this, he though he found deeper levels of what she wanted, too. Maybe things she didn't think he was ready for, but also maybe levels she didn't think she could demand, but that she needed. He was here to serve her. Give her everything she needed.

Moving toward someone on his hands and knees wasn't all that degrading to him, since there were plenty of times he'd had to move across the ground like a snake, keeping his ass down. But there was a psychological component to this impossible to ignore.

When he was her guard, he entered her chambers standing, dropped to his knees at her feet. When he was the sex slave, summoned to the queen's quarters, he never crossed this threshold except on his knees.

Christ, she'd planted the suggestion with her fantasy of him naked in a marketplace, but he'd just taken it further. It summoned in his mind the days he and his buddy Kyle had role-played being soldiers, knights, heroes of every stripe. They'd built a fort/castle in the backyard one summer. Lawrence had been the one to add a queen to the story. Beautiful and remote, sending them out to defend the castle to win her favor. Back then, she'd had an anatomy that made Dolly Parton look like a pre-pubescent girl, but being a twelve-year-old boy had its privileges.

He remembered masturbating to his image of that queen, and though her shape helped him reach climax, what really did it was imagining her ordering him to his knees, to bestow her favor on him because he'd done well...

He'd reached her. She had her legs crossed, so he stopped at the point of her dangling toe. He laid the leash and collar on the cushion next to her hip, then sat back on his heels and bowed his head.

"Explain yourself," she said coolly.

"I want..." No, that wasn't right. What he wanted was irrelevant, and it was the wrong word anyway, for what he felt. *Felt*. That was the key. "I feel like it's my Mistress's choice to put the collar and leash on me."

The words were heavy, stark, separated by the tight breaths he was taking. He'd agreed to her terms, to allow another of his hard limits to be breached. He was about to jump down the rabbit hole with nothing to stop his descent but her, and his accelerating heart knew it.

"Keep your head down. You looked very handsome, coming toward me on your hands and knees. The mirrored wall gave me a nice view of that from the back."

She had something else in her hand. A head mask. He remembered the one from the first night, only this one wasn't mesh. As she fitted it over his head, everything went dark, though it had openings for the nose and mouth. A tremor went through his muscles, a fight or flight instinct. In interrogation training, they taught them how to control it, think through it. He used that, but he realized the coping method needed to be different with her. He wasn't supposed to be looking for an opportunity for escape, using lethal force against the enemy if necessary.

She must have sensed the volatile response option, because she paused after she set the mask in place. She stroked his shoulder. "You're safe. So am I. I'm here. Trust me."

He nodded, a quick gesture. She waited another moment or two, letting him get used to it. Waiting to see if his anxiety over it would escalate. It wouldn't matter if he safeworded or not. If she thought he was losing it, he knew she'd call a stop to it. She'd proven it already. He could trust her.

That thought helped him power through, return to baseline again. He wanted to please her.

She'd picked up the collar, because he felt it in her hands, beneath his jaw. She wrapped the wide strap around his throat, worked the buckle.

"I'm going to lock this, Lawrence. Do you understand? Only I will be able to take it off, but I will before that door is opened."

"Yes, Mistress."

His cock jumped outright as she tightened the collar one more hole, a snug hold that didn't constrict his breathing.

"Now lie down. As you saw, there's a space under the throne. Slide forward slowly, put your face under the chair. There's a hammock beneath. Put your head in it."

Even as she delivered the instructions, she helped guide him so he lowered his head the proper amount to avoid hitting it on the seat edge of the throne. He found the hammock with his hands, and settled his head into it. It put his face a couple inches from the seat above. If it was a normal queening chair, there'd be a platform directly beneath her that could be shifted, giving her access to his mouth, his face. The denseness of the air around him told him she hadn't done that yet, which meant his head and neck were inside a box closed on every side but the one he'd pushed his head into.

After the sub was in place, some of these chairs had a piece to close that side. It would curve over the neck and enclose the head completely. He was glad this one didn't have that, because this was razor close to what he could handle without losing it. She kept touching him, murmuring to him. Keeping him connected to her and the situation.

Her feet came down on either side of his chest, her heels pressed against his rib cage. She grasped one of his wrists, wrapped a cuff around it, and attached it to something on the outside of the box that held it there. His elbow was bent at a ninety-degree angle, his wrist flush against the wood. She did it to the other one, so he was held in place.

Then she moved to his lower body. Bending his legs at the knee, she kept them spread with a bar strapped at the top of his calves. Then she bound his ankles in cuffs and chains.

Fuck, he was shaking. He couldn't stop it. He wanted to tell her he wasn't afraid, not really, but the words weren't coming easy now. He didn't want to break her rules about talking, or ask to speak. Things were swirling around, dark and dangerous, in his head. He wanted to warn her, he should have warned her…fuck, his mouth still worked. He could safeword…

But how could he hurt her? She'd bound him. He literally couldn't move more than a couple inches. It was like all that dangerous power and strength were turning inward, creating a cyclone of energy. It needed to go somewhere.

He should have realized his Mistress would think of that.

She was doing one of her rope wraps around his cock. Moving much more quickly over it tonight, fast and dirty, but just as thorough, encasing it, cinching the rope around his balls. She ran the excess around his upper thighs, and a couple more lines up to the collar. Every small movement of his head and body, every twitch of his legs, would create a tug on his cock.

He'd known keeping his legs up, even during the harnessing of his cock, was intentional. She made a humming noise, her hand doing a quick stroke on his thigh as a slippery tip touched between his cheeks. He'd said it wasn't his thing, and then he'd discovered that wasn't exactly true, when it was attached to her body. But it wasn't attached to her body now. He twitched, tightened in apprehension.

There was a different message to her touch right now, though, and in her voice as she spoke to him. It told him she was going to be obeyed.

"Relax and take it, sailor."

This rubber cock was bigger than what she'd used the other night. Once the lubricated shaft got through those rings of muscles, she used additional straps to hold it into place, and connected those to the web of restraints upon him. Every movement of his body was going to pull on something in his ass, on his cock, against his flesh. The plug was pressing against something that already had his hips twitching, wanting to move, thrust.

She tsked, gave his cock a light slap, which sent a jolt through his balls. Her fingertips gathered the wetness at the tip, played it along his corona. "My slave swore he would give up the reward of a release, if that was my pleasure," she said reprovingly. "An oath means nothing if it's not tested."

His cock was an iron bar, his balls were already simmering, locked and loaded, and she was still in the prep phase. Tested was a massive fucking understatement.

The platform slid out of the way, and he felt the change in the air which said there was an opening above his face. Her fingers reached down, touched his mouth, and they were wet. He smelled some of himself, but she'd wet them elsewhere, too. With her honey.

He licked at them eagerly, but she took them away faster than he wanted. He lifted his head out of the hammock, wanting to reach for heaven above, and fire erupted in his cock.

Fuck, he'd forgotten about the cane. When she hit his dick with it, his legs jerked, his hips and shoulders jerked, and all of those lines pulled in different directions on his cock, sending a barrage of sensations through him. The tightening of his muscles on what was in his ass only added to it. The mix of pure, sharp lust and discomfort were so in balance he realized, with a spike of sheer male terror and animal anticipation, just how experienced she was at keeping a man on the edge of release without letting him go.

"You don't lift your head from that hammock without my permission. You don't move your mouth or your face without my permission. You do nothing without my permission. And that includes..."

She enunciated each of the next words with a strike of that cane on his cock, his upper thighs, in a succession of blows that had his body dancing for her. "Letting. Any. Other. Woman. Touch. You. You will answer me. Repeat the words to me."

"Yes, Mistress. I don't do anything without your permission."

Another strike of the cane. Fuck. "Including...letting another woman touch me."

She might just be getting started, but with that strong opening, what had happened earlier in the day surged up, boiled over. But what boiled over could also begin to flow away, becoming a place in the distance, falling away in the rearview mirror.

"Say it again."

Christ. She made him do it three more times, with the cane in the mix, and his cock and thighs caught on fire. She wasn't playing. He almost thought about safewording, but some part of him knew, however much it hurt, she wasn't doing him permanent damage.

The only thing that was being broken, destroyed, was his world paradigm. It was realigning, putting her at the center of his orbit.

He trusted her. Fuck, he trusted her. The most important and significant words he'd ever said or thought in his life, because he'd never truly grasped that golden ring with someone he was in love with.

He knew that was what this was. There was no room to worry or wonder if she felt the same way. It didn't matter how she felt. She owned him. He was hers.

CHAPTER TWENTY

*O*nce she was familiar enough with a submissive, Ros could let herself get more lost in a session with them. At that point, she would be more instinctively keyed in to danger spots, the wrong kind of discomfort, how often she needed to check certain things.

This was an extreme scene for a man who, before her, had never willingly let anyone take away his ability to move, to see. Then there was what had happened earlier in the day, with Sally. Her crime on its own hadn't touched his heart or soul, but it had stirred what lay in the debris of his relationship with his ex. It had also dug into his transition from the SEALs, that loss of core self that had left him vulnerable as he learned to cope without it, like the absence of a limb or vital internal organ.

All these things, plus danger signs Dale had warned her about in topping someone special ops, had her paying closer, more conscious attention to him. But for the first time in her life, the connection she and this man had forged in such an insanely short time was allowing a side-by-side experience. She was being conscious of his care, of what she was doing to him, at the same time her soul and heart were taking the ride with him.

And what an incredible ride it was becoming.

She adjusted the hammock straps, bringing his head up closer to the opening, where she was now comfortably sitting. When his lips pressed against the lace crotch of her panties, she felt his mouth tremble with the effort not to move against what was there. His nose was buried in her labia, and it made her quiver, too.

She was watching his powerful shoulders, muscled arms. Hell, his whole body, trained to be an instrument to accomplish the impossible. It was here, given to her, at her service. His awareness of that full submission was overwhelming him. She saw it in the tremor that swept him from head to toe. When he'd responded to her, promised to never let another woman touch him with such disrespect, the way Salma had, his voice had broken.

It was these moments that told a Dominant what power truly was. Willingly bestowed, it only remained a gift if it was treated as such.

She rose from her seat and removed the panties, stepping easily from one side of him to the other. Then she knelt over his torso, sitting on his chest, facing his feet, her legs bent on either side of his rib cage. Leaning down, she pursed her lips into a kiss shape she landed on the tip of his cock. Teasing her tongue over the slit, she pressed in, swirling around as she opened her mouth and closed it fully over the corona, including some of the slim ropes tied around it. She bit those ropes, tugged on them as her tongue played, as she opened her mouth wider to take him fully, work her way down and back up, teasing him between the twine.

The shuddering of his thighs increased. She put her palms on them, spreading out her fingers, her thumbs on the crease between thighs and testicles. Her knuckles caressed that rounded area, even as she dug her nails in, and then moved upward, leaving four red lines on either leg. She pinched as she played her mouth over him.

He was moving with her, as her damp cunt rubbed against his chest, his upper abdomen, marking him with her arousal. Those well-developed muscles only added to the sensations against her clit and labia. She let him know that with tiny sounds of pleasure against his cock. She heard his response, a bitten off groan, muttered oaths.

In a similar situation, she might have sat a distance away and looked at him, taunted her sub with her proximity without him being able to see or reach her. But what she was asking of him now was truly one of the most difficult things she could have demanded of him. His body was responding to her, but there was a restlessness beneath it, an unease reined in with a frayed tether.

Knowing he was trusting her this much was something she

wouldn't be abusing. She wanted him to know, to be certain, she was here, she was fully in control, and he really didn't need to be. Her touch, her closeness, was the best way to do that.

She rose, and sat back on the chair again. He obeyed her earlier mandate, not to move his lips against her, though they were right on her wet flesh, but she reminded him. "No moving until I say." Then she began to move.

Slow rotations against his mouth and nose, letting little gasps escape her at the friction. She watched the hands in the cuffs clench into fists, his body rigid, a guard against the desire to open his mouth, to actively pleasure her. His cock was flushed that pleasing mauve color. When she'd had her mouth on him, he'd been steel, but now he might have thickened even more, pressing the limits of those ropes.

She judged he could go a little longer before she'd need to loosen them, but not too long. While technically the body's self-defenses should kick in, deflating the erection as the discomfort and restriction grew too much, her SEAL was a stubborn sort. While men and women were both animals, men were even closer to their beast side when their cocks were in the center of the mix.

Her lips curved at the thought, and she moved one foot, placing the toe on his upper abdomen, the heel on his chest, so he felt the bite.

"Now, Lawrence," she said at last. "You may move your mouth upon your Mistress."

She closed her eyes, her hands gripping the arms of the throne to anchor her as he opened his mouth and devoured. The growl that vibrated against her flesh was as close to a wild animal's as she'd ever heard. She'd pushed him where she'd wanted him. Now she wanted to take them further.

With a hand she had to steady with a superhuman act of will, she picked up the cane, flicked it across his stomach. Then further out, a glancing blow to his erection, his upper thigh. Every movement of his lower body would move the plug inside him, tighten and release the ropes, while the movements of his jaw would do the same. A domino effect of sensations that would become more overwhelming as he shuddered toward that climactic edge.

She was right there with him, because despite being tied down, he was after her orgasm like a predator stalking prey. Every movement of his mouth on her was insistent, demanding, while his hunger to serve her, obey her, kept pace. The amazing duality of the alpha sub.

She put down the cane, one of several tools she'd laid out close to hand, and picked up the flogger. Nearly fifty individual strands, three feet long. About half of them had sparkling beaded tips that would sting. The others would feel like a caress until the skin became sensitized, and then it would be a warm burn broken up by sharper sensations, thanks to the beads.

She started working it over him. His body was as mesmerizing as a tiered waterfall, response flowing from one part to another, all of it a powerful, unstoppable force of nature responding only to the laws of gravity.

The flogger was a prudent choice, more forgiving of random throws, since he was destroying her focus with his mouth. Time to see just how obedient her sub could be.

"Draw back, Lawrence. Stop moving your mouth, but keep it against me, as before."

Her voice was unsteady, breathless. He heard it, didn't want to listen. She didn't repeat herself, but she went completely still, seeing if he would get the message. *I won't respond if you don't obey.*

Her response would be what mattered to him. More than anything else. She knew it like she knew her own soul.

His fists clenched hard, his body reflecting the same, returning to that fierce rigidity. Ten seconds, and his lips lay still against her cunt like a sweet, firm cushion.

The confirmation of what she knew about him made her take a moment. She closed her eyes again, her hands tight on the flogger. "Very good." She made sure he could hear how pleased she was.

She'd used a modified ball gag on a sub in this position before. The ball part went into his mouth while the other end, a nice thick phallus, was pointed up. She'd ridden the phallus while he held the ball in clenched teeth. When she'd climaxed, the response had trickled down, touched his lips.

She had a gag like that with her, had placed it next to the other toys, but that wasn't what she wanted. She rose on trembling legs. If his hands had been free, and he could see, she was sure he'd have noticed and closed his hands over her ankles, her calves, making sure she was okay on her feet.

But in this moment, she was in charge. Of her own self as well as him. Entirely. It was important that one of the messages he received here was that was okay. That he could be certain, even when she enjoyed his care, wanted it, even craved it, she didn't need it in a session until she asked for it. His understanding of that would be his gift to her.

She took off the heels, unhooked the corset, and stood over him naked, surveying him. She kept her legs on the outside of his so he felt where she was. Then she knelt between his spread feet, before his bent knees, and began to remove the restraints on his legs, the ropes from his cock and body. The only thing she left were the cuffs holding his wrists to the base of the queening chair, the collar around his throat, and the plug, held inside him by the press of his ass to the floor.

Her touch alone was bringing him even closer to the brink, because that glistening fluid escaping his slit, the convulsive movements of his cock, were only increasing. When she removed the ropes, she bent, pressed her mouth to the shaft. Not with the intent to tease. Not this time. She kissed it all over, his testicles, the length of his cock, over the head, little touches of her lips. His quivering briefly stilled, but returned as a more intense vibration. She was unlocking the parts of him she wanted to access.

She lifted her head, her hands resting on his stomach and upper thigh. "Are you still with me, Lawrence?"

He didn't know where else in the universe he'd be. He didn't even know there was anything other than her. When this had started and she put that hood on him, locked him down, he hadn't been sure he was going to be able to do it. She'd gotten him here, with her firm, calm manner, with her awareness that he needed her to stay close, right with him, the whole time. Then she'd provided an incredible boatload of distractions.

He was way more comfortable untied and able to see, but the things she was doing to him...fuck, he couldn't really think it through at this point. Comfort was nowhere near as important as serving her.

His cock was aching to fuck her, his mouth wanted more of her sweet cunt. Every muscle, every atom, wanted more of her.

He managed a nod, then the proper response. His voice didn't sound like his. It belonged to something that came out of the depths of a jungle with glowing eyes and sharp teeth. "Yes, Mistress."

"You're all beast right now, aren't you? I'm going to fuck you, Lawrence. I don't mean have sex, make love. No nice words for this. I'm going to fuck you and take. Because I'm angry. I'm angry that another woman touched what was mine. I am going to make sure that even if your brain and all those calculations it makes ever hesitate over this point again, it won't matter. Your cock will remember, and it will take over and tell you exactly how to respond to someone who touches what belongs to your Mistress."

All of the other stuff leading up to this, behavior that in comparison seemed nice, civilized, regular conversation, negotiation—these emotions had been running beneath it. His Mistress was like fire beneath a lake, ready to explode forth and burn.

"The first session we did, you almost came from me hitting your cock barehanded." Her tone went from aching fire to brutal ice. "You get aroused by cock and ball torture, but you respond in a very special way when it's flesh to flesh. You will not come. I don't care what you have to do to keep yourself from it, but you will, because this is a reminder, and I want you to remember it as torture, something you don't want to have to go through again. Understand? No coming until I say, and I may not say. I may decide your punishment is going to be no release until I'm over being pissed."

Christ, he might never get to come again.

"Tell me you understand in a way I believe."

"Yes, Mistress." He licked his lips. "I don't deserve to come. You're right. I failed you."

Whoa. He wasn't expecting the flood of feeling that came in behind that. Or the additional words it pulled from him. "I...don't want to fail you. I can't handle..."

He couldn't handle failing another woman he loved.

He managed to bite that one off, but it was too late. She could hear all the emotions, and would know they involved more than this moment. That unease was back, threefold, and he pushed against the restraints. He was trapped in too small a space, needing more room to breathe, move.

"Lawrence."

Her voice was firm, her hands resting on his biceps. She straddled him, her ass and cunt on his quivering stomach.

She leaned into that throne opening above his head, and her mouth met his. A nuzzling of his lips, a stroke of her tongue. She kept it going as if she had all the time in the world, while her fingers kneaded his muscles. Her backside bumped against his cock, the erection still at full strength despite his sudden surge of panic.

"I didn't say you failed me, Lawrence," she said, as she finally lifted her lips from his. "I am teaching you my expectations. That's very different. You are beautiful. I wish you could see yourself through my eyes. Your powerful warrior's body, restrained by your willing submission, your desire to serve me. We're in this really safe place, just you and me. It's all about you and me. Even though many things, many people, brought us here, right now what sits at the top of that crest of experience, the foundations of past relationships, is just you and me. You understand?"

"Yes, ma'am. Yes, Mistress." He responded quick, desperate, needing to believe her. It wasn't his usual way. He usually thought complicated things through before he answered her. She knew it, and so she kept kneading, kissing him, before she drew back to ask again.

"Do you understand?"

He took a deep, erratic breath. "Yes, Mistress."

She brushed her mouth over his, over his nose. "I like smelling my cunt on your mouth. What is my name, Lawrence?"

"Rosalinda."

"Good. You better not call me Ros, not ever again, or I'll shove an umbrella up your backside and open it."

"Isn't that what's up there now?"

The smartass was still there, ready to be called on in extreme circumstances. Fuck, he wasn't supposed to talk. Maybe she wouldn't catch it.

"Forgot yourself there, didn't you? It's all right. I'll help you remember, so you don't forget the rules again."

She slid away, back down his body. A rustling sound, and her hand closed over his naked cock. The release of the ropes had been pure bliss, but her hand... The rustling sound had been gloves. Silky thin, but still there, a barrier.

"The gloves I'm wearing are black, and go up to my elbows. There's something very erotic about a woman wearing gloves, the way she can feel things through them. I'll take them off in a moment or two, but first we do it this way. Can you feel...this?"

She'd merely been clasping his cock, but now she ran her gloved palm lightly over his flesh, and he felt it. Prickly.

"These are a very special style of vampire gloves. They have tiny barbs, little bigger than hair width, so small they're like getting a splinter you can barely see. You don't even realize they're there until right after...this."

She slapped his cock. For a second, he only felt the sting of the blow. A few seconds later, his cock throbbed, like flesh with a light sunburn.

"Why am I going to do this, Lawrence?"

"So that...I won't ever let another woman disrespect what's yours."

"Very good." Honeyed satisfaction was in her voice.

Then she went after him, no more preface than that. She hit him on the spread upper thighs, the balls, the shaft of his cock. That light burn became more and more intense. She reached between his cheeks and started playing with the plug, pushing on it, twisting it, bringing it partway out and then thrusting home again.

Christ Almighty. Mother, Mary...what the fuck. She'd said torture, and she meant it. By telling him *he* had to hold back, he became both torturer and victim. He called on every endurance technique he had not to let the climax boiling in his balls like the end-of-times come spewing forth.

He almost despaired, thinking he was going to fail her, no matter what she said, but he dug deep. He remembered ops where he'd thought he didn't have anything left, and then they'd all keep moving forward, every member of the team on the same page with it.

Even when you think you have nothing left, you do. A SEAL never has an empty tank. His strength comes from his will, not his body. And the will is a goddamned bottomless pit.

In this case, his strength was coming not just from his own will, but his Mistress's. Her desires. He'd rather suffer a million tortures than her disappointment.

Fuck, that burn was getting overwhelming. He was trying not to move too much, but everything was reaching up toward her, his back bowing, hips lifting. Then she took off the gloves. Literally and figuratively.

She was right. He wasn't sure he wanted to dive too deeply into the why of it, but whenever she slapped his cock and balls with bare hands, particularly his cock, he'd nearly shoot on the first blow. So he pushed himself like he never had before, drawing on the reserves he'd found after swims through impossibly cold waters, hikes over rocky terrain, firefights where the team had been outnumbered.

He would prevail, persevere. Survive. For this moment. For her. He was panting, his lungs burning, heart hammering, chest rising and falling like a bellows. The plug in his ass kept shifting with him, adding to the torment.

She stopped. A groan of pure bliss wrenched him as she put a condom on him, positioned herself over his burning, aching cock and slowly slid down it. Fuck, she was so wet he would have thought she'd just climaxed, except he could feel the tightness of her tissues on him, the aroused tension of her legs, the clamp of her pussy.

"Oh...yeeess. Lawrence, you gorgeous, wonderful man."

She rose and fell, hands on his stomach, those nails digging in. She liked to mark and scratch. He expected the ones on his thighs would be with him a few days. Feeling her all over him, marking all the ground that someone had invaded without permission...it made it all better. But God, he would have killed to put his hands on her right now. He understood, though. This was a punishment, a reminder. All that mattered was obeying his Mistress.

That was the spot in his mind where his tortured body could find an edge to grip, hold onto control, long past when it should have seemed possible. Her body rose and fell, rose and fell, her breath getting more labored. She was going to come. She was going to climax on him, and he was just going to fucking die from the mixed bliss and utter torture of it.

"Now, Lawrence," she managed in a gasp, her voice elevating as the climax swept her. "Go with me."

He seized the chance and made the leap, his hips jacking up hard, thrusting deeper into her, giving his Mistress even more pleasure, which propelled his own. She cried out, and her body was rippling, rolling over his like a wave as he bucked beneath her. He was vaguely aware of the complaint of the chair as the flex of his arm on one side stripped a couple screws, and lifted the chair up, but he couldn't think about that now. He'd fix that. He'd fix everything for her.

Hoarse rutting noises ripped from his throat. The climax was so strong everything else disappeared. There was just a dark, spinning universe, the clamp of her silky soaked cunt, the breathy feminine notes of her cries, the clasp of her hands on him to hold herself, his body providing her balance and an anchor. He liked that.

The climax slammed him through a bunch of walls, no slowing down. He'd never felt anything like it, pumping up in him well past the amount of time he would have expected. Every ripple of her body, every sound from her throat, took him even higher, until he thought it wasn't possible, they could go no farther. But they did.

Then, at last, they were over the crest. Coming down took awhile, her body still moving in a rhythm on his, his responding. The boat that had been buffeted by storm winds and powerful crashing waves rocked slowly down into easier surf.

He really had no brain cells to do anything, but he realized he was pulling against the bonds in almost the same rhythm as the sex itself. The D-rings on the cuffs made a clinking sound as he tried to reach her. Needed to reach her. Touch her. The one side was loose where he'd stripped it, only two of the four screws holding the cuff.

She unclipped the hooks, guided his trembling hands to her. He clasped her bare waist, her hips, felt the cuffs still on his wrists press against her, a reminder of his bond to her. Like a slave with permanent cuffs to always remind him he had a Mistress, an owner. He would like that. He would. He'd wear them everywhere, like the collar to the marketplace and nothing else, like she'd said.

His brain was obviously a tangle of sentimental, crazy goop nonsense. He was even mumbling some of it. He needed to stop. She hadn't given him leave to talk.

But this was different from that. She knew it. She tugged gently on him and he adjusted clumsily, scooting downward so now his head was no longer under the chair. Freaking astonishing was how he wasn't sure he wanted her to remove the hood or collar, return him to that awareness of the world where it wasn't all about her. But she made that transition okay. Though she removed them, she gave him an order, in a whisper soft voice. "Keep your eyes closed."

She lay down on him, and he banded his arms around her, holding her close. Her mouth was against the side of his neck, her hair brushing his face. He could still feel the imprint of the collar on his throat, beneath her lips.

"I've got you," she said, curving her palm over his throat on the other side. She moved her hand down, clasping the cuff, tugging it against his wrist. "My slave."

"Yes, ma'am." He'd never wanted to be anything in his whole life the way he wanted that. It should have scared the shit out of him, but it didn't. Not in this moment, not when everything was exactly the way it should be.

They should have been sleeping, but neither of them was. They lay in the bed upstairs, looking out the big window where the snow was falling into the dark shapes of the forest, the glitter of the lake. He imagined how quiet snowflakes hitting the water were. One part of his mind was always listening, in case anything sounded out of place, but the rest of him was completely at peace. So her murmured question didn't disturb that peace.

"Valentina wasn't a Mistress. But did you sometimes try to actively treat her that way? Like how you kneel to me, kiss my leg?"

She'd come back to the idea several times since their first meeting, always asking the question a different way. Which prompted one of his own. "Can I ask...why do you want to know that?"

"Because it comes to the surface so beautifully in you, Lawrence. Even if you haven't been consciously thinking it, it's been there, crafting a million different scenarios where it can show itself."

What he was with Rosalinda was so very different than what he'd been with Valentina. However, he wasn't sure if *no* was the right answer. He remembered a worse-than-usual fight with her. She'd told him how she didn't deserve him, how she was total shit. He'd tried to kneel at her feet, put her hands on his head, a purely fucked-up, impulsive emotional need to tell her he was here for her, he'd do anything for her, to make things better.

She'd drawn back as if he'd shot her and cried harder, as if he'd confirmed that she was crap, that she didn't deserve his devotion. So he'd ended up merely sitting next to her, holding her until she cried it out and the whole fucked-up cycle could reset and begin again.

He told Rosalinda about that, in halting terms. Her hand moved over him, easy, fingers combing through his chest hair. She had her head on his pillow, at his shoulder, her forehead pressed to his throat and below his ear, so her breath caressed his chest. His arm was around her and it tightened as her hand went down to his groin, stroked through the hair, teased his cock, then started up the track again.

When she was awake, his Mistress wanted him on his back, where she could play with him. It wasn't until she slept that she liked the spooning position, him curled around her. He thought of how she'd tangled her sash around his wrist the other night. Thinking about that made what he'd just told her better, kept any bad feelings from rising as he waited for her response to it.

"Everyone has some Dom and sub in them," she said. "It's just the way we are, as humans. It's not always a sexual orientation, like for you and me. That said, do you think Valentina had submissive tendencies?"

The question surprised him. But as he rolled it over in his head, considering Valentina in that light, sifting through the information, he couldn't offer an unequivocal no.

"A submissive wants to be useful to another, worthy of their lover through their own service." Her voice stayed soft. "You kneeling to her when she had fucked up so much, brought that mirror so much closer. She knew she was breaking your heart. Yet you remained even more committed and devoted to her. It would have torn her to shreds, the ultimate evidence of how unworthy she was, how she wasn't serving you, wasn't submitting to your desires, because she couldn't love you the way you could love her. She'd failed. And with her alcoholism, she was already failing in so many other ways."

He'd never thought of it that way. Which meant his behavior, no matter how well meant, had made things worse.

"Hey." Rosalinda propped herself up on an elbow. Her tousled blonde hair coaxed his fingers to play with the dark tips. She allowed it, dipping into his touch, but she kept her gaze on his face, her hand coming up to stroke his throat with a firm touch. "Don't tense up. Love is difficult, and messy. If we're going to misstep, I think we'd all rather do it because of love, kindness and care, rather than cruelty, ignorance or indifference. We do the best we can."

He tried for a smile. "Unfortunately, SEALs don't believe we've done our best if we've failed."

"Maybe you shouldn't think of it as failure, then. Maybe every step in this life, every lesson we learn in love, is only part of the mission. You don't reach the mission end until you leave this life, and that's when you find out if you succeeded or failed. If you try to learn and grow, and care for those you love, all the way through, I'm betting the tally at the end says you did everything you were supposed to do."

"Easier to say than to feel, when the person you love turns into a total disaster."

"I know," she said softly.

He studied her. "Laurel."

"Yes and no." She tilted her head into his touch, closing her eyes. "I don't want to talk about that right now."

"Okay. But if and when you do...I'm a good listener."

"Yes, you are. You're good at so many things."

She reached for the hand on the opposite side of his body. A cue that reflected his thoughts of only moments ago, and spread a poignant warmth through him. He turned with her, bringing his legs up behind hers, cradling her sweet backside against his groin as she pillowed her head on the arm he put beneath it for her. She tucked his other hand over her breast, letting his palm cradle the curve and nipple as she nestled her head down, her lips on his knuckles.

She'd hold onto him through the night like that, because once she slept, she didn't move. His arm would fall asleep, but that was okay. Brad Paisley was right about that part, in that song he'd done. Long as it was in no danger of falling off, depriving her of its use in the future, Lawrence would keep his arm just where she needed it.

When he'd knelt at Valentina's feet that night, he'd known he was going to lose her. He'd never fully had her heart, and the booze had been like a cancer, taking it over, cell by cell, pushing him to the outside. That kneeling moment had been an act of desperation, a silent plea. *Please fight. Fight it, and I will never stop standing by you, helping you fight, even if it finally backs us into a corner and there's nowhere else to go.*

The thought of a heartbroken man who couldn't rationally figure out how to make it work anymore.

Now he had a contrast. A woman who took his submission, his service, and cherished it. Respected it, respected him. Demanded that he value himself, care for himself, as his responsibility to her.

It was the difference of night and day. And it brought another realization. He knew now why so many songs of love and faith circled around one vital message.

I was lost, but now I'm found.

CHAPTER TWENTY-ONE

"*F*uck."

Abigail heard Bastion muttering it under his breath as his swift stride brought him toward her office. Though there were any number of things their infallible office manager could be irritated by, something about his tone had unease trickling through her, even before he appeared in her doorway and she saw his troubled, tense expression.

"Abby, I fucked up." The words were spoken as if every syllable cost him. "Someone may have our personnel information. I called Dale Rousseau, which is what Lawrence told me to do right away for anything that affected our security. That was about fifteen minutes ago, while I was double checking everything, hoping I was wrong. He's already here."

Dale's response time would only have deepened Bastion's concern, as it did Abby's now. However, no matter her own personal demons, when it came to TRA, Laurel Grove and any of the people she and Ros considered theirs to protect, she knew how to keep her head in a crisis.

"Tell me what happened," she said evenly.

Bastion glanced behind him. He'd been only a few steps ahead of Dale. The retired SEAL moved into her office, and he wasn't alone. A tall, lean male with quiet, steely eyes was with him, and he carried the same special ops stamp that Dale and Lawrence did. With a few days' growth of beard stubble and a Swamp Rats Bar ball cap pulled low over his brow, he reminded her of a Hemsworth, possibly Liam. His serious and intent gaze held hers an extra beat before she pulled herself out of it and returned her attention to Bastion.

"I keep a password book," Bastion said miserably. "It's handwritten. It's just a small, dog-eared notebook. I lock it up when I go home, but during the business day, the drawer's unlocked. I know all of them pretty much by heart, though, so I don't even pull it out that often. Last time was two days ago."

"I know all that, Bastion," Abby said, trying not to be impatient with him. "Why do you think someone has gotten access to it?"

"Because it's gone," Bastion said. "I'm pretty sure it had to do with a delivery kid who came through here a day and a half ago."

"Well, how would he—"

"Do you trust this man's judgment?" the tall man asked.

Bastion stiffened, and Abby's gaze snapped back to Dale's companion. "Without question," she said sharply.

Dale raised a hand. "Neil isn't questioning Bastion. He's saying if you believe him when he says he thinks the information has been compromised, questions about how that happened and how to prevent it in the future aren't the immediate problem."

"And what is?"

"The passwords give the thief access to Ros's personal information, like her travel details; hotel, rental car."

"The address of the cabin," Bastion said, meeting her gaze.

Cold gripped her. She rose from her chair and circled around her desk. She had a small table with two chairs, for quick one-on-one strategy meetings. She put her fingertips on the back of one of those chairs now, because it was drenched in sunlight and the warmth immediately penetrated her fingers.

Daylight. The afternoon sun was streaming, steady and warm, through the full wall of windows in her office. Ros had given Abby the office with the most room, the most light. She'd told Abby she preferred the space at the back corner that was slightly smaller. It still had a lot of natural light, but less than this west facing one. Afternoons were harder for Abby than the mornings, because she could feel the approach of night.

Neil had shifted a pace closer to her, his brow creased slightly. As if he thought she was going to faint, she thought, and snapped her spine straight, shooting him a searing look. His own held hers without any answering challenge, just a seemingly immutable steadiness.

She slipped into session mode, where everything was clear, straightforward, and she was totally in control. Even if it was a fucking illusion, she could do more with an illusion than most people could do with their own reality.

Abby knew the meeting had concluded early at Rainbow Foods and why, since she and Ros had talked about it that same day. But it meant Ros had gone to the cabin last night. A remote location. Isolated.

Bastion had already anticipated her question. "She's not answering her cell, but I know it's spotty out there. I tried the landline. No answer."

Which could mean they were out hiking, or on one of the boats. She didn't doubt Bastion, but it was kneejerk to want to do it, to be sure, to hope this could all be resolved as a simple misunderstanding. Abby turned and reached for the phone on her desk, dialed the number.

If no one had answered, she would have held onto the same hopeful theory. But something else happened. She listened to the message, hung up, dialed again. Her gaze moved to Dale's watchful expression. "It says the number is out of service," she said. "How long ago did you call, Bastion?"

"Fifteen minutes ago. It rang through to the answering machine then. I left them a message to call us back."

She considered that, nodded. Looked toward Dale. "What's our next step?"

Dale and Neil exchanged a look. Whatever communication passed between the men, they were in agreement, because Dale took out his cell. "Be ready with that cabin address."

A few minutes later, he had the Bloomington police on the line. "I'm in charge of personal security for the renter at 611 Lakeview. She went there with her bodyguard yesterday. As of fifteen minutes ago, the landline isn't functioning. She has protection due to an active gang threat, and we believe there's been a security breach here at her New Orleans office." He provided a few more details, listened, nodded.

"I'd appreciate it. I'm not telling you your business, but send more than one car out there, with lights going and sirens blazing. The gang she pissed off won't hesitate to shoot a sheriff's deputy doing a drive-by house check. If everything's fine, the commotion will give the neighbors something to talk about. If it's not, you'll be ready." Dale paused. "Sheriff, if you want my gut feeling, here it is. Get them out there fast, or you'll be cleaning up bodies."

Abby's hand convulsed on the chair, and damn it, her knees weakened alarmingly. Fortunately, maybe no one noticed, because Neil had somehow moved so he was right next to her. A hand with intriguingly long, strong fingers wrapped themselves around her elbow and upper arm, cradling as much as holding it. As she glanced up at him and was caught in his gaze again, she was reminded of standing next to a tree whose roots could never be ripped free of their hold on the earth.

"Dale doesn't mean Ms. Thomas," Neil said helpfully, a dangerous glint in his slate-colored eyes. "He means whoever tries to get to her through Lawrence."

The afternoon sun sparkled on the snow as Ros stood out on the slope by the cabin. Snow was a rarity in New Orleans, and when it happened, it was a soft powder, gone almost as soon as it fell. She was almost childishly delighted to be crunching along in a few inches of substantial ice-crusted white stuff. Thank goodness, she'd brought a quilted coat, good for inclement weather. She hadn't thought to bring gloves, but she had pockets.

In the Southern climes, snow shut down everything when it happened, but Indiana was prepared for this kind of thing, with snow-plows and de-icers. When they left, they shouldn't have any problems. While navigating the winding roads under snow conditions could be challenging for a normal person, she'd have a trained combat driver at the wheel.

If she turned, she'd likely be able to see that driver through the windows. He was in the living room, taking an extra moment to check some Texas football scores on the sports station. He'd checked their surroundings at least once last night and this morning, even after a session that would have put most submissives in a coma for the full night. Seeing him enjoying some down time now pleased her. It suggested he might be semi-relaxed.

She'd made them breakfast, which they'd shared with leisurely pleasure. Afterward, they'd hung out on the couch together, watched a B movie on cable, discussing the pros and cons during the commercials. She'd taken a post-breakfast nap, an indulgence she rarely granted herself. He'd dozed some with her as well.

After the movie, they'd hiked down to the water to get their appetite going for the thick sandwiches he'd made them for lunch. This afternoon, they'd watched girls' softball. He said his friend Neil had gotten him hooked on it. By the time they'd reached the final inning, he'd had her appreciating it in a way she never would have expected.

They'd have to come back here when she wasn't under death threats. It had been awhile since she'd been somewhere so devoid of city sounds. In New Orleans, even when it "seemed" quiet, there was always an undercurrent of noise.

Though she wouldn't question Lawrence's diligence, checking the property last night and this morning, privately she believed he could relax. It wasn't like someone attacking her could blend into the crowd, unless they were disguised as a moose, or a bear. If one of those appeared on the slope below her, coming out of the dense forest, she would be delighted. Though she'd prudently retreat toward the house.

She heard the back door close, his shoes crunching up behind her. He didn't have snow boots, but he was wearing serviceable work shoes with thick treads that would give him good traction in this environment. He'd need it.

Hiding a smile, she stopped hot potato-ing the snowball from one cold palm to the other and spun on her toe, firing it in his direction.

He nearly dodged it, but she had the element of surprise, and it hit his shoulder. And she had more. Despite her lack of gloves, she'd amassed a pyramid-shaped arsenal at her feet and scooped up two more, shooting them his way.

He dove behind an outside woodpile, and returned fire far more swiftly than she'd anticipated. The man had good aim. She ducked one, but not fast enough, shrieking as it thudded against her chest. She ran for the cover of a gnarled tree with a wide trunk. While she had to abandon her stockpile, fortunately the ground was covered with plenty more ammunition.

But then her man went for shock-and-awe, surging out from behind the stack of wood and charging across the field at her. He was undeterred by her hail of snowballs that found their target more often than not. Until one exploded right in his face when he was six feet from her. She bolted for the house, laughing at his expletive.

Those shoes gave him the definite advantage. Her block heeled boots were far more practical than the shoes she normally wore, but they weren't made for full out running across uneven terrain, in the snow. As he grabbed her around the waist, she twisted, trusting his strength as she shoved at him. She sent them tumbling into a snow drift.

His face was wet, with snow crystals in his clipped beard and eyebrows, and his green eyes were fired with a devilish pleasure. When he leaned down to kiss her, she flattened her hand on his chest, holding him back.

Since she'd met him a handful of days ago, she'd been exploring the Mistress and sub connection outside the walls of Progeny. Within those walls she had plenty of room for improvisation, like within the boundaries of a swimming pool. With Lawrence, it was more like an ocean, with endless directions. If she followed a current, or rode a wave, there was more room to see where it went, and the current could shift or change, the waves get higher or lower, depending on where her moods went.

He was good at figuring out those moods. He glanced down at her quelling hand, then up at her. His mouth tightened. He'd wanted to kiss her, and he didn't want to be denied that, but he restrained himself without getting growly about it. She'd reward him for that.

As she pushed herself up on an elbow, she increased the pressure on her palm until he understood and laid back. It reversed their positions, her leaning over him. She sat up. "Put your arms out to your sides. Like you're making a snow angel."

"Don't need to. Already got one of those."

He could make her smile, even as he made other things get serious and intent inside her. He put his arms to his sides. He was wearing a black toboggan cap, and she pulled it off, liking the way his silky hair flitted in the breeze, how it felt as she stroked through it. She touched his brows, teased the snowflakes from his beard. As her fingers passed over his lips, he kissed them. She leaned back down to take advantage of that tempting mouth.

"Don't move anything," she murmured. "Just your lips."

"Some things move, even if I tell it not to," he responded. "It's all your fault."

She smiled again and closed the distance between them. Oh, his mouth. The man had such a mouth. Always warm, even if initially the weather gave her a pleasing cool contrast. He parted his lips so she could find his tongue and teeth with her own, and her blood surged at the heat and hunger she could feel from him. Instantly there, all hers to call. These were the moments she knew what it felt like to be a goddess, the most awe-inspiring elements of nature at her fingertips, able to call a storm to her. The turbulence of a man's desire.

She'd started the morning astride him, wanting to feel that nice, thick morning erection stretching her tender tissues. She'd rocked upon him, her hand pressed on his chest, her eyes on him, watching and absorbing everything as they both gave themselves to that intense edge. And now she wanted him again. She thought she could take him every other hour and not get enough.

She'd put one hand on his shoulder, his chest, but had left the other braced on the ground, in the snow, until her aching skin could take no more. When she broke the kiss, she stayed close to his face, staring into his eyes. She threaded her fingers under his coat, found the hem of his flannel shirt and her way beneath it. She laid her ice-cold palm on his bare, muscled abdomen.

He stiffened, and made a sound against her mouth, another oath, but he stayed still. Even when she reversed course, slipped the button of the jeans and tunneled under them and his briefs, her intent obvious. When she closed her fingers over his cock, she found he was right about not being able to keep one part of himself from moving. His already stiff cock jerked in her grip as she closed her cold fingers over it. He arched into her touch, this time a definite half-protest, half-growl of desire rumbling from his throat.

"I've heard SEALs aren't fond of the cold," she said. "But I thought that might be because you haven't had the right experience with it. I was right."

"How's that?" he managed.

She gripped, squeezed, stroked. "No cold shrinkage here. Not a bit."

Wry humor rippled amid the lust. "I want to move my arms."

She shook her head. "Bend your knees. I want your jeans and underwear pushed off your ass."

He looked like he thought she'd lost her mind, but he complied, bracing his legs so she could tug on the denim. "Back down," she said.

He sighed through his nose, but did it, putting his ass in the snow with only a slight flinch. She unzipped his jacket, unbuttoned the shirt and spread both open, passing her hands over the light mat of chest hair. She followed the narrowing arrow of it down to where his cock rested against his lower belly. As her gaze fell on it, it twitched again, telling her his reaction to her obvious pleasure.

She stood up, one foot between his spread legs, the other on the outside, and opened her own jacket. As his gaze rested on her, following everything she was doing, she opened the buttons of her gray cotton long-sleeved blouse, revealing black lace. The blouse had loose, angel wing sleeves and tapered tails that framed her hips like butterfly wings. She'd brought jeans, but she'd had a plan when she went out in the snow, so she'd chosen the warmest skirt she'd brought, a silk-lined wool tweed. It was worth the cold legs as she inched it up, almost to the matching black lace panties, but she worked them off beneath the tweed without showing him what they were uncovering.

At least until his throat worked on a hard swallow, and he spoke low. "Please show me, Mistress. Allow me to look."

Not a demand, but not a plea. He was so good at straddling that line. She paused, considering, and then she brought the skirt up to her waist. She straightened her back, and felt a tingle of sensation through her cunt when his gaze went there, lingered. A trickle of reaction dampened her labia. She thought about straddling his face, but she'd demand that from him later. She wanted something different out here in the cold and snow. Wanted to defy the elements with the heat of their joining.

She dropped the coat off her shoulders, and the tails of the gray shirt fluttered away from her body. The coat landed on his shins. "You'll be cold," he said.

"No. I won't." She unhooked the bra, threaded the straps out of the blouse sleeves so the cups fell loose and her nipples puckered from

343

the weather. But she didn't feel that either, except as a reaction to his hot eyes coursing over them.

As she came down over his cock, she rubbed her damp folds on him. Not damp. Wet. She fished in his jeans pocket for where she knew she'd find a condom, but he tilted his head, his lips parting.

"I'm clean, Mistress. Always safe. If you want me without anything between us."

She did. And he was giving her his trust, not because he was being foolishly impulsive, but because he did trust her care for him. It was in his expression, a gift beyond words.

Since she'd been on a backup birth control for some time, and hadn't had sex without protection in years, she could give him that, too. She showed him, with the soft curve of her lips, a matching expression in her gaze that fired the need in his. She squeezed his bare hip and shifted to align herself with his erect member.

His cock pressed in past her gate and found the well of arousal waiting. She took an inch of him inside.

"Don't move," she reminded him, as she felt his muscles tighten. "Who's in control here, Lawrence?"

"You are."

She treasured hearing the raw words. All those muscles that could overpower her in a heartbeat went to drum tightness beneath her. She knew his ass had to be cold, but his cock was ready to serve her.

The sun was getting lower, the sparkles around them divided into bands, thanks to the shadows cast by the trees. As she lifted her head, snowflakes touched her face. They were coming from the branches as the wind picked up. Tiny kisses of moisture as she sank down on his cock, letting it fill and stretch her.

Bliss. His gaze was drinking her in, and she imagined what he was seeing, the paleness of her throat, the gleam of her hair, the desire and need in her eyes, locked on him. The wind gusted, and she shivered.

"Let me move my hands, Mistress. Touch you one place."

She nodded, and he lifted them. Unlike her, he'd donned gloves, but now he pulled them off. A typical man, he chose to put his palms on her bare breasts, but not for typical reasons. She welcomed the heat of him as he cradled the nipples, the curves. That he was enjoying the sensation, she had no doubt, but the kneading movement wasn't the pinching or fondling she would expect. He was warming her.

She cupped her hands over his, drawing warmth for her hands too as she rose and fell. When they'd first arrived at Rainbow Foods, he'd held the door for her. The car, the front door of the building, the conference room. The elevator. Reinforcing with every gesture his desire to care for her.

She'd been very conscious of the women's glances at him, that amiable female envy. Ros's response to it in a politically incorrect world would have been, "You bet your ass I'm tapping that. Do I look insane?"

Vera would have rolled her eyes, even as her Mistress side would have understood completely. Just as she would have understood how different and far away that possessive feeling was from Salma's transgression.

Context, and the glorious give and take between Mistress and sub, was everything.

Ros embraced a clean, strong wave of lust. Her body was already shuddering with every stroke. Though she hadn't commanded it, he thrust up into her, and she allowed it, because he was following the needs of her body, not his own, though it served both.

"Oh..." Her cry started low, a composition of notes that became more and more intense as the orgasm built. He held his own, obeying her mandate of never releasing without her permission. In this case she expected the cold helped with the restraint. For the most part.

When she finally gasped out, "Now," he was only a stroke or two behind her. His grip fell from her breasts to her waist and hips, holding that anchor so he could drive into her with a strength she welcomed as much as the look of uncontrolled desire on his face. As he jetted into her, his hungry eyes never left her.

God, the feeling of it, nothing between them, made it all the more intense, and it had already been world-rocking, each time before. When she came down on him as they both finished, she could barely coordinate her limbs. Though still quivering with his aftermath as well, Lawrence found a corner of her coat and threaded her arms into it, covering her against the wind.

Her reaction to that, to everything, told her she was falling in love with him. How could she not?

He helped her rise by lifting her, and got himself up, hiking up underwear and jeans, fastening the latter. She helpfully dusted off his ass as he sent her an amused glance. She batted him away as he tried to do the same for her, with far too grabby hands, and he grinned.

They didn't say much, but he put his gloves on her hands, despite her protest. He closed his bigger hand over one of hers, now cocooned in the pillowed fabric, to guide her back up the slope toward the house. "How about I build up the fire?" he asked.

"Thought we just did that." She chuckled. "Sounds good, though. Supposedly, Abby keeps the area's best hot chocolate stocked in the kitchen. I'll make us some."

"I like that idea."

She turned to look at the sun on the snow once more before all that light disappeared behind the forest cover. Despite all the negatives the world could throw at them—Laurel, Valentina...Salma, Snake, the reasons Lawrence was her bodyguard— today had been a perfect day. And if not for Snake, there might not be a Lawrence. She wasn't going to give Snake any karma points for that, but it was a reminder that the good often came with the bad in life.

She was ready to go enjoy more of the good. Lawrence was a few steps from her, leading the way back to the house. She smiled at him, reached out a hand.

Snow kicked up to her left, close enough to spray her. For a heartbeat, she didn't understand, but then she registered the sound that had come with it. Sharp and close enough to spike fear up her spine.

Gunshots. Someone was shooting at her.

CHAPTER TWENTY-TWO

"*Move. Run.*"

Lawrence barked the command with such force that she responded with knee-jerk obedience.

It wouldn't have mattered if she'd resisted, though. In the moment he snapped out the command, he'd closed the distance between them and propelled her forward with a rough shove. As they raced toward the cabin, he kept her in front of him while staying so close behind, she realized he was creating a partial shield, making it more difficult for the shooter to lock onto her.

A moving target is harder to hit. Self-defense 101.

They reached the house. Still wearing the oversized gloves, she fumbled the knob, but he took over and turned it, then he was pushing them inside. As he closed it, he spun and covered her, pressing her to the wall next to the door as the glass in its upper part shattered. She shrieked. He was moving them again, into the depths of the kitchen, cutting off lights as he went. He put her between the refrigerator and the opening to the living room.

He'd reversed their positions, shielding her in front, his gun out and ready. She had a moment to wonder where he'd been carrying it, if he'd been lying on it while she was straddling him. The thought was completely irrelevant, but her mind was doing the trauma thing, scrambling for pointless inanities.

"Stay right here. Don't move."

He stayed low, moving swiftly to check the other rooms before he was back with her. Where he'd put her kept her out of the direct line of any windows, yet he could see all entry points. Fortunately, they were in the log cabin part of the structure, with thick walls that would stop bullets. She hoped.

"Most gangs don't employ military-grade snipers," he said. "But there'll be more than one shooter. Gangs don't do anything alone."

He'd already checked his cell and hers, pulling it from her pocket. He'd retrieved the handset from the counter but swore and tossed it back up there as soon as he checked it.

"It's not working," she said.

"No. It's not."

She'd removed the gloves, so when her hand fell onto his knee, gripped him, he closed his own over it. His strength and heat reassured. Though his expression remained cold, hard, she drew reassurance from that, too.

He went back to the bedroom, again moving low, and was back with a case. He flipped the top open, revealing the pieces of a rifle he assembled and loaded in the time it took her to digest what it was.

"Good thing we didn't fly commercial."

He shot her a glance, gave her a wry smile that didn't dilute the deadly expression. There was also another handgun in the shaped foam of the case, additional magazines. As he readied all of it, donned a shoulder harness for the second gun, and pocketed an extra magazine, his tense body pumped heat. She spoke through stiff lips.

"What should we do?"

"I'm going to go out there, drive them off or drop them."

He was leaving her in the house alone. She shoved the cowardly thought aside. "Won't someone have heard the gunshots and called the police?"

She didn't wait for an answer to that, the absurdity obvious. They were out in the hills. If anyone heard gunfire, they'd think someone was hunting or target practicing. "Doesn't it make more sense for you to stay here, make them come across the open ground to the house?"

"We're going to lose the daylight in a matter of minutes. They likely have night vision goggles, something you can get practically anywhere now. They'll use them and close in."

"Do you have any?"

He lifted the ones he'd put next to him that she hadn't noticed. She usually prided herself on her attention to details. "Me going out there is the best way to reduce their numbers," he said. "Try to keep them from getting into the house. Understand?"

She nodded, though it felt like her head was on a taut string. She'd brought her Walther, and that was something else he'd retrieved from the bedroom that she hadn't noticed. "Tell me you practice with this regularly."

"Gun range once a month. Draw drills at home at least once a week."

"Good." He handed it to her, butt first. "If anything goes south for me, this is a good defensible point. You've got visual on all entry points to your location. There's no cover for a vital couple seconds once they show themselves. Wait for your shot, make sure it's not me, and then put your finger on the trigger. You don't put your finger there until you intend to shoot. When you do, take the second to aim, and remember to squeeze, not pull."

Goes south. He could die. He was her bodyguard, her personal security. Since the break-in at her house, the shooting at the diner, her focus had been on the risk to her, her people. Now suddenly, she saw those sights lining up on the man putting himself directly between her and bullets. As the thought sank in, she had a hand clamped on his wrist, but she wasn't the one in control right now.

"Keep your head, don't panic," he said. "That's the most important weapon you have, even more important than the gun. You're tough, Mistress. Don't pussy out on me now. I'll be back." A quick, rough hand on the back of her neck, his lips fast and heated on hers, and then he was gone, moving into the back of the house.

She looked down at her hand. Blood. There was blood on her palm. She checked herself fast, then realized it wasn't hers. She'd put her hand inside his coat, against his shoulder. He'd been shot.

She reminded herself his color was good, his eyes and voice steady. If he had been shot, it hadn't impaired him much. Not that she could tell.

But he'd been shot.

That thought alone could have frozen all her brain cells, but she remembered that last moment, his look. That statement, a challenge designed to get her back up. *Don't pussy out on me now.*

Prick. Tears tried to squeeze up into her eyes from her aching chest. She tightened her fingers on the gun. One thing she knew for sure. If anyone did get in here that wasn't Lawrence, she wasn't going to hesitate.

This was a planned, serious attempt to kill her. Which meant Snake *would* have killed Pria if she'd crossed him the wrong way. A nineteen-year-old girl carrying a baby. Whoever was shooting at her now was guilty by association.

Anger was better than fear. She hunkered down. She couldn't get away from the fear, but she could manage it. She would focus on the tasks he'd given her. Watch all approaches, stay calm. Be ready to react.

She wouldn't think about the blood she'd smeared on her tweed skirt, but it was impossible for her not to think of the man who'd bled for her.

They were getting out of this. She refused to consider any other outcome.

His Mistress had balls of steel. When he'd told her the plan involved him coming out here, he'd seen her flash of raw fear. Then she'd gotten on top of it.

He'd hated leaving her side more than anything he'd done in his life.

In the movies, the bodyguard stayed with the target, to get those intimate exchanges, the funny and brave one-liners. In the real world, if you were a one-person security detail with no support coming, it was about getting the upper vantage point, taking out as many as you could before they reached the target. Maybe they'd give up before that threshold was breached. If not, he'd whittle the numbers down and come in behind the remainder.

The house being on a steep slope, requiring the car to be parked a quarter mile down the drive, had eliminated the option of the enemy rolling right up on the door and using their vehicle as a shield. So they were on foot. The first shot had struck closer to him than Rosalinda, and the second one had hit him in the shoulder as he shoved her at the door. They thought if they took him out, they had her.

They were underestimating her, but if they got to her, they *would* take her down. She would use that gun, he had no doubt, but firing it under stress was a hell of a lot different from doing it at a gun range, and smart criminals knew it.

If the plan was to take out her bodyguard, Snake wanted her alive. He wanted to play with her before killing her. He might bring her back to New Orleans so he could make an example of her. Torture her in some back room, gang rape her. Teach her how little power a woman held in his world.

Lawrence put all that out of his head. The only thing that mattered right now were calculations, logistics. Keeping them from achieving their objective.

He was guessing at least five enemy. That seemed about right for a long-distance job. They'd be NOLA boys, not used to the terrain. He dearly hoped Snake had made the mistake of coming with them.

Lawrence found his first target moving through the shadows of the forest at the base of the hill. He trained the rifle on him. People could bitch about the American military all they wanted, but no one who'd ever gone up against them, particularly their special ops units, disagreed when they were called some of the best trained forces in the entire world. He wasn't a sniper, but he was trained for accuracy at five hundred yards, and this was plenty less than that.

He squeezed, and the man went down. He was quick to surveil, and sure enough, he'd flushed another two-legged rabbit, about fifty feet away. He took him down, but the guy struggled back up, so Lawrence's second shot finished him.

Two down. Then he heard shots from inside the house. A woman's scream. Not a yelp of fear. A battle cry.

He slipped back into the shadows. Everything in him wanted to run across open ground. However, his goal was to keep her alive, and that required him to do the same. He wouldn't make the mistake those two had just made. Plus, if he was right and Snake wanted her alive, they wouldn't kill her right off. Unless she made keeping her alive too much trouble.

Lawrence moved through the woods, swift as a snake, all energy focused on foiling his enemy's objective. Not on the way that cry echoed in his gut like a knife wound.

When she heard glass shatter in the rear bedroom, Ros already had her gun up and pointed that way. Her back was still shielded by the refrigerator and bank of kitchen cabinets. The man who charged out of the bedroom had to take those vital couple of seconds to find her, just like Lawrence had said. Unfortunately, her thudding heart, her untrained reflexes, needed those seconds too, so he'd found her, was running at her, yelling, his gun pointed straight at her, before she got her act together.

She fired, and kept doing so, as he fell. She hadn't even seen the man right behind him, who came over the body like it was as important as a log across a forest path. Before she could jerk the gun toward him, he'd closed the distance and punched her in the face, driving her to the tile floor. He kicked the gun away and yanked her from the floor by the hair, pulling her in front of him, putting his back to the same cabinets. It was Snake. The stench of his preferred cigarettes clung to him, male sweat.

Three seconds. Lawrence had said that was how long most gunfights took. Her mind was reeling, her heart hammering, breath caught in her throat. She tried to thrash, struggle, and Snake hit her temple with the gun. Pain exploded, making her see stars.

"I'll bust your fucking head open if you don't stop," he told her. "Tobias," he shouted.

A crash from the other bedroom. Then nothing. Until Lawrence stepped out of that room, the rifle on his shoulder. She would have felt relief, except Snake was on his feet, dragging her up with him, his grip so tight on her throat that the stars in her vision were replaced by widening black spots. She was choking, her toes barely touching the floor. She tried to kick with her heels, but she had no purchase. She couldn't think what to do with her hands. The lack of air was everything.

Lawrence adjusted the muzzle, and she saw his eyes narrow, focus. Fighting for air, those spots pinwheeling, she still knew what he was going to do.

You just think *you're a predator, Snake.*

Snake shouted in pain, his grip loosening. She dropped. As she did, she thought she'd felt the heat, the displaced air of the bullet. So loud.

She was on the floor, holding her throat, coughing, as Snake slumped to the ground next to her. He was still holding his gun, but his fingers were loose, his eyes losing focus. She reached out, shoved the gun away from his convulsing fingers as his dark gaze became permanently fixed. A death stare.

Sirens. There were sirens. Lots of noise. Why was there so much noise, yet everything in her head was silent, like she was way under water? What she saw around her was choppy, like a slide show instead of a movie. The front door crashed open. Lawrence had placed the rifle against the threshold of the bedroom door, raised his hands and dropped to his knees.

The way he did for her. While that wasn't the reason he'd done it now, it felt like it was, because he kept his gaze locked on her when he did it.

Over so quick. So quick. Yet it had taken so long. She didn't realize she was saying the words, or that it had been over for some minutes before she focused and found herself being held by Lawrence. He'd moved her away from Snake, into the living room. He was holding her in his arms as he sat against a wall, her cradled between his bent knees. Her head was on his shoulder. An EMT was saying something to him. About her. Was she okay?

Of course she was okay. That wasn't the point. She found her words, even though they came out raspy and high.

"Shoulder. He's been shot."

Maybe more than once. But as she struggled to move out of the EMT's way and Lawrence sent her a vaguely irritated look, she reclaimed more control over herself. Enough to let the second EMT help her into a chair while the other one got Lawrence out of his jacket and checked the wound.

"It went through," he was saying. "Didn't hit anything too bad."

But she saw him wince when the EMT checked it. "Hospital...X-ray..." were the words she caught. When Lawrence shook his head, she overrode him.

"He's going." Meeting his eyes, she found she could string words together again, no matter that they sounded shaky. "You're going. Security risk is over. Back in my territory now, sailor."

His lips twisted. "With you, the security risk is never over. It just doesn't always involve life-or-death things."

353

Adrenaline was wonderful. It kept you from feeling anything. Mostly. Her teeth were chattering. He was on his feet and kneeling by her chair, no matter the EMT's protests. He had his uninjured arm around her, holding her.

"It's okay," he said.

"You could have died."

"That's the job."

"No. *No*. I forbid that to be the job."

"You need to check the bodyguard job description."

The EMTs were talking about a gurney. They had zero chance of getting him on it, or into their ambulance, without her help. Maybe even with it, given the steady, no-bullshit look he was giving her now. "If it comes down to you or me dying, Rosalinda, it's going to be me."

But then he sent her a considering look. Infused with an almost boyish hopefulness "But...since you didn't die and I got the bad guy, I think I've earned a bonus."

She strangled on a chuckle. "You're using our life-or-death scenario to leverage sex?"

"Nope. Yep. Maybe. My choice of the sex. Me on top, eye to eye, holding you in my arms."

"I come first," she managed.

His lips curved. "That's a given. I still serve you. Just want to serve you in a way I've fantasized about."

"Missionary sex is your fantasy?"

"What can I say? Vanilla is my closet kink."

"Stop. Just stop." He was making her smile, but it was also making her heart hurt and her eyes burn. She put her arms over his shoulders, crossed them behind his head, laid her forehead on his shoulder. He turned so his jaw pressed against her ear, the warm rasp of his breath. His arm tightened around her waist, held her close.

"We're okay," he murmured. "It's all okay."

"It's so not okay, I don't even know where to start."

He curled a lock of her hair around her ear, a soothing movement. "This is just another day in the neighborhood," he said. "A twisted Mr. Rogers show."

She imagined the trolley in New Orleans like the little train on Mr. Rogers' show, trundling by right now, to pick them up and carry them back to Jackson Square, to her office. It was a silly bit of nonsense that made sense in some distant, non-scrambled part of her brain.

She needed to pull it together. She'd survived. Snake hadn't. Pria would no longer have to worry that he would be coming after her or their child. She took a breath, rose from the chair as Lawrence stood with her. She gave him a short nod, telling him she was okay. He was still holding her hand, because her own was clutched around his so tightly. Yet when she made a conscious effort to release him, he held on, kept her close to his body, those intent eyes. He spoke in a voice meant only for her ears.

"It wasn't leverage," he said. "Just something I wanted. Just wasn't sure how to ask for it before."

"If you ask me the right way, Lawrence, I'll give you anything." Maybe even her heart and soul.

He tried a smile, didn't make it. His eyes had become an intense dark green forest. "Did I ask the right way, Mistress?"

"You did. In every way. But you're going to the hospital first."

The local sheriff had told them they'd been alerted by a call from Dale in New Orleans. So while Ros kept an eye on Lawrence in the ER, she called Abby, brought her up to speed. Dale and Neil were with her, so Ros gave them all the details they wanted before Abigail took it off speaker phone and apparently sent them away so the two of them could speak privately.

"He's dead, Abby," Ros told her. "It's done. It's over. Tell Pria before she hears it elsewhere. She has no love for him now, but she did at one time."

Everyone thought about the could-have-beens, after all.

"I will," Abby said. "Once you get home, you might have to punch Bastion. He's taking way too much of the blame for this. A cousin of one of Snake's guys is a delivery courier. He regularly brought us packages, so he knew some of the routines here. Probably saw Bastion with the password book a couple times. They leaned on the kid to get the information about where you were, so he stole that book a few days ago."

"Tell Bastion it all turned out the way it should," Ros said. "Snake is dead. But from here forward, he locks that drawer even when the office is open."

"I think he plans to keep it in the firesafe. How about from here forward, we also consider not incurring the wrath of a local gang?"

Abby had sounded cool and collected on the speaker phone, but now, just the two of them, her voice became strained.

"That's asking a lot." Ros held the phone a little tighter, as if she was squeezing her friend's hand. "I love you, by the way. It's all good."

Abby paused a long moment. "Take your time coming home, because if you get here too soon, I'm going to hold onto you like an idiot who can't ever let you go."

Tears gathered. "I could use that kind of hug right now. He took care of me, Abby. He..." Ros paused, stunned where her mind went. Her voice had become even less steady than her best friend's.

"Sounds like we might have some things to talk about," Abby said, calmer. "Take care of your man. Maybe send me a text about every fifteen minutes until my heart returns to a normal rate."

Ros's pulse was thudding in her throat, but she pushed past the enormity of what had just filled her mind, summoning humor in its place. "If you hint a local threat is still pending, those two good-looking SEALs might hang around the office longer."

"Dale's married and a Dom, a double-non-starter. And how do you know Neil is good-looking?"

"I could tell from your voice, when you and he took turns talking. Something about him intrigues you."

"Shut up. You're in shock and delusional."

"Defensiveness. Suspicion confirmed."

Abby hung up on her, which made Ros feel better. She knew Abby meant it, about that hug. A situation like this brought up memories neither of them wanted to experience. They both remembered getting the call about Laurel.

While Ros held out little hope that Abby would explore some-thing with Neil, she kept hoping a man would come along who would make her take a second look. Who would fight for her, even if the biggest obstacle he faced was Abigail Rose herself.

A problem for another day. She returned to the curtained section of the ER where Lawrence was. He was shrugging back into a clean button-down they'd brought from the cabin. The nurse was giving him the fisheye, as if she'd tried to help and he'd warded her off, but Ros wasn't taking no for an answer. She took over, helping him get the shirt on, and then brought the nurse back into it for the sling they'd provided to give his wounded shoulder full support.

He didn't want it, she could tell, but she sent him a look that told him he'd have a full fight on his hands if he resisted. His lips tugged into a rueful smile. After the nurse stepped back, he used his free hand to stroke his fingers through Ros's hair, which probably looked like a bird's nest. He also touched the swelling on her face from Snake hitting her.

"I would have dropped him for that alone," he said.

The fantasy of a man who would kill for a woman and the reality of it, from a man who knew the weight of a death on the soul, drove the words even more deeply into her. She put her hand over his, and gave him that understanding. "I wish it had never come to that," she said. "But thank you for saving my life."

"You talk to Abby and Dale?"

"Yes. And Neil. They were at the office. I'm sure Dale will want you to call them, provide the military speak version."

He shrugged. "'Bad guy dead. VIP safe.' A text will cover it. Where do you want to stay tonight? Even with that nice fireplace going full blast, those broken windows are going to let in a pretty substantial draft."

Abby's property manager would handle the repairs, but he was right. "If you're up to an hour drive, with me driving," she sent a pointed look at his shoulder, "how about a night at the Ironworks in Indianapolis? Bastion booked us the Founder's suite. Double TV partition wall, sixty-inch screens, terrace, spacious shower. And a very large bed."

"That's all you had to say."

"Sixty-inch screen?"

He chuckled. "That, and the other thing. The bed."

"You do look tired."

"Protecting a hard-headed marketing executive is pretty challenging. But I have some energy in reserve. SEALs have unlimited stamina and endurance, remember?"

He was teasing her, but she suspected she wasn't wrong. Once the buzz of having survived wore off, he'd need sleep. So would she. She also knew he'd give her anything she asked, even if it was his last ounce of energy.

His phone started buzzing. He fished it out, laid it on his leg, glanced at it. His expression told her what it was about, and the knowledge didn't please her. But she wasn't going to give him crap about anything right now. "You can answer that if you need to."

"Later. Tomorrow." He shut the phone off. "You're here with me. That's all that matters. Let's get out of here."

But as he rose, the stiffness in his stance and grimness around his mouth, neither caused by his injuries, cast a shadow toward her earlier thought.

Yes, he would give a woman he loved everything she asked. No matter if she had no damn right to ask that of him.

There were some things a Mistress couldn't fight or fix. She just had to decide if she could live with it.

But not tonight.

CHAPTER TWENTY-THREE

*T*he Ironworks was everything Abby had told her it was. Her CFO had stayed here several times. Once inside the room, it was as if they'd entered a cocoon. Turn of the century industrial décor was combined with all the amenities one desired in a hotel suite, even a firepit on the terrace, so they could enjoy sitting out in colder weather. She noted it when she wandered to the windows to look at the city view.

Lawrence, having checked the suite in his usual thorough way, now watched her from the center of the room. She turned away from the windows, gazed at him. She saw a tired man who'd saved her life. Who'd given her so much of himself in the space of a handful of days, a few key sessions. Thinking of what she'd said to Abby, she had to add one more thing to that list.

He'd captured her heart.

Up in the halls of heaven, was a story like theirs mapped out? If so, then the strength of their feelings, so miraculous to the two of them after such a short time, wouldn't be surprising to the angels at all.

You've been falling in love for decades, they would say. It was a process that had started long before they'd ever met one another. Every relationship they'd had before was part of the story, every experience making it possible for them to realize the person who had what they each needed, what they'd needed all along, had finally arrived.

Like opening the door of a house they'd been building for years, to become their forever home.

Ros was articulate. She was an intelligent woman who knew how to put words together in persuasive ways. Yet when it came to something like this, her core self rose up, and it was all about emotion, passion. Strength. Feeling, overwhelming feeling, always made her want to act.

She moved across the room to him. Put her hands on his chest, slid them up to the sling. She detached the Velcro pieces to take it off, and began to unbutton his shirt.

"You need a shower," she said. "The amenities for this suite include a very luxurious rain shower spigot."

He lifted his hand to her face, her hair, stroked through it. "Will you take one with me?"

"Yes," she said simply.

She ran her hands up over his chest, the soft hair, the hard muscle. She stopped short of his injured shoulder, but he clasped her wrist, laid her palm fully over the bandage. His lips tightened at the pressure, but his eyes said he wanted her to touch him however she wanted.

She wasn't going to deliberately aggravate the injury, but the gesture closed her throat, kept her from being able to speak at all. So she let him unbutton her shirt one-handed, then shrugged it off, leaving her in lace. She placed his hand on her chest, just above her breast.

"You can touch me how you wish, Lawrence."

He paused, acknowledging the significance. Then he trailed his touch over her flesh, to the pocket at the base of her throat, onward to the side of her neck, following the line of her shoulder. He slid his fingers under the bra strap, eased it off her shoulder. Then he let his fingers travel down her biceps, his thumb reaching and then coursing over the upper rise of her breast. His palm molded against the side of the curve held in shaped lace and satin.

His green eyes had become more intent, the set of his mouth firmer. He knew how to be in charge, make life-or-death decisions. Yet he would wait for her permission to touch her. He craved her control when it was about this. It would bring a whole other level of response out of him, something anyone who'd only had vanilla sex with him would never have tapped or recognized. No matter how much he'd fantasized, she was the first.

There was a charge in that, but she realized, with that little belly flop she'd experienced on the phone with Abby, that being first wasn't nearly as important to her as possibly being...the last.

No. She wasn't freaking herself out tonight. She was keeping this in the here and now. There was plenty of feeling just for that.

She opened his jeans. He'd removed his shoes, and now his hands left her to remove the pants. He had to sit down in the chair to do it. She watched him, her eyes coursing over every inch of him, as Mistress and woman, which made the journey contain an element of pain. Seeing the bandaged shoulder, the seep of blood staining the gauze, enhanced the terrifying significance of the other scars he bore on his body. She could have lost him before she ever knew him.

He rose and she moved around him, sliding her fingers over the older bullet hole marks. Her gaze flicked down to the scar tissue on his calf, above his ankle. She thought of his limp, that day when he'd snapped at her, and then later told her why. Life had beaten the hell out of him, and yet it hadn't diluted the passion inside him, as warrior, lover, submissive...remarkable man.

She removed the rest of her clothes, took his hand, and guided him to the shower. Turning on the light activated a heater to take the chill off the bathroom, so she left it on for now, started the water.

They'd given him plastic and medical tape so he could cover the wound for bathing. She helped him with that, and then they stepped under the blissfully heated spray.

Once in there, she pressed him down on the bench. While a water-resilient material, it had the look and texture of wood, edged with pewter-colored accents. He looked up at her breasts, nearly in front of his face. At her gently reproving look, he half-smiled before he lowered his gaze, giving her the gift of his submission, his understanding that she was in charge here.

She washed his hair, ran soap over his shoulders and back, chest. She gave him the bar then, and began to clean herself with another one she'd picked up from the sink. His eyes came up, clung, as she cupped her breasts, soaping her nipples. She moved down, working in between her legs and buttocks, creating a slippery and fragrant foam on her glistening skin.

He was barely moving his soap over himself. When her gaze dropped deliberately, encouraging him, he gripped himself, soaped his cock with slow, easy strokes that had her heart accelerating.

She washed her hair, rinsed, working around him, stepping between his feet. He rinsed where he was sitting. When he laid his head back against the wall of the shower to gaze at her, his eyes were half-slits. She was glad she'd made him sit on the bench. SEAL or not, being shot took its toll.

Exhaustion was riding close on her, too, but she didn't lack the energy to play and tease, lighten the darker feelings about the day's events that hovered within reach.

There was an additional sprayer with a long flexible tube. She detached it from the wall and moved the flow of heated water over him. His eyes closed completely.

A moment later, his hands lay in slack curls on his thighs, and his shoulders had lowered. He'd drifted off. He felt safe enough with her to do that. To trust her. It only increased her tender feelings of protectiveness, and the desire to care for her submissive.

She shut the water off, retrieved two towels. After easing him away from the wall, she put one around his shoulders. While the wall heater was making the bathroom toasty, she wanted to be sure he stayed warm while she dried off. When she finished, she coaxed him to his feet.

"Let's get you up and dried."

He rallied enough to try and take over, but she told him to stop and did it herself. When she at last drew him into the bedroom, she took the plastic off the bandage, made sure it was still dry.

"Time to go to sleep, sailor."

"We had a deal." He looked at her, the exhaustion and willingness to let her care for him not eradicating evidence of her stubborn, strong male. "I want to be inside you."

She grazed fingertips over his mouth, and wasn't surprised when he teased them with his tongue, sending sensation swirling through her, head to toe.

"You had a request," she said, with a faint reproof. "I might agree to it. But first we rest."

He nodded, but stood there, gazing at her, until she drew him to the bed, made them both lie down. She curled up against his side, inside the span of his uninjured arm.

"I'm here. I'll be here when you wake."

It was the last thing Lawrence heard. Some parts of the shower had been dreamlike, his subconscious recognizing everything was secure enough to allow recharge. His body had grabbed that with both hands, leaving him little say in it. The ability to take rest when and where he could get it was a life-saving mechanism, but the hunger in his gut didn't care. It wanted her.

But she'd said she'd be there. When he woke later, he had a gnawing ache in his gut. After the usual quick acclimation to his surroundings, he confirmed she was still next to him. The feeling eased.

Lying on the shoulder hadn't been an option, and lying on the uninjured side put pressure on it, from the downward pull of gravity. On his back had worked, especially because Rosalinda had arranged pillows under the affected arm.

She was curled up against the shoulder that wasn't sporting a bandage. Her head was on her pillow, breath soft and even. She was beautiful all the time, but at rest, here in the bed with him, both of them safe, he thought he'd never seen a woman so breathtaking.

She'd laugh at him, but it didn't change anything; he meant it. His cock stirred, wanting. He trailed his fingertips down her face. She was sleeping so peacefully, though, and it had been a horrible night for her. A glance at the clock said it was near dawn.

Her eyes slowly opened. She did that thing they had in common, coming awake between one blink and the next.

"I want you," he murmured, before he could stop himself. "The way I said. On top."

"Can you do that without harming yourself?"

It was probably going to hurt like a son of a bitch, but he could handle pain. Pain was far easier than loneliness, than this vast emptiness that said he needed her. Now.

"Yes." He shifted, turned on his side, cupped her face. "I want to make love to you, Mistress. Spread your sweet legs, put myself between them. Lie on top of you, feel you move beneath me. May I?"

Her fingers curved over his biceps. Exerted downward pressure. A sweet, nonverbal *yes*.

He closed the distance between them, kissed her. Kept kissing her as her fingers flexed on him and she made that sound in her throat that said she was pleased. She was relaxing into things, would give as much as she would take. He needed both from her, and wanted to offer the same.

He slid the arm she was holding beneath her, ignoring the screech from the sore muscle. When it came to injury, movement was a man's friend. Not too much or too little; that was how he'd heal. He understood the limits of his body, and knew he could have this.

He pressed her into the mattress and pillows as he moved from her mouth to her throat. She tipped her head back, her hand drifting over his shoulder, down his back. Every inch of him that felt her touch sent sensations to his brain and back again, affecting all the rest of him, not just the steel of his cock against her hip. Her fingertips teased over it, and he knew the tip would have dampened her fingers. As he lifted his head, she put those fingers in her mouth, her eyes on him as she tasted him. His heart skipped a beat.

He went back to her throat. He loved that slim column, the pulse beneath his lips. Then her collar bone, to the rise of her breast. He was glad she'd slept with him naked, nothing between them. He teased the curve with his lips and tongue. He lingered a second over the crescent scar. She'd get tense if he stayed there too long, but he gave it caring attention with his mouth as long as he could. It was a reminder that he accepted every part of her.

He worked his way to the taut nipple and put his mouth on that, suckling deep. A moan slipped from her, her hand in his hair, digging in, as the other slipped over his back restlessly, nails dragging over his flesh. Her thighs were shifting, and he knew she'd be wet.

He wanted to take a good, sweet, long time with this. He kept suckling, his other hand closing briefly over her waist, her hip before his fingers drifted down her upper thigh and across. Her legs parted for him so he could cup her pussy, feel that wetness on his palm. He worked the heel of his hand slow against her clit as he sucked her nipples, and she became a wave, moving against him.

He wanted to taste everything. He let go of the nipple and slid his mouth over the curve, down her upper abdomen. She took care of herself, his Mistress. She was firm and strong, with enough soft flesh to remind him she was all woman.

He was close enough to the juncture between her thighs to smell her arousal. His Mistress loved to have him serve her with his mouth. He could put his mouth there, and wanted to, but he wanted to be inside her even more.

He moved back up, and shifted his body over her. That first moment, cradled between her legs, his cock sliding over her gateway, was as near to paradise as he could imagine.

She parted her lips, working for air, as he put the head of his cock to her heated wetness. "Now," she whispered, and he slid in, slow and strong, any pain he was feeling overcome by something far more important. Fuck, he could stay there forever, especially when, as he pushed all the way into the root, his Mistress arched, a flicker of surprise on her face swallowed by ecstasy as she climaxed, just from the friction of their joining.

Every medal in the world wouldn't have meant as much as seeing that reaction, just from penetrating her, bringing himself into her.

He moved, a deliberately easy rhythm, as she raked him, cried out, her response building. He watched every change in her face as she did it. His cock was hard and aching, but he wouldn't have lost this moment for anything, even his own release.

His slow movements kept that climax going strong, and when she finally stopped, her eyes were locked on his as if she'd never seen anything like him before. Her blue eyes glittered through her lashes.

"Come for your Mistress, Lawrence," she whispered.

He obeyed.

He'd reached the limits his body was going to tolerate, and she knew it, even if he didn't. Ros eased him to his back, readjusted the pillows under his shoulder and arm again to support it, and curled up against his other side.

Later, when he was healed, she might decide it hadn't been fair to give him his bonus when he was still injured and couldn't enjoy it as long as he wanted to do so. So she'd let him do it again. She was generous that way.

They gazed out the windows at the city view, talked low about random things. The casual conversation would more easily lull him back to the sleep he needed, which was good.

"What were you like as a kid?" she asked. "Did you have a nickname?"

His chest rumbled in a half chuckle. "You would ask something like that. Yeah. Deadhead."

"Deadhead?"

"Yeah. Zombies. I loved zombies. I had action figures, T-shirts, made them out of clay, did zombie video games... My mom used to tease me, said most teenagers were already zombies, just grunts and moans, shuffling along." He considered her. "Where are your parents?"

"Currently living the expatriate life in Costa Rica, with maximum tax benefits and an open-air home. The rainforest within walking distance is for my mother. The three bars, just as close, are for my father."

His hand, sliding along her back, paused, then continued. "You see them much?"

"My mother comes back to the States twice a year to visit me and my sister, who lives up in Oregon. She stays with each of us for a month. We go there in January for about a week." She moved the subject back to him. "So, you were all about zombies. Did you have a best friend back then?"

A pause, and she felt a slight tension, held then released. "Yeah. Kyle. We both decided to go into the military. He said I signed up for SEAL training to prepare for the zombie apocalypse. I told him he joined the Marines to get girls."

"And both could be true."

"Exactly. He said it wasn't fair that all this media hype came along, making SEALs seem sexier than a jarhead."

She scraped a nipple with her teeth. "That's totally what made me decide to have sex with you."

He twisted, his arm tightening around her. "I figured. Frog hog."

"What a terrible term." She slid her hand over his chest, to his biceps, careful to avoid the bandage, then circled back. Dropped more small kisses on his flesh. "I'm sorry he's gone."

He hadn't said that Kyle had died, but it was in his voice. "Yeah," he said, after a pause. "Add up all the conflicts from the nineties forward, we've lost a fraction of the soldiers who died before that. And yet he manages to be goddamn one of them."

Lawrence sighed. "He was nineteen years old. Both of us still wet behind the ears. I got the details from some of his buddies in his unit. 'Tell my mom I really, really love her.' Last thing he said."

Lawrence's throat got tight as he remembered Mrs. Madison. A very attractive blonde with a pin-up figure, yet it was her sad eyes that had stuck with him, the way she shrank in the presence of Kyle's dad, who acted like he was always trying to prove how much more important he was to Kyle than her. Yet anything about Kyle would light her up like a sunrise. He remembered being in their kitchen plenty of times, her listening to the two of them talk about zombies, school, whatever, while she made them snacks.

He told Ros about that. "Did anyone in his unit ever tell her what he said?" she asked.

"I hope so. I always meant to swing back and visit her. Something happened to Kyle around the time we were in high school. He and his dad got really tight, and she got pushed even more to the background. Kyle started talking shit about her when he talked about her at all, and we didn't go to his house much anymore. At first, I didn't have the perspective to do more than agree with him, but eventually my critical thinking skills expanded beyond zombies and unconditional acceptance of my best friend's bullshit. Especially when I spent the weekend with him and his dad at the beach, shortly before we graduated. Seeing the two of them together..."

He stopped, realizing that sick grip in his lower belly for what it was. He wasn't going to go there, though, not after that damn near magical moment with Ros. "I told Kyle that his dad was an asshole, and if he wasn't careful, he could turn into the same. I remembered nothing but good things about his mom, so I couldn't imagine she'd changed that drastically. Whereas his dad was clearly becoming a bigger asshole all the time.

"After that, we both got caught up in things, me with the SEALs, and him in the Marines. But I did get a chance to see him once more, about a month before he died. He had changed. For the better. It made me glad."

"I expect your conversation helped."

He shrugged. "Can't say, but being in the military definitely did. Got him away from his dad, let him see the world from a different viewpoint."

"Makes sense. Skye says we can live in a one-room house with no windows, or in a garden with no fences. Which one we choose is determined by how open we are to what the world has to teach us."

"She says this?"

Ros smiled against his flesh. "She used her Judi Dench voice. She has a whole library of celebrity voices on her phone and computer."

"They're an interesting bunch, your circle."

Ros's conversation with Abby returned to her mind, as well as Abby's response. *Sounds like we might have some things to talk about.* They'd both known what she meant, and it was deeply unsettling. Not necessarily in a bad way. Ros had never gone down that road with a man. Even the few times she'd taken things outside the club boundaries, it had been light-hearted, a conscious add-extra-spice-to-the-relationship decision they both enjoyed. What she was thinking about now was way the hell different.

"You remember the night you asked me for exclusivity?" she asked slowly. "You challenged me, asking if it was okay for you to be with other Mistresses."

"Yeah. I remember." He stroked her back, rough fingertips playing along her skin. "Your eyes shot actual sparks at me."

She decided to ignore that comment. No matter how true it was. "You might remember I said my *no* to sharing you was a qualified no."

When she said nothing else for a few moments, he filled in the silence. "Does it have to do with the top shelf women?"

"What?"

"It's what I call your executive team in my head, because their offices are all on the top floor."

"Ah." She'd been debating how to say aloud something she never had to a man. She went with blunt. "We have an agreement. When one of us finds the man she wants to keep, to belong to her always, we bring that man to all of us. To share."

The startled look that flashed across his face wasn't unexpected. It was followed by that deep core thoughtfulness he had. Not an outright rejection. More a mix of emotions. Then he latched onto the significant part.

"Has that ever happened...for you?"

"No. Not for any of us. There've been times a couple of us have shared a sub at Progeny who enjoys being tag-teamed. But that's different. This is something we decided...after Laurel."

She touched the scar over her breast. His gaze went to it, his eyes darkening. She'd told him that maybe one day she'd tell him the story. It was time to do so.

"Abigail was the one who suggested it..."

Laurel hadn't left any written guidance on her preferences. Not unusual for someone who didn't expect to die so young. Those details fell to the circle of five friends who knew her best, since she had no close blood relations.

Ros had been her maid of honor and was now her executor. Two things that should never happen within the same decade. Laurel had once mentioned a preference for cremation and a celebration of life, not a casket and a funeral, so they went that way with it. They knew her favorite songs, the charities she would have wanted people to send memorials to, in lieu of flowers.

Ros and her inner circle of women made donations, but they also made sure the church where they held the celebration of life was decorated with Laurel's favorite kinds of flowers. So many it looked like a garden.

Afterward, they took her ashes to Couturie Forest, one of Laurel's favorite places in New Orleans. But Ros couldn't go back to the car after the scattering. She walked away, taking one of the flagstone paths deeper into the forest, skirted with heavy undergrowth along the sides of the path. A storm was blowing up, the skies heavy. At a certain point, Ros realized she'd walked far enough she'd be drenched before she could get back to the car. That was fucking fine with her. She planted herself, and sent the silent challenge to the heavens.

Bring it.

She didn't have much patience for religion, but she'd always considered herself spiritual. A person had to be a clueless idiot not to recognize the patterns that lay beneath everything, the energy that fueled life. Which only made her angrier. She'd never doubted there was an order out there far bigger than herself, but today, her anger was large enough to immolate whatever that energy was.

She didn't remember when she started shouting at the trees, threats, taunts, accusations, promises of retribution. Or when words became primal screams of utter rage that stripped her vocal cords, took her heart up to a painful gallop in her chest, and drove her to her knees. That made her mad, too, that her body would buckle under her fury instead of using it to explode into a force of nature that could level everything that had brought them to this moment.

"If you want my heart, just take it. Don't take her."

She scrabbled on the forest floor, manic, and her fingers closed over something hard and sharp. An old arrowhead, like a message from the gods, her challenge answered. Great. She didn't care what it was. She would have used a tree branch. Or her fingernails, come to that.

She ripped open the neckline of her blouse, set the arrowhead's rough point to flesh and went after it like a wild animal's fangs. Then someone was on the ground with her, holding her, grabbing her wrist, making her drop the dirt-caked rock.

Cyn had broken her hold, while Abby had her arms around her from the other side. Skye supported her from behind while Vera knelt in front of her. The four of them contained her in that circle, kept her from shattering.

Why, why, why, why... The pain broke through rage, and she was howling. Later she would understand why keening was a ritual for some cultures, but she didn't want ritual. She wanted to run through the forest and destroy everything in her path, but their touch, their presence, seemed to drain her strength. She collapsed in Abby's arms, sobbing, while the others closed in tighter, shielding her from the watching eyes of the gods she'd challenged.

"Sshh..." Abby started making the soothing noises at the exact moment Ros was ready for them. She was good at that. And only when Ros started to get herself together, the keening dying away, did Abby speak actual words against her temple.

"A goddess gets angry when fate steals something precious from her."

The tender humor couldn't conceal Abby's pain. It reminded Ros she was the head of their family. They needed her. They were all suffering.

So Ros gripped Abby, held her. Eventually the others drew back. Not far, still within arm's reach, but they knew Ros's tolerance for coddling would run out far quicker with an overabundance of it.

When Ros had her wits about her enough to look at all of them, she spoke. "Never again," she said hoarsely. "We never let one of us get that deep again, not without us being in just as deep. That way no one can be taken like this, not ever again."

She wasn't sure what she was saying, but Abby plucked the meaning out of her soul in her usual, clear-eyed way. She was the strongest, smartest person Ros had ever met.

"All right." Abby looked at the rest of the women, pulling them a step closer. For the pact. "If any of us finds the one we want to keep, then we make him belong to all of us. Open him up so every one of us has stood in his heart and soul, and knows him. Agreed?"

There was no hesitation, no questions. They all understood, in that way they did, when it mattered most. Hands fell upon Ros's shoulders, so they were all connected.

"Agreed," they said. United in resolve...and grief.

Bringing herself back to the present, the sanctuary of their hotel room, would have been far more of a struggle if Lawrence hadn't sat up, had his hands on her face, cradling it, brushing away the hard-won tears, kissing them with his warm lips.

"I'm all right," she said.

"I know you are. Abby's right. Goddesses don't like it when other forces fuck with what belongs to them."

She curled her hands over his, pressed her face to his. She needed to finish it, but she needed this too.

He picked up on it, not easing back down for some moments. When he did, she laid next to him, put her hand on his chest, her cheek on his shoulder.

"We agreed if one of us found the person we wanted forever, we would share him with the others—for one night. It would give each of us a full sense of his soul. We'd be as sure as we could be that he'd do his utmost best to love the one of us who chose him, who wanted to give her heart and soul to him in exchange for the same."

Said aloud, she expected it sounded insane. In the years since then, no one had reached that point with a submissive. Time should have made them dismiss the agreement as an overly dramatic, grief-saturated moment. But now, looking at Lawrence, the memory was clear and sharp, and she felt just as certain of it as she'd been then. When she'd inadvertently hinted at it with Abby on the phone, her friend had picked right up on it, too, as if the pact had been made last week, instead of years ago.

There was more than herself to consider, though. She tapped him. "There are still things we have to learn about one another, Lawrence. I don't know that we're there yet. We haven't known one another for long. And I'm only speaking for myself."

He put his hand on hers. "No, you're not."

She could feel the heavy thud of his heart like the intensity of his eyes, impacts that hit her soul and stayed. She nodded, but made the effort to speak calmly.

"However it shakes out, whether we get there or not, I wanted you to know about it. I want to say it's not a deal breaker. But I'm not sure I can. There's something inside me that says, if a man is to one of us what he seems to be ...he'll understand. Understand and embrace that night as a blessing. Not as a going-forward, open invitation to share what belongs to that woman alone."

He shifted to touch the scar, trace it. Sometimes it felt like a wound that had never healed, which was why she didn't like it to be touched. Except right now, when he cupped it, giving her the heat of his hand, and the shelter it offered. "How many stitches did you need?"

"I let them clean it, give me antibiotics and an updated tetanus, but I refused stitches. I wanted the reminder to be there, as ugly and jagged as it was when I made it."

She drew circles on his chest, thinking. Her original intent had been to keep the conversation focused on tidbits, like his childhood nickname. But her course with Lawrence hadn't ever followed the path she'd intended, had it? Being an experienced Mistress had taught her the best journeys with a sub resulted from not mapping them out too strictly, but sometimes being with him was like being a bird in flight, riding air currents. Exhilarating, but she could end up places she hadn't expected, good or bad.

He felt thoughtful, not tense. So did she. Then he surprised her, by handling things. He tipped up her chin. "There's a time to go over the mission details, and a time to let the brain rest," he said. "I've heard everything you've said, Mistress. How about we leave it there for now, and enjoy this nice hotel room?"

"Trying to tell me what to do?"

He smiled, his green eyes serious and warm at once. "I'm not brave enough to do that."

Yes, he was. He hadn't given her a direct answer about the outlandish thing she'd sprung on him. But now she thought he did, with a simple declaration.

"I love you, Rosalinda."

CHAPTER TWENTY-FOUR

*S*he knew he meant it. He didn't say what he didn't mean. And he hadn't asked her to say it back before he drifted to sleep, which made it all the more unsettling.

One part of her heart reacted to his statement as if she'd been given the only key in existence to a collar he'd don just for her. She'd always been a woman with an above average libido—maybe because she spent quite a bit of time expanding it—but it still surprised her, how much she could want him.

After they slept some more, they started the day with her straddling him, taking advantage of his morning erection as he moved from half-sleep into a full awareness of her. His hands found her hips, flexing on her, pushing her down while she drove them. As the climax rose, she kept her eyes on his, all the way through his release—right after hers, of course.

In the shower about a half hour afterward, he'd tried to take her up against the wall, that typical he-man behavior to prove he was capable of protecting his mate, no matter that he'd had a bullet put through his shoulder.

But she'd already noticed that the hand belonging to the injured side had gripped her far less strongly in bed than the other one. So in the shower, she sat him down on the bench, straddled him again and rode him to completion, his mouth suckling and tugging on her nipples, her hands cupped around his nape. He'd come inside her with a shuddering need that seemed as endless as her own.

Once they recuperated from that, he left the shower to shave, using the sink. He had a towel wrapped around his hips, that look she liked, the way it split at the thigh and outlined his buttocks. When he was done, with a sweetness that charmed her, he pressed his hand to the frosted shower door, meeting palms with her. Then he slid out of the room to find some clothes, leaving her to finish shaving her legs.

After she got out and dried herself with another of the thick, fluffy towels, she noticed he'd cleaned the sink after he'd shaved. His razor and shaving cream were next to it. Neat, domestic things that touched her oddly, like his palm on the glass.

Intimacy. Things shared unconsciously. It made her think of her call to Abby yesterday. How she'd become so choked up over all of it. Which led her back to what she'd told him before dawn, the pact she'd made with her circle of Dom sisters. Also driven by strong emotions. In broad daylight, she should be able to put all of it into proper perspective. But she found her feelings on it hadn't changed.

But all that aside, Ros didn't make hasty decisions, and this one was a life-altering one. A paradigm she'd never expected to shift at all, let alone so quickly. So some slow-down was warranted. In more than one way.

She considered their options. They didn't have to go home right away. They could transfer their afternoon flight a couple days out, and enjoy the area. Enjoy each other. See what was real and what was the result of an intense and dangerous situation.

She donned the hotel robe. She still needed to dry her hair, but for now she just combed it out and went to see where he was.

She expected to find him dressed, maybe checking what was on cable on one of those sixty-inch TVs. Instead, he was standing on the terrace, the towel still wrapped around his hips, showing her the muscular terrain of his back and shoulders. He hadn't put the sling on, but he had the arm close to his body, guarding it.

He was on his phone.

Before she reached the open door, she knew the call involved his ex. One of the many things that bugged her about anything related to Valentina was how his situational awareness diminished. If he knew Ros was only a few feet behind him, he didn't show it. She'd like to think that was a sign of his trust, but he would have at least glanced at her, acknowledged his Mistress, if he knew she was there.

He hadn't closed the door, so he hadn't intentionally tried to keep her from overhearing him. Stepping out onto the terrace had likely been prompted by an agitation requiring movement.

"What are the doctors saying?" he said. As he listened to the answer, he lifted his head to look up at the sky, his hand tightening on the phone. "If she gets better, she could detox there. She's done that before, though... Yeah, I get that this would be a longer recuperation period, so it could take hold... That would be good, Zoey. But..."

He stopped. She couldn't hear the words, but it was clear Valentina's mother was hitting him with a rush of words. He was holding the phone a couple inches from his ear, probably because of the vehemence projecting through it. When she moved closer, she could hear the woman.

"I know you're not together like that anymore, Lawrence. But you told her you'd do anything for her." Her voice was rough. The sound of a woman close to breaking. "I'm so sorry. I shouldn't be saying something like that to you. I know that. But as much as you've gone through with her, I've been through worse. I'm still here for her. I'll always be here for her. I'm her mother. But...I don't have much left. It's you she believes in."

His shoulders locked, knotted. Under another set of circumstances, Ros would have reached out, rubbed, reminding him to relax so he didn't aggravate his injury. But she'd gone still, inside and out, listening.

"If you can help make this happen for her, she'll have more faith that she can make it work. Please promise me you'll at least come see her when you get back into town. I know you can't do much about the other problem, but at least...please. I know you said you had to walk away, and I know you're trying to establish distance...but you still love her, Lawrence. She's not drinking now, not in that place. You know she's so easy to love when she's not drinking."

If he was wrapped in chains and being beaten with rubber hoses, she thought he would look less defeated. When his shoulders lifted in a hard sigh, he flinched from the pull on the injured muscle. "Okay, Zoey. I'll call you when I'm back in town."

He clicked off and moved closer to the rail, staring out over the city. Ros stood there, looking at him, but she wasn't seeing him. She was seeing another impossible situation. Hearing Laurel's voice. If she stood here long enough for Lawrence to turn toward her, she knew she'd see that same look in his eyes she'd seen in Laurel's. So distant and yet so close, if Ros could simply figure out how to bridge that distance. But she hadn't then. And she wouldn't now.

You told me you'd stand by me, no matter what... You can't put conditions on it... I'm not as strong as you.

As heartless you mean. I can see it in your face.

It's not that. You're just...you can walk away from things other people can't, Ros. You never tear your heart open for anyone. You never get all the way down in the mud to really love them.

Hurtful words that Abby said Laurel hadn't really meant. It didn't matter. The point was cycles. Fucking cycles, always coming back to the same goddamn starting point.

She wasn't so self-absorbed as to think other people's situations, their conflicts, were the gods aiming a direct shot at her, but hellfire, she had to wonder if the gods liked fucking with her as a side hobby. Maybe they found it funny, putting people into the path of same shit, different day, and seeing how often those people fell into that same pile of manure.

She'd said she wouldn't get lured there again, and here she was, as susceptible as anyone else. But this time, she didn't have to see it through to the inevitable end. She hadn't missed her exit. Only flirted with passing it by.

"Time to go home."

He turned. Knowing the look would be there didn't make it hit her any less hard. Her heart cracked, but she wasn't going to ignore the obvious. She saw the combination of heart-sinking regret, pain and soul-deep weariness that told her what he was going to do. Even if he didn't know it himself.

Enablers had a sickness worse than the addicts they propped up. Her mother and Laurel had taught her that.

"It's a hard place to leave," he said, but she could see he was relieved he didn't have to tell her he had to go back home. He didn't realize that it was his phone call that was making her cut the trip short. A few minutes ago, she would have happily stayed here with him a whole week.

She turned, heading back to the bathroom. She closed the door, locked it. A minute or two later she heard him approach the door. Stand there.

She donned travel clothes. White blouse, black slacks. Last night, when she'd hung up her clothes, she'd seen his eyes linger on the red scoop neck knit she'd brought, a different choice for the slacks, one that would have revealed a tasteful swell of her breasts above the neckline while outlining them under the form-fitting fabric. He'd like her in that, she was sure. She would have worn it for a nice dinner out on the town.

Instead she went with the monochromatic choices that sent a message of uncompromising resolve. But because she was her, she coupled it with blood red lipstick and a pair of heels checkered in multiple gleaming colors, including a red that matched the lipstick. The corners of the diamond pattern on the shoes featured tiny studs in a dull gold.

He hadn't moved from the door, but he hadn't spoken, either. She wondered what he was thinking about, and then he moved away. She heard him rustling around the room. Probably doing what she was doing. Donning clothes. Was he thinking of it as armor, like she was? She doubted it, though it made her think of that first night at his place, when he'd been the one to initiate the raising of walls by getting dressed. Some ways of protecting oneself were universal, no matter how flimsy such methods might be.

She packed up her toiletry bag. It wouldn't take her long to put her overnight bag together. She checked her makeup and hair once more, stared at herself in the mirror.

She needed to get back to New Orleans. Into a normal routine. It was too easy here to tell herself lies about what she'd just heard, what it meant.

When she stepped out, he was standing by the window, staring out. Wearing jeans and a T-shirt. His shoes. Oddly, it was the significance of the shoes which hit her hardest. It called to mind his reason for wanting to remove her shoes at the cabin, see her bare feet.

It means a lot, that they're walking the same earth as me.

"What's happening with Valentina?" She forced out the words. She was expressing concern, as a friend should. She and Lawrence were at least that, though the thought was almost as repellant to her as him calling her Ros.

More likely, she had a drop of hope left, thinking his response might allay her fears. She didn't have to believe a duck was a duck just because it presented with a beak, webbed feet and feathers.

He turned, looked at her, evaluating her appearance, her tone. While he made the same effort to seem casual, she expected he was aware of the brewing storm.

"I'm more concerned with what's happening in your mind."

"Tell me what the situation is," she said. "Then I'll tell you what, if anything, has changed for me."

His jaw tightened, but he answered. "Car accident. She was hurt pretty badly. She was responsible. Drunk, of course. No one else was seriously hurt, but she has a couple choices. Prison, or she can have herself committed to a treatment facility. Can't check out until the court-appointed guardian okays it. If she does it before then, they pick her up, take her straight to prison. A couple years minimum."

Ros blinked. "She's been busy."

"Yeah." He took a breath. "Zoey found a private place that can do it all. Coordinate her medical needs, the PT from the wreck, take her through rehab, a more supervised regimen. She thinks, with the mandatory consequences, and the reputation this place has, it might just work this time."

"Sounds good." She waited on him. Waited for the other shoe to drop. She didn't want it to do so, but what she wanted in these situations didn't matter.

"The complete program is pretty expensive," he said quietly. "Zoey put down the twenty-five thousand she had in her retirement savings to cover the first several months."

"She wants you to help? How? Are you that well off?"

He shook his head. "But there are ways I can earn more money. Overseas. Contract security in hot zones. Mercenary work, if I have no other choice."

She blinked. "Do you have a choice, Lawrence?"

His eyes went hard. "The frost queen routine is getting old. Say what you want to say."

She studied him a long moment. "Why are you interested in me, Lawrence?"

His brow creased. "I'm not following."

She crossed her arms, leaned against the door frame. "What I'm seeing is a man who wants to serve a woman who desperately needs him. Even if she shits all over you, takes everything you have."

Sparks flashed in his gaze. "It's not like that. And that wasn't Valentina on the phone. It was her mother—"

"Same difference, and you know it. Was me being under a death threat from a gang close enough to that desperation to satisfy the craving? But now that's done, and Valentina needs you more."

He stared at her. "Is this a jealousy thing?"

Her emotions were too close to the surface. She should back off, give herself time to lock them down. Instead, she crossed the room, bumped toes with him. The force of her feelings should have shoved him back ten feet. But the man could become a brick wall when he wanted to do so. "You really think that's what this is?" she demanded.

His lips pressed together. "I don't know. An hour ago, I was so deep inside you I was lost, and now there's a wall a foot thick between us." He reached toward her.

When she stepped back, the hurt in his expression struck her chest hard. As she buried it, iced it over, the first evidence of anger crossed his face.

"You think I'm giving her too much," he said. "Yet you're so determined to keep history from repeating itself and tearing up your heart, you're looking for an excuse to bail. My feelings for Valentina, your promises to Abby—"

"Don't," she said, in such a terrible voice he stopped instantly. Feelings she'd lashed down became sharp-edged glass that sliced through her resolve and boiled out.

"I had a friend I loved like a sister, and I tried to help her. Over and over and *over* again. She backed away from him so many times, made me believe she was going to kick the self-destructive habit of loving him. But she didn't. She'd go back to him, rationalize his behavior. She chose to stay with him, chose to stand next to him, long past when he deserved that kind of loyalty. She didn't protect herself."

"Rosalinda," Lawrence said, his expression full of pain. "When you love someone, you can't protect yourself."

"Yes, you damn well can. He destroyed her from the inside out, because that's what that kind of person does, until all those excuses make sense in your own head. Nothing else makes sense—not what your friends say, your family, support systems of every stripe, hell, the fucking Internet—none of it can get through."

She noted he'd tensed up. "Sound familiar?"

"You can't put people in the same boxes. Every situation is different."

"Number one on the enablers' top ten hits," she shot back. "My mother did it with my father. She's still with him, using an insanely busy social schedule to ignore the loneliness of her marriage. She tells me she's honoring the oath she made to him. An oath that doesn't mean a shit to him. Or at least nowhere near as much as having that next beer with his buddies does."

She stopped herself. It wasn't worth it. It didn't change anything. What was hurting so much was how deep she'd let herself get with him, in such a short time. She could fix that. She would calm herself down, right now, distance herself. She would step all the way back, so she viewed him over an uncrossable chasm, what lay between them far down below. In time, she would be able to mine the good feelings they'd created, bring them back into her heart and experience them again in the right, manageable way. Not right now.

"We're not going to agree about this, and I don't want to end things on bad terms. Let's let it lie." She waved her hand as if dismissing the rest. "The job is done. Time for you to move on with the other priorities in your life. I've enjoyed our time together, and I'm very grateful for what you did to protect me. When we return home, we're done. I'm sorry."

As she'd spoken, his expression wheeled through anger, defensiveness, then puzzlement. Finally, alarm, as he realized just how serious she was. "Rosalinda, you can't just end this."

"Yes. I can. Same as you can with Valentina. You can say enough is enough."

"She has a disease. It's—"

"No." She wasn't locked down enough, because she barked it at him, her hand flying up in a warding motion. "No. It's not. A disease is something you can't change. A terminal cancer diagnosis is going to kill you, no matter how many good choices you make to delay or manage it. Pouring a goddamn drink, shooting up with heroin...there is an element of decision there. Addiction is terrible, a horrible,

horrible thing, but it is *not* the same as disease. It comes with a breathtaking level of selfishness, where deliberately embraced ignorance is the only way you can't see what it's doing to the people around you..."

"It feels that way," he countered. "But you can't deny it's also like a cancer, the way it takes over someone, pushes everyone away. That isn't the point here, though. I don't want to be with Valentina. I want to be with you."

It was the only point that mattered, and he was incapable of seeing it. She jerked her head in a sharp motion. "I told you, this isn't about jealousy. This isn't about me thinking you're in love with her. If that was what was I happening, I could cut you loose without this sick feeling of dread."

She realized then she had tears running down her face. That wasn't what she'd intended, but it explained why he had tried to reach out to her, twice now. She'd moved across the room, well out of reach, creating a buffer that sent a clear *don't touch* message. He was smart enough not to follow, so they stared at one another with most of the room between them. An uncrossable space as empty as her aching heart.

"I couldn't stop that bastard from killing Laurel," she said. "I couldn't make my father love me more than a six-pack. But what I could do, after Laurel, was promise myself I'd never go down that damn rabbit hole again." The half-laugh was a harsh echo in the room. "They don't give any prizes for that. But people like you, who keep propping up someone who won't give up their addiction for anything or anyone? You're considered fucking noble, self-sacrificing, a martyr. Even as you break the hearts of all the people who truly love you. We're the ones who have to stand on the sidelines and watch you sitting in the passenger seat with an addict, driving toward a cliff."

He'd gotten all stiff again. He was closing down. She was hurting him, but him putting up walls was destroying her. She needed to stop, but she couldn't.

"You make a woman fall in love with everything about you, tell her you love her, and then you destroy that love with one phone call." Her voice broke, fuck it all.

She remembered how he'd said it last night, how his arms had felt around her. This was it. That wasn't going to happen again. Might as well burn the bridge. "It's total bullshit, and I'm walking away from it. Go take care of Zoey and Valentina, live your life at her bedside. She's your Mistress, whether she is one or not. You never left her behind. You just took a breather, but now you're back in it. I don't play in another woman's sandbox. Got it?"

A long moment, no oxygen in the room. No color or life. Just the death of something that had barely gotten started. As vibrant and colorful as a bouquet of flowers was, they were dying from the moment the stems were cut.

He looked carved from granite. Slowly, he took the rental car keys out of his pocket, laid them on the dresser. "You can take the car to the airport. I'll find another way home."

She should be concerned about him driving himself with his shoulder in that shape, but he was a grown man. He'd figure it out. She nodded. As he moved back out onto the terrace, stared out at the view, she bolted into motion. She packed the rest of her things up, unplugged her phone charger and did a quick glance around the room. The weight in her chest felt like a boulder sitting on it.

She told herself she'd been through worse, and she had, but some decisions felt like a return to the scene of the crime, the perp still an unsolved mystery.

She picked up the keys, shouldered her bags, moved to the door. Waited. She was sure he'd been watching her out of the corners of his eyes, and he had, because now he turned, stepped back into the room and looked at her, not saying anything.

Even that first day on the mezzanine, before they'd met formally, his eyes hadn't been as shuttered and remote as they were now. But he'd been open to the possibilities between them then. So had she.

"I don't regret our time together, Lawrence," she said, letting the raw honesty show. "It's just time for it to be done. Vera will ensure you're paid for the remainder of the job."

Heat flashed behind his expression. If he didn't have the iron self-control she knew he did, she was pretty sure he would have put a fist through the wall. "I don't want any of your fucking money."

"You did a job, you get paid for it," she said with a calmness she didn't feel. She was glad she hadn't eaten any breakfast because she would have thrown it up. "You earned it. You saved my life, you took care of the threat to Pria. That's separate from this."

"Rosalinda..." What was in his voice could break her. He was staring at her like he didn't understand, but really wanted to. Even as he was also filled with a helpless anger and deep anguish that told her some part of him *did* understand. It was why she had to be done with this.

Ros didn't know exactly when it had happened, but at some point a certain resignation had entered Laurel's gaze. Not until her death had Ros recognized it for what it was. The knowledge, conscious or not, that she would never truly leave her abusive husband, and everything she'd wanted for herself would perish at his hands.

If you couldn't stop someone from self-destructing, there was no reason they needed a witness. She opened the door. She told herself to just go without anything further, but she couldn't do it. She looked over her shoulder at him.

Misery held him rigid, but what held him in place was something different. He'd spent his life serving duty and honor first. Not love. Like most people, he'd never imagined a situation where those things wouldn't be on the same track. He didn't love Valentina anymore, not that way. Ros didn't doubt that. But he didn't know how to be one bit less honorable and committed to the mission than he'd been trained to be. Even as he was being torn apart between what he wanted and what he perceived as his duty.

"You're a good man, Lawrence," she said softly, pain in her voice. "A noble, honorable man. A hero. No one will ever tell you differently, even me. Thank you."

CHAPTER TWENTY-FIVE

"*D*ale Rousseau is here to see you, Ros. Says he doesn't have an appointment, but it's important."

Ros managed not to curl her lip into a snarl at her speakerphone. But why should she react any differently to that than anything else? She'd arrived home several days ago, partly convinced Bastion that what had happened in Indiana was not his fault, and reassured the others she was fine. Life could move on, and there was plenty of work to be done. She'd told Abby she and Lawrence were over, but she wasn't ready to talk about the whys yet. Truthfully? She really didn't want to talk to anyone about anything.

The important thing was she'd put everyone back on track, including herself.

Lindi was doing her revised presentation later today. Maybe she should excuse herself from it, else the poor girl might hang herself from the gazebo with one of her ponytail scrunchies.

Her meeting with Dale might run over, so the decision would be made for her. But even that grimly happy thought couldn't dissipate her resentment about him being here. What he wanted to talk about was personal. This was work. But courtesy was courtesy.

"That's fine, Bastion. He knows how to get to my office. You don't have to escort him."

"You are no fun at all," he said. Though his personality hadn't yet recovered its usual snap, that pat response should have made her smile. She should have playfully retorted that, at his command center, Bastion would have the optimal rear view of Dale walking up the curving staircase.

Instead, it only made her think of Lawrence's tight backside. In jeans, in slacks, in a wrapped towel. In nothing at all, as she marked it with her teeth, a cane.

If the only problem with his absence was sexual, she could manage that. But every one of those thoughts elicited an emotional reaction, and other kinds of images. The tilt of his head as he smiled at her. The hard look before he left the house to protect her, after he'd been shot. His tenderness, his hunger, his warrior fierceness, his craving to submit to her, surrender everything to her demands. Even his goddamn nobility toward a woman who'd once had his heart.

Fuck, fuck, *fuck*. Resisting the urge to hurl her butterfly- in-amber paperweight and knock a chunk out of the wall, she took a couple deep breaths. Then Dale was in her doorway. She pasted the same pleasant, bland look on her face she'd kept close to hand since her return. Yesterday Cyn had suggested if she had a cosmetic surgeon inject her face with concrete, it would save her the effort of holding her facial muscles in that unnatural position.

Ros had told her to fuck off.

"Dale. Come in. To what do I owe the pleasure?"

He surveyed her office with his serious blue-green eyes. "Nice digs. I'm not here to waste your time with bullshit. Don't waste mine with questions you know the answer to."

Oh good. Someone who wanted a fight. She was so there. "You brought your ass up here to my office," she pointed out. "I didn't request a meeting."

He shut the door. "He's in trouble, Ros. You know he is."

"Not my job to save him, Dale. He's a grown man, who has more than earned the right to fuck up his life."

Dale's gaze narrowed. Their eyes held that lock for an extra beat, and then his expression changed from combative to thoughtful. He glanced at her guest chairs, arranged with a sofa by the windows. "Mind if I sit? And would you join me on this side of the desk?"

He'd recognized some of what she was feeling, and responded to that, rather than the combative front she was projecting. It was what savvy Doms did. She'd done it herself, plenty of times. To Lawrence as well as other subs.

Karma was a raging bitch.

He fished in his shirt pocket, produced a pack of Big Red. "I have gum. You can have a stick."

She managed a halfway real smile. "Asshole."

"Yeah. I get that a lot."

She came around the desk, took the gum, but laid it on her side table for later and sat down on the sofa instead. He settled in one of the chairs. For a moment they didn't say anything, the two of them gazing out the window at the gazebo and landscaped area behind the office. Strangely, for the first time in several days, it was the closest she'd felt to peace. The why wasn't rocket science. She was sitting with someone close to Lawrence. One degree of separation, which was closer than she'd been before Dale entered.

"Tell me," she said at last.

"He's flying out of New Orleans tonight. He's signed with a private security firm for a contract in the Sudan. It's lucrative. If he survives it. It's high risk work, no government oversight."

"You tried to talk him out of it."

"Hell, yeah. So did Neil. Until he gets over his attack of stupid, we thought about knocking him out, chaining him up in a basement."

"You do know how to tempt a girl."

"Yeah." Unsmiling, Dale met her gaze. "Tell me what you're thinking on this, Ros. We're out of ideas."

The ache in her chest expanded. "It's his decision, Dale. You can't save someone who doesn't want to be saved. He thinks he owes her, because he loved her. Because she depended on him to be there. For a submissive with a deep service personality, there's nothing harder than to cut that tie. We both know that. It's hard enough for someone who doesn't have that orientation, who simply loves the person."

She sighed. "I should have picked up on how strong his bond with her was and gotten clear. But I didn't anticipate feeling so much for him so quickly. I've been telling myself we haven't known each other long enough for this, but I lose that argument every time I have it with myself. I didn't want to see. Or hoped I was wrong."

Under his sympathetic and knowing glance, she allowed herself a bitter half-laugh. "For a precarious minute, I wanted to do the same pointless thing everyone does. Believe how he felt for me, and me for him, might change it. For that moment, I let myself forget that love changes nothing. Not that kind of thing."

Dale pursed his lips. He'd rolled the gum wrapper up into a tight ball, and was worrying it in his fingers. "When Lawrence became part of my team," he said, "he made the new guy mistakes I expected, but he had the right recovery and cognitive skills. Else he wouldn't have made it to a top tier team. He achieved that way younger than most, because he was so damn level-headed for his age. I still can't believe he's barely past thirty."

He raised his gaze to her. "He *can* learn and change. Evolve. He just has to believe he's not changing the core of who he is. He's not listening to me or Neil, or anyone else. But I can tell he's hurting for you. Hurting bad."

"He knows where I am, Dale. He knows how to reach out to me."

"Does he? If he thinks the only choice he has to keep you is completely cutting off Valentina—"

"It is."

Her decisive tone stopped him short. His brow creased. "Ros, he loved her for a long time. You can't expect—"

"I can." She stabbed the table in between them with a finger. "When an alcoholic goes into AA, what do they learn? They can't have a drink. It's not this gradual process. You can't go have a 'couple drinks' with friends, or one glass of wine with dinner. It kicks it all off again. No drinks, ever. Not today, tomorrow or fifteen years from now, because something in that person can't handle alcohol. They'll never stop craving it, and letting them have one only multiplies the desire. It takes over everything again. An enabler isn't much different. You can't have any ties between you and the thing that destroys you."

Dale's face had gone blank during her passionate response. He waited a beat, making sure she was done before he responded. "Is it possible you're making him pay for someone else's mistakes?"

Her expression tightened. "See, that's where people go, when you draw a line in the sand. Yes, I have direct experience with what he's handling, and yes, that informs my decisions. Because unlike the rest of the goddamn world who *thinks* they can change, I actually do."

Dale leaned forward, so the two of them were eye to eye over the table. She braced for an additional fight, but after another considering moment, he inclined his head. "Okay."

He rose, and she did, too. He held out a hand. "I apologize, Ros. My intention was not to question your judgment. Or to upset you."

"Apology accepted." She took his hand, shook. Resisted the urge to hold onto it. Maintain that contact with another Master who understood just what it was to lose your heart to a submissive. But Dale had gotten the dream. Athena loved him with everything she was. Dale had her full submission, while in her everyday life Athena was a strong, self-sufficient woman.

Dale surprised her by being the one who held onto her hand an extra beat. "You're obviously fucked up twelve ways to Sunday over him. I'm sorry, because I introduced the two of you."

She drew a shaky breath and retrieved her hand, not unkindly. "No apologies are needed for that. Lawrence was everything you'd told me he'd be, and more. The heart heals, Dale. I wish him well, and hope he'll be all right."

He moved toward the door. Once there, he paused. "Open or closed?"

"Please close it."

"See you at Progeny."

She nodded, even though she had a feeling it would be a while before she'd show up there again. Or maybe not. She could cleanse herself with a grueling session. Or pass a casual evening chatting with her Domme friends, playing it light with a low level submissive, one who was happy just being at her feet, bringing her drinks. Like Trey. Any of those options might start her on the way to clearing all this out of her head and heart.

The door closed. She should have told him to leave it open, because it unlocked the emotions he'd stirred. She sank back down on the couch, brought her feet up onto it, curling into a semi-ball as she stared out at the garden.

He was going to leave the country. He might be killed.

She told herself she couldn't react based on that. He was getting on the plane for Valentina. Or for his goddamned honor. Not for Ros. Okay, not directly. He was getting on the plane because of who he was. The type of man she'd been willing to contemplate, just for a second, keeping forever.

But he'd made his decision. She would respect it, because that was the deal. That was the way it was supposed to work.

In a decade, she'd forget how he smelled, how his hands felt, what his eyes looked like when they gazed upon her. She wouldn't hear that slow country boy way he said her full name. *Rosalinda.* With patience, with amusement, with a man's hunger, with annoyance...with love.

He'd had to tell her he loved her, the bastard.

It underscored exactly what she'd told Dale. Love didn't change a shitty situation. It just made it that much worse.

~

Yes, it was a mistake to go to the meeting, but if she stayed in her office, her thoughts would drive her mad.

Lindi looked nervous, but Ros wasn't so much in her own head that she missed the girl's nervousness had a different quality to it from last time. When everyone was settled, and Vera gave the intern the go ahead, Lindi started her laptop presentation.

The first image that appeared on the wall-mounted widescreen monitor was a burst of color. A painting done on tile, an abstract of three women dancing at an outdoor café. Their hands were joined, their clothes flowing and swirling with their movements. One had her head tipped back in laughter.

Lindi slowly flipped through three more pictures, similar subject matter, each done on a different medium. Picket fence, stone, table tops.

Before she'd started, Lindi hadn't said anything except an oddly serious, "Thank you for a second chance." The pictures were her preface.

Ros shifted her attention from the screen to the girl, noting that Lindi was studying the artwork herself. She was grounding herself in the material. Keeping her focus on what was important. When she at last turned and faced the women watching, she left the fourth picture up on the screen.

"These pieces are done by a New Orleans street artist," Lindi said. "She's been working various spots in the city for five years, and she's accumulated a decent word-of-mouth following by tourists and locals. While her subject matter captures the spirit of New Orleans, it contains an even more universal message, as these examples show. I believe the time is right for her to expand into the specialty furniture and home décor markets, perhaps even those offered in catalog sales to an upscale clientele."

She clicked to the next slide, which showed another example of the woman's art, this one applied to a giant concrete pillar supporting a city overpass. "She's also volunteered her time for community improvement projects, like this one, and on school playgrounds. When I spoke to her about her goals, she has a dream of earning enough where she can give thirty percent of her profits to improve life and self-sufficiency for those struggling below the poverty line in New Orleans."

Lindi directed them to the handout she'd sent to their tablets. Ros listened as the young woman laid out the more technical details of the marketing plan and how it would impact the artist's profit margin projections. Lindi included the woman's personality, her drive and charisma, as vital elements of her marketability. To support that, she'd filmed a short video clip of the artist. She hummed and sang as she worked. Her personable interactions with her patrons created genuine connections that drew people to her like a popular street performer.

Lindi brought her presentation to a close, and fielded their questions. Since her data had earned serious consideration, she was hit with serious questions. She knew the answers to some, but for the ones she didn't, she didn't falter. She simply said, "I don't have that information, but I can find out by lunchtime tomorrow." Or, "I can run that down..."

Ros stayed quiet, which her team would know was an excellent sign. Lindi kept looking her way, little darting glances. When the questions were finally concluded, a slight smile was playing on Abby's lips, and there was a twinkle in Cyn's eye.

"This is a very different approach than you took last week," Ros said in a neutral voice.

"I went textbook last week, the way I learned to do it in the marketing classes," Lindi said. "I didn't take any risks. But Mr. Gatlin told me that this firm doesn't do anything without being guided by the heart. Because that's how you do it, Ms. Thomas. You're the example that those who excel in this business follow. The products we're representing, the people, have to mean something. Otherwise, it's not worth doing."

She knew she was staring at the girl with a frozen expression, because Lindi colored and hastened to say, "I'm not sucking up. I mean it. I've watched Isis on her street corner for over a year. I like to eat lunch on a bench near her, and a few months back, I started talking to her. Learned about what she really wants to do with her art. She's been homeless. She lost custody of her two kids because she couldn't provide for them. But she still perseveres, in the hope she can get them back. I realized she has a sad story, but she also has a wonderful talent. There was no reason the one couldn't help the other, with the right marketing."

She stopped, squeezed her hands together, as if to keep herself from rambling on beneath Ros's cool gaze. She did meet it, though, and added one more thing. "Whether or not I'm on the right track for this, I wanted to say thank you. I, um..." She shook her head. "Sorry, still working on the *um* thing. But I wanted to say I was popular in high school. Pretty, and that made certain things easier. I didn't have to work all that hard. Since graduating, I guess I was trying to figure out how to keep being that popular girl. You made me realize...I want to be more than that. And even if you think the presentation blows and still needs a lot of work, I'm much prouder of this one. I hope I can learn from you how to make it better."

She took a breath, straightened. "So, um, thank you."

She winced at the *um*, but maintained, sweeping the table with a nod, smile and expectant look that returned to Ros and waited.

Ros gave it a couple more beats, but then she inclined her head. "Excellent presentation, Lindi. I'm proud of you, too."

The shock on the girl's face was replaced with a flush, a barely suppressed beaming smile. Ros's severe expression helped her contain it. "Don't get carried away with that. Go outside while we discuss the finer points. Then we'll bring you back in for a full evaluation."

"Yes, ma'am. Thank you."

When the girl exited the room, closing the door behind her, Vera tossed Ros an amused look. "I'm betting she just did a spin and fist pump."

"Followed by a selfie, saying 'This is me, rocking the presentation with the boss's thumbs up.'" Abby smiled. "You only get to be twenty once."

"Wow." Cyn shook her head. "Talk about day and night. We need to sign Isis. Get our fee from the earnings increase she'll realize once we promote her. That way she doesn't have to pay it up front."

"A lot of perks to this one," Skye added, in her normal recorded voice. "Since we'll be promoting a New Orleans business and artisan, putting her on a wider stage will draw interest to other artists like her. I'm willing to bet she'll be on board developing a parallel platform that connects to other artists here, cross promotes."

"Ros, you set the nail and Lawrence drove it home," Vera said. "You made a serious impact on that girl's career path."

"Unless our boss is just setting her up to rip her young dream to shreds," Cyn said. "After which, Lindi will give it all up, use her pretty hair and cute body to find a rich old husband. Become a bored trophy wife addicted to prescription drugs."

Ros rolled her eyes at her. "The presentation was excellent. She did well."

That was true. But her lips were numb. Her chest was tight. Her hands were cold.

This firm doesn't do anything without being guided by the heart. Because that's how you do it. Lawrence had said that about her. About the business she and Abby had built.

Big deal. She already knew he admired her business, who she was. But he'd told someone that, which meant more, no matter how she denied it. Or maybe it was simply the timing.

She didn't need to get mired down in this. Lindi was waiting outside, probably biting her nails to stubs. Since Ros didn't say anything further, after a beat, Vera glanced at Abby and Abby nodded. "Let's bring her back in, then."

But Skye lifted a finger, drawing their attention. When she had it, she readjusted the finger, so it was pointed right at Ros.

All eyes turned to her. She didn't want that attention. She rose, starting toward the door. "You all have this. Move forward. I'll be in my office. I'll tell Lindi to come back in."

She put her hand on the door latch. Through the stained-glass panels, she could see Lindi moving up and down the hallway. Waiting.

Ros looked down at her hand on the knob. A manicured hand, a competent hand. One fully capable of opening doors, real and metaphorical. Yet now she stood there, not turning the actual one in her grip.

She hadn't been looking for him. Her focus was Abby. It had to be on Abby. Didn't it? He'd said she'd done that to give herself an out. Even if there was some truth to that, it didn't make the decision not right.

But that wasn't what was holding her in place right now. That thought was merely a tiny screaming thing at the bottom of a black hole.

She turned and looked toward Abby. "Why didn't Laurel realize we loved her more? We were her fucking family. Not him. He was with her in the end. Not us. Why?"

Abigail's eyes filled with pain. But not for Laurel. Abby had made her peace with that long ago. She started to rise, but Ros was having none of it. She made a sharp gesture with her hand and stomped back to the table. Out of habit, she picked up her pen, pointed it in Abby's direction, swept it around the table to include everyone.

"No. I don't want to be petted and handled. Guilt doesn't change anything. Regret's a useless fucking emotion, because it means you're sorry, but you didn't know what the hell to do to fix anything. Maybe that's forgivable when you're talking about a goddamned marketing problem, but when it's other people shredding the people you love? No. Just...no."

She was aware of the exchanged glances. They were probably having a *what the fuck* moment, thinking their boss was losing it, but she was on a roll now.

"She didn't want my help. Fine. She's an adult. I couldn't support her decision to be with the guy who ultimately killed her. I can't support my mother's decision to waste her entire goddamned life with a man who'd prefer to have his ass parked on a bar stool rather than spending time with her. I walk away, because I can't accept that kind of self-defeating bullshit, and that makes me the bad guy?"

"Ros," Abigail said.

"Don't. Bring Lindi back in. Pet her, stroke her, tell her she's done good. Maybe she'll stay on the right track, not hook herself up to a choice, a person, who will derail her whole life."

"Rosalinda," Abigail said sharply.

She'd forgotten there was someone else who did use her full name. Abby, on the rare occasions when she realized nothing else was getting through. But this time Ros wasn't prepared for the strength of her own reaction to it.

"Don't call me that," she snarled. She stabbed the pen into the table, hard enough to chip the stain. "Not now, not ever again."

The room went to post-nuclear detonation stillness, but she didn't take her furious gaze off her best friend. Abby held her gaze with a steely one of her own. "Do you love him?"

"What the hell does that have to do with anything? Does no one ever listen to me?"

"All right. Do you love me?"

Trust Abigail to jam a stick in the wheel spokes, sending Ros in a header over the bicycle basket. "I assume that's a rhetorical question, and you're about to wow me with some other insight into the fucked-upness of human nature."

The change in Abby's expression, Vera's slight unconscious shift away from her, reminded Ros that Abby had an even more formidable temper than Ros and Cyn combined. She just let it loose far less often than either of them did.

Abby fortunately contained her reaction, though she spoke between gritted teeth. "If I was standing on the top of this building, about to jump, you'd stay up there, say and do everything you could to get me not to do it, wouldn't you?"

"I don't—"

"You wouldn't follow me over," Abby persisted, talking over her. "But you'd do everything you could to stop me, until I stepped off. Wouldn't you?"

She snapped the last part, that temper firing through her hazel eyes.

"Watch the tone," Ros warned. "But yes. Of course."

Abby nodded with stiff dignity. "Has he stepped off, Ros?"

They stared at one another as Dale's words went through Ros's mind. *He leaves tonight.*

"I'm not going to run him down, try to keep him from doing something he obviously wants to do."

"But he doesn't want to do it, does he?" Abby sighed, pinched the bridge of her nose before tossing her head back up and locking gazes with Ros once more. "Every time I met Laurel for lunch or a shopping trip, when she was going down those same destructive roads with Todd, I had to staple my tongue to the roof of my mouth. But I kept thinking, if there is one opening, one lifeline, I will be there, ready to take it, to throw it."

She held up a hand and pushed on before Ros could retort. "I'm not saying I did the right thing, any more than I'm saying you did the wrong one, by withdrawing when she refused to leave him. I'm saying you're sabotaging your own happiness by refusing to consider this another way."

Ros closed her hands into fists, knuckles pressed into the table. She didn't want to, but she would listen. She might be pissed, but she'd listen.

"You don't accept it when people don't live up to their potential, their intelligence," Abby said. "When you know they can do better, be better. Because you don't accept it in yourself. You don't understand failure, Ros. You don't understand giving up. You think a bad outcome could always be avoided, handled differently, fixed. It's why you succeed at so much. But I think it also makes you blind to some important things."

She leaned forward as Ros waited, her gut churning. "What upset you so much wasn't that she wasn't as strong as you. It was that she *was*. Just in an entirely different way. She saw something in him and couldn't let it go. She wasn't a victim, she wasn't helpless, she had a support network. But she wouldn't give up on her love for him. She wouldn't accept defeat."

A smile touched Abby's mouth, so painful it cut. "She refused to believe there couldn't be a better outcome, Ros. When you love someone, you do that."

Ros crossed her arms, a defensive movement, but also one that helped contain the anguish inside her that Abby's words were creating. Ruthlessly, Abby pressed on.

"It was Laurel's fight. It's Lawrence's fight. It's your mother's fight. But sometimes, just like with Lindi, people need both. The person who kicks them in the ass, tells them to stand up for themselves, but who also stands in their corner, tells them they'll love them, believe in them, no matter what."

Abby's gaze softened. "You're that for me. You love me enough to stand with me, even if I get knocked down."

"Because you never stop trying to stand," Ros said flatly.

"But eventually that choice will be out of my hands. The wave will come that knocks me down hard enough I can't get back up. You know that, same as I do."

The quiet that had reigned while they were volleying achieved a new level of still tension. But Abby's gaze didn't falter. It was Ros's heart that clutched, that screamed in protest as her best friend acknowledged yet another fight that wasn't going to be won.

"Every battle isn't won the same way," Abby said, following her thoughts. "You'll win that one, Ros, simply by loving me. That's all I need. To know that you, and the people in this room, love me. Whatever strength I have is built on that. When my strength fails, it won't be from lack of love. So I won't be defeated. The battle is already won. Do you understand?"

Abby reached out, tapped the table. If Ros's hand had been there, she would have gripped it. Abby was one of the few people Ros would allow to touch her when she was in this kind of mood.

"Try to understand Lawrence, not from where you're standing, but from where he is. And then ask yourself this. As much as you hate the actions he's taking right now, are the things driving those actions what made you fall in love with him? Do you love who he is, or who you think he should be? And if the answer is what we both know it is, is ending it between you two really the right thing?"

Ros turned away, faced the door again. An exit, an escape, but one that wouldn't let her get away from anything. The emotions swirling inside her would merely erupt and strangle her, once she separated herself from the buffer of her friends. A reminder that she'd decided to come to this damn meeting mainly to get away from the increasing unbearableness of her emotions about Lawrence.

Love. It all came down to love. Too much, too little, wrong timing. She so often tried to put it together like a weapon that she could clasp and use to protect those who mattered to her. But in the end, it came down to this stupid Zen shit about open palms, and water flowing through the fingers.

"He's on the ledge," Abby said. "Do you really want to turn away before he jumps?"

She didn't know if she stood there for a minute or a half hour, thinking about that, but when she tuned back in, Skye was playing music on her laptop. Soft, but the tune was distinguishable.

"Rosalinda's Eyes." Billy Joel.

Ros turned around. Despite the choice creating a series of faint smiles around the table, Skye's expression was serious. She had a brilliant mind, and used her hands and technology to communicate all sorts of complicated, multi-layer thoughts. Whether it was about a marketing project, the meaning of the universe, or what color Ros should paint her kitchen. It made her simplest thoughts all the more powerful. She signed one of them to Ros now.

He matters. So do you. You can have him.

Ros looked toward Vera. Her expression reminded Ros of an ancient priestess. Somewhat detached, because Vera knew how to step back and adopt a fathomless world view, even as she acknowledged all the pain and joy in a life worth living. Cyn, just across from her, was the warrior who would advocate embracing that life to the fullest, with the energy of a tornado, and damn the consequences. No regrets.

"He's the one," Ros said. "He's mine."

Abigail nodded. The revelation obviously didn't surprise her. Ros's heart twisted hard in her chest. She went to Abby, dropped to her heels next to her. Ros gripped the arm of her chair. "I didn't want it to happen."

"What?" Abby laid a cool, slim hand against her neck, bent to brush foreheads with her. Her eyes were brimming with emotions, but what curved her lips was almost playful. "Find a man who wants to fully belong to you? Open your heart to him? I knew you would be first."

Ros shot her an exasperated look. "How the hell could you know that?"

"Because you're always the first. The brave one. The trailblazer. You're our leader. The boss. The queen." That smile deepened. "No one here gets their soulmate before you find yours."

"Abby." Ros gazed at her. "Abigail."

Tears gathered in Abby's eyes, but she visibly shoved them back with a fierce look that reminded Ros that Abby might seem more fragile, softer, but when it came down to it, she was every bit as tough as Ros. Probably tougher.

"You know what would really, really piss me off, make me far madder than you can imagine?" Abby took her hand, their fingers interlacing. "That you gave up your chance at this because of some fucked-up idea that you're abandoning me. Are you?"

"No. Never." Ros let it show, in her expression, her grip. "I will honor every promise I made to you. My love for you will never change. It will only grow stronger. No matter how much of a bitch you are, and a total pain in my ass."

"That's what I thought. You can do that by giving your heart to him fully. For both of us." Abby gave her a knowing look. "Besides which, I've met the man. He'll settle for nothing less. He deserves nothing less."

"Yeah." Ros rose, moved back to her chair. As she sank into it, she kept Abby's hand, their intertwined fingers resting on the table surface between them.

Ros let her gaze sweep the room. In the steadying boat of her emotions, she knew she'd made her decision. It roused the Mistress side of herself, bringing it to the top, ready to act. The others recognized it too, that same core identity reflected in their rapt attention.

"If I make him mine, then he's also ours. Yours. In the sense that each of you will watch out for him, care for him the way a Mistress should for a submissive. He will be part of this family. I want...what we discussed that night, in the forest. That we hammered out in more detail, when we took our memorial trip for Laurel to the Bahamas."

"A formal acceptance," Skye signed. Ros nodded.

"We had a lot of tequila that night," Cyn remembered.

A few chuckles went around the table, and Ros smiled faintly. "Yes, we did."

The women shifted, looked toward each other. He would be the first. Uncharted ground. Ros saw anticipation, speculation, some concern. "Will he agree?" Vera asked.

"If he and I resolve what we're dealing with right now, yes, I think so. This circle knows my true self, knows what I value, what tenets govern my life. Following through with that ritual would give me comfort. I think it would be good for him as well. He had a team of brothers for a long time. Though he's still connected to that, he no longer stands fully inside that circle. It's a hole inside him. Bringing him inside our circle will help with that loss."

"But that's not why you're doing it," Cyn said.

"It's part of it, because caring for him that way is what I want to do. But the other part of it is I want him to know he's mine in every possible way, no question in his mind. Or mine."

Which might help a lot of other things, for both her and him.

"Fuck civilized behavior," Vera said. Her full lips tilted, her pale eyes like moonstone. She toyed with the silver pentagram she wore, fingers tapping lightly on her breastbone. "Women have joined hearts and hands in circles of friendship and faith for centuries. For all sorts of reasons, but the most important one is to strengthen the bonds between them, acknowledge the power and energy they can raise. If he's yours, I want him to have no doubt he's ours, too. In a way that honors what's between you and him. And all of us."

Skye nodded in agreement.

"You had me at 'fuck civilized behavior,'" Cyn said.

Abigail squeezed her hand, drawing Ros's attention.

"Go get his ass," she said.

"If you need reinforcements," Cyn added, "no one at this table is against kidnapping a man for the right reasons. Even Vera. No matter what she says."

CHAPTER TWENTY-SIX

*T*here were several things to handle first. Their intern, for one.

After they invited Lindi to return, Ros tempered her earlier praise with the right cautions about keeping her focus and not getting too full of herself. When they sent Lindi back to work, Cyn pointed out the interns practically wet themselves if Ros raised her voice, so Lindi getting too full of herself wouldn't be a problem.

"We all wet ourselves when Ros raises her voice," said Morgan Freeman. "Just for different reasons."

Ros shot Skye a look. "I told you, no Morgan Freeman voice for sex jokes. It freaks me out."

"Better Morgan Freeman than Alvin the Chipmunk," Vera wisely noted.

As the meeting disbanded, the ladies headed out to do whatever tasks remained in their day, Ros noted Abby shot her a parting look. One that clearly said: "Don't talk yourself out of this."

Yeah, yeah. Ros returned to her office, shut the door. She sat on the couch another half hour, thinking, before she retrieved her phone. Since they'd gone their separate ways at the Ironworks, she hadn't texted Lawrence. Respecting her decision—the asshole—he hadn't broken that silence. He'd also obviously been up to his eyeballs in shit with Zoey and Valentina. Including plans for going to the ass-end of the planet to get himself killed.

I'd like to talk to you. Where can we meet?

The response that came back was automated.

Not an active number.

Her stomach dropped. He'd de-activated the phone. Which was what one likely did when going overseas to work a sensitive op that could take an unspecified amount of time.

She dialed the number once more just to be sure. Then she texted Dale for more info on Lawrence's flight and if he knew anything on his whereabouts. She could have called, but she was past wanting more conversation. She also didn't want to set up false hope. She wasn't completely set on what she was going to do. Or how this would all end up.

Dale fortunately understood, responding with a more detailed text than his norm. *Took us out for beer last night. Now dropped off radar. Probably went to gear up with our Baton Rouge supplier. Maybe left his duffel at his place to pick up before NOLA flight.*

He sent the flight details, plus another unexpected piece of information. *Back door key in airline pilot zombie head. Backyard garden.*

She didn't remember zombie heads in Lawrence's backyard, but a detailed study of his outdoor living space hadn't been her top priority when she was last there.

Circling behind the townhouse once she arrived involved skirting along the back edge of the yards of the flanking townhouses, but fortunately no one noticed her. She found nearly a dozen zombie heads planted at the back edge of Lawrence's yard, along the buffering tree line between this strip of townhomes and the ones behind it. The heads were fashioned out of concrete, and painted with surprisingly complex detail. Here and there a hand was coming up out of the dirt, suggesting bodies were attached to the staring heads, bared teeth. One of the zombie heads bore a pilot's cap. Beneath his bulging eyes and bone-exposed nose, he had a cigar clenched in his sparse but blood-stained teeth.

It was official. The jerk had made her love him.

She found the key in a cleverly concealed compartment she wouldn't have found without Dale's help, an additional text having explained the opening mechanism.

She let herself in the back, closed the sliding door.

There was a hushed emptiness to a house when someone was

gone, and not just for the work day, or a trip to the grocery store. She didn't have to look for the duffel to know Dale had been incorrect. Lawrence wasn't coming back here. In fact, he wasn't planning on returning at all.

As she moved from the kitchen into the living room, she saw he'd packed up his personal items, and the boxes were neatly labeled. Kitchen, Living Room. The painted tiles in the kitchen were gone, replaced by beige ones that matched the generic walls. New caulk held them in place.

Maybe he intended to establish physical as well as emotional distance between himself and whatever happened with Valentina and the money he sent her. She couldn't see him leaving New Orleans, moving away from Neil and Dale, but he could accomplish that distance by moving out of the place they'd shared.

She went up to the bedroom. The neatly made bed had solid-colored throw pillows on it. It confirmed her thoughts, since it looked like Lawrence had staged the townhouse for a realtor to show it, once the boxes were removed.

There was another reason to box everything up. A practical one. Due to the risk of what he was doing, he was making sure no one had to come in here and gather up his stuff once he...

No. She wasn't going there, damn it.

She noticed there was an extra bed pillow. It had been left off the bed, propped in the side chair. From the creases in it, she imagined him leaving it there by accident, after sitting against it for awhile, thinking. Saying good-bye to all of it in his quiet way.

She sank down on the chair, picked up the pillow. There was a note pinned to the top. *TAKE* was written on it in black marker. Because she wanted to torture herself, she hugged it to her, hoping to find the aroma of the man himself. If he'd left any shirts in his closet, he was going to lose a couple at least, even if she chided herself for it later as a weak moment.

She did detect his scent, but someone else's, too. Hers. She smelled her shampoo, the fragrance of her moisturizer.

Rising, she bent over the bed. Inhaled. The linens on the neatly made bed had been laundered.

It was the pillow that had been on the sofa, the night she was here. He hadn't washed the case. When he returned—not if, damn it—and reclaimed his things from whatever storage place he was leaving them, was he hoping her scent would linger?

She sank back down on the chair, smoothed her hand over the pillow, the note. A heartbeat later, she froze. Something about the house's stillness had changed. As she rose from the chair, clutching the pillow like a shield, a tall man stepped into the room.

He had a gun half-lifted, but he immediately lowered it, tucked it away. "Sorry about that," he said, in an easy Louisiana drawl. "I'm Neil. I came to get the boxes."

Her pulse was racing. She guessed recently being in a lethal gunfight had made her edgier about such things. Neil waited on her, staying at the door, his expression concerned and caring, but giving her space. She appreciated his sensitivity, the time to put it together in a logical way.

She'd left the sliding door unlocked. He would have noticed that, because he probably had his own key. She hadn't heard him enter, cross the kitchen or come up the stairs. How did they teach them to move that quietly? She'd have to ask Lawrence.

She took a breath and a closer look at the active SEAL. She didn't see anything that displeased her. Lean muscularity, a slate-colored gaze beneath a bill cap pulled low on his forehead. Stubble dusting the strong jaw.

But Ros's mind was on another man. "Have you heard anything from him?"

An unhappy expression crossed Neil's serious features. "Not since last night. He texted me before he dumped his phone. Said he'd be back in touch once he got where he was going and picked up a new one."

"Are you going to the airport to see him off?"

"We thought about it, but decided no. He's done talking. He didn't give us his flight info. Dale had to find it out another way. Even so, he'll anticipate we did that, check in as soon as he gets there so we can't intercept him. It is what it is, Ms. Thomas." He shook his head. "I told him even though I don't agree with his decision, I have his back, however he needs it."

"What did he say?"

"Thanks, and pick up his boxes if I had the time. Put them in my storage unit. Stubborn idiot."

Neil pointed to the bed, and she nodded, confirming she was over her fright and fine with him moving further into the space. He removed the cap, stuffing it in the back pocket of his faded jeans, and sat down on the edge of the bed, met her gaze. "How about you? You going to try and catch him at the airport?" The corner of his mouth quirked. "I'm guessing Dale sent you the flight details."

"Haven't decided yet."

He nodded. "How's Abigail doing?"

At her bemused look, he shrugged. "You're not going to talk about where you are on this, and Lawrence is done talking. Figured I'd ask about something less set in stone."

Ros snorted. "Mount Rushmore has heads softer than Abby's."

"Yeah, I got some of that." That smile became deeper, with an intriguing sensuality that explained why Abigail had seemed distracted when the man was in the room with her. "She sure is a pretty little thing, though."

The exaggerated drawl surprised laughter out of her. His smile became an easier grin, though it didn't dilute what she saw in his eyes. He was hurting, same as her. This was one of Lawrence's best friends.

"Will he be okay?" she asked.

His jaw flexed. "Munch is always okay. He's steady as a lake, and he doesn't change direction, as long as he's sure he's on the right course."

She looked down at the pillow still in her arms. "You're worried, though. Which means it's not about his state of mind. It's the physical side. What he's doing is dangerous. More than usual."

When Neil considered his response, she gave him a look. "I don't need handholding. Just the truth."

Neil lifted a shoulder. "What we do is dangerous. We accept that. But we do it as a team. We train together, we work together. He's going to a place where it's a bunch of other guys being paid top price to do a job. Most will be former military, so they'll recognize the practical value of watching each other's six. But they're still new to one another, to the rhythm of how they work. The reason they're paid high dollar for these jobs is the risk is comparable, no safety nets. I can't be there to have his back. That bugs the shit out of me. I have faith in his training, his intuition down range. But skill only gets you so far. You need luck, too. And luck can be a pretty unpredictable thing."

He met her gaze. "Then there's the will to get home. Sometimes that's more important than anything else."

"You know I cut him loose."

"He told me you made the right decision. 'No point in tying herself to a boat stuck in the mud.' His words, not mine."

She bit back a curse. "That wasn't what I meant. I told him he could stay tied to a woman destroying him, or he could be with me. Choice was his."

Neil inclined his head. "He didn't give me any other impression, Ms. Thomas. It was the right call."

"I don't need you to tell me that."

His mouth tightened slightly at her sharp tone before he blinked at her with those calm eyes. As she registered the firm set of his jaw, the deliberately loose curl of his hands on his thighs, she recognized some latent Dominant in the pose and reaction. That alone would have made her warn him off Abby as a lost cause, yet there were some other things there, too, nebulous things, hard to pin down.

Since Abby wasn't willing to entertain a long-term relationship with anyone, Ros might as well let him run with his infatuation, see where it went.

"You haven't told me if Abby's doing okay," he mentioned, as if picking up the direction of her thoughts.

Yes, definitely some Dom. Or SEALs were just that damn intuitive. Lawrence had surely proven himself to be, often anticipating the direction of her thoughts.

"Yes, she's fine now." She remembered Abby's expression in the board room, the earnest anguish, her desire for Ros to find love, a permanent center. Ros rose, making herself put the pillow down in the chair. "Though don't take my word for it. You should check with her yourself."

Neil cocked his head. "She won't thank you for that."

"No, she won't. But being friends means we look out for one another, even if we sometimes trample on what our friend claims to want."

"True enough." His expression became somber again. "He doesn't want this. Not even close. But life is mostly about what needs to be done or faced, with a smattering of what you really want to do, and a whole lot of wild card thrown in. What you don't expect, good and bad."

He rose, too. He was so tall, she had to look up, even in her heels. "Did you give him the Munch nickname?" she asked.

That serious smile came easily to him, enough that when he wasn't doing it, she saw the lines for it embedded in his handsome features. "I don't remember who called him that first. He calls me Twizzler. Twizz for short. Before I built muscle for the SEALs, I was just a skeleton with skin. He saw a picture of me as a kid, when I'd gotten a wretched sunburn. Licorice red, he said. Name stuck."

She ran a critical gaze over him, knowing the Mistress in her was showing. It was so much a part of her, she didn't bother stopping it, most times. "You did a good job putting muscle on the bones."

"Thank you, ma'am."

The courtesy, the familiar rhythm of it, was as painful as a bullet through the chest. She knew it reflected in her face when he closed the step between them.

She stopped him before he could reach out, offer physical comfort. She couldn't handle that right now, with so much pending that could go wrong.

"As you said, there's no point in going to the airport, not if he's going to check in first thing," she said.

"Unless you get there first and can head him off at the gate."

"I don't chase men."

"You're not chasing." Neil grinned. "You're stalking. Hunting."

"Neil, you have a peculiarly good understanding of my perspective on life."

"I listen and learn. Not so hard to get what you want if you anticipate and prepare. Know your quarry."

She couldn't argue with that. She moved around him to the bedroom door, but stopped there and turned. "If you reach out to Abby again...I think that would be good."

"Nice to have an ally in my corner."

"Don't go crazy," she said dryly. "I don't know you well enough yet. But Lawrence wouldn't be bound to you the way he is if you lacked his integrity."

A Mistress was a different animal. She wasn't like Cyn, whose measure of right and wrong often equated with whether or not she

could get away with something. However, Ros did believe the boundaries of the heart and soul were far wider than people liked to pretend
they were. In this case, Ros was less concerned about integrity, and far
more about achieving her objective.

"Neil?"

"Yeah?"

"Tell me something about him." Something to remind her he was
real, that he hadn't yet slipped between her fingers.

Neil considered. "He was a fat kid. He'd lost the weight by the
time he got into BUD/S, but we still threatened to call him Gordo
when we saw old pics."

"Are you taking the zombie heads?"

"Are you kidding? He'd kill me if I didn't. He left them outside
because they'll have dirt on them. I'll wrap them up and transport
them in my pickup bed."

"Need any help with the loading?"

"I've got this." He gave her a look. "Sounds like you have a plane to
catch, ma'am."

She did at that. But she had one more question. "The horse in
front. The one turned ass-end. What's that story?"

His eyes darkened. "Valentina picked it up at some secondhand
shop, planted it there one day when she was mad at him. He kept it,
never turned it around."

"Sounds like it needs to have an unfortunate accident on the way
to storage."

His eyes flashed approval. "Accidents do happen."

Now what? Though she found the idea mortifying, she expected the
only strategy was the tried and true rom-com one. Go to the airport,
camp out at the security check-in, try to catch him there. Since
Lawrence's flight would depart at nine p.m., at least she had enough
lead time. So she thought.

She hadn't counted on getting a call from the police.

Francesca, one of their shelter residents, had experienced a crisis.
Ros had brought Francesca into Laurel Grove. She had a severe
learning disability, which had led to her present situation, a sixty-two-

year-old victim of a forty-two year abusive marriage. Since she only responded to Ros, Ros had to handle the matter personally.

Resolving that crisis took her to seven-thirty. Then there was the drive to the airport. When she hit gridlock within a couple miles of her goal, due to an accident that backed traffic up in every direction, her heart sank into her toes. The fates themselves seemed to have decided how this was going to go.

Yet still she persevered. She'd come this far. If it was going to be futile, she was going to give it a hundred percent. When at last she parked and yes, flat-out ran to the right desk in the airport, it was ten to nine. She did it just like one of those big screen heroines, her shoes clasped in one hand so she could have better traction.

But she was too late, even to have him paged. The employee shook her head. "I'm sorry, ma'am. That flight is already taxiing away from the gate."

Ros could barely summon a nod. She told herself the brutal pain was way out of proportion to what it should be. She hadn't known him very long. No one fell this hard that fast. The words were empty. As she'd told Dale, and the other Mistresses, she'd already had those arguments with herself and come to one simple conclusion.

He was the one.

So what were her options? Go on with her life until he eventually returned, and see what happened then? Love shouldn't be defined by the right moment or set of circumstances. It should be something inside someone, like a key for a certain lock. It didn't matter if that key showed up today or ten years from now; it would fit.

Those thoughts might slap a half-assed balm on this moment's pain, but she was a realist. "Should" didn't mean shit. Timing could be everything in these things.

She couldn't sit, things hurt too much, but she couldn't bring herself to leave, either. Here her pain wasn't under anyone's micro-scope. It was an anonymous, story-in-progress snapshot.

The New Orleans airport was a reflection of the city itself. Lots of windows, wide open spaces, palms, and margarita colors. She wandered through the central atrium that connected the three levels of the airport, and eventually found her way to the giant circular bar placed beneath an impressive skylight. Its large palms formed an umbrella over the white and soft lime green accents. The spiral-shaped arrangement of polished planks that filtered the beams of light drew the eye up toward to the skies.

She toyed with the idea of getting herself a drink, but for tediously obvious reasons, that had never been her answer to pain. Maybe a double shot of coffee instead, to keep the mental fatigue clutching her from turning into a week on her couch with ice cream. A week where she'd stay wrapped in her oversized robe and ginormous neon-blue Mike the Monster slippers the girls had given her as a joke. She kept them tucked away where no one could find them. Even Snake hadn't gotten his hands on those.

While she considered that, she let her attention drift over the banks of chairs scattered around the area. Not too many patrons were inhabiting them right now. She decided to park herself in a seat close to the windows, where she could stare at the planes sitting on the tarmac or taxiing off.

She'd sit there, let the world pass by, and think. Or maybe not think at all. She was still holding her shoes in one hand. Someone would eventually tell her she needed to put them on, but right now she didn't have the energy. And maybe no one would notice. She was so deep in her head, it felt like she'd disappeared into a bubble of invisibility. She was good with that.

More potted palms with wide, thick fronds were scattered around her chosen seating area. Which was why she didn't see there was another occupant of that section until she was only a few feet away.

It was Lawrence.

He was sitting in the chair she would have picked, end of a row, close to the window. His duffel was beside him.

Her heart had accelerated to a five hundred mile an hour gallop. That speed left behind every rationalization she'd told herself in the past five minutes:

He didn't matter as much as she thought.

It was okay that she hadn't caught him before he boarded.

In a few days, she would laugh at herself for letting herself get this carried away.

She took a moment to let things settle. While she did, she took in everything about him from a safe distance. Just a guy in jeans and dark T-shirt in a brooding sprawl on the seat. His short hair was spiky, and she suspected he hadn't touched up his shave this morning. Maybe for a few mornings. He looked kind of scruffy, really.

It didn't matter. The fit body, something about the energy around him, would draw a woman's interest even if she couldn't figure out what had done it. Until he turned his green eyes toward her; then she'd be a goner.

Well, that bitch could roll her carry-on right on by. Ros saw way more to pull her in, hold her. Everything they'd shared was there, mapped on him like ink only she could see.

Despite the time of night, he wore sunglasses. They hid his eyes, so she didn't know where they were looking. The angle of his head suggested he was staring at the planes. His body looked made of stone.

Then that situational awareness kicked in. He shifted, turned his head and saw her.

She put her shoes on, holding onto the pillar next to her. Thanks to the glasses, his expression was unfathomable. If she got close enough, she was taking them off and stomping on the damn things.

He hadn't moved. Hadn't even twitched. Did he not want her here? He'd made the decision to not get on the plane, but for all she knew, he'd simply changed his flight schedule, and him sitting out here wasn't significant at all.

Regardless, she had access to him right here, right now. Neil and Dale had honored the guy code, leaving it alone. They knew they couldn't change his mind.

They weren't his Mistress.

As she closed the distance between them, he straightened in the seat, pulling his legs in from that sprawl. He did her the courtesy of rising before she stopped in front of him. "Take off the glasses," she said.

Maybe starting with an order wasn't the best idea, but he didn't refuse. He pulled them off his face, folded and hooked them in his pocket. His gaze looked emotionally bruised. Sad. Torn. Resigned. The deadness in his expression alarmed her, more than a little bit.

Her gaze coursed over him. He looked tired. It hadn't been long enough for him not to be wearing the sling, but she was sure he'd dumped it at the hotel. She didn't consider herself a particularly nurturing sort, but as his Mistress, she'd ream his ass if he didn't take better care of himself.

"Did you miss your flight?" she asked.

"Yeah. And no. I started to check in and then..." He lifted his uninjured shoulder. "I changed my mind."

Her erratic pulse sped up again. The ups and downs were making her light-headed. She warred between a cautious gladness at his decision and the desire to slap him for worrying her. Followed by an alarmingly strong urge to stretch him over a luggage cart and beat his ass in front of the world. Then ride the stupid, stubborn male behavior totally out of him.

Bet those rom-coms didn't usually include that scene.

"You remember that first night, when you told me to hold the sink?" he said slowly. "At one point, I reached back and took your hand."

She did remember that. It had been an intriguing move, one that had touched her with the depth of emotions it revealed.

She sank down in the chair next to him. As he sat back down, she laid her hand on his thigh. It quivered, his eyes flickering at the contact. Her palm tingled, her body gravitating toward his. It knew this was the man she wanted most. Her man.

"Yes." She managed to sound calm. "Tell me about that. And why you didn't get on the plane."

She'd come to the airport for him.

When he'd first seen her, he was certain he'd mentally pasted her face on someone else, because Rosalinda Thomas would never chase a man down. He came to her or it was done.

But no one else had that ball busting stare. Made his heart hammer against his rib cage as if it wanted to tear loose, throw itself at her feet. And no one else wore shoes like she did. Today's pair were open-toed white lace, tiny charms hanging from the buckle of the rhinestone studded ankle strap.

As she'd moved closer, the mask had slipped, and he'd glimpsed something that made the hammering worse. This was beyond pride, or Dom/sub stuff. She'd come for him, she would fight for him, and, being Rosalinda Thomas, she had no intentions of losing.

That was what had made him think of the night in the kitchen. Lawrence didn't know if he could explain it to her, but it was part of why his heart was tearing itself up now. That night he'd reached for her, letting go of the sink, he hadn't realized it consciously, why he'd done that. But he figured out some of it later, as they did more together. Now, sitting here together, he had no reason to doubt the truth.

With Valentina, coming home from being down range hadn't been what home was supposed to mean. She'd been so caught up in her own shit that she didn't notice the well of love he was offering had become a one-way channel, and she was draining him dry of everything. Heart, soul, will to live. He'd refused to see it himself, believing if he loved her enough...it would be enough. That well could be refilled.

"You chose sanctuary as my safe word from the very beginning," he said slowly. "It's like you knew I hadn't had that in a relationship, not in a really long time. And it's not that I want or need you to take care of me all the time. But just knowing you want to, that you consider that part of the relationship...it changed my thinking on things."

He leaned forward, clasped his hands, stared at the floor. Rosalinda's hand stayed on him, though, and he was glad to have it there. "That kind of epiphany sounds really good, you know," he said, squinting out at the planes. "Like something you'd say at an Al-Anon meeting before everyone claps. And yet I say it and I see Valentina's face, her hands reaching for me, her voice, pleading, and I feel like the world's biggest shit. Even when I *know* it's fucked up. Mission failure. Nowhere else left to go to make it better."

It was a constant weight on his chest. Sometimes it would ease. It had, with Rosalinda. But every time the phone had rung and he'd seen Valentina's number, or Zoey's, it had brought it back, twice as heavy. It defeated him in ways nothing else could.

He lifted his gaze to hers, his expression miserable. "I was supposed to take care of her. Help her."

He hadn't intended to say all that, afraid he'd drive her off again, but she'd wanted to know why he hadn't gotten on the plane, and it had spilled out.

He'd never seen her eyes so sharp and pain-filled. Or so open to him. "That was your job," she said. "And you tried everything you could to do it. But you weren't the lead on that mission, Lawrence. She was."

She moved her hand to his shoulder, stroked. "When we're together, you protect me. You make me feel safe." A smile touched her mouth, poignant. "But I want to do the same. I want to guard your heart, hold your soul in my hand when you surrender to me. It's time to let it go, sailor."

He stared back down at the ground, processing it. She moved her stroking hand from his shoulder to his back, kneading the muscle there. He was full to the brim with the suffering of the past, his struggle to believe her, to accept and move on. She could see it, for she laid a hand on his face, sharpened her tone in a way that had everything in him turning in her direction.

"Accept me as your Mistress, and let go of what's no longer yours to control. Because the truth is, you never controlled her. You can't control another person. Only with their consent, their willing surrender, which is far deeper than something in your head saying yes or no. It's a release, a letting go."

She turned her hand, trailed her knuckles down the side of his throat. The touch was sexual, possessive, and yet a reassurance, all at once. "Remember that first day when I said I wanted to work you over until you were exhausted, so you'd simply collapse in my arms, let me care for you? I wanted you to let go of everything but my strength, the surety that I've got you. I've got you, Lawrence," she repeated. "Just like you've got me. And I promise I will never ask you to be responsible for me. Only to me."

Her eyes sparked. "That, too, draws from Al-Anon, but I think it works very well for just about everyone. Right?"

He nodded. He swallowed. Looked away. His hands closed and unclosed on his knees. Her words had shifted something inside him. Something alarming. Her hand moved from his throat, to his shoulder and back. He dropped his head down, but that shoulder and back terrain remained rigid. Then he rocked slightly, his body moving, gravitating toward hers. It took a couple movements, a couple shifts, like a lame horse trying to turn without using the injured foot. But he managed it, turned in the circle of her arm and placed his forehead against her shoulder. His hand found her other one, clasped it.

He was fighting what was coming up inside. He needed to warn her. He wished there was a way he could hold it back the way he held back a release until she said it was okay, but that was exactly what she did now.

"Let it go, love." She cupped his head, pressed her lips to the top of it, stayed there. "Let it go. It's okay to grieve for the journey you took together. You cared for her with your whole broken heart. You can let it heal now. I'll help you."

A hard shudder went through him, and when he would have broken away, mortified, she tightened her grip. "It's okay, baby," she whispered. "It's okay."

He banded his arms around her, hard, almost too hard, but she didn't say anything. The chair arm between them pressed into his stomach, but that was okay.

"Trust me," she said. "You can be whatever you need to be in my arms, Lawrence. It won't make me love you less. Just the opposite. I know who you are. I know what kind of man you are."

The words broke him down, and Lawrence couldn't hold it back. Her arms were too strong and welcoming. He didn't make a lot of noise, but the tears came. He squeezed out stingy, bitter ones for the loss of a woman who'd meant something important to him, in the arms of the woman who now meant everything.

She stroked his head, spoke in a wind-quiet voice. "Sometimes it feels like an infected wound that's never going to get better, doesn't it?"

Hammer to nail, and she drove it in place on the first strike. He stood at a crossroads of who he was and who he wanted to be. He was being torn in two.

She made that reassuring noise, kept her hand moving over him. "When my mother pushed my father into a corner where the drinking problem was staring him in the face, he'd lash out at her. Choose the cruelest things to say. 'If you didn't nag me about it so damn much, maybe I'd drink less.'"

Valentina had said things like that to him. Way more than once. And things like it. The more he tried, the worse she was.

"In that kind of world, love hurts way too much." While her voice

415

remained easy, just a flow of conversation, he knew diving into those kinds of memories couldn't be easy for her. He wanted to tell her she didn't have to go there, but some part of him needed that acknowledgement, taking away the sense of isolation.

He needed to let the threads of his life and stories intertwine with hers, draw him away from the path with Valentina, and onto Rosalinda's instead.

"I thought I wanted someone to save," he admitted. He sounded bone tired. He cleared his throat, tried to fix that. "Until I found someone I couldn't."

She caressed his face, lifted it, and he found her blue eyes close, so serious and full of emotion. "Maybe what you need is a woman who can take care of herself." She brushed her mouth over his cheek, his jaw. "But who also has total faith that if she does run up against something where she needs saving, needs care, you're the person she can depend upon."

A light smile touched her lips. "Like a queen depends on her captain of the guard. She has confidence that he knows his job. It's like the comfort of her house around her. Her castle. But she doesn't need him to run the country. That's her job."

The queen in her castle. His heart tightened at the childhood memory.

She let him ease back, anticipating his need to get himself together. Crying in a fucking airport, for God's sake. But she'd intended to open him up and she had, because he couldn't seem to refuse her much of anything.

"I'm sorry I said you use Abby as an out, in relationships."

His Mistress wasn't too proud to allow balance in the give and take between them. "Your aim was off," she said, "but you correctly realized there are reasons, both good and maybe not so good, that I've chosen not to get involved in the messier side of relationships. Workaholics often become so because work is the only place they don't feel like a total fuckup, even if the world doesn't see them that way."

She flashed a smile with teeth. "Not me. I'm well-rounded. A great CEO, a creative and inspired Mistress, and a good friend. I'm well-read, always seeking new experiences, and I prefer to have a man kneeling at my feet, with no apologies for it."

"I don't disagree with any of that. Particularly the well-rounded part."

Her lips quirked, showing she was glad he was feeling better enough to banter. Though it was a fragile thing. He expected she realized that, too, because her hands stayed on him, his thigh, his shoulder near his throat, stroking. Then those hands stilled. She was thinking, a crease on her brow. She took out her phone, tapped in a text. Sent it.

She didn't say a word, and something about her demeanor kept him silent, the two of them gazing at each other until the response came, about a minute later. It didn't lessen the crease on her brow, but she pocketed the phone and put her full attention on him again.

"I'm going to tell you about Abigail."

She shifted her attention to the windows, obviously sorting it in her mind. Tension settled on her shoulders, shadows gathering in her eyes.

"You don't have to—"

When she looked his way, he realized she was offering him something important. He bit back the words and instead waited. She inclined her head.

"Thank you, Lawrence." She took one of those steadying breaths. "Abigail's grandmother and her mother both had paranoid schizophrenia. Abby has an eighty percent chance of it happening to her."

Christ. Lawrence instinctively reached for her hands, now folded on her lap, and took one, cradling it. Her gaze shifted to the contact. Something softened around her mouth, even as her eyes became more brittle, her face set. Proof that she wouldn't back down from anything. Even if a tidal wave of emotion was rising in front of her, she'd stand through it.

"Abby's mother suffered third-degree burns when she was twelve. She'd come into her mother's room because she'd had a nightmare. Grandma Rose thought she was a monster, trying to eat her in her sleep. She went after her daughter with a hot iron she kept plugged in at night for just that reason, to fight the monsters she believed would come for her out of the shadows."

Rosalinda swallowed. "Once she reached adulthood, Abby's mother self-medicated to deal with her fear of inheriting her mother's condition. Her erratic health plan didn't include consistent birth control. Abby's father was some random somebody she slept with when she was high, and Mother Rose didn't change her drug habits during the pregnancy. Abby was born at twenty-seven weeks, with a twenty-five percent chance of surviving. She did survive, though, to become the brilliant, amazing woman you've met. But her childhood didn't make that journey any easier."

Rosalinda shook her head. "She tried to drown Abby in the bathtub. Twice. Once when she was six, and again when she was nine. Those were two of the less horrible episodes of her childhood."

Lawrence remembered what he'd told Rosalinda about Abby, the first time he'd met her. *...the kind of fragile beauty that goes hand in hand with pain ... they always look like they're standing on a dock watching a ship sail away, carrying all their dreams with them.*

He lifted her hand to his face, kissed her knuckles. She laid her other hand on his head. It felt good, but the reason he kept his head bowed, pressing against her touch, was the same reason he'd knelt by her chair in the darkness, the night she'd talked to Abby on the phone. He was here. He was hers. He could be her rock.

Which brought another realization, an overwhelming one. It was done. He'd committed himself to Rosalinda, a hundred percent. Moreover, she'd accepted that. She wouldn't be telling him this otherwise. He took a tighter grip on her. "Did anyone in family services try to get her out of the home?"

"Abby refused to tell anyone what happened to her." She nodded at Lawrence's stunned look. "She kept the house cleaned up, made sure she looked the way she should, so the child services people would think everything was fine. Abby figured out at an astonishingly early age that her mother was sick, and took it upon herself to be her primary caregiver. But a child can only hide so much. Her mother was eventually institutionalized. After ten months, she strangled herself and ended her own torment."

"Ah, God."

Rosalinda nodded, her expression tight. "Abby believes if her mother had been living with her, she could have stopped it. One of many weights she carries that she shouldn't."

His Mistress traced a pattern on the top of his hand with her free one before she continued. "Paranoid schizophrenia can happen at various ages, usually younger or older, but there are always exceptions.

It fully manifested in her grandmother by age thirty-eight. For her mother, it was thirty-two. Abby is thirty-five."

Resolve set into her voice. "I promised to take care of her, Lawrence. For the rest of her life if needed. Which isn't as long as it sounds."

The next part was obviously even more difficult to say, though he couldn't imagine how it could be worse until she revealed it.

"When she starts to see evidence of the symptoms, she's planned for a legally assisted suicide. She won't let me talk her out of it, so I made her promise that she'd let me accompany her, to be with her. She won't ask it of me, but I know she needs me there. I won't let her die alone."

Damn it all. He rejected the idea vehemently, and not just because of his impression of Abby, her beauty and kindness, the strength in her, her obvious love for Rosalinda. He also thought of the three women in the wedding photo and imagined Rosalinda standing alone, the last of the trinity. The toll that would take on her.

"So you see," she said carefully, as if not trusting her voice to hold steady, "It isn't exactly my promise to her I'm making sure is kept. It's Abby's to me. Though it's all the same in the end."

This was ground she'd likely covered a million different ways. She didn't need an argument from him. That wasn't why she'd told him. What Abby would or wouldn't do, what Rosalinda intended, those things weren't his call. He could step up for what was, though.

"All right," he said. "When and if it happens, I'll come with you."

She blinked. "I won't hold you to that. You won't know what it's like until you're in it."

"Neither will you. But you love her enough it can't matter." He squeezed her hand. "You said we take care of each other. Simple. If you have to be there for her, someone is going to need to be there for you. Your friends will be that, sure. But you're their leader. Their strength. That's important to you. Maybe part of what gives you strength is knowing you're their strength. So I can be the one who can hold you when you cry and you think you can't ever stop, because it hurts so bad. You're my Mistress. It would be my fucking privilege and honor to earn the right to be the pillar you can lean against. Today, tomorrow...maybe always."

She wasn't the type of woman who asked anyone to be there for her when the darkness closed in. But that didn't mean she didn't need that. They all did. It was something she'd taught him, right? He could give her back the same gift.

While he'd spoken, her eyes had filled with a tangle of emotions, but he had more to say.

He took a breath. "As my Mistress, you should be able to expect that. I hope me almost doing this, almost getting on the plane, hasn't lost me your trust, your willingness to lean on me. And yeah, maybe I am a magnet for women like Valentina, because of how much…I want to serve."

The next part hurt to say, but he got it out without looking away. "Without me, you'd for sure survive, thrive, find happiness elsewhere. Just like with or without me, Valentina will continue to be who she is, until she kicks her habit. I can't be the one who props her up anymore. I want to be with you, and I want to be the kind of person you can want, even if you don't need me."

Now her lips parted, those emotions spilling forth in her expression, the grip of her hand on his, the way she leaned forward. "Oh, Lawrence," she murmured. "I do need you. I need you very much."

The truth of it, plain in her eyes, stunned him. Humbled him. How could he have ever thought of choosing anything other than standing by her side?

As he put his free hand over hers, sandwiching it between his and gripping hard, he couldn't find words. Wry humor touched her beautiful blue eyes. "You think I came to the airport for the beignets?"

"Well, yeah," he managed hoarsely, after another steadying beat. "My Mistress would never chase after a guy. For one thing, any man who ran from her would have to be a fucking moron. So I figured you being here was a big coincidence. The beignets explain it all."

She found her way under the neck of the T-shirt, caressed. "That's the official story, sailor. I expect you to stick to it, even under torture."

"Yes, ma'am."

Then she leaned closer and kissed him.

Maybe she'd intended it to be a quick thing, but the second her mouth was on his, he needed to dive deep. He savored that feeling, the grip of her hands on his shoulders, the way she let him clasp her waist. She made a little noise as he brought her over so she was sitting on his lap, but she slid her arm around his shoulder, the other cupped on his face as their lips moved on one another.

His reaction to her ass on his groin was inevitable, and from the little shifts of her body against it, she was feeling the same. Their strong, instantaneous response to one another was fueled by something far deeper than just the friction of two bodies, though.

When she at last broke the kiss, she didn't speak for a long moment, keeping her face pressed close to his, lips nuzzling his cheek. Which led to another long kiss, and another. He was dazed with them, all hers, when at last she put a firm hand on his chest, holding him back.

"We're going home. And when we cross that threshold, you'll show me just how far you'll go to earn my forgiveness."

CHAPTER TWENTY-SEVEN

*O*ver the next couple weeks, he adjusted his world view, served his Mistress's limitless and creative desires, and handled the closing chapters of his life that involved Valentina. Most of that involved good things. One or two of them were difficult enough he hoped never to face them again.

He'd helped implement some final security upgrades at Rosalinda's office and home, and received his last check for those services. He'd decided to take an open coach's position at the rec center he'd mentioned to her. The current coach's family was relocating, so the position was available at the beginning of next month. The job didn't pay much, but he didn't need much. And he'd already signed up for the counseling courses that would supplement his natural talent for connecting with the kids, a talent he'd already demonstrated as a volunteer. Dale, Neil and Max had all thought it was a great idea.

Rosalinda also had approved the choice. "I know you're not concerned about the money," she'd said. "But if it doesn't ruffle your manly pride, remember you have a rich Mistress. You're not going to starve."

As far as the Valentina stuff, he'd gone to see Zoey the day after he'd decided not to take the overseas job. Telling her he couldn't provide the money had been hard. She'd tried guilt, passive aggressive insinuations about abandoning someone he'd promised to love forever.

She'd accused him of wanting to see Valentina go to jail. Then she'd cried and he'd held her.

He'd told Rosalinda he needed to do that one alone, and she'd respected that. He was afraid she'd insist on a replay of the whole thing, but she didn't. She'd taken one look at his face when he came home that night, and put him through a grueling session. It had wrung him dry, but had also emptied out all the poisonous crap the meeting had churned up inside him. As they lay in bed together later, she'd told him she was going to meet with Valentina and Zoey together. Without him.

He wasn't sure how she'd gotten him on board with that idea, but she had. The very next day, they were at the treatment center, her inside, and him waiting in the car. Thoughts had ricocheted off the inside his head like bullets in a metal tank. Just when he'd decided fuck it, he was going in, she emerged.

She strode out as confidently as she always did, her supple body looking good in her dark blue blouse and gray slacks, her pumps a matching blue. Only the set to her features and his ability to read her told him what she'd handled inside the building.

As she crossed the parking lot, he was already out of the car, opening her door for her. A hundred questions were in his head, but before he could voice one, she reached out, kissed him. Thorough, deep, possessive. A hint of anger, frustration. Need. She'd left bruises on him last night, marks she'd made him beg for. He had a feeling tonight would be a memorable more of the same.

He was down for that. Because just as she'd drained the bad things from inside his heart and soul, he could do that for her, too.

When she drew back, she touched his face, her own less tense. "I gave Zoey some advice about other court-approved facilities, when Valentina's time here runs out. They're decent places. Through Laurel Grove, I have contacts who will help."

"You didn't…" He grasped her wrist then, a firm hold. "Tell me you didn't foot the bill on this. I mean it, Rosalinda. I won't tolerate—"

"There it is. My alpha sub's steel core." She gave him a look, flint to flint. "No, I didn't. I respect you too much to do that. But re-think using that tone with a woman who can put a wide variety of spiked high heels up your backside."

She dropped her hand and fondled his balls through his slacks, following that up with a sharp squeeze and a warning look. Fortunately, the position of the car and her body didn't let anyone else see what she was doing.

Not that he could summon a reason to really care about that.

~

Later that night, she not only made him pay for that pushy remark by slapping that multi-ringed thing on him, she made him wear it while giving her several orgasms. She wouldn't let him come until she believed his apology was sincere. That took a while.

It brought balance to them both. When they finally settled into a relaxed aftermath, she was ready to talk to him about what they'd discussed, that night at Ironworks.

About sharing him with the other Mistresses.

As a SEAL, as Valentina's lover, he'd agreed to things he didn't really want to do because they had to be done. This wasn't that kind of thing, but he had a lot of mixed feelings about it. Life had taken him some strange, exotic places, but he wasn't sure he could have anticipated this one.

"Vera, Cyn, Skye, Abigail and I are a family," she told him. The two of them were curled up in her bed. The ceiling fan was a light breeze against his still damp skin. She played her hand over him, slow strokes, explorations, tiny bites with the nails. He was pretty sure she was going to get him hard so she could take one more ride before bedtime. The woman was insatiable.

How would it feel to be at her mercy and that of four other Mistresses, with possibly similar appetites? He supposed there were worse ways to go.

"That family relationship hits a lot of levels," she continued. "But in the BDSM community, within groups, there are sometimes tiers. A submissive might belong to one Dominant, but he might also be part of a 'family,' where he's considered under the care and supervision of other Dominants as well."

She tipped her face up to his. Her hair was mussed, her lips full from how often they'd kissed. With her naked body sprawled so loosely over his, she reminded him of a lioness who'd had her way and was pleased with everything within her domain. He brushed his fingers over her face, her mouth, down across her pale shoulder. Cream and softness.

"Are you listening to me?"

"Family relationship. Dominants, submissives. Yes."

Her lips tugged in a smile. "The post-coital male brain. It has the retention of a soaking wet sponge."

"You're being kind. I'd say a soaking wet napkin. The cheap, flimsy kind."

"I'm not in a kind mood." She curled her fingers into his chest hair. "Put your hands over your head."

As he complied, reluctantly, she dropped her hand to his cock and began to massage. Her toy to play with, it responded to her almost instantly, despite having given everything to her only a short time before.

"Close your eyes and listen to me."

"I like looking at you, Mistress."

"I like denying you." She gave him a hard squeeze. "Particularly right now. Am I your Mistress?"

"You and no other." He shut his eyes. Her voice filled him as her hand continued to work him.

"The night I offer you to them, a lot of sexual play will happen. But you won't be having sex with them. They will not be having sex with you. No strap-ons. You will have a plug up your ass, sizeable enough to keep you mindful of who you serve, and it won't be removed until the session is over. When it is, the one who put it in will be taking it out."

He remembered how he initially thought taking anything up the ass wasn't for him. Then she'd hurdled over that by having him regard those plugs as an extension of her will, or part of her delectable body, like her clit, her pussy, her breasts, the slim line of her throat. Her incredible ass.

The other night, while she'd lain on her stomach, typing on her tablet, she'd allowed him to put kisses on that part of her, tease it with tongue and teeth, then lay his cheek on the small of her back while he watched the news.

Hell, with the kind of pictures she was painting, it was hard to slow his mind down, keep it focused, and he'd been trained for focus. Yet from the edge in her voice, she needed his attention. Even if that hadn't worked, her next words did, transforming every one of those random thoughts into a sharp arrow, pointing toward her.

"At the end of the session with them, I will collar you, brand you, and you will be mine."

Her close attention, the sudden stillness of her hand on his chest, palm pressing against his heart, told him this wasn't just a passing comment, like telling him she was going to use a crop in a session versus a flogger.

The words played and replayed in his head. This was something permanent. A commitment.

His startled gaze met hers. She regarded him like that dangerous lioness in truth, her voice a silky purr.

"Did I say you can open your eyes?"

He shut them again, though his arms were tight, his hands clenched as she slid her body halfway over his, covering him. Her knee was against the base of his balls as she bit his nipple, moved up and nipped at his chest, his throat, then paused over his parted lips. His heart thundered beneath the press of her breasts against his ribs.

"You're making me want to be uncivilized, Lawrence," she whispered. "Until the night I give you to my ladies, I want to lock you in a cage, or make you sleep on my floor. Keep you naked, make you depend on me for everything, food, water, all of it, so that by the time that night comes, you're already completely mine, your entire focus on me and what I want. The collar and brand will be afterthoughts."

"Not to me," he managed.

While some of the pictures her words were putting in his mind might be pure fantasy, something real was driving them, something that called to who they both were.

Her hand dropped, closed around his cock, now fully erect. She stroked, pulled, as he held still with effort, his body quivering.

"What do you think, Lawrence? How would you like it if I did all those things I just described?"

It might seem a weird moment for it, but everything she'd said about how she viewed him, and him her, came together. Respect, love, submission. Caring for one another, in the way they both best needed it. Which was her as a Mistress, totally owning his ass. And him, serving her with his last breath because she deserved his devotion.

Because she loved him.

That was exactly what a collar and a brand meant to her. As well as sharing him with her team under those controlled conditions she'd just outlined.

So strong were the feelings, it took a couple tries to summon words. "Safeword on the cage. The rest of it...whatever you want, Mistress, it's my pleasure."

He felt her approval through the brief easing of her hand, the tender, teasing stroke up his engorged shaft.

"Good thing for you I don't keep a cage here. Do you have any other questions right now?"

No. He didn't want to ask any. He could feel her urgency to have him all over again, as blatant as the state of his cock. He had a sudden, strong desire to never make her wait, not for anything she wanted.

"No, Mistress."

She nipped him again during the next kiss, a sharp little bite. Her hand slid over his waist to his buttock, her nails cutting into the meat of it. He kissed her with want, with need.

"Open your eyes," she whispered. "And be still."

Though his cock was hard and aching, he obeyed, gazed at her. He might not have had the words for what he was feeling, but he knew what she saw in his eyes would please her. She could read him like that sign language Skye used when she didn't use her automated voices.

At long last, she took her hands from him, laying one on her hip and propping her head on the other. She reclined before him with only inches between their bodies, but gazed at him with that remote Mistress kind of look that put him back in his head, made him seek what was there. What he could give her.

Because he wanted to fuck her—Jesus, he thought he could do that until his heart gave out and he had nothing left—but that wasn't what would serve her. And what his heart told him to do before anything else was serve his Mistress.

She could read him like a book sometimes. "What is your heart telling you to do?" she murmured.

He rose from the bed. It was tough leaving the pleasure of her body, particularly with her lying there in that decadent way. Her sweet breasts that she loved to have suckled were like firm fruit begging to be palmed. The trim pelt around the petals of her sex still gleamed from her arousal and his seed. He'd been inside her less than a half

427

hour before, watching her ride him, her head dropped back. She'd be wet again now. Wet and hot. Those killer legs were ready to wrap around him, the strength of her arms holding him, her fingers digging into his flexing ass.

Her eyes slid down to his cock as it twitched. Damn thing was like a dog begging. Her lips curved, and he saw the hint of her tongue. She liked tying him down and sucking him. She'd tease his cock to near orgasm, then go read a book, answer emails, and wait for it to settle down and start again.

But for all his body's responses, he was a man who knew what really drove his cock and satisfied everything. Not just his body, but his heart and soul, too. So he picked up one of the pillows from the bed, dropped it on the floor.

As she propped herself up to peer over the edge and see what he was doing, he knelt next to the bed, bowed his head. Then he stretched out on the Persian rug that would be his sleeping spot until she shared him with her sisters.

As he settled himself, a rustling came from above. The quilt she kept folded at the foot tumbled down, landing upon his chest. He smiled, spread it loosely over his hips.

His Mistress did know how to be kind. In just the measured kind of way he liked.

He'd anticipated it happening at the club, but the following day she didn't mention anything more about it. Because she forbade him to ask her about the subject unless she brought it up, it was in his mind, a lot. All the possibilities kept that part of him that obeyed her will, craved her dominance, in a state of agitation that resulted in even more enthusiastic responses to her demands over the next couple days.

To burn off the extra energy, on top of the other things he was doing, including volunteering at the center and working out with Max, he did handyman jobs and yard work for her. He did the latter under Freak's window view supervision. Though the cat wasn't overly thrilled when Rosalinda shut him out of the bedroom during the sex part of the evenings, Freak had accepted Lawrence, with a bolstering level of trust. The night Lawrence had rested his head on the small of Rosalinda's back, the cat had jumped on the bed, stretched out against his side like a long, furry caterpillar and fallen asleep, his purr so loud Lawrence had to bump up the volume a couple notches.

He'd spent years learning that he could wake up with a plan for the day and two hours later be on a plane to a remote country. Trips to the grocery store, plans to hit a new comic book store, all that would be swept off the table by tactical considerations and strategies for taking out targets, collecting intel, rescuing hostages.

That acceptance of unpredictability should have been useful right now. It was, mostly. But he had a tough time restraining the urge to introduce the sharing thing into the conversation in a way that could coax out more details, a timeline, without seeming to break her rule. Like that would work.

She'd started her day those past couple of mornings by inviting him from the floor into the bed, straddling him, bringing herself to climax. She let him come the first morning, but not the second one. Today she slipped out of bed, standing over him where he was on the floor, straddling his shoulders. She wore a silky black nightgown that was short, but shadowed what was between her thighs way too much. He pressed his mouth to her ankle, their current version of a good morning kiss. As he did that, she picked up her robe, slipped into it, freed her hair from the collar and gazed down at him. "Blanket off," she said. "You don't have my permission to look at me."

Well, that sucked. He loved looking up at her first thing in the morning. But he pushed the blanket out of the way and stretched out so she could see his morning erection, the readiness of his body to please her. She nodded after a long look but moved away, her words drifting back to him.

"Use the guest bathroom if you need it," she said. "After that, come back here, kneel by the master bath door. No clothes. Fists pressed to the floor, eyes down. If I approach you, you will immediately go to a back straight, hands laced behind your head posture, presenting your body and your cock. No talking, no looking at me.

"Until I'm ready to leave, those are the rules you follow. This morning you're fully my slave, Lawrence. I own every thought you have, every word you speak. The right to wear clothes, to move, to speak, all of those are my privileges to give or take away. Do you understand?"

It was going to be today. Or, at the very least, she was putting him in the starting gate with the strict protocol. His mind flooded with thoughts, questions and images, but before he could run away with that, his brain barked at him like a BUD/S instructor having a bad day.

She'd demanded something from him, and she was waiting for his response. He'd vowed to never make her wait for what she wanted.

"Yes, Mistress."

When he returned from the bathroom, she'd finished brushing her teeth. Though he didn't meet her gaze, he felt her regard as he knelt where she'd ordered. The sharper anticipation in the air told him her want for him this morning was strong. That want was contagious. Especially as he knelt naked, waiting on her pleasure.

She didn't ease up on that want as she got ready for work. After she left the shower and moved for her closet, which had her passing right by him, he remembered, snapping his spine straight so he could lace his hands behind his head. She stopped briefly, bent and gave his stiff cock a light, playful slap.

Playful to her, but she knew what that did to him. His cock leaked clear fluid, and she tsked, but he knew she wanted to see him wanting her.

She did it almost every time she passed in front of him. A total of eight times. When at last she was ready, she stood before him in her silver gladiator shoes. His kneejerk possessive and jealous reaction to her wearing them out in public around other men was proof she was turning him into a mindless animal.

"You won't leave the house today," she said. "Tonight I share you with my Mistresses. That requires preparation of your mind and body to please them, and me, to the extremes we'll demand."

He'd intended to do some errands. Neil had been called out for a mission, but he'd had plans to work out with Max. He'd be rescheduling.

"I'll send a car for you at six-thirty. Eat when you need to do so today, but keep it light. I want you a little hungry. The rest of my instructions are downstairs on the kitchen counter. You'll go look at them immediately after I leave. You don't have permission to do anything else first, which means you stay naked. Now kiss me good-bye."

He leaned forward, put his mouth on her ankle again. As he did, she lifted the other foot, braced it on his curved back, just behind his nape. She had good balance, his Mistress, but he couldn't help but be protective, putting his hands behind her knees, sliding them up behind her thighs. Yes, to keep her steady, though there was nothing under his hands he didn't want.

She could punish him for it as an infraction, but she understood the things in him that had to protect, to care. And she welcomed them.

"See you tonight. Behave."

He had to grin at that, his lips curving against her leg so he could give her a hint of teeth. She made a reproving noise that had a smile in it, and she was gone, her heels tapping down the hallway, down the steps. He heard the door close, but he waited until he heard her car pull out, until she'd officially "left," to follow her next instructions.

There was a precise way she did certain things that was familiar to him, like taking orders, working within a command structure. Was that the kind of Mistress she'd been before him, or had she integrated elements of that into her approach, because it called forth deeper responses from him, something she wanted?

He'd ask her sometime, or maybe not. There were things about her being a Mistress she didn't allow him to plumb. Probably because keeping some of that to herself was like the class distinction protocols observed at Progeny, which helped establish the mindsets that bound Doms and subs together in the way they craved.

He headed down the steps. In broad daylight, it felt odd to walk through the house without clothes. She had some big windows, so he hoped the sunlight was obscuring the interior view. It probably was, because embarrassing him wasn't her thing. Anytime she'd touched him in public she'd done it discreetly. He liked that about her. He guessed he didn't have much of an exhibitionist side outside of a place like Progeny, though he wasn't all that modest. Wasn't much room for it when he was on a mission, but he wasn't into flaunting it either.

He found her directions on the counter, along with a bright, shiny apple. The apple made him smile.

The kind of apples she bought were a mix of tangy and sweet. The first time they'd shared one, he'd really liked it. She'd since then decided that was his reward food, when she was exceptionally pleased with him. It had started as kind of a joke, but in that way she had, tapping into what was inside him, she'd turned it into something meaningful. Seeing the apple next to the note was a message. She was anticipating he'd earn that apple by following her direction.

A few days ago, they'd shared pillow talk about whether the strength of his feelings might be because she was his first Mistress. Like a kid thinking his first sex was his forever love.

He knew this wasn't that. He thought things through. He wanted her. The night she'd suggested he consider that possibility, he'd demonstrated his singular devotion in ways intended to leave her no doubts about it. He got into some trouble for walking that line of topping from the bottom, but he'd gotten an apple for breakfast. While he cut it up and shared pieces, she'd sent him looks from beneath her lashes that reminded him of a satisfied cat.

He focused on the note, on handwriting as elegant and controlled as the rest of her.

No clothes until the time indicated. Go back to bed until eleven o'clock (sleep in the bed, not on the floor). Even if you can't sleep, lie there. I want you well-rested. When you get up, sit on the screened back porch for an hour. Read the book I left for you out there, relax and listen to nature. Don't turn on the television.

Starting at one, masturbate at the top of every hour for five minutes. No condom. Don't allow yourself to come, but get as close as possible. No half-assed effort to keep yourself in control. I'm in charge of your control.

At three, take a thorough shower. Keep masturbating once an hour. At six o'clock, put on what I've left in your closet, and only that. Don't look until six. The car will pick you up at six-thirty.

Putting on the clothes should only take ten minutes, so from 6:10 to 6:30, kneel by the door and stroke yourself, again restraining yourself from coming, but getting yourself as close to it as possible.

Once the car arrives, you will not speak unless you are asked a direct question.

PS – I took Freak with me.

Hell. How was he supposed to sleep after reading that? But he followed direction. Once in the bed, his body nested in the mattress that bore her scent, face pressed to her pillow, he surprisingly found he was able to drift off. However, he slept on his back with the covers off, worried friction might give him a wet dream. He knew Rosalinda Thomas. No way would she accept involuntary orgasm as an excuse for giving away something that belonged to her.

Except for the five minutes of torture every hour, he figured the rest would be easy. He was quickly reminded not to underestimate the diabolical nature of an experienced Mistress.

Out on the screen porch, when he wasn't reading the graphic scenes she'd marked in the novel she'd left him—*Corporal Johnson's Punishment*—*Christ*—he was staring mindlessly at the backyard while a host of erotic scenarios played through his head. By the time he gripped his cock at one, he was seriously doubting he was going to be able to do this without coming.

He made it, but at four minutes and fifty-nine seconds he had to put a death grip squeeze on the base of his dick to stop the pulsing need to spew.

After that, he wandered the house, made a repair to a small crack in the sheet rock. He'd never done home maintenance naked, but desperate times called for desperate measures. He appreciated the foresight that had motivated her to take Freak to the office. Wandering around, sitting or lying down with things hanging out that could catch the cat's attention would have been somewhat unnerving. Cue the Robin Williams' joke about Mr. Happy waking up before Robin did, and the cat deciding it was a mouse.

She would have laughed her ass off at that. And at him taking everything out of her linen closet, dumping it on the bed and refolding the items with military precision.

He leafed through the photo album she had on the shelf in her living room. For a while his heart was able to distract him from his libido, seeing pictures of her childhood, her college days. At her high school graduation, she stood with her mother and father. In her mother's face, he saw the clues Rosalinda had given him. Mrs. Thomas looked like the typical middle-class wife. Any evidence of disappointments, hard choices or an unhappy marriage was concealed by an iron-clad practiced smile. Her dad had the likable salesman look, face with the telltale ruddiness, arm placed around his wife's waist with genuine affection.

There were more pictures of her, Laurel and Abby. When he saw one of the ribbon cutting at TRA, he lingered, studying the women laughing together, their hands on one another. Tonight, their hands would be on him. According to what Rosalinda had said, she was his, but he would also be theirs, from here forward.

It should have gone two ways in his head. Either a *yeehaw*, purely male reaction to having five women handle him sexually. Or a self-preservation terror, thinking of how extreme a session with five Mistresses could be. But the truth lay somewhere in between, in the understanding that these women loved Rosalinda, and she loved them. This was about bringing him inside that bond. He didn't know what that looked like, but he was going to find out.

It was his feelings for her—his trust—that made him not only willing, but want to go there.

It was now two o'clock. He set the album aside, knelt in the kitchen—a precaution—and took hold of himself again.

"God...damn..." He'd thought he'd done a good job of distracting himself, but his grip reminded him of hers, her demands, and his cock was ready to go, his balls wanting to boil over. He kept working himself, because she'd told him he couldn't do it half-ass, but he had a hell of a time. He played every mind trick in the book with himself to keep from caving to the orgasm that demanded to be released.

He made it, just. After the five minutes were up, he stretched flat out on the cold kitchen tile. Damn if that didn't make him think of the two of them in the snow in Indiana, her hand closing around him after their snowball fight.

He made himself think of what had happened after, far less sexy thoughts. But he did remember how well she'd held it together. Even shot one of her attackers. The man hadn't died, but it had been a near thing. Lawrence wouldn't have been sorry to hear it, but he was glad his Mistress didn't have that hanging over her. The gang member would spend a long time in jail, and she was satisfied with that.

When a civilian was part of a mission, he calculated how they would handle themselves if things got dicey. Could they be left alone to follow instruction, would they hold it together and be able to help, or would the panic of a life-or-death situation make them freeze? He'd had no doubt of what to expect with her. He'd known she wouldn't freeze. She'd been scared, but she'd done what he told her to do, and then given him hell for risking himself.

His mind stayed with that, and the photo album, as he left the kitchen, walked up the stairs. He ended up in her closet. All her shoes were arranged the right way. He smiled at the many different colors and shapes, thought about how her legs looked in the heels. Which brought him back to the gladiator shoes, and the way those had made her legs look this morning. Her skirt had been the classy two inches above the knee style that on her was even sexier than a much shorter skirt, though he couldn't explain why.

Pausing at the blue-green sneakers, he picked them up, cradling them in his palms. She said she was an average shoe size for a woman, but they were narrow. Slim feet. He thought of her painted toenails, gripping the edge of her chair, her knees drawn up, when she sat on the screen porch and reviewed work stuff on her tablet. Usually while drinking the morning coffee he'd made the way she liked it.

Several weeks ago, they hadn't even met. Now his belongings were here. Neil hadn't taken his boxes to their storage facility. He'd told Lawrence he'd had a feeling he'd just be pulling them back out again. Rosalinda told Lawrence to put his boxes in her guest house, a former one-car garage shed she'd converted into an extra room. It had a bathroom, bedroom and small sitting area. His boxes fit in a few neat stacks along one wall.

She'd told him he could use the space until he decided if he needed to get another place. He'd been fully prepared to treat her house as a separate residence, with him knocking or calling ahead to visit her. Instead, it had been, "Let's make dinner. What's on TV? Come to bed..."

He was living in the house with her, because that was where she wanted him. The only thing she'd said that suggested otherwise was what she told him the first night they were making dinner together, him chopping vegetables while she put together the makings for lasagna.

"Unless you need your space or I need mine, I expect your full attendance to my needs and desires. Understand?"

He wasn't sure he did, not the full scope, but she was offering him the invitation to find out. He'd accepted. She had him put his zombie heads in her yard, helping him choose the best arrangements for them among the flowers and shrubs. He couldn't imagine a more direct declaration of love from a woman than that.

Her closet—which was an odd name for a room the size of his townhouse living room—had two parts. One was for the shoes. The other was for her clothes, set off in a section that more closely resembled what he considered a walk-in closet, though about twice as wide. It had a cozy, hushed feel, and something even better.

He stopped in the middle of it. Inhaled. He was surrounded by an intense cloud of her scent, that womanly fragrance of well-tended, expensive female. His lips curved as he imagined her reaction to that.

Did you just imply I'm high maintenance, Lawrence?

If the shoe fits... And he was really glad it did.

He sat down against the wall, beneath the section of closet that held her shirts. He pulled his knees up, linked his hands loosely over them, put his head back and closed his eyes to breathe her in.

Before her, he'd had a lot of fantasies but no clear idea of the day-to-day of being a man who wanted to serve a woman like this. Now, just like his reaction to the apple reward, and this, sitting in her closet, there were limitless avenues to what he wanted to do, say, feel.

In the non-D/s world, a man saying, "I'm a submissive," was interpreted with judgment as "I'm a submissive male." Something pretty damn different, but without her guidance it was part of what had kept him from going down this road for so long. Since he hadn't been able to figure out exactly what it looked like in his own head, he wasn't willing to let the world define it for him. Serving her had cleared that up for him. He knew what he was.

He was hers. He was a man who knew what he wanted and had no problems going after it. He also was a man who wanted to love a woman with everything he was. It was something he wanted more than anything in the world. Even more than the ability to be an operator again, and that really was saying a whole fucking lot.

Leaving his team had been like carrying a knife blade in his gut that sawed at him every minute. Being a SEAL had defined the best parts of who he was for so long. He hadn't realized a whole other part of him had been growing along with that definition. And he was ready to embrace it now.

He would never stop being a team guy, one who could have Neil's back, or Dale or Max's, when the moment called for it. But those moments could be on civilian ground, as their friend. He'd never stop missing the impossible-to-explain camaraderie of an active relationship built in those circumstances. But he was finding something here that meant just as much.

When Neil's time came, as it did for all of them—if fate let them live to see it—Lawrence would be there to help him find that kind of meaning, too.

A chime reached his ears. Her bedside clock. It was the top of the hour again.

He wanted to prove his devotion to her directly. In her absence, being surrounded by her clothes, her shoes, her scent, was the closest he could get to her. But without permission to use a condom, he had to take some wise precautions. If he lost control in here, she'd bury him among his zombie heads.

She had a set of narrow wooden shelves for her purses, a basket of scarves and other female things. On one of them was a box of tissues. He claimed a handful of them, and clasped them over the end of his cock as he began to stroke.

He'd kept his phone with him, not just in case she had further instructions, but so he could time himself for this hourly torment. He was pretty good at counting down seconds in his head, but the distraction made it easy to drop a couple seconds, and he wouldn't chance not being sure and making himself go longer, just to be sure he hadn't cheated, no matter how inadvertently.

Oh, God. It felt too good, to handle himself while the soft scents, textures and colors of his woman cocooned him in this dark, quiet corner of her home.

His phone buzzed, a text popping up. His eyes fell on the words, devoured them, even as his hand never stopped moving, jerking up and down his cock.

I'm in my office, thinking of my sub. On his knees, handling himself, suffering for his Mistress. My legs are spread over the arms of my chair, my heels braced on the edge of my desk. I have my hand on my cunt, stroking. I've brought myself to climax in my office twice and I'm already wet again.

Son of a bitch. His cock convulsed. *No, no, no...*

It was a good thing he'd used those tissues. Even if she didn't want to risk a murder charge, if he'd sprayed her clothes and shoes, his house privileges would have been revoked. She'd have put him on a chain under the porch, just like a yard dog in one of those ASPCA commercials.

Only unlike them, she'd say he deserved it.

~

He'd tried so hard to choke back his release, even all the way through it. But whether that effort deserved any consideration or not would be his Mistress's call, and mercy would depend on her mood and purposes.

As he showered, he tried to put aside the frustration. He'd wanted to be able to tell her he'd complied with all her instructions. Then he thought about the timing of that text and realized maybe he'd given her exactly what she'd wanted.

After he finished bathing, the next several hours became three of the longest he'd spent in a while. He did push-ups, tried to read again. He'd never read the stock reports in the paper, and today he did, ticking off the numbers. If he'd been clothed and not showered, he might have grabbed garden tools from her shed and done some yard work she'd mentioned having her landscapers handle. A naked guy pruning her roses might cause issues with the neighbors, though.

He found a notepad, drew zombies. Which made him think about Kyle. Who and where he might have been now.

The sexual frustration was expected. His emotions and thoughts going in all different directions, with her closet, her photo album, spending time with his own head, wasn't.

Inevitably, his mind went to Valentina. He'd gone to see her one more time, the day after her visit with Rosalinda. He'd told her he would never regret being with her, and that he'd hope for her happiness every day.

She'd cried, and they'd held each other. At one point, her head had come up, their faces so close, and he'd seen the woman he'd fallen in love with. But even if she got her life together tomorrow, reclaiming the vibrant, self-deprecating, eccentric artist she'd been at the street fair where he'd met her, he wasn't the same person. He loved her, but he was no longer in love with her, and never would be again.

Maybe she felt that, too. Because though he'd felt drained afterward, the way a caregiver did after they left the funeral of a person who'd suffered from a long illness, he'd felt at peace about it.

But there was still sadness there, for the way the world worked out sometimes. For her and him, for Kyle. For his father. Daddy would have loved Rosalinda. He would have danced with her, plied her with romantic, lyrical streams of Spanish, made her laugh. He would have teased Lawrence with a threat to steal her away, while Mama would have shaken her head at his harmless flirting. Though he never in a million years would have been unfaithful, his father had a strong appreciation for the fairer sex.

The clock chimed. Five o'clock.

This was part of it, wasn't it? Everything she was doing to him was to open him up to what would happen tonight.

He needed her. He needed her mind, her heart. Her arms.

By the time he reached six o'clock, a day's worth of the physical and emotional breakdown had taken its toll. His movements were jerky, his head not focused. His cock was almost permanently erect and all he could think of was her pussy. Wet, hot, pink, legs spread on the bed, her sharp nails beckoning to him, her voice commanding him to serve her.

He wanted to eat her out, rub his face in her scent, ram his cock into her and feel her body close over it like a tight glove. Yeah, he was being crude, but he wasn't feeling particularly silver-tongued.

Her eyes would lock on his as he pounded into her, her hands on him, so light and easy. Still in control. He wouldn't want to leave her body for days. Food, water...none of that mattered as much as fucking her. He now understood why rutting stags looked half out of their minds at the height of the heat season for does.

Time to get dressed.

She'd given him a guestroom closet and dresser for his clothes. He'd amused her when he filled the dresser with jeans, socks and underwear, and barely took up a third of the space in the closet for the limited amount of hanging clothes he drew from the guesthouse boxes. "If I'd needed any proof you were a straight male," she'd said, "this would be it."

He didn't figure her choice of outer wear for him would be too terrifying, since she wasn't into the exhibitionist thing, and someone was picking him up. What she might want him to wear *under* his clothes was the real worry.

When he opened the closet, he saw she'd set out a pair of jeans she particularly liked, because of the way the broken-in denim held him.

The shirt was a surprise. It was one his cousin had given him for Christmas a couple years back. She had to have retrieved it from the guest house when he was off at the rec center or meeting Max for his workout.

It was a nice shirt, black, soft and fit well, but it had the Navy SEAL Trident emblazoned on the back in bold colors. He didn't really advertise himself that way. Most of the guys didn't. He suspected it was her sense of humor that had prompted the choice, since a common SEAL mantra, "All in, all the time," was scrolled on a crimson ribbon winding around the Trident.

A velvet bag hung on the rack with the shirt. When he looked inside it, his lower body's coiled state received an additional twist. She'd left a printed diagram, so he'd know just how the handful of metal cuffs and slender chains worked. A good thing, because the current scrambled state of his brain made it look as complicated as defusing a bomb.

The solid silver cuff went just behind the head of his cock. Another one clasped at the base, above his balls. The two cuffs connected with a double length of chain that wrapped in a spiral around the shaft.

Putting it on with a full erection wasn't easy, especially without pinching the skin of his cock in the clasp of the cuffs, but fortunately having his skin pulled drum tight over his erection helped. The wrapped chain cut into his sensitive flesh. It wasn't unbearable, but it was a distinct reminder that his cock, and everything attached to it, belonged to a very possessive Mistress.

Donning the jeans and shirt, socks and shoes, no underwear, took only a couple minutes. She'd correctly gauged a ten-minute prep time, with the cock harness taking the biggest part of it.

Now for the next hurdle. Sitting by the back door and working his cock for twenty fucking minutes. God help him.

This morning, he'd thought sending a car was unnecessary. He could drive himself. But she had insisted, no flexibility on that mandate. Now he knew exactly why. A person blowing the hell out of a blood alcohol limit was in better shape to drive than him.

He knelt by the door, jeans open, his hand working up and down the steel rod of his erection, which pulled on those chains, rubbed them against his sensitive flesh. He still got thicker, even as the hold of the cuffs made him wince. At least they made it less likely he'd lose control. He was revved up, aroused as hell, but he was also uncomfortable enough to keep it balanced. His heart was pounding, his palms damp, the top of his cock wet, but the lava in his balls stayed there. His muscles were as tight as when he was pushing himself through an obstacle course.

Right at six-thirty, a car pulled up to the back of the house. He could see it through the kitchen door's upper window and adjacent screened porch.

He put himself back in his jeans, carefully zipped himself up, and thanked God his Mistress hadn't said anything about tucking in his T-shirt. His cock was continuing to scream for release from its manacles, and anyone with eyes would notice that.

But when he rose and took a closer look at the car, his mind took a sharp right turn away from his sexual frustration. His heart jumped in his throat, his stomach flipflopped.

He'd assumed she'd send an Uber or taxi. He hadn't anticipated a Kensington limo.

One driven by Max himself.

Oh, hell no.

CHAPTER TWENTY-EIGHT

*H*ow did you safeword to a Mistress who wasn't present? Why the hell had Rosalinda sent Max, instead of some anonymous driver? He was too wound up, too out of control, to put the best face on this. Telling himself there was a big difference between a submissive male and a submissive, and feeling all confident about that, sounded good...in her fucking closet. But thinking Max might know some of what was happening here, that was a huge, unbalancing shove. He wasn't ready for that.

Nor for what happened next.

Max circled the limo and opened the front passenger side. If he'd brought Dale, Lawrence was not coming out.

The thought showed just how confused his mind was. Max would no more open a car door for MC than Dale would keep his ass in the car, waiting for him to do it.

Janet stepped out. She wore a skirt and jacket, the female version of a suit, in form-fitting hunter green. A supple leather-looking trim followed the lines of breasts and hips, drawing the eye to all those curves. Though Janet was slim and petite, a ballet dancer in a former life, she wasn't the type of female anyone would call delicate. Except maybe Max. Stunning, charismatic, striking-looking. Those would be the words to describe her. While one look could send the male libido into overdrive, a second look would tell him to mind his manners, unless he wanted to lose his balls. She was so obviously a Mistress,

Lawrence couldn't believe he'd ever doubted the answer to that question.

The idea of a Domme having to come all the way to the kitchen door to fetch him lit a fire under Lawrence's reluctant ass. Muttering a *fuck it*, he stepped out onto the porch, locked the kitchen door and headed for the stoop.

Max had given Janet her his hand to navigate the uneven root-cracked driveway in her black heels, until she reached the smoother walkway to the back porch. He didn't look toward Lawrence. Instead, his hard-to-read expression stayed on Janet. She laid a hand on his chest, spoke low. Max covered that hand, nodded, his gaze warming on her.

Releasing her, he returned to the car and took up position by the passenger door. It was how he'd behave if he was waiting on Matt or one of his guys to conclude some business that didn't concern him. Exercising a peripheral vision and studied detachment that made his presence non-intrusive, projecting an attitude of privacy and protection both.

Since Lawrence was juggling possible ways to handle this awkwardness, he found himself evaluating Max's behavior in a different light. He was demonstrating all the signs of a man respecting a Mistress's authority. Even as Max *still* didn't give off any kind of sub vibe. Their next workout was going to be an interesting conversation.

"Lawrence." Janet gave him a cool nod as he came down the steps to her. "I told Ros we would give you a ride to TRA, since Max and I are going to a concert at Audubon Park."

Lawrence *was* a submissive, and Janet's expression required one response only. It was out of his mouth before a blink had passed.

"Thank you, ma'am."

A little smile flirted around her usually unsmiling mouth, and she glanced at Max. He sent her a wry look, with more than a little possessive heat behind it.

She offered Lawrence a nod, then pivoted. Max was already back at the walkway, taking her hand again. He helped her into the front seat, closed the door.

As Lawrence moved toward the car, Max cocked his head. Lawrence narrowed his gaze. "Open the door for me, and I'll kick your ass."

Max smiled. "Wouldn't think of it, Munch."

~

Shit. He didn't think of it until he was in the car, but he'd broken one of the rules, speaking to Max out of turn. He'd have to report that to his commanding officer, so to speak. Along with the loss of control in the closet. But the saving-face comment had helped, as well as seeing the understanding and relaxed grin on his friend's face.

He did want to ask Max a lot of stuff, but not now. Now was the time to be in his head, letting things settle into a river, the current going one way. Toward his Mistress.

It seemed they'd been read into the no-talking part of Rosalinda's instructions, since they didn't engage him in chitchat once they were on their way. That was a relief, even as Lawrence hoped they weren't privy to the rest of that note.

While Max drove, he clasped Janet's hand, resting on his thigh. She glanced toward Lawrence periodically, and it wasn't intrusive. She was judging his mental state, he realized. Watching after him. As a Mistress, she obviously still recognized he wasn't in his usual headspace.

Max's being here with Janet might be Rosalinda's way of telling him he had two families watching after him now. It wasn't a bad thought.

He laid his head back, closed his eyes. His cock's enthusiasm hadn't been dampened by Max's presence. It was ready to go off like a water hose with a backlog of pressure against it. He needed to focus on keeping that reaction dammed up, while still responding to his Mistress's demands. She excelled at teaching him how to do that. A couple days ago, he'd told her so.

"Thank you, Lawrence. But the will of the submissive is equally key to learning that skill. Your denying your own desires and gratification, holding my will above them, is a sign of deep respect for your Mistress. It's appreciated, and a deep pleasure to reward."

He thought of that ribbon-cutting picture again. Skye, bringing him an ice pack. Cyn, with that unsettling stare that promised a man pain, the good kind that Mellencamp wrote a song about. Abby, her thoughtful dark eyes and shrewd advice about not being a dick. He believed she'd known, well before him or even Rosalinda, where this was going between the two of them.

Vera, that day they'd entered the contract with him. She'd instructed him to wander and familiarize himself with the offices while she handled her conference call. She'd had a way of talking to him that made him think of a matriarchal ruler talking to her beloved yet unruly and slightly misguided subjects. With kind firmness and a steely gaze that missed nothing.

Thinking of each of them made him nervous as hell, but it didn't deflate his response to being at their mercy at all. If he did start to get nervous about it in the wrong way, he remembered the gym, when Cyn had overstepped. Not only had Rosalinda called her on it immediately, but Cyn had offered a sincere apology. These were women who wouldn't be abusing his submission, and if there was an inkling of it, his Mistress would be on it.

He wasn't a man who asked for protection. But as she'd taught him, everyone needed protection. Care.

He would answer that tonight with everything; head, heart, cock, soul. He was dedicated to showing her his respect and devotion, focused as he'd never been focused on anything before in his life, all on pleasing her. He would be like he'd been in BUD/S, where everything became about achieving the next moment, so at the end of the day, he knew he was one step closer to being everything he intended to be.

They were here. As they pulled up to the front, Max glanced at him in the mirror. "She said you should use the security code to get through the gate and front door, and go straight to the board room."

"Roger that."

Lawrence glanced toward Janet, nodded. "Ma'am."

She returned the nod, that light smile on her face. "Your Mistress is very fortunate, Lawrence. Take care of her."

"Yes, ma'am."

Then he was out of the car, stepping out into a clear evening. When the sky darkened to full night, they should have a good scattering of stars overhead, those that could penetrate the dome of city lights. The blooming bushes landscaped around the entranceway provided a light fragrance that reminded him of his Mistress. He wanted to be with her. He'd missed her all day. Some of that ache came from the conditioning she'd put him through, but a large part of it was just there whenever he was away from her, for any reason.

All quiet in the lobby. No sign of Freak, so he wondered if the cat was sleeping in her office. She kept a cat bed here for when he was visiting, and set it on top of her credenza, in a nook between the printer and the wall. Lawrence re-secured the door, then moved to the curving staircase. At the top, he found a note, handwritten in her lovely script. She'd told him she'd loved calligraphy as a kid, and had always considered handwriting like being asked to draw a picture.

Take off all your clothes. Leave them here. Come to the board room. Get on the table, stretch out on your back. Put on the blindfold. Legs spread to shoulder width, arms out to the sides. Then wait.

Note: Remember your first job is protecting your Mistress's property. Since it's better but not fully healed, keep your shoulder at the angle most comfortable for it.

Tonight, I'm demanding your full trust, Lawrence, even if it takes you far out of your comfort zone. You will be tied down, and there will be much you will not be able to see coming. Safewords are always an option. But I ask you to do your very best to trust tonight's direction. Trust where I can take you.

Trust me.

He wanted to take pleasure in what was done here, because that would please his Mistress. Being alone with her in a secured room, she'd helped him handle being restrained, his vision restricted. He wasn't as sure about accomplishing that in this situation.

But she was simply asking him to try. He could do that.

He removed his clothes. Doing that in an office building where he was used to thirty people swarming around like a creative beehive was unsettling. Especially knowing there were people other than Rosalinda here. But he did it, folding everything and leaving the clothes at the top of the stairs.

His cock was back to a straight up position again, pulling against the chains and swelling against those silver cuffs. It didn't have any reservations about tonight's agenda.

He padded down the hallway. It was warmer up here than usual. They'd ensured he wouldn't be cold. A sign of care among her more inflexible demands.

He did a doubletake at Skye's office when he realized she was in it. She was typing on one of her monitors, but she looked his way as he passed, giving him an appraising look before she went back to what she was doing. Like seeing a naked guy in a cock harness walking around was normal.

Then Cyn of course, her boots up on her desk, talking low into her earpiece. Again, she didn't change position, even break the conversation, but her gaze fastened on him, raked him from head to toe, and a devilish smile touched her mouth.

He had a feeling he'd turned beet red. His knees were feeling a little weak. Now he knew where they'd all be. Abby was making notes on a pad at her desk, and Vera was looking through one of her file cabinets. Yet they all stopped, turned, remained in that silent, watchful pose until he passed. Like running a gauntlet.

Rosalinda's office was closed, the only woman he didn't see. But the stained-glass board room doors were wide open. Though no one was in there, the sense of being watched was. There was a camera in here, he knew, because he'd helped with that upgrade. He didn't doubt it was activated.

The table was covered. Black vinyl, easy to wipe down and handle messes. It had one those elastic hems that fit it snugly to the table. A cushioned black mat was in the center, long and wide enough to support his body as he lay upon it.

Rosalinda had told him they'd never done this before, honored the pact they'd made in Laurel's name. He hoped they'd likewise never had a man stretched out on this table, but he put that aside. It shouldn't be his focus right now.

The lights were set on dim. The shades to the tall windows, normally open to let in lots of sunlight, were closed, giving the room a closer, more intimate feel. Like a club dungeon. Fat ivory-colored candles were grouped on a side table, the flickering flames adding to the room's ambiance, the sense of hushed heat. A mix of vanilla and some kind of heady spice reached his nose.

There were other things on the side bar, too, but they'd been draped in a dark cloth, so he couldn't see what they were. He didn't really like that, but he remembered her words. *Trust me.*

He wasn't going to delay seeing her as soon as possible. Moving to the table, he hiked himself onto it and shifted to the center, stretching out on the mat. The thing on his cock stretched too, sending arousal and discomfort shooting through his lower belly and upper thighs.

As he lay down and spread himself for her, everything got more worked up. His breath shortened, his heart accelerated. He had to see her, now. But then he remembered. The blindfold.

It was black, too, folded and left on the vinyl covering. He might have missed it if he hadn't brushed against it.

He didn't want to put it on. But she wasn't going to appear until he did. Yet as he tried to lift it to his face, his hands weren't listening to him. There were two entrances to this room, multiple entrances to the building. There were at least five people here. He hadn't cleared the entire structure.

Trust me.

He paused, took a breath. Swept one more look around the room, then wrapped the blindfold around his head, lacing it down the back and pulling it secure, so it molded to his eyes, the bridge of his nose, his cheekbones. He couldn't see anything.

His night vision goggles had malfunctioned on one mission. Crouching down in the forest, fighting the sense of being a blind, neon-lit target, he'd calmed everything inside him. He'd remembered that hunters had known how to hunt in darkness, long before they had ways to see through it. He'd centered himself, steadied. Listened. So he heard his target's footsteps, moving along the forest floor. Smelled the faint tang of the regional blend that clung to a smoker's clothes. The man had been moving slow, almost silent...but not silent enough.

A much better sound disrupted the memory. A feminine heel on the wood floor, the squeak of a door opening. And her scent, something he would know anywhere. She'd put on a sea salt and jasmine hand lotion this morning before she left, and she'd taken the bottle with her. He expected she'd put it on her hands right before she came in here, a message just for him. Even before she spoke, the wrong kind of tension in his stomach started to settle.

"Thank you, Lawrence. Your trust means a great deal to me. I won't abuse it. You're secure here. You're safe."

If he had permission to speak, he'd assure her what bugged him most was not being fully prepared for a threat against her. The truth was, it might take years before he was remotely okay with this level of sensory deprivation. His life, and the lives of his brothers, or whomever they were protecting, extracting, had hung in the balance too often. Having access to the full range of his senses, instincts and training, had been the difference between success or failure.

But she'd introduced him to an idea so foreign to him he couldn't believe he was standing within it, considering it with some relative degree of calm. He could let go in this situation, submit, and let himself be guided by her desire to control all the variables.

It reminded him of a HALO jump, the airplane door opening, the rush of air inviting him to leap, spin through the air, fly. Once that jump was made, that letting go feeling flooded the senses. Feeling it here startled him enough it almost worked in reverse. Before his nerves could act up, her hand was on him. She stroked his face, his neck and shoulder, down over his chest, his flank. She didn't touch his cock, though the mindless thing convulsed, in case she didn't notice how eager it was. No manners at all.

She made a soft noise. "I like the way my jewelry looks on my property. You followed my direction. That pleases me."

He swallowed. "May I speak, Mistress?"

"You may."

"I spoke to Max once, out of turn. And when you texted me, at two...I tried hard not to, but I couldn't stop myself. I'm sorry. I disappointed you."

"The apology is necessary. But telling me how I feel about your infraction, is that proper behavior from the man who serves me?"

A punch in the gut. "No, Mistress."

"A lesson to consider. Be silent now."

She wrapped a cuff around his wrist, and he felt the pull on his arm as she secured it to something, maybe a hook beneath the table.

"I've thought about you all day today," she said. "Everything about you, every moment we've spent together."

She was moving around the table, her fingertips whispering over his hip bone to his upper thigh. He shivered under her touch, a ticklish reaction, but other things, too. She circled around to his other side, caressed her way back up his body, until she reached his injured shoulder. It was much better now, thanks to exercises he was already doing to get the muscles back in shape, but there was still some tenderness. She bent and put her mouth there. He felt the brush of her hair against his skin.

"Mistress," he murmured, moved. Then remembered he wasn't supposed to talk.

The one word was apparently okay, because she didn't chastise him. She cuffed this wrist, secured it, but there was more give. "I've given you a couple inches of movement to adjust for comfort. You'll tell me if you need more."

Fingertips headed back down, stopping at his upper thigh. "Bend and spread your knees, brace your feet."

Cuffs around his ankles, and a bar between them that spread his bent legs out about three feet. A further loss of mobility and increased vulnerability. He did the same calming mind exercise, even though it was more difficult this time. She was good at providing distractions, though.

"Take a breath, let it go and push out."

He knew what was coming. She'd said his ass was hers and hers alone tonight. The heated tip of an oiled-up rubber phallus pressed against his entry point. As he obeyed her directive, she began to ease it in, directing him with a firm tone. "Keep relaxing, keep pushing, open up to me. Relax the muscles...relax..."

It was larger than what she'd used in the past. She took her time, but he supposed a little panic was making his muscles too rigid. She merely wrapped her fingers around his cock and began to play, working her thumb over his slit, spreading the fluid over the head, teasing the coronal ridge above the cuff.

Only the control he'd had to practice all day kept him from shooting off to the moon. That and the burn going on in his ass, thanks to the stretch of that monster. She took such time with it, though, kept working him, so that his reaction mixed equally with need and desire. Finally, it was seated. Where she'd placed it offered additional sensation with every move he made.

His bent legs were quivering, and his cock was leaking on her hand. "That's my boy," she murmured. "My gorgeous man. My sailor. This ass is mine. The way this cock is mine. I'll let my sisters play with you tonight, but I chose a size that would remind you who your Mistress is, no matter what they're doing to you. Do you understand, Lawrence?"

"Yes, Mistress. I'm yours."

"He pushes the boundaries of your rules, Ros."

Cyn's crisp voice, coming from the right. He suspected she'd been standing in the doorway watching. He still jumped at the evidence of her presence.

Rosalinda stroked him, a reminder. *I'm here. You're safe.*

"You told him not to speak unless spoken to," Cyn continued. "But he calls you Mistress when you first touch him. And now, you asked for a yes or no answer and he had to add to that as well."

"True. He gets caught up in his devotion." His Mistress's tone was warm, indulgent. "Would you like to remind him that orders should be followed to the letter?"

"I would."

"I'm going to sit down and watch, then."

"There are no bad views on this one." Cyn touched his shoulder, his uninjured one. A very different touch from Rosalinda. His Mistress didn't believe in a warm-up. She was starting him off with the scariest Domme of the group.

Cyn caressed his biceps with obvious pleasure, moving down to his wrist, fingertips playing over his palm, an unexpected intimacy that made his fingers twitch. As the night progressed, he suspected he'd learn to recognize every woman's touch.

He jumped again, startled, when a wet mouth enveloped his cock, sucked it hard, pressing the chain and cuffs against him. A tongue swirled over his shaft as suction and the sheer physical response to the stimulation damn near pulled his hips up off the table. Almost as soon as he lifted his ass, the mouth was gone. He grunted as something whip sharp struck his cock. The sting vibrated through his shaft. His knees jerked, and suddenly he was way more aware of that spreader bar, keeping all of him exposed and vulnerable.

"Did I tell you that you could move?" Cyn's voice was silky sex and pure menace.

"No, ma'am." He was trying to marshal his thoughts here, but she didn't give him a shot at that. She grasped the flared base of the big dildo inside him, rocked it, pushed a little harder, played over his prostate as his eyes nearly crossed from the wave of pleasure. His cock was so close to wanting to detonate, and he fought it, fought it...

He snarled as what felt like a crab's claw snapped down on his right nipple. The pain jerked the orgasm back, which should have been a relief, but it was as jarring as being clotheslined at a full run.

This was too crazy, too...he was yanking against the bonds without realizing he was doing it, and a low-level panic was trying to get away from him. But then Rosalinda's mouth was on his, her hand on his face, fingertips stroking through his hair.

She was making a crooning sound in her throat, that hum she did. The movement of her mouth on his, escalating from gentle wet heat to more demanding pressure, the deeper penetration of her tongue, made his ass vibrate and his balls and cock ache. It also created a fixed center in the chaos of his mind. Her.

That ache in his nipple was being soothed by another mouth. He couldn't tell whose, except he knew it wasn't Rosalinda's, and he didn't think it was Cyn's. Too gentle. That mouth played around the clamp's hold, making it better and worse at once. Then it moved to his other nipple, worked it up into a tight bud, and another clamp was put in place. Like tiny clothespins, sending shards of pain and a mix of twisted arousal to all his nerve centers.

As that was happening, Cyn cupped his balls. Every touch brought more knowledge, and disturbingly, hers reminded him of a trained interrogator. There was a detachment to it that was a lie, because the thought going on behind that touch was fully focused, ready to dive deep and tear apart anything in the way of her goal.

He grunted as she pinched up the small spot of loose skin between his balls and his stretched rectum. He bucked as something clamped him there. He was being simultaneously tortured and pleasured, such that his brain was having trouble keeping the wires straight.

Crazy stuff exploded in his head, images and thoughts, none of them in a straight line. His body was straining, rocking, even as he tried his best to stay still.

More pinches along his balls, a curved line of them. Cyn's touch was all over his cock as she applied them, while the mouth was back on his nipples, playing around the clamps there. A hand slid down his stomach, attached to whoever was paying attention to his nipples. He'd never thought of himself as having highly responsive nipples when it came to sex, but he'd never had someone play with them with this level of thoroughness.

That person's hand wrapped around his cock as Cyn relinquished it. Pulled and stroked.

It had to be Skye. No sound, no spoken word. Just a focused intensity that made her presence as palpable as the two women who could speak.

"They want to devour you," Rosalinda whispered against his mouth. She moved to his temple, his ear, to his pulse beneath it and set her teeth there. Her hand curled around his throat, squeezed, and then spread out, fingers fanned, and played over his bound nipples. He groaned against her, his body jerking, and the sound that came from her throat was pleasure.

"You should see the way they're looking at you. We may never let you off this table. Just keep you here for days to play with you, make you come over and over. Service us with your mouth and cock in between meetings."

She tightened her grip on his throat, her tone abruptly fierce. "I want to use you until you know nothing but serving your owner, your Mistress. Total devotion to me is the only thing that matters. Every inch of you mine, no walls between us. Will you give me that?"

A question. She needed him to answer, and he almost barked it, like he would to a drill sergeant. "Yes, Mistress."

He wanted to add, fucking hell, yes, but Cyn and Skye's clamps had him really mindful of the rules. Christ, they hurt. Yet his cock was swelled to full capacity against that metal yoke she'd had him lock onto himself.

His voice went up on the last syllable because Cyn rocked that dildo in his ass again, pulled it out an inch or so and then slowly thrust it back in. He jerked restlessly against the bonds and then he snarled, swallowing further curses as Cyn hit his cock with that sharp sting, following it up with quick, fiery flicks over his balls, his nipples.

He couldn't stop groaning against Rosalinda's mouth as she came back to his again and again. Her hair brushed his face as she moved her lips to his throat, his temple.

"Ladies," she said suddenly. "Step back, please."

The throbbing of the clamps remained as their hands and mouths withdrew. Rosalinda lifted his head and unlaced the mask, removing it. His field of vision was suddenly filled with just her, bending over him. Her blue eyes had the fire of a goddess, her mouth the resolve of a sensual predator.

She let his head rest on the table again, but kept her other hand on the side of his neck, stroking. "Your cock is mine to command, isn't it?"

He nodded. "Yes, Mistress."

"And you are my slave."

"Yes, ma'am." There was nothing outside this room, in any part of his life, that wasn't about her.

"Then come for me, Lawrence."

Her eyes upon him, her hands stroking his face, his chest. Her words expanding inside him. *Mine to command, mine to command.*

His hips jerked, his thigh muscles tightening as he fucked air. No friction except what was provided by the cock harness and the pull of his muscles, straining to obey her command. All against the discomfort of the plug in his ass, the pain in his clamped balls and nipples.

It took far less time than he expected. A few dry humps of the air, a couple mental echoes of the sharp command, the fixed attention of her eyes, and he was lost.

Stars and black spots mixed in his vision, and he growled the strangled, broken sound of an animal pushed past endurance, tumbling, tumbling...

A mission had markers to tell them how close they were to the objective, even though a hell of a lot could happen to knock it in a different direction. He had a feeling he'd only passed the first couple markers. He still had a long way to go to meet his Mistress's expectations of him tonight.

He was the one who'd told her SEALs had limitless endurance and stamina.

He was an idiot.

CHAPTER TWENTY-NINE

She hadn't put a condom on him, so when his release fountained over him, Skye's hand was there, capturing the fluid and spreading it over his ridged abdomen, his chest. As the orgasm was still happening, she was rubbing it into his nipples, around the bite of the clamps, adding to the sensation.

He saw her intent look, the sharp cut of her hair on the one side, the straight fall of it on the other, framing her soft, rounded face. She wore a laced medieval faire style embroidered vest with nothing under it, hinting at plenty of touchable, tempting curves. A cuff on her ear looked like a dragon, the claws against the top shell of her delicate ear, the tail wrapped along the bottom and held with a black diamond stud. The stud held his glazed attention, sparkling as his body bucked with aftershocks and he gave himself to what his Mistress wanted.

When he was finally twitching at a slower pace, Rosalinda bent over him, making her his full view. She came close enough to speak against his mouth once more.

"They've made all those beautiful muscles glisten," she observed. "I want to give my ladies a gift for taking such good care of you tonight. Don't disappoint me."

Never. He would never disappoint her. She withdrew, though, and he missed her keenly. Then Vera was there. Ros offered her a hand, and she ascended what he assumed was some kind of stool to stand on the table over him. She wore a black corset, and a draped black skirt.

A fall of silver stars from each ear lobe were accented with rings up the shell. The pentagram she'd worn at his initial job interview with them gleamed in the valley between her raised breasts.

That stern matriarch look was there again, but it belonged to a powerful, sensual Goddess, not June Cleaver. When Vera straddled him, sank down, she returned the world to darkness, spreading the flowing skirt over his face, chest and shoulders. It was like being draped by the petals of a large, dark flower. Her fingers slid beneath it to grip his hair.

"Serve me, slave," she murmured, bringing her unclothed pussy to his mouth.

Three words that triggered him in ways he couldn't have imagined. He got down to it, working his mouth over her, teasing the labia, the clit. He took his time, making it clear he liked eating pussy, was turned on by it. It didn't matter that he'd just come. Arousal was more than a physical reaction. She had a spicy scent, like earth and a musky cologne mixed.

Those clamps were hurting bad. He took their distraction as the enemy he had to defeat, to prove they wouldn't keep him from performing as ordered, and with full enthusiasm.

Vera let out a hum of pleasure. "Oh, Ros. He's got a very talented mouth." She raked strong fingers through his hair as her hips worked. She rubbed herself over his mouth, his nose, his beard, taking advantage of all the sources of friction he could offer.

But at length she slowed, her hand moving to touch his lips, rest on his throat as she stopped, an unspoken order to stop moving his mouth. She stayed pressed against it as she spoke again. "Are you listening to me, Lawrence?"

"Yes, ma'am."

She shifted at the movement of his lips. The heat of her response to his mouth was in her voice, but it didn't subtract anything from the intensity she put behind her words. "You're not just serving Ros's inner circle at her command. You know what this is, and not only because she explained it to you. Words don't tell us what something means, do they? Every act demanded of you tonight by your Mistress proves your devotion to her. But it also proves it to us as well, that her care will always be your top priority. Won't it?"

"Yes. Yes, Mistress." He knew that was how he was supposed to address every one of them tonight. Because they were all claiming him, just as Rosalinda had said.

"Good." Vera caressed his throat, then withdrew her hand. She began that dance upon his mouth again. The sleek glide of her wet labia against his mouth and face, the pleasant taste of her, inspired him to greater effort, no matter the throbbing in his genitals and nipples.

"Don't stop until she's come." Rosalinda's voice now, a warning. "No matter what else is happening."

His ankles, spread with the bar, were being lifted, the clamps pulling on his balls enough that he had to muffle a groan against Vera's flesh. Two sets of hands guided him so he bent his knees to a ninety-degree angle and maintained that position, calves parallel with the table. They were given extra support by the grip of those hands. One pair might be Skye. Which would make the other set Abby's, because Cyn was playing with that dildo in his ass. He now knew Cyn's hands, Skye's mouth, Vera's cunt. As far as Rosalinda...he knew her touch anywhere, no matter what part of her was making contact with him.

He suspected she'd withdrawn it for now because she was moving around, watching from all angles. Watching over him. From head to toe, every sensation he was experiencing, every feeling, was hers to notice, to react to, adjust as she felt necessary.

"Keep going," Cyn reminded him, following it up with a sharp pop on his buttocks. He flinched, but a heartbeat later, another strike came. She paused just long enough between strikes that the pain radiated, spread out before the next came, multiplying the situation. Even so, they were coming steady and fast, striking his ass cheeks in a lot of different places. Every jerk went through those clamps, then one or two strikes landed right on his clamped balls and perineum, sending that electric bolt up through his core. He cried out, even though he tried to strangle it back.

Vera made noises of pleasure against that vibration. She was working herself against his mouth, her pace and fervency increasing, responding to the involuntary movements of his body and the rising climax in her own. No matter the pain, he was helpless not to respond to serving a Mistress. His cock was coming back to life, even as he knew the mindless thing was just making itself a bigger target for —*fuck*—another strike with whatever Cyn was using.

Tight coils of emotion in his chest and belly exploded and reformed.

"Lawrence. Are you paying attention?" Cyn's voice. Sharp. "If you're hearing me, put your tongue inside Vera, fuck her with it. Deep as you can go."

Vera made a guttural sound of pleasure as he obeyed, and the walls of her cunt rippled against him. She was close.

"You're welcome," Cyn said, not to him. But her next words were. A continuation of the conversation Vera had started.

"Everything you endure, everything we demand of you tonight, is to see how deep your submission to Ros runs. What is she, Lawrence? What are her desires, her demands? If you are truly her slave, you know the answer to that. Find it. *Find it*. There's no mission more important."

Her tone made it clear the question was vital, yet she didn't want an answer now. Vera let herself go, her climax tiny, sweet spurts against his tongue, her nails biting through his scalp. She cried out as she danced upon his mouth, his tongue, his lips. Victory gave him a brief, chaotic satisfaction, a savage animal pleasure. His thoughts lost cohesion as he spun in the dark, mouth working, nose inhaling Vera's arousal.

He had a provocative, cock-stirring thought that Ros might require him to service all four of the other women before he could do the same for her. He wanted her now, but he knew he'd do anything to earn that right.

Then, as if she'd known he really needed the reminder of his Mistress's presence, Vera slid away from him. The ceiling was there and then Rosalinda's face, her curtain of hair. Her mouth was on his, tasting from his lips what he'd tasted.

He growled with need, trying to devour her, but she only gave him her mouth for a moment. As she straightened, gazing down at him, he saw the detached magnificence of a queen, one whose passion was like wildfire in her eyes. Not only was she in control here, but what she wanted most was total control of him.

"I know the clamps hurt, Lawrence, but they're not damaging you, I promise. Can you bear them a few moments longer?"

"Yes, Mistress." Though the pain was killing him when he didn't have a distraction, if she wanted him to bear it longer, he would.

She gave him a measured glance, verifying he was telling the truth. Then she turned, offered her hand to Skye the way she had to Vera. Hell and heaven, and every fucking thing in between, he'd apparently guessed right. Though helping each woman onto the table was a prudent safety thing, it was more than that. By guiding each woman to him, Rosalinda reinforced the message that he belonged to her.

A brief glimpse of that dragon ear cuff and then the multi-layered skirt Skye wore, a mix of watercolor hues, floated over his face. His Mistress knew he didn't care much for a prolonged blindfold, but a woman's skirt, draped over his eyes to give him access to the treasures beneath? She knew how to bait the trap and make him welcome its hold. Or not mind it nearly as much as he'd thought.

Skye was a different set of scents. Powder. Lemon cake. A strong undercurrent of female desire that called to the testosterone in him like a lure. He was inundated with pain and overcome with arousal, both taking him places he'd never imagined anything sexual could go. With these women, sex contained whatever had created the universe, in one incredible violent explosion.

Skye leaned back, bracing herself on his upper abdomen so she could undulate against his mouth, sensual and graceful. It put her soft ass right up against those nipple clamps, increasing his pained awareness of them. She spoke to him with her body, the way a rider talked to a horse, teaching him how to move with her. After several moments of moving together, she increased the pressure of her thighs, telling him to be still, but to keep his head up. Now she moved against his open mouth and available tongue, the motionless objects she was using to pleasure herself. Well, mostly motionless. Being used this way had everything quivering.

She shifted, pressing his head back down to the table, putting her pussy directly over his mouth again. At the same time, she reached behind her, grasped one of the nipple clamps in gentle fingers. Another hand gripped the other. The hand he thought was Abby's. He had less than a second to dread and anticipate it, an *oh shit, no*, and then the nipple clamps were pulled off.

White hot fire went through him, and a hoarse scream ripped from his throat. Suddenly mouths were on him. Vera and Abigail were holding his legs in that ninety-degree position, so it had to be their mouths on him, soothing that burning feeling with tickling care.

JOEY W. HILL

Cyn went after his still clamped balls with that whip again, increasing both her striking speed and the vulnerability of her targets. While his first thought was *what the fuck*, the different kind and source of pain distracted him from the throbbing in his nipples, getting a bit better under the ministrations of those heated female mouths.

Skye was moving in figure eights against his, demanding he pay attention, give her the same pleasure he had Vera. Having a task, a mission, helped bring some balance again. Something had broken loose in him though, because the grunts of incoherent need he made against her wet cunt were a strange kind of plea.

Skye's fingertips kept sweeping the area behind her, over his chest, above the nipples, along his biceps. Her backside pressed into his body below his collar bone, her buttocks flexing with her rhythm. Every touch from the women marked him with their scent. An imprinting.

Skye's breath became erratic and, a dozen heartbeats later, she reached her climax. He followed her movements, giving her pulsing tissues their full due, savoring the sound of her little gasps, the clutch of her fingers upon him. There was something about the vulnerability even the toughest woman experienced during such a moment that made him want to protect and care and be everything she needed.

Though Skye had not spoken aloud the way Cyn and Vera had, he received her part of the message as if it had been delivered straight from her mind to his soul. It was a two-way street. If he belonged to them, they'd belong to him. Rosalinda was his Mistress, but he would protect and care for these women, these Mistresses, with as much of his skill and ferocity as they ever needed.

He couldn't...fuck, he could only go on. He'd never been over-whelmed by so much sensation. He held onto Cyn's question, Vera's direction, Skye's body language. Most importantly, he held onto his Mistress's presence.

When he'd had to keep going far beyond what most people's physical and mental capabilities could handle, he'd thought of it as a grind. Grind was the wrong word for this. This was like earning his way into Heaven by being handed over to a quintet of fierce-eyed angels. The brush of their wings delivered bliss and feathery caresses in one direction, fiery pain on the return stroke. Yet all of it took him soaring.

He didn't know how it was possible, let alone how to find the ability to stop it, but he was close to climax again. Skye moved down to his abdomen, rubbed her bare backside against flesh still sticky from where she'd spread his last release. She sent him a mysterious, playful look, her cheeks flushed, eyes bright, lips parted. Her fingers teased the sectioned muscles of his abdomen with obvious appreciation. She kissed a sore nipple with tender lips.

She dipped her head toward Cyn, drawing his eyes to the Domme dressed in severe black. Form-fitting slacks, sleeveless tank. A studded belt low on her hips. Cyn held the weapon she'd been using, something that looked half cane, half single tail. He expected it allowed her to alternate between the rigid rod and flexible whip ends, depending on her preferences.

"Are you still thinking about my question?" Cyn asked. "Do you even remember what the question was? Do you need a reminder?"

"No, ma'am," he said hoarsely, then admitted he was brain damaged with his next words. "Unless you want me to need it."

Skye sent him a cool smile, revealing a core that could be just as ruthless as Cyn when needed. Then she left his field of view. He was blinking, bleary-eyed, his jaw aching, his heart thundering in his ears, his balls throbbing from the clamps, the harness around them and his cock.

"Stare up at the ceiling," Cyn said. "You don't have permission to look at us, even when you're not blindfolded by cloth or pussy."

He'd wanted to pinwheel his gaze around the room, find Rosalinda, but they anticipated everything, didn't they? Cyn started up again, her strikes making all of it a mass of aches. He didn't know if he could go on. Even gave some thought to using the word *gray* to take break. Then something better happened.

Rosalinda's face was above his, blue eyes staring down. "Now, Lawrence. Again."

No way. There was no way. Yet some part of him he didn't understand responded to her and obeyed.

She didn't even touch him. The only touch he had was Cyn's whip, driving him on, which made him think of Ros slapping him bare handed. He spurted through the pain because his Mistress's eyes were locked on him, telling him he damn well better obey her.

His mouth was open and working, wanting to say things to her.

She picked up the blindfold, held it where he could see it a moment before she brought it to his face. His lips parted, an attempt to protest, but the climax was thundering through him, taking any sound but animal-like growls and deep groans. She kissed his snarling mouth, probably tasting Skye there as she had Vera.

Before he disappeared into that darkness, he saw something he could cling to. Her eyes, alive with desire and approval, said he was pleasing her. Pleasing her better than anyone ever had, because she whispered it to him. Told him it was true, and he believed her.

As passionate as she was in that declaration, the steadiness of her hand upon him brought its own unexpected reassurance. She controlled everything. She had him. Nothing mattered but what was happening right in this moment, and she was in charge of all of it.

"Abigail." Cyn spoke.

The whip stopped for a blissful moment. As it did, the last spurt of climax left him shuddering and weak. His legs were brought down, his straining thigh and calf muscles massaged with capable, brisk hands. His legs were straightened, and the ankle cuffs were attached to tethers binding him to the table. As his ass was pressed to the black vinyl, the unyielding wood beneath pushed that plug deeper into him. The spreader bar wasn't removed, so he was now bound spread eagle.

Skye's fingers whispered over his shoulders, checking tension. His arms were adjusted in a position that eased those muscles. More reminders they were still watching out for him. His Mistress was still watching out for him.

It brought him back to Cyn's question, the one they obviously wanted to keep beating into his brain. At some point, he would be asked for an answer. Every intense training had its reckoning moment, and this was definitely like training.

What is she?

He knew the answer wasn't simply his Mistress. The way Cyn had delivered the question, the anticipation that swept the room around him, told him they were trying to get him to an important truth. One that underscored exactly what tonight meant.

What are her desires, her demands?

Abby's hand was resting on his thigh. She had cool fingers, thinner than the others. He felt the vibration as Cyn mounted the table at his feet, and she walked her way up, stepping between his legs, putting the toe of her boot beneath his clamped balls. "This is going to hurt, Lawrence. But pain brings truth."

A change in pressure from that toe, a press of her knee on his other thigh, told him she was squatting over him. Then, in one swift, smooth movement, like pulling down a zipper, she pulled the clamps off his balls and perineum.

He'd been shot before. Stabbed. He wasn't saying those pains didn't hurt worse, but something about this being done when it was done, how it was done, sent echoes of pain into far deeper places than he'd ever felt it before. Places where Valentina lived, and the loss of his father, and his blood-tinged moments of utter despair and confusion about how fucked-up the world could sometimes be.

He screamed. He might deny it later, but it was echoing in the room. He couldn't not say it, he had to say it, he needed...her. His body could handle anything, but his soul, his heart, they were being ripped open.

"*Gray...gray*... Mistress."

"Sshh. It's all right." Her hand was on his chest, her other one down between his legs, massaging, soothing. His cock stirred weakly, but the breath sobbing in his throat, the exploding bomb of his heart, held sway over any other physical reaction. "I'm here. Easy, sailor. Sssh..."

His hands were opening and closing, reaching, yanking against the tethers. She unclipped one, and his hand was immediately upon her, holding her forearm in a death grip as she stroked his hair with the other hand, her fingers whispering over the blindfold, over his mouth.

"We're taking a break," she said. "You're doing so wonderfully, Lawrence. So wonderfully. Taking such good care of my sisters. I'm very proud of you."

He sucked up the approval like a kid in the front row of the class, but he accepted that, like he accepted the comfort of her breasts pressed to his face as she curved her arm around his head. She had slipped fully onto the table, was reclined on her hip next to him.

He was aware of the whip sliding over his chest, his abdomen. Cyn, still moving it over him, but not to hurt. Just a warning caress, keeping his head in the game, reminding him this was a pause, that there would be more. The others were taking off the spreader bar, unwrapping the cuffs to massage his legs again, bend them, work his hips. The dildo was still in his ass, the metal harness still on his dick, but all the other things helped ease those discomforts. Plus his Mistress's fingers, playing over his cock, cupping his testicles, was the best balm of all.

"Just wait until I get you pierced here. So I can tug on it all I want."

He didn't know which part of his equipment she meant, but either one might be a hard *sanctuary* call when the time came. Or she might just be messing with him.

But she had told him that at the end of this night she would collar him, brand him. Was that how she planned to do it? Or had she meant an actual collar, an actual brand? He wanted to ask questions, but he didn't as well. The part of him she understood so well, and he was starting not to question, even if he couldn't fathom it, didn't want to have the right to ask, not unless she actively invited the question.

"Cyn wants your mouth, now. Then Abigail."

"What about...my Mistress?" His voice had that broken, hoarse quality. He wouldn't ask about a ring being driven through his dick, but he wanted her to know she was still his top priority. Her pleasure.

"You are serving me with everything you're doing. When you're done, I will mark you as mine again. Never fear. Can you continue, Lawrence? Much as I love that side of you, don't be mindlessly obedient right now. Think about the question, then answer."

He didn't know how to tell her that his ability to think might be shot for the near future, so he did his best. He didn't want to go on, in some ways. But when he thought of stopping things now, when he still needed to prove himself worthy of Rosalinda's ownership to two more Mistresses, the answer was plain.

"Yes, Mistress. I can continue."

She brushed her lips over his, tasted him, let him feel the slight quiver of her lips. "I love you."

It was the first time she'd said it, straight out. The words stayed with him as her hand slipped from his face and she lifted herself away from him. As she moved back, her hand dwelled briefly at his cock, massaging and stroking. Then it disappeared and Cyn shifted forward, bringing her toned thighs down on either side of his head.

Cyn didn't want his mouth like the others, though. No surprise, she wanted more control than that. She strapped something around his jaw and chin that he realized as she handled it was a phallus. She'd brought her own dick to the party, a grimly amusing thought that only confirmed his harrowing impression of Cyn as a Domme.

She'd straightened above him, and the slacks she'd been wearing thumped down over his thighs, telling him she'd taken off whatever clothing interfered with her objective. "Just move your mouth on my clit," she ordered. "I'll fuck myself the way I want. And I'm still waiting for an answer to that question, Lawrence."

She'd unthreaded her belt and now slid it behind his head, gripping it two-fisted to do as she'd indicated. She sank down on the rubber cock with a growl of pleasure and began to ride it like an unruly mount, working it in and out with the tension of the belt that directed the movements of his head.

His body strained to keep up with her. Since they'd re-cuffed his ankles and tied his legs down straight, those movements only increased the harrowing sense of his cock being stretched inside the two steel cuffs and spiral of chain around the shaft.

He found her swollen clitoris with tongue and teeth, trying not to help thrust, despite the tempting, wet sounds of her cunt on the phallus. She must be signaling, because the couple times he couldn't keep his head still enough, a cane hit his upper thighs, his cock, a very effective way to flatten the learning curve. He had no idea who was wielding it, but she was as accomplished as Cyn. For some reason, he thought it might be Abby.

Feeling Cyn fucking the dildo, rising and falling against his mouth, made him imagine his Mistress doing the same. He'd get off on seeing that, though he also expected it to set off a territorial raging in his cock, fighting mad to do it better for her.

When she'd asked if he could continue, it wasn't the pain and extreme demands of this that had made him hesitate. As pleasurable and out of this world as all this was, everything was starting to be about wanting Rosalinda. This was a fantasy, yes, but he wanted the reality. Her brief touches, her few words, weren't enough.

Someone's mouth closed over his cock, over the metal, playing with the flesh. Their hands cupped his sore balls, kneading. Skye again, her other hand on his abdomen. She raked him with those nails, hard enough to draw blood, because this group liked to mix the bitter and the sweet.

He zeroed in on his ankle a heartbeat later because his Mistress's hand was on it, stroking, telling him she was there, watching it all. As if she knew where his head and heart were, how he was starting to flounder.

Fortunately, Cyn came in almost no time, telling him she'd been worked up. He knew the feeling, intensely, but unlike his situation, no one told a Mistress she couldn't come whenever she damn well wanted to do so.

Cyn unbuckled the contraption from around his head, and then rubbed her thumb over his mouth. "They're right. You're good at this. If you were mine, I'd have your head locked beneath a queening chair every night when I came home from work."

She sat back on her heels, on the slope of his chest, and he felt her regard like a rifle scope on his face. "Time to answer me, Lawrence. What is Ros? What are her desires, her demands?"

She tapped his forehead above the blindfold. "If you're meant to be hers, the answer is there, in that abyss. You want to prove you're hers? That you'll serve her like no other?"

Cyn's voice became razor sharp. "Give us the right answer. Make us believe this isn't just bullshit to get at her pussy. Or a commitment that lasts only as long as it makes you feel warm and fuzzy."

"Cyn." A quiet murmur, from Abigail.

"No," Cyn said. "It's over the top beautiful, tying down a gorgeous sub and having our way with him, but there's more to this. He knows it. If he can't answer the question, he hasn't been torn open enough, broken deeply enough. Or he doesn't really feel it and hasn't earned the right to kneel at her feet. Isn't that right, Lawrence?"

The personal was mixed with the mission. He could hear it in her voice. Cyn sounded suddenly ready to rip his heart out of his chest with her bare hands if he didn't find the answer. He'd focused on Laurel, what she'd meant to Rosalinda and Abby, but tonight was about more than that. This was also about what Rosalinda meant to the women in this room. To Cyn in particular, in this moment.

Cyn was the guard dog, the kind that would hang onto the throat long past when the attacker's breath was gone. He could appreciate that kind of dedication and single-minded ferocity.

He fought through the chaotic haze of tonight's reactions, through the roller coaster of emotions, to think about the question. Consider it from every possible angle. He thought again of Laurel, the extraordinary pact these five had made, to watch over one another so no one like Laurel's husband could get inside their guard, not ever again.

With a tiny spurt of panic, he realized he wasn't sure of the answer. It was there, maybe, just past another door, yet he didn't know how to open it. Or maybe he did. He was spinning around and around, disoriented. Because Cyn's question ate at his gut, it started opening some bad places inside. She needed an answer he didn't have, and that answer was obviously of path-altering importance to them.

"I need Rosalinda," he said. Forgetting safe words, permissions, all of that. This was a direct peer-to-peer communication, between him and Cyn. And a beacon sent out to his Mistress.

"Back off, Cyn."

That firm directive came from Abigail.

Cyn said nothing more, but she rose, moved off of him. As he heard her slide off the table, he didn't get Rosalinda in her place. Instead, Abigail's fingertips trailed through the last release he'd had, which was still puddled, half dried on his abdomen. She made circles, easy patterns.

He heard faint squeaks, the movement of chair wheels, suggesting one or all of them had sat down. Everyone had stepped back, probably watching Abby do what she was doing. Which included his Mistress.

Since she controlled all of this, this was her response to him asking for her. It wasn't what he wanted, but the switch of intensity from Cyn to Abby helped him steady, find patience where he'd been sure he had none left.

Abby leaned in, breathing on his cock, a featherlight touch. Whereas everyone else had handled him there, he didn't think she had. Stroking his legs, arms, yes. Sketching her fingers through his release, putting her mouth on his nipple, yeah, those were intimate things, but she hadn't crossed that line.

"The purpose here tonight is an important one, Lawrence." Abby's voice was even, serious. "It's making sure you realize she needs you. And how seriously every one of us takes that. If you're not fully committed, fully in, you need to safeword and be done. Because she's ready to give you her heart and soul."

Hearing it said baldly like that, knowing she was listening, endorsing it with her silence, hit him hard in the chest. His fists closed above the cuffs.

"The only thing standing between that and you is us," Abby said. "Us making sure you are worthy of that gift."

"I will be. I will."

"Easy words when a man's cock is stirred up, so his heart and soul are spilled out on the table like this." Now only one finger continued to move, to create patterns. "But that mess can be cleaned up in the morning light. Made to disappear."

Abby had to be on the table, her legs folded beneath her, because she came so close, her breath was against his ear. No one would be able to hear her but him, unless they were right next to her, and he only sensed himself within hearing distance.

"I need to be sure you'll love her like you've never loved anything in your life. That you will love her even more than I do, Lawrence. Don't speak. Your words don't mean anything right now. You're stretched out on this table at her pleasure, for our pleasure, and it's something unforgettable to us. From tonight onward, you will be ours. We will have your back, we will watch over you, even if you think you don't need that. That bond will hold even on the days you and Ros might be fighting, on days less blissful than this one, because we know being in a family isn't always easy. Love doesn't guarantee never-ending happiness."

She paused. "But care is a double-edged blade. Let go of everything that was before, whatever doesn't contribute to your feelings for her. Do it now. Simply be still, let the thoughts flow. Don't worry about the right answer, don't resist anything. Let it come. It's not in your head. It's not a test."

Her hands continued their movements, but now there were other hands on him. All of them. Stroking, playing, teasing, rubbing. The only pair missing were the ones he wanted most of all.

"Rosalinda."

"She's here. She's listening. She's not sure she likes us going down this road with you, but we know what we're doing when we protect family. Think, Lawrence."

A mouth against his leg, then on his cock. Another teasing over his abdomen, tasting him, flicking at his nipples. Someone stroking his arms, his stomach and shoulders.

He was dissolving into sensation again, but he was grabbing at that darkness, trying to get a handle on the question they wanted answered. All of it rose up, receded, came back again. Dark and light, dark and light.

"Do you see it? What is Ros, Lawrence?" Abigail's hand was on his face again. Firm, tender, ruthless, drawing it all together, taking away the wrong kinds of pain and leaving stark, heartbreaking truth. "When she is deserving, what is the Mistress to the slave? Her needs, her demands, everything."

That clicked, and suddenly it was there, just waiting. His vibrating, bruised, aroused body recognized it. The answer to the question, the explanation for every hard path taken, the connection he'd been seeking ever since he came out of the womb. The connection he'd despaired of finding, the way lost, when he'd taken the wrong road with Valentina.

The words themselves were overused, a cliché. But that was the thing with words. When you really understood what they were supposed to mean, it was like it was the first time the universe had ever heard them.

He spoke them aloud, in a raw, determined voice, wanting his Mistress to hear.

"She's the reason for my existence."

Why he breathed, lived, had made the choices he'd made.

Rosalinda was his Mistress, and he was her devoted slave. She was the reason he'd survived. The reason he would live now, and for however long he was given.

Live *and* love.

CHAPTER THIRTY

A significant pause, and the hands withdrew. He groaned as his Mistress's mouth was on his again, drawing deep, holding a lingering caress between their lips, before she pulled back, spoke. Not to him.

"We'll talk about this."

"No," Abigail answered. "We won't. There's no need."

Rustlings, the sound of movement, doors closing. There was a murmuring, an exchange of instructions. Then a quiet descended on the room.

It was just the two of them.

Rosalinda slid her hands over him, and he shuddered in relief. Until now, he hadn't realized how much tension he'd been holding, even as he wasn't sure he'd ever been so aroused, for so long, in his life.

He was still tied to the table, but she removed the cock harness, blissfully working his length in her hands without the bite of the cuffs and chain. Freed of all encumbrances, the organ responded to her, no matter the workout he'd had. Christ, how many orgasms could a man have in a night?

Rosalinda hadn't had him service Abby the way she'd intended, the way he'd done for the others. He'd ask her about that later. Right now he was just seeing what the lay of the land was. She hadn't sounded unhappy with Abigail, just mildly reproving, as if their initiation hadn't been intended to go quite that deep. Obviously, Abby disagreed.

He had no thoughts on it, one way or another. No real thoughts at all, because his mind had been tested, shattered, and now he was simply quiet, waiting to see what his Mistress desired. She freed his hands, his legs, removed everything except the blindfold. The plug she eased out as gently as she'd put it in, but the withdrawal made his balls contract and cock stir at the wave of sensation. *The one who put it in will be taking it out.*

"Leave your hands and legs where they are."

She stretched out full upon him, and she was completely naked.

Violent need gripped him, because he wanted to see her, touch her, but somewhere he found the will to obey, not lift his arms. She curled her arms around his head and began to kiss him. Long, deep, needy kisses that got his heart hammering and every muscle, every fiber, wanting to strain toward her.

By the time she rose, his ability to not reach for her, hold onto her, was tested like it never had been before. An ounce of self-control he shouldn't have left kicked in to keep him still.

She took off his blindfold, set it aside, and there she was, kneeling above him, her blue eyes as full of him as he felt of her. Her blonde hair, the dark tips, framed her precise features. Her mouth was soft with approval, and an emotion he didn't think he'd ever seen there. His Mistress was a confident, successful woman who enjoyed her life thoroughly, so she wasn't unhappy. But he hadn't known what deep-from-within happiness looked like on her face, in her eyes, until now. She'd let go of something that had kept it from finding its way there, and he'd been able to help with that.

He'd spend his life making sure it didn't get lost again, because she'd given him the same. When she backed off the table, he reached for her, closed his fingers on her wrist.

"I don't want you that far away." His voice had that growly sound to it that said it had been strained as much as the rest of him tonight. He was okay with that.

Those lips curved, her eyes heating. "Don't get demanding on me now, sailor. I could knock you on your ass with one of my pens."

"You could probably spear a ninja with one. I've seen you wield those things."

He tightened his grip. Why he was getting all alpha on her right now, he didn't know, but there was no disrespect intended. He just didn't want to let go of her.

Reading it fortunately for what it was, she let him get away with it. She nodded. "I want you to come off the table with me. Move slowly."

Since the world tilted all kinds of crazy directions when he lifted his upper body, she obviously had more common sense than he did right now. As he put his feet on the floor, he thought he was pulling it together. Then he tried to stand, and his knees gave out as if they weren't connected to the rest of his body.

"Shit." He grabbed for the edge of the table and managed to have most of his weight end up there, but she had him around the waist and back, her body leaned into his. She gazed up at him, her eyes amused, soft.

"You're floating, Lawrence. It's okay. I have you. How about you go to your knees for me?"

He wouldn't say he oozed to the floor. Anyone else would, but fortunately it was just the two of them. He made it to his knees, and then had to drop forward, brace himself with a hand as the world spun. Her fingers drifted over his hair, his nape. "There you are," she said. "Just take it slow."

She squatted beside him, letting that hand slide down the valley of his spine, curve over his buttock, then back up. She was studying him, seeing everything. All he could do was sit there, be quiet, trying to figure out why the world wouldn't expand beyond the immediate surroundings, which was her, a bit of carpet. It was as if they were in a cloud.

"May I speak, Mistress?"

"You may."

"Okay. Good to know." He didn't have anything to say. He just wanted to know it was all right when he did. Her eyes glittered with amusement, and she rose, leaving her fingertips on his shoulder. "Follow me. You can stay on your knees. We're not going far."

He followed her for a few, stumbling steps on his knees, and then he registered another cushioned mat on the floor. She applied pressure on his shoulder, bringing him to a stop, and then turned. Backing up a couple steps, she gracefully stretched out on the mat. She laid it all out before his appreciative gaze, her slim limbs, gorgeous breasts, the apex between her thighs. Her tousled hair and penetrating eyes.

She lifted her arms. "Come lie upon me, Lawrence."

Heaven just kept getting better and better. He moved between her legs, bent and brushed his lips over her abdomen, the sweet curve of one breast. Something shuddered through him and he tilted his head up, meeting her gaze. She lifted her legs, one curving over his thigh, moving him forward as the other folded over his back.

"It doesn't matter that you're on top, does it?" she said, her voice silk along his skin. "Why is that, Lawrence?"

"Because I belong to you, Mistress. I exist for your pleasure."

Her lips curved. She hadn't gotten herself an army, but she did have herself one sole sex slave, a guardian who would protect and serve her with his last breath.

It could be the drama, the erotic intensity of the moment, but despite the frisson of humor the thought brought him, in the depths of his gut, he knew it was true. So did she, because when she cupped his jaw and spoke, her voice had a fierceness to it, just like the queen he imagined her to be.

"It's a gift I will never abuse, Lawrence. But if I do, I expect my slave, my submissive, to tell me. That's his job, too, every bit as impor-tant as any other. Tell me you understand."

"I understand, Mistress."

She stared at him a long minute, then nodded. "I think it will take time for your heart to believe it, because it's your nature to defend others, not yourself. I'll help you with that. I love you, Lawrence."

Twice in one night. With the intensity and emotional power of all the rest, it hit him even harder now, and the first time had been world changing. "Rosalinda."

She smiled. "Come down here, Lawrence. Don't keep your Mistress waiting. We're not done yet."

He lowered himself upon her, and she wound her arms around him. She lifted her hips and his cock pressed into her wet heat, the mindless thing miraculously ready to be called to duty once more. Until he was old and doddering, he expected that was one part of him he wouldn't ever have to worry about letting down his Mistress. Not when she was so good at making him think of nothing but the desire to be inside her.

473

He slid in, all the way, and braced himself by her head. The position also allowed him to gaze down into her face. Strength, feminine power, and that fragility, a human vulnerability, that made him want to love and protect her with everything he was.

"I love you," he said. The words almost didn't seem necessary, and her response confirmed it.

"Everything you did tonight proved it, Lawrence. Show me how much you want to serve your Mistress, please her."

He could do that. He started to move with her, calling on reserves of strength he knew were running dangerously low, but he could manage this. If they were standing, his calf, the damaged tendons, might have been complaining more after their workout on the table. But his knees and thigh muscles wouldn't fail him.

She was checking on other parts of him, though, one hand on the healing scar on his shoulder, her fingertips resting lightly on his biceps, likely testing the steadiness of that arm. He shook his head at her, lifted his other hand for a brief moment to clasp hers, kiss it, guide it to his chest instead, a firm squeeze. She was his Mistress, but he wasn't going to be babied. Not in this moment. She was his to care for, too.

She gave him a look, but let it go for now, sliding her hand around to his waist and then down, nails digging into his buttocks to pull him deeper, urge him on. He rocked inside her, felt those heated, damp tissues contract on him, squeeze. He reveled in the sound of her caught breath, how her gaze lost focus as the climax built within her. Her body moved against his, nipples brushing his chest, hips lifting up to his. He watched all of it, the beautiful feminine dance of a woman lost in pleasure. He didn't care if his shoulder caught on fire or his leg knotted up. He wouldn't miss a moment of this. Every second with her was a different kind of gift.

The climax rolled through her, and she tipped her head back, making those feminine cries that could keep him hard or take him over the edge, whichever was her pleasure. The grip of her hands told him, the insistent kneading of his pumping buttocks, the bite of the nails, the jerk of her arms as the climax went higher, got more volatile.

"Now..." she managed, and he followed her, sliding one arm around her back to hold her up against him, giving him more leverage to take it higher, deeper. Her mouth was against his neck, her breath sobbing there. He closed his eyes, the sensations and emotions tied together in so many perfect knots it would take the universe a millennium to untie them. He hoped. He hoped for so much with her, and hope had been out of his grasp for so very long.

As the world slowed, he was spinning again, still floating, but that was okay. He had his Mistress in his arms. She eased back, but brought him down with her, insisting this time. He lay upon her, but he did keep one elbow propped by her head to take some of his weight. When he brushed a light kiss over her crescent-shaped scar, she ran her hand up and down his other arm. It was quivering.

"You overdid," she said, mild reproof in her tone.

"It was worth it," he said.

She gave him an intent look. "I made a promise to you, about how this night would end."

"I don't want it to end."

She smiled at him, her eyes full of emotion. "Sub-brain," she teased gently. "How did I tell you I would *finish* this session with you and my ladies?"

That was when the smell of smoke, of fire, touched his nose.

At the end of the session with them, I will collar you, brand you, and you will be mine.

"I meant it, Lawrence."

Her other hand rested loosely on his back, the upper rise of his ass, but now it pressed into his flesh, warning him that they were about to be not alone again. As the door opened, before he could look in that direction, Rosalinda curved her hand over the side of his face.

"You won't look toward them. Only at me. Do you object to me branding you, Lawrence? Speak now, or forever hold your peace."

She was going to mark him as hers. The fantasy of it was about to become the reality. He heard nothing from his mind but vehement approval. "I'm yours, Mistress. Do whatever you wish to mark me that way."

As female footsteps drew closer, the scents of the women he recognized, her throat tightened on a swallow. She gripped his shoulder, fingers brushing the side of his throat. "You are too good to be true," she said softly. "Thank you, Lawrence."

"Spread your legs." That came from Vera, now kneeling at his side.

Rosalinda adjusted her own limbs higher on his back as Lawrence obliged. Skye's hands were on his left leg, adjusting it outward, having him expose more of his inner thigh, telling him where they were going to put the brand.

"You need to hold still," Cyn said. "It doesn't take long, but it will feel longer."

Rosalinda still had his gaze in that lock. "He won't move," she said. "Do it."

Endless different images flashed through his mind. The past, the present, the possible futures.

Heat pressed against his inner thigh, close enough to his balls to give them a moment of *holy shit*, especially as that initial touch became a whole fucking lot of heat. All his muscles locked, his face set in a stone rigid expression of endurance as that fire erupted and told him he needed to jerk away, but he wouldn't let himself do it. Wouldn't...

Then it was gone, and the fire was just from the skin's reaction to being burned, etched with his Mistress's mark of ownership.

"Keep them spread." Vera's hand was on his lower back, fingertips resting partially on Rosalinda's crossed calves. "I'll leave care instructions at the front desk. Follow them to make sure you care for your Mistress's mark, and her property, with as much vigilance as you care for her. The sooner it's properly healed, the sooner you can feel her hand upon it, as often as she wants to touch it."

"Yes, ma'am." He didn't look toward her, because it was clear Rosalinda didn't want him to look away, but he injected a full dose of courtesy in the acknowledgement. Vera's hand whispered along his back. Skye squeezed his ankle. Finally, a cheerful, stinging swat on his ass. Cyn, he was sure.

"I'm leaving the box on the table." Abby's voice, somewhere off to the right.

Rosalinda nodded, but her attention remained on Lawrence. Her hands swept over him, caresses, possessive touches. From the urgency in that contact, he knew the branding had aroused her emotions. His own chest was tight in reaction, not just to the fire against his thigh, but what it meant, to both of them.

"Change places with me, Lawrence. I want you stretched out, your legs spread so I can stand over you and see."

He pushed himself up on his knees, took her hand and helped her to her feet. Her thighs showed traces of his seed, and her limbs were shaky, like his. He held her, steadying her, and she cupped her hands on either side of his neck. Her eyes were vibrant.

"Down on your back, sailor."

He complied, and spread his thighs. As he did that, she moved to the table and retrieved her heels, putting them back on. He expected she'd removed them to get on the table with him earlier.

They weren't the gladiator shoes she'd been wearing when she left him this morning. These sandals had ankle straps made of braided gold ropes, looking like snakes with winking amber eyes. They spiraled around her ankles and a few inches up her leg.

Since she wore the shoes and nothing else, he'd never seen something so fuckable and worth worshipping at the same time. She cocked her hip, bracing the toe of one shoe just below the brand, making him adjust the leg out wider. Her gaze passed over it, then followed all the terrain in between, up to his face.

"It says *Hers*, Lawrence. When it heals, it will be even bigger. When it eventually starts to fade, I may choose to have it re-etched as a tattoo."

She lifted the box he assumed Abby had mentioned. It was a velvet jewelry case. "Stand up."

He did, taking it slow as he knew she'd advise, but he was steady enough to stand before her. He gave her a half smile. "You didn't have to buy me jewelry. I'm more of a flowers and chocolate kind of guy."

She flicked her nails under his sore nipple and he winced, but didn't withdraw. "Smartass," she reproved. "Dale warned me about that."

It had been awhile since he'd embraced his knack for it. Fortunately, her barely suppressed smile said she wasn't really mad. Then the grin left his face, replaced by far more serious emotions, as she opened the box and removed its contents from the silk-lined interior.

It was a custom dog tag. His name, rank at time of discharge, and military branch of service was stamped on one side. On the other was the etching of a rose with a curving thorn-laden stem. The stem underlined *Property of Rosalinda Thomas*.

The chain was shorter than the military standard. When she put it on him, reaching behind his head to clasp it, the dog tag lay against his chest, a couple inches below his collar bone.

"When I play with you at a club, whether you wear a bracelet or not, between this and the brand, there will be no mistaking you're taken."

She leaned fully into him and he closed his arms around her, holding her. Her beautiful, naked body, his beautiful Mistress.

When he murmured that one word into her ear, she tightened her arms around him in answer. "You'll wear this at all times, unless I tell you to take it off," she ordered.

"Yes, Mistress."

Things were building in him again, emotionally, physically. He'd lost his mind, because he couldn't possibly...and yet.

That light, mysterious smile was in her eyes, and she pressed more intently against him, feeling his reaction. "Your friend Neil said life was a whole lot of wild card. If I gave you that wild card right now, what would you do with it?" Her eyes darkened, primal understanding. "Show me."

He banded his arm around her waist, hiked her onto the board room table and shoved into her, all in the same rough motion. It was a miracle he didn't topple them both, but the savage need inside him had a source of strength beyond the body. A sound escaped him, pure animal relief and satisfaction at the feel of her, at her feminine gasp. It drove the needed blood back into his abundantly-used cock to accommodate the desire he saw in her face.

"My Mistress..." he said. The words contained every bit of possessiveness toward her that her brand and the dog tags declared for him. Her eyes glowed.

"All yours," she agreed, with a cock-teasing breathlessness. Her surrender to his strength only made him need to take more. Take all she was giving, because he needed what she offered. Needed it with a hunger in his gut that was a little frightening.

Fortunately, nothing scared Rosalinda Thomas.

He might not have a climax left in him, but he'd make sure he gave her one before his legs gave out entirely. He wanted to watch her shatter with it. He also wanted to hold her tight, his face pressed to the side of hers, as he showed her exactly how much he loved her.

How much he was going to love her.

EPILOGUE

$\mathcal{R}$os moved to the window of the bedroom. Lawrence was sitting on a bench in her backyard, head cocked as he listened to the birds. His arm was stretched out along the back of the bench, as if inviting her to join him.

Tempting, but she was also looking forward to their plans for the day. He was waiting on her to join him so they could head to a barbecue at Dale and Athena's house.

All her ladies would be there, as well as Matt Kensington, his boys and their wives. Max and Janet. Neil, too. He was back from his latest mission and, despite a new scar on his forearm—a shrapnel graze, according to Lawrence—he was no worse for wear.

Abby had asked about that injury, way-too-casually, but refused to be baited by the others' teasing about it.

If they were here, Ros figured she might be the target of some teasing herself. Though she told herself she was just taking a moment watching him through the window, she honestly could do this for hours.

Today he wore a pair of those jeans that held him just right, never failing to tempt her to fondle and squeeze. A short-sleeve button-down dressed it up some, not because it was a dress-up event, but because festive events with friends sometimes made a person want to wear something a little different. She glanced down at herself. Case in point. She wore a dress he hadn't yet seen, but she thought he'd like it.

479

That mattered to her, and not just because of the Mistress side of her that liked to get his motor going. As a woman, she liked wearing things he obviously enjoyed. It still took her by surprise, how her feelings for him grew every day, and in how many new directions they went.

Not only did she have the right to stand here and ogle him, she could require him to be any way she wished while she did so. Clothed, unclothed. Tied, untied. Kneeling, standing, chained. He still wasn't comfortable with a heavy level of restraints, but last weekend he had let her tie his wrists to the headboard of the daybed and spent an afternoon lying there, not a stitch on him, as she read a new book she'd been anticipating downloading to her tablet. She'd put earphones on him, connected her iPod and set it on an audiobook, a steamy Mistress/sub book. She'd enjoyed watching his cock and body tighten in response to it, as she guessed which scene he was hearing. A couple hours later, she finally rode him to a strong finish.

She thought back to her meeting with Valentina, shortly before the turning-point night in her board room where she'd branded him. When she'd told Lawrence she was going to meet with his ex and her mother, Zoey, she knew Lawrence hadn't wanted her to do that. As he'd driven her to the facility where Valentina was being held, he'd been tense, but to his credit, he hadn't tried to argue with her about it. When she told him he had to stay in the car, she thought that was about to change, but in the end, he'd simply nodded, his expression granite hard.

Valentina had a fragile yet brittle beauty. Ros could easily see how Lawrence had loved her, had even detected the hints of the woman she'd been before drink had destroyed her. Ros wasn't there to exercise pity or compassion, though she possessed both for Valentina. Laurel Grove had housed more than one substance abuser.

Ros had sat at her bedside and laid it out.

"You figure your shit out, that'll be great. But he's no longer available. He's mine. He protects me, shelters me. He's given you enough. Time to stand on your own, heal yourself."

Valentina had said little, but what she did say, told Ros she understood. As Ros had risen to leave, she'd seen the misery in the woman's eyes, the despair in knowing how many times she'd failed to fight a foe who seemed insurmountable. After a moment's hesitation, Ros put a firm hand on her shoulder. The exhausted brown eyes lifted to meet hers.

"I'm going to take care of him," Ros said quietly. "His wounds will heal. Let that be one thing you can let go. He loved you, so the best gift you can give him is to take care of you, get better. I'm going to tell him he can come see you one more time, to say good-bye, but that's it. It's done."

She'd left it at that. She believed that discussion had helped make Lawrence's final one with Valentina better, because he'd looked easier after that happened. As there'd been no more calls since then, either from Valentina or Zoey, it told Ros it truly was done. He was all hers.

She gave Freak, sitting in the window seat, an ear rub and then existed through the back. As she emerged from the porch, Lawrence was already looking her way, so she saw the way his eyes lighted up at her appearance. The crocheted sundress had a blue liner at the bodice and skirt, the open mesh in between revealing her midriff, back, and her legs from the upper thighs down, in a mixed pattern of blue and yellow yarn. She wore a straw hat with yellow and blue roses. For her, the shoes were pretty low-key, low block-heeled sandals with a yellow rose pattern upper. Blue straps double wrapped the ankle.

The dress clung to her curves, and though the V-neck was modest, the dress had no back. She paused, enjoying the anticipation. Last night, she hadn't allowed him in her bed, hadn't allowed him to shower with her, to keep it a surprise. But she had made him mastur-bate while looking at her doing the same, enjoying that male hunger, held back only by her command.

His desire to serve was limitless, his ability to control himself overwhelming, especially when she knew how to break that control. He trusted her more every day, and the feeling was mutual.

"You look beautiful," he said. "Though I need some new words, because you're beautiful every day."

"When you say it like you mean it, it *is* new every day."

He'd stood up as she arrived, and when she stretched out a hand, he took it. The restrained power in the grip conveyed his banked sexual frustration from being denied her bed, her body. But he truly was a well-behaved submissive, never pushing her the wrong way, even as that avid gaze was incentive all its own, testing her resolve.

Her attention slid to the open collar of the shirt, and she reached out to play with the dog tag. The brand had healed, so every time he stripped, she had the pleasure of putting her hand over it, sometimes her mouth. Sometimes she had him eat breakfast with her naked, and made him spread his legs as he sat in his chair, so she could see it.

"Did you pack my swimsuit and yours?"

"Bag's in the car."

"Which swimsuit did you choose for me?" She'd left it up to him.

"The blue one with the dangly things."

Her most revealing bikini. She chuckled at him as he gave her an unrepentant grin. "Will you help me retie the neck of this thing?" she asked.

"Sure."

She pivoted. She'd piled her hair up off her neck, to give her gift a better presentation. He'd started to reach forward already, anticipating, but then he stopped. Looked.

She waited, her head dipped, and then closed her eyes as his fingers touched the area along the outside of the tattoo. She'd taken off the plastic this morning, figuring the backless dress would be okay to give it more air. Since it would be a couple weeks before chlorinated water was okay for it, she wouldn't be able to submerge herself in the pool or hot tub at Dale and Athena's place, but it was a small price to pay for his still regard now.

She'd never contemplated having a tattoo, but with Lawrence, she got the craziest impulses.

"He's bringing you back to a part of who you were before Laurel, before all of it," Abigail had pointed out. "He's letting you be that girl inside of all of us, falling in love in the way we all want to fall in love. You're in love with him, but you didn't let yourself indulge all the 'fall in love' moments. Now you're doing that."

She expected Abigail was right, because she couldn't deny it was a young girl's butterflies going mad in her stomach as he touched her, as she imagined the look in his eyes.

The tattoo was one of the most popular SEAL mottos, *The only easy day was yesterday*. It was an appropriate reminder for a man in a relationship with a demanding Mistress. The tattoo was enclosed by blue roses. Worked into their design was a tiny etching of his initials, *LBG*.

"Mistress," he murmured.

482

When she turned, he was staring at her with wonder, contentment, pleasure, a mix of everything he wanted to do to her, even as
they were both content to stand there, just feeding off one another's
emotions.

Yeah, the others might laugh at her, but they knew what it was.
The thing Abby had said it was. *Soulmate.* Nothing else could explain
how they'd fallen for one another, so hard, so fast. So truthfully.

He picked up her hand, kissed her palm. She let him, but then she
backed away, moving toward the bench. When she reached it, she put
her knee up on the seat, her hand on the back, and used the other
hand to gather the skirt, bring it to her thighs.

"I want you inside me, Lawrence. Right now."

He stepped to her, his hand already on the fastener to his jeans.
She didn't invite a man to fuck her from behind that often, but she
wanted Lawrence to be gazing at that tattoo with every stroke, understanding everything it could mean.

"Take it slow, sailor. We have a few minutes. I want to enjoy your
cock like this lazy, lovely spring day."

While she could see him from her window, at ground level the
overgrown azaleas and trees provided a good screen to the neigh-
boring views. She'd never been gladder for the decision to let those
azaleas grow so wild and beautiful.

Lawrence put his hands on her shoulders, slid them along her
back, framing the tattoo, then down to her waist, her hips. He took
over holding the skirt up for her, and then he was hooking her
panties, pushing the crotch out of the way and putting himself in their
place, slowly easing a very thick cock inside her. She closed her eyes, a
sound of pure pleasure humming out of her throat.

He bent forward, pressing his lips to the left of the tattoo, and
kept his mouth there as he pushed in, withdrew. Slow. Easy. Their
breath became more erratic, their hearts pounding as he drew the
feeling out just as she'd demanded.

The quiver in his limbs told her his desire to become more insistent was increasing, though. Her sailor. So powerful, but submitting to
the hold of her leash when she tightened her grip on it. Her cunt
spasmed, wanting the approaching climax, but she held herself back,
too. This was too good to waste.

The only easy day might be yesterday, but Ros had never cared for easy. Easy things weren't worth keeping.

Fuck easy.

Or rather, fuck what wasn't easy. Often and thoroughly.

As she arched back into him, murmured his name, savored his grip, the press of his body, she felt all the love he had for her cocoon her, shelter her in every important way. She thought of the stepping stones outside Club Progeny. The ones with all the different quotes on them.

Her latest favorite was one close to the door. She never stepped directly on it, respecting the message, the import of it for people who crossed the threshold. People seeking what might seem different from what the rest of the world wanted, but it was really all the same.

Let love be genuine. Romans 12:9

The most powerful rules of the universe were always the simplest.

∾

The End

AUTHOR'S END NOTE

Matt Kensington's story, as well as those of his four-man executive team—Lucas, Peter, Jon and Ben—were told in each of the award-winning Knights of the Board Room series books. The series also included Max and Janet's story (*Willing Sacrifice*).

The success of the KBR launched the Mistresses of the Board Room spinoff series. While his book is a "non-series" title, Dale is obviously intimately connected to this world. His and Athena's story can be read in *Unrestrained*.

You can find a full series list and links in the end matter of this book. And if you don't want to leave this world quite yet, read on for the first chapter of Janet and Max's story!

If you liked Rosalinda and Lawrence, stay tuned for other Mistresses of the Board Room books. Neil and Abby's story should be up next, unless the muse decides she wants one of the other ladies to take the lead!

WILLING SACRIFICE

Summary

Janet prefers her men submissive, her relationships confined to a club environment. Which is why her attraction to former Navy SEAL Max doesn't make a lot of sense. There isn't a submissive bone in his honed, muscular body, suggesting that her interest in him is best indulged as a private fantasy. After a crisis situation reveals a different side of them both, the attraction becomes mutual, explosive and undeniable. They take the plunge, willing to see if the give-and-take of their unexpected relationship can satisfy their deepest desires. Unfortunately, ghosts from their past might take the reins from them both, destroying the balance of power before their love can find a way to tip the scales.

CHAPTER ONE

"*R*andall, is Max in yet?"

"Yes and no, ma'am."

She paused by the security desk, arching a brow. The head of K&A security pressed a button on his console, calling up the needed camera angle on the top covered level of the parking deck. "He's not on until noon, but most mornings, this is where you'll find him. He won't mind doing anything you need, as long as you don't mind he's not in uniform. Want me to buzz him? He's wearing his pager."

"No. I need to stretch my legs. I'll go to him."

Randall nodded, waited until she was a safe distance down the hall, then murmured, "And fucking fantastic legs they are. Ma'am."

Janet paused at the elevator, a good fifty feet away, and glanced back at him, a glint in her eye. Randall cleared his throat, paid close attention to his monitors and didn't let out a breath until he heard the elevators close. Jim, the desk guard, gave him a grin. "You're a brave man. Mr. Kensington says she can hear through concrete walls."

"Why do you think I added the 'ma'am'?" Randall responded wryly.

"Should we give Max a heads-up she's coming?"

Randall shook his head. "The moment she steps into the parking-deck elevator, he'll hear it engage. He'll be tracking where it stops."

Jim studied the video dubiously. "He looks like he's asleep."

"Trust me. He can tell you how many bugs have scurried across the parking deck in the past half hour, *and* give you their current coordinates."

"Since she can hear through walls, sounds like they're made for each other."

Randall pursed his lips. Imagining Janet Albright, Matt Kensington's terrifying admin, and Max Ackerman, his head limo driver, as a couple wasn't as unlikely a vision as he'd expected. In fact, it might be a mighty interesting combination. 'Course, an explosion was interesting—if you were outside the blast zone.

Janet stepped off the parking elevator, careful not to snag her heels on its metal threshold, and headed toward the back corner of the parking deck. Her glossy brown pumps made a crisp echo on the concrete. Glancing over the wall at the New Orleans business district, she drew in the faintly smoky air, pleased to detect the cool scent of fall beneath the city smells. But as she made the turn toward that back corner, other scenery captured her attention.

Randall had said Max wouldn't mind running her errand as long as she didn't mind he wasn't in uniform. She wasn't sure there was a red-blooded woman alive who would mind that. He looked handsome in his various uniforms, everything from the traditional chauffeur's suit to the more informal black dress jeans and crisp black placket shirt with the embroidered K&A insignia. However, in the blue jeans and dark-blue T-shirt he wore now, he was pure sex.

He had his muscled arms crossed over his broad chest, his back braced against his windshield in his reclined position on the hood of his battered Ford Ranger pickup. The jeans were classic Wranglers, worn down to that soft cling that drew the female eye to all the right points of groin, thighs and ass. Despite the covered parking deck, he wore sunglasses, which made it impossible to determine if his eyes were open, but she knew they were. She suspected they'd opened as soon as she stepped off the elevator.

Max had been working for K&A for over six years but had taken over management of the fleet after less than two years with the company. He oversaw maintenance of the vehicles and management of the rotating staff of eight drivers. One of his important secondary duties was being Dana's driver, taking her to and from her job as assistant pastor at one of the local churches. Peter and Max looked enough alike that the other men teased Peter, telling him he'd provided his wife a surrogate for the frequent times he had to be out of the country, dealing with their Central American plant operations.

The physical features of the two men were remarkably similar, dark-blond hair and gray eyes, both over six feet and possessing a large-boned build wrapped in a lot of military-trained muscle. However, to Janet's way of thinking, their respective personalities gave each man a unique stamp. They both had the discipline and strong moral code of many servicemen, but there was a silent core to Max, seemingly impenetrable. When he met her gaze, she felt pulled into that silence, and it wasn't a bad place to be. A gray, overcast day, no break in the cloud cover, somber but comforting, like a blanket being wrapped around the earth.

She'd dreamed a lot about those eyes in the past six months. They'd gotten in the pleasant habit of interrupting her occasional nightmares, driving them away with their tails tucked between their legs.

The limo he usually drove was parked in its spot along the back wall, pristine and gleaming, the way he made sure all vehicles in the fleet were kept by the team he supervised. Though his older-model pickup truck had seen some fender benders, it was equally clean and polished. His sturdy, thick-tread work shoes were crossed at the ankle but projected over the edge of the hood, not making contact with the paint. He not only took good care of what he was paid to maintain, but his own belongings as well, no matter their age or condition. A woman noticed such things.

Music was wafting out of the truck window, and the selection surprised her. *I'll Never Find Another You* by the Seekers. The poignant, innocent sound of it made her think of waltzing across the concrete with him, her hand curled on his neck, a faint smile in her heart.

Ever since Savannah had given birth to sweet Angelica, the idle fascination Janet had with the limo driver had grown far stronger. The man had been positively heroic, getting Savannah to the hospital under trying circumstances. It would have made any woman's heart trip faster. But Janet knew he'd intrigued her for quite a while before that. That day, as now, she reminded herself she'd kept her distance for several intelligent reasons.

Yet here she was, seeking him out for something any of the other on-duty drivers would be happy to do for her. It told her she'd reached some kind of decision in her mind. It was an intuitive thing, not fully formed, which wasn't the same as being impulsive or rash. She'd mulled it over for well beyond those six months, yet recently realized the reason she couldn't get a clear sense of her intent with Max was because she needed more information to sift. So this was a planned direction, even if the road ahead was murky.

Matt had told her Max was a former Navy SEAL. After looking up considerably more specific information on it, she'd learned that meant he'd left the SEALs before reaching the twenty-year retirement mark. Even so, she wasn't sure if the term "former" or "retired" truly applied to a SEAL. The quick reflexes and cool nerve he'd demonstrated the day they had to get Savannah to the hospital had underscored it. It was also why she knew his eyes were open behind those glasses, though he hadn't yet moved. Not until she turned with purpose in his direction. Then he slid off the hood in one powerful motion, taking off the glasses and hooking them in his shirt. She waved at him with the folder she carried.

"No, don't come to me. I'm coming to you."

She issued it as a command, and he simply nodded. "Ma'am." But he still took a couple steps toward her, showing he wasn't entirely comfortable waiting for her to do all the work to get to him. She really needed to sit in on hiring interviews one of these days. She was fairly certain Matt Kensington had the HR department subject all male applicants to a super-secret chivalry test handed down since Lancelot's days.

"Were you sleeping?"

"Just a short nap, ma'am." He nodded at the folder. "Do you need me to take that somewhere?"

"No." Though it had been her excuse for coming to him, she decided then and there she would send the documents to the bank with Wade later today, when he took Matt to his lunch meeting. She didn't dissemble when it suited no purpose. "Max, do you dance?"

He wasn't expecting that. She experienced a small spurt of satisfaction at the flicker of surprise, and amusement when it turned to wariness. "Not really, no."

"I'm on a break. May I join you?" She nodded to the hood of the truck. "You made that look very comfortable."

Actually, she visualized using his body the way he'd used that truck, leaning back against his chest, her body ensconced in the cradle of his thighs, her hand caressing one as she put her head back on his shoulder and they gazed at the rectangular panorama of the city. He'd be warm, she was sure, a good contrast to the touch of cool air wafting over the business district. She wouldn't miss the sweater she'd left on her chair.

There was a reason she connected so well with the K&A men. She herself was a sexual Dominant, one who regularly enjoyed playing Mistress to willing submissives at Club Progeny. As such, she was direct with men, in or outside a club. Her senses were tuned to evaluate how they responded to the unexpected. Max glanced at the hood of his truck, then at her pale-pink silk suit, his gaze lingering on her stocking-clad legs revealed by the just-above-the-knee hem. The short slit in the back offered a glimpse of her thigh, which she knew was what had caught Randall's eye. She dressed for business, but she also thoroughly enjoyed being an attractive middle-aged woman. She had no problem highlighting her better features within the tasteful boundaries of professionalism.

"I'll need a boost," she said. "And you'll need to take off my shoes once I'm there so they don't scratch your truck. Of course, you still haven't said whether you mind ten minutes of company."

"I'm just trying to keep up, ma'am." He had a little bit of a Texas drawl, just like Matt. It was entrancing. "Why did you want to know if I dance?"

"I teach a ballet class for teenagers at the community center. We don't have any male dancers at the moment, and the girls want to learn some basic lifts. When a dancer first starts learning lifts, confidence in the strength of your lifter helps you focus on your form. You seem more than capable of lifting teenage girls. But it does require some grace and agility, which is why I asked about the dancing."

She gave him a critical look. "You move well, though, so even if you don't have any dance training, I think it will still work. If you're willing, it pays nothing, and it will take up a night of your time. Given your looks, I'm sure it will also gain you the slavish adoration of a dozen underage girls. While I promise not to give them your social networking links, I can't guarantee they won't find them anyhow. A fourteen-year-old has ways of ferreting out information the CIA only wishes they knew."

Putting the folder on the hood, she held out her hands. "Want to prove you can lift something heavier than a teenager?"

"If I see something that is, I'll do that, ma'am."

She chuckled. "Charm serves a man well, Max." She kept her arms out. She knew he couldn't let her stand that way for long without it becoming awkward or embarrassing for her, at least to his way of thinking. Sure enough, within a blink, he stepped forward to close the distance between them. When his hands settled on her waist, he met her gaze. If he'd wanted to keep it more impersonal, he wouldn't have done that, so that alone gave her another intriguing piece of information about where this might go.

First intentional physical contact was a critical sensation, where she logged her own reaction as much as his. Heat swept out from where his hands closed over her waist. She felt the strength in his restrained power, saw the biceps flex as he tightened the grip and prepared to lift her. Then he stopped himself. "Hold on a moment." Releasing her to open the truck's door, he twisted his upper torso to reach behind the front seat. He came back with a rolled-up quilt in a brown-and-green camouflage pattern. He untied the straps, folded it into a rectangular cushion and put it on the hood where he'd been about to place her.

"It's clean enough for me, but not that." He nodded to the pastel color of her suit. "I don't want you to get anything on it."

She didn't think there was a speck of dust on the truck, but she appreciated the consideration. Now he lifted her. She'd expected his display of easy strength, but her reaction when it swept through all her nerve endings startled her. During that effortless suspension, short as it was, she was catapulted to a memory of lights, a crowd's breathless attention as she bounded lightly across the stage, leaping into the capable hands of her partner, who lifted her high above his head.

Jorge had given her that moment. She couldn't deny that gift. He'd also been the one to take it all away.

"Ma'am?"

She opened her eyes, realized she'd simply gone away, too much like that night in the hospital bathroom. Her hands were gripping his on her waist, nails digging into his skin. He'd put her on the truck hood, on the quilt. His hard abdomen was pressed against her knees as he held on to her, obviously not wanting to let her go until he was sure she was all right. Maybe for other reasons too, but it was a little too soon for that. She wasn't given to fanciful romanticizing. Then she thought about how she'd imagined lying inside his embrace on top of the truck and realized he'd already taken her down that road. Men didn't usually do that to her. Not anymore.

"Yes. You did that very well. In fact, now I'm not sure the girls will be able to focus on their form at all. You'll make them think they're swans, about to give flight. Which is actually what it feels like, when it's done right."

"You dance too?"

"I did. Now I teach." She gave his hands a functional pat, a signal to let her go. They reflexively tightened, a brief squeeze, then slipped away, leaving her tingling. "Thank you. Please remove my shoes. You take very good care of this truck. I don't want to cause any scratches."

"It's had its share of those." He paused. Wondering if he would kneel to take off her shoes, she played with that fantasy, but of course the truck was too high to make that necessary, and he wasn't that type of man. She already knew that much about him, one of the intelligent reasons she hadn't pursued anything with him. She liked her men submissive, and limited to a club setting. At least, she had, until Max started visiting her waking thoughts as much as he did her dreams.

He slipped off one of her pumps, his fingers sliding along her arch. She quelled her visible reaction to the arrow of sensation that went right up her inner thigh, but she savored it behind a neutral expression. When he touched the other arch the same way, she was sure he was testing her reaction, because he looked up at her, meeting her gaze once again. Setting the shoes carefully by the front tire, he leaned on the hood next to her, propping his elbow by her hip. He laced his fingers together, but his knuckles were a tempting distance from the modest section of thigh her seated position revealed.

When she glanced down at that small space, a weighted pause drew out between them, inundated with sexual awareness. She'd introduced it by requesting a personal favor, suggesting physical contact, both of which encouraged a new level of intimacy between them. Now she waited to see what he would do with those signals. Studying her leg, his head bent so she could gaze upon the dark-blond strands across his crown, Max loosened his fingers. He allowed one to slide along her stocking, to the hem of the skirt and just under it, encountering the lace top of her thigh high. He stayed within that short range, his finger going still as he lifted his head to meet her gaze.

Nothing so sexy as a man who didn't doubt himself. She thought of the cameras, but where he was, his broad shoulders were blocking the lens. To Randall or anyone watching, Max was leaning against the truck, talking to her. Perhaps they were closer than the usual personal space boundary, but he'd just lifted her onto the hood.

She had no doubt he'd shifted into this position to ensure their privacy. It made her ache for more contact than just that casual fingertip. As a general rule, she wasn't impulsive when it came to desires. She might be guided by intuition, but it was disciplined and directed to enhance her own pleasure and that of the man she was controlling. However, this time her intuition was taking her down a path where things were far less calculated. "You always call me 'ma'am'," she said. His finger might be motionless, but since it was still beneath her skirt, resting on the lace top of her stocking, her leg was in danger of catching on fire. "Whenever I tell you to call me Janet, you just nod and say, 'Yes ma'am. Janet'."

His expression was somber. Though his attention returned to her leg, it wasn't as if he'd lowered his gaze, not the way she was used to a man doing around her in a sexual situation. It was as if he was absorbing everything happening beneath and around his touch, sensing the simmer of her blood, the delicate ruffled shape of her clit swelling to ripe reaction. She thought of his mouth there and nearly shuddered.

"Just the other day," she continued, "I overheard you leaving Ben's office. Alice asked you something and you said, 'No problem. See you later, Alice'. You call Alice by her name, Max. Yet you call me ma'am."

"You prefer ma'am. You like it when men call you that." His gaze lifted then, and there was a heat in those gray irises. "Your eyes get more focused, like now. It reminds me of a hawk. I like it. I think that's why you and Matt get along so well. You're both birds of prey."

She blinked. "Will you join me for the ballet class?"

"When is it?"

"Next Thursday, seven to nine."

He nodded. "I'll drive you, if you like."

"We'll see." She should meet him there, keep things on a controlled footing. Letting him drive might be relinquishing too much, sending the wrong message, but it took more than one detail to upset her balance of power. "I'd also like you to consider coming to Club Progeny one night, as my guest."

He straightened, taking his hand away to hook his thumb in his jeans pocket. He braced his other palm on the truck hood. A polite withdrawal. "I don't know much about that world."

She lifted a brow. Matt, Lucas, Jon, Ben and Peter regularly took their women to Club Progeny, as well as Club Surreal in Baton Rouge. Despite her religious vocation, Dana was the most hardcore submissive of all the wives, and would be until Ben and Marcie decided to marry, since Marcie even eclipsed Dana in that department. Rachel was a close runner-up to Dana. Savannah and Cassandra were softer in that regard, but still very much in tune with their respective husbands' Dominant sides.

"Given the places you've taken Matt and the others after hours, it doesn't say much about your eye for detail."

A smile tugged at his firm mouth. "There's seeing a world and knowing it."

"Are you interested in an inside look?"

"Not so much. Except when you talk about it." His gaze slid over her, then back up to her face. "I might like to see how you see it. But I don't do so well with getting more personal with people."

"Neither do I."

"We could start with coffee," he suggested.

"There's a nice coffee shop on Progeny's viewing deck. It even has a separate entrance and exit for those who want to observe but not participate. Street clothes only allowed. It's like being outside an aquarium, where you get to watch all the exotic life swim around." She cocked her head. "But you already know that. Lucas says you've hung out there some nights, watching the public sessions, until they're ready to go home."

He didn't say anything. He didn't ask the obvious, if she'd been checking up on him by fishing for information from Lucas. He just waited her out, probably to see what other information she'd volunteer. He wasn't a nervous talker. That silent core, she reminded herself. It impressed her. As a result, she was willing to give him an idea of where her interest in him had been taking her.

"I've been reading about Navy SEALs. One thing that caught my interest was a description of what it was like to be down range, on a mission, in enemy territory. The SEAL who wrote the article said it was like being on a different plane, everything high intensity, hyper alert, every detail mattering." She glanced down at her leg, recalling for them both that single touch, his close attention to it.

"It made me wonder if you like watching the public sessions because a Dom and sub are exploring that intense immersion in detail. Their mission is this one focused goal, a goal the Dom always has to keep in sight, yet the journey to that goal is indescribable. The immersion itself is a drug, something you miss when you no longer have it. No matter how brutal or bloody it can be, how it tears you open or pushes you past your boundaries, you always want to go back for more."

She had his full attention now. Interestingly, that was all she had. Everything else had closed up, reminding her of a coiled snake, so close his fangs could reach her if he chose to strike. She could vividly imagine what it would be like if Max struck. Passion was a form of controlled violence, and she expected Max did controlled violence very well, if the quick shift from gray cloud to molten steel in his piercing gaze was any indication. Though he hadn't moved, he felt much closer, the way something did when it became far more dangerous.

"Why haven't you tried it, since you like watching?" she asked.

He lifted a hand toward her face. She intercepted it, a simple lift of her hand. When she pressed her knuckles against his palm, her long nails gleaming, she didn't push it away, just held enough pressure against it to keep him from touching her face. He let the hand stay there though, hovering near her lips, her lifted chin.

"You want to play it out this way?" His voice was a rumble.

"Do you?"

He closed his hand, put it back down on the truck hood next to her leg. "I'm not the Master type. I'm protective enough, but I couldn't tie up a woman or strike her. Even spanking. It's not how I roll."

"Yet I'll bet you've psychologically dominated every woman you've been with. Just taken her over with that alpha vibe and made her surrender. You've got the conqueror in you. Of course, sometimes you find that in a sub as well."

He chuckled at that. "I definitely couldn't be on the other side, ma'am."

"Most of us could be on either side. And you'd be infinitely fascinating either way." She closed her hand over his thick wrist, the one attached to his braced hand. "Notice when I touch you like this, everything between us gets still, focused, intent. What am I about to do? What are you reading from me, and me from you? There's an intensity to it. You're trusting me to care for you, watch your back, no matter what. And I'm trusting you to do the same for me. Because whichever one is holding the reins, we both hold one another's souls, even if it's just for a short space of time."

He lifted his gaze, locked with hers. It recalled the night at the hospital, when he was holding Matt, yet the two of them couldn't look away from each other. That was really what she'd been unable to forget or dismiss, wasn't it?

He put his other hand over hers, fingers sliding over her knuckles, a lingering caress. Then he squeezed it, stepped back, taking both his hands away. "Maybe I'll come in sometime when I'm bringing Matt or one of the others. Just see if you're there and go from that point. It feels like it needs to be that way. More unplanned."

"Less controlled."

"Is that a problem?" She detected a hint of challenge in his tone, and met it with a cool gaze.

"Not for me." She glanced at her shoes, bemused when he immediately understood her desire. He retrieved them, sliding them back on her feet, his fingers once again sending those lovely ribbons of sensation spiraling around her calves and inner thighs.

When she put her hands on his shoulders, she indulged the desire to slide her fingertips from the broad span up closer to his neck. His grip on her waist increased, his thumbs caressing her hip bones beneath the skirt, which sent a definite arrow of reaction between her legs. Her nipples tightened beneath the lacy bra. This man would be a thorough, overwhelming lover. That wasn't usually what she was seeking, but maybe her tastes were evolving.

"I still have your shoes," he said as he put her on her feet. "From that night at the hospital."

There were only a few inches between them, and he hadn't let her go. With the truck behind her, she was pleasantly enclosed between two very masculine, large objects. Lifting a brow, she slipped out of that narrow crevice and tapped him with the folder she retrieved from the truck hood. She wondered what he'd do if she swatted him on his very fine ass with it, and expected he might swat her back. It almost made her laugh. Then she registered his words.

She pivoted to face him again. The intensity of his expression made her feel like she was flush against him. "And you haven't had the opportunity to get them back to me in six months?" she asked lightly.

"You haven't asked me for them."

They studied one another. "Max, I want my shoes."

He cocked his head. "There it is. That female hawk look."

She understood what he meant. She knew the feeling when it took her over, that sense of command, exercised over a male eager to experience her power. She didn't feel that eagerness from Max. More like intrigued curiosity, another type of raptor perched on a different branch, watching her with abiding interest.

He moved to the limo, opening the front door. Oblivious to what viewing the stretch and bend of that powerful body could do to her, he leaned across the seat, withdrew her shoes from a side compartment. She noticed he'd wrapped them in a towel to protect them, and he took that off now, bringing her the dainty pumps, the sheen of the white-gold insoles a contrast to the polished outside walnut color. The shoes had ankle straps, but he carried them under the arches, rather than letting them dangle.

When he brought them to her, she closed her hands over the straps, pinching the back of the shoes between forefinger and thumb. As his hand slid away from the soles, her arches tingled, remarkably. What did the man wear? He had a scent like sea water and cotton, plus that musky heat that was distinctly male. Looking up at him, she saw he was staying put, less than a foot between the rise and fall of her breasts and his chest.

He lifted his hand, but this time she didn't stop him. He didn't reach toward her face. He slid beneath her bent arm and pressed his palm against her back, just below her shoulder blade. As if he was about to begin a proper ballroom waltz. She was always aware of her body's movements, particularly in relation to the give and take of a man's, and the way he eased them together was like clouds, a drift that seemed effortless.

As he bent toward her, he kept his eyes open. So did she. When he put his mouth on hers, she saw the flicker in the gray, a reaction to how her lips parted, releasing a soft sigh into his mouth. He held the contact there, a bare touch, then he drew back, pressing his lips together.

"I was wondering if that gloss tastes the way it smells. Like honeysuckle. It does. There was a honeysuckle bush behind the house where I grew up."

She imagined him plucking a blossom, drawing out the threadlike inner stem, bringing that single drop of honey to his lips. Her body responded in the same manner. She felt the tiny blot of cream dampening her panties.

"I have other flavors as well. But honeysuckle is my favorite." Turning, she moved back toward the elevators, making sure she kept her steps efficient and even as always, the sound of the heels against the concrete just as crisp. She'd had twelve-hour rehearsals that required less effort than such nonchalance took.

She lifted the shoes out to her side, not turning. "You better not have stretched them out. And I hope you wore them with proper stockings."

At the elevators, she looked over her shoulder to see him leaning against the truck, watching her, one foot hooked around his ankle. The position made the most of every inch of his hard, powerful body.

His gaze sparked with humor. "Yes ma'am."

AFTERWORD

Did you enjoy spending time with Joey's characters? If you did, then we ask that you share your experience with at least one other book-reading friend. Or mention the book on a Facebook page, at a book club meeting or online forum, on Twitter, in an Amazon or Good-Reads review, or wherever you feel comfortable. You, the pleased reader, are the best marketing strategy authors can have. If you do just one of those things to spread the word about our work, we will be very grateful! And thank you again for taking the journey with our characters.

READY FOR MORE?

Check out Joey's website at **storywitch.com** where you'll find free excerpts, buy links and news about current and upcoming releases for all of her books and series.

Love her series and want more? Revisit your favorite characters through FREE novellas and short stories, available on her website. Just choose the Cantrips (Vignettes) menu item on her website and find them in all the popular download formats. You can also go under her Books menu to choose Cantrips (Compilation) and buy the compendium volumes of these stories.

Here are some other places to find out more about Joey and her work!

- **Website:** storywitch.com
- **Facebook:** JoeyWHillAuthor
- **Twitter:** @JoeyWHill
- **GoodReads:** JoeyWHill
- **Pinterest:** jwhill23
- **YouTube:** youtube.com/storywitchpress
- **Bookbub:** bookbub.com/authors/joey-w-hill
- **Amazon:** amazon.com/Joey-W-Hill/e/B001JSCIW0
- **E-Mail:** storywitch@storywitch.com

ABOUT THE AUTHOR

Joey W. Hill writes about vampires, mermaids, boardroom executives, cops, witches, angels, housemaids...pretty much wherever her inspiration takes her. She's penned over forty acclaimed titles and six award-winning series, and been awarded the RT Book Reviews Career Achievement Award for Erotica. But she's especially proud and humbled to have the support and enthusiasm of a wonderful, widely diverse readership.

So why erotic romance? "Writing great erotic romance is all about exploring the true face of who we are – the best and worst – which typically comes out in the most vulnerable moments of sexual intimacy." She has earned a reputation for writing BDSM romance that not only wins her fans of that genre, but readers who would "never" read BDSM romance. She believes that's because strong, compelling characters are the most important part of her books.

"Whatever genre you're writing, if the characters are captivating and sympathetic, the readers are going to want to see what happens to them. That was the defining element of the romances I loved most and which shaped my own writing. Bringing characters together who have numerous emotional obstacles standing in their way, watching them reach a soul-deep understanding of one another through the expression of their darkest sexual needs, and then growing from that understanding into love - that's the kind of story I love to write."

ALSO BY JOEY W. HILL

Made in the USA
San Bernardino, CA
11 June 2020